THE ACE OF SKULLS

THE ACE OF SKULLS

A Tale of the *Ketty Jay*

Chris Wooding

GOLLANCZ
LONDON

Copyright © Chris Wooding 2013

The right of Chris Wooding to be identified as the author
of this work has been asserted by him in accordance with the
Copyright, Designs and Patents Act 1988.

First published in Great Britain in 2013
by Gollancz
An imprint of the Orion Publishing Group
Orion House, 5 Upper St Martin's Lane,
London WC2H 9EA
An Hachette UK Company

A CIP catalogue record for this book
is available from the British Library.

ISBN 978 0 575 09810 7 (Cased)
ISBN 978 0 575 09811 4 (Trade Paperback)

3 5 7 9 10 8 6 4 2

Typeset at The Spartan Press Ltd,
Lymington, Hants

Printed and bound by CPI Group (UK) Ltd,
Croydon, CR0 4YY

The Orion Publishing Group's policy is to use papers that
are natural, renewable and recyclable products and made
from wood grown in sustainable forests. The logging and
manufacturing processes are expected to conform to
the environmental regulations of the country of origin.

One

The Optimist – Stormriding – Jez is Distracted –
Women's Intuition – A Majestic Decline

C aptain Darian Frey was accustomed to long odds; his whole life, he'd been an outside chance. Lacking the ability to win in a fair fight, he survived instead by guile and the illogical optimism favoured by gamblers and drunks, which made the riskiest of plans seem like a good idea at the time.

That was how he found himself flying through the heart of a thunderstorm, on the trail of a target he couldn't even see.

The *Ketty Jay* shuddered and bucked, shoved this way and that by crosswinds as Frey wrestled with the flight stick. Bulkheads groaned, fixtures rattled, thrusters clawed the air. Tatters of cloud flapped at the windglass like angry black ghosts.

Frey bullied the *Ketty Jay* onward, teeth gritted. Lightning flickered somewhere, a dull flare muted by the intervening murk, briefly illuminating the darkened cockpit. Frey winced in anticipation of the thunder, and cringed when it hit. His ears were still ringing when he felt his stomach plunge and the *Ketty Jay* was sucked down into an air pocket.

Ordinarily, he'd have left this kind of flying to Jez. She had uncanny night vision and a way of reading the wind that was nothing short of eerie. But that was before. These days, he didn't trust her to fly at all.

'Will you just *give it up*?' he yelled at the storm in exasperation, as he hauled back on the flight stick hard enough to pop a shoulder joint.

As if at his command, the cloud flurried away and the *Ketty Jay* broke out into clear sky. The last light of dusk painted the night soft and bloody. A full moon shone down on a mountainous world of looming thunderheads, piled masses sliding past, borne on an invisible current.

Frey eased off on the flight stick and listened suspiciously as the

1

thrusters settled back to their usual tone. The peace had come so suddenly that he suspected it was a trick.

When no immediate disaster occurred, he slumped back in his seat and allowed himself to relax for a moment. These last few hours had been hard on his nerves. He knew he shouldn't be out in the open, but he needed the respite.

His eyes roamed the massive shelves and canyons of cloud, looking for a sign of their target. As expected, he found none. They'd be hiding deep in the storm, riding it as far as it would take them. Lightning lit up a distant cloud; a crackling grumble rolled across the sky.

He searched for Pinn and Harkins, but he couldn't see them either. 'You fellers alright up there?' he asked.

'Bored,' said Pinn immediately, the pilot's voice transmitted to Frey's ear via his silver earcuff. 'Haven't you found it yet?'

'I . . . er . . . actually I like it up here,' said Harkins timidly. 'It's . . . er . . . well, it's sort of nice. Quiet.'

'*Quiet*?' Pinn scoffed.

'I'm just saying . . . I mean, why shouldn't I—'

Frey pulled off the earcuff before they could get to bickering, cutting the connection to his outflyers. 'Jez. What can you hear? Jez?'

When there was no reply, he leaned round to look over his shoulder. The only other occupant of the cockpit was his navigator, sitting at her station in shadow. A small woman in shapeless overalls, black hair tied back from her face. She was staring at a set of charts on the metal desk in front of her, but she wasn't seeing them.

'*Jez!*' he snapped.

Her head jerked up and she fixed her gaze on him. Moonlight reflected from wide pupils, discs of bright white like the eyes of a night predator. Wolf's eyes. Frey felt an icy chill pass through him. Ever since Samarla, just being around her made him uneasy. She'd changed. Sometimes he dreaded being alone with her in the cockpit.

'Can you hear it?' he asked her, keeping his voice firm.

She looked at him blankly. He ran out of patience. 'The freighter, Jez! What's wrong with you?'

Realisation crossed her face, and she looked momentarily ashamed. 'I'm sorry, Cap'n, I . . .' She shook her head, waved it away. 'Hang on a moment.' She closed her eyes and listened. 'We're close now, but we've drifted. Drop to nine thousand, heading oh-fifteen. They're about twenty kloms from us.'

'You're sure?'

'I can hear the engines,' she said. 'Cargo freighter and . . . five or six outflyers running escort. They shouldn't be flying through this kind of chop with craft that small but . . .' She shrugged.

'But they're Awakeners,' Frey finished for her. She managed a wan smile at that. A joke among the crew: the Awakeners were crazy. You had to be, with a maniac for a messiah.

Jez rapidly checked her calculations. 'We'll be over the wetlands in a couple of minutes,' she said. 'Time to make our move.'

'I need you here on this, Jez,' he told her. 'Concentrate.'

She gave him a look that he couldn't read, then a resolute nod. He hoped his reminder would be enough to keep her mind on the job.

She could hear the engines. At twenty kloms, in a storm, over the bellow of the *Ketty Jay*'s thrusters. She'd always had good ears, but this was something else.

What else do you hear when you go away like that? Frey thought. *What's happened to you, Jez? What are you listening to?*

'Doc!' he shouted over his shoulder, through the open door of the cockpit. 'We're getting close! Stay sharp!'

'Right-o!' Malvery called. He was up in the autocannon cupola, a blister on the *Ketty Jay*'s humped back, set above the main passageway which ran along her spine. Probably keeping himself warm with a bottle of rum. The doc reckoned his aim got better when he was drunk, but Frey had never known him to shoot sober, so he had nothing to compare it with.

Frey vented a little of the ultralight aerium gas from the ballast tanks to bring the altitude down. An anvil-shaped thunderhead loomed over him. He steered the *Ketty Jay* towards it and let it consume them.

Back in the dark, Frey felt the tension take hold of him again. His fingers flexed nervously on the flight stick. All he could see ahead was his own face reflected in the windglass, underlit by the glow of the dash gauges. Black hair, a stubbled jaw, handsome features that he counted as his only blessing of birth. Frey was not a man unfamiliar with his own reflection, but tonight it surprised him. He looked lean and hard. Haunted.

You can do this, he told himself. *One freighter and a few shabby outflyers. Not even professional pilots. And rich pickings when we're done.*

He'd coughed up a lot of money for the information, buying from a reputable whispermonger who told him the target's route and cargo. This time, he was determined there would be no surprises. He was doing things right these days. No more shady tips or jobs that seemed too good to be true. No more corner-cutting, no more screw-ups.

And he had reason to be confident. The last two operations had gone like clockwork. It didn't matter that they were simple takes, small vessels with minimum escort caught sneaking through the volcanic passes over the Hookhollows. It didn't matter that they hadn't been carrying much, and most of what Frey stole he'd used to buy the information for this run. What mattered was how they'd executed their plans. His crew had been disciplined, efficient, and despite their bitching they'd worked as a team.

Encouraged by that, he'd decided it was time to step up to bigger prey.

The Awakeners had been stormriding ever since the civil war became official and the Archduke declared open season on their aircraft. For most freebooters, it took great persistence and a healthy dose of luck to catch a freighter in the winter storm channels over Vardia. But most freebooters didn't have a half-daemon navigator on their side.

Even knowing their target's route, it had taken a lot of searching before Jez picked up the trace. But now they were on the hunt, and closing in fast.

The *Ketty Jay* began to shake gently as the winds picked up again. Frey readied himself for another fight with the flight stick, but the battle he expected didn't come. Instead, the shaking grew steadily more pronounced. He peered through his own reflection, willing the clouds to part. They refused. And still the shaking grew.

'Jez? Is one of the thrusters coming loose or something?' he asked. A vibrating aircraft was never good, in his experience.

Jez didn't reply. He swore under his breath, turned round in his seat and found her gazing emptily at the wall again. She'd never been as bad as this before.

'Jez, damn it!' he barked. 'Wake up!'

She jolted out of her trance, looked at him, looked *past* him. Her expression turned to horror as light washed into the cockpit.

'Frey!' she shrieked.

He twisted back, saw the black cloud ahead turn to bright fog, a dozen burning suns lighting it from the inside. 'Oh, bollocks,' he muttered.

Floodlights.

He shoved the flight stick forward and wrenched the lever to execute an emergency vent of the aerium tanks. The *Ketty Jay* plunged as the clouds finally parted and the vast blunt snout of the freighter pushed through, bearing down on them like some titanic god of the storm. Frey yelled as he saw it and leaned on the stick, putting every ounce of his strength into the dive.

Not like this, he couldn't die like this, not till he'd done what he had to do, what he'd *sworn* he'd do!

A wall of black metal roared towards him. The engines screamed as they forced the *Ketty Jay* downward. Malvery added his own bellow of incoherent fear from the cupola.

Come on come on come on!

And then they were beneath it, the freighter's belly thundering overhead, shaking the *Ketty Jay* hard. Faster craft shot past them, tiny lights in the cloud, whipping by like fireflies.

In seconds, they were gone, swallowed up by the murk.

Gasping, Frey fed aerium gas back into the tanks, levelled the *Ketty Jay* out and then began to climb. No way he was staying in this damned cloud a moment longer. The gauges went momentarily dark and the engines stuttered as they were struck by lightning. He paid no attention; he didn't even flinch when the thunder hit. He didn't stop till they broke through the top of the thunderhead, and out into clear sky.

'Cap'n,' said Jez, her voice weak. 'Cap'n, I'm sorry, I—'

'Stow it, Jez. We've got a job to do.' He was angry, and scared, but mostly he was determined. They'd seen the freighter. They couldn't let it get away now.

He raised his voice and called up to the cupola. 'Doc? What's the situation?'

'Situation is I ain't drunk enough for this bullshit!' Malvery called back. 'And we got fighters breaking cloud behind us. Escort's giving chase. There's one . . . two . . . ah, bugger it, I'm just gonna shoot at 'em.' Any further conversation was prevented by the steady thumping of the autocannon as Malvery got to work.

So the escorts had abandoned the freighter to take care of the danger. Good. That was exactly what Frey wanted. Out here in the open, he could deal with them.

'Looks like we scared them as much as they scared us,' said Frey, feeling a little bravado returning. 'Pinn! Harkins! Get down here!'

He listened, but there was no reply. 'Harkins! Pinn! Is *anyone* on this crew awake?'

'Earcuff,' Jez reminded him.

Frey looked down and saw the earcuff lying in the hollow of the dash where he'd thrown it. He cursed and clipped it back on his ear. 'Pinn! Harkins! Get here now!'

'On our . . . er . . . I mean . . . Coming!' Harkins babbled.

Frey glanced at the silver ring on his little finger. It was thralled with a daemonist trick, linked invisibly to a compass in Harkins' cockpit. The needle of the compass always pointed towards the ring. That was how the outflyers would find him in the storm.

He tried not to think about who was supposed to be wearing that ring. Now wasn't the time.

The Awakeners opened up with machine guns and Frey threw the *Ketty Jay* into evasive manoeuvres. Even if they were as green as the whispermonger had promised, five or six pilots on his tail was no laughing matter. He couldn't see behind him; the *Ketty Jay* was too big for that. All he could do was to make himself a hard target till help arrived.

His aircraft was more agile than her bulk suggested, but even so he couldn't avoid the barrage entirely. Bullets ripped across the hull and Frey banked hard in the other direction. Tracer fire burned away into the distance and was lost to the night.

'Doc!' he shouted, during a pause in the firing. 'How many?'

'Five!'

'Right,' said Frey. 'Let's see if we can't improve our situation a little. Hang on!'

Frey hit a flurry of pedals, levers and valves, venting aerium gas and opening the airbrakes to maximum. The sudden increase in weight made the *Ketty Jay* sink hard just as the airbrakes killed her speed.

Wind roared past them, as if they'd run into a hurricane. Frey was thrown forward towards his dash, but his restraining straps held him back. Jez scrabbled to keep her charts pinned on the desk before her.

There was a howl of engines, and three of the five fighter craft shot overhead, caught out by their target's sudden deceleration.

Frey disengaged the airbrakes, boosted the thrusters and fed aerium gas back into the tanks. The *Ketty Jay* surged forward. He pressed down the trigger on the flight stick, and her underslung machine-guns clattered. His aim was good. The tail assembly of his nearest target was hammered into shreds, before a bullet hit the fuel tank and the explosion tore the craft apart.

The remaining fighters panicked and swerved off in two different directions. As they banked, he saw insignia on their wings and fuselages. A cluster of small circles connected by a complex series of lines. The Cipher, symbol of the Awakeners.

Frey couldn't chase both, so he picked the biggest one, a battered old Kedson Stormfox, and went after it. At least he only had three behind him to worry about now. Maybe they'd be a bit more wary from here on in.

'Pinn! Harkins! Where *are* you?' he demanded.

'Cap'n,' said Jez from behind him. 'They're lining up on you. Pull left when I say . . . *Now!*'

Frey banked to port, and a salvo of machine-gun fire ripped through the air where he'd been a moment ago. He glanced over his shoulder at her. 'How'd you know?' he asked, almost afraid of the answer.

She grinned. Her teeth looked ever so slightly sharper than normal human teeth. 'Women's intuition,' she replied.

'*Ya-hoo!*' Pinn yelled in his ear as he and Harkins came swooping down from overhead, machine-guns rattling. 'It's dying time, boys!'

Frey winced. Pinn had a habit of delivering lines like that on his way into combat. Presumably he thought it made him sound like some kind of action hero from a pulp novel, but really it was just embarrassing.

Frey opened up with his guns on the Stormfox. The pilot swerved, but only into the path of Harkins. The Firecrow's guns raked across the Stormfox's flank and shattered the cockpit canopy. It went into a dive, leaving behind it the awful ascending whine of an aircraft heading uncontrollably earthward. Then it disappeared into the storm and was gone.

'Pursuit is scattering, Cap'n!' Malvery reported.

'We can deal with this lot,' Pinn told him through the earcuff. 'Go get the freighter.'

'On it,' said Frey. He pushed the *Ketty Jay*'s nose down and looped around to head back the other way. Above him, his outflyers were chasing the freighter's escort all over the place. Pinn in his gull-winged Skylance, Harkins in his new-but-second-hand Firecrow that Frey bought him after he thrashed the last one to extinction. Mentally unstable as they were, they were both exceptional pilots. Given the quality of their opposition, four to two wouldn't give them much trouble.

The murk closed in over the *Ketty Jay*, and the wind began to shake her again. 'Some directions would be good,' Frey suggested.

'They're above us,' said Jez from behind him. 'Oh-thirty-five.' She was frowning, a faraway look in her eyes, listening to something he couldn't hear. 'They've broken cloud, heading for another thunder-head.' She focused again, and became excited. 'Boost it, Cap'n. We can catch them in the open if we're quick.'

'How in damnation can you tell that from—' Frey began, then stopped himself. 'Never mind. Women's intuition.'

He opened up the thrusters and the *Ketty Jay* drove onward and out into clear air. They found themselves in a canyon in the sky formed by the sides of two clouds, with the night above them and the ground far below. The shallow lakes and waterways of the Ossia wetlands shone in the moonlight.

Ahead and slightly above the *Ketty Jay* was the freighter, a dark slab in the storm, its thrusters aglow as it pushed across the canyon towards the slowly swirling wall on the other side.

'Where are the aerium tanks on a thing like that?' Frey asked Jez, as the *Ketty Jay* powered towards its target. She was the daughter of a craftbuilder: she tended to know these things.

'On the underside, set central, one ten metres fore of the tail assembly and one just aft of the nose.'

Frey gauged the distance between him and his target. 'Only gonna get one shot at this before we lose it in the cloud again,' he muttered.

'Then don't miss it,' said Jez, helpfully. A smile touched the corner of Frey's mouth. That was more like the navigator he knew.

The trick to bringing down a freighter was to hole the ballast tanks. Once it was leaking aerium, it would become too heavy to stay in the sky. As long as the leak was slow enough, the pilot would be forced to land. But if the hole was too big, they'd drop too fast, and there wouldn't be much left to salvage afterward. Frey didn't have more than a passing concern for the people on board – they'd signed up with the enemy, after all – but he was very keen on keeping the cargo intact.

The gap between them closed up fast as he came at it from below. Either the freighter crew didn't see him, or it didn't have any guns worth firing. The Awakeners must have been stretched thin on resources to trust their treasures to such a light convoy.

Doubt brushed him. Too easy? *Too late now.*

Frey picked his spot, zeroing in on the aft tanks. There was nothing there to suggest a vulnerable point; it was only Jez's knowledge of aircraft that guided him.

Closer, closer, and the freighter's nose had almost reached the cloud.

Now.

The *Ketty Jay*'s machine guns rattled and a barrage of tracer fire whipped away through the night. Bullets scored the underside of the freighter. Then it slid into the cloud, and was lost to sight.

Frey throttled back and pulled away. He wasn't chasing that thing in there, not after the scare he'd got last time. 'Did I get it?' he asked Jez.

She held up a hand to shut him up while she listened. Frey waited impatiently. Pinn's triumphant whooping in his earcuff told him that his outflyers had polished off the escort.

'Jez?' he said again, when he could stand it no longer.

'She's losing altitude,' Jez said, and gave him that ever-so-slightly frightening grin again. 'She's going down!'

Frey let out a little laugh, half of triumph, half of amazement at their triumph. 'She's heading for the deck, fellers,' he said to his out-flyers. 'Come and watch the show.' And he put the *Ketty Jay* into a shallow dive, thankful to be heading out of the storm at last.

Below the clouds, the Ossia wetlands spread out beneath them, a glittering muddle of weeds and water, of wide, shallow streams and islands shaggy with trees. Far to the east was the shore of Lake Atten, barely visible, stretching from horizon to horizon. Overhead, the procession of clouds following the storm channels flashed and grumbled. Lightning jabbed at the ground in the distance.

The freighter sank through the floor of the storm and kept sinking. It was a huge, ungainly thing, without wings, only stumpy ailerons for steerage. Something more like a whale than an aircraft, something that didn't look like it belonged in the sky at all. Frey watched its grand, slow trajectory towards the earth. There was something majestic in its decline.

'Will you look at that?' said Frey. He felt expansive in the aftermath of the battle, taken by a new appreciation of the world. 'That's kinda beautiful.'

'I bet the hundred or so people panicking inside it don't think it's so beautiful,' Jez observed.

'Hey, we gave them a soft landing,' Frey protested, pointing at the wetlands below. 'Besides, it's their fault for being Awakeners. There's a civil war on, y'know.'

'A civil war that we kind of, er, started.'

Frey didn't need reminding of that. 'It was going to happen anyway,' he said, as he'd said to himself many times over the past three months. 'We just made sure the good guys didn't get taken by surprise.'

'Get your retaliation in first,' Jez said, quoting one of Frey's favourite maxims.

'Damn right.'

Pinn and Harkins joined them as they descended, following the freighter down, predators tracking their wounded prey. The Awakener pilot managed to keep his craft mostly level right until the last moment. Frey held his breath in anticipation as they reached the ground.

Bring her in safe, he told the pilot.

The freighter touched down, landing on its belly and skimming across water and turf, raising huge fins of spray to either side. As its weight gathered, it ploughed deeper into the earth, the back end fishtailing out, a colossal slow-motion skid accompanied by the hiss of water and the screech of tortured metal. Even from up high, and far removed from the chaos, it was awe-inspiring.

When the water settled, the freighter lay still. Partly submerged, missing a few parts, but almost entirely intact.

It had worked. Their plan had worked. Frey could scarcely believe it.

'Alright, boys and girls,' he said. 'Time for the hand-to-hand. Let's get down there and rob the shit out of 'em.' He flopped back in his seat. 'Somebody wake up Bess.'

Two

The Intruder – Sentinels – Crowd Control –
Marinda – Pinn Receives a Prophecy

From the darkness, a monster emerged.

It loomed into sight, filling up the passageway: a shadowy hulk, hunched and massive. The crash had shorted out the lights of the Awakener freighter, but emergency backups flickered fitfully, providing horrific glimpses of the intruder.

It was an ogre of tarnished metal and chainmail, standing eight feet high and five broad. Its face – if it *had* a face – was set low between its enormous shoulders and hidden behind a circular grille. Two malevolent and inhuman eyes peered out, cold chips of light shining in a void.

The Sentinels crouched in doorways or took what cover they could find. They were the guardians of the Awakeners, soldiers for the cause. They wore grey cassocks with high collars and the emblem of the Cipher emblazoned in black on the breast.

They aimed their rifles and let fly. Bullets sparked off the creature's armour. It flinched, bellowed, then came stamping onward with a roar. The foremost of the Sentinels broke cover and ran. Seeing him falter, others followed, backing away in fear. One man, full of the zeal of the faithful, stepped bravely out into the centre of the corridor.

'Stand your ground!' he cried. 'For the Allsoul!' And he fired his rifle at point-blank range through a gap in the creature's face-grille, right between its eyes.

He hit nothing. There was a series of sharp, metallic echoes as the bullet ricocheted about inside the monster's body. The Sentinel had only an instant to wonder how an empty armoured suit was storming an Awakener freighter, before he was backhanded into the wall with the force of a steam train. The other Sentinels lost all taste for the fight then, and they fled shrieking. The monster thundered off in pursuit.

When the coast was clear, Frey and his crew stepped into the passageway, revolvers and shotguns in their hands. They followed warily in the monster's wake, pausing only for the captain to examine the spread-eagled form of the dead man, who was still embedded in the wall in the midst of an artistic splatter-pattern. He was wearing a startled expression, as if surprised to find that he was a corpse.

'Good ol' Bess,' Frey said approvingly.

'She ain't subtle, but she gets the job done,' Malvery agreed.

Grayther Crake, the *Ketty Jay*'s daemonist and the man behind the monster, felt vaguely sick. Bess's rampages never failed to distress him. It wasn't the sheer ferocity with which she maimed and crushed her opponents. It was because she took such childish glee in the carnage.

The whole crew was here, with the exception of Harkins, who was even more useless with a gun than Crake was. Leading the way was the Cap'n, sporting a daemon-thralled cutlass and a surplus of charm to hide his many and varied flaws. Next to him was Malvery, a man of great size and enormous mirth, with a ring of white hair and round, green-lensed glasses perched on his wide nose. Silo, the *Ketty Jay*'s Murthian first mate, walked alongside. Bringing up the rear was Jez. Jez, half Mane and getting more so every day, in Crake's opinion.

There was a jostling at his elbow, and Pinn pushed past him down the corridor. Oh yes, he'd forgotten Pinn. He had warm feelings for the rest of the crew, even the cowardly Harkins, but Pinn he didn't like at all. Crake was a man who valued intelligence, and Pinn was only slightly more intelligent than yeast.

'Are you coming?' Pinn asked impatiently, eager to shoot something.

'After you,' said Crake, barely concealing his disdain.

Pinn went off up the passageway. Behind him, the man embedded in the wall peeled away and slumped into the corridor. Crake focused all his concentration on keeping his supper where it was meant to be.

He found Ashua at his shoulder, the ginger-haired, tattooed girl from the slums and most recent addition to the crew. 'Don't worry,' she said. 'You know Awakeners. They're pushovers.'

'Unless they've got Imperators on board,' Crake said.

'On a craft like this? Doubt it,' she said. She gave him a pat on the shoulder. 'Besides, that's what we've got you here for, isn't it?'

13

Crake laughed nervously and stepped over the dead man, doing his best not to look.

They caught up to the others just as they were preparing to burst into a room off the passageway. The door was shut, and Frey and Malvery had taken position on either side. Bess was around the corner, terrorising those Sentinels who hadn't run far enough the first time.

Frey gave the nod to the doctor, who pulled the sliding metal door open. Screams of fright came from within. Frey peered inside, then relaxed and waved to the others. Silo, Ashua and Jez covered the passageway while Frey, Pinn and Malvery went in. Once Crake had judged it was safe, he followed.

It was a small assembly chamber, with benches arranged in rows and screwed into the floor, facing a low platform. Huddled against one wall were a group of Awakeners. They were mostly women and old men, wearing the beige cassocks of Speakers, the Awakeners' rank-and-file preachers. Each of them had the Cipher tattooed on their forehead.

'Calm down,' Frey was saying, as he checked between the benches. 'No one's getting hurt. We're just after your stuff.' He had one hand held up reassuringly, while the other pointed a pistol at them. It was a rather contradictory message, in Crake's opinion.

'We don't have anything!' protested one young woman. 'We're Speakers. We only spread the word of the Allsoul.'

'Really?' Frey cocked his head. 'Word has it you lot have been transporting all your relics and valuables from your hermitages to a hidden base on the coast, 'cause you're afraid the Archduke will get hold of them. You wouldn't have any on board, would you?'

The group stayed quiet. Frey and Malvery slipped between the benches and approached them.

'Listen,' said Malvery, in a friendly fashion. 'We're gonna ransack the place anyway. Save us some time, eh?'

'Those relics are the property of the Allsoul!' snapped one old man, bald and wrinkled like a turtle.

Frey grabbed him by the collar and pulled him out of the crowd. 'And you just volunteered to tell me where they are.'

'I'll never tell!' he declared shrilly.

Malvery cranked his lever-action shotgun and pressed it to the side of the old man's head.

'Follow the corridor! Third door on the left!'

'Thanks,' said Frey, giving him a slap on the shoulder. He turned to Pinn. 'Keep an eye on 'em. We'll go get the loot.'

Pinn looked appalled. 'Why me?'

'Because you're who I asked. Just do it. Can't have them running about all over the place.'

Pinn cursed and kicked one of the benches, then went very quiet, bit his lip and tried to pretend he hadn't almost broken his toe. Frey and Malvery headed off out the door. Crake moved to follow them.

'You!' said the old man suddenly. Crake realised that the Speaker was pointing at him. 'Are you responsible for that *thing* out there?'

If only you knew how responsible, thought Crake. But the old man's tone inspired defiance and a quiet anger. He turned calmly to face his accuser. 'Yes,' he said. 'I am.'

The crowd muttered in horror. The old man sneered. 'I thought so. None of these others had the look. How do you live with yourself, daemonist? What bargains have you made with the unnatural?'

'Your own Imperators are daemons,' Crake said. 'Haven't you heard?'

'Lies, perpetrated by daemonists like you,' said the Speaker, waving a gnarled hand to brush the words aside. 'You've always despised and feared the Awakeners.'

'You have hanged quite a lot of us,' Crake pointed out. Then he grinned nastily, and his gold tooth glinted in the faint glow of the emergency lights. 'Unfortunately for you, you missed one.'

Pinn listened to the distant gunfire with a resentful scowl on his face. The others were all out there having fun while he was stuck with guard duty. On top of that, his toe hurt like buggery. It was all so bloody unfair.

He leaned against the wall of the assembly chamber, shotgun cradled in his arms. The Speakers watched him fearfully, huddled together like sheep. He glared at them, blaming them for the whole woeful situation.

One of them, a man in his sixties who still had a full head of blond hair, cleared his throat. 'We're not men of violence, friend,' he ventured.

'Well, maybe you should learn,' said Pinn. 'Stop people like us robbing you.'

'What I mean is, there's no need for the gun. We won't cause any trouble.'

Pinn hefted the shotgun in his arms and made a show of studying it. 'What, this? You want me to put it away?'

The blond Speaker nodded hopefully.

'But what if I want to shoot one of you?' Pinn asked.

The Speaker's face fell, and some of the women gasped. Pinn's lips curved into a nasty smirk. He wasn't above enjoying a little cheap bullying now and then.

'I'll tell you why you won't give me any trouble,' he said. He brandished the shotgun to show them, patting the barrel for emphasis. 'Because this little baby will put a hole in you big enough to—'

He was interrupted by a deafening boom as the shotgun went off in his hands, blowing a chunk out of the bench next to him. The Speakers all began to scream at once, falling over each other in their desperation to get away from him. Pinn was no less panicked. He chambered a new round and pointed his weapon at the crowd.

'*Stop screaming!*' he screamed, desperate to shut them up. But all they saw was a pudgy red-faced man waving a shotgun at them, and that made them scream all the more. They scattered across the room, scrambling for cover, tripping over their cassocks.

Not knowing what else to do, Pinn ran away. He fled clumsily over the benches, through the door, and yanked it shut behind him.

Out in the passageway, he leaned against the wall, catching his breath. He needed a moment to get over his fright. The freighter was quiet and deserted in Bess's wake. Even the gunfire in the distance had stopped. He listened as the screams from the assembly room gradually died down.

A movement to his left made him bring up his shotgun sharply. But it was only Silo, sauntering round the corner. He regarded Pinn with a long, slow stare. Emergency lights reflected in dim arcs from his shaven skull.

'Cap'n asked me to check on you,' he rumbled.

Pinn raised a hand. 'All under control,' he said breezily.

Silo stared at him a moment longer, then turned and disappeared without a word.

Pinn blew out his cheeks, waited a few moments, then opened the door again. There were yelps of fear from the cowering Speakers. He held up one hand as he entered the room, the shotgun dangling from the other.

'Everybody calmed down a bit?' he said. 'Good.'

He shut the door behind him, then walked over to the low platform where he could command a good view of the room. The Speakers' eyes followed him from their hiding places behind the benches.

'Now, as I was saying,' he continued, in a soothing tone suitable for explaining things to infants and particularly dull domestic animals. 'This shotgun here, it'll put a hole in you big enough to fly a frigate through. So if everyone will just—'

Someone shrieked in the audience, and one woman slumped to the floor in a dead faint. Pinn looked down and realised he was patting his shotgun again.

'Oh, right.' He stopped patting it and held it up instead. 'Hair-trigger. Very sensitive. Better watch out.'

At the far end of the room, one of the Speakers slowly stood up, her hands in the air. She had a cloth satchel hanging from one shoulder. 'May I approach?' she asked.

Pinn had never had anyone ask him that before. It made him feel rather grand. 'If you like,' he said.

She made her way out from the benches and walked up the aisle on one side of the room. As she got closer, Pinn got a better look at her. She was young, about his age, with chin-length strawberry-blonde hair and wide, honest eyes. Despite her lack of make-up and the unflattering cassock she wore, Pinn decided she was really quite attractive. It was a pity she had a great big Cipher tattooed in black on her forehead. It seemed like a waste of a good face.

She lowered her hands as she came closer, and spoke softly. 'What's your name, brother?'

'I'm not your brother,' Pinn replied. Mostly because it would make the things he was imagining into incest.

She smiled anyway. 'We are all brothers and sisters in the Allsoul. Each of us is connected, each a part of its great code, its wonderful communication.'

Pinn meant to tell her to shut up, that he couldn't stand the Awakeners' religious babble and he wasn't interested in becoming a convert. But she was cute, so the words came out as: 'Really? Tell me more.'

'I'll show you,' she said. She laid a hand on the cloth satchel she carried. 'If I may?'

He waved his assent with the barrel of his shotgun. To her credit, her flinch was barely noticeable.

She stepped up onto the platform and joined him. 'My name is Marinda,' she said.

'Artis Pinn,' he replied absently. He was curious to see what she was going to do next.

The other Speakers watched from behind the pews as Marinda drew out a small, shallow wooden saucer, a metal flask and a long needle. She knelt down and poured some of the flask into the saucer, until it was full of milk.

'A saucer of milk?' Pinn asked, confused. 'Is your god a cat or something?'

'Silly,' said Marinda indulgently. She picked up the saucer and held it in one hand, fingers spread underneath. In the other hand she held the needle. 'The Allsoul isn't a *god*. Gods belonged to the old, primitive religions, in the days before King Andreal dictated the Cryptonomicon. The Allsoul is the wind and the water, the harmonies of song, the flight of butterflies and the stirring of the earth. The Allsoul is the great system of interconnectedness, a being formed of all the processes of the world. It is the planet we live on, and we are its greatest triumph.'

'Not a cat, then?'

'No. Well, yes, I mean, cats are part of the Allsoul too, just like birds and—'

'So your god *is* a cat?'

The slightest hint of frustration crept into her voice. 'Not *just* a cat.'

'So why the saucer of milk?'

She took a deep breath. Pinn had the distinct impression that she was silently counting to ten. When she was done, she smiled sweetly and held up the needle.

'I need a drop of your blood.'

Pinn was startled. 'What for?'

'The will of the Allsoul makes itself known to us through signs. Things that seem random are not random at all. A Speaker has learned to interpret those signs. Some do it by calculating important numbers in your life. Some do it by turning cards. The Allsoul speaks to me through the swirl of blood in milk. Give me a drop of your blood, and I will tell you your future.'

Pinn snorted. 'You're gonna tell my future?'

'You don't believe me,' she said, with a knowing quirk of her mouth. 'That's alright. You will.'

The confidence in her voice unsettled him. 'Listen, right. You're pretty and all, which is the only reason I've listened to you this far, but if you think I'm going to let you stab me with a—'

'Thank you,' she said.

That stumped him. 'Thank you for what?'

'It's kind of you to say I'm pretty.'

'Well,' he shrugged. 'Still, I—'

'It's a pity you have someone waiting for you.'

Pinn gaped. 'How did you know about Emanda?' He felt almost guilty to be reminded of his sweetheart when he'd just been thinking deviant thoughts about the woman in front of him.

Marinda just gazed at him with those wide, honest eyes, letting him draw his own conclusion. Then she held up the bowl and the needle.

'Give me your finger,' she said. 'Don't be afraid.'

'I'm not *afraid*,' he scoffed. She waited expectantly. Pinn realised that, having said so, he was now required to prove it.

'Fine,' he sulked. He looked out over the assembly room. Suddenly he felt like the unwilling victim of a stage magician. He brandished his shotgun in one hand. 'Don't anyone try anything! Remember what this gun can do! Big enough to fly a frigate through!'

Once he was satisfied his audience was sufficiently cowed, he held his finger out to Marinda. She positioned the wooden saucer beneath it and aimed the needle at the tip of his finger.

'Hold still,' she said, and jabbed him.

Pinn had never been stabbed in the fingertip by a needle before. The pain was unexpectedly enormous. He yelled an elaborate curse at the top of his lungs, and only just managed to rein in the impulse to shoot her.

She ignored him, stepping back, her eyes fixed on the saucer. There was considerably more than a drop of his blood in the milk. His finger was squirting enthusiastically. He stuck it in his mouth.

'You pierced my damn artery!' he cried, but she couldn't understand him because he was sucking his finger at the time. She held up a hand and Pinn shut up. Half of him was convinced he was dying of a mortal wound, but the other half wanted to know what kind of prediction she was about to make.

'You're going on a journey,' she said, studying the saucer. 'Somewhere you've never been before.' She frowned. 'I see death.'

'Death?'

'Death.'

'The good kind, or the kind that happens to me?'

'Don't interrupt. I see death. That's all.'

'Okay,' said Pinn, although privately he was a little put out. The specifics were sort of important.

'I see a stranger with dark hair.'

'Is she hot?'

'It's a man.'

'Oh.'

'You will find something. Something important. Something you never knew was there.'

Pinn was relieved. 'I reckon I can't be dead, then. Not if I'm busy finding stuff.'

Her face turned grave. 'Tragedy will fall on someone you hold dear.'

He was suddenly worried again. 'Is it Emanda?'

'The signs are unclear. But one thing is certain. When all these things have come to pass . . . *you will believe.*'

Their eyes met. Pinn felt himself held, caught by the certainty within, the challenge he saw there.

Then the door of the assembly chamber was suddenly pulled open, and someone called his name. He jumped and discharged his shotgun into the platform at his feet with a terrifying roar. Marinda recoiled from him with a shriek, blood and milk spilling everywhere. The Speakers disappeared behind the benches like rabbits into their holes.

Frey was standing in the doorway. He surveyed the scene with one eyebrow raised. Pinn became suddenly aware that he was standing at the head of the room as if he was the leader of a congregation.

'I won't ask,' Frey said. 'We're done here. Let's go.'

Three

O n the western side of the Hookhollows, in the depths of the Forest of Aulen, lay Timberjack Falls. At that spot, several rivers gathered into one great flood before plunging into a horseshoe-shaped valley hundreds of feet below. The base of the valley was shrouded in mist, and the noise was never-ending. Birds winged in groups through the red winter evening, silhouetted against churning walls of water.

At the top of the falls there was a town, divided among three forested islands connected by arched bridges with gates set at their midpoints. Mansions hid among the evergreens. In the narrow, cobbled streets where the shops and markets clustered, lamps were being lit. The only noise to be heard over the rumble of the falls were the cries of water birds which made their home here, or the sound of a motorised carriage as it rattled along the winding lanes.

The Broken Anchor sat on the island nearest the lip of the falls. It was the only island of the three with a public landing-pad for aircraft, and the only point of entry for visitors passing through the town. That third island was where all the unseemly commerce of freebooters and merchants took place, out of sight of the rich folk across the bridges; and the Broken Anchor was the hub of it.

'Three Dukes,' Frey said, laying his cards on the table in a fan.

The other players cursed and tutted. Frey's opponent, a burly man with a port-wine birthmark on his neck, tossed his cards down in disgusted resignation. Frey scooped up the pile of money that lay between them, careful to keep his satisfaction off his face.

'Getting all the luck tonight, aren't I?' he commented innocently.

'Luck's only gonna get you so far,' muttered a pinch-faced man whom Frey had been bluffing off the pot all game.

21

Frey gave a helpless little shrug, calculated to annoy, as if he just couldn't help winning no matter what he did. He pushed away from the table. 'Sitting this next one out, fellers,' he said. 'Never play a hand after a big win, that's what someone told me once.'

The man he'd just beaten shook his head in anger, robbed of his chance for immediate revenge. Let him stew awhile, Frey thought. A frustrated man was apt to do something stupid.

He took a swig of grog and tipped his chair back, surveying the bar with the kingly air of a satisfied man. The gas lights were low, woodworm-ridden ceiling beams mere shadows in the tobacco haze. The room rang with shouts and laughter. Harmless drunks jostled with dangerous strangers. Just his kind of dive.

We did it. We took that freighter down. And it was just as loaded as the whispermonger promised.

Frey could hardly believe they'd pulled it off without any of the crew getting hurt. Despite their close shave in the clouds, all they'd suffered was a few bullet-holes in the *Ketty Jay*'s hull. In return, they'd come away with a haul of trinkets and artefacts which would see them right for a good while, once they flogged them to a fence. And that was *after* he'd deducted what he needed for tonight's little investment. All in all, it was the kind of success that warmed a man's heart.

His crew were sat round a table on the other side of the bar, visible in glimpses through the press of bodies. Some were deep in conversation, some were raucously drunk. Harkins and Jez looked like they'd rather not be there at all, but they'd made the effort for the sake of their companions. It had become a tradition to celebrate together after a score, and Frey didn't want anyone left out.

Even Silo had joined them, drawing unfriendly stares from people nearby. Murthians were a slave race ruled by the Samarlans. Many Vards still remembered them as enemies from the Aerium Wars; others considered them potential spies for their masters. In the past, it had been sensible for Silo to keep out of sight. But he was no one's slave these days, and he refused to hide in the *Ketty Jay*'s engine room any more. It had caused a scrap or two over the last few months, but Frey's crew didn't shy from a good scrap, and anyone who messed with their first mate ended up regretting it.

Frey watched them across the bar while a new hand was dealt without him. Malvery was drunkenly explaining something to Crake, who'd leaned close and was nodding gravely. Frey could guess what the subject was. The civil war, as ever. Awakeners versus the Coalition. Those who sided with Vardia's dominant – and only – religion versus those who sided with the Archduke. All over the land, people were fighting and dying for their god or their country. Frey thought both were pretty absurd things to die for.

The crew of the *Ketty Jay* might have been instrumental in starting the war, but Frey was doing his level best to ensure they didn't get tangled up in it. They owed nothing to either side, as far as Frey could see. It wasn't their fight.

Malvery and Crake would disagree. Malvery was a patriot – he even had a medal from the First Aerium War – and Crake had a misplaced sense of civic duty that probably stemmed from being born with a silver spoon in his arse. Both of them had been grumbling about profiteering from the war when they should be fighting the Awakeners. Frey had patiently explained that they *were* fighting Awakeners by depriving them of their valuables, but his paper-thin veneer of morality didn't fool anyone. They were pirates, at the end of the day. Frey was alright with that.

Jez was sitting at the end of the table, talking to no one. Her gaze darted about the room like that of a wary animal; her whole body was tensed. She'd never been the sociable sort, but these days she could barely handle crowds at all.

Frey worried about her. The crew had been able to accept a half-Mane in their midst because she only flipped out on rare occasions. The rest of the time, she'd just been . . . well, just Jez. And they all used to like Jez. But now it was different. Now she unsettled everybody. He noted Harkins' petrified glances, and the way the crew unconsciously moved along the table to be further away from her. They sensed the change in her.

He hated to admit it, but Jez – loyal, reliable Jez – was becoming a problem.

Her head snapped around and she stared at him, right into his eyes, across the width of the room. Frey's blood ran cold.

As if she heard what I was thinking.

'Oi! Are you playing this hand or not, Mr Lucky?'

It was the angry man with the port-wine birthmark whose money Frey had just taken. Frey turned back to the table, grateful for the distraction. He coughed into his fist, took a swig of grog, and waved them on. 'I'm in,' he said. 'Deal.'

The cards came out, three for each player. Frey peeked at his cards. Two Dukes and an Ace of Crosses. A good hand, a *very* good hand. He bet big. Port-Wine and Pinch-Face matched him, while the last player dropped out.

The middle cards were dealt, three face up and three face down. Frey felt a flutter of excitement as he spotted the Duke of Fangs. The thought of beating Port-Wine with Three Dukes twice in a row was too much to resist.

He was first to pick up. He took the Duke. Port-Wine took the Four of Wings, and Pinch-Face took one of the face-down mystery cards.

Frey bet big again. He knew Port-Wine would match it. That man had too much pride to fold, and it was going to cost him.

Port-Wine more than matched him. He pushed all his money in.

Oh, damn, now he's made me think he's got something.

Pinch-Face dropped out, as Frey had known he would. He was easily intimidated. But now Frey had Port-Wine to deal with. What could he possibly have that could beat Frey's Three Dukes? All he could think of was that Port-Wine had picked up three fours in his original hand, and added a fourth, but the odds against that were ridiculous.

He just wants to beat me. He wants to see me fold.

Frey pushed his money in too. 'Show 'em,' he said.

Port-Wine laid down his cards. Frey felt a little bit sick.

Four fours.

Port-Wine leered smugly. He knew before Frey showed his cards that he had the hand sewn up. Frey thought of all the money on the table, and resisted the urge to punch his opponent.

'Reckon you need another Duke,' said Port-Wine, running his finger through the air above the two face-down cards on the table. 'You think it's one of these?'

'It ain't,' said Pinch-Face. He flipped over a card from his own discarded hand. 'I had it.'

'Well,' said Port-Wine. 'That just leaves the Ace of Skulls.'

The Ace of Skulls. The most dangerous card in Rake. It could turn a winning hand to shit or make a losing hand unbeatable. Frey reached out, let his hand hover over the cards, as if he could sense through his palm which of them could save him.

Probably none, he thought. He flipped a card.

'Oh, look,' he said with a smile.

Port-Wine had to be physically restrained by the other players. Frey gathered up the money on the table and left before the urge to gloat got him shot. His impoverished opponent was still yelling abuse when Frey was intercepted by a tall man with waxed black hair, polished leathers and a shoulder cloak.

Frey raised an eyebrow at the stranger's attire. He took care of himself far too well to belong in a place like this. 'Reckon you're Pelaru's man.'

'I've come to ensure his payment arrives safely,' came the reply. 'There's transport outside.'

'Right you are,' said Frey. He looked over at the table where his crew were carousing. 'Silo! Jez! Doc! We're going! The rest of you . . . I dunno, amuse yourselves.'

Ashua raised a mug to him. 'We'll manage!' she shouted.

The three he'd called got to their feet. As they walked over, the men and women in the crowded bar drew away from Jez like oil from a drop of soapy water.

'Pinn? Artis Pinn?'

Ashua looked up at the two shambling drunks who'd just materialised at the edge of the table. They were gawping at the *Ketty Jay*'s outflyer with something akin to awe in their eyes.

'Did I hear someone say you was Pinn?' asked one of them.

Pinn looked around the table, unsure whether he was in some kind of trouble. Nobody else knew either. 'Might be,' he said neutrally.

'Artis Pinn the pilot? The man who beat Gidley Sleen in that race at the Rushes? Who brought his craft down out of the sky with no engines and lived to tell about it?'

Ashua felt Harkins go tense next to her.

'Yeah!' said Pinn, brightly. 'Yeah, that was me!'

'We'd be honoured if you'd come join us for an ale,' the other drunkard gasped.

Pinn beamed, his tiny eyes almost disappearing in his chubby cheeks. 'Why not?' he said magnanimously. He squeezed his short, round body from out behind the table. ' 'Scuse me, everyone,' he said. 'Some fans want to say hello.' He disappeared into the sweat and heat and murk.

Ashua turned to Harkins. His narrow, hangdog face had gone a strange shade of purple.

'Didn't *you* do that, not Pinn?' she asked him.

'*Yes!*' Harkins fairly screamed it, before his voice wobbled back to normal pitch. 'Yes, that was me! But I . . . I had to fly under *his* name . . . It was . . . I mean . . .'

Harkins gave up speaking. He looked like he was about to strangle on his own neck veins.

'Why didn't you stand up for yourself, then?' Ashua asked.

'Oho!' said Crake, who'd been watching with wine-addled amusement over the rim of his cup. 'Now that's quite a question to ask our Mr Harkins.'

'I . . . you . . . I mean . . . It's not as *simple* as that, now, is it?' The ears of his battered pilot's cap flapped about his unshaven cheeks as he waved about in agitation.

'Why not?'

He seemed stumped. 'It's . . . er . . . I don't know! I just can't! I never could, alright?'

'He never could,' Crake agreed, nodding sagely.

Ashua blew out her lips to show what she thought of that. 'How'd he get to be such a good pilot when he's such a chickenshit?'

'I'm *not* a chickenshit!' said Harkins.

'You sort of are,' Crake commiserated, and took another mouthful of wine.

'Yeah,' said Ashua. 'What about that time when Pinn burped behind you and you jumped so high you fell down the stairs in the cargo hold?' Crake had broken apart laughing before she was halfway through the sentence.

'But he *pushed* me!' Harkins whined, a protest so pathetic that nobody believed it now or then.

'*I* heard,' said Ashua, then took a gulp of rum because she'd momentarily forgotten what she'd heard. '*I* heard that you were a pilot for the Navy in *both* Aerium Wars. That you shot down *dozens* of Sammies. Didn't you?'

'It was different then,' Harkins mumbled.

'How was it different?' Ashua asked. The *Ketty Jay*'s crew were usually a closemouthed lot, but she was drunk enough to be nosy.

Harkins squirmed. He didn't like to be on the spot. 'I . . . er . . . it's . . . well, I suppose . . .'

'Come on, it must be *something*,' she said. 'What was different back then? What did life in the Navy have that life on the *Ketty Jay* doesn't?' She tried to think of the most obvious thing. 'Discipline?' she guessed.

Crake snapped his fingers and pointed at her. 'Discipline,' he said, as if she'd just solved a puzzle.

'Discipline . . .' Harkins said thoughtfully. 'Er . . . yes, actually. I mean . . . you know, getting up at the same time every day, I sort of liked that. Train with your squad, everybody together. Nobody in the spotlight, nobody better than anyone else.' A little smile broke out on his face. 'And people like Pinn . . . They'd never let someone like him in. I mean, they would at *first*, but the sergeant would knock all that stupid cockiness out of him. He'd stick to formation or he'd be cleaning latrines! Back then we were a team; you cheered your team-mates on instead of trying to steal all the glory. And when you were out there on a mission together, I mean, they had your life in their hands, and you had theirs in yours, and it was . . . I don't know, it was just . . .' He shrugged. 'Safe. Not like *safe* safe, I mean, we were at war, right? But safe like home. Everything in its place and you knew what you had to do and you knew who everyone was and they knew you.'

He took a quick sip from his flagon and nodded to himself. 'Yeah. Safe. That's what it was.'

Crake was staring at Ashua in amazement. 'You know he's never spoken that much about anything, ever?'

'Maybe you never bothered asking?' she said cheerily. She felt rather pleased with herself. No one paid attention to Harkins, except Pinn, who tormented him. Ashua had an affinity for outsiders and underdogs, especially when she'd had a few.

She slapped Harkins on the shoulder and for once he didn't flinch. 'Harkins, your idea of happiness sounds like my worst nightmare, but I'll drink to it anyway.'

They all raised their mugs, and afterwards Harkins looked a little bewildered. But he was smiling, and none of them saw that too often.

She left Harkins with Crake and went to relieve herself, swaying a little as she wound her way through the crowded room. She was feeling good, still on a high from last night's victory, and there was nothing to concern her in the future. Life on the *Ketty Jay* had turned out better than expected. She'd bargained her way on board in order to evade her enemies, but she'd always intended to leave when the moment was right. These days, she wondered if she really wanted to.

They were a good lot, in all. She was fond of Malvery and liked Crake, and the others were a decent bunch too, even the Cap'n. She'd pegged him as a bit of a sleaze when they first met, but to her surprise he hadn't made any advances on her since she'd joined. In fact, she'd warmed to him as a person, against her better instincts.

Careful, she told herself. *Don't get too attached to this crew. You know what'll happen, sooner or later. What always happens.*

Ashua was used to looking out for herself. It was how she'd survived as an orphan child on the bomb-torn streets of Rabban. She made alliances when it suited her and ducked out when things got rough. The only one she'd ever put her trust in was Maddeus Brink, a dissolute aristocrat and drug dealer who'd adopted her in a fit of drunken charity. He'd been like a father to her for many years until, with characteristic callousness, he exiled her from his home and sent her out on her own again.

She learned her lesson from that.

Maddeus, she thought, and a heavy sadness came upon her. Maddeus, rotting in the heat of Shasiith, his poisoned blood killing him slowly as he passed his last weeks in a narcotic haze. Was he dead now? Perhaps. But he'd made his wishes clear, and she had enough respect for him to keep away. Besides, he'd sent her out of Shasiith for her own safety; she wasn't foolish enough to go back.

Respectable ladies might have found the toilet of the Broken Anchor disgusting, but it took a lot to disgust Ashua. When she was done, she pushed her way out and back into the noisy bar.

'Ashua Vode?' said a voice by her side.

She had her pistol out and pressed into the man's belly in half a heartbeat. Being recognised was rarely good, in her experience.

She didn't know him. He had a plain, nondescript face, folded and rucked with middle age. But it was his scent that alarmed her. A smoky, woody blend of spices and blossoms. The kind of smell that often clung to rich Samarlan merchants.

It was a smell from Shasiith, from her past. And that meant trouble.

'I'm no enemy, Miss Vode,' said the man, calmly. She was standing close to him, her body concealing the weapon in her hand. The other patrons of the bar were oblivious.

'I'll decide that,' she said.

'I bring news. Jakeley Screed is dead.'

'That's a lie.'

'I assure you it's not.'

'Then who are you?'

'My name is Bargo Ocken. You remember Dager Toyle, of course?'

'Of course. I also remember that Screed killed him. What's he to you?'

'I'm his replacement.'

Ashua stared into his eyes. 'So you say.'

'Miss Vode,' he said levelly. 'If I wanted to kill you, there are better ways than approaching you in a crowded bar. I don't work for Screed. I work for the people who killed him.'

She sized him up. He was Vardic, educated, probably from minor nobility by his accent. If the softness of his belly was anything to go by, he wasn't much of a physical threat.

She put the gun away. Ocken let out a little breath of relief. It was the only sign that he'd been tense at all.

'Over here,' he said, gesturing towards a small table tucked in the corner. She followed him, and made him wait while she checked the table and chairs for concealed weapons. Danger had sobered her up fast.

'You're very suspicious,' he observed.

'So would you be,' she said. 'Sit.'

They settled themselves. She regarded him in the dim light of the gas lamps. Night had fallen over the town now, and the windows were dark. She could feel a slight tremor though her legs: the thundering falls nearby.

'How did he die?' she asked, as quietly as she could over the noise in the bar.

'Our people caught up with him. You don't need to worry about him any more.'

'The others?' Ocken gave her a blank look. 'The others that worked for Dager Toyle,' she elaborated.

'I hope you don't expect me to name names.'

'Are they all dead?'

'Not all.'

She drummed her fingers restlessly, thinking over the implications of Ocken's news, wondering whether to believe him. It had been Screed she'd been hiding from when Frey first encountered her, skulking in a den of drug addicts. Her hired muscle proved to be a useless defence. If Screed had found her before Frey, she'd be dead by now.

'What do you want with me?' she asked.

'I want to resume our relationship,' said Ocken. 'Toyle might be dead, but the organisation is not. Cut off a limb' – he spread his arms as if to say: *Here I am* – 'and it grows again.'

She sat back in her chair, never taking her gaze from him. 'I've got a new thing now,' she said.

'Yes, the *Ketty Jay*. I hear they're doing moderately well these days. Don't worry. It rather suits our purpose that you stay on the crew. Look on us as, well, something on the side. Insurance. In case it all goes wrong somewhere down the line.'

Ashua thought about that for a time, but in the end she shook her head. 'You let me down before. Screed wouldn't have been after me if you hadn't screwed up.'

'We understand. You deserve compensation for what you've been through. That's why we intend to treble your retainer.'

That was enough to give her pause. Money had never been the guiding force in Ashua's life, but it was a lot of money to someone who'd never had much.

'First payment up front?' she asked.

'Naturally. And subsequent payments every quarter-year, for as long as we need you. And as long as you provide what we want.'

Tempting. A little insurance never hurt anyone. And after all, what did she know about what the future held? She might be kicked off the *Ketty Jay* tomorrow, and then where would she be? She knew from experience that it was naïve to rely on others. They all let you down in the end.

She leaned forward across the table. 'Keep talking,' she said, and Ocken smiled.

Four

The Thacian & Jez – A Necessary Change –
A Meadow – The Small Hours

Pelaru the whispermonger lived on the most exclusive of Timberjack Falls' three islands. Frey and his companions were taken there by motorised carriage, after first picking up their delivery from the *Ketty Jay*. The bridge guards eyed the scruffy passengers suspiciously as they approached the gates to the island, but they knew Pelaru's man and waved them through.

The villa was set back from a woody lane on a steep hill. Evergreens rustled in the night; nocturnal animals chirruped and hooted from the undergrowth. The carriage was met at the entrance to the grounds by several men who checked Frey and his crew for weapons. After that, they were taken up a sharply sloping drive which wound past ornamental rock pools and skeletal arbours to the house itself.

The villa was designed in what Frey vaguely recognised as a foreign style, adorned with domes and porticoes. It was asymmetrical to accommodate the rise in the land, and surrounded by multi-layered gardens containing fountains and sculptures bizarre to his eye. A summer place, built for warmer times. On a still winter night in Aulenfay, it just looked bleak.

Pelaru was waiting for them outside the main door, along with a pair of discreetly armed bodyguards. He was a tall, straight-backed man in his thirties, with the statuesque, arrogant features typical of Thacians. He had olive skin and neat black hair, and was wearing fashionable trousers and a waistcoat that looked far too light for the weather.

The carriage pulled to a stop and Frey stepped down from the passenger seat. Pelaru walked over to greet him.

'Captain Frey,' he began, in the lilting accent of his people. 'It's my pleasure to—'

He trailed off as he caught sight of something over Frey's shoulder. Frey looked back, following his gaze to the carriage. Malvery and Silo were climbing down, but it wasn't them he was staring at. It was Jez. And Jez was staring at him, an intense, mesmerised stare, and *oh, damn it* her eyes were shining in the moonlight.

I knew I shouldn't have brought her.

'You want to see your payment?' Frey prompted quickly, to distract him. 'Silo, Malvery, show the man what we brought him.'

Pelaru seemed to notice he was there again. 'Ah, er . . . Forgive me, I don't seem to be . . . quite myself tonight.' He shook it off and focused. 'Captain Frey, we must talk. Walk with me.'

'Don't you, er . . . the relics, though?' Frey motioned towards the heavy chest which Silo and Malvery were manhandling out of the trunk.

'Ah, yes, the relics,' said Pelaru, not in the least bit interested. He put his hand on Frey's arm and steered him away. 'Come. We have things to discuss.' He took one last look at Jez, who'd evidently unsettled him, and then led Frey towards the side of the villa, leaving Malvery and Silo holding the chest between them.

'Oi!' Malvery yelled after them. 'What are we supposed to do with this?'

Frey gave him a helpless shrug. *Your guess is as good as mine.*

'Well, that's just great,' Malvery grumbled. He was sobering up and getting ratty. Frey winced as he dumped his side of the chest on the ground. The crash that followed probably halved the value of its contents.

He followed Pelaru along a path through the courtyards and round to the back of the villa. The whispermonger seemed deep in thought. Frey hoped he hadn't been too disturbed by the sight of Jez. He'd known she might be a risk, but he'd needed her along in case things went bad. They might not be able to carry weapons into a whispermonger's house, but Jez was a weapon herself.

Behind the house was a tiered cliff garden overlooking the vast, rushing river. The sound of the falls was loud, rumble and hiss, and when the wind blew against him Frey could feel water mist on his face. He could see another island half a klom away, a black hump in the water, dotted with friendly lights.

Out here, it was hard to imagine there was a civil war going on at all. But the war was young, and Vardia was vast. Frey wondered how long it would be before it reached even remote spots like Timberjack Falls.

Pelaru walked to the edge of the garden, where a twisted metal railing guarded against the drop. Frey joined him warily. He wasn't sure what was going on, but he knew one thing: if the whispermonger tried to pitch him over that cliff, he was bloody well coming too.

'There a problem?' he asked. 'I thought we had a deal.'

'We did,' said Pelaru. His face was impassive and serene as he gazed out across the water. 'I'm changing it.'

'You're changing it,' said Frey flatly.

'Yes.'

Frey looked out over the vista and took a long breath. The beauty of his surroundings did little to calm the anger boiling up inside him. The whole reason he'd started dealing with high-level people was to avoid situations like this. He'd had enough of betrayals.

'You're a whispermonger,' he said. 'A whispermonger. You're expensive as gold-plated cowshit and you live and die on your reputation. That means you don't spread secrets you aren't paid for, and you *don't change deals.*'

'I think my reputation will survive one disgruntled freebooter,' Pelaru said. 'But for all that, I am sorry. It is necessary.'

His infuriating calm broke through Frey's last shreds of restraint. '*Necessary?*' he shouted. 'I couldn't give half a damn about *necessary*! Tell me where she is!'

His voice rang out into the night and was swallowed by the churning waters. He shut his mouth, feeling suddenly exposed. Had his crew heard that on the other side of the house? Had Jez, with her inhuman perception?

As far as any of them knew, he was busy locating their next target, just like he'd located the last. In a way, they were right. But the target wasn't what they imagined.

It wasn't riches he was hunting. It was Trinica Dracken.

Pelaru was studying him with new interest after his outburst. 'She means a great deal to you,' he observed. 'I didn't see that before.'

Frey gave him a hateful glare, then turned his head and spat over the railing. He'd given himself away. She'd always had the power to make him do that.

'She owes me money,' he lied.

Pelaru didn't say anything.

'What do you want?' Frey asked at length.

'You can keep the relics,' said Pelaru. 'Sell them as you wish. Instead, I want your help. If you play this right, you'll not only come away with the information you seek, you'll be a great deal richer.'

'Or I could just go to another whispermonger,' said Frey.

'You could,' said the Thacian. 'You could give up the money you've already paid me and leave. But Trinica Dracken is a hard woman to find. She is a pirate, after all, with a hefty price on her head. Suffice to say there was a certain amount of good fortune involved in tracking her down. Another whispermonger might take longer than I did. By then, she may be somewhere you'll never find her.' He turned his pale green eyes on Frey. 'I suspect you don't want to take that risk.'

He suspected right. The past three months had been dedicated to the search for her, even if the crew weren't aware of it. But Trinica could be anywhere in the known world by now, and having a civil war to deal with didn't help. His chances of finding her by chasing rumours were close to zero. That was why he'd employed Pelaru.

Since they returned from Samarla, every score had been made to bring them closer to this moment. First he had to raise the money to set Pelaru on the trail. Then he'd paid a different whispermonger for the tip-off on their last job, in order to get the remainder of Pelaru's fee. He'd done it *right*, damn it, he'd done everything right! But now this. And three months was already too long.

'What's the deal?' he asked.

Pelaru walked away from the cliff edge, wandering slowly into the gardens, where marble statues waited in the moonlight. Frey rolled his eyes and followed, as he was meant to. Everything about this man annoyed him. He was so damned *poised*. Frey wanted to trip him, just to see him stumble.

'You may have surmised that I have an interest in Awakener artefacts,' Pelaru said. 'You would be wrong. I think they're childish junk, relics of a transparently manufactured religion created by Royalists in order to make a hero of their last mad King.' He shook his head. 'You people and your Kings and Dukes and Oracles.'

'Yeah, yeah,' said Frey in a bored tone. 'Thace and its wonderful republic, I know. Except while you've all been sitting on your arses playing lutes and drawing each other naked, your neighbours in Samarla have been tooling up to invade the rest of the world. Lot of good all that culture's gonna do you in chains.'

Pelaru ignored the insult. 'My business partner is the collector,' he said, as if he hadn't been interrupted. 'Two days ago, he located a site where he believed there was a cache of great value. He immediately set out with a group of men to find it. He has not returned.'

Frey waited. 'So?'

'So I need you to go after him.'

'You're serious? This is a *rescue?*'

'If he's alive.'

'And if he's not?'

'Then I want to know.'

Frey thought this over. 'Y'know, if one of my crew was a day or two late coming home, I'd just assume they were drunk or they'd found a willing member of the opposite sex to have a bit of fun with. I think you're just overprotective. You'd better hire someone else to do your babysitting.'

'I *can't!*' Pelaru snapped.

Frey allowed himself a small smile. A crack in that armour of serenity. Frey had a talent for pissing people off.

'He means a great deal to you, doesn't he?' Frey said. 'I didn't see that before.'

Pelaru scowled, his features twitching with suppressed emotion. 'There's no *time* for anyone else. The cache was in a buried shrine in Korrene.'

Frey stopped walking. Pelaru went on a few steps before noticing.

'Korrene,' said Frey. 'You want us to fly into a warzone.'

'It's *because* it's a warzone that I need you at all,' said the whisper-monger. 'The shrine was situated in an uncontested area of the city. Now the battle fronts are closing in on that position.' He gave Frey a steady gaze. 'I have to find him before then.'

'*You* have to find him? I thought *we* were taking all the risk?'

'No. I'll be going with you.'

'Ah,' said Frey. That made things interesting. He folded his arms. 'Now why would you want to do that?'

'That's not your business,' Pelaru said coldly.

'On my craft it is,' he said.

'That's not what I heard. I heard the *Ketty Jay* was the kind of place where a man might not be asked awkward questions.'

That was true enough, though perhaps less so now than in the past. But he could guess Pelaru's motives anyway, so he didn't push it further. Whoever this business partner was, he was important. Pelaru wanted to be there to make sure they did everything they could to save him. Or maybe just to bring back his body.

'You can come,' said Frey. 'Alone. I'm not having hired muscle on my craft. That's how hijacks happen.'

Pelaru opened his mouth to protest. Frey cut him off.

'That's the deal, or there's no deal at all,' he said. 'Seems like we're both looking for someone. Difference is, I only have your word that you've found Trinica. I'm not flying my crew into a warzone for that. So you come alone, and the moment we find this man of yours – dead or alive – you tell me what I need to know. And if I don't like what I hear, if I don't believe you, I swear I'll shoot you right there and then.'

Frey saw the conflict on Pelaru's face, and felt a small, private sense of triumph. He'd learned this tactic at the Rake tables. Don't let someone else dictate the play. Always be the one asking the questions. You only learned what a man had when you pushed him. The whispermonger had shown weakness. He hadn't given away all the cards in his hand, but he'd given away the best one.

Now he'd see what Pelaru's information was worth, and whether he was willing to guarantee its value with his life.

'Done,' said Pelaru. He sounded disgusted at himself.

'We keep whatever we find inside this shrine, too.'

'Done!' Pelaru cried.

'Alright, then,' said Frey. 'Be at the docks tomorrow at ten.'

'Tomorrow?' Pelaru said, but Frey was already walking away.

'Half my crew are drunk and I need to sleep. You think you can find a better crew faster, be my guest. Otherwise, I'm the captain, and we set off when I say.'

Frey waited for a response. Pelaru didn't give one. He took that as capitulation. *That's what you get when you try to screw me, you sneaky Thacian bastard.*

He felt a little better now that he'd clawed back some advantage, but he was still disappointed and angry about the way it had turned out. He felt bad enough about deceiving his crew this far. They were making a healthy profit, it was true, and if this job came off they'd make a lot more of it; but he didn't want to put them in further danger. He wanted to be straight with them. He just couldn't.

The whole thing was too personal. Frey had never been comfortable talking about emotions, and certainly not to the gang of piss-takers and reprobates that he shared the *Ketty Jay* with. He knew what they'd say, if they found out what he was up to. They'd say he was deluded. Trinica had made her feelings perfectly clear last time they met. She never wanted to see him again. Aside from that, she was a dangerously unhinged pirate captain who dressed up like Death's bride, and she'd stabbed him repeatedly in the back. On paper, she wasn't much of a potential mate.

But he'd made a promise to himself. A promise to make right what he'd done. And he had to find her, before it was too late, before she forgot who she was, what she'd been and how she loved him once.

Korrene, he thought. *How am I ever gonna explain this one to the crew?*

WANTED FOR PIRACY AND MURDER

Frey sat on his bunk, his back against the metal bulkhead, a straining hammock full of luggage suspended above him. He was staring at a creased handbill, its edges bent and pinched from thoughtless storage. Beside a list of his crimes, a younger Darian Frey stared back at him. The ferrotype was a close-up of his face, a little blurred due to cheap ink and paper. He wore a smile that managed to be both posed and genuine. Not the face of a pirate or a killer. Hard to believe he'd turned out that way.

Frey wasn't much for mementoes. He'd never seen the point in recording his experiences; he'd always looked forward rather than back. But these days he found himself wishing he'd taken better care of the past. This portrait of himself, smiling and accused, was the closest thing he had to a picture of Trinica.

'Come on! Quick! Quick!'
Breathless hurry. The whirr of the camera timer.
'Here! Stand there! Smile!'
'It's not even pointing at us!' he said.
'Oh! You're right! Left, left, quick!'

'Right, you said? Over here?'

'Left!' Laughing now. 'Quick! Quick!'

She pulled him to her by his arm, he flashed his teeth, and the camera shutter snapped, biting off that moment, preserving it on a plate. Of all of the ferrotypes they ever appeared in, that one was most perfectly them. Later, the authorities would take that picture and cut Trinica out of it, leaving only the face of a criminal-to-be. But in his mind, the picture was whole, and would always remain so.

He was there with her now, as she squeezed him and kissed him, then ran off towards the camera. He watched her go, her light summer dress blowing about her pale legs as she hurried across the meadow. The sun was hot on his neck that day, but there was a cooling breeze from the mountains at his back. She went to the camera and worried at it, as if she could open it up then and there and find the moment they'd caught inside.

'I want to see!' she said.

'All things come to those who wait,' he told her sagely, because it was something her father would say, one of a thousand jokes they shared.

'Oh, you're no fun!' she said, in tones that suggested the opposite. 'And you've never waited for a thing in your life!'

'That's right,' he said. 'When there's something I want, I go right ahead and take it!' He chased up the meadow towards her, and she squealed like a little girl and fled. When he caught her, he picked her up and lifted her, and with her face turned down to his she kissed him, her long blonde hair falling across his cheek.

Was it like that? Was it truly the way he saw it in his memory? Had the sunlight caught the floating dandelion seeds and turned them to gold? Had the grass smelt so fine? Did he realise the perfection of the moment at the time, or was it only perfect through the lens of loss?

The lovers that day had no idea of what was to come, the betrayal and tragedy that would turn their happiness to grief and send them both spinning out into the world, shattered and bitter, careering towards a violent future. That day, they knew nothing but the moment. Perhaps that was how they should have stayed. If he'd loved more fearlessly, instead of poisoning their joy with doubt, then they'd still be together now. But then, maybe it couldn't have been any other way. Maybe they had to break apart to know each other.

Once upon a time, before the days of guns and drink and treachery, he'd run in a meadow with a woman he loved entirely. Those days were gone. He wanted them back. It had been that way once; he had to believe it could be so again.

If he could find her.

If he could change her mind.

It had been more than five years since Jez last slept. She didn't miss it. She'd never been much of a dreamer anyway.

Her favourite time was the small hours, when the crew were usually asleep and the *Ketty Jay* was full of ticks and creaks and large empty silences. Then it was only her and the cat and the rats in the hold.

Sometimes she joined Slag in the hunt, her thoughts mixing with his as he stalked his prey through the vents, ducts and secret places. She shared in the kill and tasted the blood on her tongue. Other times she chose the rats, melting into their hot busy minds.

When the mood took her, she'd take control of a rat, replacing its instincts with her commands. She'd guide it through the ducts to the spot where Slag lay in wait, and stay with it as it was torn apart. Those sharp, sharp claws sank into her back as they sank into the rat's, and the pain was almost beyond endurance. But she hung on to those death agonies until there was nothing left to hang on to, and when it was over she felt fiercely alive, her mind clear, and the voices were silenced for a time.

But they always came back.

She crouched, perfectly balanced, on a walkway railing that over-looked the *Ketty Jay*'s cavernous cargo hold. She liked to be high up. The way her crewmates moved bored her: walking on the floor, labouring up stairs, following paths laid out for feet. She wanted to leap from perch to perch, zigzagging through her environment. She wanted a three-dimensional world, not one restricted to flat surfaces and prescribed routes. When she was in company she resisted her impulses, knowing how it disturbed the others. But at night, alone, she was free.

She had more in common with the cat than the Cap'n these days. Sometimes that concerned her, sometimes it didn't.

Ashua was asleep below her, wrapped in a sleeping bag and tucked up in her little nest, a padded nook in the bulkhead. Jez could hear the sigh of her breath, the slow beating of her heart. Elsewhere, she heard the soft chink of Bess's chainmail parts moving in the faint breeze from the *Ketty Jay*'s air circulation system. The golem was dormant and still, an empty suit standing in Crake's makeshift sanctum at the back of the hold, hidden by a wall of crates and a tarpaulin curtain.

There were other sounds too, sensed rather than heard. The mutter and babble of dreaming minds. The distant call of the Manes, a plaintive howl like a wolf-pack missing a member. Loudest were the thoughts of the pilots, labourers and customs officials who walked the docks outside. They came to her in a whispered susurrus, a confused mess of voices on the edge of understanding.

She could listen to them, if she wanted, though it was frustratingly hard to make sense of what she heard. It came as stitched-together patches of nonsense, windows of clarity in a shifting haze. She made it a point never to consciously spy on the crew's thoughts, but she couldn't help overhearing some things. She knew the Cap'n's concerns about her. She shared them herself.

At least he thought it was only her uncanny hearing he had to worry about. If he knew the truth, he'd kick her off the *Ketty Jay* for sure.

Frey had wondered how she knew so much about that Awakener freighter in the storm. Things that couldn't possibly be accounted for by hearing alone. The truth was, she'd been listening to the mass of thoughts from the people it carried, gleaning titbits from the muddle.

'. . . *should have told her when I . . .*'

'. . . *emember to fill this up before . . .*'

'. . . *is he now? What is he . . .*'

'. . . *not my problem anyway, no matter what they . . .*'

'. . . *feel sick. Been a month now since I've felt right. Should see a . . .*'

She brought herself back to her body with an effort. It was perilously easy to lose herself in other people's worries and desires. Too many minds nearby, even at night. During the day it was worse. In a crowd, it required constant concentration just to keep herself together. She felt that if she let go, she'd scatter like light, flying away in a thousand directions at once.

I'm losing it, she told herself. *Losing myself.*

Riss had warned her. The more she tested herself, the more she practised her newfound Mane abilities, the more like them she'd become. She'd accepted that. She'd chosen to change. But it was hard to let go of what she once was, what she'd always been. It was hard to let go of the world that surrounded her.

She'd drifted into an unknown sea, with no shore to navigate by and no lights to guide her. She was becoming estranged from both her companions and herself, and getting closer to nobody. It frightened her.

Then she saw Pelaru.

The thought of him focused her mind. The voices from outside faded. She saw his face, clear as if he was standing there beside her on the walkway. His olive skin, the sculpted hauteur of his features, the curve of his mouth, the straight set of his shoulders.

Beautiful.

Beautiful, in a way that startled her. Beautiful like an infant saw beauty as it stared in wonder at the sunrise. Incomprehensible, overwhelming, penetrating to the core.

What did it mean? What had she seen, when she saw the whispermonger?

Jez had always been detached, even before that day in Yortland when the Manes came. She'd yearned to connect with others but never could. She had friends and family and partners, but the deep, passionate link that she craved in her adult life had always eluded her. Aspects of human relationships that other people seemed ready to kill and die for had never seemed that important to her.

Once she'd slept with a man forty years older than her just to get the Cap'n's neck out of a noose. Most people would have been appalled by the notion. For her, it was simply the most expedient way of getting something done. She hadn't been defiled by the experience. She hadn't felt much of anything about it.

Maybe there was something wrong with her. Maybe she wanted to feel more than she had a right to, more than she was capable of. That was why she'd chosen the Manes, in the end. They promised togetherness, companionship, the kind of unity that was beyond anything she'd experienced before.

But now this. Was this what the Cap'n felt when he thought of Trinica? This astonishing, stunned sense of *wanting*? Was she in love? And if that was so, was it too late to turn back from the path she'd chosen?

Was it too late to choose to be human?

Five

T he city of Korrene lay at the feet of the Hookhollow mountains, on a stony hill that afforded a commanding view of the plains to the west. In the days before the Third Age of Aviation and mass-manufactured aircraft, it had been an important gateway for travellers and merchants making their perilous way up to Vardia's vast Eastern Plateau.

Those days were long gone.

'Damn,' said Frey, peering through the windglass of the *Ketty Jay's* cockpit. He looked across at Ashua. 'And I thought *your* city was a piece of shit.'

Crake couldn't help but agree with the sentiment. Rabban, where Ashua grew up, had been bombed to rubble during the Aerium Wars and still hadn't been adequately rebuilt. But the destruction in Korrene was of another order of magnitude altogether.

The ancient city had been literally ripped apart. An enormous crooked chasm ran through the heart of it, separating the western third. Smaller cracks radiated outwards; the streets slumped into them. Broken stubs of towers jutted from the wreckage of palaces, shattered arches lay in pieces, winding lanes and terraces had folded and crumbled. The river that had run through the city was dry now, choked off by the cataclysm.

Fifty years since the final quake. The city had endured many shocks over thousands of years, but this last one had been the end of it. The survivors left and never returned. Once the scavengers had picked it over, not even the pirates wanted to stay. It became a ghost city, a bitter reminder of the savage nature of the land they lived in.

But the ghosts had been stirred up by the civil war, and the city wasn't so empty any more.

42

'Somebody tell me why they're fighting over that heap of bricks?' Ashua asked. She was leaning against a bulkhead, hands in one of her many pockets. Her expression, as was usual, suggested she was deeply unimpressed by everything. A black tattoo swirled around her left eye, reaching over her cheek and onto her forehead. Rabban gang fashion, from a time when the borders of that smashed city were the limit of her world.

When nobody answered her question, she looked at Pelaru, who was standing near the doorway. The cockpit was crowded, as it often was these days. Usually the Cap'n was easily annoyed by people pestering him while he was flying, but Crake got the sense that Frey didn't like being alone with Jez. Nor did any of them, for that matter.

'How about you?' she asked the whispermonger. 'Isn't it your job to know everything?'

Pelaru gave her a faint smile. 'And if I gave it away for free, how would I eat?'

'Oh, I'm sure you'd eat just fine,' said Frey, with the merest hint of sulkiness. 'Fighters coming in.'

There was a Navy frigate to the south of the city, hanging in the early evening sky. Several small shapes had detached from it and were approaching. They were hard to make out against the mountains, but since it was a Navy frigate, it was a safe bet they were Windblades.

Frey touched his earcuff. 'Nice and easy, Pinn. We're all friends here, remember? Stay off the trigger.'

Crake shifted uneasily and his gaze returned to the city. He didn't like the idea of going down there, and not only because of his lifelong aversion to getting shot. It was something deeper than that, something that had been nagging him for weeks now.

It wasn't the idea of stealing from the Awakeners that bothered him. It was the aristocratic sense of honour that had been instilled in him by a stern and industrious father. There was a clear enemy here, a threat to the nation and his way of life. He felt he should be participating in this war rather than living off it.

Besides, it was in his own interests to see the Awakeners defeated. They'd persecuted daemonists for more than a century and poisoned the populace against them, forcing them to practise the Art in secret or risk being lynched. If the Awakeners won, the persecution would only get worse.

But if they lost, if they were driven out . . . well, what might that mean for daemonism? What great strides in science might they make if daemonists were allowed a university, a library, a place to share their views without fear? Maybe then their profession wouldn't be so fraught with danger.

Maybe then no more daemonists would have to suffer the tragedy that he had.

'Ready on the heliograph, Jez,' said Frey. 'We want to let 'em know we're on their side.'

Jez, hunched over her desk, reached for the press-switch by which she could send coded messages. There was a signal light on the *Ketty Jay*'s humped back, bright enough to be seen on all but the brightest day. Most aircraft didn't have the daemon-thralled earcuffs that the *Ketty Jay*'s pilots used. It gave the crew an edge that had saved their lives more than once. Crake felt a small sense of pride at that.

Frey picked up a mug of coffee from the dash and sipped at it, watching the windblades approach without much concern. 'So what do we tell 'em, Pelaru?'

'Tell them that I am aboard, and I have important information for their leader. He knows me.'

'Oh yeah? Who's in charge down there, then?'

'Kedmund Drave.'

'Shit! Shit! Ow!' Frey hissed as he spilt burning coffee over his fingers. He put down the mug and flapped his hand in the air to cool it off. 'You could have told me that before!'

'You didn't ask. You and he have some history, then?'

'Few years ago, Frey emptied a shotgun into him, point blank,' said Ashua with a wicked smile. She liked that story.

'Suffice to say I'm not his favourite person,' said Frey. 'Jez, do the business.'

Jez began tapping on the press-switch, signalling to the approaching Windblades. She hadn't looked up from her desk since Pelaru had entered. The Thacian was making such a show of ignoring her that his interest was obvious to everyone.

What's going on between with those two? Haven't they only just met?

Crake cleared his throat. 'Any, er, any other Century Knights down there apart from Drave?' he asked Pelaru, as casually as he could manage. Frey cackled knowingly, and he felt his cheeks growing hot.

'Some, I believe. Morben Kyne. Colden Grudge. Samandra Br—'

Frey clapped his hands and twisted in his seat to grin at Crake. 'You hear that?'

'One word, Frey . . .' Crake warned.

'What?' Frey protested innocently. 'You should be happy. That girl's a knockout.'

Crake hurried out of the cockpit, face burning, Ashua's laughter in his ears. Samandra Bree. Spit and blood, just the thought of her made his heart beat faster. Samandra, who he hadn't seen since she decked him in the Samarlan desert. Samandra: loud, vulgar, wonderful.

As he headed for his cramped quarters, he began calculating how much time he had before landing. Enough to trim his short blond beard and do what he could with his hair. Enough to pick out his best coat and apply a little scent. Enough to make sure his hands were clean and his fingernails clipped.

Samandra.

The dangers of Korrene had paled into insignificance all of a sudden. Today, he was both the happiest man alive, and the most terrified.

The Coalition's forward base was near the eastern edge of the city, set around a cracked landing pad surrounded by a clutter of ruined buildings and broken streets. There were a dozen craft there, tough military models, Tabingtons and Besterfields. Shuttles flew back and forth from the freighter to the south. Portable anti-aircraft guns scanned the sky.

Half the pad was taken up by the camp. Tractors pulled trailers loaded with crates between the tents. Generals debated over maps. Squads of blue-uniformed men smoked and waited restlessly.

The Windblades escorted the *Ketty Jay* down. Pinn and Harkins landed their fighters alongside. They'd barely touched the ground before a half-dozen men came heading over, led by the formidable figure of Kedmund Drave.

'Let's get out there and meet our fans,' said Frey, who seemed rather jolly at the prospect of an argument.

They assembled down in the cargo hold, all but Bess, whom Crake had left dormant and hidden in the back. He thought it best if she stayed asleep: she wasn't much help in delicate negotiations.

Silo pulled the lever and the cargo ramp opened up. The stink of prothane and aerium gas slipped in from outside, along with the noise of men and machines.

'Best smiles, everyone,' said Frey, and they followed him down to meet the welcoming committee.

Kedmund Drave was a man with a fearful reputation. He was the Archduke's attack dog: stern, implacable, ruthless. They said he could smell treason; they said he could look into a man's heart and root out a lie. And when you saw him, you believed it. He had a face that looked like it had never known a smile, cheek and throat scarred, eyes grey as stone, cropped hair the same colour. He wore close-fitting crimson armour beneath a dust-stained black cloak, a two-handed sword across his back, pistols at his waist.

'Captain Frey,' he said. 'Just when I thought I had trouble enough.'

'There's always room for a bit more,' said Frey. 'How are you, Drave? Been a while.'

'And haven't you been busy since?' said Drave, with an unmistakably dangerous insinuation which Crake didn't much like.

Crake's eyes went to the man standing nearby. Many of the Century Knights were familiar to the public through ferrotypes and broadsheets or children's trading cards. Morben Kyne's was a picture that nobody forgot.

He was cloaked in black like Drave, but his armour was even finer, delicately moulded to his body, the colour of burnished copper. A large-bore pistol that was more like a cannon hung at his hip, along with a pair of exquisite shortblades.

But it was his face that was most arresting; or rather, the lack of it. A deep cowl hid him partially, but Crake could still see the bronze mask beneath. It was smooth but etched with rows of tiny, strange symbols. The mouthpiece was rectangular and protruded slightly, like the radiator grille of a motorised carriage, giving him a mechanical look. And indeed, he might have been some kind of automaton, for there was not a millimetre of skin to be seen. Artificial eyes shone from the shadow within the cowl, pallid green glitters in the dark.

'Pelaru,' said Drave, switching his attention to the whispermonger. 'Didn't expect to find you keeping such company.'

'Captain Frey graciously agreed to escort me to you,' Pelaru replied. 'I have information.'

'Don't you always? And what's your price?'

'That we can discuss in private.'

Crake stopped listening to the conversation as he caught sight of the woman striding purposefully towards them across the landing pad. His insides fluttered with delighted fear.

It was her.

She was dressed with typical practicality. Grubby coat, scuffed boots, hide trousers. Twin lever-action shotguns, a cutlass at her belt. And that tricorn hat, made famous by the Press and ten thousand ferrotypes. She walked right up to him, ignoring Drave and the others.

There was intention in her step. He suddenly realised she was going to hit him again.

'Miss Bree,' he began to protest in an embarrassingly high voice. 'I think you should—'

She swept off her hat, her dark hair falling free, then grabbed the back of his head and kissed him on the mouth. After a moment she let him go, stared hard into his eyes.

'You,' she told him firmly, 'are late.'

Frey laughed. Drave made a noise of exasperated disgust. Pinn called him a jammy turd.

'Mind if I borrow him?' she asked Frey. 'You kept him from me long enough.'

'Be my guest,' said Frey, smiling. 'Just bring him back in one piece.'

'Comin'?' she asked Crake, and before he could reply or even get over the shock, she was away. He looked awkwardly around at his company and then followed.

By the time he'd caught her up, he found his voice again: 'I tried to see you.'

'I know you did,' she said, still walking. 'Adrek at the Wayfarers told me you'd been by.'

'Three times,' he told her, getting breathless from keeping up. 'Whenever we were near Thesk. I sent you letters.'

'I got 'em,' she said. 'That was sweet of you. Meant to send some back, but I'm not too much for writin'. This damn war, I been all over everywhere, barely had time to—'

'Hey!' He grabbed her arm. It seemed an unconscionably brave thing to do once he'd done it. She stopped and spun back towards him, looking faintly surprised. After that, there seemed no elegant way out of the situation but to seize her and kiss her properly.

Happily, she didn't batter him for the liberty.

They slowed down a little after that, took their time, got used to one another again. Crake was still in something of a daze. He was used to being wrongfooted by her lack of propriety, but he'd never been so glad of it as today.

They walked through the camp, stepping over bits of uncleared rubble and cracks where weeds had pushed the stone apart. The air was still and cold, taut with expectation. A medical tent was being prepared – last night's casualties had all been ferried to the frigate by now, Samandra explained – and scouts hurried here and there with messages. All around the edge of the landing pad, the crumbled city pressed in. They were an island in a sea of ruin.

'Quite a thing we started, ain't it?' Samandra said, looking over to the west where the sun was sinking through a long wing of feathery cloud towards the shattered skyline. Crake wasn't sure if he meant their relationship or the war, so he made a noise of agreement and waited for her to clarify.

'We ain't found the Azryx tech yet,' she went on. 'We know the Sammies were selling it to the Awakeners from those records Malvery found in the city, but that's about all we do know. Not how much, not what it does, nothin' like that. Even if they got something we should be scared of, might be they don't have the first clue how to make it work. Still, it got the Archduke and his lady going. Final straw, as far as they were concerned.'

'They took their time doing something about it. The Awakeners have been a plague on this country for years.'

'Politicians, huh?' She grinned. 'Reckon they were a bit wary of ticking off half the population.'

'It can't be *half* of them fighting for the Awakeners. The country would be a bloodbath.'

'Half of 'em are believers,' said Samandra. 'But there's a long way between a believer and someone willin' to fight and die for a cause. Specially when you're fightin' against somethin' you don't much want to.'

'They're siding with us? Even in the country?'

'You should've seen the parades in Thesk when the Lady Alixia was born. They love the Archduke and Archduchess, and they love having a new heir. Most people've had it pretty good since the Coalition took down the monarchy. Besides, it ain't the *belief* in the Allsoul we're tryin' to stamp out. People can believe what they want. It's the sons of bitches stealin' from their pockets we're tryin' to take down. The ones at the top.'

'I imagine Maurin Grist's research that showed the Awakeners were employing daemons in their ranks must have shaken things up a bit, too.'

'Some of 'em are scared by that,' she agreed. 'Rumours been flying since midsummer. They're beginnin' to think it just might be true.' She jammed her hat back on her head and adjusted the tilt. 'People ain't stupid. It's just the fanatics we're fightin'. Don't matter what you tell *them*.'

Crake found himself lost in admiration for her penetrating insight into the popular attitude. Then he shook himself and realised that he was probably just in love.

'And what are the Awakeners doing here?' he asked, waving a hand to indicate the city all around them.

'That we don't know. But whatever they're up to, we caught 'em on the hop. Been driving 'em back towards the chasm. Soon they're gonna have to run for it or we'll push 'em off.'

'Can't you just fly over the top, get behind them or something?' Crake said.

'They brought anti-aircraft guns. Not like ours, but enough to take down anythin' overhead. So we have to fly at night, and then you can't see a damn thing among the broken buildings. They've got the chasm at their back, so gettin' over that way would be more trouble than it's worth.' She pursed her lips in consternation. Crake found that unbearably pretty. 'They're dug in tight. Question is, what are they doin' here in the first place? Where's the sense fightin' over Korrene?'

'Because the Allsoul told them to?'

She gave him a wry look.

'I'm serious,' he said. 'They believe in predictions and patterns and all of that. I mean, they really *believe* the Allsoul can show them the future. Maybe one of the Grand Oracles just flipped the wrong card and they ended up invading this heap of rubble.'

'So what would've happened if they flipped the right card?'

'They'd have tried to invade the sea.'

She laughed at that, a loud and indelicate laugh not at all befitting a lady. It was music to his ears anyway. 'I'd love it if they were that dumb,' she said. She tipped back her hat and scratched under the brim. 'Anyway, probably we'll never know. Goin' in for a big push in a few hours. If this don't drive 'em out, nothin' will.'

She looked him over as if something had occurred to her. 'Wait, why are you here anyway? I mean, not that I ain't glad.'

Frey had told them to keep it quiet, but Crake had promised himself he wouldn't deceive Samandra again. Not after last time. It was an easy decision to make.

'Officially, we're escorting that whispermonger, Pelaru. Unofficially, we're looking for his business partner. He disappeared in the fighting, while he was searching for treasure or something. Honestly, I didn't ask too much. It's important to the Cap'n, that's all I know.'

'Huh,' said Samandra. 'Frey and his schemes, eh?'

'You have to admire his sense of adventure.'

'That you do.'

'Well, no doubt you'll be able to get in there and get your hands dirty if that's what you're after. We've already got half the Shacklemores working for us, nobody's going to say no to a few more guns.'

Crake felt his mouth go dry. 'Half the—?' he began, and then stopped.

'Yeah. Shacklemores. Look.' She pointed over at where a group of men were bivouacked on the edge of the landing pad, dressed in dour trench coats and low black hats, cleaning their shotguns. 'Lot of bounty hunters have gone merc for the Navy. Pay's better in these troubled times.'

Shacklemores. Spit and blood, after all this time I'd almost forgotten they were after me.

Samandra became concerned. 'Oh, hey, you've gone all pale. You worried about the fight? I forget how shit you are with a gun sometimes.' Then she grinned and slapped him on the shoulder. 'Don't worry about a thing, you brave little daemon-botherer. I'm gonna be needed on the front line, but you got your friends to look after you. Come the mornin', this'll all be over, and after that I'm damn well due a couple days off.'

When he didn't reply, she nudged him. 'Well? How about it?'

'How about what?'

'Two days. Leave. Go somewhere?' She rolled her eyes. 'Do I got to *throw* myself at you?'

It suddenly clicked into place. 'Oh! Er . . . yes! Yes, of course! And if the Cap'n has a problem with it, well, I'll just quit or something.' He gave her an unsteady grin.

'Well, alright then.' She smiled. 'So you just keep yourself safe till then, you hear?'

Crake glanced at the Shacklemores one last time, then looked away before they could notice his attention. 'I aim to,' he said.

Six

Harkins Takes Flak – A Warzone –
'Now We Got a Problem' – Dynamite – Jez Is On Her Game

Harkins screamed as the night sky exploded in front of him. He banked away from the blast, his Firecrow rattling and shuddering as it was battered by concussion. Shrapnel pinged off the canopy, inches from his head.

All across Korrene, the darkness was lighting up. Anti-aircraft guns spat explosive shells at the half-seen shapes slipping low over the city streets. Tracer fire drifted up from colossal autocannons. The Coalition aircraft flew without lights, sallying out from the safety of the forward base. They were ferrying hundreds of soldiers to strategic drop-points in the heart of the shattered city. From there, they intended to encircle the Awakener troops and drive them out for good.

Harkins didn't care about their grand plan. He was only concerned with making it to tomorrow.

Another shell exploded close by, shaking him violently in his seat. He screamed again.

'Will you *shut up*, you brown-arsed pansy?' Pinn yelled at him through the earcuffs. 'I can't think straight with you howling in my ear.'

You can't think at all, you fat moron. Harkins imagined himself saying it, pictured the look of shock on Pinn's face. Maybe he'd be so angry he'd choke on his own porky cheeks and fly into a building. Wouldn't that be fun?

But Harkins didn't say anything. Pinn would only come back with something worse, and double his humiliation. He'd long ago learned that defiance got you nowhere.

The flak eased off as the guns aimed at other craft, and now they were all but invisible again. He looked for the *Ketty Jay*, having lost her momentarily, and found the glow of her thrusters in the dark. Pinn's Skylance was somewhere nearby, tracking the larger craft just as he was.

Harkins tried to ignore the explosions and concentrated on following the Cap'n. He wasn't too sure where they were going – he didn't concern himself with stuff like that – but he wasn't too happy that the whispermonger was calling the shots. He didn't like newcomers at the best of times, and especially foreigners, who were not to be trusted. Even Silo, whom he'd known for years, made him uneasy on account of being Murthian.

Then again, most people unsettled him for one reason or another. And none more than Jez, nowadays. He couldn't believe he'd actually *fancied* her once upon a time.

Another explosion lit up the *Ketty Jay*'s lumpy, ugly form in silhouette. She slewed away to port and Harkins followed, his teeth gritted with the effort of keeping quiet. He'd flown through much heavier fire than this before, but it distressed him nonetheless. At least you could see your enemy in a dogfight. With anti-aircraft guns, you were just waiting for a shell to come from nowhere and blow you to pieces. The tension was awful.

He tried to reassure himself. *It's not so bad. Looks worse than it is.*

And it was true. Muzzle flashes lit up small patches in the broken sea of buildings beneath them, but there were not many guns, and their shots were speculative. Already he saw Coalition craft sinking down towards the streets, their belly lights coming on as they dropped below the flak, easing themselves into their designated landing spots.

'How'd he get to be such a good pilot when he's such a chickenshit?' Ashua's words from last night. He thought she was probably trying to be kind, but she had a rough way of showing it which he didn't like.

You'd be scared too, if you'd seen what I have, he told her in his head. Two wars. Friends shot down, and then more friends. So many brushes with death that he'd lost count. It was enough to crack a man, and it had.

He heard engines growing to starboard, and looked over as a troop carrier slid through the sky twenty metres off his wing. A distant flash threw light on its flank, illuminating the insignia of the Coalition Navy. Just for a moment Harkins was back there, back in the war, back in formation. Flying into battle against the Sammies with that

familiar cold fear in his gut, but also the strength that came from cameraderie, the knowledge that he was part of a unit, the pride of fighting with his companions for a cause. In that world there had been no ambiguity, no uncertainty, no questions. He had a purpose and a place.

Something warm swelled in his chest at the memory. He wasn't always a coward. He'd been brave once. He could be brave again.

The *Ketty Jay* banked off to port, heading away from the Coalition craft. Harkins followed, and the troop carrier faded into the dark.

The sight of that Coalition insignia had lasted only an instant, but the feeling took a long time to fade.

The Cap'n put the *Ketty Jay* down in the courtyard of a half-demolished mansion. The walls of the yard were mostly broken and had slumped into heaps of rubble and brick, but they were still high enough to provide concealment on three sides. Belly lights came on as they neared the ground, flooding the cracked square in harsh whiteness. They descended fast and landed with a jarring thump.

'Everybody out!' Silo yelled, as he opened the cargo ramp. They moved at his command, hurrying down into the yard, where they took up defensive positions, their breath steaming the air. He went out with them, surveying the area for signs of the enemy. As soon as Pinn and Harkins had landed, the Cap'n killed the lights. His outflyers' engines faded to silence. Silo listened, and heard distant gunfire over the sound of autocannons and anti-aircraft guns. Nothing moved in the shadows. They were well hidden; it was a good spot.

Frey, Jez and Pelaru made their way down the ramp. Some of the crew were carrying backpacks, all but empty except for ammo. They'd be used to carry loot. Crake's pack was heavier, full of daemonist equipment. Bess stamped and clanked along behind him. She seemed agitated; the sounds of combat in the air had excited her.

Pelaru gave her a glance, but no more than that. Silo watched him narrowly. Most people were more than a little fazed by their first sight of an eight-foot metal golem. That meant he either knew about her already, or he was used to stranger things.

Ain't sure about that one, he thought. *Ain't sure at all. There's somethin' between him and the Cap'n. Him and Jez, too.*

Harkins and Pinn had clambered out of their cockpits and joined them on the ground by now. 'Harkins,' said the Cap'n, 'you stay here with Bess, make sure no one gets near the craft. They're our only way out of here, and I don't plan on getting stuck in this dump.'

'Yessir!' said Harkins, saluting. Frey gave him an odd look. If it had come from anyone but Harkins, he might have suspected he was being mocked. Nobody saluted on the *Ketty Jay*.

'We're not taking Bess?' Pinn complained.

'You reckon she can climb over these?' Frey replied, indicating the piles of rubble that surrounded them. 'She's too clumsy for this terrain. She'll hold us up. Besides, the idea is to stay out of any fights.'

'You picked an awfully strange location for it, then,' said Crake, who was watching the explosions overhead.

'No sense standin' about. You heard the Cap'n. Get movin'!' Silo barked, ushering them towards the ruined walls.

'Think I liked him better when he didn't speak,' Pinn muttered to Crake as he trotted off.

They clambered over the precarious rubble pile with a certain amount of knocks and bruises. On the other side was a narrow street, narrowed further by the slopes of bricks and debris that had fallen into it. There was nobody about, but Silo could hear pistols and rifles not too far away. The ground troops had engaged.

'Which way?' Frey asked Pelaru.

The whispermonger consulted a small cloth map and compass. After a moment of deliberation, he pointed.

'That map accurate?' Frey asked doubtfully as they headed off. It looked hand-drawn.

'It's a copy of the one Osger was using,' Pelaru said. 'He believed it was. So do I.'

The whispermonger glanced at Jez then, and quickly away. He didn't show much beneath his unflappable veneer, but Murthians were the same way, and Silo was adept at picking up small signs. He saw the slight flush of Pelaru's cheek, a hint of anger, the way his pupils dilated fractionally.

Reckon he likes her, he thought, and was faintly amazed. *Reckon he likes her and he don't like that he does. What's that all mean?*

They headed up the street, shotguns and revolvers at the ready. The night was crisp and brittle. Black and broken buildings rose up on either side, silhouetted by flashes in the sky. The sound of gunfire and autocannons had them all on edge. They ran with shoulders hunched, expecting to be shot at.

Silo wasn't sure what the Cap'n was up to, bringing them to a place like this, but he had his suspicions. The Cap'n hadn't mentioned Trinica once since she left him back in Samarla. That was evidence enough that he was hurting about it. He'd chased that women to the North Pole before. He'd taken on the Manes to save her. Only a fool would think he'd given up now.

Silo understood. He knew what love might make a man do. And better this than following some patriotic dream of joining the war on the Coalition's side, as Malvery would have it. The civil war wasn't their fight: Silo and Frey agreed on that. They might have helped start it, but that didn't mean they had to die in it.

Yet here they were. The Cap'n had assured the crew that the heavy fighting was elsewhere in the city, and even though this was supposed to be a rescue mission, it was really all about the loot they'd find in that temple. But that was only a sweetener to justify the risk they were taking. There were easier pickings than this to be found, and they all knew it. It was a measure of their loyalty to the Cap'n that they went along with it anyway.

Frey consulted with Pelaru at a junction, and they turned a corner into a wide street. They were in a newer part of the city, where the stones were not as ancient as the twisted, winding lanes at its heart. Here, some walls and buildings had resisted the last quake. They survived partially or in sections, mazy with creepers. But now the explosions overhead were disturbing the fragile structures. Huge pieces of stone came tumbling down from a crumbling tower that overlooked the street.

'Watch yourselves,' said Frey quietly.

They moved on. The ground had split and bucked in chunks and slabs, and they were forced to navigate their way through the uneven terrain.

'Just like home,' Ashua murmured, slipping up alongside Silo, her eyes scanning the darkness.

'Someone's gonna turn an ankle on this ground,' Malvery grumbled.

'If that's the most we have to worry about,' Crake said, 'I'll be—'

He was cut off by a volley of gunfire. Stone sparked and puffed. Silo felt a bullet whip past him.

'Down!' Frey yelled, and they scrambled for cover as more bullets came their way. They crammed themselves behind rubble shields and made hasty barricades of tipped-up blocks of road.

'Up the street!' Ashua called. Silo saw gun flashes there; dark figures with rifles peeped out of concealment. He aimed and loosed off a blast with his shotgun to keep their heads down for a moment.

'I see four!' said Ashua.

'Five,' Jez corrected.

One of their attackers went scampering across the street, switching cover for a better angle. Ashua leaned out and fired her pistol. There was a squawk from the darkness.

'Four,' Ashua said.

'Cap'n,' Silo said. 'They in cover. Ain't good. We can go back, work our way around.'

Frey thought about that for a moment. 'Right,' he said. 'Scout it out. Find us a path.'

Silo grunted and headed back along the street, keeping low. Once, there had been a time when he wouldn't have raised his voice. Once, he'd been content to take orders and take no responsibility for anything. Those days were past. The Cap'n had made him his second-in-command, and he took his new position seriously. He wasn't the man he'd been when he came on board the *Ketty Jay*, starving and running for his life. He had the Cap'n to thank for that. Most of the others had similar reasons to thank him.

The Coalition weren't his people. The Awakeners weren't his people. Even the free Murthians back home didn't much want him any more, now that Ehri was leading them. His people were the crew of the *Ketty Jay*, and it was his job to keep them safe.

So keep 'em safe.

He made his way back to the corner and looked around to check the coast was clear. It wasn't. He saw a half-dozen men coming warily up the street, no doubt drawn by the *Ketty Jay*'s landing. Men with rifles, closing in on their position. If the crew were caught between the two forces, they'd be cut to pieces.

Mother, he thought. *Now we got a problem.*

★

Malvery popped up from cover and let fly again with his shotgun. He didn't have much hope of hitting anything, not with the enemy scrunched down like that. It didn't stop him trying, though.

Silo was signalling from the corner. 'Ashua, Pinn, Crake!' Frey said. 'Go help Silo. I could do without more Awakeners crawling up my arse.'

More gunfire came their way as they scampered off. Malvery listened to the zing and whine of ricochets. Wasting bullets, the lot of them. They were trapped here for the moment. He took a pot-shot anyway, for something to do. He had to let off the tension somehow.

'What are we here for, Cap'n?' he snarled, suddenly angry. 'What are we really here for?'

Frey looked across at him. So did Pelaru. Neither said anything.

'Better be bloody worth it,' he growled.

He wasn't even mad at the Cap'n, not really. He'd been getting these little fits of frustration more and more often lately. Malvery was usually a jolly sort, slow to anger and quick to forgive, and he didn't like himself when he got in these moods. It was just this whole damn war. This war, and his part in it.

A new battle started up on the corner: Silo and his team scrapping it out with the Awakeners coming up behind them. Malvery kept his mind on what was ahead of him. He peeked out from hiding, saw nothing up the street but a jumble of broken shapes. The artillery fire overhead was petering out, and the night crackled with pistol shots. Most of the Coalition craft were down now, their troops storming the Awakener positions.

Something bounced near him and rolled to a halt near his feet. Something bright and fizzing. Dynamite.

'Oooooohbollocksbollocksbollocks!' he babbled as he scrambled towards it. He scooped it up in one meaty hand and lobbed it away. A second later there was a dull *bang* in his right ear and he was knocked flat. Suddenly everything was muffled, except for a high-pitched whistling that seemed to go on and on. He looked about, dazed, not quite sure where he was until Frey seized him and pulled him down.

'Doc! Doc! You alright?'

Malvery managed a nod. Dimly, he heard somebody shooting. The

Awakeners must've managed to sneak closer than they thought if they were within throwing range.

Beyond Frey, Pelaru was firing over a barricade at somebody up the street. Malvery frowned. Something was wrong. It took him a moment to realise what it was.

'Where's Jez?' he asked, his voice sounding thick inside his skull.

Frey looked around. 'Where *is* Jez?'

There was a sharp *crack* from somewhere nearby, and a cry. An Awakener came stumbling out from cover, holding his back. He was a Sentinel, dressed in a grey, high-collared cassock. Pelaru sighted and shot him neatly through the head.

For a whispermonger, that feller can certainly handle a gun, thought Malvery. He was coming back to himself now, the shock of the dynamite fading. Thankfully it hadn't been too near when it went off. Or the fuse hadn't been cut half a centimetre shorter.

There was another *crack*: a rifle shot. Frey looked up and Malvery followed his gaze.

'*There* she is,' said the Cap'n, with a little smile on his face.

She was crouched in the remnants of the ruined tower, sighting through a gap in the wall at the street below. How she'd got up there so fast, Malvery couldn't say, but she had an elevated position now, which made the Awakeners' cover all but useless. When she was on her game, Jez was a phenomenal shot. And she was on her game tonight. Another shot, and a scream from the darkness.

'Come on,' said Frey. 'Let's give her a hand.'

They opened up with their weapons, blasting away down the street. It was more to cause chaos than anything, because Jez was handling the sniper work. She took out another Sentinel. The last one was flushed out and fled. Frey shot him in the back, which was his preferred angle of approach when it came to killing someone.

'Silo!' Frey yelled. 'How we doing back there?'

'Got 'em pinned down,' came the reply.

'Leave 'em. We're clear this way.'

Jez hopped out of the tower onto the lip of a wall and dropped four metres to the ground, landing like a cat. Pelaru stared at her. She stared back, her head tilted, like something feral studying a curious new find.

'Good one, Jez,' said Frey.

'Yeah,' said Malvery, mustering up a camaraderie he didn't really feel. 'Nice work.' He slapped her on the shoulder, and her head snapped round. He thought for a moment she was going to attack him.

'Thanks,' she said, without the slightest emotion in her voice.

Malvery took his hand away, unsettled. He harrumphed and headed off after the Cap'n, eager to be away from her. He liked Jez, he really did. He just didn't know how long he could handle having her on the crew.

Silo and the others caught them up as they reached the end of the street and found a five-way junction. One side of it had caved in, but most of the buildings were still standing. Pelaru checked his map again again scanned his surroundings intently.

'Do you actually have any idea what we're looking for?' Frey asked impatiently.

Pelaru's face cleared, and he pointed at a doorway with an ancient coat of arms still barely visible above it. 'That,' he said.

Seven

The Pumping House – Fictions – Crake Loses His Dignity –
A Precipitous Crossing – Wards

Pelaru led them across the junction, once they'd established that there were no troops around. Frey hurried everybody after him. He wanted to get off the street. The Awakeners that had been fighting with Silo's team would come up on their rear if they weren't quick.

The doorway was the entrance to a tall, narrow building which stood at the junction between two roads. Its roof had fallen in and chunks of the façade had broken off, but the structure was intact otherwise. Frey glanced at the coat of arms as he approached. It belonged to some duke or another, possibly the symbol for the Duchy of Banbarr, within whose borders Korrene lay. It didn't look very grand, so it was likely some kind of municipal building. There were letters carved across the frontage, but the stonework was too shattered to guess at the words.

The door had once been stout wood, banded in iron, but it had rotted and warped and now stood half-open on rusted hinges. They squeezed past it and found themselves in a chilly corridor scattered with broken tiles and chunks of stone that had fallen from the cracked ceiling.

'What is this place?' Frey asked the whispermonger.

'An old pumping station,' Pelaru said.

'The relics are here?' Frey said doubtfully.

'If it were that easy, don't you think they'd have been found by now?' Pelaru replied. He was impatient, eager to get on and find his partner. Frey let him lead.

You'd better know what you're doing.

They made their way along the corridor. It was bare and lightless, and they had to break out gas lamps from Crake's pack. A nearby

61

explosion made the building shiver, and dust sifted down from the ceiling. Frey looked uneasily at the cracks in the wall, and wondered just how stable this place was.

They passed doorways that led into small rooms containing decayed office furniture, and chambers crowded with flaking pipes covered in levers and turn-wheels.

'I tried to stop him,' Pelaru muttered, almost to himself.

'Your partner? Osger?' Frey prompted. He was keen to get Pelaru talking. The Thacian had volunteered precious little information so far, but Frey had the sense he wanted to unburden himself. Whisper-mongers were renowned for being ruthless in their dealings, acting without emotion, respecting only money and taking no sides. But beneath his calm exterior, Pelaru was agitated and distressed. Even Frey could see that.

'Osger was obsessed with Awakener relics,' Pelaru said. 'When he heard about this place, there was no reasoning with him. And you can be sure I tried.'

'So he went looking for this shrine? What's so special about it?'

Pelaru cast him a glance, with that haughty expression on his sculpted features that made Frey feel that he was being looked down on.

Thacians, he thought. *So very punchable.*

'If the story is true, this shrine has been hidden away for a century. Even before the quake hit, it was only a rumour. Afterward, it was thought lost, if it had ever existed at all.'

'So what's changed?'

'An explorer,' said Pelaru. 'Godber Blinn. He claimed to have found the shrine, and had with him a relic as evidence. Nobody believed him: the relic could have come from anywhere. But when Osger heard about him, he had me find the man and we listened to his story. He was demanding an exorbitant amount to reveal the details of its location.'

'Sounds like a con artist to me,' said Frey.

'That was my reaction. Though he'd always been honest in his dealings in the past, as far as I could determine. Regardless, Osger believed him. In the end we made sure the information stayed exclusive to us.'

'Oh yeah? How?'

Pelaru gave him a long, reptilian stare. The kind of look that said: *Don't ask.* And you didn't need to, after that. Frey wondered if he'd underestimated this man. Maybe he was bluffing, or maybe he was a damn sight colder than Frey had given him credit for.

'Why didn't Blinn just loot the place and sell the treasure himself?' Frey asked.

'Because he was scared.'

'Of what?'

Pelaru's face hardened slightly. 'Fictions,' he said, and wouldn't say any more.

The corridor ended in a spacious rectangular hall, dominated by several huge pumps, their pistons and screws drab with dust and shadow in the lanternlight. Most of the ceiling had fallen in, and the floor was cluttered with debris.

'Look for a way down,' said Pelaru. 'It'll be here somewhere.'

They split up into three groups and made their way through the hall. Ashua went with Frey and Pelaru. Frey noticed Pelaru glancing in Jez's direction as she moved off with another group.

There it is again, he thought. *This man has way too many secrets.*

The darkness brought on an instinctive hush, and they moved quietly. Outside, they could hear the crackle of gunfire and the occasional explosion. The fighting was not far off.

'I worked it out,' said Ashua to Pelaru. 'Why the Awakeners are here. This Korrene place is dead, right? No strategic value, no resources worth taking, not even a particularly good place for a stronghold. Only one reason they're expending so much effort here.' Her eyes shone slyly in the lanternlight. 'They're after the same thing Osger was, aren't they?'

Frey watched Pelaru closely. The same thought had crossed his mind.

'I can only guess at their intentions,' said the Thacian. 'But yes, it seems likely. Blinn told a lot of people what he'd found in Korrene before we found him. But he told only us the exact location.'

'So they came here to find it,' said Frey. 'But the Coalition got wind of their movements and intercepted them. Now the Awakeners are trying to hold out long enough to find this shrine.'

'They must really want those relics, huh?' said Ashua.

'Maybe,' said Pelaru. 'Maybe they just want to be sure no one else gets to them.'

Frey grabbed Pelaru's arm and pulled him round roughly. He stared hard into the other man's eyes.

'I'm sick of games, Pelaru. What's in that shrine?'

Pelaru held his gaze a long time, not in the least intimidated. 'I don't know and I don't care,' he said. 'Osger was excited but he wouldn't tell me why. He said it would be a surprise. He was the one interested in relics, not me.' He shook off Frey's hand and looked away into the dark. 'I want to find him. That's all.'

'Hey!' called Malvery. 'Over here!'

They converged on the doctor, who was standing near the top of a caged spiral staircase which drilled downward. Frey went first. After dragging his long-suffering crew into the middle of a warzone, leading from the front was the least he could do. It took the edge off the guilt a little.

'As long as I don't abuse their loyalty, I can look at myself in the mirror. The day I do is the day I don't deserve to lead them. Same applies to you.'

Trinica's words, that she'd spoken to him during one wonderful night in a restaurant in Samarla. She'd been talking about her crew, the crew of that rot-damned frigate she was shackled to. The crew that she'd chosen over him, in the end. Because her feelings for him were putting them in danger. Just as he was doing now, with his crew, for her.

I should give it up, he thought. *I've got a good thing here. Good friends, good times. We can ride out the war in style and we'll still be standing at the end of it. Forget Pelaru, forget Trinica. Turn around now, fly into the sunset and enjoy the rest of your life.*

But he couldn't. He just couldn't.

As he descended, he noticed a foul smell, growing stronger with each step. A stench of wet decay, of slime, of shit and things un-imaginably worse. By the time he reached the bottom, it was making his eyes water. He could hear groans of disgust from the men above him.

'Come on, fellers,' he said, summoning up some brio. 'It's not that bad.'

'Cap'n,' said Malvery steadily. 'It smells like I just buried my face in Pinn's cavernous arse flaps.'

Pinn's riposte was a pointedly vicious fart, more eloquent than anything he could have managed with words. Ashua broke into hysterics somewhere up the stairway.

Pelaru gave Frey a flat look: *This is your crew?* Frey grinned at him and shrugged.

At the end of a short corridor was a heavy iron door, standing open. The stench was emanating from there. Frey poked his lantern through and looked out into the sewers.

They were at the end of a narrow tunnel. Light from Frey's lantern shone on damp brick. Droplets glinted in the light as they oozed free and plopped from the ceiling. There was a stone walkway on the near side, raised above the level of the scummed and foetid water. It had been stagnant for fifty years, and the stink was appalling. Clumps of unidentifiable muck bobbed near the mouldering body of a massive rat. Further up the tunnel, globules of congealed fat had formed a small white island.

Frey looked back at Pelaru. 'You're sure this is the way?' he asked, rather hoping for a negative.

Pelaru brandished another piece of cloth with another map on it, this time a sketch of the sewer network. 'Perfectly sure,' he said.

They made their way into the sewers, sticking to the walkway. Crake hadn't gone ten metres before he had to stop and throw up into the water. When he was done, he stood there wheezing, leaning on his knees, wiping his mouth with a handkerchief.

'You alright?' Frey asked him.

Crake gave him an accusing glare. 'I thought I'd given up all dignity long ago when I joined this crew,' he said. 'But this? This is a new low, Frey.'

'It's character-building,' said Frey. 'Does you aristocrats good to get down in the shit with the rest of us every now and then.' He gave Crake a comradely slap on the back of his pack, which inspired the daemonist to bring up what little was left in his stomach.

Pelaru led them deeper into the sewers. They passed through junctions and over little arched bridges that crossed the still water. The dark was oppressive, but it held no terrors for Frey, who'd seen plenty worse. Rats squabbled and splashed out of sight. The conflict in the streets above was too far away to be heard. Once, Frey spotted a pair of shining eyes watching them from beyond the range of the lantern light, and his heart jumped in his chest; but it was only Jez, who'd dropped behind and was tailing them.

Frey's reservations about the mission began to fade. There didn't seem to be any Awakeners down here. If darkness and stink were all they had to worry about, then maybe it wouldn't be so bad after all.

He was about to say as much when a dreadful howl echoed through the sewers. It rose and fell like a klaxon; a bone-chilling, deathly sound that sawed at the nerves and set their teeth on edge.

'Um,' said Ashua, when silence had returned. 'What was that?'

'The wind?' said Frey. It was a wishful suggestion at best.

'That,' said Crake, 'was *not* the wind.'

Frey looked at Pelaru. 'You said something about fictions?' he prompted.

'Tales,' said Pelaru. 'Rumours. That's all.'

'Enlighten us,' Crake said.

'Ever since the quake, people have told stories about this place. A ghost city must have its ghosts.'

'But Blinn believed in them,' Frey pointed out.

'Blinn believed in a lot of things. Not all of them were real,' Pelaru snapped, suddenly harsh.

'Might be you thought that before,' said Silo, his deep bass voice echoing in the tunnel. 'Might be you were wrong.'

Pelaru cast him a poisonous glance, but said nothing.

'Eyes peeled, everyone,' said Frey, and they made their way onward.

They hadn't gone far before they found a fissure in the tunnel wall, wide enough to enter one by one. Pelaru headed inside without explanation, and Frey went after him, holding his lantern up. He heard Crake struggling through, the pack on his back clanking, and Malvery squeezing in with a grunt.

'Least we're getting away from that damned stink,' the doctor said, huffing out his moustaches.

The fissure widened quickly, opening out into an underground grotto. As their lanterns came through and light swelled, they saw that a chasm split the grotto from side to side, ten metres wide at its narrowest point.

Then Pelaru cried out, and Frey swung his lantern round to see what had excited him. Strung across the chasm were two thick ropes, one above the other. The first was set at shoulder-height, secured by pitons in the walls of the grotto. The other was at ground level, wrapped around spikes driven securely into the stone floor.

'They were here!' said Pelaru. He hurried over to examine the pitons. 'Yes, yes. This is Yort metal; he had a set of these. It's him!'

Malvery had gone over to the edge of the chasm and was looking down doubtfully. Silo tested the ropes, yanking on them hard, and tried his weight on the lower one.

'Looks secure, Cap'n,' said Silo.

But Malvery shook his head. 'Uh-uh. You're not gettin' me on that. Not a chance.'

'You scared of heights or something?' Pinn sneered.

'Nope,' said Malvery. He was looking at Frey. 'Just don't fancy trustin' my life to a piece of rope. Not when I don't see the point of it.'

Frey saw the defiance in his eyes. There wasn't much discipline on the *Ketty Jay*; it was loyalty that made them work well together, not fear of punishment. But Malvery's loyalty had been eroded of late, with the civil war and all of that. The doc was giving him a push, to see what he'd do.

Frey recognised a man who was trying to start a fight. Malvery's battle wasn't with him, but with himself. And Frey wasn't about to make anyone do anything they didn't want to.

'Fine,' said Frey. 'Stay. That goes for anyone else who doesn't want to come. We'll pick you up on the way back.'

'Wait, *he* gets to stay?' Pinn complained. 'Alright then, I'm staying too.'

'Scared of heights?' Ashua asked sweetly.

Frey made a noise that indicated he didn't much care whether Pinn came or not. 'Anyone else?'

Ashua looked at the rope bridge and shrugged. 'Looks pretty safe to me.'

'Ain't much of a thing,' said Silo.

'Between certain death and Pinn's conversation, I know which one I'd choose,' quipped Crake.

'You've got sick in your beard,' Pinn returned spitefully.

Jez took a running jump and cleared the chasm in a single bound. That shut them all up. Frey let his head sink into his hand.

'Jez,' he said. 'You remember we had that talk about keeping your, er, *condition* under wraps?' He waved a hand vaguely towards Pelaru, who was wearing a look of amazement on his face.

'Sorry, Cap'n,' she said, her eyes white discs in the dark. 'Thought I'd save some time.'

Pelaru opened his mouth and closed it again.

'Don't ask,' said Frey. 'Let's go.'

He left his lantern with Malvery and Pinn and walked over to the rope bridge. Not long ago he'd have let someone else take the risk of going first, but of late he'd developed a certain doggedness that surprised even himself. Anything that got between him and finding Trinica was an obstacle to be overcome, and the faster he got on with it, the better. He had a promise to keep, a purpose at last.

It was just a rope bridge, after all. With what he'd been through, it wasn't that much of a challenge, surely?

The chasm wasn't wide, but the black drop beneath his feet made it seem wider. He held on to the upper rope, which was taut, and tried the lower one with his feet. It was thick and as stable as he could hope for. Shuffling carefully side-foot, he made his way along it, hanging tight to the upper rope in case he slipped.

'Don't look down!' Pinn called helpfully.

Frey, being a contrary sort, did exactly that. He regretted it immediately. The abyss sucked the courage out of him. He felt the heat drain from his body, his strength leaking away. Suddenly he was weak and frail and his position seemed terribly precarious. Until that moment, it had been possible to ignore how slim the margin for error was. Now he was reminded that one misstep would see him plunge into the chasm. And it was a long, long way down.

He tore his eyes away, doing his best to keep his face composed. The most important thing was not to look scared for the others. He knew they were watching him.

'No problem!' he said, with a forced cheeriness that sounded fake even to him.

His steps became miniscule, shifting his boots centimetres at a time. His hands clutched hard, and refused to let go, so that he had to drag them along the rope and burn his palms on the hemp. He felt very cold, and yet he was sweating.

Centimetre by centimetre. *Don't look down,* he told himself, echoing Pinn. And then, just to be bloody-minded, he did so again. It was even worse the second time. He swallowed and faced forward.

'Go on, Cap'n!' said Pinn. 'You're almost halfway there!'

Frey felt his heart sink. Almost halfway. He'd thought he was nearly at the end. There was more of this torment to go. How did he get himself into these situations?

Slowly, with infinite concentration, he moved along the ropes. They were stout and stable, but even the small amount of give they had sent him into flutters of panic. As long as he kept his feet and hands connected to the rope, he'd be alright. As long as the rope didn't break.

When he reached the other side, he was genuinely surprised. He stepped off the rope, moved a safe distance from the edge of the chasm. Suddenly, all his misgivings were forgotten, and his bravado reasserted itself. What had he been worried about, anyway? It was easy! If it had been half a metre off the ground instead of hanging over a bottomless pit, he'd have practically run across it! He'd never been in any danger of falling for a moment!

He grinned at Jez and then waved his hands over the chasm at the others. 'Come on, fellers!' he called. 'Nothing to it!'

It took some time, but soon they were safely on the other side, with Crake looking more than a little relieved as he adjusted his pack. Frey looked back to Malvery and Pinn, hunkered down in a circle of light.

'Shout if you see that bloody awful thing we heard earlier, eh?' he called maliciously.

'Right-o,' said Malvery, not concerned in the least. 'You too.'

'Wait, I forgot about that!' Pinn said. 'Hey, Cap'n, wait a minute! I'm coming!'

'You made your choice, Pinn!' Frey said. 'See you later.' He led them off down a new fissure, with Pinn's increasingly frantic protests echoing in his ears.

Pelaru was becoming visibly agitated now, hurrying them along when he could. He sensed they were getting closer, and his Thacian composure had all but deserted him. Shortly afterwards, a break in the fissure wall led them into a corridor of dank brick, evidently an underground passageway of some kind. It was partially collapsed, but a way had been cleared, and there were fresh bootprints in the dust.

'Come on,' said Pelaru. 'Not far now. It's not—'

'Wait,' said Crake, holding his hand up. He frowned.

'What's up?' Frey asked.

Crake said nothing. Instead he took a lantern from Silo and began poking around the rubble. He picked up a brick and examined it closely.

'Crake?' Frey said again.

'He's right, Cap'n,' said Jez. 'Something's wrong here. A feeling. Like . . . *crawling* on my skin.'

Crake held out the brick so Frey could see it. There were markings carved on one side. 'There are other bricks around here, with more markings.'

'What are they?' Frey asked, bemused.

'Well, from what I can make out, they look like wards. Daemonist wards.'

Frey felt a trickle of ice pass down his spine. He'd had enough of daemons to last several lifetimes. 'Meaning what?'

'Meaning there was a wall here covered in wards,' said Crake. He tossed the brick aside. 'Powerful ones, too. I can still sense them, even now. Probably the wall came down with the quake.'

'And whatever they were keeping out got in,' said Ashua.

'That, or the other way round,' Silo added.

Pelaru looked pale. Frey thought of the howl they'd heard earlier. 'Great,' he said. 'That's just bloody marvellous. Crake?'

'I've got some tricks in my pack, Cap'n,' he said. 'Can't be sure they'll—'

He was interrupted by a cry from Pelaru. The whispermonger pushed past them and up the corridor, disappearing beyond the range of the lantern light. Frey ran after him. A few metres on, he caught up, and found Pelaru staring at something on the ground.

There was a body there. The upper half of one, anyway. It was lying face-down across the corridor, having been roughly ripped in half.

Pelaru wore an expression of anguish on his face. 'I . . .' he began, but then his mouth dried up.

Frey walked up to the corpse. 'Calm down, it's not him,' he said. 'Look how withered he is. He's been dead for ages. There's not even any blood.' He hooked his toe under the shoulder of the corpse and flipped it over.

Then it was Frey's turn to yell.

The body flopped onto its back. The head lolled. An emaciated face, frozen in a yawn of sharp and crooked teeth. Glaring yellow eyes staring blindly.

Frey scrambled back behind Pelaru, almost crashing into Silo in his haste to retreat.

'It's a Mane!' he said. 'There are Manes down here!'

But Pelaru staggered forward and dropped to his knees by the body. He slid his arms around the grotesque thing on the ground and cradled its head to his shoulder like it was a baby.

'Half-Mane,' he whispered. 'He was only a half-Mane.'

Eight

Osger's Infection – The Flux Thrower –
A Glamorous Life – The Broken Gibbet

'That's Osger?' Frey asked, barely suppressing his disbelief. 'That's who we've come to find?'

Pelaru didn't reply. He rocked slowly back and forth, hugging his partner's severed body to his own, trembling with the effort of keeping his emotions contained. Crake didn't know whether to be appalled or touched by the bizarre lantern-lit tableau before him.

'Well,' said Ashua chirpily. 'Mission accomplished, I suppose.'

Jez hissed at her, baring her teeth like an animal, making Ashua jump. 'Not the time for jokes,' she said, and suddenly she seemed terrifying. 'Look at him!'

'Your . . . partner was a half-Mane?' Frey asked. And looking at the Thacian now, Crake realised now that Osger must have been more than just a business partner.

'Yes. What of it?' said Pelaru, without raising his head. 'So is your navigator.'

Of course, thought Crake. *He knew the signs. No wonder he was so interested in her.*

'Did he always, er, look like that?' Frey asked.

'Of course not, you fool!' Pelaru snapped. He seemed about to say something else, but he reined himself in, brought himself under control again. His eyes became sad. 'This isn't him,' he said quietly. 'This is his infection.'

He laid down the body on the ground. It was hard to look at, but not frightening. The daemon was gone. What remained was merely a lump of warped meat. Pelaru seemed to think so too, for when he stood up he didn't look at it again.

'Do we need to take him back, bury him or something?' Ashua

asked carefully. She was still a little cowed by Jez. It took a lot to intimidate her, but Jez could do it.

'There's no need,' said Pelaru, suddenly cold. 'But I ought to find the rest of him.'

He walked off up the corridor a little way. Jez almost went after him, then caught Frey's look and didn't.

'What now, Cap'n?' Silo asked.

'What do you think?'

'Reckon we can't be far from that shrine. Ought to take a look while we're here. Seem to remember loot was part of the deal, yuh?' He fixed the captain with a steady gaze. 'Can't think of no other good reason why we'd be down here.'

'Plus one for looting,' said Ashua, raising her hand.

'Whatever you want, Cap'n,' said Jez distractedly.

'Crake?' Frey turned the daemonist.

Crake's instinct was to get out of there as fast as they could. He ignored it. Marshalling all his bitterness, he said 'I want to see what the Awakeners were up to in there.'

But that was only half the truth. For while the others hoped to avoid the thing that had torn Osger apart, Crake hoped to meet it.

Three months ago, he and Frey had faced down a powerful Azryx daemon known as the Iron Jackal. With the help of a Yort explorer called Ugrik and the daemon thralled to Frey's cutlass, they'd trapped and destroyed it. Previous to that, Crake's experience of daemonism had been confined to the sanctum, where he could deal with daemons in a controlled environment. In order to save Frey's life, he'd been forced to take on the Iron Jackal in the field. And he'd won.

Inspired, he'd begun working on more techniques for field daemonism. Instead of lamenting the lack of a good sanctum on board the *Ketty Jay*, he'd embraced it. No longer would he be chained to cumbersome machines and elaborate lairs; no longer would he hide away in the dark as daemonists had for so many years. He'd conduct his research out in the open. His passion for the Art had returned, and he felt like a new man because of it.

But research was no good without testing. And for that, he needed daemons. Terrifying as it was, this was an opportunity not to be missed.

He took off his pack and readied it. Most of the space inside was taken up by a chemical battery. The rest was occupied by a modified resonator, into which he screwed a set of cylinders tipped with a pine-cone arrangement of rods. Then he took a controller from the side pocket of the pack and connected it with wires to the resonator. The controller was large and inelegant, too big to easily hold in one hand. When he hefted the pack onto his shoulders again, the wires ran under his arm and into the pack, and the rods poked up higher than his head. It was clumsy, but it would do.

'Ready,' he said.

'You look like ridiculous,' Frey observed.

'What is that thing you've been lugging around, anyway?' Ashua asked, cocking an eyebrow.

'This,' he said proudly, 'is a flux thrower.'

'A *flux* thrower?' Ashua said. 'Isn't flux, er, when you get sloppy diarrhoea?'

Crake reddened. 'The *other* kind of flux. Sonic flux! You see, the frequencies change constantly and that causes—'

'I'm just saying,' Ashua went on, her voice curving with suppressed amusement. 'Back in the slums, kids used to go down with the flux all the time. Something in the water.'

'There's more than one kind of flux! This will allow me to narrow down on a daemon's primary frequencies and pull it out of phase with our senses, actually send it back to the aether, and—'

''Cause I want to be sure, you know? If that thing's gonna be flinging diarrhoea around, I plan to stand well back.'

Frey was in quiet tears of laughter. Crake shut his mouth. He gave Ashua a glare that communicated the level of betrayal he felt. That she should turn her vicious wit on him. On him!

Pinn came puffing up the corridor. Evidently he'd decided he didn't want to be left behind. Crake was disappointed to see that he hadn't fallen into the chasm.

'You're all bastards,' he told them sullenly.

'Doc not coming?' Silo asked.

'Does it look like he is?'

'What's that on your back?' Pinn asked Crake.

'It's my shit-thrower,' Crake replied primly, before anyone else could get in first. Ashua and Frey fell about in hysterics. Pinn just looked puzzled.

Pelaru returned, dragging the lower half of Osger. He dumped it next to the rest of him, and his expression killed their laughter. Pinn opened his mouth to ask what he'd missed, then didn't bother.

'We're going on,' Frey told Pelaru.

'Alright,' said Pelaru.

'We'll talk later about payment,' said Frey. Crake saw the look that passed between them, the hidden meaning there. Then Pelaru nodded. He seemed defeated.

Some private matter of the Cap'n's, no doubt. Crake wasn't too curious. He had private matters of his own, namely the Shacklemores he'd seen roaming round the camp earlier.

Come the mornin', this'll all be over. So you just keep yourself safe till then, you hear?

Yes. Once they were done, he'd go to Samandra. The thought of it made him thrill with anticipation.

Come the morning. Until then, he had work to do.

Pelaru led them up the corridor, where they found more bodies. These were human and, unlike Osger, they'd bled. The corridor was thick with the stench of them, and dismembered parts were everywhere. Crake wanted to be sick, but he'd already brought up everything he had in the sewer.

What a glamorous life I lead, he thought to himself, and retched.

'You'd think he'd seen enough bodies by now,' Frey said to Silo, as they stepped over the dead.

'Oh, I'm quite alright with the ones that still have their skin on the outside,' Crake replied.

A set of steps joined the corridor, heading upward. Pelaru took them. At the top they found an arched doorway that had previously been blocked by a heavy wooden door. It had been smashed long ago, and only rotted chunks remained. Above the door, their lanterns revealed a symbol etched into the stone. The interlocking lines and spheres of the Cipher.

'Huh,' Frey said. 'Maybe that explorer was on to something.'

They stepped into the shrine and raised their gas lanterns to get a better look. A ruined hall was revealed. There were hints of the grim grandeur it might have once possessed – a section of cornice here, the groin of a vault there – but calamity had spoiled it. The building above had fallen through the ceiling in places. Huge pieces of masonry had tumbled in and smashed the floor where they hit. Piles of rubble were heaped up higher than their heads. One wall had burst and the bedrock had thrust in from the side. It smelt of must and decay and something else, something subtle and insidious that made Crake's senses prickle.

Crake had never been inside an Awakener shrine. None but Awakeners were allowed in. Only they were privy to the inner mysteries of their order, sole keepers of the secret knowledge. Only they could interpret the will of the Allsoul. That way, their believers always needed them.

He hated them. Hated everything they stood for. Daemonism was a science – poorly understood and dangerous, but a science nonetheless – and the purpose of science, in Crake's view, was to further the knowledge of all mankind, not just a select few. The Awakeners hoarded knowledge for their own gain, jealously exterminating their rivals. Perhaps they feared what would happen if people saw what was behind the veil. There was no better example than the Imperators of that.

'This isn't exactly the wealth of riches I was hoping for,' Ashua said, surveying the chamber.

'Split up, dig about a bit,' said Frey. 'Damned if I'm leaving empty-handed now.'

They made their way between the rubble piles, brandishing guns and lanterns. Restless shadows slid among the stones as they passed. Crake saw his companions pulling things from the rubble: once-fine cloth now dusty and ripped; broken icons; a battered gold cup that was still good enough to salvage.

They found bones too, and pieces of skeletons. Some were buried under rubble. Others weren't, but they were broken nonetheless. Crake wondered what had happened to them, and whether it was the same thing that happened to Osger many decades later.

He didn't trouble to search. He wasn't interested in riches. He'd been born with them, and they hadn't done him much good in the end. He was after something else, something he could use against his enemies. Something that would damage them.

What he found was a machine.

It was huge, occupying one end of the hall, where it had been hidden by the dark. Half of it was destroyed, crushed by a cave-in from above, but what was left was enough to get a sense of it. It was a great apparatus of pipes and wires and diodes, of valved tanks and banks of gauges and dials. The stark design and the bulk of its parts told him it was old, perhaps thirty or forty years older than the quake that had destroyed it.

Eighty or ninety years ago, then. That's when they built this machine. He began to put the story together in his head, his scientist's mind assembling and examining the evidence. *And later they sealed up the place with daemonic wards, until it was opened again by the quake. But there are still relics around; they didn't take them when they left. That implies they left in a hurry.*

He looked at the machine. There, at the centre, was a narrow cage somewhat like a gibbet, shaped to fit a person inside. The bars on one side had been bent and twisted by some enormous force.

And then he knew.

Spit and blood. Imperators. They were creating Imperators here.

It all fit. The timing, the secret location. Long ago, a group of daemonists, full of hubris, attempted a grand summoning and accidentally unleashed the Manes. The Awakeners heard what had been done, kidnapped the survivors, and learned how they'd managed it. They refined the technique, and soon after the first Imperators appeared.

They took their most faithful servants and put daemons inside them. And they did it using apparatus like this.

He studied the machine and did some calculations in his head. This wasn't one of the original devices. It was too advanced for that. Imperators had been around for twenty or thirty years by the time this was built, though their powers were cruder then, by the accounts of the day. But this shrine must have been an important place, judging by its size and location. Perhaps they were up to something here, something more ambitious than simply creating more of their terrible enforcers.

He looked at the broken gibbet.

Something that went badly wrong.

Encouraged, he went looking for more evidence, while keeping a wary eye on the darkness beyond his lantern. Whatever was in that cage had escaped, and he'd lay odds that it was the same thing they'd heard howling earlier. Perhaps it was nowhere nearby, or perhaps it was already watching them.

He rounded a huge stone, larger than he was, and caught sight of Pelaru. The whispermonger had found something in the debris, it seemed. He'd put down his lantern and was holding a large grey metal casket in his hands. There was a frown on his face as he examined it. As Crake watched him, the Thacian's expression slackened in realisation. Then he turned his head, and saw that he was being observed. His features became a carefully composed mask again as he met Crake's gaze.

He recognises it, Crake thought. *Damned if he doesn't recognise what he's got.*

But the thought fled his mind as a new sensation crept over him. He recognised this feeling, this faint sense of detachment and unreality, this increasing paranoia and unease. He'd felt it many times before, in the presence of daemons.

He looked around frantically. 'It's here,' he said, his voice echoing up to the roof of the hall.

'You what?' Frey called from elsewhere, loud enough to make Crake flinch. 'You say something, Crake?'

'It's here!' Crake yelled. 'The daemon! It's here!'

From the darkness, something screamed.

Nine

Gristle & Hide – Daemons –
Crake to the Rescue – Running in the Dark

Frey went cold at the sound of that scream. He dropped the relics he was carrying, pulled out his cutlass with one hand and a pistol with the other. Backing up, he scanned the hall, saw nothing.

Suddenly he wished they'd got out of here when they had the chance.

Ashua came hurrying towards him from another direction. 'Cap'n,' she murmured. 'That doesn't sound much like something I wanna meet.'

'Me neither,' said Frey. He raised his voice. 'Time to leave, fellers! This junk's not worth gettin' killed over. Let's leave the nice monster alone, shall we?'

The others were nowhere to be seen, lost amid the rubble. Frey was glad of Ashua by his side. The presence of a woman necessitated bravado, and it helped him to stand firm. Otherwise he might have just legged it. He bloody hated daemons.

That sound again: a tortured shriek, inhuman, possessed of some terrible quality that went across the nerves like a rusty saw. And the *fear*! Damn it, that was the worst. It was what they did to a man, these Manes and Imperators and daemons, that made them so hard to tackle. Just being near them inspired a feeling as unreasoning and primal as a child's terror of a dark wardrobe.

Something moved, up on top of a rubble pile. He whirled and aimed.

Nothing but the skitter and bump of stones and rocks as they tumbled down the slope.

He thought of Osger, and the other bodies out in the corridor. Torn to pieces. Was that what awaited him and his crew?

You should never have brought them here, you selfish son of a bitch.

Silo and Pinn came into view, weapons held ready, and joined them in their retreat towards the door. Silo exchanged a glance with Frey. They didn't need words. They'd been in enough spots like this before. They knew how bad it was.

'There!' Ashua cried. They caught a glimpse of a dark shape dropping through the air. It landed with a heavy thump in front of the door, compressing to a crouch, blocking their path.

It raised itself to its feet. Frey's mouth went dry.

He'd seen Manes, and he'd seen Imperators unmasked. He'd looked the Iron Jackal in the eye. But this was the most horrifying yet, this grotesque, malformed, swollen wreck of a thing. The very sight of it appalled him.

There was enough humanity in its form to see how it had started out, but it was far from human now. Piled cords of veined muscle bulged unevenly all over it, gathered into huge straining knots. One of its arms was three times as thick as the other. Its back was twisted beneath a lopsided hump of gristle and scaly hide. Tendons stood out stark on two-fingered hands.

He'd seen how daemons could change a person, but there had always been purpose and symmetry in it before. This one was a wild jumble of flesh and bone, as if its insides had grown unchecked and in all directions, barely contained by the stretched sack of its skin.

It opened its jaws and shrieked again. Its face had slumped. One eye faced forward; the other was a third of its size, and sat low on its cheek looking sideways. Half its mouth was toothed, the other was bare. Saliva dripped from its gums.

'Cap'n?' said Pinn quietly.

'What?' Frey croaked.

There was a pause. 'Aren't you gonna say hello to your mum?'

Ashua snorted with suppressed laughter. The tension dissipated. Leave it to Pinn to get a dig in at a time like this. He was too stupid to be afraid of death.

'Hi, Mum,' he said, and opened fire.

The daemon shuddered and jerked as a hail of bullets tore into it, sending it staggering back towards the doorway. The crew's faces were lit up by muzzle flashes, teeth gritted, eyes hard. They emptied their chambers, and when they were done, the monstrous thing lay on the floor in a heap, tattered and torn.

Then it groaned and, slowly, it began to get up.

'I bloody knew it was going to do that,' said Frey, as the crew backed off and began to scatter. 'Crake! Where are you?'

But the daemon was on its feet now. Its skin was ripped and its flesh full of holes but it didn't bleed and it didn't appear any the worse for wear. It fixed an eye on Frey and snarled.

'Don't come after *me*!' Frey cried. 'Eat Pinn, he's fatter!'

His generous advice fell on deaf ears. The daemon came lumbering towards him, accelerating as its powerful legs drove it forward. Frey darted to the side, hoping to put a pile of rubble between him and his pursuer. It angled to intercept him, smashing through the edge of the pile and causing a landslide behind it. The impact barely hindered it; it bore down on him like an express train.

Frey vaulted a rock and hit the ground running, looking for an escape route in the broken maze that surrounded him. The rest of the crew were yelling, trying to distract the daemon. A shotgun blast tore away a chunk of its shoulder. None of it mattered. It was intent on him, and nothing was going to stop it.

He turned, switching his cutlass to his good hand. The blade sang faintly in his mind, the daemon in the blade responding to the presence of another daemon. It had killed daemons before, and was eager for another taste. But as the creature powered towards him, screeching, Frey felt his confidence waver. There was no way he was winning a fight with that thing, cutlass or no cutlass. It would swat him like a fly.

The creature was suddenly thrown sideways as a blurred figure crashed into its flank. It tumbled and skidded away in a dusty muddle of limbs, entangled with its attacker. The two of them came apart as they rolled. One of them landed catlike on her feet.

Jez, and yet not Jez.

This was the thing that lurked beneath the surface of his navigator. This was the thing they were all afraid of. The change was subtle but its effect was great. A shift in aspect, a look of naked savagery in her eye, the feral way she moved. The sense of unease she inspired had sharpened to a terrifying pitch. She might be wearing the shape of the woman he knew, but she had the feel of a nightmare. This was her Mane side, unleashed.

She launched at the daemon, crashing into it before it could get to its feet. The impact sent it flying away and into a wall of rubble. As she came at it again, it lashed out with its oversized arm. Jez seemed to flicker in Frey's vision, as if there were three of her at once in three different positions, and suddenly she was half a metre to the left of the spot where she'd been, and the creature swiped through thin air.

She seized its arm and flung it. It shot through the air, missing Frey narrowly, blasting his hair against his face with the wind of its passing. Jez sprang after it, not letting up for an instant, a hungry shriek escaping her.

Someone grabbed Frey's shoulder, making him jump. He turned to see Ashua's urgent eyes.

'Let's make tracks, huh?'

Frey stuck his cutlass in his belt, looked back at Jez. Deserting her felt wrong. She might have the creature on the ropes for now, but that thing was twice her size.

'You can't help her!' Ashua told him.

She was right. He couldn't. Not against that. And yet . . .

'Wait, wait! I can handle this!' called Crake. He came hurrying into sight, labouring under the weight of his pack. The pinecone-shaped metal rods waggled above his head, and he clutched his makeshift controller in both hands, struggling with the wires that tangled around his arm. 'Teething problems, that's all!'

The daemon was thrashing about nearby. Jez was on its back, having sunk her sharp teeth into its neck from behind. She was trying to get a grip on its head to wrench it off.

'She's doing alright, Crake,' said Ashua. 'Now let's *go!*'

'Yes, yes,' said Crake. 'Just give me a moment and . . .'

He thumbed a switch on the controller to activate the flux thrower. Frey immediately got a splitting headache. There was no other effect that he could see.

'Ow! Will you turn that bloody thing off and stop messing about?' he cried.

'It just needs tuning!' Crake protested, twiddling with the dials. 'Should be about . . . here!'

Jez screeched, her body going rigid, teeth tearing free from the daemon's flesh. Released, the creature took advantage. It reached over its shoulder with its huge arm, clamped its fingers round Jez's leg, and flung her away. Frey watched in horror as she spun through the air and hit the side of a rubble pile with enough force to smash the rocks to powder. The side of the pile collapsed, burying her. When the dust blew clear, all that was visible was a hand and part of a knee.

Frey felt time slow down as the enormity of the moment hit him. He had no idea what she was capable of surviving, but that would have killed a normal woman several times over.

Oh please no.

Crake was agape, face slack as he realised what he'd done. The daemon turned its deformed head back towards Frey, a dreadful purpose in its gaze. Ashua surreptitiously edged away from him.

'Crake . . .' Frey said quietly.

'I . . . It's not . . .' Crake began, then snapped his mouth shut and set himself to frantically twiddling the dials on his controller. The daemon started loping towards Frey. Whatever Crake was doing, he wasn't doing it fast enough. 'Cap'n, I can't! Run! Cap'n, run!'

Frey took his advice. The door to the sanctum was close now, and his way was clear. He turned tail and ran for all he was worth.

Jez. Oh, shit, Jez.

But all thoughts of his friend were swept away in the storm of instinctive terror that propelled him towards the door. If Jez couldn't stop it and Crake couldn't stop it, what hope did he have?

The daemon had built up speed now, heedless of the crew's renewed attempts to distract it. Frey sprinted through the doorway. Too late he realised that he wasn't carrying a lantern, and the corridor was lightless. Heels skidding down the twilit stairs, he reached the bottom and found it pitch black. It didn't stop him. Going by memory, he ran into the darkness.

The daemon followed. He heard it come crashing down the stairs, carried into the far wall by its own momentum. It squealed, a sound like the maniac hunger of the damned, and then came thumping after him. His running feet kicked something aside, and he felt wetness spatter his face—

a severed limb. blood.

—but he went on blindly, heedless, as fast as he dared. The same instincts that made him run warned him against colliding with something unseen or breaking his leg in a hole. His hand trailed along the wall to his right, seeking an exit, looking for the cleft in the rock that he knew would be there.

Come on, come on!

He remembered Osger's corpse an instant before he tripped over it. He went over hard, kicking apart the piled halves of the body. Pain blazed across his hands and forearms as he hit the floor. He pushed himself up again, his boots scrabbling at the floor, driven to his feet by desperation. The beast was behind him, thumping through the dark, so close that he thought he could smell its breath.

Not this way not now not yet!

Stumbling onwards, his bloodied hands scraping the wall to his right, searching for the nothingness that would lead him into the fissure, searching for—

There!

And he slipped inside, heading through the split in the corridor and into the narrow passageway of rock. Here he could run both hands along the wall, get a sense of where he was. He could only hope that the daemon was as blind as he was and that it would miss the fissure in the dark.

It didn't. He heard it howl close behind him, and knew that it was inside the fissure with him. He gave up all care and redoubled his speed. The beast thumped and scraped and panted behind him, and damn if it wasn't getting louder, damn if it wasn't catching him up. His shoulder hit a protrusion of rock and sent him bouncing off, but he ignored the pain and kept going. He wouldn't end up like Osger. He wouldn't die down here in the dark.

Then: light! A faint glow up ahead, illuminating the end of the fissure. And he remembered Malvery, sitting there with his lantern in the cave where they'd left his stubborn arse. And he remembered the chasm. And he knew he'd reached a dead end.

He cast a terrified glance over his shoulder. The light fell on the face of his pursuer. It filled up the gap between the walls, a bulging, twisted mass of muscle, so close it could almost reach out and grab him.

Frey burst from the mouth of the fissure onto the ledge beside the chasm. On the other side of the gap, he saw Malvery, holding up his lantern, shotgun in one hand and a look of alarm and surprise on his face.

The creature howled as it reached for him, running full pelt in pursuit. Frey gave everything he had to put himself beyond it. A heavy claw glanced off his back, pushing him forward, off balance.

The momentum was too great to stop now. Stumbling, skipping, he leaped across the chasm.

He couldn't have made the jump even on his best day.

For a heartbeat, he was airborne, gaping emptiness below him, the dread of death in his gut. His arms and legs flailed wildly in the air. He screamed, high and raw and despairing.

And then his hands closed on one of the ropes that spanned the chasm. His flight arrested, his legs whiplashed out beneath him and his grip came loose. He fell, but instinct made him reach out, and the lower rope slammed into his chest and armpits and somehow, *somehow* he held on to it, clinging to that last slender thread that kept him from extinction.

Something flying through the air towards him. Something huge. He pulled his feet out of the way just in time to avoid the daemon's reaching hand, and it plummeted past him with a shriek, tumbling into the chasm where it was swallowed up in the dark.

That shriek went on for a very long time before it stopped.

'Cap'n! Cap'n, take my hand!' Malvery was reaching across the chasm towards him, but he was too far away to be of use. Frey had the rope under his armpits but he wasn't strong enough to pull himself up and the damn thing kept moving. He swung his leg up to hook his boot heel over the rope. On the third try he made it. He tried to get himself upright but balance was impossible. He began to panic.

'Cap'n! Hang off it and crawl towards me!'

Malvery's directions were less than clear, but Frey got the gist. He hooked his other foot over the rope. His hands were almost too painful to hold it, but he gritted his teeth and made them grip.

Laboriously, inch by inch, he crawled towards Malvery, moving hand over hand and sliding his crossed legs up behind him. The doc reached down and he grabbed on, adding Malvery's not inconsiderable strength to his own. He scrabbled and struggled and found himself at last with solid ground beneath him, where he lay collapsed for a while, joyous with the various hurts of being alive.

Malvery sat next to him, panting. 'That was, er, quite a scream you gave, Cap'n,' he said. 'Almost girly, you might say.'

Frey's cheek was pressed to the stone floor and his eyes were closed. 'Not a word to the crew, Doc,' he said out of the side of his mouth.

'Right-o,' said Malvery, and patted him heavily on the back.

Jez. Spit and blood, Jez. Please be alright. Please.

Crake dug frantically into the rubble pile, pulling out rocks and tossing them aside. Pinn, Silo and Pelaru worked with him to uncover the small figure beneath. She looked less than fearsome now. Covered in dust, her overalls torn in several places, she seemed terribly fragile.

I've killed her. Oh, no, I've killed her.

He'd been so eager for the opportunity to try out his new techniques. He hadn't thought how it might affect Jez. Clumsily sweeping the frequencies like that, he was just as liable to hit her as his target. Caught up by pride in his new machine, keen to show it off, he'd messed everything up. And now she might be dead. *Really* dead.

Just like what happened with Bess.

He plucked out stones, threw them away and went back for more. He'd already lost one person close to him through meddling with forces beyond his control. He couldn't bear to lose another.

They pulled her out and laid her on the floor. She looked wan in the lantern light, but then she'd always been pale. There were cuts and scratches, but they didn't bleed; they just lay open and red.

'Is she breathing?' he asked frantically.

Pinn gave him a look. 'She wasn't breathing *before*, thick-arse.'

Crake was so distressed that the absurdity of Pinn mocking his intelligence passed him by. He crouched down next to her, and was about to listen for a heartbeat before he remembered that she didn't have one.

'She's already dead! How do we know if she's alright?' he asked helplessly.

'Any bones broke?' said Silo.

Crake hesitated to touch her; it felt improper. Pinn had no such compunctions, and began mauling her all over until Pelaru pulled him away.

'Have some respect,' the Thacian told him harshly.

Pinn shook him off. 'Last I checked, you weren't shit to me, mate,' he snarled. 'Put your hands on me again, I'll kick your face off.'

'This isn't the time!' Crake snapped. Pinn reluctantly subsided before Pelaru's infuriating calm.

'She always went like this after she flipped, yuh?' said Silo. 'Out for a while. Might be she'll be alright. Just needs time.'

Pelaru knelt down next to her and laid his hand gently on her forehead. He seemed to be listening. After a moment, he drew back, with a deep breath of what might have been relief.

'She's alive,' he said. 'Or as much as she ever was. She'll recover.'

'Are you sure?' Crake asked. 'How do you know?'

'I knew Osger for a very long time,' he said. 'I know the signs.'

Relief flooded through Crake. There was such certainty in the Thacian's voice. Crake didn't question his assurances. He wanted to believe, so he did.

Ashua came hurrying through the doorway to the hall, holding up a lantern. Her face was alight with amazed happiness.

'The Cap'n's okay!' she said.

'What about the daemon?' Crake asked.

'He killed it!'

Pinn spluttered. 'He bloody *killed* it?'

'That was pretty much my reaction. How's Jez?'

'Hard to tell,' said Silo. He thumbed at Pelaru. 'This feller says she'll be alright.'

'Good, good,' said Ashua absently. She wasn't all that bothered. She hadn't been with Jez as long as the rest of them. The others recalled with fondness the Jez of earlier days, before she became frightening. Ashua had never really known those times.

Pelaru picked up Jez, hoisted her over his shoulders, and picked up his pack with his free hand. 'I'll take care of her,' he said gravely.

No one argued. 'Cap'n says we're to grab what we can and get gone,' Ashua told them.

The others headed off to fill their empty backpacks with treasures. Crake had no interest in that. He just wanted out of this place. When Pelaru left to carry Jez back to Frey, Crake went with him to carry the lantern.

They followed the corridor past the ruined bodies of the expedition members, and finally came to Osger's body. The two halves were scattered now. Pelaru looked at the horrifying corpse for a long moment. Then he stepped over it and walked on.

When they reached the chasm, they found Frey and Malvery on the other side, swigging from a bottle that the doctor had brought along 'just in case'. Frey looked shaken up, but the news that Jez would survive cheered him.

After some deliberation about how they were going to get Jez across, Pelaru had them tie Jez to him with a pair of belts, and he crossed the rope bridge while bearing her on his back. Then he came back for his pack. The man seemed to have a gymnast's strength and balance: the rope bridge bothered him not at all, nor did he show any strain from carrying Jez. Crake noticed as he picked up his pack that there was something heavy in it, and he thought then of the casket that he'd seen the whispermonger examining.

I'll have a word with him about that once we're out of here, he thought.

The others arrived, bearing loot, and crossed the chasm with only minimal complaining from Pinn. Frey told his story about the daemon as they sorted themselves out. Frey's version cast him as heroic. Malvery told them how he'd screamed like a girl.

When they were done, Pelaru picked up Jez once more. 'We ought to get her to safety,' he said, his voice flat.

Crake frowned at him. 'Are you sure you want to leave your partner's body lying back there? I mean, you seemed rather upset when we found him.'

Pelaru gave him a steady look. 'We should be concerned with the living now,' he said, and walked off, taking Jez with him.

Ten

Frey's Confession – Ambushed –
Picking Sides – Crake Turns Back

They made their way back through the sewers and up to the pumping station. Frey waited at the top of the caged spiral staircase for the rest of the group to catch up. The old mechanical pumps loomed half-seen in the lantern light, disapproving guardians in the dark.

He tapped his foot nervously. He was on edge. The doc's rum had helped him out, but not much. It felt like there was some pressure inside him, growing steadily, and only an effort of will could keep it in.

The daemon had scared him witless. The run through the dark had been worse. But it was hanging over that abyss that had done him in. When he'd clung to a rope above that appalling chasm and only the failing strength of his arms had stood between him and the end.

He looked at his hand. It was shaking.

Malvery joined him and they watched Pelaru carry Jez past. The Thacian didn't look at either of them.

'Was it worth it?' Malvery asked.

The tone of his voice made Frey bristle. 'Don't. Let's do this later.'

'No, I reckon now's a good time,' said Malvery. 'Before she wakes up and you forget again. You oughta look at her. Look how close we came.'

'I see her, Malvery. I'm not blind.'

'When's it gonna stop, then? When one of us is *really* dead?' Malvery rumbled. 'How much treasure do you want?'

'It's not about the bloody *treasure*!' Frey cried, his voice echoing through the pumping house. He was too loud, and he drew the attention of the others. Suddenly he found he had an audience.

'Then what is it about, Cap'n? Why'd you bring us here? Reckon you owe us that, at least.'

89

His crew watched him, waiting for a response. He felt isolated and hunted, *accused*. Anger came quickly. His fragile control faltered, and he turned on Pelaru. 'This is your mess, not mine!' he snapped at the whispermonger. 'You brought us here! You strong-armed me into it! Tell them! Go on! Tell them why we're here.'

The accusation sounded feeble even to him, and that made him more frustrated. He just wanted to lash out at something. He was sick of secrets; he'd be reckless, and damn the consequences. If the crew wanted to know so much, he'd give them what they wanted. And if they didn't like it, they could all just suck it up.

Pelaru just gazed at him calmly. He didn't address the crew, but spoke directly to Frey. 'Trinica Dracken is with the Awakeners,' he said. 'She has been working as a mercenary for them since the conflict began. Presumably, their previous relationship and the death sentence hanging over her from the Coalition side made her choice easy.'

Frey was aware of the silence from the crew. Suddenly he wasn't sure he'd done the right thing at all. But he was committed now. 'Where is she?' he said.

'The Awakeners have a base in the Barabac Delta. It is hidden in a vast area of bayou, hundreds of miles wide, without track or trace. She is there. But you won't find her, Captain Frey. Nobody knows where that base is. The whole area is laden with anti-aircraft guns. Even the Coalition Navy don't dare fly over it.' He adjusted Jez's weight on his back. 'And now I believe our business is concluded.'

'It's not *concluded*!' Frey said. 'You were supposed to *find* her!'

'I did,' said Pelaru. 'I've told you where she is. How you get to her is your—'

He hadn't finished his sentence before Frey had his revolver out and was pointing it at his forehead. 'I'm not in the mood, mate.'

'Hang on,' said Malvery, apparently oblivious to the fact that Frey had a gun to another man's head. 'Am I hearing him right? Did he just say that you dragged us into the middle of a warzone and risked all our lives on account of your hopeless romantic fantasy? Tell me it ain't true, Cap'n. Tell me you got more respect for us than that.'

Frey rounded on him furiously. 'You're getting paid, aren't you? Between these relics and the last lot we lifted off the freighter, we'll make a fortune! Isn't that what you lot want? Didn't I get it for you? So where's the bloody problem?'

There was something like pity in Malvery's eyes. 'You think I stick with you for the *money*?'

'Only reason I'm here,' Pinn volunteered.

'You shut your cake-trap,' Malvery said. 'No one asked you.'

'Well, *I'm* asking me,' Pinn retorted.

'Can we have this little family spat later, d'you think?' Ashua put in. 'Right now we need to get back to the *Ketty Jay*.'

The attack came so unexpectedly that Frey didn't register what it was at first. He heard a *crack*, and Crake lurched forward and crashed to the ground. Then Ashua shouted 'Gun!' and it all fell into place.

Suddenly everyone was moving. Malvery had Crake by the hands and was dragging him away along the floor. The others scattered for cover. Frey threw himself against the corner of a pump, Silo alongside him, searching for the source of the attack.

'Here! They're over here!' yelled a high voice from the other end of the hall. Frey caught sight of a shadowy figure running between the pumps. He aimed quickly and loosed off a shot. There was a scream – he sounded like a young man – and the figure stumbled, fell and rolled out of sight behind cover.

'One thing I hate more than daemons, it's grassers,' said Frey. 'Doc! How's Crake!'

'He's fine!' Malvery called back. 'Got a leaky battery though!'

The news, and Malvery's jocular tone, made Frey feel better. They fell easily back into the old banter and camaraderie in a gunfight. What differences they had were soon forgotten when danger threatened. Frey was big on sweeping things under the carpet.

They heard footsteps approaching. Ashua tossed a flare out into the hall. Red light swelled with a hiss of sparks, painting the chamber bloody. Frey spotted movement: a robed Sentinel with a rifle, and a couple of grizzled old men. He pointed them out to Silo as they took cover behind a pipe.

'Same lot we were shootin' on earlier,' Silo muttered. 'Must've been lookin' for us.'

'They don't learn, do they?' said Frey. He leaned out around the corner and fired a couple of times. Bullets sparked off the pipes. He drew back as more gunfire came their way.

'Silo,' he said while he waited for them to stop shooting. 'About what I just said . . .'

'I figured, Cap'n,' Silo replied. That was why he liked Silo. The man understood him.

'Think the crew'll be okay?'

'Most of us here cos there's nowhere else'll take us, Cap'n. They'd follow you. Maybe they're hurtin' 'cause you weren't straight with 'em, but they'll get over it.' He thought for a moment. 'Ashua, she don't got that loyalty, but she's happy long as you provide. Just the doc and Crake you gotta watch for. They got issues with conscience, and you ain't helpin'.'

'What about you?'

Silo leaned out of cover, aimed his shotgun and fired. Half the Sentinel's head erupted in a mess of red mist and bone shards.

'I ain't got no issues,' he said. 'Ain't *my* people killin' each other.'

'You lot out there!' Frey called. 'We're not with the Coalition! Your fight's not with us! So why don't you go home before you end up like your mate?'

Frey waited for a response. He didn't get one. Instead, he heard the scuffling of feet, and the two old men went running off back towards the pumping house entrance, and away.

Frey was actually quite surprised they'd listened to him. 'Well,' he said. 'That wasn't so bad.'

They heard a muffled groan from a little way away: the sound of someone trying to stifle their pain and failing. Once it was clear there were no more attackers, they made their way over. There they found a young man lying crushed up against the pipework, wrapping a tourniquet round his thigh that he'd fashioned from the ripped arm of his thin coat. Dazed by the pain, he didn't hear them approach. When he did, he lunged for the pistol lying nearby. Silo got his boot on the pistol first, primed his lever-action rifle with a crunch, and aimed it at the man's forehead.

'Nuh-uh,' he said.

The man drew his hand back. He was scared rigid and pretending he wasn't. Under the dirt, he had a look of rustic freshness about him, blond hair falling in a cowlick over his forehead. He couldn't have been more than twenty.

'You ain't Coalition,' he stated defiantly.

'Like I said,' Frey replied. 'And you're not an Awakener. What's your name?'

'Abley,' he said, finding no reason not to give it.

'I'm Captain Frey, of the *Ketty Jay*. What are you doing in Korrene?'

Abley eyed him mistrustfully. 'I'm a pilot,' he said. 'Used to do crop deliveries between Lapin and the wheat belt.'

'How'd you get tangled up with the Awakeners?'

'I weren't tangled up in nothin'! I'm one o' the Allsoul's men.' The rest of the crew had gathered round now, looking down at him. He appealed to Ashua, the only woman present who wasn't unconscious. 'Please, I need help.'

'Didn't you just shoot at my friend here?' she reminded him, indicating Crake. His pack sat on the floor next to him, oozing battery fluid from a hole near the bottom.

Abley began to get desperate. Blood was seeping through his tourniquet, and he was clearly suffering. 'Look, they came to my town, alright? Everyone believes out there. I know they say they don't in the cities much, but out in the country we all do. And the Speakers started callin' everyone off to war. I didn't wanna go, most of us didn't wanna go, but you can't say no, not when everyone else is an' they got Imperators stalkin' around in the background. You're either with us or against us, they said. Pick a side.'

'Looks like a pretty bad wound you got there.' Frey said. 'Malvery?'

Malvery made a show of considering the injury. 'He ain't gonna last too long if we leave it,' he said. 'It'll fester. He'll lose the leg, even if his mates find him.'

'Mmm,' said Frey. 'That's a shame. Well, they did say to pick a side.' He shrugged. 'Come on, fellers.'

'Wait, you can't!' Abley cried, fear making his voice high. 'There won't be no one comin' to find me!'

'But surely the Awakeners look after their faithful, don't they?' Crake said, with an unpleasantly snide edge to his voice.

'They're pullin' out! That's what they say! There won't be anyone to find me!'

'The Awakeners are pulling out of Korrene?' Frey was suddenly very interested. 'Tonight?'

Abley gritted his teeth as a fresh wave of pain from his wound swept over him. Sweat was dampening his hair. 'Yeah. They had enough. Word is . . . *aaah* . . . word is they were planning on it anyway, and now with the assault . . .'

'Suppose whatever they were looking for here wasn't worth taking on the Coalition for,' Ashua opined.

'The machine,' said Crake. 'They wanted to make sure no one found it. It's evidence they've been putting daemons into people to make Imperators. The kind of evidence that might make the blinkered idiots that fight for them start doubting.'

'I ain't no idiot!' Abley snapped. 'Least I believe in something!'

'So do I,' said Crake. 'I believe in leaving you here to rot.'

Frey wasn't sure if Crake was serious or not. He wasn't very understanding where Awakeners were concerned. But Abley's information had given him an idea.

'The Awakeners. We know they have a base in the Barabac Delta. You wanna tell us where it is?'

'I don't know! How would I know?'

'Because it's the only reason I can think of to waste my doctor's time and supplies on fixing you up.'

'You're a doctor?' Abley said, gazing beseechingly at Malvery.

'Sorry, mate,' said Malvery, backing Frey's play. 'Can't do a thing 'less the Cap'n lets me. Pick a better side next time, eh?'

Silo picked up Abley's gun, and they began to walk away. Frey mentally counted down in his head.

'Stop!' Abley cried after them, right on time.

Frey looked back at him. He cut a desperate figure, lying there wounded in the dark.

'I know this!' he said. 'I know they're going there now! That's where we're retreating to, when we leave Korrene!'

'You *know*?' Frey asked, staring at him hard. Abley's expression was that of a man pathetically eager to please. 'You're lying.'

'I *think* they are, I *think*!' he babbled. 'They gave us a rendezvous point. We meet up and go from there. There were rumours, that's all, but the rumours said—'

'What's to stop any old aircraft turning up and following you back?' Ashua interrupted. 'How do you know who's on your side? The Awakeners have been picking up flotsam from everywhere.'

'Flotsam?' asked Frey, who'd never heard the word before and was frankly getting a bit sick of the fact that half his crew had a better vocabulary than he did.

'They give us a code,' said Abley. 'It changes every day. If we're challenged, we flash it on our electroheliographs. That way they can pick out intruders in the fleet.'

'And you know today's code?' Frey asked.

'Yeah! Yeah, I do!' His face lit up as he saw a future that didn't involve bleeding to death in the dark. 'I can tell you, if you help me!'

Crake came over to stand next to Frey. 'You'd better not be thinking what I think your thinking.'

Frey raised an eyebrow at him. 'Don't you want to strike a blow for the Coalition?'

'This isn't about that, Frey, and you know it! This is about you and *her*!'

Pinn looked confused. 'What am I missing?'

'Besides your frontal lobes?' Malvery said. 'Seems to me the Cap'n wants us to join the Awakeners.'

'Oh,' said Pinn. 'Well, can't see the harm.'

'No,' said Crake. 'No, that's too damned far, Frey.'

'We're just going to *pretend*, for shit's sake!' Frey cried. 'No one's asking you to swear eternal fealty to the Allsoul.'

'No, Frey! No!' Crake's voice was rising in anger. 'This is a bit beyond a spot of light piracy and occasional theft. You want us to *infiltrate the Awakeners*? I thought you didn't want to get us involved in this war?'

'I thought you *did*?' Frey replied. 'Don't you hate them and everything they stand for?'

'That doesn't mean I'm willing to die for it!' Crake was shouting now. 'Have you forgotten that I'm a daemonist? You know what they'd do to me if they found out? I'm not getting my mind torn apart by an Imperator for the sake of your doomed bloody relationship! Let her go, Frey! She doesn't want you! Spit and blood, just let it drop!'

Frey boiled over. His recent brush with death, the frustration of being separated from Trinica, the guilt he felt about Jez; all that bubbled up into rage, and he couldn't hold it in any longer.

'Stay, then!' he yelled. 'Stay, if you want to! I'm not making you come with me! But last I checked, the *Ketty Jay* was *my* craft, and *she* is going wherever Trinica is. You can come along, or you can piss off; it's all the same to me! Just as long as you shut up while you're at it!'

Crake's face was red with anger and indignation. He opened his mouth for a heated retort, then mastered himself and closed it again. He drew himself up with the affronted dignity of an aristocrat and said, very calmly, 'Goodbye, Cap'n.' Then, picking up a lantern, he turned and walked away towards the entrance of the pumping house.

'Fine!' Frey called after him, when he saw that he really did mean to leave. 'Fine! Go!' He turned on the rest of the crew. 'Anyone else?'

Malvery stepped close to him, his bristly white eyebrows gathered in a frown above the rims of his round, green-lensed glasses. 'Cap'n,' he said sternly. 'That woman is turning you into an arsehole. Stop it.'

Frey swallowed a retort. He could see by the faces of his crew that he'd done wrong. Even Abley looked startled. Crake was his friend, and they'd saved each other's lives many times. He didn't deserve the short shrift he'd got. And he must have been plenty offended to storm off in the middle of a warzone.

'I'll go get him,' said Silo.

'No,' said Frey, holding out a hand. 'I'll go. You lot get back to the *Ketty Jay*. Malvery, can you see to the lad? We're gonna need him.'

'Right-o,' said Malvery. The others readied their packs and picked up their bits without further discussion, more subdued than normal. Frey hurried off through the pumping station after Crake. He was glad to get away from them, to hide his face from their gazes.

There was no sign of anyone when he emerged from the pumping house. The junction where five roads met was quiet except for the distant chattering of gatling guns. He turned off his lantern and left it in the doorway for the others to find, then stepped warily out into the junction.

Crake was nowhere to be seen. Frey cursed under his breath.

There was only one thing for it, then. This place was far too dangerous to call out his name, so he picked a random direction and set off to search.

Crake. Where are you?

Grayther Crake, several streets away, was already beginning to regret his decision. The reality of his situation cooled the heat of his anger. He found himself alone in a broken city, with Coalition troops on one side, Awakeners on the other, and neither likely to ask questions before they opened fire. He didn't even know which direction he should be heading in to find safety.

You're a fool, Grayther Crake. A scared, prideful fool.

He was already ashamed of his outburst in front of the Cap'n. He didn't like to lose control. Crass emotional displays weren't his style. But the incident with Jez had disturbed him, brought back terrible memories of Bess, his beautiful niece whom he'd stabbed to death with a letter knife while under the control of a daemon. On top of that, he was humiliated by his latest failure. His daemonist skills were the one thing that set him apart from the arrogant, vapid elite that he came from. Now he'd made himself a laughing-stock. He felt angry and wretched, and Frey's comment had been the last straw.

Where could he go now? The Cap'n wanted them to join the Awakeners. No, he absolutely wouldn't do that. Even if it was in order to infiltrate and hurt them. He hated them too much, opposed them too squarely. What if they made him undertake some sort of initiation to prove his faith in the Allsoul? It would be too much a betrayal of himself. The others might possess a more elastic moral fibre than he did, but he wouldn't be swayed.

And yet, he couldn't help wondering if that was really the reason. *'Don't you want to strike a blow for the Coalition?'* Frey had said. And he *did* want that, he *did* want to strike. For the Coalition, but more importantly, against the Awakeners. Wasn't this his chance to do that? And wasn't he turning his back on it?

Since the civil war began, he'd fretted about whether he should be joining in. Now that he had the opportunity, he realised that he really didn't *want* to get involved. Much as it pained him to admit it, he was scared. He wanted to sit out the war and let somebody else deal with the Awakeners. In the end, he was no better than Frey, or any of the others.

He stopped, turning this way and that. The smashed and shadowed streets watched him malevolently. Fear wormed its way into him.

'You have no idea where you're going, do you?' he asked himself.

And then, with a shock, he remembered Bess. Not the girl he'd killed but the golem he'd made of her. In all his self-absorbed fury he'd forgotten that there was someone back on the *Ketty Jay* that relied on him. Spit and blood, what a selfish creature he was! If his thoughts weren't of himself then they were usually of Samandra. And where did that leave the golem in his charge?

No choice, he told himself. *Go back.*

No way was he going to any Awakener hideout, but the Cap'n would surely drop him and Bess off at the forward base. Or somewhere safer than this, anyway. They'd both have to swallow a bit of pride, but Frey wouldn't refuse him that.

And then he could go to Samandra. He wondered if he'd have stormed off at all, if he hadn't known that she'd be waiting for him.

Taking a deep breath, he turned around to retrace his steps.

There was a man in the street, walking purposefully towards him. A tall man in a trenchcoat and a black hat, carrying a shotgun. Crake's heart leaped in his chest. He had no idea who that man was, or what side he was on, but he knew that he didn't want to meet him. He spun to go the other way.

And found himself staring down the barrel of a revolver. The man on the end of it was young and clean-shaven, and gave him a crooked smile.

'Grayther Crake,' he said. 'We're from the Shacklemore Agency. And you're comin' with us.'

Eleven

A New Recruit – Pinned Down – Minor Surgery –
The Cupola – A Peach of a Shot

Frey flinched as the sky overhead erupted with a boom louder than thunder. Running in a half-crouch, he scampered along the street, staying close to the walls for cover but ready to flee if any looked like falling on him. The anti-aircraft guns had started up again in earnest. A few streets away he saw a ragged old Westingley lift itself above the broken parapets of the ancient city.

The Awakeners were pulling out, under covering fire from their guns. If the *Ketty Jay* didn't get going soon, they'd miss their chance to infiltrate the Awakener fleet.

Damn you, Crake. Why'd you have to run off now?

The street ended suddenly at a chasm, an enormous rip in the earth, twenty metres wide. Parts of buildings still hung precariously over the abyss. Frey decided that Crake was unlikely to have gone this way, unless he'd secretly developed the ability to fly. He backtracked and tried a side-alley, but that turned out to be blocked by a fallen house.

Frey spat on the ground. Dead end. He must have picked the wrong road back at the junction. That meant Crake could be any-where. Searching for him was all but hopeless.

But he wouldn't give up. Not yet. Not when it was his fault that Crake was out here. The crew always became unbalanced when one of them went missing. They were a team, and they needed each other. And what about Bess? He didn't want to think how she might react when she twigged that her master wasn't coming home.

His eyes fell to the silver ring he wore on his little finger. Crake usually carried the compass with him on expeditions, just in case Frey managed to get himself lost. Had he brought it this time? Frey wasn't sure. But the compass meant Crake could always find him, if he wanted to.

The problem was, he didn't want to.

He heard running footsteps coming from a side road. He cast around for a way to get out of sight, but he wasn't quick enough. Three men came into view. Two of them wore a Sentinel's cassock and carried rifles. The other was a middle-aged man with a broad, plain face and a cauliflower ear.

One of the Sentinels stopped in front of Frey, ushering the other men past him. More were coming up behind, ten or twelve at least. Three of them carried the various parts of a gatling gun. 'Come on!' the Sentinel urged Frey. 'There are Coalition troops right behind us!'

Frey didn't miss a beat. He'd always been an agile liar. 'Thank the Allsoul, brother! When I lost my unit, I thought I was dead!'

'Get going!' the Sentinel told him, and Frey ran off with the rest of the Awakeners, who were conveniently hurrying in the general direction of the *Ketty Jay*.

The recruits were mostly rural folk, by their dress. Some wore stitched Ciphers on their clothes, others didn't. Some were grimly determined, some looked scared. The Awakener army was a rag-tag mob of untrained recruits. No match for the disciplined Coalition forces. The Archduke's men could mop these fellers up without the help of people like Frey.

He kept pace with them, waiting for an opportunity to dump them and get away. It occurred to him that he might stay with them, and get to Trinica that way, but there was no chance he was leaving the *Ketty Jay* behind. Rot knew what would happen if Jez got at the controls, and she was the only other crew member who could fly her.

The street they were following ended in a small square with an ornamental fountain in the centre, long dry. The houses on all sides had been shaken to pieces by the quake. Weeds grew thick among cracked flagstones and piles of broken bricks. Flashes of light from above gave them brief snapshots of the ruin that surrounded them.

They were halfway across when a dozen Coalition soldiers ran into the square from a road to their left. The soldiers were as surprised as the Awakeners, and for a moment no one did anything but stare. No one but Frey, who threw himself over the stone lip of the fountain just before both sides let loose on one another.

Rifles and pistols snapped, men shouted, some shrieked as they were hit. Frey kept his head down while the rest of the Awakeners came piling into cover around him. Some of them had gunshot wounds. One man was shot in the back while trying to help another over.

The Sentinel who'd first spoke to Frey ended up next to him. 'Get that gun firing!' he yelled at a group of men down the line. They began hastily assembling the gatling gun. Then he glared at Frey. 'What are you waiting for?' And he aimed his rifle and started firing.

Frey pulled out the revolver that he'd emptied into the daemon back at the shrine, and began loading bullets into it. He had a full one in his belt, but he wanted time to think. He wasn't keen on shooting at Coalition troops. That seemed like the kind of thing that might get a man into trouble. But he'd had no bright ideas by the time he was loaded, so he popped up and loosed off a couple of shots to look convincing. He aimed wild on purpose. The Sentinel was too busy to notice.

No way I'm dying with these losers, he thought, as he looked around for a way out. The Coalition troops had retreated into cover at the edge of the square. To his right, Frey could see a gap in the rubble, perhaps an old alley or something. It would take some clambering to get to, but it was an exit and, most importantly, it was sheltered from Coalition fire by a collapsed house.

There's my way out, he thought. *Now I just have to get there.*

It wasn't far, but it was far enough. If he broke out of cover he'd be a target for the Coalition soldiers. And once the Awakeners saw him deserting, he had little doubt they'd shoot him in the arse.

He hunkered down again as bullets chipped the stone fountain, showering him with speckles of grit. Damn it, he had to get to Trinica! He didn't have time to get pinned down in a fire-fight!

The Sentinel next to him took advantage of a break in the shooting to pop his head up and aim again. Frey heard him take in a sharp breath and saw his eyes widen. 'By the Code!' he said. 'That's—'

He was rudely interrupted when his head blew apart, spraying Frey with blood and strips of gelatinous muck that used to be his brain.

'Ewwww,' Frey groaned. Getting covered in bits of other people ranked among his least favourite things. He wondered what the Sentinel had seen before he died, but he wasn't curious enough to stick his head up and find out.

'You men who fight for the Awakeners!' roared a commanding voice. 'Put down your arms and surrender!'

The gunfire petered out at the sound. Frey closed his eyes in silent despair. He knew that voice, and it meant he was screwed.

He found a crack in the fountain wide enough to peer through, and put his eye to it. It only confirmed what he already knew. There was Kedmund Drave, standing boldly before his troops, a smoking pistol in one hand.

Frey cursed his luck. If he was caught by Drave in the company of Awakeners, the Century Knight would string him up for sure.

'This is your only chance!' Drave shouted. 'There won't be another!'

A gunshot ran out, followed quickly by a second. Two shooters on the Awakener side, trying their luck. Drave thrust out his open hand, palm first. The first bullet sparked off his armoured glove, his hand moved with incredible speed, and the second one whined away too. His pistol came up, he fired twice, and the two shooters went down dead.

Thralled, Frey thought. *His gloves have been thralled by a daemonist, just like my cutlass. No wonder the Century Knights seem superhuman, with tricks like that.*

As quickly as it had stopped, the gunfire kicked up again. Drave ducked away into cover: even *he* couldn't deflect that many bullets. Frey hunched down near the dead body of the Sentinel, shots flying all around him. He was getting desperate now. Maybe he could make that gap. Better than ending up in Drave's hands. But it seemed an awfully long way between here and there.

He holstered his pistol, took a deep breath. Then he took another.

Ready, he told himself unconvincingly.

Then, from further along the fountain, came a sound that brought hope to his heart. The harsh rattle of a gatling gun. The Awakeners had got their shit together at last.

The Coalition forces retreated into cover as the gatling gun sprayed rounds across the square. Frey squeezed his hands into fists. This was the best chance he was going to have. Now, while their heads were down.

Now!

He scrambled to his feet, ran low around the fountain and vaulted over the lip before any of the Awakeners could react. Now he was out in the open, his feet pounding the flagstones, arms pumping, wild-eyed and afraid. It would only take him seconds to reach cover, but they were long, long seconds, and he could only hope that the everyone was too preoccupied to notice him.

'Frey!' roared Drave. Frey looked over his shoulder in terror to see the Century Knight rising out of cover, heedless of the bullets flying all around him. He was sighting down the barrel of his pistol at Frey, and Century Knights didn't miss.

Frey didn't stop running. His hand went to his belt and his cutlass leaped into it. It guided his arm, moving faster than he ever could. He twisted in mid-stride just as Drave's pistol fired, and threw the blade up between them.

The cutlass absorbed most of the impact, but not all. There was a jolt up his arm, a shower of sparks in front of his eyes, and he tumbled. But he tucked into a roll, shoulder-first, and came back up on to his feet. He sprinted the last few metres into cover before Drave could work out why his target wasn't dead.

You're not the only one who can deflect bullets, he thought.

Sheltered now from the Coalition forces, ignored by the Awakeners who had their own concerns, Frey went scrambling through the gap in the rubble towards the street beyond.

'Frey!' Drave yelled from somewhere behind him. 'I'll see you dead for this! You damned *traitor!*'

'Hold still,' said Malvery to his patient. 'This is gonna hurt like buggery.'

Abley nodded, his face pale and sweaty. He lay on his belly on the operating table of the *Ketty Jay*'s grubby infirmary, a folded belt gripped between his teeth. A bloody trouser leg had been thrown on the floor nearby.

The bullet had gone into his calf and lodged in the muscle there. It wasn't as bad as it must have felt, but Malvery had been telling the truth when he said it would fester without attention. He aimed with his forceps, gripped Abley's ankle, and dug in. Abley screamed and passed out.

'Ain't so delicate as I used to be,' Malvery muttered apologetically, as he dropped the bullet into a pan. He cleaned the wound of fabric shreds, swabbed it with antiseptic and put in a couple of stitches.

Abley came back to consciousness and started murmuring nonsense as Malvery was wrapping his dressing with gauze.

'Easy there,' said Malvery. 'Done in a jiffy, son.'

Abley took the belt from his mouth and swallowed to wet his throat. 'Thanks, Doc,' he croaked. 'Thanks for not leaving me there.'

'You just be sure to thank the Cap'n by giving him that code you promised,' said Malvery sternly.

'Aye, I will. I ain't stupid,' Abley said weakly. 'This craft gets shot down, so do I.'

Malvery said nothing more as he finished up. There was a familiar sensation in his chest, a strange mix of pride and sadness that he used to feel when stitching up young soldiers on the battlefield. Pride that those big hands of his could help to save a life or a limb. Sadness that they needed to at all.

Abley was just a lad. Strong, handsome, an honest look about him. He probably radiated an aura of robust health when he wasn't half in shock. He ought to be charming the girls in some rustic village, getting up to no good in the old watermill, eating half his weight at some harvest festival somewhere. Wasn't right that he'd been dragged into this.

Malvery didn't much care what anyone believed, as long as it didn't get in anyone else's face. But he cared about Vardia and her people. This lad never wanted to fight. Despite his protests, that was plain as day. He just wanted to believe in something that made a bit of sense out of a chaotic world. But war had been forced upon him by the Awakeners. Him and hundreds of thousands like him. He was lucky he'd ended up in such merciful hands.

Malvery wasn't sure if Frey would really have left Abley in the pumping house. The Cap'n could bluff with the best of them. But Malvery wouldn't have left him. And if the Cap'n had tried to make him, he'd have quit the crew right there and then. Because while the Cap'n and most of the others seemed to believe that the civil war wasn't their fight, Malvery was quite sure that it was.

He heard the whine of hydraulics as the cargo ramp closed, hurrying feet and voices in the corridor. Silo and Ashua.

'Cap'n's back,' he told her.

'Is Crake with him?' she asked.

Malvery occupied himself with making Abley comfortable as he listened to the hubbub outside. He should check in on Jez, who was lying in her quarters. Wouldn't do any good, though. He didn't know how to treat her when she dropped into one of her comas. Best thing he could do was to leave her and hope she woke up.

Frey came up the stairs, barking orders while Ashua asked questions. They were leaving right now. No, he didn't find Crake. No, they weren't going back to look. Because Kedmund Drave was on his tail.

'Kedmund Drave!' cried Ashua. '*Now* what've you done?'

'Well, he sort of got the idea that we joined the Awakeners for real.'

'He *what*? How?'

'Never mind. Tell the doc to get on the autocannon. I'll need eyes behind me if we're going up there.'

Frey hurried off towards the cockpit. Ashua appeared in the doorway of the infirmary.

'I heard,' said Malvery. He waved at the patient. 'Keep an eye on him, will you? Give him two of those pills on the table, too. Wound might go septic otherwise.' He headed out past her before she could argue. A few metres down the corridor was a ladder bolted to the wall. He pulled himself up it.

The cupola was cramped for a man his size. A battered leather chair hung in a metal cradle that sat at the butt end of a large autocannon. The cannon barrel poked through a hemisphere of windglass within a reinforced steel frame. The whole assembly could pivot and tilt to give a field of fire covering everywhere but directly above. Mechanical locks prevented the trigger being pressed when the cannon was in certain positions, to prevent him accidentally blowing the *Ketty Jay*'s tail off.

He climbed into the seat and settled himself. This small space was his domain, perhaps more so than the infirmary, since no one ever came up here. It was chilly and musty and smelt of him. Partly empty rum bottles, old broadsheets and battered books were stuffed into spaces in the bulkhead. He rummaged around till he found a bottle that was quarter full, pulled the stopper and raised it to the night sky, which was flashing and thundering with anti-aircraft fire.

'Stay safe, mate,' he said to Crake, and drank deeply.

A maudlin mood settled on him. Crake was gone. Just like that. No doubt he was capable of taking care of himself, but still. Stalking off that way. Wasn't like him. And now they'd been forced to leave him behind.

Still, you had to admire the feller. Man took a stand for what he believed. That was more than Malvery had done. And now Malvery was off to join the Awakeners, the bloody *Awakeners*, and as far as the Coalition were concerned he was a genuine turncoat, too. All he'd wanted to do was join the war on the Coalition side, but it was too late for that now. Bridges had been burned. They'd never let him join up even if he asked them, and what did they want with a fat old alcoholic anyway, Duke's Cross or not?

The thought of it curdled the rum in his stomach. He drank some more to wash away the taste.

Should've done something, he told himself. *Should've taken a stand*.

But Abley had needed him, and by the time he'd seen to his patient the chance had gone. His fit of pique back at the underground chasm seemed churlish now, an act of defiance that only served to make him feel better. He might have protested, but in the end he hadn't mustered the wherewithal to do anything about it. He always did go with the flow a bit more than was good for him.

He took another swig of rum. It helped take his mind off it.

The *Ketty Jay* trembled as the engines powered up. There was a soft buzz through the hull as the electromagnets got to work, extracting gas from liquid aerium, pumping it into the ballast tanks. The *Ketty Jay* creaked as she became lighter. She stood up on her skids and floated uncertainly off the ground.

'Doc? You in position?' the Cap'n's voice came faintly from below.

'I'm here!' called Malvery. Then, quieter and to himself: 'Always here.'

The sky cracked and flared with explosions. Tracer fire slid up into the night. Coalition Windblades shot by overhead, chasing down Awakener craft that were lifting off from hidden places all over Korrene. To the right of the *Ketty Jay*, the Firecrow was rising. He saw Harkins in the cockpit, intent on the controls, his pilot's cap jammed low on his head and his scarecrow legs visible through the bubble of windglass on the nose of his aircraft. Pinn was ascending alongside him, his pudgy face underlit by the dash of his sleek Skylance. Inside the cupola, Malvery felt insulated from it all, as if it were some show happening far away with no power to affect him, and which he was equally powerless to affect.

An explosion close overhead shook the *Ketty Jay* and made him spit his rum all over his crotch. Suddenly he felt a lot less detached.

The *Ketty Jay*'s thrusters kicked in, pushing her forward. Her outflyers kept pace alongside. Frey flew them low over the city to avoid the worst of the flak, but it still seemed uncomfortably near to Malvery.

Coalition forces were swarming now. They were determined to inflict some casualties on the scattering Awakeners. Now the *Ketty Jay* was airborne, Malvery could see that the anti-aircraft fire was much lighter than on their way in. In some areas, it had diminished to almost nothing, as the gunners joined the retreat.

'Doc! How we doing back there? You still keeping your eyes out?' Frey called. He had a tendency to nag during a battle. Not being able to see behind his craft made him anxious.

'Apart from all this sodding flak?' Malvery called back. 'Just fine.' He stopped as he caught sight of something moving in the dark, then bawled: 'Eight o' clock high, Cap'n! Fighter! Incoming fire!'

Frey reacted immediately. The world lurched and tilted outside Malvery's cupola. A flurry of blazing tracers whipped past him and flew away earthwards to be swallowed by the streets. Malvery stuffed the bottle of rum into a gap in the bulkhead so as not to drop it into the corridor below.

'Where is it now?' Frey called, wrenching the *Ketty Jay* back and forth in an evasive pattern. Harkins and his Firecrow swung into view and away. Malvery craned his neck, trying to spot the fighter against the night. A flash of anti-aircraft fire lit it up just as it unleashed another barrage. This time gunfire lashed across the *Ketty Jay*'s hull, pocking the metal with bullet holes. Something deep inside the craft groaned. A pipe burst and steam hissed out into the corridor below him. He heard Silo come running to fix the leak.

'It's on our six, Cap'n! Still above us!' he yelled over the noise.

'Well bloody shoot it then!' Frey yelled back.

'It's a Windblade!' he protested.

'*Do I sound like a man who gives a shit?*' Frey screamed.

'I ain't shooting at Coalition!'

'They're attacking us! You want to die for your damned patriotism?'

'Why not?' Malvery roared. 'You want us to die for your damned woman, don't you?'

The Cap'n was momentarily defeated by that. There was silence from the cockpit as he formulated a comeback, but then a fresh salvo from the fighter put a few new holes in their wing, and Frey gave up trying to be witty.

'Just do it!' he shrieked.

Exasperated, Malvery grabbed the handles of the autocannon. The cupola swivelled with the gun. 'Keep her still, then!' he shouted. Frey stopped jinking about, and Malvery brought the target into the centre of his crosshairs.

It was a peach of shot. The Windblade was lining up on them, encouraged by the lack of return fire. The pilot, thinking only of the kill, wasn't even trying to dodge. Both of them were in each other's sights.

'Malvery!' Frey yelled.

The first one to fire would destroy the other.

'Malvery! Take the shot!'

Malvery's finger hovered over the trigger. He thought of all the people on the *Ketty Jay*. Of the Cap'n and Silo and Ashua, especially, who he was inordinately fond of. All the people who'd likely die if he didn't shoot.

'Malvery!' Frey screamed, loud enough to threaten imminent prolapse. *'You horrible fat bastard! Fire!'*

Malvery took his finger away, sat back in his battered leather chair, and sighed with something like satisfaction. What would be, would be. But he'd be damned before he shot down a Coalition aircraft.

A moment later, the Windblade exploded, ripped apart by tracer fire from out of the night. Pinn's Skylance slashed through the air and away.

Malvery watched the flaming pieces of Windblade fall towards the city below. They'd outrun the flak now. There was no more pursuit that he could see.

He pulled out the bottle of rum and emptied the remainder down his gullet. Then he hauled himself out of his seat and went down into the steam-filled corridor in search of another. He was going to get plenty drunk tonight.

Who says I can't make a stand?

Twelve

Pinn's Women – Signals –
The Interloper – A Horror

rtis Pinn, thought Pinn to himself. *Hero of the Skies*.
He rather liked the sound of that. He pictured the title on
the cover of the novel they'd one day write about his adventures. Maybe a few more exclamation marks here and there. *Artis*
Pinn!!! Hero of the Skies!!! Yes, that would do. Make it stand out a
little. The cover had to be good, since he'd never actually read it. The
important thing was that it looked impressive in the window of a
bookshop.

The flight from Korrene had left him time to daydream. *Or should*
it be nightdream? he thought. *It's dark, after all.* He congratulated
himself on his own wit and wiggled his butt in the seat of the Skylance
to dig a more comfortable dent in the padding.

They'd been flying without lights for hours, heading southwest.
The glow of the *Ketty Jay*'s thrusters, the steady roar of his aircraft
and the long period of inactivity had lulled him into a half-drowse.
His mind, such as it was, wandered freely.

The Coalition Navy had been long left behind them. Crake too,
and good riddance to the pompous arsewipe. If he wanted to flounce
off in a strop like a girl then let him. Pinn wouldn't miss him one
bit. In fact, he'd have his biographer write Crake out of the book
altogether. He didn't want the reader distracted from the real focus of
the story. Artis Pinn. Pilot, lover, rogue.

He glanced at the little picture frame that hung from the dash,
swaying gently with the motion of the aircraft. A ferrotype of a
middle-aged woman looked back at him, with long curly hair, slightly
crooked teeth and a formidable bosom. In the past, he'd spent hours
staring at that portrait, but she didn't look quite so good tonight. He
struggled to remember her name, and was alarmed to find that he

couldn't. It might be important, he thought. What if his biographer needed to know?

Emanda, he thought, with the kind of relief he normally associated with unloading a particularly troublesome bowl of oats in the *Ketty Jay's* head. Yes, he remembered her now. The woman from Kingspire. He'd spent a few heady days with her, gambling and drinking and shagging like champions. Inevitably, she'd succumbed to his charms, and told him she loved him. She was a bit hammered at the time, but he'd leave that part out. Anyway, he'd known at that moment that she was the one for him, and he left her that night with a note of explanation. He was going to find fame and fortune, and then he'd be back. When he was worthy of her. When he was a hero.

Except, well, all of a sudden he just wasn't that keen on her.

A thought occurred to him. He held the flight stick awkwardly between his knees to keep it steady, then took the frame from the dash and opened it up. He took out the portrait of Emanda and tossed it aside. Jammed in the frame behind it was another ferrotype. He took that one out too. A blonde, eighteen or so, with a wide, plain face and big innocent eyes. A smile free of guile or intelligence. He frowned as he stared at her. Who was *she*?

Pinn was a creature of the moment. Seven years was a long, long way back for him. It took time for the memories to seep apologetically through the armour of his consciousness.

Lisinda!

At last he had it. His biographer would want to know that one. His first great love, a girl from his home town. Pinn had slept with other local girls during the tenure of their relationship – men had urges, of course – but never with her. He wanted to keep her pure. That kind of consideration was probably why she adored him, and why she'd ended up telling him she loved him. He left her soon after, with a note of explanation. He was going out into the wide world to seek his fortune. He'd be back when he was worthy of her.

Pinn dimly discerned a pattern there for the briefest of instants, but the thought was slippery and he lost it.

Lisinda. She'd promised she'd wait for him. Well, actually, she *hadn't*, he just expected her to, since she'd told him she loved him. Seven years wasn't that long. But anyhow, she'd gone and married someone else or something, so she could piss off now. He'd found out in a letter she'd sent him. A letter! She didn't even have the decency to tell him to his face! Faithless wench.

He crumpled up her picture and stuffed it in his pocket so he could deface it later. Then he took up the flight stick again. Lately, a notion had been growing in his mind. Maybe all this heroism and fortune-hunting wasn't getting him anywhere. Maybe there was something bigger than all this. And maybe there was another woman out there for him, a woman far more intelligent and beautiful than Lisinda *or* Emanda. A *spiritual* woman.

Stuck to his dash was a piece of paper. Written on it in barely legible script were several short phrases in pencil:

Jurny.
Deth.
Dark hared stranger (not hot)
Find sumthin important
Trajedy on sum-one deer (emanda?)
You will beleeve!!

The first three lines had been crossed out. He reckoned that Korrene counted as a journey to a place they'd never been to. The dark-haired stranger was obviously Pelaru. And death was probably to do with Osger, since he was dead. Pinn couldn't understand why Pelaru had been so broken up about some shit-ugly half-Mane with a face like a maggoty bollock, but Thacians were a strange lot.

'There's the fleet,' Frey said in his ear, startling him out of his reverie. He lifted his head and saw a knot of lights on the horizon, above the cloud line. It seemed like their hostage's information about the rendezvous was good.

He dug around for a pencil and crossed out the fourth line. Find something important? That was surely the Awakener base they were heading for. He stared at the paper and shook his head in amazement. This prophecy stuff was really pretty incredible. There had to be something behind it. After all, how did she know?

He looked at the next line of the prophecy.

Tragedy will fall on someone you hold dear.

He stared at the words with an expression of deep thought, then slowly lifted one of his buttcheeks and farted.

★

'Here they come,' said Frey.

Ashua watched the Awakener cruiser approach through the wind-glass of the cockpit. It had broken away from the main mass when they turned on their lights, and set course towards them. This fleet didn't have anything as big as a Coalition frigate, but they had guns enough to blow up the *Ketty Jay* several times over.

'Stay due north of the fleet. That's the approach pattern for today,' Abley told Frey. He was sitting in the navigator's chair, within easy reach of the press-switch that operated the electroheliograph.

'Don't try anything,' Ashua warned him darkly. 'They try to board us, I promise they're gonna find you with a hole in the back of your skull.'

Abley didn't say anything. He looked cowed enough, though. Ashua was a big believer in threats. You had to make sure people knew their situation. Hostages got it into their heads to try the stupidest things when their backs were against the wall. Their consciences made them brave, so they screwed it up for everyone, and almost invariably ended up dead. She'd seen it happen enough on the streets.

Ashua wasn't a big fan of the Cap'n's latest plan. She didn't want to take sides in this war. Having grown up in the violent slums of Rabban and later in Samarla, she didn't feel she owed Vardia much. Archdukes or religious fanatics, rulers were all the same to her. Her inclination was to sit back and see who was going to win, then join them.

But the Cap'n called the shots, and he wanted his pirate lady. Ashua had only ever met Dracken briefly, and then Dracken had threatened to have her nails pulled out. Ashua didn't know what the Cap'n saw in her. Still, she must be quite a woman, with all that Frey was willing to go through to get her. That, or he was just desperate.

Well, at least while he was after Dracken, he wasn't after her. That made for a more pleasant travel experience all round.

A light began to blink on the cruiser's electroheliograph mast. Abley watched it closely. Ashua watched him, just as closely. She was good at spotting liars and tricksters. She'd been surrounded by them all her life.

When the blinking stopped, Abley set to work, tapping away. With

Jez still out of action, they had no way of telling what he was communicating. Of those in the cockpit, only the Cap'n had any knowledge of EHG code, and he'd relied on navigators for so long that he was abominably slow at it. Ashua exchanged a glance with Silo, who was standing next to her, his arms crossed. No sign from him to betray his emotions, of course. If he was tense, she couldn't tell.

Abley finished up. They waited. Then the cruiser began flashing again. Abley picked up a pencil and scribbled down the message. Then the cruiser swung away from them, heading back towards the aircraft hanging in the distance. Ashua noted that several of the bigger craft were departing the fleet and heading away, going dark as they left the main mass.

'They've accepted the code,' said Abley, his shoulders slumped in evident relief. He held up a piece of paper. 'These are the coordinates for the next rendezvous. Looks like it's due west of here, over the Splinters. We have to be there by dusk.'

'The Splinters?' Ashua said. 'I thought we were meant to be going to the Barabac Delta.'

'I don't know! That's just what they told me!' Abley protested.

'Can't move a whole fleet all the way 'cross Vardia by daylight,' Silo rumbled. 'Least, not without someone takin' note.'

'So everyone makes their separate ways to the rendezvous,' Frey mused, thinking it over. 'Then they fly down the length of the Splinters by night. Lights off, no one'll see them.'

'Makes sense,' said Ashua.

'Looks like we've got an appointment to keep, folks,' said Frey. He waved a hand at Silo. 'Put the lad somewhere he can't cause any trouble, will you? We'll sort out what to do with him later.'

'You said you'd let me go!' Abley protested, as Silo pulled him to his feet.

'We will, if you behave,' Frey replied.

Abley hobbled away with Silo. Ashua, deciding that the danger had passed, went with them down the corridor, then split off and headed to the cargo hold.

She emerged on a walkway overlooking the dim, echoing chamber that had become her home. Below her she heard thumping and clanking: Bess, restless, as she'd been ever since they'd taken off.

Ashua spotted her stomping about near the lashed-up crates of Awakener relics they'd pulled off the freighter a few days ago. The weak hold lights reflected from her dull and battered armour.

'He's not here, Bess,' she said quietly to herself. 'He left you behind. People do that.'

She was a little sad about Crake. She'd liked him. Maybe it was his aristocratic style, but he reminded her of a younger, finer Maddeus, before he'd wasted away. Now he was gone, and Malvery wasn't half as much fun since he'd started brooding about the war. The others were still along for the ride for now, but she wondered how much longer they'd stick with the Cap'n if he didn't find Trinica soon. Or maybe the Cap'n would dump them once he got his woman. Being saddled with a bunch of reprobates was hardly conducive to romance, after all.

Better look out for herself, then. She wasn't sure how much longer this crew was going to hold together.

She made her way down the steps to the floor of the hold. Bess spotted her and came thundering over with such speed that Ashua almost had to jump out of the way. The golem only just stopped in time. She stood there, looming over Ashua, regarding her with those sharp glimmers of light from behind her face-grille. Then she thrust out a hand.

The armoured glove was holding something. A large red leather book, slightly battered by her grip. Ashua just looked at it. Bess proffered it again, cooing impatiently. Ashua got the hint that time, and took it.

Stories for Little Girls.

Ashua didn't quite know what to think. She raised an uncertain eyebrow at the golem. 'You want me to have this?'

Bess poked the book with a heavy, urging finger. Then Ashua remembered hearing the faint murmur of Crake's voice from behind the tarp curtain at the back of the hold, and she figured it out. 'You want me to *read* this to you?'

Bess cooed eagerly. Ashua made a face. 'Oh, Bess, you've got me all wrong. I'm not the mothering type. Sorry.'

She handed the book back to Bess. Bess took it and clutched it to her chest. Despite having no features, she somehow managed to look hurt. She sloped away, moaning disconsolately.

Ashua felt a pang of guilt. Crake had always been evasive about the exact nature of his guardian, but sometimes it seemed almost alive. A passing anger took her, that Crake would abandon his golem this way. She reminded herself that it wasn't her problem.

She made her way to the nook between the pipes where she slept. She'd fashioned herself a cosy little spot there, lined with tarp and blankets, scattered with what meagre possessions she had. There was a fabric curtain for privacy. She liked her little den; in fact, she'd turned down the chance of a bunk for it. Having grown up sleeping on floors and in corners, she didn't get on with beds. She enjoyed having the whole cargo hold as her domain instead of the cramped quarters upstairs. The pipes kept her warm at night, and soothed her with their creaking and tapping.

She rummaged through her bedding until she found what she was looking for. She'd hidden it away well between the pipes. She didn't want anyone asking any questions. They wouldn't understand.

She brought out the object that Bargo Ocken had given her back in Timberjack Falls, and studied it. It was a brass cube, small enough to sit in her hand. On the upper face was a button. On one of the adjacent faces was a small circular opening, covered with glass. That was all. An innocuous-looking thing, but an important one. With this, she could work her way to a small fortune.

She saw Bargo Ocken's face as he sat across the table from her in a smoky bar. She heard his slow, measured voice. *Look on us as, well, something on the side. Insurance. In case it all goes wrong somewhere down the line.*

She began tapping the button on top of the cube. A code, a language she'd memorised long ago, created for just this purpose. With each touch, a light came on behind the glass circle on the side of the cube.

When she was finished, she waited. After a short while, it started blinking back at her.

Slag, the *Ketty Jay*'s moderately psychopathic cat, clambered out of the ventilation ducts and into the engine room. He was battered, scratched and bloodied, but he was triumphant. Another battle had been won deep in the guts of the aircraft, another blow struck in his lifelong war against the rats. It was all he'd ever known, this conflict. He was a warrior to the core.

The engine room was a noisy, rattling place full of machine smells. Neither the noise nor the stink bothered him: he was more at home here than he ever would be in a field or garden. The pipes and walkways that surrounded the huge engine assembly were Slag's jungle. Right now he wanted somewhere to rest, somewhere that would put some heat into his ancient bones and tired muscles. He picked his way to his favourite spot atop a water pipe, tested the temperature and found it just right. There he settled to lick his wounds.

In days gone by the breeders in the depths had turned out monsters, huge rats to test his mettle. These were the challengers to his supremacy. The fights were vicious and terrible, but always he put them down. His many years of experience, his strength and speed told out in the end. He reddened his claws on the best of them.

This rat had not been the best of them. Big, yes, but nothing like the legendary enemies he'd defeated in his prime. And yet he'd struggled. He'd killed it, but he'd struggled.

Slag was an old cat. Tough as a chewed boot, but old. And of late he wasn't as strong as he had been, nor as quick. He lived in a world of instinct and not reason, but even so, on some level he was dimly aware that his body was failing him.

The knowledge meant nothing. He could conceive of no other life but this one. His world was the *Ketty Jay*, its ducts and crawlspaces and pipes, and there he was a tyrant. He'd been beaten only once, by one of the huge two-legged entities that wandered around in the open spaces. The vile scrawny one had lured him away from his territory once, and defeated him there. But never on his own turf. Here, he was still supreme.

He lifted his head. A strange smell came to his nostrils, the merest whiff in amongst the acrid stench of aerium and prothane and oil. It was gone in a moment, but it was enough to put a suspicion in him. Ignoring the pain of his wounds and the aches in his joints, he dropped down from his perch and went prowling.

There it was again. He followed his nose, padding along metal walkways, up and down steps. It was no human smell that he knew, nor a smell of machines or rats. Soon he found a spot where it was strong, a particular corner he liked to spray on to mark his territory.

But there was a new scent there now, over the old. He sniffed. Something about it stirred a sense-memory from a time before the *Ketty Jay*, when he was only a squirming kitten in a litter. It took a few moments for everything to fall into place.

A cat. He was smelling another cat.

And it was on board the *Ketty Jay*.

Jez's eyes opened. A crushing sense of loss settled on her. She was back on her bunk on the *Ketty Jay*.

How she dearly wanted that unconsciousness back. For that precious time, she'd been formless, drifting, and all around her had been music. The voices of her kin calling, their thoughts flashing everywhere, the great communication of the Manes. And in the darkness of non-thought she'd been with them, *connected*, and they'd welcomed her and begged their reluctant sibling to stay, stay, come and join them and be one of them for ever. She'd felt the enormity of belonging, and it was like a glowing coal in her heart.

But the memory was fading faster than a dream. She was back in the world, back in that place of limited senses and limited desires. Back to the drab, cold torpor of isolation.

'You hear them, don't you?'

Pelaru's voice made her turn her head sharply. He was sitting in the dark by her bunk. She felt a flood of nervous joy at seeing him there, washing away the sadness.

'Yes,' she said. Her tongue felt unfamiliar. She had trouble shaping the word. It was sometimes like this, when she returned. It got harder and harder to remember how to be human.

Pelaru shifted himself. He seemed discomfited. 'Osger heard them. All the time, he said. Tempting him. Drawing him away from me. Sometimes he . . .' The Thacian's voice drifted off. 'What is it like, to be so close to them?'

'It's . . . wonderful,' she said. His expression tightened, and she knew she'd said the wrong thing. But she couldn't lie.

'Do you think he's with them now?'

'I don't know.'

Her eyes roamed over his face in the dark. His grief suited him, made him seem nobler; but she longed to see him smile.

'He was always . . . torn,' said Pelaru, and then he did smile, but not in the way she'd wanted. A bitter smile, recognising the irony of what he had said. Osger had ended up in two halves. 'I could never understand. Why would you give yourself up that way? Give up your humanity? To be one of *them*?'

He spoke the last word with such hatred that Jez almost feared to answer. How could he love a half-Mane and yet despise them so? 'It's not like giving yourself up,' she said at last. 'It's like *opening* yourself up.'

'By turning yourself into a horror,' Pelaru sneered, and the disgust in his voice wounded her.

She sat up in bed. She was fully clothed, still covered in stone dust, her overalls torn at the arms and legs. She looked a mess, but she didn't care. 'Is that what you think I am?' she asked. 'A horror?'

'No,' he said. 'No, and that's the worst of it. I . . . *feel* for you, Jez. From the first moment I saw you, I felt something. Something as strong as that which I felt for Osger. Even seeing you that way, back in the shrine . . . as a Mane. It doesn't change a thing.'

A sensation both hot and cold and blessed spread through her, like the touch of some benevolent deity. She tried to make herself speak, but found that it was hard, although for different reasons than before.

'I . . . I feel that too,' she said clumsily.

Agitated, he flung himself to his feet. 'What is it?' she asked, fearing that she'd done something wrong, that she'd repelled him. How was she supposed to act? She'd never done this before, never anything *like* this.

'This shouldn't be,' he said, his voice thick. 'Osger is not a day dead in my mind and yet . . .' He clenched his fists. 'This shouldn't be!' he said again, angrily. Then he walked out of Jez's quarters, and slid the door shut behind him.

Jez was left sitting on her bunk, the joy of a moment ago withering to an ashy despair.

'Why not?' she asked the darkness, quietly.

Thirteen

Arrival – A Welcoming Committee – The Prognosticator –
Ashua Gets Creative – The Allsoul Speaks

T he sun was breaking over the horizon when they reached
the Barabac Delta. Strawberry light cut low across a colossal
mangrove swamp that stretched from horizon to horizon. Frey
rubbed tired eyes and gazed out over the endless expanse before
him. Bayous and mighty rivers cut channels through the greenery,
glistening in the dawn light. Hills rose steep and sharp from the
watery murk, shagged with tropical trees. Vardia was a land so
enormous that the weather from one end to another differed drastic-
ally. Here on the south coast, not far from the Feldspar Islands, the
chill of winter was never felt.

It had taken them a day and a night to get here. Frey had reached
the first rendezvous in the early afternoon, well ahead of the slower
craft in the fleet. He'd landed the *Ketty Jay* in a mountain valley and
caught up on some long overdue sleep while the rest of the Awakeners
gathered. When night fell, Silo woke him and they took off again.
There was another round of identity checks, for which Abley's
assistance was needed once more, and then they all headed south *en
masse*, without lights.

It was a dangerous business, night-flying with an undisciplined
mix of volunteers and conscripts. Most of them had never flown in
formation in their lives, and certainly not in the dark. Even though
they kept very loose, with plenty of distance between each aircraft,
there were a few accidents. All of them were fatal. *Wonder if their all-
seeing Allsoul saw* that *coming?* Frey thought uncharitably.

As they flew, Frey had begun to hope. He was heading towards
Trinica at last. The thought energised him, and anticipation made the
long night flight bearable.

He knew he'd put his crew through a lot. He knew he should have told them what he was up to in the first place. But he happened to think he'd been doing a pretty fine job of treading the line between what his crew wanted and what he wanted. Maybe Malvery and Crake had issues about the war, but everyone else wanted to stay well out of it. Maybe some of the crew didn't think Trinica was worth risking their lives for, but they'd risked their lives for Frey on plenty of other occasions, so why was this different? And he was making sure they all got paid: there was a pile of Awakener treasure in the hold that Pelaru had forfeited as part of their deal, plus everything they'd nabbed from the shrine beneath Korrene.

He still wasn't sure if they were chasing phantoms. He still wasn't sure if Trinica would even see him, if he ever managed to track her down.

But he had to try. It was as simple as that.

During that long flight he thought of Crake as well. Frey hoped he was alright. He hoped he'd make contact again, sometime soon. He hoped a lot of things, but they were all out of his hands now. Crake had gone, and while Frey felt guilty, he didn't entirely blame himself. It had been one moment of thoughtlessness that had driven his friend away. If Frey beat himself up every time he did something thoughtless, he'd be in a wheelchair.

It occurred to him belatedly that they still had Pelaru aboard. But the whispermonger had shown no signs of wanting to leave, and Frey hadn't had the opportunity to drop him off anywhere. As long as he kept quiet, Frey didn't mind overmuch. Information being his business, he might even turn out to be useful.

Once they were over the swamps, the fleet dropped down low to follow a river. The bigger craft travelled in single file while the fighters buzzed around them. Though much of the land was submerged, there were many islands and bluffs, and the trees grew high and thick. In this terrain, and with anti-aircraft batteries supposedly concealed everywhere, it was no wonder the Coalition had been having trouble tracking down the Awakeners.

You could search for ever and never find someone in this place, Frey thought. Which, he reminded himself, was entirely the point.

The heat began to grow as the sun rose higher in the sky. Brightly coloured birds winged across the convoy's path. Twisted trees spread roots like hag's claws into the torpid water. Reptiles slid between them, half-submerged.

The river branched and branched again, and finally it came to a kind of open-ended valley between two island peaks that thrust out of the waterlogged earth. Then they rose up, over the trees, and below them Frey saw their destination.

The base, such as it was, spread over kloms of swampland. Dozens of clearings, some natural and some man-made, were hidden between the trees. Thousands of aircraft ranging from tiny to mid-sized stood in them, raggedy old crop-dusters and sleek pleasure craft alike, all getting kitted out for war. Anti-aircraft guns lurked nearby, watching the sky.

A small makeshift town had been constructed in one of the largest clearings near the centre. Ramshackle huts had been built and large tents put up. Most of the people seemed to be there, Frey noted as they flew over it. Presumably that was where they distributed supplies and information.

Frey hadn't expected much, but he still thought it was a dump. The Awakeners didn't have half the resources and organisation the Coalition did. He couldn't imagine how they hoped to win, the way things stood.

Well, at least the ground was above water level, he thought, as the fleet leader signalled and the craft began to land. Frey looked for the *Delirium Trigger*, but there was nowhere nearby to hide such a massive craft. That worried him slightly, but he wasn't to be deterred. He'd simply make his way to the town and ask around.

He brought the *Ketty Jay* down in a small clearing shared by a couple of freighters that looked like they'd been assembled from junkyard scraps and cutlery. He powered down the engines and flopped back in his seat in relief.

Trinica, he thought. *Here I am at last.*

'Trouble, Cap'n,' Silo called down the corridor from the cockpit.

Rot and damnation, what now? Frey thought. He'd been staring critically at himself in the grubby mirror above the metal sink in his quarters. There were heavy bags under his eyes. He'd only snatched a few hours' sleep since they set off for Korrene the day before yesterday. After flying all night, he looked fit for the knacker's yard. Not the face he wanted to present to his long-lost love.

He tore himself away from the mirror – even at his worst, he found a ghoulish fascination in his own reflection – and went to see what the matter was. He found Ashua dragging Abley up the corridor at gunpoint. His hands were tied before him with rope.

'I warned you, didn't I?' she told him. 'Cap'n, where can we shoot this little bastard where he'll make the least mess?'

'Whoa, whoa! Don't anyone shoot anyone till someone tells me what we're shooting people about,' said Frey.

Ashua pulled the terrified Abley to a halt, and pressed a pistol to the side of his head. 'There's a bunch of armed Awakeners out there, that's what. And they want to come in. I call that quite a bloody coincidence, don't you?'

'Where's Harkins and Pinn?'

'Here! Here!' Harkins said, stumbling out of his quarters in his long johns, with the imprint of a pillow stamped into one side of his face. 'Thought I'd catch some sleep. Er, it was quite a long flight. Sorry, Cap'n.'

'And Pinn?'

From the door behind Harkins, there came an intake of breath as if someone were cranking up a ballista, followed by a despairing wheeze like the lamentations of the damned.

'Is he snoring or dying in there?' Frey asked.

'Er . . . well . . . when he's asleep, it takes a bomb to wake him,' Harkins said. Then he dropped his voice, glanced back through the door and covered one side of his mouth. 'It's probably because he's an enormous lazy turd,' he added bravely.

Well, that put paid to the idea of flying off. He wasn't going to leave the Skylance and Firecrow behind.

Silo came out of the cockpit and into the corridor. 'They lookin' pretty impatient, Cap'n,' he advised.

Frey was beginning to feel flustered. First bags under his eyes, and now this? 'Where's the doc, then?'

'He won't be getting up, Cap'n,' said Jez, who'd appeared out of her quarters. 'He was drinking pretty hard yesterday.'

Frey was glad to see her up and about. She'd put on new overalls and washed, and she looked more focused than he'd seen her in a while. That, at least, was heartening.

He made a quick decision. 'We'll have a pretty hard time explaining away a dead man if they come aboard,' he told Ashua. 'Bring him. Silo, you too.'

He headed into the infirmary. Ashua pushed the prisoner along after and Silo followed. Frey picked his way through Malvery's medicine cabinet until he found a bottle with the right label. 'Hold him still,' he said absently.

'I didn't tell them! I swear! I did what you said!' Abley was wailing, as Silo wrapped strong arms round him to secure him.

Frey found a wadded rag, tipped some of the bottle on it, and then slapped it over Abley's nose and mouth. 'That's enough out of you,' he said.

Abley struggled for a moment, but not hard enough to break Silo's hold. His eyelids fluttered as he breathed in the chloroform, and then he went limp.

'Give me a hand,' he told Silo. Between them, they hauled Abley to the operating table and left him there.

'If he's shopped us, Cap'n, I'm coming back to shoot him, unconscious or not,' Ashua promised.

There was a banging on the cargo hold door, faintly heard. Frey straightened, arranged his hair a bit, and went back out into the corridor. 'Ashua, Silo, come with me. Jez, find Pelaru, make sure he stays quiet. I don't trust him not to sell us out. Harkins . . .' He waved at the air, unable to think of anything useful that Harkins could possibly contribute. 'I don't know, get dressed or something.'

'Cap'n!' Harkins saluted smartly and disappeared back into his quarters. Frey shook his head. He couldn't get used to that saluting thing.

They made their way down to the hold. Frey thought their numbers were thin for a confrontation, but he didn't want a firefight here, which was why he'd given Jez a job to keep her out of the way. He didn't need her making everyone nervous. And anyway, if it came to that, they always had Bess.

Oh, damn it. Bess.

He could hear her clanking around as they came down the stairs to the floor of the cargo hold. Without Crake's whistle to put her to sleep they were going to have trouble hiding the fact there was a daemonist's golem on board. And that would take some explaining to a bunch of Awakeners.

'Ashua. Go back there to the sanctum. See if you can shut her up.'

'How am I supposed to do that?' Ashua protested.

'I don't know. You're the smart one. Be creative.'

Ashua muttered something about how creative he'd feel with a rusty fork rammed sideways up his arse, but she did what she was told.

So now there were two of them. The captain and his first mate. He smoothed his rumpled clothes as Silo went over to the lever that opened the cargo ramp.

'Let's look like we've got nothing to hide, eh?' he said. Silo pulled the lever and then returned to stand by his captain.

There were a dozen of them waiting outside, and most of them were carrying rifles. There were Sentinels in grey cassocks, an Acolyte in beige, and an assortment of men who looked like mercenaries. At the head of them was a tall man in a black cassock, high-collared and single-breasted like those of his companions. He had a long flowing moustache and a shaven skull, with the Cipher tattooed prominently on his forehead.

'Brothers!' Frey called out happily, throwing his arms wide.

'That,' thundered the man in black, 'remains to be seen.'

They came up the ramp and into the cargo hold, spreading out to cover the area with guns. Frey didn't count that an encouraging sign. The man in black walked up and stood squarely before him.

'My name is Prognosticator Garin,' he said. 'And you are Captain Darian Frey.'

'I'm pleased that my reputation precedes me,' he said, though in this case he really wasn't. If word had got back that he'd been robbing Awakener vessels, this wouldn't go well.

'We recognised your aircraft,' said Garin. He glanced at Silo, then turned his attention back to Frey. 'And now I'm wondering why you are here.'

Frey thought about playing the religious conversion angle, but he knew he'd never make it stick. So he went with what he knew. The best lies were closest to the truth.

'Look, mate,' he said confidingly. 'I know you lot are into your

Allsoul and stuff, but to be honest, that's not for me. The idea of my destiny being mapped out before me and all that, I don't much like it. I'm a simple man at heart. But I see the way the common folk rally round your banner, and I think, well, whose side do I want to be on? The Dukes and all those pompous city types? Or down here with the salt of the earth?'

'Don't try me with speeches, Captain Frey,' said Garin, his arms folded.

'Sod it then. We're here for the mercenary work,' said Frey, shrugging. 'The only mercs the Coalition are hiring are Shacklemores. They want everyone on their side all disciplined and legal. Their loss. We reckoned you fellers might put up some coin for a few fighting craft and some experienced pilots.'

'And so you found your way here. Very enterprising. I can't imagine that would have gone down very well with the daemonist on your crew. A man by the name of Grayther Crake?'

Ah. That's what this is about.

'It didn't,' said Frey. 'So we kicked him off. Bloke was a pain anyway.'

Garin raised an eyebrow. 'That's interesting. Rumour has it you were fast friends.'

'Rumour has it your Imperators are all daemons,' Frey replied. 'Don't believe everything you hear.'

A smile touched the side of Garin's mouth. 'You're far from the first pirate to join our ranks,' he said. 'It's regrettable, but in order to fight the Archduke's persecution, we'll take the measures we must.' His smile faded. 'But if a man allies himself with the faithless, he'd better be ready for betrayal. You won't object if we search your aircraft? Just to see if you're telling the truth about your daemonist.'

The thought of Awakeners crawling all over his beloved aircraft, poking through his possessions, made Frey want to punch that stupid moustache off Garin's face. But he didn't see that he had much choice in the matter, so he hid his feelings behind a broad smile. 'Of course,' he said, with admirable control. 'Take a look around. Silo, why don't you go upstairs and warn the crew that men with guns are going to be there shortly?' He looked at Garin. 'Don't want an incident, do we?'

Silo did as he was told. Garin motioned to some of his men to follow the Murthian. 'Keep the crew up there until I'm done with the Captain,' he instructed them. He told the others to search the cargo hold.

'What's through there?' he asked Frey. He was pointing towards the back, where crates and tarp separated off a section.

'Crake's old sanctum,' Frey said. He saw no point in lying. He also saw no point in mentioning Bess.

Immediately, Garin strode off across the hold towards it. Wrong-footed, Frey stood there a moment, said 'Er,' and then hurried after him, frantically thinking of ways he could explain the golem away.

The Prognosticator pushed aside the tarpaulin curtain and stepped into the sanctum, with Frey at his shoulder. Frey's heart sank a little at the sight of it. It didn't look good, with that weird daemonic circle drawn on the floor and the chalkboards covered in formulae and all the books and equipment and stuff. The whole thing looked like a cross between a mad scientist's laboratory and the domain of some-one who should be in a padded cell.

'Hi, Cap'n,' said Ashua chirpily, straightening up from a bookcase with an armload of books. 'I was just packing away Crake's stuff, like you told me to. Who's this?'

I could kiss you, you wonderful thing, Frey thought. 'This is Pro-gnosticator Garin. He just wants to make sure we don't have any daemonists on board.'

Ashua smirked. 'Not any more!' she said.

'He got sort of snippy about leaving,' said Frey. 'Some rubbish about money we owed him. So we kicked him about a bit, then threw him off.'

'No honour among thieves, eh?'

'We prefer to think of ourselves as wealth distribution experts.'

Garin studied the room sceptically. Frey glanced about and found Bess in a shadowy corner. She was standing entirely motionless. He narrowed his eyes and peered closer. Two little glimmers peered back at him from the darkness behind her face-grille. Frey looked away quickly as Garin turned to him. The Prognosticator gave him a penetrating glare.

'I'm not at all sure that what you're telling me is the truth, Captain Frey,' he said. 'But I've ways to find out. Follow me.'

He swept out of the sanctum. Frey pointed at Ashua on the way out. *You*, he mouthed, *are amazing*. Ashua did a little curtsey. Bess tried one too, creaking and squeaking as she did so.

'What was that?' Garin called from outside.

'Just Ashua tidying up!' Frey replied hastily, slipping through the tarp.

They walked back to the far end of the cargo hold, where the Acolyte had assembled a small brazier from pieces in his backpack and was in the process of lighting it. 'Are we having a barbecue?' Frey asked, mildly confused.

Garin ignored him. One of the Sentinels came down the stairs into the hold. 'Can't see any sign of him, Prognosticator,' he said. 'We're looking through the engine room now, but there aren't too many places to hide on a craft like this.'

'I see,' said Garin. On a piece of cloth, the acolyte laid out a brush, a small pot of ink, a pair of tongs, and a white oval stone the size of a hand. 'Anything else?'

'There's an unconscious man in the infirmary.'

'Abley,' said Frey. 'He took a bullet through the leg when we were fighting the Coalition in Korrene. It was a bad one. We had to put him out.'

Garin seemed to have lost interest. He picked up the brush and began painting something in black ink on the stone.

'What's in here?' asked one of the Sentinels, rapping the butt of his rifle against the lashed-up pile of chests in the centre of the hold. Frey didn't turn to look, but his heart sank a little. The relics. All the relics they'd stolen were in those chests.

He pretended to ignore the question. Garin hadn't noticed. There was nothing quite so withering than when you spoke and no one listened.

The Sentinel didn't repeat his question. He gave one of chests a cursory jiggle but found it closed tight. Eventually he wandered away, slightly embarrassed.

Frey let out his breath. He needed these people off his aircraft. What was Garin *doing*, anyway?

'Hold this,' said Garin, passing him the stone. 'Careful. The ink's wet.'

Frey held the flat stone in his hands. Written on the stone were two words. Darian Frey.

127

'Say it aloud,' Garin instructed him.

'Er . . . Darian Frey,' he said. 'That's me.'

Garin took the stone back carefully and put it over the brazier. The Acolyte, a young carrot-headed boy, watched eagerly. Some of the other searchers began returning to the hold, having found no trace of Crake. They gathered round the brazier, fascinated.

'What exactly are you doing?' Frey asked, when he couldn't stand it any more.

'I am asking the Allsoul whether you are a deceiver, or whether you truly want to aid our cause.'

'I truly want to aid it if you *pay* me,' Frey corrected. 'I presume your little barbecue can handle the difference?'

'I'd not be so flippant if I were you. Your freedom, and likely your life, rests on this.'

One of the Sentinels primed his rifle. Frey suddenly wished he hadn't allowed himself to be separated from his crew. If it came to it, perhaps Ashua and Bess could help him, but not before he got shot.

There was a quiet *crack* from the stone. The Acolyte picked up the tongs, but Garin signalled him to wait. There was another crack, and a pop. Garin motioned to the Acolyte, and the stone was taken off the brazier, turned upside down and laid onto a wadded cloth on the floor. The Acolyte picked up the cloth with the hot stone in its centre and presented it reverently to Garin. Garin began studying it intently.

Frey peered over his shoulder. The stone had been split by the heat. Crooked black lines spread across it, intersecting each other.

'Are you getting something from that?' Frey asked.

'There are many ways to know the mind of the Allsoul. This is the way that chose me,' Garin said.

'The pattern means something?'

'The pattern means *everything*,' Garin said, frowning as he studied the lines. All eyes were on the Prognosticator now. Frey saw wonder and amazement on their faces.

You're all being duped, you bloody idiots. It's a carnival trick! he thought. But he wasn't quite as sure as he pretended. The slim possibility that there might be something to this Awakener mumbo-jumbo had him nervous, and the Prognosticator certainly *looked* like he knew what he was doing. Soon he was as mesmerised as the rest of them, as he waited to learn his fate.

Finally, Garin folded the cloth over the stone and handed it back to the Acolyte. 'The Allsoul has spoken,' he said. The Awakeners repeated his words in a low mutter, their eyes cast down to the floor. Garin turned to Frey, and stared at him long and hard.

'So what's the verdict?' Frey asked. The tension was killing him.

Garin laid a hand on his shoulder. 'Welcome,' he said gravely. 'We will accept your aid in our righteous cause. See the quartermaster in the town about payment.'

Frey managed to keep the relief off his face. 'Glad to be here,' he said. *And glad you're a massive charlatan with it,* he added mentally.

Garin walked away. The others called down their companions who were guarding the crew, and then followed him out, leaving the Acolyte to tidy up the brazier. Frey waited patiently till everyone was gone, then shut the cargo door behind them.

'Everythin' alright, Cap'n?' Silo enquired from the walkway above.

'Just fine,' said Frey, as he was heading towards the sanctum at the back of the hold. 'We're in!'

He pushed open the tarpaulin curtain and looked in on Ashua. He found her sitting cross-legged opposite the golem, who'd plonked down on her butt like a baby. Ashua had a large red leather book open in her lap.

'How'd you manage to get her to keep still like that?' he asked in amazement.

She lifted up the book to show him. *Stories for Little Girls.* 'Bribery,' she said. 'Works a treat.' Then she turned her attention back to Bess. 'You ready? Alright, here we go. "*The Duchess and the Daisy-Chain*".'

Fourteen

Hooded – Crake's Return –
A Bloody Reading – Pinn the Convert

hree years. Three years and they've finally caught me. I suppose it's
true what they say, then. The Shacklemores always get their man
in the end.

Grayther Crake sat on a metal bench in the back compartment of a small aircraft, contemplating his impending death. At least, he guessed it was small, by the sound of the engines. It was hard to tell with a sack over his head.

The past twenty-four hours had been a terrifying and humiliating ordeal. The Shacklemore Agency had a reputation built on professionalism and a gentlemanly veneer intended to put rich clients at ease. Shacklemores were polite, well-dressed and efficient: the acceptable face of bounty hunting. But scratch the surface, Crake had discovered, and underneath you'd find mercenary thugs like all the rest; proud members of the biggest gang in Vardia.

'You won't be using that tooth on us, mate,' they sneered when they caught him. That was when they put the sack on, and it had hardly been off since. They cuffed his hands behind his back and pulled him, blind and helpless, through the streets of Korrene. Distant guns and nearby explosions made him shudder and cringe in fear, but they tugged him onward mercilessly until they reached an aircraft. When he felt them taking off, he knew he was lost. There was no hope of rescue after that.

He spent a day and a night in a cell, tormenting himself with thoughts of what was to come and what he'd left behind. He thought of the crew, and wondered how they were faring, and wished he'd never been so foolish as to leave. He thought of Samandra, and burned with shame. Better that she thought he'd run out on her and missed their rendezvous, or that he was dead. Better that than the truth.

He thought of Bess . . . But no, he couldn't think of Bess. Bess, the golem he'd abandoned. Bess, the little girl he'd murdered. He'd evaded justice all this time, but he couldn't evade it for ever.

They left the bag on his head and kept him manacled like an animal. It only came off when they fed him. One man would spoon stew into his mouth while two others stood by with guns in case he should try any daemonist trickery. He ate what he was given. He didn't have the heart to protest his treatment. He deserved it.

'Don't worry. You'll be on your way soon,' they told him. 'We're just waiting for someone to take you off our hands. You weren't even supposed to be our catch, but Rokesby here remembered your warrant from the newsletter, didn't he?'

Rokesby, the clean-shaven young man who'd caught him, gave a proud little smile. 'Should've kept a bit more of a low profile, I reckon,' he said, filling up another spoonful of stew for his prisoner. 'Not many people ain't heard of the *Ketty Jay* these days. Victim of your own success, ain't you?'

Crake didn't care for their explanations. *Just get on with it,* he thought. *Just get it done.*

Early in the morning, his escorts arrived. They took him from the cell and walked him to an aircraft. He could smell food cooking and heard the rough conversation of men nearby. It occurred to him that the flight from the spot he was taken had been short; they were probably in the Coalition's forward camp, where Samandra had kissed him not two days past. A wild thought came to him, filling him with sudden hope: he should shout out for help! But the notion died as soon as it was born. Who would help him? He was a legitimately guilty man. Why would anyone, Samandra most of all, intervene to save a criminal from the law?

He stayed silent. They put him on the aircraft and took off. He didn't need to ask where they were taking him.

They were taking him home.

I'm going to hang, he thought, as he felt the aircraft touch down. He'd thought it many times since they caught him. Grief and despair, panic and resignation all visited him in their turn while he waited in his cell.

But there were worse things, even, than the prospect of a short sudden trip to oblivion. Worse would be his father's silent, grief-stricken disappointment. His sister-in-law Amantha's hysterical shrieks. And Condred, oh, Condred, whose daughter he'd stabbed to death. It didn't matter that he knew nothing about it till afterwards. It didn't matter that the whole thing was an awful accident. He'd still have to face the distraught wrath of his brother before they sent him to the gallows.

After some time, he heard the aircraft doors open, and they came for him. They took him outside and walked him along a path. Even blind, he suspected he knew where they were. When it kinked right and went up a shallow incline, he was sure. He'd walked the route from the Crake family's private landing pad a thousand times.

Ahead of him and to his left was the mansion he'd grown up in. Behind him, across the grounds, was Condred's house, where Crake had spent his post-university years playing the layabout while studying daemonism in secret. Condred had taken him in as an act of arrogant charity. He thought it would improve his idle brother's attitude to live with a family that knew the value of duty and hard work.

No doubt he'd regretted his charity since.

They took him into the foyer and along a route he recognised, though he'd seldom travelled it. The study was his father's sanctuary. After Crake's mother died, Rogibald took to it more and more often, until he was seldom seen elsewhere except for meals and business. His sons knew not to bother him there. Rogibald disliked being interrupted when he was working. Or thinking. Or doing pretty much anything, for that matter.

He'll make an exception for me now, I'll bet, Crake thought. Even in the midst of his misery, he could summon a touch of bitterness where his father was concerned.

They opened the door without knocking and led him inside. He felt a key in his cuffs and his wrists were freed. Then they pulled the bag from his head.

He blinked at the morning light streaming in through the high windows. The room was as he remembered it: expensive fixtures and furniture gone comfortably shabby with age. There were many books but no ornaments. Rogibald was not a man for sentiment, nor did he appreciate art.

His father was sitting in a high-backed red leather chair, facing the hearth. All Crake could see of him was one arm of a houndstooth suit jacket. A butler that Crake didn't recognise was just delivering a glass of brandy on a silver tray. There was an identical chair next to Rogibald, this one unoccupied. A fire had been newly lit to fend off the chill of winter in the hills.

'Sit down, Grayther,' Rogibald said. His voice was worn and weary. Not at all the tone that Crake was used to hearing from him. 'Everybody else, get back to your duties.'

One of the Shacklemores, a young fellow with a pencil moustache, seemed uncomfortable at the idea. 'Sir, perhaps we should stay? To ensure that the fugitive doesn't get out of hand.'

'I have nothing to fear from my son,' Rogibald snarled. 'Get out!'

The butler opened the door and invited them to leave. They did so. The butler left with them, and closed the door behind him.

Crake sat down in the empty chair. His father was thinner than he remembered. He'd always been lean, but now the flesh was falling off his bones, and his once stern face was gaunt. He seemed to have shrunk inside his clothes, and there was the sour smell of the old about him. But for all that, he was still Rogibald Crake: solemn, erect, intimidating.

'Hello, Father,' said Crake.

Rogibald didn't reply. He rarely indulged in pleasantries. He was a big believer in the idea that a man shouldn't speak unless he had something worth saying.

Crake had never been able to suffer those silences for long. He needed something to fill up the space. 'You have a new butler,' he heard himself saying. 'What happened to Charden?'

'I got rid of him,' Rogibald said. 'I got rid of all the servants. Amantha insisted, after . . .' He waved a hand. 'You know.'

Yes, thought Crake. *I know perfectly. But neither of us can say it.*

'She used to fly into a rage at the sight of them,' Rogibald said. 'Blamed them for not seeing it coming, not watching Bessandra closely enough, not locking the doors, or some such thing. She cleared out her own household, then started on mine. I let them go, to keep the peace. But Charden . . . that was hard. That man had been with me twenty years.' He shifted in his chair and folded his legs. 'She was insane,' he said. 'We just didn't know it then.'

133

'Where is she now?'

'The sanatorium at Clock Shallows. We sent her there a year ago. I don't think it's made her any better, but she seems happy, at least. She has come to believe that Bessandra is there with her. Nobody is inclined to discourage the notion.'

Crake felt his throat close up. His brother's wife in a sanatorium. His doing. He'd never liked her, but that hardly mattered. Her ruin lay at his feet.

'Damnably difficult, keeping any servants these days,' Rogibald went on. 'They're a superstitious lot. People in the village talk. The way they tell it, the manor is cursed and all of us with it. Not many servants stay long after they hear that.' He sipped his brandy. 'Superstitious lot,' he said again.

Crake couldn't bear listening to his father talk this way. He was usually so direct, a no-nonsense man who got to his point instantly. To hear him working up the courage to address the real subject was awful. Only then did Crake realise how much pain he'd inflicted on a man he'd thought incapable of feeling.

'Father. I know there are no words that can—'

'No,' he said. 'There aren't.'

Crake shut up. All of a sudden, he wanted to cry; but that would never do. It was unthinkable to shed a tear in front of Rogibald. Condred had always followed their father in all things, but Grayther had been a disappointment. Rogibald had always said he'd bring shame on the family.

Well, at least he could take solace in the fact that he'd been proved right. For Rogibald, being right was everything.

Crake looked hard out the window, to gather himself. Trench-coated Shacklemores walked the lawns in the crisp morning light, or patrolled near the wall that surrounded the grounds. They carried shotguns. It seemed a lot of firepower for a single fugitive.

'The bounty hunters?' Crake asked, when he found his voice again.

Rogibald said nothing.

'Father?' he prompted.

'I'm sorry, was that a question?'

Crake had forgotten how wilfully obtuse his father could be. When he wasn't being infuriatingly literal, he was being pedantic. It was his way of maintaining superiority.

He tried again. 'Why are there so many Shacklemores here?'

Rogibald's jaw tightened at that. He stared into the fire. 'The rabble hereabouts.'

'The villagers? The farmers?'

'All of them. The Awakeners have stirred up the countryside, Grayther. Turning the common folk against the gentry. If we don't declare for their cause . . . Well, I wouldn't be the first to be strung up because I won't bend the knee to their nonsense. Many of us have gone to the cities, but I'll not cave in to ignorance.' He turned to Crake, and there was a feverish anger in his eyes. 'I won't, you hear? No matter what the cost!'

Crake had the sense that there was some meaning to Rogibald's words that he was missing. But he had other questions, and he couldn't take the suspense any more. His father's feelings be damned; he had to know.

'Where is Condred, Father?'

Rogibald flinched as if struck. He seemed to diminish, and shrank back into his chair, where he took a swallow of brandy.

'Father, where is he?' Crake persisted. 'He took the contract out on me, didn't he? Why did they bring me to you and not him?'

'Your brother . . .' said Rogibald, his voice heavy with a melancholy disgust. 'He cancelled the contract two years ago.'

Crake just stared dumbly. Two years ago? All this time he'd been living under a shadow, and there was no contract on him? No wonder the Shacklemores hadn't been on his back. He'd always thought it strange that they hadn't been more persistent.

'We kept the murder out of the courts, for the family's sake,' Rogibald said. 'Condred wanted to deal with you himself. But after a year . . . After Amantha . . .' The tiniest of frowns crossed his brow: a sign of what his next words cost him. 'It would have been a hollow victory, he said. To exact vengeance on his brother. No matter what you did.'

Crake's hands began to tremble. A torrent of muddled emotions threatened to overwhelm him. Relief and guilt came all together. Was he reprieved? Would he live after all? And if so, where was his justice, his retribution? He couldn't believe that his brother would ever have forgiven him for what he did. And yet . . .

'If he cancelled the contract, why did the Shacklemores bring me here?'

'Because I told them to,' said Rogibald. He finished the last of his brandy, grimacing as if he'd swallowed something rank. Then, venomously:

'Because I need your help.'

Pinn hurried across the clearing, his heart beating hard in his chest. The sun was low and yellow as it pushed through the swampy tangle at the clearing's edge. Insects swam in clouds in the early evening swelter.

There were a few hundred people here, gathered round a haphazard collection of dirty tents. A couple of light cargo freighters, ugly Ludstrome craft, loomed in the background. From the tents, he could smell food cooking. A dozen voices sang tonelessly over the strumming of a stringed instrument and some clattering percussion. A small group had gathered outside an open tent painted with the Cipher on its side. Pinn headed for that one.

The Awakener base was spread out over many clearings, and beyond the central 'town' at its hub there were smaller gathering-places like this one. Pinn had tramped around plenty of them since he woke up. He was hot and bothered and his buttcrack was so sweaty that it bubbled whenever he farted. But none of that mattered now, because his search was at an end at last. Stumpy legs pumping, he hurried over to the tent and looked inside.

There she was. Young and pretty, her hair in a strawberry blonde bob, wearing a white Speaker cassock with red piping. A group of people were watching her, fascinated, as she held a needle to the upraised fingertip of an old woman. Beneath the woman's hand was a pedestal, on which sat a wooden saucer to catch the blood. Her tattooed forehead was creased in concentration, her wide blue eyes intent as she aimed.

The sight of her made him want to burst with joy. 'Marinda!' he cried as he rushed into the tent. Marinda jumped violently and stabbed the needle right through the old woman's hand.

'Oh! Oh my! I'm sorry! I'm so sorry!' Marinda gasped. The old woman stared at her hand, took a breath, and screamed. Suddenly everyone in the tent was on their feet, crowding round, yelling advice and accusations.

Pinn fought his way through to stand behind Marinda. She was bending over the old woman, who'd sunk to floor in shock. The woman's hand was held up in the air by the men who crowded round her. People were arguing about what to do with the needle. Someone grabbed it and pulled it out. Blood squirted in thin jets everywhere, on Marinda's face and all over her crisp white cassock.

'Hey!' said Pinn, trying to get her attention over the ruckus. 'Hey! Don't you remember me?'

'Call for help!' she shouted. 'We need a doctor!'

'Pinn, remember?' Pinn continued. 'From the freighter? You read my future?'

But Marinda, panicking, wasn't even looking at him, let alone listening. 'She needs a bandage!' she cried. Someone ripped off a sleeve of their shirt and began wadding it together. The old woman was wailing like a cat with its tail stuck in a door.

Pinn tried a new tack. He dug in his pocket and pulled out the piece of paper that had been stuck to his dashboard. 'Look!' he said, talking a bit louder. Someone shoved past him rudely, but he wasn't to be deterred. He brandished the piece of paper over her shoulder. 'Look, I wrote down your prophecy!'

She snatched the piece of paper from his hand, glanced at it a moment, and threw it away. 'That's no good, I said a bandage!'

The man with the ripped shirt seized the old woman's hand and wrapped his sleeve around it. 'Get her to the doctor!' someone cried, and the old woman was pulled to her feet.

Pinn was a little put out by what had happened to his precious piece of paper, but he forged on regardless. 'Isn't this crazy?' he asked. 'You and me, here? What are the chances? I mean, I know there's a lot of Awakeners gathered here, but still . . . Whew! If that's not the Allsoul's will, I don't know what is!'

The old woman was being bundled away by the spectators now. Marinda tried to go after her but a glare from one of the helpers stopped her. 'I'm sorry! I'm so very sorry!' she called. 'Oh, my! Oh my, this is terrible!'

'Hey!' Pinn said, with more than a touch of annoyance now. 'It's me!'

She whirled on him, a flash of anger in her eyes. 'What do you wa—?' The words froze in her throat and her face went slack with horror as she recognised him.

He threw his arms wide. 'That's right! Artis Pinn, Hero of the Skies, ace pilot, at your service! And I'm pretty handy with a shotgun, too!' To prove it he pulled out his shotgun and spun it round with his finger through the trigger guard. He thought he hadn't primed it, but obviously he had, because it went off with an ear-shattering boom and blew a hole in the roof of the tent. There was a muffled honk from above, and the world's most unfortunate goose thumped heavily to the turf just outside the entrance.

'Yep. Pretty handy,' Pinn said, to break the shocked silence that followed. His memory was already rewriting history, and he wasn't entirely sure whether he'd aimed for that bird or if it had been an accident. In five minutes' time there would be no doubt: he was quite the marksman, after all. At least in his own mind.

'You . . .' Marinda began, gaping. She had a very pretty gape. 'You robbed us, you monster!'

'Never mind that!' said Pinn, a stupid grin plastered on his chubby face. 'I'm an Awakener now!'

'You're a . . . What? How?'

'I just am! Look!' He bent down, picked up the piece of paper, and gave it to her. It was a bit muddy.

She looked around for help, embarrassed and not a little afraid. People were staring into the tent, drawn by the gunshot, but nobody dared come near. She brushed her hair behind her ear and read the piece of paper, frowning as she struggled to cope with Pinn's mangled scrawl and his appallingly tortured Vardic. 'What is it?' she asked.

'It's your prophecy!' said Pinn. 'Look, it came mostly true. Except the tragedy bit, but I reckon that's coming up.'

Marinda's frown deepened as things began to fall into place. 'Do the Sentinels know that you crashed an Awakener freighter, killed two dozen people and stole the artefacts on board?' she asked.

'Oh, yeah. Some Proboscitator feller came on board, cleared it all up.'

'A Prognosticator? And he said it was alright?' she asked doubtfully.

'More or less. Why else would they let us stay here, right? He let us off, 'cause we're Awakeners now.' Pinn wasn't sure if this was true or not, since it had happened while he was asleep, but it seemed to make sense.

'Oh,' said Marinda, disarmed. 'Well, I'm . . . I suppose I'm very glad, then. That you've decided to join us. Now I should go and see to that lady I hurt.' She was already halfway to walking off, but Pinn grabbed her arm before she could escape.

'It was you!' he said, leaning close with the manic sheen of the determined molester on his face. 'What you said to me, it . . . It changed my whole way of thinking! It changed my life!'

'Well, that's kind of you to say, but—'

'What's going on here?' demanded a shrill voice. An elderly man in a black cassock was striding towards them across the tent. 'Speaker Marinda, what's all the commotion?'

She stepped away from Pinn, blushing. 'I'm so very sorry, Prognosticator. I was attempting a reading, I was clumsy, and . . .'

'She converted me, Mr Pugnostrilator!' Pinn declared. 'She showed me the Allsoul!'

Marinda looked awkward. 'I explained, um, some of the nature of the Allsoul to this man. He has decided to join our cause.'

'But I need to know more!' Pinn said hastily. 'There's so much I don't understand. All that stuff about the cat god and the saucer of milk!'

'Our god is *not* a cat!' Marinda snapped. She thought for a moment, then added: 'Or a god!'

'Temper does not serve a Speaker's purpose well,' the Prognosticator chided her. 'It seems you have an enthusiastic pupil here. Is not the task of the Speaker to spread the word of the Allsoul?'

'Yes . . . but . . .' Marinda began. She had the expression of some adorable and harmless animal that could sense the door of its cage swinging shut.

The Prognosticator looked up at the hole in the tent roof, then raised an eyebrow at Pinn.

'Misfire,' said Pinn. 'Won't happen again.'

The Prognosticator turned his benevolent gaze back to Marinda. 'You should atone for your mistake, Marinda,' he intoned piously. 'Our greatest challenges are sometimes our greatest lessons. Teach those who would be taught.'

'Oh, yes!' said Pinn, with a grin that oozed smugness. 'Teach me.'

Fifteen

Preparations – A Poor Idiot Indeed –
The Watchpole – What Happens to Pirates

'Cap'n. Cap'n!'

Frey jerked awake. The shreds of a nightmare flurried away from him into the darkness of his quarters. Silo was standing there, a lean shadow, outlined by the dull electric light from the doorway.

'Yeah, yeah,' he murmured. He sat up, blinked, rubbed a hand through his sleep-mussed hair. 'What's going on?'

'You got a visitor, Cap'n. Crund. He's waitin' outside with a shuttle.'

Frey's head still wasn't working right. He had no idea how long he'd slept, but he felt like he could have done with a lot longer. It took him a few moments to work out who Silo was talking about. When he did, he sharpened up fast.

'Wait, Balomon Crund? Trinica's bosun on the *Delirium Trigger*?'

'Yuh. Says Trinica wanna see you.'

'Now?'

'Looks that way.'

Frey scrambled out of his bunk. 'Shit, I gotta freshen up first. I'm not seeing her like this. Tell him I'll be there soon as I can.'

'Reckon he'll figure it out,' said Silo, and then left, sliding the door closed behind him.

For the next half hour Frey flurried about the *Ketty Jay* in a panic. He showered in the communal bathroom next to the head, faffed about with his hair for a while and pulled on some clothes that looked suitably un-thought-about. Malvery scowled at him as he hurried down towards the cargo bay. The doc was in the grip of a mind-shattering hangover, but he knew what Frey was up to. The whole crew had heard by now.

Well, damn what he thinks. Damn what any of them think. We're here now.

By the time he left the *Ketty Jay*, he was geared up for the confrontation to come. Trinica had heard of his arrival and sought him out, but that didn't mean she bore him any tender feeling. Likely she was ready for a fight, so he would be too. He couldn't imagine what he'd say to her, and he knew it wouldn't be easy, but it needed to be done.

It was late afternoon when he emerged. The sun beat down and the air was thick and humid. Balomon Crund waited in the clearing next to a tiny shuttle that was only big enough for four people at most. He was a short, ugly man with a scarred neck and dark, thatchy hair that hadn't seen soap in a couple of decades. He sneered at Frey as he arrived.

'You took your time,' he said. His expression conveyed what he thought of Frey's rakishly unkempt attire.

'You can't rush perfection,' said Frey breezily, and flicked an imaginary bit of lint off his shoulder. Crund rolled his eyes, climbed into the pilot's seat and didn't say another word.

They took off and flew away over the grasping tangle of trees. Below, he caught glimpses of the clearings which made up the Awakener base, but even from close by they were well concealed amid the foliage. There were no large craft in the air and he could only see one other in the sky at all, which was a shuttle like the one he was riding in.

Ahead of them a low wide island rose out of the swamp. Crund steered for it and put them down in a glade on its southern slope. Frey could see nobody about.

'The Cap'n will meet you here,' Crund said. 'I'll be back in an hour.'

Frey got out. Crund pulled the door shut behind him and took off, leaving him behind.

Frey was slightly disconcerted. He'd assumed he'd be taken to the *Delirium Trigger* to meet Trinica in her cabin. Instead he found himself in a pretty glade surrounded by lush green jungle. The grass sloped down towards the edge of a small lake which nosed out from beneath the trees, surrounded by rocks and rushes. Brightly coloured dragonflies hung in the air, and somewhere a chorus of frogs were burping away merrily to themselves.

Well, Frey thought. *At least it's nice here.*

With nothing to do but wait, he wandered down towards the lakeside, looking for a suitable spot to perch. Halfway down he heard a familiar voice.

'Darian Frey,' she said.

It was Trinica, but not the one he was expecting. This was not the dread pirate Trinica with the white face and the black eyes and the torn hair, like a sickened ghoul from some delirious hallucination. This was his Trinica, the Trinica of old. She was still wearing the black outfit and boots that she wore on the *Delirium Trigger*, but she'd removed her fearsome make-up. That blonde hair was still short but it was longer than he'd ever seen it.

Just the sight of her locked up his senses and, for a moment, he simply stared.

'Am I going to have to kill you to get you off my tail?' she asked, as she walked out of the trees.

'Uh . . .' said Darian. 'Yeah, pretty much.'

She was smiling. She'd come without her defences up, without the shield of make-up and artifice that she used to deceive everyone else. She'd come as he wanted her.

Gradually, it dawned on him that he might not be in for a fight after all.

'I can see that's what it's going to take,' she said. She stopped in front of him, looked up into his face. 'What happened to the layabout boy I used to know? The one who drove my father mad because he was always late on haulage runs?'

'I'm still kind of a layabout,' Frey said with a grin. 'Wait, was this whole thing just some plan of yours to instil some ambition in me?'

'Yes, Darian,' she said, gently sarcastic. 'Because the whole world revolves around you.'

'Well, who else would it revolve around?'

He wanted to touch her, but he didn't dare. Just seeing her made his chest go light. The three months they'd been apart seemed an age; his search for her felt like an epic. And now here she was, and she actually seemed happy to see him. It was more than he could have hoped for.

'You look beautiful this way,' he said, because he had to. The thought was so strong that it wouldn't be contained.

It was clumsy, and he expected a rebuff, or at least a jibe. She gave none. 'Well, I'd have dressed more appropriately, but I can't be away for long,' she said.

'That outfit actually looks pretty good on you, without all that shit on your face,' Frey said.

She laughed. 'You've a silver tongue, Darian. But your compliments need work.'

She led him to a smooth rock at the edge of the lake. There they settled themselves and looked out across the water. The surface was busy with midges, glowing as they were caught in the glare of the sun. Brilliant motes of golden light appeared and disappeared in a frantic dance.

They sat together in contented silence for a while. Frey was fine with that. He feared to break the spell that had brought her here, as if one wrong word would turn her into the chill ghost that had haunted him these past years. But to be so close to her and not to know her mind was hard for him, so in the end he had to speak.

'How's your war going?' he asked.

She stirred, almost surprised, as if his voice had brought her out of deep contemplation. 'Well enough. Yours?'

'Not so great. The Century Knights think I'm a traitor, I lost Crake, and Malvery's going to mutiny as soon as his hangover clears.'

'You lost Crake?'

'Literally lost. We had an argument, he stormed off and I couldn't find him before we had to bail out. He's probably okay, though. Safer than he'd have been with me, at any rate.' He thought of Prognosticator Garin, and wondered what would have happened if Crake had been on board. Frey's hasty plan might well have got him hanged, and the rest of them too. Frey wasn't the only person on the crew to have worked that out.

But he wasn't here, Frey told himself. *Be grateful for that.*

Trinica sensed something of his thoughts. 'It's difficult to be a captain and a friend,' she said. 'Usually they want you to be one or the other.'

Frey made a neutral noise. 'It'll be better now, anyway.'

'Why?'

'Because we found you. At least they can tell themselves that. Rot knows what would've happened if this had been a wild-goose chase.'

'Ah, I see. It seems that neither of us are good for each other's crews.'

He opened his mouth to argue, but closed it again. She was right, of course. His single-minded pursuit of her was driving wedges between the crew, and Frey's mere presence undermined Trinica's authority among the cutthroats she led.

Her crew knew her as a tyrant, a cruel goddess to be worshipped and obeyed, distant and untouchable. That was what she'd made herself; that was how she kept them in line. They were crude men who respected brute strength. They wouldn't let themselves be led by a woman otherwise.

But where Frey was concerned, she was not as ruthless as they demanded. Frey had killed many of her crew, and yet later they found themselves risking their lives to help him. Several of them had died on his behalf. That was what tore them apart the last time.

Frey thought of the trip over here. 'You trust your bosun to keep quiet to the crew?' he asked. 'I'd have thought he'd be the first to . . . You know.' He stabbed an imaginary knife in her back.

She laughed. 'You always were so eloquent,' she said. 'No, Crund is the only one whose loyalty I can be sure of. He has no desire to lead, and he's done more to keep the crew in line than anyone. He knows the value of secrecy in these matters. But even he has never seen me like this.' She waved a hand at herself, the woman beneath the mask. 'I don't trust him *that* far.'

'I think the poor idiot's kind of in love with you,' Frey said confidingly.

'Ah. Then he is a poor idiot indeed,' said Trinica, but she gave Frey a knowing look that warmed him.

Well, she'd have to pretty blind if she hadn't figured it out by now, he thought.

'The Awakeners, though?' Frey asked. 'You're working for them? I mean, didn't you learn your lesson the first two times?'

She laughed again. 'I rather think it is they who haven't learned their lesson. Duke Grephen was hanged, and Grist's little treasure was lost for ever. I'm hardly their lucky charm. But they do pay so very well.'

'You certainly know how to pick the wrong side.'

'I'm confused. Aren't we on the *same* side now?'

Frey found a stone and skimmed it across the lake. 'Yeah, well. Appearances can be deceptive.'

'You plan to fight for the Coalition, then? You think they'll take you now?'

Frey threw up his hands. 'I don't want to be on *any* side. I didn't even want to be part of this war!'

'War has a way of making you part of it whether you like it or not,' she said. She looked back out over the lake. 'Darian, I . . . shouldn't have left you. Back in Gagriisk.'

He felt something tighten in him at her sudden change of tone. It was the voice she'd used whenever they'd talked about their relationship in the past, and it had always inspired a certain amount of terror. Events of emotional importance were something he'd never be comfortable with, because you couldn't just shoot an emotion if it all got a bit tricky.

'After what happened . . .' she continued hesitantly. 'The lives of those men who died on your behalf . . . That was on my head, do you understand? What I felt for you, it *killed* those men. And it killed *me*.' She turned to him, her eyes roaming his face. 'But I turned my back on you, when I knew you were in mortal danger. And once I'd done that, I couldn't take it back. I didn't even know where you went after Gagriisk and you had . . . what was it, a day? Two days to live?'

Frey stayed silent, certain that if he spoke he'd spoil things somehow. Was she *apologising* to him? Of all the ways he'd envisaged this meeting, this had never occurred to him.

'Then when I heard . . .' she said. 'I heard you were in Vardia again, getting up to rot knows what, and . . . Spit and blood, Darian, the *relief* I felt, it was . . .'

She stopped, gathered herself a moment. He couldn't remember the last time he'd seen her struggle like this.

'I'm so very sorry,' she said at last.

Frey was aware that his shirt was sticking to his back in the swelter of the day. The chatter of the jungle seemed suddenly loud. He picked up another stone. It was a good, flat pebble. He turned it over in his hands, examining it, and thought for a long while before he spoke.

'It's weird,' he said. 'I never blamed you for that. Or if I did, I don't remember. When you left me, I was . . .' He felt his tongue thickening, words coming harder. It was so difficult to avoid saying the wrong thing. 'I mean, I was kind of a mess, and I hated that you were gone, and the whole situation felt . . . I don't know, *unfair*. But I never blamed you for not being there to help me. I can take care of myself.'

He threw the stone out onto the water. It skipped three times before it sank.

'Besides,' he said. 'The Iron Jackal? Kicked its puppy arse.'

He'd meant it light-heartedly, but it brought to mind a horrible memory. As he'd prepared to strike the final blow the daemon had taken the form of Trinica, hoping to stay his hand with pity. But it had chosen the wrong Trinica, the dread pirate with the white face and black eyes. If it had been the image of the woman before him now, he probably wouldn't have been able to drive his cutlass into her.

She seemed grateful for his attempt to lift the mood. 'Tell me what happened, then,' she said. 'After I left you.'

And so he told her about the Iron Jackal and the Azryx city lost in the Samarlan desert. She was an amazed audience. After he described the Juggernaut they'd unleashed, he had to spend several minutes convincing her that he wasn't just spinning a yarn. She was more sober when he told her how they discovered that the Samarlans were selling Azryx technology to the Awakeners. Incredible as that was, it was nothing to what he'd already told her.

When he was done, she was thoughtful again. 'Come with me,' she said. 'I have something to show you.'

She led him around the edge of the lake, and then headed off into the trees. Frey followed her as they made their way upslope along a narrow dirt trail. Under the leaf canopy it was stifling hot and thick with roots and creepers. Insects hummed loudly. Things that sounded uncomfortably large moved in the undergrowth.

'It's a relief, in a way,' Trinica said.

'What is?'

'Well, for years there have been rumours that the Samarlans have struck aerium. They have huge resources to build aircraft but pitifully little aerium to keep them in the air.'

'I gathered that, Trinica. We fought two wars about it, remember?'

She gave him a gentle smile over her shoulder. 'Darian, you know as well as I do that you're fully capable of fighting in a war without having the faintest idea what it's about.'

Frey had to give her that. 'Yeah,' he said, and swatted a midge on his neck. 'I suppose I don't trouble myself with the big picture much, do I?'

'Anyway, even with the smuggling through the Free Trade Zone, our most pessimistic estimates say that the Samarlans couldn't keep a sizable fleet in the air for long. Not long enough to sustain a proper war, anyway. We were all worried that might change. But it's Azryx technology they found, not aerium.'

'And you think that's better?'

'It is if they don't know how to use it.'

'They made the whole city invisible!' Frey protested. 'They had some kind of interference field that made me crash the *Ketty Jay*!'

'No,' she said. 'The Azryx did that. It was probably on when they got there.'

'Well, they must have dealt with it somehow. A guard told us they saw Sammie aircraft flying in and out every so often.'

'That is troubling,' said Trinica. 'But the fact remains: if the Samarlans don't have aerium, they can't mount a full-scale invasion. So instead they're helping the Awakeners.'

'And when the Awakeners are in power, they'll lift the embargo and sell aerium to the Sammies again.'

'Exactly.' She shrugged. 'See? A relief. At least there won't be a Third Aerium War.'

'Yeah, that is a relief,' said Frey. 'We'll just live in a country ruled by fanatics instead.'

'It'll be just like having the old kings back,' Trinica quipped. 'Ah, here we are.'

They came out of the trees onto a narrow strip of clear land at the lip of a cliff that overlooked the southern flank of the island. Here, the ground was too stony for anything bigger than wild grasses to take root. Standing near the edge of the cliff was a triangular pillar roughly three metres high. It was covered in strange designs, and it appeared to have been fashioned from dull grey metal, now rusty and weathered with dirt and time.

'That's, er, unusual,' said Frey.

He went over to look at it more closely. The designs were hard to make out, and heavily stylised, but they seemed to be depicting events of some kind. In one, three people walked through a desert towards a mountain. In another, a grieving figure held a dying man, with other dead figures in the background. Near the bottom there was a panel that showed men labouring while robed figures watched them from a tower. There was writing amid the designs which looked vaguely familiar, but it wasn't Vardic or Samarlan or any other alphabet he'd seen with any frequency.

'What is it?' he asked.

'They call them watchpoles,' said Trinica. 'They were quite common on the south coast once, but many have been taken away for study, and many more have been broken or stolen. You can still find a few here and there, in remote places. The language is Old Isilian.'

Now Frey knew why he recognised it. It bore a passing similarity to writing he'd seen in the Azryx city.

'Look on the south side,' she said. 'The one facing the cliff edge. For some reason they always built them with one side facing south. The other two sides show scenes of history or myth, but that one . . . well, see for yourself.'

Frey did. The flat side was mostly worn away below chest height, but he could make out the topmost shape. It showed a creature standing on all fours, facing outward, with fearsome eyes but a mouth in a perfect O.

Then he realised. No, it wasn't a mouth. It was supposed to be a tube. A *cannon*.

'That's a Juggernaut,' he said. 'That's what it looked like.'

Trinica was watching him closely, eyes bright with excitement. 'You're sure?'

'Sure as I can be.' Frey was recalling that monstrous beast, flesh and machine fused, striding over the city in its last moments, before it was consumed in a ball of silent lightning. He'd seen some strange things in his time, but not much stranger than that.

'This pillar is about nine thousand years old,' she said. 'The people who made it were the first settlers in Vardia, as far as we know. They shared the legend of the Juggernaut with the early Samarlans. The Samarlans remember, but we have forgotten.'

'Yeah. I remember you talking about it, back in Shasiith. The Nameless and all that, right?'

'You *did* learn something, then,' she said, with a smile to show she was teasing. He grinned at her. Damn, it was good to be with her when she was like this. Her moods were treacherous at times, but when she was happy, it felt perfect.

He walked to the cliff edge and looked out across the island. His attention had been dominated by the pillar thus far, but now he saw something he hadn't noticed at first. At the foot of the cliff, the island dropped away into a massive sinkhole, a gaping maw of rock, its edges shaggy with foliage. Anchored inside the sinkhole was the dark bulk of the *Delirium Trigger*.

The sight of it dimmed the day a little. Wherever Trinica was, the *Delirium Trigger* wasn't far away. He wondered how many craft the Awakeners had like it, tucked away in secret niches all over the delta.

'The Samarlans see the Juggernauts as the gods' punishment for their ungratefulness,' Trinica said. 'But these people,' she touched the pillar reverently, 'they see them differently. They believe that their civilisation was once poisoned, corrupt, oppressive. The Juggernauts set them free.'

'How? By destroying everything in sight?'

'Sometimes you have to burn a house to the ground before you can rebuild it,' said Trinica.

Frey felt grim unease edge into his heart. 'Is that why you showed it to me?'

She didn't reply. He could see men moving about on the deck of the *Delirium Trigger*. He watched them for a time.

'What do you feel, Trinica?' he said. 'About us?'

'That might be the first time you ever asked me that,' she replied. 'You're normally so afraid of the response.'

'I'm still afraid of it,' he murmured.

She laid a hand on his arm, briefly. He turned to face her, and she withdrew it, as if to touch him had committed herself too far. But she didn't answer him, and so he felt he had to speak, to try to make her understand something of why he'd followed her here.

'What I did back then . . .' he began. 'Leaving you on our wedding day and . . . everything that happened after . . .' He felt his throat closing up as he thought of it. The child that would never be born because of him. Because of her. 'I just . . . I . . .'

'No, Darian,' she said quietly. 'We've both done terrible things. But we were young. We were so very young. What we did then, we can perhaps forgive ourselves. But what we've done since?' She took a breath, and tears stood in her eyes. 'Look at us,' she whispered. 'We're ridiculous.'

He wanted to say something to that, to offer her comfort, but her expression hardened and she became angry. She swept away from him, away from the cliff edge.

'What do you want for us, Darian? A house? Children? A soft life in the country? Do you think either of us could live that way after what we've seen, what we've *done*?'

'I don't know!' said Frey. Her anger aroused his own. He followed her back towards the trees, shouting after her. 'I don't care how we live! Why are you always trying to stop this from working? I want to be with you, that's all! Why does it have to be complicated?'

'Because I have a crew! And so do you! We have responsibilities! I thought you understood that?'

'They're not your dependants. If you walked away, they'd get on fine.'

'And me? How would I get on? What would I be then?'

'You'd be Trinica Dracken. As you are now. Not the woman in the make-up, not the pirate captain. And you could do whatever you wanted!'

The heat went out of her as fast as it had come, and she saddened. 'I've been a pirate for a long time now,' she said. 'Everything I wanted was given to me, until the day I left home. From that point on, I fought for every damned thing that I've got. I won that craft and I won its crew—'

'And someday someone will take it from you,' said Frey. 'You know what happens to pirates in the end. They don't live out their lives counting their ducats. They don't retire to Retribution Falls. They hang on too long and they bloody *die*, whether it's fast from a bullet or slow from the grog.'

She went silent. The look on her face made him feel that he'd been cruel, and he decided not to press his point. He walked over to her, wanting to hold her, not knowing how.

'Sorry,' he muttered.

'They can sense weakness,' she said quietly. 'They're like wolves with the scent of blood in their nostrils.' She raised her head and looked at him, and he was shocked to see fear in her eyes. 'I thought turning my back on you would make it better, but it didn't. Not two weeks ago, I had Crund haul up a man in front of the crew and I had him hanged. Once that would have cowed them. Now it's made them hate me.'

Suddenly she clutched herself to him, pressing herself hard against his chest.

'They *know*,' she whispered.

Her body was warm, so wonderfully warm, but Frey had gone cold. He felt cheated. He'd waited so long to have her in his arms again, but not like this. He'd dreamed of affection; he found desperation instead. He sensed real terror in her, and that inspired terror in him too. He felt a powerful need to comfort and protect her, but he wasn't sure if he could. So he held her, and her arms tightened across his back.

He knew what she feared. He'd thought about it enough. It wasn't dying. It was the loss of her world, the world that had sustained her and kept her stitched together after the horrors she'd suffered. Attempted suicide, the loss of a child, her kidnap and the dreadful ordeals that followed. She'd become steely and cold and vicious because that was what it took to survive and thrive in the hell where she found herself. But change was threatening, from within and without. That was worse than any bullet.

'Don't go back,' he said to her. 'Come with me. We'll get on the *Ketty Jay* and fly out of here, and damn them if they try to stop us.'

She gave a cynical little chuckle, and he knew that he'd lost her. His time was up. She broke away from him gently, and when she did she was different. More bunched, more businesslike.

'The Awakeners have a compound a few kloms northeast of the main base,' she said. 'They've invited me and the other frigate captains to visit it tonight. I expect they intend to share their plans with us. There are rumours that the Lord High Cryptographer himself has been seen, the supreme leader of the Awakeners. If there is any news of Azryx technology, we may well hear it there.'

Frey was disappointed by the change in her. She'd withdrawn. Not all the way, not into sharp pitilessness, but she'd closed up all the same. 'And after that?' he asked.

'Then I will decide what to do next. I am not going to die for the Awakeners' coin. Unless they have some great plan in store, it's hard to see how they can win this war. I suspect other captains feel the same, and the Awakeners are keen to keep the bigger craft on side. So we shall see what we shall see.'

'That wasn't really what I meant,' Frey said.

'I know.' She softened a little. 'As to that, I can't say. Every time we meet it's different. Every time we meet it all begins again.'

'Yeah,' he said. He understood that strange sense of renewal and reset each time they were brought together. 'Yeah, that's how it is.'

She walked back to the cliff edge, and looked down at the *Delirium Trigger*. 'You should go,' she said. 'Crund will be back at the clearing soon to pick you up. I have to change.'

She meant it literally. Not her clothes, but herself. The crew wouldn't recognise the beautiful woman before him. They only knew the ghoul in the make-up with the black, black eyes.

He wanted to stay with her until everything was resolved. He feared to let her out of his sight. But she wouldn't have that. Her moment of weakness had been only a moment. So he could only do as she said, and take what she'd given him. It had already been more than he dared to dream. She still felt for him, that was clear. That would have to be enough for now.

'Will you see me again tomorrow?' he asked.

'Yes,' she said, without turning around. 'I'll see you tomorrow.'

Sixteen

The Patient – A Man of Science – Unwelcome Modifications –
A Bit of Breaking & Entering – Slag Defends His Territory

Crake stared down at the inert form of his brother. Condred lay there on the bed, pale and still, dressed in a red silk gown. His hair, once dark, was now white peppered with grey. Even in repose the folds around his mouth were deep, and he wore a troubled look.

Crake could not match the figure on the bed to the one in his memory. Condred was a man who strode into a room and demanded attention, a man with all the hauteur of their father but none of his modesty or restraint. He was high-handed, patronising and infuriating, and Crake had all but hated him.

Yet he'd given up his revenge. Even after Crake had cost him his wife and child.

Why didn't you want to punish me? Crake thought. The Condred he knew would have been full of wrath. He'd have pounded the table and demanded satisfaction. Crake would have done the same, in his place. But Condred had called off the Shacklemores instead.

Why?

Two burly orderlies and a nurse were standing in the doorway of the bedroom. He motioned to them.

'Bring him,' he said.

The orderlies carried in a stretcher and busied themselves with loading Condred onto it. The nurse hovered nearby.

'They say it's a plague, sir,' she said. She was a mousy woman in her middle forties with a nervous disposition. 'There've been cases all over. Master Rogibald had all the best doctors in, but as you can see . . .' She gestured at his brother.

When Crake didn't offer a reply, she asked: 'Begging pardon, sir. Are you a doctor?'

153

'Of a sort,' said Crake, and left it at that.

The nurse stayed to tidy up while the orderlies took Condred from the building and across the grounds. Crake walked ahead of them. Gardeners stopped to stare when they saw him. Servants watched from the windows. More than one of them made a sign against evil as the procession passed.

Superstitious lot, Crake heard his father say. His eyes went to the Shacklemores that patrolled the manor grounds. *Is this how bad it's got out in the country?*

It made him angry to see his father so diminished, hiding behind armed guards for fear of the locals. Rogibald was a man who'd built an industrial empire from modest beginnings. Even though Crake had the misfortune to be his son, he respected his father's drive. It was wrong for a man like that to be threatened in his own home by the ignorance of the common folk, baying at the call of those damned Awakeners. It offended his sense of order. Vardia's aristocracy was far from perfect, but they deserved better than that.

And his father had fallen far indeed, if he'd called on the Shacklemores to bring him Crake. The very sight of his second son was loathsome to him. It was the act of a desperate man, and he must have choked on his pride to do it.

The servants knew it too. He saw it in their faces. They might not have been here at the time, but they'd heard the stories. *Murderer,* they thought. *Daemonist.* They'd never thought to see him back, not without a noose round his neck. Yet here he was, leading a pair of orderlies, bearing their master's son away from the mansion and back towards the house where Crake had once lived with Condred and his family.

Back towards his sanctum.

As they approached the house he kept his features stony to disguise the fact that his insides were turning to water. His hand went to his pocket, felt the weight of a heavy brass key that he'd once kept close to him at all times. The key to the wine cellar. The place where all his nightmares began.

His skin prickled as he stepped into the foyer. A mirror showed him his reflection, hollow-eyed and haggard. A clock ticked on the wall. Everything had been dusted, everything was in its place . . . but nothing was right.

At first he thought it was just old memories reaching for him out of the past, but it was something more than that. Long years practising the Art had honed his instincts. Paranoia lurked on the edge of his consciousness. Something sinister hung in the air.

Had he done this? Had he poisoned the house with his crime, turned the very walls and floor evil?

Stop it, he told himself. *You're a man of science. Act like one.*

The orderlies hesitated at the threshold. Perhaps they sensed it too. 'What are you waiting for?' he snapped at them, and he stalked into the house.

It had been two weeks since Condred fell asleep and didn't wake. Servants still lived here, but the house felt chill and unoccupied nonetheless. And still, that sense of faint but pervasive dread lingered.

A narrow set of stairs led down to the servant's quarters. In an out-of-the-way alcove near the bottom was a door. It was heavy and small and made of dark oak. Crake stood before it for a long moment before he drew the key from his pocket.

He should have warded the door. It would have been easy to fashion something to deflect attention. But Condred and his wife had always been sneeringly dismissive of their lodger's mysterious experiments, and the servants had been ordered not to pry, so there didn't seem much point. Besides, he was afraid of getting it wrong and drawing suspicion upon himself. They thought he was nothing more than a budding and inept scientist; better to let them keep thinking that. A locked door was enough.

But a locked door hadn't been enough to keep a curious child out.

Maybe he'd got complacent and left the door unlocked. Maybe Bess had found a spare key somewhere, in an old drawer or on a peg in some dusty recess. Maybe it was just some sick twist of fate, some awful alignment of coincidence that brought her to his sanctum on *that* exact night, at *that* exact time. He'd never know. It didn't matter.

He became aware of a scullery maid standing at the end of the corridor, agape. She was watching him with terror in her eyes.

He put the key in the lock and turned it. She gasped and fled.

Well might you run, he thought. The orderlies had seen her reaction and caught on to her fear, but they were big men and not given to retreat. He pushed the door open before they – or he – could change their minds.

Beyond the doorway, steps led downward into darkness. He reached inside and found the switch with his fingers. An electric lamp sputtered into life, illuminating stone arches and brick pillars, an island of light in the darkness. By that flickering, fitful light he saw a mess of cables and rusty devices, overturned poles and broken bulbs and a large brown stain on the floor which he dared not look at. In the centre was large metal chamber like a bathysphere. It had been dented outward as if struck by some great force from within, and its door hung open.

He heard a wet clicking noise, so clear that it seemed momentarily real. That sound had troubled his nights for years. The sound of his niece trying to draw breath into punctured lungs.

He wanted to be sick. He wanted to turn and run and never have to return to this place. But he couldn't, because he owed Condred more than he could ever pay. Everything he suffered, he deserved.

'Follow me,' he told the orderlies, and he stepped into the dark.

'What in all damnation is going on here?' Frey cried, as he jumped out of the *Delirium Trigger*'s shuttle and went hurrying across the muddy clearing.

The *Ketty Jay* and her outflyers were the centre of a mass of activity. Engineers in overalls were fiddling about inside the cockpit hoods of the fighter craft. Teams of men swarmed over the *Ketty Jay*, pasting enormous decals onto her flanks. A team of Sentinels stood by with rifles.

Frey stormed over. Harkins was being restrained by Pinn, crying in strangled agony as his beloved Firecrow got a massive blue Cipher pasted on to its underwing. Malvery went stamping past the other way, his face like thunder. He ignored Frey's attempts to hail him.

'Well, that's just great, that is!' he fumed. 'If that ain't just the bloody *limit*!'

Frey looked about for someone to strangle. Prognosticator Garin presented himself.

'Will you tell me what in the wide world of buggering shitarsery you are *doing to my aircraft*?' he yelled.

'Calm down, Captain Frey,' said Garin. 'You're making a fool of yourself.'

'Nobody messes with the *Ketty Jay* without my say-so!'

Several Sentinels with guns walked over to stand next to the Prognosticator, alerted by the tone of Frey's voice.

'You weren't here,' said Garin. 'There are a lot of aircraft waiting to be assimilated into the fleet. We don't have time to wait around for permission. I take it you do still *want* to join the Awakeners?' The question had a sinister and ever-so-slightly threatening edge to it.

Frey saw the trap and thought fast. 'I haven't even spoken to the quartermaster about pay yet!'

'If you wanted to quibble about your price, you should have done it before you got here,' said Garin. 'This is a secret base, Captain. Nothing bigger than a shuttle gets airborne without permission. If you try to fly out, we'll shoot you down.'

Frey looked over his shoulder to see the *Delirium Trigger*'s own shuttle taking off. Of course: a shuttle wouldn't be able to fly far enough to escape the delta. He couldn't be sure, but could swear he could see Balomon Crund grinning at his discomfort.

'What are you doing to the engines?' Frey demanded.

'Trust in the Code, Captain,' said Garin benevolently.

'That's no bloody answer!'

'A harmless modification. You won't notice it.'

'What does it *do*, Garin? My men will be flying those aircraft, I can't have them—'

Garin held up a hand. 'I have my orders, as do we all. The answer will be revealed to you in time. Until then, it's not the business of a soldier to know the plans of his superiors. The Lord High Cryptographer will guide us.'

Frey narrowed his eyes. 'You don't know what it does, do you?'

Garin just stared at him. Frey swore loudly and stalked off towards the *Ketty Jay*.

Silo met him on the cargo ramp and walked inside with him. Ashua came rushing up anxiously. Engineers were descending the stairs into the hold, carrying bags of tools.

'They been up in the engine room, Cap'n,' Silo advised him.

'You gotta get rid of them,' Ashua murmured urgently. 'Don't know how much longer I can keep Bess quiet.'

'You done?' Frey shouted at the engineers that were coming down the stairs. 'Good! Now piss off!' He stormed over, seized one by the shirt and practically threw him across the cargo hold towards the exit.

The others hurried after him. When they were gone, Frey hit the lever and shut the ramp behind them.

'You let them on the *Ketty Jay*?' he cried, rounding on Silo.

'They got armed Sentinels with 'em, Cap'n. Reckoned we wanted to look co-operative.'

'They're messing with our engines!' Frey cried.

'Ain't nothing they can do I can't undo,' Silo said.

The Murthian's unflappable manner took the edge off Frey's rage. He saw the sense in that, but it was the *principle* of the thing. He felt defiled.

'We oughta go see what they been up to,' said Silo.

Ashua made to follow, but Frey stopped her. 'Keep Bess busy till the Awakeners have gone, will you?'

'Sure, sure. Not like I've got anything *better* to do,' she grumbled as she headed back to the sanctum.

The engine room was an oven, warmed by the south coast sun. They made their way among the pipes and gauges until Silo spotted what they were looking for. It was a rectangular metal case, thoroughly sealed and bolted to the frame of the engine. There were no markings on it beyond a meaningless identification code.

Silo poked around at it. 'Don't look like it's even connected to the engine, Cap'n. They just stuck it here. Don't see how it gonna affect anythin'.'

'Could it be a bomb?'

'S'pose,' he said. 'Don't see the good of it, though. Need a bitch of a transmitter to set it off at a distance. And if it's on a timer, well . . .' He shrugged. 'If they wanted to kill us, reckon they'd have done it.' He tapped the case with the end of a screwdriver that had appeared from his pocket. 'Let me get into, Cap'n. I'll let you know.'

'Later,' said Frey. 'I need you downstairs.'

By the time they opened the *Ketty Jay* up again, the Prognosticator and his men were packing up and heading off. Frey glared at them till they were gone. Harkins was flapping about the Firecrow, gibbering in horror at the sight of all those Ciphers. Pinn was complaining about people messing with his engine.

'Alright, alright! Get in here, you lot!' Frey called.

The crew assembled in the cargo hold. Pelaru materialised from the gloom. Jez jumped down from the walkway many metres above to land expertly on top of a pile of crates, where she crouched, watching them with shining eyes. Once the ramp was shut, Ashua came out of the sanctum with Bess tramping after her.

'Swear I need double pay for being her bloody mother on top of everything else,' she grouched.

'Ciphers on the *Ketty Jay*,' Malvery muttered. 'Insult to injury, that's what it is. Never thought I'd see the day.'

'Settle down, everyone,' said Frey. 'I've got some information.'

'Oh yeah? Get it from your sweetheart, did you?' Malvery was in a foul mood.

'Clam it, eh? You'll want to hear this. Might stop you carping for two seconds.'

When he had everyone's attention, he began. 'So I was talking to Trinica—'

He was interrupted by a chorus of groans.

'—*talking to Trinica*,' he continued pointedly, 'and she told me the Awakeners have a hidden compound a few kloms from here. They're planning on inviting a bunch of captains over there, her included. Sounds like there's something important on the boil. I want to find out what, and take a look at that compound while we're at it.'

'Bit of breaking and entering, Cap'n?' Ashua asked, with a wicked look in her eye.

'Might come to that,' he said.

'Why not just find out from Trinica?' Pelaru asked.

'Because, believe it or not, she might not tell me the truth,' Frey replied, irritation creeping in to his voice. 'Now let's get something straight, everyone. Despite appearances, we are *not* on the Awakeners' side and we sure as shit aren't gonna fight for them. But right now we've got a chance to find out what they're up to and I for one don't plan to waste it. Might even get us back in the Coalition's good graces if we've got a juicy bone to throw 'em. Right, Doc?'

Malvery crossed his arms, reluctantly mollified. 'Yeah,' he sulked. 'S'pose.'

'Harkins,' said Frey. 'I reckon you should—'

'Yes, sir! Staying behind to look after Bess, sir!' said Harkins with a smart salute, his chin outthrust.

'Er . . . good,' said Frey, who'd been about to suggest exactly that.

'I would like to come,' said Pelaru.

'If there's information to be found, you want in, huh?' said Frey. 'Alright, you can come.' Privately he was relieved: he worried what Pelaru might get up to and didn't trust Harkins to deal with him if he proved troublesome.

He held out his hand to Jez. 'Lend me your earcuff, will you?'

She plucked it from inside her overalls and dropped it down to him. 'What happened to yours?' she asked.

'It's in Trinica's pocket. I slipped it in there when she hugged me. As long as we're close enough to receive, we'll be able to hear everything the Awakeners tell her.' He winked at them. 'Still got it,' he said with a grin, and then walked away from his amazed crew, snapping his fingers in the air.

Oblivious to the furore, Slag prowled among the pipes and panels of the *Ketty Jay*'s maintenance ducts. He was angry. A challenge had been made to his supremacy, and that would not be borne. It could only end in blood.

The smell of the intruder was everywhere. It seemed he could scarcely pass a corner without finding that the foreign cat had rubbed against it, impressing its scent over his own. It maddened him and made him murderous.

Slag was not capable of any emotion as subtle as indignant outrage, but his instincts provided a pretty close approximation. The *Ketty Jay* was *his*. He allowed the puzzling and noisy big ones to share it, but only because they knew their place and paid him tribute in food (and occasionally booze). Otherwise he found them generally inoffensive. But the intruder's scent dredged up hot new sensations that compelled him into action.

The wounds from his fight with the rat hadn't entirely healed, and the bruises were still making themselves known. In his younger days he'd have shaken them off, but he wasn't young any longer. He did his best to ignore the aches and twinges, obsessed with the need to eradicate this pretender to his territory.

The intruder was elusive. He'd neither seen nor heard it on his patrols. But now he was on the trail.

He stopped and sniffed at the edge of a vent. The scent was strong. Fresh. He listened. His ears weren't as keen as they once were, but they were good enough to hear faint movement up ahead. And it didn't sound like a rat.

He crept slowly forward, hackles rising. At last he had his prey within reach.

The vent became a crossroads up ahead. The sound of movement came from around the corner. It was his enemy, rubbing up against something. He knew the secret ways and hidden routes of the *Ketty Jay*, and he knew that was a dead end. The other cat had no way out.

Slag stalked closer, eyes fixed. Small red lights provided illumination in the warm, close ducts. He sneaked silently through the glow, a dark pile of muscle and mange.

Not silently enough. He heard the enemy freeze, tensing up in alarm. He lunged towards the corner, but the other cat flashed across the junction in front of him. Slag hissed as he went in with his claws, but the intruder was small and fast, and it went darting away down the duct to his left.

Claws scrabbling, Slag gave chase. There was no way he was letting that cat get away.

Down the air ducts they went, over and under pipes and obstacles, sprinting where they could. Slag's blood was up now; by the size of it, the other cat was no threat at all, and he threw caution to the wind. He pursued it here and there, and though it was agile it didn't know this territory like he did, and it didn't have his fury. They thumped and thundered through the narrow metal passageways, Slag yowling like a thing possessed.

Suddenly it skidded to a stop. He caught his first good look at it then, as it bunched its haunches to spring, eyes fixed on something above. It was a thin, ragged, ugly thing, fur a muddle of black and orange. He raced towards it, hoping to bring it down before it jumped, but he was too slow. It disappeared just before his unsheathed claws could find it, leaped upward through a shaft in the ceiling of the vent. He heard a scrabble, and then it was gone.

Slag's pounce had taken him a half-metre down the vent. He found his feet, turned about and ran back. The shaft above him looked impossibly high. When he was in his prime he could have got up it, but he hadn't attempted a jump like that in years.

Still, the invader had managed it. And he wouldn't be outdone.

He screwed himself down on his haunches, wiggling his hind-quarters as if to build up power for the leap to come. His gaze never left the shaft above. He ignored his aches and tiredness and the weakness of age, and let anger lend him strength. Then, with a mighty surge, he sprang.

His jump took him to the lip of the shaft, but only barely. His forepaws cleared the edge; his claws tried to dig in, but there was no purchase. For a terrifying instant, he began sliding back towards the drop. Then his back paws found a grip against the side of the shaft, and propelled him over, and he was triumphant.

There was the intruder, backed into a dead end. It was pressed down low, eyes wide with terror, ears flat against its head. Slag approached with his back arched and hackles up, crooning danger-ously. There was no escape for it now. He moved slowly closer, ready to exact retribution.

But just as he came close enough to strike, he felt a new and puzzling feeling wash through him. His anger began to dissipate. There was something in the newcomer's scent, something . . . interesting. He'd detected it before but hadn't known what it was. He'd been isolated from his own kind for so long that he hadn't anything to compare it with. Now he was up close it was overwhelm-ing, and instinct told him what he should have known all along.

The intruder was a female.

Confused, Slag came closer, sniffing at her. He hadn't encountered a female since before pubescence. Powerful, unfamiliar sensations swept through him. He didn't want to sink his claws into her any more, he wanted to sink his—

The female lashed out with a hiss, and a stunning burst of pain startled him as she scratched him across his sensitive nose. She squirmed past him and back down the shaft. By the time he recov-ered, she was long gone.

Slag blinked, and licked at his nose. The wound was nothing. The newcomer . . . that was something else. A female? On board the *Ketty Jay*? What was he supposed to do now?

He looked around as if to check no one was watching, then began to groom himself uneasily with his tongue.

Seventeen

The Compound – A Fearful Encounter –
The Infiltrator – Mercy

Trudging off into a swamp in the middle of the night had seemed like a good idea at the time but, like most of Frey's ideas, the reality fell short of the concept. A few kloms from the base to the Awakeners' hidden compound didn't sound like much, but Frey hadn't accounted for the terrain. After a couple of hours of ploughing through sucking mud and reeds, he was ready to admit they should have abandoned stealth and gone for a good old full frontal assault instead.

It didn't help that he was a tiny bit lost. Trinica's directions had been vague at best, and he was beginning to worry that they'd missed the base amid the dense foliage. He'd sent Jez to get some bearings, and she'd sprung off into the dark like a wild animal loosed from its leash. It worked out for all concerned. She moved faster without them, and the group felt better when she wasn't around.

It was hard to see anything, even with the moon up. A white mist lurked in the hollows and lay on the water, curling between the twisted roots of the mangroves. In the dark, things slithered and moved, some of them unpleasantly large. Insects hammered the hot air with percussive taps and whistles that ranged from mildly annoying to painfully loud.

Malvery in particular was being driven to distraction. His hangover had rallied with the din, and he looked ready to murder somebody. 'Think we've got enough bullets to shut up every bloody living thing in the delta?' he asked hopefully.

'I'm up for trying,' said Pinn, who was equally unimpressed with their situation.

'Come on, you two, where's your spirit of adventure?' Ashua said. 'Get a lungful of that swamp air! Ooo, I think that was an alligator!'

Pinn and Malvery had been griping ever since they set off, only pausing when one or the other of them tripped and splashed into the brackish water. Ashua, on the other hand, seemed to be rather enjoying her field trip. Frey knew she'd spent most of her life in cities, but the way she talked you'd think she'd never seen a tree before.

Silo was uncomplaining, as ever. Frey was glad to have him by his side. The Murthian's solid presence helped to anchor him somehow. That was a man he always knew he could count on.

Pelaru followed along silently behind, picking his way through the hot soggy undergrowth. Frey kept a suspicious eye on him. What was his angle? Whispermongers were famous for their neutrality, but Frey couldn't help feeling the elegant Thacian had some agenda here. The sooner that man was off the *Ketty Jay*, the better, but there hadn't been a safe place to offload him yet, and Frey certainly wasn't going to leave him unsupervised while they were busy playing double agents in the heart of Awakener territory.

Annoyingly, Pelaru was the only one of them still clean. Frey and the others were sweaty, grimy and tired, but he'd somehow escaped with only mud spatters on his boots, and he wasn't even out of breath.

Thacians. Even in a swamp they're so rotting superior.

'Cap'n,' said Jez by his ear. He jumped and clutched at his heart.

'Don't do that,' he gasped.

'Sorry, Cap'n,' she said, but her voice was flat and she wasn't sorry at all. She looked through him with those shining wolf eyes of hers. 'I found it.'

Relief soothed Frey's unease at being so close to her. 'Nice work, Jez,' he said. 'Lead on.'

They spotted the lights of the compound soon after, hazed by mist in the distance. It was surrounded by a perimeter wall, surmounted by electric floods that illuminated the dank swampland all around. Once they got near, they cut across in the direction of the main gate and found a dirt road leading back towards the base. Silo picked out a likely hiding spot which overlooked the road and the gate, and there they settled in amid the mud and roots and scuttling things.

Frey eyed the defences uncertainly. The gate stood open, but it was heavily guarded. The wall was metal, discoloured by the wet air and patched with lichen. This compound had been constructed with care and attention, not at all like the ramshackle hotchpotch of dwellings in the main part of the base. There was no way they'd cobbled it together since the war kicked off. That meant the Awakeners had been up to something in the Barabac Delta long before anyone realised there was a base here at all.

'Strikes me, Cap'n,' said Malvery, adjusting his glasses. 'Strikes me we might just've taken this road all the way from the base instead of arsing about in stinking bogs and whatnot.'

'Wouldn't have worked,' said Ashua. 'I asked about while I was off procuring a few bits.' She slapped the pack on Silo's back, one of three that were stuffed with items which Ashua had stolen from the camp, and which Frey dearly hoped they wouldn't need. 'They've got guards all up and down this stretch.'

'Besides,' Frey put in. 'I reckoned you and Pinn could do with working off a kilo or two.'

'Oi!' said Pinn, patting his belly. 'This is prime steak, you twat!'

'Good of you to be thinking of our health, Cap'n,' said Malvery.

'I'm considerate like that.'

Everyone felt better now they had the compound in sight. Even Malvery's grumbles were light-hearted. The doc was glad to be doing something to ease his conscience, striking a blow for the Coalition. Frey enjoyed seeing him a bit more upbeat. He'd been in a downer ever since the civil war began, and Crake's departure hardly helped matters.

Crake, you'd better be alright, you idiot.

Thoughts of Crake reminded him of his earcuff. He hadn't been wearing it in the swamp. He found voices in his ear distracting, and he was only capable of concentrating on one thing at a time. Now he took it out, clipped it on and listened.

At first there was nothing. He began to worry. What if Trinica had found the earcuff in her pocket? What if she'd changed clothes? But then he heard a muffled voice. He frowned and focused on the sound over the racket of the swamp. Soon he could make out words.

'. . . arriving at the compound soon, eminent captains.' It was an oily voice that he didn't recognise. Some random fundamentalist nut-bag, no doubt. 'I beg of you your complete discretion in the matter of the things we are about to show you.'

Frey let a little smile touch his lips. Oh, she could be discreet if she wanted. But he'd find out all the same.

Trinica was going to kill him when she eventually discovered the trinket in her pocket. That, or she'd laugh and tell him how clever he was. It depended on the day, really; he'd take his chances. But her talk of the growing threat from her crew had disturbed him deeply, and he wanted to keep track of her. He wouldn't let her get away again.

She'd be hurt that he didn't trust her, perhaps. But he was smitten, not stupid.

'They're on their way,' he told the others.

Shortly afterward, two vehicles came rumbling up the track, each rolling along on six huge wheels. A pair of Renford Overlanders, armoured all-terrain transport vehicles. Frey had only seen a few before; flying was almost always preferable to land travel in a country as vast and varied as Vardia. But Ashua had told them there was a no-fly zone overhead, and a ring of anti-aircraft cannon ready to enforce it. Obviously the Awakeners didn't even want to risk shuttle traffic here.

Definitely up to something, Frey thought to himself. *Something big.*

'She in one of those Overlanders, Cap'n?' Ashua asked.

Frey nodded.

'You've really got a thing for her, haven't you?' she said.

'You have no idea,' muttered Malvery.

Ashua nudged the doctor. 'Leave him alone. I think it's kinda sweet. Never pegged him as a romantic.'

'Fellers, can we stop discussing my love life?' Frey complained.

'Or lack of it,' Pinn put in. 'When was the last time you got your pods jiggled, Cap'n?'

Malvery coughed to suppress a laugh. Ashua, who wasn't suppressing it quite so well, said, 'Yeah, Cap'n. Spill it. When was the last time someone, er, jiggled your pods?'

'I'll have you know my pods have been jiggled by some of the finest bloody females in the land!' Frey said. 'Now shut it, I'm trying to listen.'

Malvery leaned over to Ashua, covered his mouth and pointed at the vehicles on the road below. 'Saving himself,' he stage-whispered, loud enough for everyone to hear. Even Silo smiled at that.

'Swear I'm gonna dump you all at the next port,' Frey murmured, shaking his head.

The vehicles halted in front of the gate and a pair of Sentinels emerged from the guardhouse. After a brief exchange with the driver of the first vehicle, they waved them through. The second vehicle stayed where it was. The passenger door in the flank slid open, and a dark figure stepped out.

Oh, shit, thought Frey, as his stomach sank.

It was an Imperator.

He was dressed head to foot in close-fitting black leather. A smooth black mask showed beneath the cowl of his cloak. The eyes were the only evidence that there was a person inside there at all, but Frey had seen beneath an Imperator's mask before, and he knew they were not people. They were more daemon than man, the husks of the faithful turned rancid by monstrous symbiotes from the aether.

The Imperator stood in the middle of the road, bathed in the harsh light of the floods, alone. Slowly, suspiciously, he turned his head, scanning the swamp on the side where Frey and his crew were hiding.

He senses us, Frey thought, and panic burst in his mind at that. *He's gonna find us!*

Fear sank down upon him, pressing him into the undergrowth. It wasn't just a desire to remain unseen, it was a *need*. He wanted to dig into the mud and disappear. Anything to avoid that dreadful accusing gaze. He was guilty, an unbeliever, a heretic, and if the Imperator saw him it would be as if a light shone through him, turning him transparent, exposing his soul in all its filthy grotesquery. He clawed at the ground and whimpered like a child.

The others felt it too. Their faces were distorted in horror, despair in their eyes. How could they possibly triumph against this kind of terror? Frey knew this feeling to be caused by the power of the Imperators; he'd felt it before. But knowing that didn't lessen the fear one bit.

He looked back over his shoulder, and saw Jez there. On Jez's face was not fear but rage. Her teeth were bared, and seemed sharper than before. Her eyes rolled like a maddened beast. She was turning; the daemon in her was forcing its way out. But it couldn't, it mustn't! Even though Frey had seen her kill an Imperator before, it seemed inconceivable that she could fight the force that oppressed them.

Driven by one fear to overcome another, he grabbed on to her wrist to hold her back. Her head snapped round and she glared at him as if she was about to rip his throat out with her teeth. Then another hand closed round her other wrist. Pelaru's. Of all of them, he seemed the calmest, the least affected. He stared hard at Jez, and she stared hard back at him, and the intensity between them was such that Frey felt almost ashamed to witness it, as if he was intruding on something intensely sacred and private.

But Jez stayed where she was, pinned by that gaze, and she didn't move.

The Imperator's searchlight gaze swept away, and the fear lifted from them. Frey lay there panting. He heard the door to the Overlander close and the vehicle drive away. He didn't dare lift his head until silence had returned and the road was empty again.

'What was *that*?' Ashua asked, her eyes round.

'That's what we're up against,' said Frey. 'That's what we'll get if the Awakeners win.' The experience, now that it had passed, made him feel angry. That wasn't the first time he'd been humiliated by an Imperator. Suddenly he was very keen to prevent the Awakeners doing that shit to him again.

'What about your woman, Cap'n?' Silo asked.

Frey was reminded to listen to the earcuff again. He put his hand over his ear to block out the noise of the swamp and listened.

And heard nothing.

His face clouded. 'These things have quite a range, right? I mean, we use them when we're flying around, don't we?'

No one needed to answer that.

'I can't hear anything,' he said, and panic fluttered anew in his chest. 'It's like she's disappeared.'

'Well,' said Pinn. 'That's Plan A buggered.'

'We've got to get in there,' said Frey. 'Something's wrong. It shouldn't just have gone dead. Something's—'

Malvery's hand landed heavily on his shoulder. 'We're with you, Cap'n,' he said. 'Let's have a look inside, eh?'

The swamp teemed with life. The dark was thick with a thousand sounds and sights and smells. What seemed a bewildering barrage of noise to the others was a wonderful complexity to Jez. She heard everything: the flutter of a sleeping bird stirring in its roost; the footsteps of something many-legged as it rattled through the undergrowth; the squeal of a frog as it was caught up in a predator's jaws.

Insects burrowed through detritus; night-midges were busy over the torpid water washing down towards the sea.

So much life, and she, dead, in the midst of it.

Yet she didn't feel dead. Her body rang with the presence of the Imperator. Her daemon had stirred inside her, risen close to the surface, and still it lurked there. She felt the power of it. Once she'd feared it, but now she knew it was not something to be feared. It was simply a part of her.

Beyond the swamp, she heard the distant howling of the pack. The Manes, in their cities beyond the Wrack, the great cloud-cap that shrouded the northern pole of the planet. It was like music to her, igniting a yearning, a promise of home. Each surrender was easier. She'd given up her resistance outside the Azryx city, and since then the change had gathered speed and she'd embraced it.

But then came Pelaru.

She shook her head. *Concentrate. The Cap'n gave you a job. Concentrate.*

She crouched in the branches of a gnarled tree, high up in the dark. Before her was the wall, and beyond it the buildings and tents of the compound itself. Floods cast pockets of rude light, driving back the shadows. The air was moist and close.

There were Sentinels on the wall, enough to make it impossible to approach along the ground unseen. But the branches of the trees spread wide and leaned close, and nobody looked up at them.

The floods faced outward, shining on the swamp. The Sentinels were shadows by contrast. Once the crew were in behind the lights, they'd become shadows too, and nearby guards would find it hard to spot them. But first they had to get up the wall.

The perimeter of the compound was uneven, built to follow the landscape. She'd chosen a place where the wall bulged out, where the foliage helped screen it from the other guards. Here there was a single Sentinel, standing idly, having ceased even any pretence at patrolling. He leaned on the wall and smoked, looking outward. The tip of his roll-up glowed behind the blinding shine of the floods.

When she judged the moment was right, Jez moved. She raced along the branch and leaped, passing silently through the air to land on the walkway atop the wall. The guard saw something move out of the corner of his eye, but he didn't appreciate the danger until he saw her running towards him. Not until he saw the look on her face and the glitter of her eyes, and he saw her teeth bared like an animal. She pounced on him and broke his neck before he could utter a word.

She crouched next to the corpse, a savage grin on her face. The exhilaration of the hunt filled her. That had been worth the wait. Now she wanted more.

But no. She had a task. *Stay focused.*

Looking around quickly, she saw that she hadn't been observed. The walkway was protected on both sides by a parapet. As long as she stayed low, no one could see her. Secrecy was the thing. She remembered that.

What now, then? The rope. Yes, the rope, so the slow ones could follow her. She tied it up and dropped it over the wall, then forgot about it. She turned instead to the dead man, took his chin carefully and tilted his head this way and that, studying his face. Blank eyes stared upwards. She tried to feel something and couldn't. This corpse was meaningless. Would hers be as unimpressive?

Malvery came clambering over the wall, huffing like a bellows. Just like Jez, he was dressed in a beige cassock, though his barely contained his belly. His omnipresent glasses were missing, his bald pate gleamed with sweat, and the sign of the Cipher had been carefully painted onto his forehead in blue ink.

He stood with his hands on his knees, heaving in breaths. 'Ain't never gonna live this down,' he wheezed.

He flopped down against the parapet, looked over at Jez, and then at the dead man. His expression became grim.

'You really have to do that?' he asked.

Jez was puzzled. 'He was in our way,' she said.

'He was just a boy. You could've knocked him out.'

Jez thought about arguing, but the words wouldn't arrange themselves. Speech was clumsy and irrelevant and tiresome when she was like this. She turned away instead. What was his disappointment to her? He didn't understand. None of them understood. Except perhaps Pelaru.

She watched as the whispermonger slipped lithely over the parapet. He didn't so much as glance at her. But he knew she was there.

She'd expended a lot of thought on Pelaru but come up with very little. He'd taken a half-Mane for a lover, yet he left his sundered corpse to rot when they found him. He'd carried her out of the shrine in Korrene – they'd told her about that – and he'd as much as said that he loved her, yet he was so angry about it that he could hardly bear the sight of her.

She'd never been at home with strong emotions, never knew how to talk her way around them. She couldn't decipher him. She wanted to explore this new and painful and wonderful sensation, but she felt she lacked the ability.

Pelaru was a blank to her. She caught snippets of the others' thoughts now and again, mental monologues drifting unbidden into her mind. But not Pelaru's. He was a blind spot. Something was clouding her perceptions, keeping her at a distance.

Who are you?

Once they were all over the parapet, they threw the rope over the other side and threw the corpse off after it. The edges of the compound where it ran up against the wall were poorly lit, and a building screened them from the camp. They climbed down. Jez untied the rope and dropped down after them.

She found them stashing the corpse in an out-of-the-way spot. They were all wearing the cassocks that Ashua had stolen for them. Some wore the white-and-red of Speakers, some the grey of Sentinels. Real Speakers had the Cipher tattooed on their foreheads, not painted, but they'd pass as long as nobody looked at them too closely. She noted that Frey had gone for one of the Sentinel robes, which meant he only had a Cipher stitched on the breast rather than displayed on his brow. Captain's privilege. His vanity wouldn't suffer the kind of disfigurement he'd put Malvery, Jez and Pinn through.

The only one who'd escaped the humiliation was Silo. He'd been forced to remain outside, watching the gates. A Thacian could pass as a Vard with a bit of luck, but a Murthian stood out anywhere outside of Samarla. They left him with Pinn's earcuff, just in case, but they had little doubt the signal would be lost once they got inside.

When they were ready, Frey addressed them. 'Alright. We're here now, so let's get out there and poke around. Try to look like you belong here. Jez . . .' He gave her a pitying look. 'You're kind of giving us away, Jez.'

She realised that she was standing in a predatory crouch. 'Sorry,

Cap'n,' she muttered, and stood up straight. It was so hard to keep her mind on things.

They stepped out into the open. Storage depots and garages clustered nearby. A dirt road ran inward from the gate, splitting off in different directions to head away across the sprawling compound. There were several more Overlanders parked up, and some smaller buggies and tractors.

The buildings they could see were a mixture of old and new. Some had been here for a while, long enough for mould to grow and the rain and sun to weather them. Between them, clumps of tents alternated with simple prefabricated portable cabins, flown in on freighters. Men and women passed this way and that. All of them wore cassocks. Outsiders were not permitted inside the compound, it seemed.

'What are they up to in here?' Malvery wondered aloud.

'It takes a lot of paperwork to run a war,' said Pelaru.

'You think this is the command centre for the Awakener forces?' Ashua asked.

'It may be,' said Pelaru. 'Their strongholds are too obvious a target. They have no air superiority. Their best tactic is to hide themselves.'

There was a sense of fevered industry in the air. The Awakeners walked with hurried steps. Jez noticed it, and the Cap'n did too.

'Trinica told me the Lord High Cryptowhatever might be dropping in,' he said. 'Maybe that's why they're hustling.'

Ashua whistled and looked aside at Frey. 'The boss? When you get us in the shit, you really get us in the shit, don't you, Cap'n?'

'Never let it be said I don't take you to the best places,' Frey said. 'Let's find Trinica. Wherever she is, that's where the answers are.' He listened again to his earcuff, but evidently heard nothing.

'How do you reckon we're gonna find her in all of this?' Malvery asked, surveying the compound.

Jez pointed. 'There,' she said.

They followed her gaze to a blocky stone building, rising above its neighbours on another side of the camp. It was ugly and simple, with sloping sides and an imposingly martial look to it.

'Any special reason?' Frey asked.

'I can . . .' She stopped. 'I can *feel* something from it.'

She couldn't find the right word, but that was the gist of it. There was something unsettling about that building. Something that buzzed at her consciousness. She didn't like it.

They others looked at her sceptically, unconvinced. Then Pelaru said 'She could be right. I mean, it's the logical place if you want to impress somebody. And that is the purpose of summoning the captains, isn't it?'

Unexpected as it was, Pelaru's backing was enough to convince the others, who had no better ideas. They took a roundabout route towards the building, skirting the edge of the compound. They saw other Awakeners, but they were only one group of robed figures among dozens and nobody paid them the slightest attention.

As they got closer to the building, the buzzing in Jez's head got stronger, and she knew that she was right. Her skin prickled. There was a power in there, something sinister, daemonic. It was strong enough to muddle the weak daemon thralled to the earcuff in Trinica's pocket. If Trinica was in here, that would explain why they lost contact.

'Something . . .' she said, but once again the words didn't come easily. The daemon in her was still too close to the surface, roused by their encounter with the Imperator and now this new threat. 'Something bad ahead,' she said, her voice strained.

'Ain't there always?' Malvery commented, gazing up at the building. He glanced at Frey. 'Hate to be the one to bring this up, Cap'n, but you might want to consider the possibility that we're walkin' into a trap. Wouldn't be the first time Trinica stitched us up.'

'You don't need to tell me, Doc,' Frey replied. 'First sign of anything dodgy and we're outta here.'

'Wasn't that the first sign right then?' Ashua asked, pointing at Jez. 'I mean, a half-Mane just warned us there was something bad ahead. I'd say that counts.'

Frey rolled his eyes. 'Alright, *second* sign of anything dodgy. How's that?'

Ashua shrugged. 'Just saying.'

The entrance to the building was guarded by four Sentinels. A pair of Overlanders were parked outside, which Jez took to be the convoy they'd seen earlier, along with several other vehicles.

'Anything from Silo?' Malvery asked.

'I think I can hear something,' Frey said, covering his ear with one hand. 'It's really faint, but it's . . .' He became excited. 'Not Silo. I can't make it out. But I can hear voices.'

'Well, we're not getting in through the front without a firefight,' said Ashua. 'Let's take a look round.'

Staying out of sight as best they could, they circled the building at a distance. They saw no other entrance, but at the back they found a spot where another building pressed up close and there were no floods. In that dark alley was a sheer wall with windows at the top.

'Jez? You think you can get up there?' Frey asked.

Jez showed her teeth in what passed for a grin. She snatched the coil of rope from Pinn, slung it over her shoulder and launched herself upward. Splayed hands gripped the wall with inhuman strength. There were no handholds, but she climbed anyway. The tiniest cracks were purchase enough. She scaled the wall with a fierce joy in her heart, glad to be free of the crew for a moment. They slowed her down. Everyone slowed her down.

She slipped through the window into a corridor floored with gridded metal and bright with electric lights. It was quiet, but the sensation of strange power in this place made the air feel raucous. She secured the rope and dropped it down, then headed off scouting, unable to wait for the others.

She investigated to the end of the corridor, but found only closed doors. Her senses were too muddled to detect anything nearby, so she made her way back, in time to find Malvery hauling himself over the sill.

'. . . ever going to notice me? Don't I do my devotions? Don't I . . .'

She froze. A streamer of thought had curled through her mind. Not Malvery's. Someone else's.

A door was opening up the corridor. She ran. A Sentinel stepped through, a young blond man with a pudding-bowl haircut. His rifle was slung across his back. He had only an instant for surprise before Jez pulled him through, seized him by the throat and slammed him up against the wall.

The Sentinel hung there, heels kicking uselessly at the floor. His eyes bulged in terror, face turning red. Jez glared at him, a snarl on her face.

She could squeeze. She wanted to squeeze. The bones in his neck would crack like a bundle of twigs.

Then she lashed a fist across his face, and the Sentinel dropped in a heap, out cold.

She looked down at the man at her feet. A heavy hand landed on her shoulder. For once, she didn't flinch.

'Attagirl, Jez,' said Malvery, and there was a warmth in his voice that she heard too rarely nowadays. 'Attagirl.'

Eighteen

The Dark – Diagnosis –
The Man In Black – Blame

Crake felt the dark pressing close at his shoulder. Beyond the light of the electric lamps lay ghosts and dreadful memories. No matter how he tried to shut them out, they whispered at him from the blackness.

He hunched over the tome on his desk, ran his finger across the formulae to fix them in his mind. Then he stood up and took a breath. *There's nothing behind me.*

He turned around. No phantoms waited there. Only his brother, clad in a red silk gown, lying still upon a bench.

The summoning circle was ready. The air was taut with the barely perceptible throb of the resonator masts that surrounded it, throwing out a cage of frequencies that a daemon couldn't pass through. This time, he was determined that nothing would escape.

He checked his instruments meticulously. An oscillator sat in the centre of the circle: a plain metal hemisphere, wired to a trolley rack outside the circle that held a modulator, a pair of resonator boxes and an oscilloscope. He scanned the array of gauges and dials on their faces, then checked the backup generator was running properly in case the electricity failed. Lying next to the oscillator, attached by wires to the second resonator in the trolley rack, was an iron band about a foot in diameter. He checked it was properly connected.

Lastly he glanced at the echo chamber, the great riveted bathysphere that lurked at the edge of the light. He'd not be needing that, he thought. It would take a lot to make him turn that damned contraption on again.

They'd shut the cellar up after the tragedy, and left his belongings virtually untouched. The law hadn't been informed. The affairs of the Crakes were kept within the family: Father's business was too important for scandal. And so Bess's death was reported as a tragic fall, and the cellar door was locked, and the Shacklemores employed, who could be trusted to keep their mouths shut. The servants knew, of course, but no one would take their word over a powerful aristocrat like Rogibald Crake.

For almost three years the wine cellar lay undisturbed. Waiting like some malevolent creature, crouched and patient. Waiting for him.

'Stop it,' he said aloud to himself. His voice echoed around the pillars and came back hollow. He wouldn't bow to terrors of the past. Bess was dead. He'd accepted that. All that remained here were memories.

It had taken him most of the night to prepare. He pored greedily through his old books, intoxicated by them. It was a store of knowledge that he'd thought he'd never lay hands on again. So engrossed was he that for a time he forgot why he was here, and when he remembered, he was ashamed. Once, the Art had been an all-consuming passion, and though he'd turned from it after the tragedy, it drew him back like a moth to a flame.

His preparations complete, he set to work at the dials, searching the frequencies of the aether. His formulae gave him a range to search in. His instincts would do the rest. This wasn't a particularly tricky summoning, but he'd never attempted it before. Ridiculous of him, really. Of all the many uses a daemon could be put to, he'd never used one to heal.

The doctors were baffled by this strange disease that put people into a coma. But doctors didn't have the tools he did.

The first stage was the easy part. He'd bring in a daemon to diagnose the patient. Theoretically, once it had had been introduced to Condred, it would provide him with a set of frequencies that would enable him to bring a more powerful daemon to bear, one targeted to the illness. With luck, it would cure whatever ailed his brother.

Daemonist lore had it that the most appalling wounds could be healed this way, and maladies of the brain and nervous system that were beyond medical science. A skilled practitioner might bring somebody back from the brink of death. That, at least, was the rumour, but confirmation was hard to come by in the secretive world of the daemonists.

If only he'd been that skilled, he might have saved Bess. But he could save Condred. Perhaps.

A hum began to build as he moved through the frequencies, probing, searching for a nibble from beyond. There! The needle of one of the high-end gauges jumped. He set about penning the daemon, setting up interference patterns round it so it couldn't slip away from him. His concentration sharpened with the thrill of the chase. He'd become good at this. No longer did he clumsily fumble about the aether. He was deft and decisive, trammelling his quarry and then shrinking the cage until it had nowhere to run to. After that, he found its primary resonance and pinned it, spearing it with sonics. Then he set about matching its vibrations with those of the visible world, pulling it into phase with what most people called reality.

The familiar sense of paranoia and unease sank into his bones. It was expected: the presence of a daemon unsettled people on a primitive level. But here in the wine cellar where he'd killed his niece, the feeling was particularly sharp. Ghosts gathered in the dark. Sweat trickled through his hair as he fought the urge to look over his shoulder.

She's not there. There's nobody there.

The daemon began to take shape inside the summoning circle. It was a wisp, nothing more. A barely conscious thing like a smudge on the eye. It curled and billowed this way and that, but the resonator poles kept it from escaping. Once he was satisfied it was stable, Crake turned to the second resonator, and set about matching the vibration of the iron ring to the daemon. The wisp was pulled, gently at first and then insistently, tugged closer to the object until it was sucked inside and disappeared.

Crake eased off both resonators steadily, keeping the vibrations matched until he was sure the daemon was securely thralled to the iron band. The paranoia receded as he did so. Finally he powered down the resonators and with that, the first summoning was done.

He reached into the circle and picked up the iron band. It looked entirely normal, but his tuned senses detected the daemonic life within.

Well, that had gone well enough. But that was the easy part. He switched round some wires so that the iron band was connected to the oscilloscope and carried it over to where Condred lay. If things went to plan, the daemon in the band would feed back readings to the gauges that he could record.

He looked down at his brother's face, and was assailed with sudden doubt. Did he really want to do this? Would it be better if Condred never woke, if he was spared the pain of seeing his daughter's murderer again?

He shook his head angrily at himself. That was cowardice talking. He was merely afraid to face his brother's justified wrath. He'd save his brother, and face his punishment. It was what a gentleman would do.

He lifted Condred's head and placed the iron band on his brow. Then he retreated to stand before the trolley rack. The daemon would already be working. Invisible tendrils were spreading through Condred's body, seeking out illness and corruption.

Crake waited. The only sounds were the soft hum of the resonator and the buzz of the electric lights that stood on poles around him. Beyond that lay the swarming dark of the cellar.

One of the lights crackled and stuttered. It flickered for a moment, stabilised again. Crake glanced over his shoulder and frowned, then returned to the oscilloscope. He should have been getting readings by now. The first hint of doubt crept into his mind. Had he performed the summoning properly? Everything had seemed to go right, but it was always hard to be sure.

The light fluttered again. He scowled at it. What was wrong with the electrics in this place? And why was it so damned cold in here?

When he turned back he saw that the gauges of the oscilloscope had come to life, needles swinging back and forth at random. He watched them with growing concern. Surely some malfunction? He tapped the side of the machine, but the needles kept swinging with no rhythm or sense to them.

Suddenly Condred bucked as if hit by an electric jolt. Crake looked up in alarm. His brother bucked again, his body jerking with the violence of it, and then went still.

Crake's mouth dried up. No, no, this was wrong! There was nothing in the procedure that could possibly harm him. The daemon in the band was as mild as the one in the earcuffs the crew of the *Ketty Jay* wore. He hit the switch to kill the oscilloscope and hurried over to Condred.

'Condred? Can you hear me?'

Abruptly Condred began to spasm. His limbs shook and juddered. His eyes flew open and his face contorted into an awful grimace. Spittle flew from his lips and his heels drummed on the bench.

Crake grabbed the iron band and pulled it off Condred's head, but the spasms only grew more violent. Crake tried to restrain him, but even in the midst of crisis, something held him back and he didn't apply all his strength. He and his brother never touched; it felt wrong.

Condred jerked and slipped off the bench. Crake only just managed to stop his head hitting the stone floor.

Spit and blood, not again! he thought as he clutched his brother helplessly. *What have I done? What have I done?*

The light that had been flickering blew out in a shower of sparks. His skin prickled with goose-bumps; fear crawled down his spine. He looked around desperately, as if there were somebody nearby that could help him. A small figure in a nightdress ran by, glimpsed at the edge of the light, gone in an instant.

His heart stopped in his chest. It couldn't be her. It *couldn't.*

Condred's shuddering was becoming ever more violent. His fists clenched and unclenched and his eyes rolled up in his head. Crake searched his mind for anything of use but came up blank. He was no medical man. He didn't know what to do.

A thin line of blood trickled from Condred's nostril. He stared at it in horror.

From the dark came a wet clicking sound. He heard it distinctly. The sound a little girl fighting to draw breath into punctured lungs.

'You're not here!' he screamed.

But this had happened before, and he was wise to the trick. He'd been tormented this way in the past. In another sanctum, beneath Plome's house in Tarlock Cove. When he'd been trying to cage a daemon.

A daemon was here. Not that tiny spark that he'd brought from the aether. Something stronger, darker, worse. But where had it come from? It hadn't been here before. Unless . . .

He looked down at Condred, eyes wide with horrified realisation. His brother thrashed and twisted, gurning and mugging blindly.

Unless the daemon was inside Condred.

Another lamp blew out, showering him in glass. He felt a dozen tiny sharp bites across his cheek and nape and the back of his hand.

There was a daemon inside his brother. It had awoken at the presence of the new daemon Crake had introduced, risen up to defend its territory. And unless Crake stopped it, it would kill its host in its fury.

A movement in the dark. He looked up and saw a bloody face, slack with anguish. The face of a little girl, gone in a blink. Crake felt his throat seize tight. He wanted to scream again.

But he didn't. He knew this game. He knew how daemons played on a man's fears, dredging up his sins and teasing out the thing that frightened him most. For Crake, that was Bess. Always Bess. Except her memory didn't have the power over him that it once had. He'd faced the truth of what he'd done. It couldn't break him now.

Condred needed him. He had to get the daemon out.

He cast around the sanctum for an answer. The summoning circle? No time. He'd have to recalibrate all the resonator masts. Condred was bleeding freely from the nose, his back arching fit to snap. No time. So what else? What else?

The echo chamber.

As soon as he thought of it, he was on his way, rushing over to the control panel attached to the metal bathysphere. He threw the switch to activate it. A sinister drone of suppressed power grew out of the silence. He returned to Condred and reached down to lift him up. Just for a moment it was Bess there instead, her white nightdress reddened and pierced with many cuts.

He squeezed his eyes shut. *Not here.*

When he opened them, there was Condred again, his lips bloodied and his eyes roving like those of a frenzied horse. Crake slipped his arms beneath his brother's, encircling his chest, and yanked him along the floor, haste making him rough.

'It hurts so bad, Uncle Grayther,' came a little girl's voice from the dark. 'Hurts so bad.'

A cry escaped his lips then, forcing its way out through gritted teeth. But he took that grief and used it, and it gave him strength. He hauled Condred towards the open door of the echo chamber, the same terrible portal through which he'd once put Condred's daughter. Condred slipped and pushed this way and that, but Crake was relentless. A hand hit him across the nose, startling him with pain. He didn't let go. Muscles straining, he manhandled his brother through the hatch. Once Condred was halfway in, he seized him by the hips and shoved his kicking legs in after.

'Hurts so bad . . .'

He slammed the hatch on his brother. A bloodied girl's hand slapped against the inside of the porthole. Crake recoiled, frightened. Then his face reddened in anger, and he surged towards the control panel. He twisted the dials, not caring where they went, building a chord of appalling disharmony.

Tiny arms slipped round his leg, and a cold little body pressed against him.

'Nice try,' he said hatefully, and threw a switch.

The echo chamber blasted Condred with a sonic barrage, a mess of vibrations and harmonics that swooped and crossed and hammered. A shriek echoed through the wine cellar as the daemon was torn apart by the flux. It seemed to come from everywhere at once: from the walls, from the floor, from inside Crake's head. It lasted a long time before it faded, receding to some unguessable distance as it did so.

He didn't let off the assault until he was sure there was no little girl holding his leg any more. Only then did he dare to look down.

He wrenched the door of the echo chamber open. Condred was there, bundled and still, his eyes closed and his mouth and chin slicked red.

Dead?

'You're not dying on me!' Crake said furiously. He reached in and pulled. He wouldn't allow Condred to be dead. He'd make it unhappen through sheer force of will. He hadn't half the affection for Condred as he'd had for Bess, but to kill them both in his sanctum would be more than he could take. It wouldn't happen. No world could be so cruel.

It took all his strength to drag his brother out of the echo chamber. Condred's bare feet slapped heavy and limp to the floor as the last of him emerged. Crake stumbled, borne down by the dead weight, and went down onto his arse. He sat there, with Condred's head in his lap like a lover's, searching that pale, slack face for a sign of life.

Condred's eyes flew open, and he screamed.

'No! Don't! Don't!' he shouted, arms flailing as he fended off invisible enemies. He lurched away from Crake, rolled over and ended up on his side, hands held defensively in front of his face. Then a wary calm came over him, like a man woken from a nightmare.

'Where is the man in black?' he whispered hoarsely. He raised himself so that he was kneeling. 'The intruder?' His eyes went to Crake. 'Is he gone?'

Crake's heart darkened at his words. No wonder he'd sensed something sinister when he'd entered this house. One of *them* had been here. A man in black. An Imperator.

'Yes, Condred,' Crake said quietly. 'He's gone.'

Condred peered at him. 'Grayther?' he croaked.

Crake felt tears welling and fought them. 'It's me,' he said.

Condred stared, his eyes widening in amazement. Then he lunged at Crake. Crake put his hands up, but he was too slow to stop Condred throwing his arms around his brother and hugging him tightly.

Crake did cry then. He couldn't stop himself. He sobbed as he held his brother, the frail shell of the man he'd known, and despite all their animosity he clutched him like someone long-lost and dear. Of all the things he'd expected when the Shacklemores had caught up with him, he hadn't expected this.

'I never thought I'd see you again,' said Condred over his shoulder. 'Spit and blood, after all I'd lost, I thought I'd lost you too.'

'Condred . . .' Crake said. 'Condred, I'm so *sorry* . . .'

Those words broke him, and his tears became hysterical, and he gripped his brother's back with fingers like claws and knucklebones stark. But while Crake was wracked with grief, no tears fell from Condred. He breathed steadily, and held his brother and was silent.

Finally, Condred released him, and they sat facing each other on the stone floor amid the scattered apparatus of the sanctum. The shadows were deep in the grim electric light, and still the darkness lay beyond. Crake waited, half in hope and half in terror, for his brother to speak.

Condred wiped the blood away from his mouth with the sleeve of his nightshirt. He was weak, and his head was evidently causing him great pain, but he didn't complain. That was his way. Their father had never liked a complainer.

'Grayther,' he said at last. 'You don't know what it means to lose a child and I pray you never do. If you had asked me before it happened, I would have said this: that I would hunt you to the ends of the earth and see you dead for what you did to Bess. But hate has a limit, at least for me, and I reached it long ago. When Bess was gone, when Amantha was . . .' he swallowed, '*gone* . . . What was the point of revenge after that? To spite myself by killing the last person I loved?'

Crake felt a jab in his chest, a physical pain. To hear Condred say a thing like that. He'd never imagined Condred felt anything more than contempt for him. But hadn't Condred taken him in when Crake needed a place to live, and made him part of the family, however reluctantly? Hadn't he done what a brother should, even though every act came bundled in scorn?

'I can't explain it to you, Grayther,' he murmured. 'I just . . . One day, I didn't hate you any more. So I resolved to let you go. There had been enough suffering. Causing more wouldn't undo a thing.'

He'd never heard Condred speak this way before. Crake didn't know what to say in return. Words seemed a pitiful tool for the purpose.

'It was an accident . . .' he said, and then stopped because it sounded pathetic.

'I know,' said Condred. 'Of course I knew. You adored her. We all did.'

But Crake blundered on. If he didn't get it out now, he feared he'd never get the chance. 'It wasn't . . .' he said. 'It wasn't me that did it, do you understand? There was a daemon in me. It was my fault, oh, spit, it was my fault but it wasn't *me* in there, it wasn't *me* that did that.' He felt tears coming again. 'I locked the door. I always locked the door. But maybe that time I didn't . . .'

'You locked the door.' Condred's voice was weary, devoid of feeling. It was as if it had all been drained out of him. He was never an emotional man, at least not on the outside, and he must have cried all the tears he ever would over this. 'I knew what you were doing down there.'

Crake looked up at him in surprise. Condred snorted. 'Living under my roof, spending all your time in my wine cellar, pretending you were working on some grand invention? You think I'd let you build some scientific contraption without my knowing about it? I feared you'd blow the house up. There was always a second key, Grayther. So when you were away, I went down there.'

He sighed, and ran his hand over his forehead, pushing back his lifeless grey and white hair.

'When I found out, I pitied you. Poor little brother with his wild ideas, never able to settle to business like I could, never able to find his place.' He shifted position, sitting up against the echo chamber with a wince. 'I thought daemonism was superstitious nonsense. I thought you'd grow out of it. But I was blind and careless, and one day I left the key out.' He managed a small, bitter smile. 'You remember how desperate Bess was to see your workshop? You told her you were making toys down there. Every so often you'd bring a toy from the city and tell her you made it. Well, she found that key. You locked the door, Grayther. It was my fault she got in.'

His head hung, though whether from exhaustion or grief Crake couldn't tell. He stared at Condred, numbed by the moment, processing all that he'd been told. If not for Condred, Bess would never have been down in the sanctum that night. If not for him, she'd be alive. And his brother blamed himself for that.

'The Awakeners did this to me,' said Condred, raising his head. 'I remember the man in my bedroom, the *fear* of him, how it crushed me. And then nothing.' His eyes narrowed in concentration. 'He was carrying something . . . He held it out towards me . . .' Then he shook his head. The memory was gone.

'Some thralled object, no doubt,' said Crake, his voice firmer now they were on safer ground. 'Perhaps a ring or a bracelet or a band. It contained the daemon that kept you unconscious. He put it on you after you were subdued, and the daemon passed into you.' His voice became grave. 'Others have fallen to this sickness. I'll wager all of them are the sons and daughters of aristocrats who refused to bend the knee to the Awakener cause.'

'Yes,' said Condred. 'I wonder if Father would have received some message eventually. Promising my recovery if he would lend his resources and support.'

Crake thought back on his conversation with his father. 'Perhaps he already did,' he said.

There was silence between them at that.

'They want the rural areas,' said Condred at last. 'That's where they're strongest. They'll get the country folk on their side, trap the Coalition in the cities, cut off their supplies.'

Crake was about to agree, but then he heard a faint sound from outside the cellar. A sound that had become familiar to him over these past years. He scrambled to his feet as he heard another, and another and another.

Condred pricked up his ears. 'What is it?'

'Gunfire,' said Crake. 'It's gunfire!'

Nineteen

A Conversation – The Prize – The Mouth of the Allsoul –
Frey Sees the Future – No Escape

'Somebody's coming!'

Jez's hissed warning sent them scampering back down the corridor and through a side door. Beyond was a small infirmary, shiny and sterile in a way that Malvery's never was. They crowded inside. Frey left the door open a crack and pressed his eye to it.

Voices were approaching. Two men in conversation.

'Then what's the effective range?'

'Ten kloms.'

'Theoretically.'

'Based on the Sammies' measurements of an identical device.'

'So, not actually tested at all, then.'

The voices were louder now, and Frey heard footsteps, walking fast and with purpose. He glanced round the room to check on his crew. Ashua was close to the door, listening, with Pinn crowding in to hear as well. Jez waited in that feral stance of hers that meant she was ready to pounce. Pelaru stood there fearlessly, arms folded; he even made a Sentinel's cassock look good, damn him. Malvery was pilfering suppies from the medicine cabinet.

'You know what we're up against,' said the first voice. 'They want it kept secret. How are we meant to test its parameters when this place has become a refugee camp for every Awakener in Vardia? We needed more time.'

'We get one chance at this, that's all I'm saying. It's our necks if we're wrong.'

Frey saw them now, as they passed the door and continued down the corridor. Two middle-aged men, one balding and with spectacles, the other with unkempt hair and an untidy beard. They were wearing the standard issue Awakener cassocks, but unusually their cassocks were brown. Frey didn't understand the significance of that. He wished Crake were there to shed light on the subject; he didn't want to ask Pelaru.

'Effective radius is ten kloms,' said the balding one. 'That's all you need to say. Now tidy yourself up. They'll hang you if you present yourself to the Lord High Cryptographer like that. Where's your respect?'

'Respect? I'm in it for the science. For the chance to work with something no one's ever seen before. You know I don't believe that Awakener nonsense.'

'When you see him, you will,' said the balding man, and with that they passed out of hearing.

'Sounds like something we should be investigating, Cap'n,' Ashua suggested.

'That it does,' Frey agreed.

Once the coast was clear, they sallied out and headed in the direction the men had come from. The interior of the building had an industrial feel to it, with steel floors and sterile grey walls. This wasn't a place meant to impress somebody, it was a place where you got things done. The question was: what?

He covered his ear and listened to the earcuff again, but the signals were frustrating. Occasional garbled voices came in faint snatches, and none of it understandable. He heard Trinica's voice once in a while, and she sounded relaxed and calm. That made him feel a little better. Probably they were all making nice, the Awakeners buttering up the captains with promises in order to secure their aircraft. But Frey wanted to know for sure; he wanted to know exactly what they were saying. This damned interference, though – he'd never heard anything like it.

Thanks to Jez's uncanny senses they'd managed to avoid bumping into anyone in the corridors so far, but Frey wasn't sure how much longer their luck would last. He was beginning to think that this whole idea was a bad one. He should have just taken a chance and trusted Trinica to tell him what she learned. But he couldn't pass up the opportunity to look around the Awakeners' base. He needed a card in his hand in case the Century Knights tracked him down, or someone stuck a bounty on him. The way events were going, it might be the only thing between him and the noose.

There was a sliding metal door at the end of the corridor, of the kind they used on the *Ketty Jay*, except considerably cleaner. Jez listened at it, then nodded at Frey. He pulled it aside.

Beyond was a small steel-walled room filled with a bewildering array of gauges, dials and instruments. A ledger lay open on a desk, full of scribbled calculations. Two half-empty coffee mugs stood cold next to it. Frey crossed the room, passing strange scientific devices of brass and glass. He could only guess at the purpose of half of them, and he didn't care to. Behind the instruments was a window, and he went to that.

'*That's* what we're looking for,' he said.

They were standing in an observation room, set high up on the side of a large circular chamber. Around the edges of the chamber were banks of instruments: cabinets that clanked and chattered, bellows that wheezed up and down, gyroscopes tilting this way and that. None of that interested Frey. The prize piece was in the centre, on a pedestal, surrounded by rods and sensors and rot knew what else.

It was a tall cylinder, twice the height of a man, encased in a mass of pipes and protrusions that looked like they'd been carved from yellowed bone. Inside the cylinder, a bruise-coloured gas swirled, and little sparks of lightning flashed and flickered. At its four corners were squat, thick towers of some brass-like material that wasn't quite brass. Their surfaces were trenched and pitted with what might have been language, or perhaps a form of subtle machinery.

He'd seen its like before. It was Azryx technology.

'Whoa,' said Ashua, who'd come up to stand next to him. Its very presence seemed to dent the world around it. 'Is that what's messing up your, y'know?' She flicked his earcuff, which Frey found deeply annoying.

'Must be,' said Frey, batting her hand away.

'It's not,' said Jez from behind them. 'Not that. Something else.'

'There's something else in this building weirder than *that*?' said Pinn sceptically.

Malvery had crowded in now. 'That must be what the Sammies

sold to the Awakeners,' he muttered. 'Whatever these buggers are up to, that's the key to it down there.'

Frey looked across at Pelaru. His eyes showed nothing as he gazed down at the machine. 'Any ideas, whispermonger? Any titbits you want to share?'

Pelaru's eyes flicked to him disdainfully, then back to the Azryx device.

'Alright then. I'm gonna take a closer look. Doc, you wanna come?'

'Bloody right I do,' Malvery said.

Frey took off his earcuff and tossed it to Ashua. 'Keep hold of that, will you? I can't handle conversation in my ear when I'm being sneaky. Everyone else, stay here. If those scientists come back, well . . .' He made a vague motion in the air. 'You can handle a couple of scientists, can't you?'

There was a hatch in the floor in the corner of the room. It was open, and they saw a metal ladder leading down into the chamber, secured against the outer wall. They descended and stepped out from among the banks of machinery, peering around warily as if someone might be hidden in here, waiting to catch them. There was a large door to the chamber, big enough to drive a vehicle through, but it was securely closed and there was no one else in sight.

Once they'd established that they were safe, they approached the Azryx machine. The coloured gas in the cylinder was hard on the eyes; it became disorientating if stared at too long. Parts of the device hinted at familiar technology, but that only made the rest stranger by contrast. Frey had seen the preserved bodies of the Azryx, and knew them to be human, but they seemed unfathomably alien nonetheless. Their works awed him a little. After seeing a Juggernaut in action, it was hard not to be afraid of what they could do.

'Buggered if I know what it is,' Malvery declared, after a cursory inspection. 'We ought to smash it or something.'

'I dunno,' said Frey. 'Remember what happened last time we tried to smash up a piece of Azryx tech? Wiped out everything within a dozen kloms.'

Malvery waited for his point.

'*We're* within a dozen kloms,' Frey elaborated, measuring the distance from Malvery to the machine with his arms.

'Never thought I'd hear you arguing against wanton property destruction, Cap'n,' the doctor said.

'Old age has mellowed me,' said Frey. It was good to hear a bit of banter from Malvery again. His mood had improved considerably since Frey had decided to infiltrate the Awakener base. Frey gave himself a mental pat on the back for his excellent crew-handling skills, then remembered Jez and Crake and stopped patting.

Malvery resumed his study of the device. 'You think the Sammies gave 'em an instruction manual with this thing?' he asked.

Frey scanned the room, searching for something that might shed light on its purpose. Habit made him check on his crew, and he glanced up at the window of the observation room. Jez was waving at him frantically. He wondered what on earth she was doing. When he twigged, alarm bells went off all over his body.

'Doc!' he snapped, racing towards a bank of machinery at the edge of the chamber. Malvery huffed after him, and the two of them hid amid the clicking cabinets and whirling gyroscopes. Not a moment too soon: the door to the chamber hissed and slid upwards, and four Awakeners trooped in.

They were unlike any that Frey had ever seen. They didn't wear the traditional cassocks of their order, but red hooded cloaks emblazoned with the Cipher, and fitted silver armour as exquisite as a Century Knight's. Their rifles were polished and top of the line, and their faces were covered with red silk masks below their eyes. On their foreheads were more Ciphers, tattoos displaying their faith.

Frey didn't need Crake to guess what they were. The Lord High Cryptographer's honour guard. The supreme leader of the Awakeners was about to make his entrance.

A half-dozen Sentinels followed, along with a red-cassocked Interpreter and the two scientists they'd observed earler. With them came a tall hooded lady in black and red walking at the side of the Lord High Cryptographer himself.

It wasn't hard to pick him out. The Awakeners dressed in an austere fashion as a rule, but not their leader. He was draped in white and gold, swathed in fine fabrics, and though he was small and bent with age he seemed to shine in the dim light of the chamber. An embroidered red mantle hung about his shoulders, and he wore a great golden collar that made his head seem tiny in comparison. That head was covered with a skin-tight white fabric mask that concealed the face totally, and across his eyes was a strange grilled visor that wrapped from ear to ear, giving him a disconcertingly mechanical look.

'That's the bastard behind it all,' whispered Malvery, clenching a fist. 'Just give me ten minutes alone with that decrepit son of a bitch. I'll kick his arse to dust.'

'Easy, mate,' said Frey. 'Lot of firepower in here. I plan to be around to see the good guys win.'

All eyes were on the Lord High Cryptographer as he shuffled into the room. There was something fascinating about that strange, anonymous figure. An *aura*, for want of a better word. He felt somehow precious and fragile. Frey wanted to protect him, and didn't know why.

The Lord High Cryptographer whispered to the hooded lady, who bowed down to hear him.

'The Lord High Cryptographer asks if all is in readiness,' she announced in a ringing voice.

'Everything is ready,' said the balding scientist, with a warning glance at his companion. 'The device has been thoroughly tested.'

The Lord High Cryptographer whispered again and the hooded woman spoke. 'The Mouth of the Allsoul demands to know how quickly his great weapon can be deployed.'

'We can have it aboard an aircraft within an hour, Honoured One,' said the Interpreter, a tall narrow man with slicked-back black hair. 'It can be anywhere in Vardia in two days.'

The Lord High Cryptographer conferred with his aide again. Frey felt a powerful desire to hear the old man's voice. He could see why some people fell for the teachings: the Lord High Cryptographer commanded the room without even showing his face. Even the sceptical scientist with the beard gazed at him with a sort of bewildered wonder in his eyes.

'The Lord High Cryptographer advises you that the time is very near,' the aide announced. 'Our triumphant assault will soon begin, and it will fall like a hammer blow upon the enemy. The Lord High Cryptographer himself will accompany the fleet in his flagship, such is his belief in our victory. By the Allsoul's will, we shall prevail over those who seek to silence us.'

'As the Code dictates,' some of the assembled muttered.

Frey exchanged a glance with Malvery. Normally he rolled his eyes at the pompous overblown language that boring people used to sound important, but this talk of hammer blows and triumphant assaults worried him. It sounded like the Awakeners were planning something big, and soon.

'The Lord High Cryptographer may rest assured,' said the Interpreter, 'the device will work as our Samarlan allies have promised. Our enemies' weapons will jam, their lights will fail, and they will fall from the skies.'

Frey felt his heart turn to ice. He knew exactly what the Azryx machine did now. He'd experienced its power in the Samarlan desert, when an identical device had disabled the *Ketty Jay* and brought her crashing down. That one was destroyed when the Azryx city was obliterated, but there must have been others. The Samarlans had got hold of one, and they'd sold it to the Awakeners.

He saw in his mind's eye what would happen if that device was activated in the middle of a fleet. Frigates, fighters, gunships, spiralling out of control or diving unstoppably earthward as their aerium tanks vented. Those that didn't crash would just hang in the air, sitting ducks for the enemy guns.

Hundreds of aircraft. Thousands of lives. Rot and damnation, it would be a massacre.

He'd been content to drift through the civil war and let it work itself out without much help from him, safe in the knowledge that the Coalition could handle itself. But matters had become a whole lot more urgent all of a sudden. He'd never really thought the Awakeners might actually *win*.

'The Lord High Cryptographer wishes to look up on the device with his own eyes,' the hooded lady announced. 'You will leave the room.'

Her peremptory demand was met at first with confusion and hesitation. Then the Interpreter clapped, and everyone outside the Lord High Cryptographer's immediate retinue bowed and left the room. The door slid closed behind them. Only the aide and his personal guard remained.

Frey and Malvery hunkered down deeper into cover and watched as the hooded lady removed the visor from the Lord High Cryptographer's eyes. Frey was disconcerted to see that the mask covered his face entirely, even the parts that were hidden by the visor. His mouth and eye sockets were mere depressions in the fabric; there was barely any nose at all. He was a blank, a ghostly mannequin.

The aide carefully slid her fingers under the neck of the mask, rolled it up and slipped it off.

The Lord High Cryptographer was ancient. His scrawny, wattled neck extended like a vulture's as he leaned forward, gazing upon the Azryx device with an expression of idiot greed. His eyes were a starburst of red and yellow, irises like a spatter of blood and pus. His bald head was liver-spotted; his nose had all but rotted away. And when his puckered mouth opened in a sigh of wonder, they saw his teeth. Teeth like needles, long and thin and sharp.

Unmasked, Frey adored him, and the feeling filled him with horror. He'd never imagined it was possible for two such polarised emotions to exist together. His mind and his body were repulsed, but his heart swelled with something atrociously close to love. He wanted to believe. Had he not been so set against the Awakener's dogma, he might have turned to the faith right then. There had to be something in it, surely? All those people couldn't be wrong? How else to explain the sense of righteousness that emanated from this man, this great man, this

daemon

He said the word to himself and it put steel in his spine. He'd seen the face of an Imperator and he'd seen Manes, and he knew they were not so different. He'd seen the way a daemon changed its host. And in the Lord High Cryptographer's face, he saw the same.

Once he'd been a man, but not any more. Like the Imperators, he had a daemon inside him. Perhaps he'd put it there himself, to acquire the powers it bestowed. Perhaps he believed his faith would overcome it. Or perhaps, more dreadfully, his own Imperators had forced him to it, turned on their master and made him one of them.

He didn't know. He couldn't guess. But he knew one thing. The Awakeners had used daemonism to create enforcers that allowed them to destroy the old religions. But somehow, over the years, it had got out of control. And the daemons were in charge now.

If the Coalition lost the civil war, Vardia wouldn't be ruled by fanatics. It would be ruled by daemons. He gazed upon the face of the

Lord High Cryptographer, and he saw the future, and it was unutterably terrible.

The creature crooned as it looked upon the Azryx device. It saw victory and lusted for it. It was a sound of such lascivious *want* that Frey had the urge to seize his revolver and shoot the damned thing right there.

But to shoot it would be suicide, and he couldn't have done it anyway. The Imperators emanated fear, but this daemon was worse. It emanated love.

He saw Malvery struggling with the same feelings. His face was locked in a taut frown and he was breathing heavily. He wondered if Malvery might really pull out his shotgun and end it now, destroy the monster and the machine, whatever the consequences. It was the kind of stupid heroism patriots were prone to.

But Malvery didn't fire, and the daemon's face was covered once more. When they were ready, the aide opened the door to the chamber once again. The others were waiting outside. Words were exchanged outside their hearing, and the Lord High Cryptographer and his retinue left, accompanied by the Interpreter. The scientists stood in the doorway with the Sentinels after they were gone, talking amongst themselves.

'We have to do something,' said Malvery.

'We have to get out of here,' Frey replied, pointing to the ladder that led up to the observation room. At the moment the Awakeners were not watching the room, but if they came in, there was no way Frey and Malvery would make it to that ladder without getting spotted.

Malvery was reluctant, his mouth set in a grim line. It didn't sit well with him, leaving something like that in the hands of the Awakeners.

'Doc!' said Frey sharply. 'Who's gonna tell the Coalition if we're dead?'

Malvery gave an exasperated sigh. Frey had got through to him with that. 'Come on,' he said.

They slipped between the banks of machinery, keeping their eyes on the scientists and Sentinels, who were deep in discussion just outside the chamber door.

Keep talking, Frey thought. He looked up at the window of the observation room, and saw that Ashua was practically jumping up and down, beckoning them.

Stealthily he ran the last few metres to the ladder and went scampering up the rungs. Malvery came more slowly behind him, blowing out his moustaches with the effort. Frey's muscles were tight with tension as he climbed higher. Surely someone would turn and see him? Surely he was so obvious that they couldn't fail to notice?

But he gained the top of the ladder and no alarm was raised. Ashua all but hauled him through the hatch and into the room, then went back to urge Malvery on.

Frey picked himself up and checked on everybody. Pinn was staring out of the window with a puzzled look on his face. He looked even more vacant than usual. Jez was in a corner, crouched, her teeth bared. Pelaru squatted before her, hand raised, like a man calming a skittish dog. He looked over his shoulder at Frey.

'The Lord High Cryptographer,' said Pelaru, and for once there was visible emotion on his face. 'He's—'

'A daemon,' said Frey. 'I got that.'

'She doesn't take it well when there are daemons about.'

'I got that too.'

Malvery clambered through the hatch, and sat down on the floor against a workbench to catch his breath. Frey went to the window and looked down into the chamber. The Awakeners were still in the doorway; they hadn't even come in yet.

'What did they say?' Ashua asked Malvery.

Malvery stared at her with a look of such despair that even Frey was affected. It took a lot to knock Malvery down, but this had rocked him.

'Give me the earcuff,' he said to Ashua. She dug it from her pocket and lobbed it to him.

'We have to get gone, Cap'n,' Malvery said. 'We have to tell someone.'

'We're going, Doc,' said Frey, clipping on the earcuff. 'Just let me check on Trinica . . .'

His voice tailed off as the sounds filled his ear. They were fuzzy and indistinct, but the words didn't concern him. It was the tone. Shouting. Protests. Alarm. He heard an impact and a crash. Trinica cried out, and it stabbed through the confusion and pierced him.

They saw it on his face. 'Cap'n . . .' said Malvery, a warning in his voice.

'She's in trouble,' he said. He looked about wildly. 'She's in trouble!'

'Cap'n, we have to go!' Malvery insisted.

'You go,' said Frey. 'Get out of here. I'm going after her.'

'This is too important!' said Malvery.

'Yeah,' said Frey. 'It is.' And with that he pulled open the door and headed off down the corridor.

Malvery swore. Ashua looked from the doctor to the departing captain in confusion.

'Are we just gonna let him go on his own?' she asked.

'Y'know, I hope he rescues her, I really do,' Malvery snarled as he got to his feet. 'That way I can punt her pasty arse to the moon.'

He stormed out of the door in pursuit of his captain, and the others had no choice but to follow.

Twenty

The Groundsman – Family Ties – Accusations –
Up on the Roof – A Long-Expected Admission

Crake pushed open the door of his brother's house, and looked out onto a battleground.

Guns cracked and snapped in the cold winter night. Trench-coated Shacklemores fired lever-action shotguns from cover, their breath steaming the air. Men were clambering over the wall that surrounded the grounds, their shadows long in the light of electric lamps. Folk from the village, from the countryside; folk who'd once been glad of the wealth and prosperity that Rogibald Crake had helped bring to the area, the amenities he paid for and the school he funded.

Crake felt outrage as well as fear. They were attacking the manor? They were actually attacking the manor? But he couldn't deny the evidence of his eyes.

The main mass of them had gathered behind the gates. He could hear the incoherent roar of their fury. Shacklemores shot at them from behind fountains and garden walls. Crake saw one man go tumbling back into the arms of his fellows, but those behind him pushed on, undeterred. The gate was stout and thick, and wouldn't give way easily. Several men were wrapping a chain around the ironwork, no doubt hoping to drag it down. Others fired back through the bars, keeping the Shacklemores busy.

There were so many of them. So many, and more coming over the wall. Some were killed, but Crake saw others drop to the ground and go scurrying away across the night-shrouded lawns, rough-dressed men carrying clubs or pistols.

Condred was at his side, leaning on him, supported by his arm. He heard his brother groan, a sound of weary despair from the depths of his being. In the flat light from the house he was haggard and wan. He was barefoot, and his red silk gown was no protection against the chill. In his face there was something like acceptance, as if he'd long known this day would come.

'They're here for you, ain't they?' a voice snarled. Crake turned and saw one of the groundsmen, a man he didn't know, advancing along the side of the house. He was a stocky, unshaven man with a cloth cap squashed down over his ears. He had a spade in his hands, and was holding it like a weapon.

'Daemonist!' he spat. Then he looked at Condred. 'And you, his puppet! What black art brought you back when no doctors could? Whatever you once was, you ain't no more.'

Crake saw fear and rage and murder in the man's eyes, and he backed away into the foyer, pulling Condred in with him. But the groundsman lunged at him suddenly, made a feint with the spade. Crake jerked away, stumbled, and Condred's weight brought him down. The two of them tripped and fell to the parquet floor in a heap.

The groundsman ignored Condred and went for Crake. He put his boot to Crake's shoulder as he tried to get up, and shoved him back to the floor. He raised his spade, edge downward, aimed at Crake's throat. Hesitated. Not so easy to kill a man. But Crake knew it was coming in a second or two, once he'd screwed up his courage.

A strange calm took him. He looked up at the grizzled face of the groundsman looming over him. His lips peeled back in a wide grin.

'Hey . . .' he said quietly, though it hurt to speak with the man's weight on his chest. 'Hey, there's no need for this.'

The groundsman stared down at him, and as he did so, his attention was caught by something. The glitter of a gold tooth. Crake saw the balled-up rage behind the groundsman's eyes loosen a little.

'Here . . .' he muttered. 'That's a nice tooth.'

'It is, isn't it?' said Crake. 'Now why don't you get off me and put down that spade?'

The groundsman regarded the spade as if he couldn't quite work out how it had got into his hands. 'Reckon I will,' he said. He stepped back, tossed the spade aside, and gave Crake a sheepish look.

Crake began to pick himself up. 'Good. Now why don't you—'

The groundsman's chest exploded, spraying Crake's face with warm flecks of blood. He fell to his knees and tipped sideways.

Standing in the doorway was a Shacklemore, a gaunt man holding a shotgun, a scattered beard on his long, hollow face.

'You alright?' he asked them, and pulled Crake up before he had a chance to reply. He went and helped Condred after. Crake wiped the blood off his face and looked down at the dead man on the floor. There was a wet hole in his back. A pool of red was spreading from beneath the body, running down tiny channels in the parquet floor.

Another dead man. Once the initial shock had worn off, he found it didn't mean a thing. He'd lived long enough in the world to shrug at a stranger's corpse.

'Let's get you to the landing pad,' said the Shacklemore brusquely. 'We're falling back.'

'I thought you were supposed to defend this place,' Crake said.

'There's two hundred people out there, or I'm a blind man,' said the Shacklemore. He took Condred's arm over his shoulder. 'We're bounty hunters first, bodyguards second and mercenaries third. Martyrs ain't on the list.'

'What about our father? Rogibald Crake?'

'The old feller? Someone's taking care of him.'

But the man was vague, and Crake wasn't convinced. And he knew his father.

'Take my brother to the landing pad,' he said.

The lines around Condred's mouth deepened in disapproval. 'Leave him, Grayther. You know him. He'll do as we will.'

Yes, thought Crake. *I know him well enough.*

But Condred saw his brother's mind, and grabbed his arm. 'You don't have to make it up to him,' he said. 'Not to him.'

'Go to Thesk,' said Crake. 'Perhaps I'll see you there.'

Perhaps. And perhaps I'll never see you again. Perhaps we'll never again be able to look at each other without being reminded of Bess.

Crake looked long into his brother's eyes, searching for something to say. Condred was thinking the same as he was. Neither knew what the future would bring. It was all too raw and new right now. In the end, he clasped his hand over Condred's, and that was enough.

'Get him out of here,' he told the Shacklemore. 'Keep him safe.'

'Will do.'

Crake turned to leave, and then stopped and turned back. 'One last thing,' he said. 'You've a pistol in your belt. I'd better have that.'

'Will you bollocks,' scoffed the Shacklemore. 'That's *my* pistol.'
Crake grinned, and his tooth glinted. 'I beg to differ.'

By the time he reached the mansion, the Shacklemores were in steady
retreat. Groups of men shot at one another from cover. Bodies lay
sprawled across herbaceous borders, bloodied hands dangling in
ornamental pools. The fighting was still fiercest round the gates, but
enough men had got over the walls to sow havoc among the defenders
now.

I did this, he thought as he ran. *They're here for me. Seeing me take
Condred to the sanctum was the last straw.*

But no. He wouldn't blame himself entirely. The Awakeners had
riled them up, filled their heads with lies and nonsense, made them
furious and frightened so the only thing they could do was hit out.
Even the Shacklemore bullets didn't stop them. All these deaths born
out of hate and ignorance and superstition, and the bastards who
started it were predictably nowhere to be seen.

He ran up the slope towards his father's house, keeping to the edge
of the lawns where there was some meagre cover, staying out of the
light. A bullet chopped into the turf nearby and he saw someone
aiming at him from over by the wall. He ignored them and kept going.
After all his time on the *Ketty Jay*, he knew they were just wasting
ammunition at that range.

*What are you doing, Grayther Crake? What do you owe your father?
The man never loved you.*

But love didn't matter. It was a question of duty. It was what a son
ought to do. And maybe if Rogibald found out what Crake had done,
maybe if he knew Condred was alright, maybe he'd smile and favour
him at last.

Foolish, he thought. But he ran on anyway.

Crake reached the mansion and went skirting along its façade,
sticking close to the building. As he reached the main door, a
Shacklemore came running out of it onto the drive, a young man
with slick black hair. He looked about, saw Crake, and then raised his
pistol and fired twice. Crake covered his face instinctively as a stone
vase smashed to pieces next to him.

'Stop firing, you moron! Do I look like a bloody peasant? I'm on
your side!'

He didn't know where that peremptory tone of command came from. Perhaps his surroundings had brought out his aristocratic side. But the Shacklemore stopped shooting.

Crake glared at him. 'Where's my father?'

'In there,' said the Shacklemore, tipping his head. 'He won't move himself. I'm going for the landing pad. If you've got half a brain you'll come with me.'

'I'll get him out,' said Crake. 'You hold those aircraft. Remember who's paying you.'

There was a shrieking noise from across the grounds. They both looked out over the lawns and saw the gates being torn off their hinges. Their attackers were using chains and a tractor to pull them down. The villagers came swarming in, and the last of the Shacklemore resistance broke.

'No pockets in a shroud, my friend,' the young man said. 'You'd best be quick.'

He sprinted off, and Crake went up the porch steps into the foyer. He knew exactly where his father would be. He hurried through the mansion to the study, and pushed open the door.

The fire had reduced to glowing embers. It had been burning all night. His father stood by the window with a glass of brandy in his hand, looking out. The decanter was on a silver platter on a side table, mostly empty.

'Father,' he said.

'Grayther,' he replied.

'Father, we have to go.'

'I don't think so.'

'They'll kill you.'

'Damned if I'll run.' His hand trembled on his glass. 'Damned.'

Crake came into the room. Even now, the study inspired respect and awe in him. His father's own sanctum, sacred and forbidden.

'Condred is awake,' he said. 'You did the right thing calling on me. The Awakeners caused the coma.'

Rogibald sipped his brandy.

'But you knew that, didn't you?' Crake said.

'It takes daemons to fight daemons,' said Rogibald. He motioned to the window. 'And here is my reward.' He turned his head and stared at Crake levelly. 'At least I have my son back. That's all I wanted.'

It was a pointed singular, pitched to wound. But Crake was no longer the man that had fled this place three years ago. His father's barbs were blunt now.

He walked over to stand next to Rogibald. Beyond the window, the gunfire continued. A pair of Shacklemores ran past. Here inside the study, he felt strangely insulated from it all. He wondered if that was how his father had always felt when he looked out on the world.

'Don't throw your life away, Father.'

Rogibald didn't reply.

'Look at me,' said Crake, and his father did so. Crake gave him a smile. He felt the cold suck of the daemon as it sapped the energy from him, saw his father's gaze move to the gold tooth. Crake hadn't slept, and using the tooth so much had weakened him, but he felt strong enough for this.

'Live to fight another day, Father. Do it for your son. The one you *do* care about.'

Rogibald watched his reflection in the tooth, then slowly raised his gaze to meet Crake's . . . and dashed the brandy in his eyes. Crake recoiled, spluttering. Rogibald regarded him with naked hatred.

'Get out!' he cried. 'You're no part of me! You're no son of mine! You were weak from the start and now you're fouled. Run! Save your own life, coward! I'll fall with my house, and Condred will have all that's left, but you? You'll have nothing. You've brought ruin upon us!'

Crake retreated before the barrage. He'd never heard his father speak that way. It shocked him and shamed him, but it hardened his heart as well. What did he care for a man who'd never cared for him? What accusation could he face that he hadn't already accused himself of? He'd done his duty; he'd tried his best. That was more than he owed this man.

He drew himself up and mustered as much dignity as he could with brandy dripping down his face. 'Goodbye, Father,' he said.

Rogibald turned back to the window without a word. Crake opened the door and left. It seemed a weak way to bid farewell for ever, but then, they'd never had much to say to one another.

He heard smashing glass as he hurried back through the house, and quickened his step to a run. He'd wasted too long on Rogibald already. It was time to look after himself.

Coward, his father had called him. Well, if he'd learned one thing from his captain, it was this: cowardice was always the last insult thrown by the brave, just before they got shot in the face.

Damn you, Father. Die if you want. I'm done with you.

He reached the foyer, headed purposefully for the door, and stumbled to a halt. Through the panes of leaded glass on either side, he saw men running up the drive towards the mansion. Men with guns and clubs, faces distorted with hate.

Already they were at the door. Seized with the fear of their vengeance, he ran in the opposite direction, up the wide staircase of polished wood. They burst in behind him, a shouting horde. Someone yelled when they saw him. Crake fled upward, and a dozen men followed. The rest scattered throughout the mansion, smashing and destroying anything they could lay their hands on.

He sprinted wildly down a corridor, not knowing where he was going, desperate only to escape from the pain and death promised by his pursuers. And yet even through his terror there was a cold sense of inevitability, a closing-in all around him. The ground floor was occupied; the landing pad was cut off. How was he going to get out now?

One villager, particularly fleet of foot, sprang up the stairs and came thumping down the corridor after him. He was skinny and blond, a chair-leg club in his hand, his teeth gritted and his face red, drunk on the blind hatred of the mob and the sense of togetherness it brought. Crake heard him coming and knew he couldn't outpace him. Instead he planted his feet, pulled out his revolver and aimed it square at his pursuer.

The villager skidded to a halt, blanching as he realised his predicament. Crake didn't even think of mercy; he was too frightened. He fired, three times at short range.

They stood looking at each other in disbelief. Then the man turned and scrambled back the other way.

Crake looked at his gun as if there was something wrong with it. But no, it was just his aim. *I should give up firearms altogether.*

Three more men came rushing up the corridor, shoving the fleeing man aside. Crake didn't dare gamble that the threat of a gun would keep them back. He turned tail and ran.

He pulled open a door and darted inside, slamming it behind him. A narrow stairwell led up and down: the servants' stairs. He hesitated:

perhaps he should descend to the ground floor? Could he get out that way? But instinct wouldn't let him. It drove him away from danger, without regard for sense or logic. So he went up instead.

The door burst open below him, and there was a shout. He fired two shots down the stairs, the revolver deafening in the stairwell. The third time the hammer fell on an empty chamber. They pulled their heads in, but it wouldn't keep them back for long. He reached the top of the stairs and came out on the upper floor of the mansion.

He shut the door behind him. If only he had his thralled skeleton key, he could have locked it, kept them back for a few more precious moments. But the Shacklemores took it when they captured him, and it was gone now.

He fled down the corridor. Voices ahead of him. *They're coming up the main stairs.* He skidded to a halt, heart banging against his ribs. There were too many to escape. He was outnumbered and trapped. Nothing he could do would prevent the end. He'd die at the hands of a filthy lynch mob, beaten to death in a flurry of blows, bones snapping as they stamped on him, teeth kicked in, a blinding jumble of agony to see him out of the world.

He searched for a way to delay the inevitable, and found a door he didn't recognise. It took him a moment to pull it from his memory. It had been repainted since he saw it last. He'd walked past it a thousand times, but had gone inside only once. He'd been a child, and he'd been beaten for his trouble.

There!

He seized the handle and turned it. It was locked. In desperation, he put his boot into it, hard. He kicked twice more, until the door frame split and it hung by a hinge. With one last kick, he was through.

The door to the servants' stairwell opened at the same time. A bearded man aimed a gun at him and loosed off a wild shot. Crake darted into the room he'd opened.

It was tiny, barely big enough to contain half a dozen boxes of tools and sundries. A wooden ladder, fixed to the wall, led up to a hatch. The roof access. He climbed the ladder, shoved the hatch.

Locked.

No, no, no!

There was a bolt on the inside. Sense cut through his panic. He slid the bolt across, pushed the hatch, and it came open. Up he went, and out into the night. He dropped the hatch behind him and backed away, looking about for something to pile on top of it.

He was near the edge of the roof. A mountainous landscape of skylights and chimneys, lit from beneath, blocked his view. Down below he could see that the grounds were aswarm, the invaders racing over the lawns. There was the occasional crack of gunfire, but the Shacklemores were nowhere to be seen.

Closer by was Condred's house. The lower windows had been smashed, and smoke was churning out of them.

They're burning the place. Those ignorant bastards are burning my home.

The sound of rising engines drew his attention to the landing pad. Already several craft were high in the sky, small with distance. The last one was taking off, under fire from a few villagers who took pot-shots at it with their pistols.

Sudden hope ignited inside him at the sight. Surely one of the Shacklemores he'd met would remember that Crake was at the mansion? Surely Condred would tell them? He ran along the edge of the roof, waving his arms.

'*Hey!*' he shouted. '*Heeey! I'm still here!*'

The aircraft swung around lazily above the landing pad, turning towards him, and for a moment he'd thought they'd seen him. But it kept on turning, swinging round to follow the other craft towards Thesk, and its thrusters lit and pushed it away. Crake watched it dwindle, and the hope in his breast burned to ashes.

The hatch burst open behind him. Crake turned and aimed his empty pistol at the burly man who came climbing through. The man hesitated at the sight; but when Crake didn't fire, a slow and wicked leer spread across his face. He kept on coming, slowly, as if to say: *I dare you.*

Crake lowered his weapon. It had suddenly become too heavy for him. His limbs were leaden. He couldn't run any more. He didn't see the point.

I should never have left the Ketty Jay, he thought. *I should never have left my friends.*

He walked to the edge of the building and let his pistol fall from his hand, over the side. It tumbled through the air and smashed to pieces on the driveway.

He closed his eyes. More men were coming through the hatch, but he didn't care. They were too far away; they wouldn't have him. He'd not be meat for the savages.

The wind blew his hair across his forehead. He felt it keenly, as if for the first time. He'd miss the wind. It seemed to get louder as he listened to it, rising to a scream in his ears as the world narrowed to a single sharp moment and his senses focused on one final and all-consuming task.

Take a step, he thought, and he felt himself become light. Even in the exquisite sadness of the end, he knew this was the right thing to do.

He sucked in his breath, put out his foot over the edge, and then the roar of the biggest damn autocannon he'd ever heard scared the shit out of him.

His eyes flew open and he recoiled from the edge, throwing himself down with his hands over his head. The rooftop was chewed up all around him; slates and gutters were smashed, skylights exploded, shards of stone went wheeling into the sky. The wind whipped at him and the bellow of engines filled his ears. He saw the men from the village throw down their weapons and flee wildly from the onslaught.

Then the cannon stopped, and he heard a voice over the chaos.

'Are you comin' or what?'

He raised his head. Hovering just beyond the edge of the roof was a shuttle. He saw the masked and hooded face of Morben Kyne through the cockpit windglass. The side door was open, and the huge bearded figure of Colden Grudge stood there, his legs planted apart and an autocannon at his hip. Next to him, leaning out and reaching with one gloved hand, was the owner of the voice.

Samandra Bree.

The sight of her brought new strength to his limbs. He surged to his feet. The shuttle swayed alarmingly towards him, driven by a gust of wind; but Samandra's hand found his and they clasped. She yanked him up with a strength greater than her size would suggest. His feet found a step, and Colden grabbed him by the shoulder. He was pulled inside, where he tumbled to the floor in a heap, tangled with Samandra.

'Shift it, Kyne!' she yelled, and the shuttle pulled away. Samandra kept an arm tight around Crake's chest as they ascended. Grudge kept his autocannon trained on the villagers on the roof until the mansion had dwindled beneath them. Then he reached across and flung the door shut, sealing them in with the sound of the engines.

Crake climbed to his feet dazedly, still disorientated. He'd committed himself to death; it wasn't easy to pull back from that. He staggered to the side door, slapped one hand against it to steady himself, and stared out of the window. Beneath him, the Crake family manor was getting smaller. He could see smoke coming from his father's mansion now, as well as Condred's house. They hadn't even waited for their companions to get off the roof before they started burning.

'You okay?' Samandra asked, picking herself up. Grudge watched him steadily.

'They're burning my home,' Crake said, his voice hoarse. Then, because he knew it had to be true, he added:

'They killed my father.'

Samandra walked over to stand next him. She looked out, following his gaze. 'Rough,' she said at length.

He turned his head towards her. In amid the shock and the numbness, he felt something new, breaching the waters of his mind with a clear and inarguable certainty. He knew there was no time to waste, no time for *anyone* to waste, and that all things might be snatched away in a moment.

'I'm in love with you,' he told her then. 'I want you to know that.'

She rolled her eyes. 'Duh,' she said, and put an arm round his waist.

Twenty-One

A Master in Action – The Prisoner –
Deadly Opposition – Frey Makes a Plan

It was all Frey could do not to run headlong down the corridor. He could hear her through the earcuff, her voice getting louder as he got closer. He'd heard her shriek – spit and pus, an actual *shriek* from her lips – and it had almost broken him. But he hadn't entirely forgotten the danger he was in. His disguise wouldn't stand up to scrutiny, and running full pelt would alert everyone he passed.

What were those sons of bitches doing to her? He needed to find her, and find her *now*.

Two female Speakers were coming the other way. He checked his stride, walked by with a quick bow in their direction. They bowed back without a flicker of suspicion. As soon as they were gone he accelerated again.

He could feel her, he was sure of it. Whether by some trick of the earcuffs or his imagination, he had some sense of where she was. The other captain's voices had disappeared now: only Trinica's frightened protests were left, muffled into incoherence.

The Awakeners had brought all the frigate captains together in order to spring some kind of trap. What did they hope to gain? To take over their aircraft, annex them to the fleet so they could put loyal Awakener captains in charge? But what about their crews?

It didn't matter. All that mattered was the tone of Trinica's voice. Very rarely had he heard her scared, especially since she became a pirate. But he heard it now. Real, mortal terror.

If they've harmed a hair on her head I swear I'll murder every last one of them.

He turned a corner, and checked himself again. Standing before a door was a Sentinel, his rifle standing upright next to him in the manner of a formal guard. There was no one else in sight.

The Sentinel looked up at him, noting his interest. 'You'll have to wait, brother,' he said. 'Nobody goes in till they're done.'

Frey carried on walking towards him. 'That's fine, brother. There was one thing I wanted to ask you, though.' He drove his knee between the unsuspecting man's legs with all the force he could muster. The Sentinel doubled over, eyes bulging, a faint whistle coming from his nose like a kettle on the boil. Frey grabbed his hair, wrenched his head up and butted him in the face. The Sentinel crumpled to the floor, eyes blank and nose bloody.

He heard footsteps and spun around. His crew had followed him. They came hurrying up when they saw him.

Malvery looked down at the guard, then over at Jez. 'Now there's a master in action,' he told her. She stared at him as if he was from another planet.

'Guns,' Frey said tersely. They pulled weapons from beneath their cassocks. They all looked ridiculous, Malvery and Pinn particularly so: fat men in too-small cassocks with Ciphers painted on their foreheads. But their faces were grim, and they were ready to do what had to be done.

It was a good crew. When he needed them, they were there.

He pulled the door open and stepped inside. The room beyond was small, with a raised Cipher pattern covering one wall and a large window dominating all. There were a dozen Awakeners in here of various ranks, seated on chairs facing the window. Some turned round as Frey came in. He stormed over to them and dragged them from their chairs before they had the chance to voice their alarm. Malvery, Pinn and the others waded in, manhandling the Awakeners to the ground, knocking over side-tables as they did so and spilling wine jugs everywhere. Only Pelaru stayed back, observing the scene calmly.

In moments, they had the room under control, with the Awakeners herded into a corner and held there at gunpoint. Jez dragged in the Sentinel from outside, who was dazed and semi-conscious, and Pelaru shut the door behind them.

'Well, there goes our cover,' said Pinn. He pointed out his shotgun to the cowering Awakeners. 'Watch out for this,' he said. 'This thing's got a hair-trigger.'

Frey walked to the window. It was another observation room,

overlooking a chamber of similar dimensions to the one that housed the Azryx device. What he saw below made the blood drain from his face.

There were two dozen Awakeners there, including the Lord High Cryptographer and his retinue, and two Imperators. They stood at the edge of the chamber, outside a circle of metal masts that were attached by cables to a control console, worked by three men. More cables ran from generators and other large brass machines he didn't recognise.

He'd seen this kind of thing before, on a smaller scale. He'd seen it in the back of the *Ketty Jay*'s cargo hold. This was an industrial-sized sanctum. No doubt this was the source of the interference that was messing with the earcuffs.

In the centre of the sanctum was a great riveted sphere, supported by struts, a hollow chamber that had been split in half horizontally. Bubbles of thick glass were set into it, windows to the interior. The bottom hemisphere was secured to the ground; the upper hemisphere was several metres above it, slowly descending on the end of a hydraulic arm.

In between was Trinica.

They'd strapped her to a grid, lying on her back, her wrists and ankles secured. Her eyes were wide and black in her corpse-white face, staring upward as the upper hemisphere was lowered towards her. She wasn't struggling: she had a kind of paralysis of terror upon her, a rabbit gone limp in the jaws of a fox.

Frey watched, unable to act, as the upper half of the sphere met with the lower. There was a hiss, and locks clanked into place, sealing Trinica within. Through one of the portholes Frey could see Trinica's face, warped and smeared by the domed glass. She lay still, gazing into the middle distance.

He turned away and seized one of the hostages, pulling him out of the group. It was a black-robed Prognosticator, the highest-ranking Awakener there. He had a shaven head, a bristling beard, and a scrawny, unhealthy look to him that made Frey want to batter him for the sake of it.

'How do we get down there?' he demanded.

'You can't,' the Prognosticator said, cringing away from the pistol Frey shoved in his face. 'The entrance is on the floor below.'

'Guards?'

'Yes! Yes! This place is just for observation.'

'Observing *what*?'

'So the young ones can see the glory of the Allsoul made flesh. The faithful attuned to the great Code through science. So that the Allsoul can enter them and leave them transformed . . .'

'I'd can the theatrics if I were you, mate,' said Malvery, who'd seen the murderous look on Frey's face.

'What. Are they doing. To *her*?' Frey said through gritted teeth, finger hovering over the trigger.

The Prognosticator opened his mouth but then closed it again, scared to say the wrong thing.

'Last chance.'

The Prognosticator swallowed. 'They're turning her into an Imperator.'

Frey felt the bottom fall out of his world. His legs went weak, and he staggered. No. It couldn't be. It *couldn't*!

His head was swarming and his skin prickled. There was a sense of building power in the room. Jez began to whine, low in her throat. She backed away from the window with her teeth bared. From the chamber the throb of generators could be heard.

He felt trapped, caged, wild. An enormous rage filled him but there was nowhere to vent it. He had to do something, he had to *save* her! She needed him!

He seized the Prognosticator by the collar, jammed the gun against his forehead. The other hostages cried out in fright. 'Stop them!' he demanded.

'I can't!' the Prognosticator blurted.

'I'll kill you,' Frey said. 'Swear to shit I will.'

'It's already begun! If you interrupt it, it'll kill *her*!' Frey cocked the revolver, and the Prognosticator's eyes squeezed shut. 'I'm telling you the truth!' he wailed.

Frey swore in frustration and pistol-whipped the Prognosticator across the face. The man collapsed and Frey backed away, face red, breathing heavily. The faces of his crew seemed strange to him now, full of suspicion and plots. They were watching him, noting his loss of control, criticising him for his foolish pursuit of Trinica. And he saw wicked amusement in the eyes of the Awakeners, as if they relished his suffering, safe in the knowledge that their ultimate victory was secure.

Paranoia. Delusion. A daemon was coming.

And they were putting it into Trinica.

He couldn't contain his fury any longer. He ran to the window, aimed his pistol down at the Lord High Cryptographer, and pulled the trigger.

The window exploded outward. Frey fired until his pistol was empty, shooting into the scattering crowd. The Lord High Cryptographer was pulled into cover by the men surrounding him. One of the armoured honour guard went down; the crimson-robed Interpreter took a bullet through the head. When Frey's first pistol was done, he jammed it in his belt and pulled out a spare.

He looked over at the echo chamber that Trinica was sealed inside. Magnified in the window, ballooned and distorted, he saw her face turned towards him. One huge black eye stared out. She pinned him with that gaze. He didn't know what he saw there – Sorrow? Resignation? Love? Or the dead cold eye of a daemon? – but in that instant time seemed to stand still, and the unutterable horror of what was to come crushed him.

Then Malvery grabbed his arm and hauled him back into the room, just as a salvo of gunfire ripped through the spot where he'd been standing.

'Come on!' the doctor was yelling. 'You can't do anything! Let's go!'

And they hauled open the door, and they ran. A daemonic shriek followed them down the corridor, a sound that was half Trinica and half something else. To Frey, it sounded like the world ending.

Malvery shoved his way past a frightened Speaker, leading the way down the corridor, his lever-action shotgun in his hands. The others came behind: Jez, mad-eyed and on the verge of turning; Frey, shell-shocked, a shattered look on his face; Ashua, alert, at home with danger; Pelaru, enigmatic and untrustworthy, not a hair out of place; Pinn, uncommonly quiet, which worried him. Pinn only ever shut up when he was about to do something stupid.

Malvery had wanted to be part of the war. He'd wanted to weigh in on the Coalition side. But he needn't have worried. He should have known the Cap'n's talent for finding trouble would get them tangled up in it eventually.

Well, we're all in it now, like it or not.

A pair of Sentinels came running round a corner to investigate the commotion. But rifles were cumbersome at close range; they didn't get them up fast enough. Malvery gunned one down without breaking stride. Pelaru shot the other neatly between the eyes.

Malvery didn't feel a thing about their deaths. With what he'd just seen, he didn't care any more. Anyone who signed up to be on the Awakener team was fair game now. They were ruled by daemons. They put daemons in innocent people. And they had a plan to smash the Coalition that sounded very much like it might work.

Someone had to get to the Coalition and tell them. At any cost. He felt a determination and purpose such as he hadn't felt since he was a young man.

They found stairs leading down, and took them. The alarm was spreading through the building now. Shouts and running feet. They had surprise on their side, but it wouldn't last for long. They had to get out, and fast.

A Sentinel appeared at the bottom of the stairs and loosed off a shot. It missed Malvery and headed squarely for Jez, but she flickered and it seemed to pass through her as if she wasn't there. Malvery opened up the Sentinel's chest with his shotgun, thumped past the falling body and out into the ground floor corridor.

They found more resistance there. A group of Speakers, who fired on them with rifles. They were forced to retreat to cover, and ended up pinned down in doorways and behind corners, trading shots while unarmed Speakers ran for their lives.

Ashua hunkered down next to him, squeezed off a few shots. 'This isn't exactly the best place to make a stand,' she muttered.

She was right. They were stuck at a three-way junction at the bottom of the stairs. Too many directions for the enemy to come from. They needed Bess to get them out of this, but she was back on the *Ketty Jay*.

Ashua looked over at Frey, who was crouching in a doorway across the corridor with Pinn. He was shooting mechanically, an empty look on his face. 'Cap'n's in a bad way,' she said.

'We're all gonna be in a bad way if someone doesn't do something quick,' said Malvery.

Fear crashed over them like a wave, dragging him under. He could barely squeeze the trigger any more; he could hardly support his own weight. Walking up the corridor were two masked men dressed in black. They were not tall, but they loomed in his mind, and dread flowed from them.

The Sentinels stopped firing to make way. They were not afflicted: they were the faithful. But Malvery, Ashua and the rest of the crew were driven into cringing heaps by their unreasoning fear of the Imperators.

He wanted to run, but he couldn't make it. He wanted to be sick, but nothing would come. He saw Ashua's face, wide open with terror, and the Cap'n pressing himself against the door jamb as if he could crush himself into the wall and disappear. He staggered backwards, turned as if to flee, and came nose to nose with Jez.

Or at least, what *used* to be Jez.

He cried out. He couldn't help it. She was right in front of him, fully Mane in aspect, a primal, terrifying savagery on her face and her sharp teeth skinned back like a snarling dog. She radiated an other-worldly fear, less intense than the Imperators did but awful all the same. Caught between one horror and another, Malvery spun away, seeking a way out, and found Pelaru.

Or at least, what *used* to be Pelaru.

The handsome, sculpted face, the olive skin and dark eyes were still as they'd always been. But now it was no more than a covering, a skin tent stretched over a something unspeakably threatening, an appalling blasphemy against the world of the sane and the real. He was hunched, eyes mad, veins standing out at the base of his neck.

'Is anyone on this crew *not* half Mane?!?' Malvery screamed.

They leaped past him in a blur, out into the corridor. Some of the Sentinels were quick enough to fire off a shot, but Jez seemed to be in three places at once and Pelaru flowed like a snake. They leaped on the Imperators, bore them to the ground, and tore at them like animals. Malvery saw Pelaru rip a black-clad arm from its socket; Jez punched at the other Imperator's chest until the ribs broke and her fist burst out of the back.

At once the fear lifted from them. Frey reacted first, and came lunging out of hiding, firing his pistol with reckless disregard for his own safety. Malvery saw a fury in him that had nothing to do with the Sentinels and everything to do with Trinica. Malvery himself was not so quick. He checked on Ashua, helped her back to her feet, and by the time he was ready the Sentinels were either fleeing or dead. Jez and Pelaru chased them, screeching.

Pinn wandered out into the corridor, looking dazed. Ashua followed, and Malvery went with her, until the four of them were standing in the midst of the battleground. The Imperators had been taken apart like dolls. There was blood everywhere, mostly from unfortunate Sentinels who'd suffered the same fate. Distantly, they heard screaming and gunshots.

'Are we going?' Malvery prompted, and that seemed to shake them all out of it. They ran off in Jez and Pelaru's wake, because they had no other direction to go.

The main doors to the building were not far down the corridor. The half-Manes had cleared the way with gory efficiency. Malvery had seen horrific gunshot wounds and injuries that would make a lesser man faint, soldiers pleading and gaping as they tried to gather their relentlessly slithering intestines back into their bodies. But there was something in the primal savagery of the Manes that frightened him more than the mechanised death which men visited on one another. The Manes were berserkers, all rage and appetite; they strewed sundered corpses as they passed.

The doors were already ajar, having been slid open to the width of a few feet. Evidently some people had already fled the building. Malvery and Pinn looked out. Someone shouted 'That's them!' and they pulled themselves back in as bullets smacked into the door, pinging off the metal. There were a couple of Sentinels out there, covering the exit. There would be a lot more arriving shortly.

Frey came up to them, and stood there panting. Malvery had a quick go with his shotgun and then ducked away to avoid the return fire.

'Cap'n,' he said. Frey didn't appear to hear him. '*Cap'n!*' he barked.

Frey jerked and looked at him. Malvery couldn't imagine what was going on in his head right now. He'd just seen the woman he loved condemned to become a monster. Malvery wasn't Trinica's biggest fan by a long chalk, but he knew how Frey felt about her.

It didn't matter. They needed a leader now. Malvery wasn't that, and Silo was elsewhere. Frey needed to get himself straight.

'We need a plan,' Malvery said firmly.

Frey nodded. Malvery and Pinn popped out and started blasting while Frey peered between the doors. They retreated at the same time, and let the Sentinels take their turn at shooting.

'Ashua!' Frey called. Ashua was looking down the corridor, in the direction that Jez and Pelaru had gone. She scampered over.

'They're on their way back,' she reported. 'Jez is out; looks like she overexerted herself again. Pelaru's carrying her.' She looked from Frey to Malvery and back again. 'Did you lot know he was a half-Mane and just didn't tell me?'

Malvery shook his head. 'Although we probably should've guessed, thinking about it.'

'Ashua. Come here,' said Frey. He pointed through the gap in the doors, careful to stay out of the line of fire. 'Think you can drive one of those?'

Malvery looked. There were two Overlanders parked out there, off to one side. Bulky, six-wheeled all-terrain vehicles: it was the convoy Trinica and the other captains had arrived in.

Ashua shrugged. 'There's not much on four wheels I haven't stolen at some time or another. Can't see that an extra two will give me much of a problem.'

'Then that's our plan,' said Frey. 'Ready to run for it?'

'Shit, why not?' said Ashua. 'Gotta die sometime.'

Pelaru came sprinting up the corridor, Jez slung over his back like a sack. With him came a wave of fear, the instinctive repulsion that Manes inspired in humans. It was the impetus they needed. Driven from behind, they went forward. They tore open the doors and let loose with their guns.

Before them was the camp, laid out muddily beneath the harsh white floods in the sweaty, buzzing night. Men were running towards them from nearby tents and buildings, two dozen or more. A few Sentinels squatted down behind a row of crates, hiding from the volley of bullets. Frey picked off a man who unwisely tried to get a pot-shot in.

The distance between the building and the vehicles wasn't far, five seconds at a run, but they were long seconds. The Sentinels were mostly taken by surprise, but some return fire came their way, and out in the open they were exposed. Perhaps it was the presence of Pelaru that saved them. He drew the horrified eyes of everyone around, and bought the crew precious seconds to reach the shelter of the vehicles.

Frey pulled open the driver's door of the nearest Overlander. Ashua slid in while the others fired round the side. Bullets came spanging off the metal around them, forcing them to duck. Malvery hauled the passenger door aside and they piled into the dark interior of the vehicle, where metal benches sat against the walls. Last came Jez, slung inside by Pelaru before he launched off and away, leaping towards the enemy.

'Is he coming?' Malvery asked, as he bundled Jez's unconscious form away from the doorway.

'Who cares?' said Frey. He slammed the door shut. Bullets smacked against the Overlander. 'Go! Go! Go!' he shouted, and the engine bellowed as it came to life.

'Hang on to anything!' Ashua called. The vehicle lurched forward and they were away.

Twenty-Two

Dangerous Driving – The Fear –
A New Passenger – Outside Intervention

Ashua hunched over the steering wheel, foot pressed hard on the accelerator, staring out of the reinforced windglass slit at the chaos outside. Sentinels fired helplessly at the Overlander. Bullets bounced off thick armour plate. The vehicle surged and bounced, six huge wheels spinning on the muddy ground as they roared away into the heart of the camp.

Awakeners ran this way and that, fleeing out of her path. She took the dirt road that led away from the building. The Overlander skidded and slipped until it found traction: it wasn't meant to be driven at speed over terrain like this. They drifted right, swung back too hard to the left. The edge of the vehicle clipped a supply tent and brought the whole thing down in a tangle of sticks and tarp.

A grin spread across her tattooed face. Here she was, dressed in a Sentinel's grey cassock, running rampant through the middle of an Awakener base. Damn, this was fun. She was usually so careful, a survivor, weighing risk and reward and looking out for herself before anyone else. She hadn't done anything this reckless or stupid in a long while.

She looked back over her shoulder at the crew, absurd in their cassocks, some of them with Ciphers painted on their foreheads. Pinn and Frey were getting into their bench seats, grabbing on to whatever they could. Malvery was crouched over Jez, keeping himself steady with one hand and trying to secure the unconscious half-Mane with the other. It looked like the aftermath of one of Maddeus' fancy dress parties, gone horribly wrong. Then again, they'd always gone horribly wrong.

'Everyone alright back there?'

'Just drive!' Frey snapped at her. He was right on the edge. They all were.

She turned her attention back to the road, just as an Imperator stepped out into it.

Her first instinct was to swerve. Her second was to plough the bastard into the earth. She went with that.

But the Imperator stood there in her path, hooded and cloaked and clad in black, face hidden behind a smooth black mask. And he looked at her through the windglass.

She knew the fear by now, and expected it. It didn't help at all. If she could have held out for a few seconds, she could have run him down. But even a few seconds was beyond her. She threw the steering wheel to full lock, and the Overlander skidded wildly, flinging Malvery and Jez against the benches. Mud sprayed up against the viewing slit. Her leg was locked down on the accelerator, glued there by terror. She felt the vehicle's centre of gravity shifting, felt it trying to tip. But those huge wheels kept it upright, and they bit into the ground again and sent the Overlander arrowing off at ninety degrees, into another supply tent.

Boxes smashed against the Overlander's nose. Tarp piled against the windglass and blinded Ashua. The vehicle bucked and jerked as it bounced wildly over unseen obstacles. Any moment they'd hit something solid, something hard enough to send her flying into the dashboard, cave her chest in against the steering wheel. She fought to take her foot from the accelerator but the panic was just too much. She had to get away from the fear, get away, get *away*!

And then it was gone. Snapped off, like a light. Out of range? She didn't know.

The tarp pulled away from the windglass, tugged under the wheels and off. Ahead, the side of a building loomed, a wall of grey. She swung the wheel, hit the brakes. Malvery and Jez went flying again. Frey was thrown from his seat. She felt herself slide across her seat as the Overlander fishtailed, back wheels swinging round to hit the wall broadside. She switched her foot from brake to accelerator, stamping down hard. The Overlander's back wheels spun, found a grip, and shoved them forward. Their wide skid took them past the building into clear ground beyond, and they came out of it steady, racing though a floodlit landscape of grim buildings and tents stewing in the swampy night.

Pinn whooped behind her. She shook her head and blew out a breath.

Unable to see the main gate, she cut back toward the road. It led to a hub in the centre of the camp where she could get her bearings. There was pandemonium all around her. Occasional bullets came their way, but she ignored them. Small arms wouldn't do them any harm. She had to get out of the camp before news of the escape reached the gate. If the guards shut it, they'd be trapped. Outrunning the messengers was her priority.

Something moved at the edge of the viewing slit, a quick blur that drew her eye. She caught a glimpse of a cassocked figure racing towards her. Suddenly it leaped through the air. There was an impact on the roof of the Overlander, making her duck. Pelaru. Rot and damn, it was the half-Mane. He'd cut across the camp and caught up with them. Now he was clinging to them, riding on top.

Well, let him, she thought. She had other things to worry about.

She saw the hub ahead, a wide dirt patch surrounded by buildings both permanent and temporary. Roads rayed out in all directions towards the walls and the doleful mangroves beyond. Awakeners scattered as she approached. She spotted an Overlander coming in from another direction, racing to cut her off.

No, you don't, you son of a bitch, she thought, and pressed down on the accelerator.

The two vehicles reached the hub at the same time, swung together, and met wheel-to-wheel with a heavy crash that almost jarred Ashua out of her seat. Malvery swore loudly behind her.

'Will you keep this bloody thing still for two seconds?' he yelled, hauling Jez up onto the bench.

'Doing my best, Doc!' Ashua called back, then swung the wheel and sideswiped the other Overlander, sending Malvery tumbling. Her opponent rebounded away from her, taking out a floodlight. A pair of Awakeners dived out of the way as it roared by, sending up fins of mud as it passed.

'Try harder!' Malvery called up from the back, exasperated.

Ashua kept an eye on her opponent. Knocking him away gave her the room she needed to aim them towards the road that would lead them out. She could see the gate some way away, a gap in the wall ahead of them. How long would it take the guards to notice the armoured vehicle roaring towards them, she wondered. Would their first instinct be to close the gate, or to leave it open? Would they think they were preventing an escape, or slowing an urgent errand, risking the wrath of their superiors?

The other Overlander had regained control and was coming back in again. It couldn't outpace her, but it seemed determined to knock her off the road. She braced herself as she saw it looming to her right. The impact rocked them, but she wrestled with the wheel and kept them on course.

The Overlanders left the hub and the road narrowed around them, lined on either side with buildings and tents and floodlight poles. There wasn't much room any more: the two racing vehicles took up the whole road.

Ashua slammed into her opponent, but she didn't have the space to deliver more than a nudge. The engine bellowed in her ears. Ahead of them, Awakeners were getting out of the way as best they could. The gate was still open.

She heard a bumping up above. Pelaru. Next time she looked, the other Overlander had acquired a new passenger. The Thacian was on top of the other vehicle, clinging on grimly, his hair blown back against his skull. All his elegance and poise was gone now: he was a primal thing, animal, savage. He crawled along the back of the Overlander with inhuman dexterity, fighting through the wind towards the cockpit.

Fascinated by the sight, Ashua was almost caught out when the other Overlander swung sharply towards her again. She met the swipe with one of her own, but hers was weaker and she was knocked away. She swung towards the edge of the road and bounced off the side of a building with a crash. Her head whipped to the side as she was flung; she almost lost the wheel. Driving more by instinct than conscious thought, she fought the Overlander's skid and somehow came out of it still on the road, and still neck-and-neck with her opponent.

Dazed but awash with adrenaline, she struggled to focus. She was close enough to the gate to see the guards running about. She looked across and saw that Pelaru had reached the front of the Overlander. The other driver seemed unaware that he was there. They realised pretty quickly when Pelaru dropped down onto the nose of the Overlander and glared in at them through the windglass.

The driver panicked and jerked the wheel. The Overlander swung wildly away from Ashua, off the side of the road, carving a shallow arc through a stack of crates and a small mess tent. She saw the vehicle coming back towards her hard as the driver over-corrected, Pelaru still hanging on to the front. She hit the brakes and turned into it.

The Overlander crossed the road in front of her, and she slammed into its rear corner, right on the sweet spot to force a fishtail. It swung right around, its back end skidding wildly, and smashed hard into the side of a building, facing the other way. Ashua raced past it. An instant later she heard a thump on the roof of the Overlander, and looked up.

Pelaru. She couldn't imagine the agility it must have taken to leap off one wildly spinning vehicle and land on the roof of another that was moving at speed. She shook her head. Manes. What a world.

They were coming up on the gate now. The gate guards were swarming. She'd expected some resistance, but there was something odd about their behaviour. Their response to her approach was chaotic rather than coordinated. It took her a moment to realise they were shooting outwards, down the road, beyond the gate. And then she twigged.

Silo. Silo was shooting at them from the cover of the swamp.

She looked back at Frey and realised he was still wearing his earcuff. Silo also had one. Despite the interference from the dae-monic machine, the Murthian must have picked up enough scraps of what was going on, and decided to weigh in.

That's it. Keep them busy. A few seconds is all we need.

She saw one guard running for the gatehouse on the inside of the wall, where she presumed the gate controls to be. He went down, clutching his leg, chopped down by a shotgun shell. A second man ran past him: this one made it inside.

Ashua put her foot to the floor. The way was clear now. It was a straight shot to the gates. The engine roared, drowning out all sound beyond the armoured shell of the Overlander.

She saw cogs begin to turn on the inner wall. Pulleys strained. The gates started to roll shut.

'Brace yourselves!' she shouted. She turned to glare at Malvery over her shoulder. 'I really bloody mean it this time!'

Malvery had Jez as secure as he could make her by now. The others hung on to whatever they could with as much strength as they were able. Ashua spared a thought for Pelaru, up on the roof, but she couldn't worry about him now. Besides, if they hit that gate at full speed, she wouldn't need to worry about anything ever again.

Come on, damn it! she urged the vehicle, willing it onward.

Bullets pinged off the Overlander's armour as some of the guards turned their attention to her. One hit the windglass, causing a spiderweb crack, making her flinch. The gap between the doors of the gate was narrowing by the second, closing in on her, and no matter how hard she pushed the Overlander it seemed like it couldn't possibly be enough. She angled them towards the centre of the gap, heedless of anything else, concentrating only on that. They rushed towards it, the gates clanking in on either side, thick walls of steel like slow jaws.

Here it comes! she thought with a sickening terror.

And the Overlander roared through the gap, its tail striking sparks from the gate as it passed. Ashua hit the brakes, half to control the skid and half because they couldn't leave Silo here. The gates crashed shut a few metres from their tail.

'Whoo-hoo!' Pinn yelled from the back, and slapped his thigh.

Frey was up in an instant, pulling open the side door, calling out to his first mate. Ashua slumped back in her seat, heart thumping in her chest. Malvery blew out his moustaches in relief.

'That was some driving,' he said, shaking his head. 'That was some bloody driving.'

Bullets came down on their roof from the guards up on the wall. Were they shooting at Pelaru? Was he still up there? She didn't care; they couldn't get to her. There was a commotion behind and Silo bundled in. Frey slammed the door behind him.

'Reckon we might have outstayed our welcome, fellers,' she said over her shoulder. 'What say we get out of here?'

She put her foot down and the Overlander tore away down the road, back towards the *Ketty Jay*.

Twenty-Three

A Little Discipline – The Returners – A Man Left Behind –
Point Blank – Evade, Evade, Evade

Harkins sat on the stairs of the *Ketty Jay*'s cargo hold, and watched Bess searching for her master. She'd taken to doing this whenever she was left unoccupied. She'd peer into corners, search behind crates and pipes. She'd adventure into the dark recesses behind the sanctum and come back again empty-handed. If she could have got into the rest of the craft, she'd have gone searching there, too. Mercifully, her size prevented her.

Harkins wondered what she thought. Did she believe Crake was still on board, on the upper decks, ignoring her? Did she think anything at all? What a strange creature she was. Strange and mis-understood and treated rather badly, in his opinion. In that, they were the same.

'You're sad about Crake, aren't you?' he said. He raised one of the ear flaps of his pilot's cap and scratched the side of his head to relieve an itch. 'I'm sad, too, a bit. I mean, he didn't take the piss quite as much as the others. And he was, well . . . he's a gentle sort. That's got to count for something, right?'

Bess briefly stopped her search, aware that he was speaking. She stared at him without any sign that she'd comprehended. Harkins sighed. He was beginning to wish he hadn't volunteered to stay behind. They'd been gone an awfully long time, and Bess wasn't much good as company. He doubted they missed him, though. He doubted they'd even noticed he wasn't there.

'You and me, Bess, we don't get much respect, do we?' he said. 'I mean, who'd respect us, right? I'm a big chickenshit and you're a walking pile of pots and pans with a mental condition.'

Bess made a quizzical bubbling sound.

'Exactly,' said Harkins.

Bess went back to her search. Harkins decided he couldn't bear watching her any more. He needed to do something to get himself out of this maudlin mood. Moping around was no fun, and Bess was bringing him down.

'Come on, Bess!' he said, getting to his feet. 'Enough of all that. We've got an important job to do here, you know!'

Bess watched him curiously, her eyes distant glimmers in the dark behind her face-grille.

'Well, the Cap'n told us to guard the *Ketty Jay*, right?' he said. 'We're making a pretty poor fist of it, though. What *you* need,' – he bonked her with his knuckles – 'is a little discipline. Like this! March! March! March!'

He went marching off across the hold, arms straight, skinny legs jerking. It felt unfamiliar and a little ridiculous at first, but it wasn't long before his body remembered. Hundreds of hours on the parade ground as a young man had left an imprint on his muscles, and he found himself slipping easily back into the rhythm.

'About . . . *face!*' he cried, and went marching back the other way.

Usually he'd have been too wary of mockery to dare anything like this, even knowing that the rest of the crew were elsewhere. Fear of being caught, detected by some secret method he hadn't yet thought of, would have kept him from it. But now he stormed up and down, throwing his limbs about, and it felt rather exhilarating. It felt good.

Bess watched him with interest as he came back towards her. 'What are you doing standing there, soldier?' he cried. 'Get in step! On the double!' He turned and marched off in another direction. Bess trailed uncertainly along behind him.

'Not like that!' said Harkins. He turned and started marching on the spot in front of Bess. 'Swing those arms!' he said. 'Legs straight!' He was enjoying himself now.

Bess clapped her hands and started stomping her feet, rocking left and right.

'Not good enough, soldier! Arms! Like me!' He swung his arms harder for emphasis. Bess copied him. 'Now your legs!'

This was harder for Bess, whose legs were short and stumpy in comparison to her body. Still, she did what she could. Her attempts at staying in time were hopeless, but soon she was wobbling and flailing about in a comical approximation of a military march.

'Good!' said Harkins. He was sweating and a big grin was plastered on his face. 'Now follow me! Quiiiiick . . . *march!*'

He spun on his heel and went off across the hold again. Bess clattered and crashed along behind him, throwing her outsize arms all over the place, kicking the air. 'That's the way!' he cried. 'That's the way!'

They paraded up and down the hold, and Harkins felt wonderful. He was so light he could almost laugh out loud. Damn, how long had it been since he was silly like this? How long since he'd done anything with such abandon? He was a red-faced, beaming fool leading a grotesque, clumsy golem around an empty cargo hold and for once, just for once, he didn't care. He wished this moment could go on for ever.

But it didn't, and when it ended, it ended in the roar of an engine and the shriek of brakes.

He knew right away that the sound meant trouble. All that good feeling drained out of him in an instant. He stopped, and Bess bumped into the back of him, sending him stumbling forward. By the time he'd regained his balance, he was awkward old Harkins again, fumbling and embarrassed.

He hurried over to the lever to open the *Ketty Jay*'s ramp. If something was going on outside, it was best to find out what. It occurred to him belatedly that this wasn't necessarily the safest or most sensible course of action to take, but by then he'd pulled the lever and the ramp was opening. He watched it descend, wondering at himself. An impartial observer might interpret what he'd just done as something other than rank cowardice. He must be getting sick or something.

He went down the ramp, and Bess followed. It was humid, warm and dark outside; the only light came from the moon and the head-lights of a six-wheeled armoured Overlander which had just pulled up next to the *Ketty Jay*. The crew came piling out. All of them were wearing Awakener cassocks, and some had Ciphers painted on their foreheads. He would have laughed, but the gravity of the situation was etched on their faces.

He saw Pelaru snatch the unconscious Jez from Malvery's hands and come racing up the ramp. The Thacian bounded past without so much as looking at him. Harkins cringed away; there was something wrong about the way he moved, the way he looked.

'Wait, is Pelaru coming with us?' Malvery asked the Cap'n as they hurried towards the *Ketty Jay*. 'You know that two half-Manes make a whole one, right?'

Frey didn't seem to be in the mood for humour. 'We'll deal with him later. Harkins! Get to the Firecrow! We're leaving! Malvery, Ashua, go drag out that bloody lad and toss him off my aircraft. We've got enough dead weight. Bess, get inside!'

Bess paid no attention, waiting eagerly on the ramp to see if Crake was going to appear. Malvery and Ashua hurried past her. Silo took position at the bottom of the ramp, scanning their surroundings, shotgun ready.

There were the sound of engines in the distance. Even at this hour, there were a few other people in the clearing where the *Ketty Jay* sat. They were mostly crewmen from the battered freighters nearby, smoking roll-ups or drinking away the night. The dramatic arrival of the *Ketty Jay*'s crew had stirred their interest, and some were walking over. Some of them looked like they had guns.

'Cap'n!' said Pinn. He grabbed Frey's arm as Frey headed for the ramp.

'What?' Frey snapped irritably.

Pinn stood there a moment, thinking. No doubt trying to assemble his moronic thoughts into some kind of coherent grunts, Harkins thought uncharitably.

Frey ran out of patience. 'There's no time! We need to get out of here!' he said.

'But that's just it,' Pinn blurted. 'I'm not coming!'

Frey stared at him. Harkins stared at him. Silo kept his eye on the people from the other freighters. One of them was calling out. 'Hey! What's the trouble over there?'

'Better move it, Cap'n,' he rumbled.

'Pinn, get in the Skylance!' Frey cried. 'You can have whatever bloody crisis you're having after we're airborne.'

But Pinn shook his head, stubborn as a mule. 'It's not right, Cap'n. What we're doing.' He pulled out a piece of crumpled paper and held it up. There were several phrases scrawled on it, all but one crossed out. 'See?' he said. 'The prophecy! Look! *Journey*: that's Korrene.

Death: that's Pelaru's mate or whatever. *Dark haired stranger*: Pelaru. *Find something important*: well, we just did! *Tragedy will fall on someone dear . . .*' He looked at Frey meaningfully, and drew his finger across the last phrase, as if crossing it out.

Frey was about to explode. 'What in the name of gibbering shit are you talking about, arse-wit?'

'The Allsoul is *real*, Cap'n,' said Pinn, his piggy eyes wide. 'We're fighting on the wrong side.'

'What are you lot *doing* out here?' Ashua cried as she came hustling out with Malvery, pulling Abley between them. The Awakener boy had his hands tied behind his back, gagged, limping and bewildered. Ashua put her boot in his arse and sent him sprawling on the turf. 'Bess! Inside!' she said sternly.

Bess trudged off up the ramp, having given up on the possibility of her master returning. Ashua and Malvery followed her inside.

'Oi! Hey! What's up over there?' called one of the approaching men, in a tone that made a friendly enquiry sound like a threat. Abley tried to yell something through his gag.

'Do what you like, Pinn,' Frey snapped, angrily dismissive. 'Do whatever you like.' He rounded on Harkins. 'What did I say, Harkins? Get to your damn aircraft!'

Harkins shuddered at the force of his voice, and fled towards the safety of the Firecrow's cockpit. A pair of Overlanders raced into the clearing, skidded to a halt and began disgorging armed men. As if that was the signal, the suspicious freighter crew opened up, and the sweltering night was suddenly alive with the snap and whine of gunfire.

Frey and Silo loosed off a few shots and then ran up the ramp, which Ashua was closing. Pinn danced on the spot for a moment, obviously tempted to follow now that he saw his predicament. But he procrastinated too long, and the ramp raised out of his reach, and in the end he fled off towards the trees at the edge of the clearing.

Harkins sprinted for the Firecrow and threw himself up the ladder that led to the cockpit. All his previous joy had faded: he was trapped in a nightmare of fear again. Halfway up, he felt his leg seized, and he was pulled away from the ladder and crashed heavily to the muddy ground. Spluttering, he tried to get up, but a dark figure put a boot in his chest and shoved him back down.

'You ain't goin' nowhere,' snarled a rough voice. 'Let's see what you been up to, huh?'

He struggled wildly, but the man was standing on him and he was pinned. He could hear the sound of the *Ketty Jay*'s engines powering up; he saw more men rushing in, and Speakers with guns in the lights of the newly arrived Overlanders. Guns cracked as they shot uselessly at the *Ketty Jay*.

They've caught me! he thought, his mind ablaze with panic. *They've caught me and they're going to kill me and they're going to make me pay for whatever the others did and I wasn't even there!*

The only thing in his mind was to get away. No matter what the consequences, no matter what the cost. His terror at being left behind to face the music was worse than his terror of anything else.

'Quit strugglin'!' said the man holding him down. Harkins couldn't even see his face: he was an elemental enemy, an opposing force without character or identity. The man took his boot from Harkins' chest and leaned down to secure him more thoroughly with his arms. Harkins writhed to one side, pulled his pistol from his belt and jammed it under his attacker's ribs.

The man froze, eyes wide in horror. Harkins was no less horrified at where he found himself. He had an instant in which to act, and only that.

He pulled the trigger.

He saw the man's face in the flash of the shot. A folded, weathered face, underlit by the blast. It was there for a fraction of a second and then gone, but it stayed in his mind, burned there like the afterimage of the sun.

He slumped towards Harkins, an avalanche of inert meat. Harkins shoved him aside as he fell, and scrambled out from under him. He heard shouts nearby, but he couldn't make out the words. The world had closed in around him. Everything had narrowed: he saw as if through a tunnel.

He blundered back to the ladder, his route to safety. The Fire-crow's cockpit had always been his sanctuary, the place where he was the master, where there was no one to mock him or make him feel small. He climbed to it, and opened the windglass canopy, and pulled it shut over him.

Dimly, he was aware of the *Ketty Jay* rising nearby. The Skylance sat silent and forgotten beyond it. Moving on automatic, he hit switches, pulled levers, strapped himself in. The acrid smell of aerium wafted through the cockpit as the tanks filled. The engine clanked and hummed as it ignited. Bullets pinged off the hull, but the sounds were dulled and he had difficulty connecting them with danger.

That man's face. He could still see it. The look in his eyes as his life blew out like a candle.

A bullet hit the windglass in front of his face, sending a long crack along it, making him jump. It shocked him back to sense. He looked about himself, and saw men swarming all around, rushing towards the Firecrow with guns firing. They couldn't harm the *Ketty Jay*, but a shot in the right place *could* damage the Firecrow.

He lit the thrusters while he was barely off the ground; he needed to present a moving target. The Firecrow moved sluggishly, not yet light enough for effortless acceleration, but it shifted enough to spoil the aim of the men shooting at him. Harkins hunkered down over the flight stick, banking and climbing slowly as the aerium tanks flooded and the craft lost weight. Bullets pinged off the underside now, and some punched through. But the Firecrow gained altitude fast, and the thrusters pushed harder as they warmed. Harkins pulled out of the clearing in a long ascending curve, circling round the *Ketty Jay*, which was rising vertically. He saw her thrusters light up, shoving her away over the trees, and he followed her.

The gunfire fell away behind them. Harkins didn't feel relief. He didn't feel anything.

That man's face . . .

The explosion caught him completely by surprise. The Firecrow was slammed sideways, swiped by a wave of concussion that sent him into a hard bank, engines screaming. The cockpit shook like it was going to come apart. He'd barely managed to react to the first blast when there was a second, lighting up the sky ahead of him, rattling the windglass. The crack doubled in size, reaching out like a lightning fork.

Anti-aircraft guns.

Blood thumped at his temples. He hit the throttle and blasted forward through the turbulent air. The engines whined, came close to stalling, then kicked in with a blaze. A barrage of detonations pounded him; the noise battered at his mind. Caught in the flashes, he saw the *Ketty Jay* climbing fast, flying without lights, reaching for the safety of the darkness high above.

Evade. Evade. Evade.

He swung the Firecrow to starboard, climbing as he did so. Evasion patterns came naturally to him. He'd always been hard to hit, slippery in the sky. Shells swatted at his aircraft. The Firecrow shuddered and jerked. Harkins barrel-rolled and banked, g-forces wrenching him around in his seat.

Still the explosions came, near at hand and then far away, immense firecrackers ripping across the night. Harkins flew between them, his hangdog face set, eyes sharp and fixed. He couldn't see the shells coming, so he couldn't avoid them if they landed on target. All he could do was keep dodging about, and make sure they didn't. His body knew what to do.

Evade. Evade. Evade.

But this wasn't the frantic panic he was used to feeling. This wasn't hysterical fear. This was cold, sharp-edged, efficient. Death was all around him. He couldn't control it. He didn't recoil from it. He just had to negotiate it.

And then, all at once, he was through. The explosions fell away, scattering, random blooms of flame in the distance. They were too high up now, too hard to see, the light of their thrusters pinpricks of blue against the stars. The anti-aircraft gunners had lost their range.

The *Ketty Jay* was there too. He could just about make it out, not far off, beneath him and to port. So they'd escaped too.

He dropped back so as to see the *Ketty Jay*'s thrusters. They'd be the beacons he'd follow. They kept climbing until they were high above the earth, and then Frey tacked northeast and they headed back towards the centre of Vardia, out of the Barabac Delta.

Harkins was calm, so very calm as he floated in the dark, cradled by his cockpit amid the warm roar of the Firecrow's thrusters. Something had changed inside him, in the crucible of the anti-aircraft barrage. He felt it. Perhaps it had been coming for a long time. Perhaps it had begun when he tried to ram a Mane dreadnought in the skies above Sakkan; perhaps when he'd beat Gidley Sleen in a pointless and near-suicidal race in the Rushes, just because he was damned if he'd lose. Or maybe it had begun even further back than that.

Once, he'd been a warrior, until the pressures of war had cracked him. He'd flown with the greatest Navy in the world and he'd fought in battles of such savagery that even the history books shunned them. Death had been at his shoulder every time he flew into combat. But one day, Harkins had turned around and seen him, caught a glimpse of what waited, and his frayed nerves had snapped.

Since then, he'd brushed past death several times. Always unwillingly, sometimes accidentally, but on the *Ketty Jay*'s crew he'd been hard pressed to avoid it.

None of it was like today, though. Today he looked into a man's eyes as he died. A man that Harkins had killed, at point-blank range. Today he looked death in the face again. Square in the face. He'd seen it there as he pulled the trigger.

And it wasn't much. Wasn't much at all.

Harkins stared fixedly into the middle distance, and thought about that.

Twenty-Four

Doubt – Frey Makes a Move – Negotiations –
Slag Finds a Thing – Half-Manes

Ashua stuffed her hands into her pockets and walked up the slope to join Malvery. He was sitting on a black crag, bundled up in a voluminous coat. Behind her, the *Ketty Jay* and Harkins' Firecrow rested silently among stony hills. They'd left the sun behind in the south, and flown back into winter. An icy wind blew around them, whistling through the rocks.

She climbed up alongside Malvery and sat. He passed her a flask of coffee. She took a swig. It was fifty per cent sugar, and forty per cent alcohol.

'Cap'n could've picked a better spot,' he grumbled.

She had to agree. Before them the hills petered out into bleak moorland, scarred with dry stone walls and clusters of skeletal trees. The sky was overcast and grey. A few desultory sheep roamed the pastures, and here and there a grim cottage sent up a twist of smoke. There was a village in the far distance with a tiny landing pad.

'In his defence, he is a bit of a mess,' she said after a time.

'That ain't news,' said Malvery. He sat back and rolled his shoulders. 'Still glad you signed on?'

'Don't remember signing anything.'

'You know what I mean.'

She looked into the distance. 'It's better than where I was,' she said.

Malvery gave her a pat on the leg. She shuffled up closer to him and laid her head on his shoulder. He encircled her with his arm. They sat there for a long time like that, gazing out over the land.

She'd never known this comfort, never known male warmth without the expectation of something more. Maddeus, the closest thing she'd ever had to a father, hadn't been a very tactile man. Affection embarrassed him. She'd been held by lovers, of course, but that

234

wasn't the same. Malvery reassured her, in a way she hadn't known she needed. He was trusty and weighty and solid.

'Is this crew gonna be alright?' she asked. 'Crake gone, and now Pinn. Are you sticking around?'

'Reckon so,' he said. 'Depends on the Cap'n, though. Depends what he wants to do with what we found out.'

'You want to tell the Coalition.'

'Course I do.'

'You reckon they'll believe you?'

He let her go and looked at her in surprise, as if that was the first time he'd thought of that.

'They think we're traitors,' she said. 'We haven't any proof. If you were them, what would you do? Launch an assault on the Barabac Delta on the word of a few random pirates? The Awakeners are dug in. Casualties would be huge.' She pulled her coat tighter around her. 'More likely they'd just hang us.'

The wind blew around them, mournful and ghostly. Malvery coughed. 'What they do with the information ain't my business. They gotta know. That's all.'

She sighed. Her warning hadn't penetrated. Malvery had faith in the system, that justice would be done and the truth would out. One way or another he was going to do the right thing. Even if it did no good. Even if it got him dead.

Malvery swigged his coffee. 'This waiting ain't solving anything,' he said. 'We need a plan.'

'Give him a bit of time, huh? He just saw the woman he loves suffer a fate worse than death. Don't tell me that wouldn't knock you on your arse for a while.'

'Bigger things than that bloody woman in the world,' he said, but by his tone she could tell he was chastened and a little ashamed.

'I'll go check on him,' she said. 'See how he's doing.'

Malvery just grunted.

She made her way back down to the *Ketty Jay*. Nearby, she could see Harkins in a hooded coat and heavy gloves, working on patching up his Firecrow. Lost in concentration, he didn't notice her.

The reassurance she'd sought was already giving way to worry. She felt the crew unravelling, and what would happen to her then? She knew nobody in Vardia. Would she go back to Rabban, pick up the threads of her past, get back in the gangs? No, she was beyond that now, and likely a new generation would have already replaced those of her youth.

Back to Samarla, then? To Shasiith? Not a good option. She knew people there, but was still wanted by the authorities. She could go to Maddeus, if he was still alive, but that would be the worst thing she could do. A betrayal and a defeat all in one. He wanted her gone so she wouldn't see him deteriorate, poisoned by the drugs in his blood. She wanted to prove that she didn't need him.

Then there was the issue of the civil war. Now she knew there was the very real possibility that the Awakeners might win. And if they didn't, there would inevitably be retribution against the Sammies for their part in it, and then all foreigners in the Free Trade Zone would be in deadly peril. So how best to handle this? Where to stand to avoid the fallout?

First thing to do was to talk to the Cap'n. He ought to know his crew. He ought to know what to do and say to keep Malvery on side. Because if the doctor left, there was no way Ashua was staying. Not with Jez and Harkins and Silo. She had no real affection for them.

And if Malvery walked, he might very well walk right into a noose.

She made her way through the craft to Frey's quarters, one of several blank metal doors to either side of the passageway that ran along the *Ketty Jay*'s spine. She knocked, and was answered by a bored 'Yeah?' from inside.

'Ashua,' she said.

Frey slid the door open. He was dishevelled, his eyes weary. He looked her over. Either he hadn't slept, or he was drunk, or both. Then he stepped out the way, inviting her in.

His quarters were grubby and poky. A sour smell of unwashed male hung in the air. A hammock bulging with luggage hung above an unmade bunk. Lying on the bunk was a creased handbill. At the top was the legend: *WANTED FOR PIRACY AND MURDER, LARGE REWARD*. Below it was a picture of Frey, young and smiling. It was obviously old, but Ashua wondered why he'd been looking at it at all. What kind of memories did it hold?

She walked past him into the dim metal room, and he closed the door behind her. When he turned back, he noticed the handbill as if for the first time, picked it up quickly and put it aside. 'Wanna sit?' he said, indicating the bunk.

She eyed his sheets. 'Thanks,' she said. 'No.'

He leaned back against the door and crossed his arms. 'What's up?'

'Just came to see if you're okay, Cap'n,' she said.

'The doc send you to make a diagnosis?'

'No,' she said. 'Wondering if you needed something, that's all.'

Frey cleared his throat and looked around the room as if surprised to find himself there. He was dazed and glassy-eyed. Definitely drunk, she thought, though she couldn't see a bottle anywhere. She was beginning to wonder if it had been a good idea, coming here. Perhaps she'd been over-familiar. She should have left him to himself.

He reached over to a cabinet fixed to the wall and pulled open a drawer. It had a key in it, but it was unlocked. From within he drew out a small glass bottle full of liquid.

Ah. Now it made sense. She felt a slight sinking feeling in her belly.

'Since when did you take Shine?' she asked.

'I like a drop now and then,' he replied. 'Haven't touched it since Samarla, but now . . .' He gave a slow, clownish shrug and a stupid grin. 'Who gives a shit, right?'

Ashua decided she'd had enough. She thought a bit of sympathy might help him out, even though sympathy was a rare weapon in her arsenal. But she knew that look. She'd seen it on Maddeus' face, and the faces of the people he surrounded himself with. The placid, empty look of the chemical escapist.

The sight of him filled her with disgust. She hadn't thought him so weak.

'You know what? I think I'll leave you to it,' she said. 'Excuse me.'

She moved for the door, but he put his arm across in front of her, barring her way. 'Stay a while,' he said. 'Now you mention it, there *is* something I need.'

And then he had his arm around her waist, and he was leaning in to kiss her. She shoved him away with such force that he fell against the luggage hammock, which snapped under his weight. He fell onto his bunk amid an avalanche of suitcases. After a moment of surprise, he burst out laughing.

'You've got some kick to you!' he said.

'Knock it off!' she snapped at him. She swatted the bottle of Shine from his hand and it smashed on the floor. 'And you can knock that shit off too! You already lost two of your crew. Pull your damn self together or you won't have any left!'

She pulled open the door and stormed out. Frey was still laughing hysterically as she left.

She went down to the cargo hold, humiliated and boiling with fury. That arsehole! She always knew he had it in him, that sense of entitlement concerning the opposite sex, that need to obtain women. She'd seen it from the start. But she'd thought he had it under control. She'd come to believe he was better than that.

Should've trusted her instincts. People always disappointed her. It was just a matter of time.

There was nobody about in the hold. She burrowed into the blanketed niche between the pipes where she slept and let the fabric curtain close behind her. The pipes gave her no warmth: the *Ketty Jay* had cooled off quickly from her flight. She lay on her back and stewed for a while. Then she rolled over, dug between the pipes, and pulled out the object that Bargo Ocken had given her. A small brass cube with a press-stud on one face and a light on the other. Her signalling device.

If the crew fell apart, if it all went to shit, it wouldn't be Ashua they hunted. She'd go free; she'd have the world before her. But she needed money, if she was to be thrown out in the cold. And with what she knew now, she could negotiate a bonus. A big bonus. Something that could set her up for a while, if she played her cards right.

A faint note of caution sounded in the back of her mind. The secrets they'd learned in the Awakener base were dangerous material. They had to be handled carefully. She remembered what had happened with Jakeley Screed. The spy game could be a deadly one, and every player took a risk.

They'd first approached her not long after Maddeus had kicked her out. Maybe it was just coincidence; maybe they knew she was in need. She'd never have agreed while she was still under his wing, but she was out on her own, and this was an opportunity.

His name had been Dager Toyle. He was a Vard in the Free Trade Zone, a charismatic man in middle age, with the kind of manner that made everyone want to be on his side. He came to Ashua with an offer.

We need your eyes and ears, he said. *Anything you can tell us. Titbits. Everything helps, and the better you do, the more we'll pay you.*

It sounded like a win-win situation for Ashua. Sounded like money for old rope. Little did she know.

And so she began to spy on the Samarlans on the Thacians' behalf.

At first she was lazy about it. She knew the underground, and there were always rumours. Toyle was interested in anything. The Thacians, long-time enemies of the Samarlans, would be arrested on sight in the Free Trade Zone or anywhere else in Samarla. They had to keep an eye on their aggressive neighbours somehow. Ashua imagined they had dozens, hundreds of people like her in Shasiith, feeding them scraps.

But the money wasn't much, and Ashua wanted more. Motivated, she tried harder. She made friends with the untouchables, the lowest caste of Samarlan society, who were so insignificant to other Samarlans they were practically invisible. And invisible people made good spies. Soon Ashua was regularly providing Toyle with good information, and her pay increased accordingly.

Eventually the good times ended. Eventually, Jakeley Screed turned up.

She first heard it through another spy in Toyle's network. He made contact with her, warned her that Toyle was dead and all his agents compromised. Ashua had warily agreed to a meeting, but he never arrived. She tracked him down, found him dead in his apartment. Frightened, she went into hiding, and while there she learned that the Sammies had employed a Vard spyhunter named Jakeley Screed. He was killing all of Toyle's agents. It was only a matter of time before he got to her.

But Frey got to her first.

In the end, it was through her connections in the untouchables that she heard about the shipment which contained the Iron Jackal. She needed the money to hire protection or to escape, she wasn't sure which. So she started gathering men for the job, but somehow a whispermonger found out and sold the news to Trinica Dracken. She sent Frey to find Ashua, which led her here. Strange how things worked out.

Her finger hovered over the press-stud. She'd only ever dealt in small-scale secrets before. The news about the Awakeners was enormous. Big enough to topple governments, start wars, save or destroy hundreds of thousands of lives. She was afraid to let it loose.

But it was like Malvery said. *What they do with the information ain't my business.*

She began to tap, and with each touch the light on the side of the cube flashed. When she stopped, it began to flash back.

So the negotiations began.

Slag had found a thing.

He found it in the vents, behind one of the grilles that led out into the big world where the big creatures lived. How it got there, he didn't know. It hadn't been there before.

He'd sensed it from some distance away, on his journey up from the depths where the rats scuttled and scampered. Like a discordant sound just on the edge of his hearing, unpleasant and nagging. Now he'd located it, the sensation was stronger. It was out of place, in some deep, instinctive way that he didn't understand. And it needed investigating.

He padded closer. The corpse of a rat dangled from his jaws. It was a feeble specimen, but quick, and it had given him more trouble than it should. Once, he'd have pinned it and broken its neck before it knew what was happening. But he'd been slow, his aching muscles responding a fraction too late, and he'd missed his pounce. Catching it had worn him out, and he still hadn't fully recovered. Where was his energy?

Every day he slept longer, moved more stiffly. Every day his strength diminished. He'd held off the depredations of age for a very long time, but he couldn't hold them off for ever. Time was taking its toll, and the price was the heavier for avoiding it.

But this wasn't the day. Not today. Today, he could still fight, and run, and kill. Today, he was a warrior, as he had been every day since kittenhood.

He dropped the rat to the floor of the vent, padded forward and sniffed at the curious object. It was a large grey metal casket. There were decorative grooves and etchings on its surface, but it was firmly closed. Slag had no idea of its purpose, but he understood that this object was only a container, and that whatever interested him was inside. He circled it warily, but after a thorough inspection, he was none the wiser as to how to get inside.

A sound. In the gloom further down the vent, he saw the glitter of eyes. She was there, also drawn by the thing. She crouched at the sight of him, unsure whether to run or stay. Her eyes went to the dead rat lying on the floor between them. Calculating whether she could snatch it before he got to her.

He moved towards her slowly, eyes narrowed: a sign of peace, a sign he meant her no harm. She backed off, confused, ready to bolt. He paused, let her relax, then moved forward again and gently picked up the rat in his jaws. Still she hovered, wavering on the edge of flight. She was hungry. She had the smell of it. A cat from outside, from beneath the sky, who didn't know the ways of the iron warrens.

He approached, moving closer still. She jerked back, halfway to fleeing; but she didn't. He saw the fear in her. One more step and he'd lose her.

He lowered his head and laid the rat on the floor. An offering. Then he retreated, backing away down the vent. He sat back on his haunches and watched her carefully.

She sniffed at the rat. Took an exploratory step forward. Then, with a lunge, she snatched it up in her jaws and flurried away down the vent in a scrabble of claws.

The scent of her lingered in the air after she was gone. Slag gazed down the empty shaft.

No, this wasn't the day. But soon.

Jez awoke in her bunk, alone.

Again, the loss. But this time it was so much sharper, so much deeper. There was no disorientation, no need to collect her thoughts. She remembered everything that had happened in the Awakener base. She'd chewed it over in the dark places of her unconscious. And she knew. Pelaru was a half-Mane; now she understood everything.

She'd been tricked. Tricked by her feelings. She thought she'd fallen in love. At last, after a lifetime, she'd fallen in love.

But it wasn't love. Not in that way. It was something she'd brushed against in other times, something she'd yearned for but never dared to seize. The love of the Manes, the sense of connection, of integration, of truly knowing another being and being accepted by them. A companionship more intimate than any she'd felt as a human.

No matter which way she turned, the Manes were there. Once she'd feared to become one. Later she thought she could exist as a human, with her Mane side held in abeyance. Later still she decided to explore it, drawn by the promise it held. Meeting Pelaru had been a reminder of what she'd give up if she left her humanity behind, the last moment when she might turn aside from her path.

But she'd been fooling herself. She'd struggled and fought and agonised over the years, but since the day she was given the Invitation, her course had been decided.

How could her heart possibly hurt this much? It was only a muscle, and it didn't even work.

She got up. She was muddy and blood-spattered and stank. It didn't matter any more. Manes didn't care for outer beauty.

Once, she'd been a human cursed with being a Mane. Somewhere along the line, she'd become a Mane playing at being human.

She slid open the door to her quarters. There was nobody out in the corridor. She could hear them all over the *Ketty Jay*, and some of them outside. She caught snatches of their thoughts. Ashua was angry about something. The Cap'n was embarrassed and befuddled. The only one she couldn't sense was Pelaru. But then, she'd never been able to hear his thoughts.

She walked down the corridor to Crake's quarters, where they'd put their Thacian passenger. She could hear his heartbeat inside. It was quickening: he was aware of her. She knocked on the door, and he opened it.

Even knowing what she knew, it didn't make a difference. The sight of him filled her. She'd thought it was his face that attracted her, his noble Thacian features, firm and beautiful like a hero from some ancient legend. But it wasn't that. It was the kinship of daemons.

'So you know,' he said. He seemed sunken and diminished somehow.

'Yes.'

He stepped aside, and she went in.

Crake's quarters were more cluttered than hers, which had almost nothing in them at all. The upper bunk was a bookshelf, with tomes of daemonism secured in place with a cargo belt. She stood there awkwardly for a moment, acutely aware of her proximity to Pelaru. Then she sat down on the bunk, and Pelaru closed the door and sat down beside her.

'How did it happen?' she asked him.

'I was in Yortland,' he said. 'It was in the early days, when I was making connections, when I had to go and meet people face to face. I had a meeting on a prothane rig off the north coast. It was my bad fortune that the mists came while I was there.'

'But they didn't take you.'

'I refused them.'

She watched him keenly. No, he wasn't lying. 'You refused the Invitation?'

'As did you,' he pointed out.

'Only because the Mane was interrupted. If it hadn't been . . .' Her eyes were far away. 'I doubt I could have resisted.'

A sour expression passed over his face. 'I couldn't resist them entirely. I'm still . . . *infected*.'

She was surprised at his tone. 'You hate what they've done to you.'

'Yes,' he said quietly. 'And I hate them.'

'But you loved Osger.'

'But it wasn't love!' he cried. 'I thought it was, but then I met you, and I felt exactly the same! Don't you understand? I thought I loved him, but they cheated me!'

Jez's head was hung. Straggles of hair had escaped her hairband and fallen across her face. 'Oh, I understand perfectly,' she said.

'And yet . . .' Pelaru seemed to be struggling with his words now. 'I know it's not real, but I still *feel* it!'

'It *is* real,' said Jez quietly. 'It's just not what we thought it was.'

Pelaru's fists tightened, but he said nothing.

'How is it that you can make me blind to you?' Jez asked. 'I can't sense your mind the way I can with others.'

'I don't know how I do it. It's different for everyone, I think,' Pelaru said. 'Every half-Mane is not the same. Osger couldn't control it. He changed at the slightest provocation. I saw him slipping away from me, becoming more like *them*. He *liked* it.'

'And you didn't.'

'I won't give them that. I won't give them an inch. They won't have

243

me.' His hands were trembling. 'But some things . . . some things I can't fight. And then the change will come.'

'Imperators.'

'There were *two* of them,' he whispered. It was almost an apology.

There was silence then, and she thought how strange it was to love the Manes and hate them at the same time.

'We're infected,' he said. 'It's a disease. Every day you have to fight it. Every day. Or it will take you.'

She stirred and raised her head. 'What if you *want* to be taken?'

'Don't say that!' He burst to his feet, sweeping an arm out angrily as if to dash her words away. 'Osger would say that! Look at me! Do I fall into a coma after I change? Do I become wild and savage and lose my mind? No! Because I won't submit to them, not even a little. Because I have it under control!'

Do you? she thought. *Is that even possible?*

He turned to her, an eager look on his face, and behind it something faintly desperate. 'Maybe I could show you. I could teach you how to suppress it so nobody even notices you're a half-Mane. I've seen how the others treat you. They flinch away; they can't help themselves. You've lost control, that's all! I could help you get it back!'

For the first time she saw him, unclouded by thoughts of love. She felt something unfamiliar then. Pity. Pity for this poor, pathetic creature who denied what he was. So what if he'd been made this way against his will? It was done. You could only deny your nature for so long.

'I don't want to control it,' she said.

She met his eyes, and saw the shock there. He couldn't believe what she was saying. But she'd never been more sure of anything. She got up, and walked past him, and went out of the room.

The last promise that humanity had offered her had turned out to be a lie. This was not a human love, but the love of the Manes for one another. Out there were her kin, ever waiting, ever faithful. They wanted her to join them. And she couldn't think of a single reason to resist them any longer.

Twenty-Five

A Rude Awakening – Wrath – The Gathering –
Divided Loyalties – Silo Steps Up

Frey dreamed he was in a metal box and someone was banging violently on the outside. Then he woke to find it was true.

'Cap'n! Get up, you dozy sod!' yelled Malvery, hammering at the door to his quarters. He jerked out of his bunk, tried to stand, and his feet went out from under him. He fell among the scattered luggage that covered the floor, bashing his elbow on the corner of his bed. He swore at the top of his lungs. Today was not starting well.

He unlocked the door and pulled it open. Malvery was standing there, holding a shotgun, wearing the grubby union suit that he slept in and heavy boots on his feet. The sight of the doctor in his underwear confused Frey for a moment. Then he remembered that he was wearing long johns himself, and he realised Malvery must be just out of bed like he was.

'They've found us!' he cried. What little hair he had left was sticking everywhere, and his eyes were cracked with a hangover. 'The Coalition's here!' And with that, he ran off up the corridor. He'd only done up one button on the arse-flap of the union suit. Frey saw something he never wanted to see again.

He stood there and rubbed the back of his head dreamily. He'd taken a lot of Shine yesterday, and everything was just a little too hectic right now. The news took a moment to penetrate.

When it did, his eyes flew open and he sprinted for the cockpit.

The sound of thrusters grew all around him as he hurried to the front of the cockpit and stared up through the windglass. He swore again as he saw what was up there. A Tabington Wrath, a heavy fighter craft, about half the size of the *Ketty Jay* but with three times the armaments. It was a brick of dark metal, bulky and brutal. It kept its nose towards the *Ketty Jay* as it swung in to land, weapons trained.

He wouldn't get off the ground before they blew him to pieces. Nor would Malvery have time to get up in the autocannon cupola and swing it round.

But he couldn't just do nothing. Drave would string him up if he got hold of him. The lethargy that grief had brought on was swept away by the need to survive.

Get outside. Fight if you have to. Flee if you can. But you can't stay here.

He ran the other way, met Silo coming up the corridor. The Murthian was dressed in engineer's overalls. He slung a pistol to Frey without a word and they headed down into the hold.

Someone had already opened the cargo ramp as they descended. An icy blast of wind flurried through and grey light seeped in. Jez was heading outside, rifle in hand; Malvery was on her heels. As he reached the bottom of the stairs, Bess went thumping past, eager to see what all the fuss was about.

Frey caught sight of Ashua, who was hovering between going outside and staying put. She met his eye, looked away in disgust, and followed the others.

Frey ran after her. He didn't have a plan. He didn't have anything. He was simply swept along in the momentum. Small arms would be no good against a Tabington Wrath, but he was damned if he'd hide inside his aircraft either. He felt stupid and reckless. He was in the mood to shoot someone.

They found Harkins and Pelaru outside. The chill hit him through his long johns and his bare feet sank into cold, wet earth. The grass was dewed with the morning. The crew had taken cover where they could find it: behind the *Ketty Jay*'s landing struts, behind the Firecrow, behind black volcanic rocks. Bess was stamping the ground; she'd been idle too long. The Wrath descended from a gloomy sky, coming in to land alongside them.

'How'd they know we were here?' Ashua cried over the roar of the engines.

'Who cares?' Frey shouted, though the question hadn't been directed at him. 'If they give us any shit, gun the bastards down!'

Malvery looked at him in disbelief. 'That's Coalition troops up there!' he said, pointing.

'I'm not going quietly to the noose, Malvery,' he called back.

'Look!' said Ashua.

The electroheliograph on the Wrath was flashing. Frey made a hopeless attempt to figure it out before remembering that Jez was with them too.

'Jez!' he called.

'I got it, Cap'n,' she replied. 'They don't want to fight, Cap'n. They're saying there's no need for the weapons.'

'We'll decide that,' said Frey.

'Hold your fire till they're down!' Silo shouted. Frey felt a momentary surprise at hearing Silo give an order. Sometimes he had to remind himself that the Murthian was his first mate. It had only been a few months since he'd accepted the job, and Frey still wasn't used to him being assertive.

The Wrath settled itself in the clearing alongside the *Ketty Jay*, and put down its passenger ramp. Frey blinked to try to clear the lingering fog in his head and sighted down his pistol at the doorway. If Kedmund Drave stuck his head out of that door . . .

'Whoa! Whoa! Don't shoot!' came a voice from inside. And out came Crake, hands held to the sky, a wide grin on his face.

The tension broke. The crew laughed and cried out in relief. They broke cover and went running over to him.

'Wait!' Frey called, but nobody was listening. 'There's still . . . I mean, Coalition craft . . . Guns . . . Oh, never mind.' And he went running over himself.

Bess led the charge, pounding across the turf. Crake had to prevent her from hugging him for fear of snapping his bones. But he hugged her first of everyone, and pressed his face against her faceplate, and whispered something that could only be an apology.

When he was done with Bess, he greeted the rest. Ashua lit up at the sight of him. Malvery roared with laughter and pummelled him on the shoulder. The others were grinning, except Pelaru, who stood apart. Even Jez got in on the joy, and Crake, to his credit, didn't flinch when he touched her. Silo clasped his arm hard. Finally Frey made his way through the press, and Crake's eyes met his.

Frey felt the warmth of new hope at the sight of his friend. Even though bleak despair lay on his shoulders, Crake lifted him. He'd come back. Frey's crew was one of the few good things he'd found in this world, and Crake was a big part of that. In the back of his mind, he'd feared the worst when he lost Crake in Korrene, and he blamed himself for it. But that, at least, wouldn't weigh on his conscience any more.

They looked at each other, both trying to find the words. In the end, none were needed. They embraced, and that was enough.

'Damned good to have you back, mate,' Frey said, with feeling.

'Seems you misplaced your daemonist, Captain Frey,' said a voice. Samandra Bree was standing on the ramp, one hand on a cocked hip, gazing at them from beneath her tricorn hat with an amused look on her face.

'Ah, he's never gone for long,' Malvery boomed.

'Not while I've got this,' said Crake, holding up his compass. As ever, it was pointing towards the silver ring on Frey's little finger.

'So you made it to the forward base after we lost you, then?' Frey asked Crake.

'Not exactly,' he said. 'Long story. But what about you? What did I miss? Did you find Trinica?'

Her name killed the mood like a curse. The happiness slid off Frey's face and he went ashen.

'Oh,' said Crake.

Samandra came down the ramp. She laid a supportive hand on Crake's back, sensing the tragedy in the air. Nobody spoke for a few moments. The wind blew between them, smelling of rain.

'Miss Bree,' said Malvery gravely. 'We gotta talk. There's some things the Coalition need to know.'

She looked him up and down. 'Well, alright,' she said. 'Can they wait until you've all changed out of your pyjamas, though?'

They gathered in the *Ketty Jay*'s mess over several pots of strong coffee. By the time they'd all squeezed in, there wasn't much room left. Colden Grudge stood against the wall near the ladder, hulking, bearded and crag-faced. Leaning in the corner was Morben Kyne, arms crossed and head lowered, his cowl hanging over his mask. Silo watched the two Century Knights carefully from where he stood on the other side of the room. He knew Grudge and trusted him well enough, but Kyne was an unknown.

The rest were jammed round the table that was fixed in the centre of the room. Even Slag had attended, sensing an occasion. The oven had been left open and he was sitting inside. He groomed his paw and watched proceedings with half an eye.

They told their stories, and Silo listened. Frey's he knew. Crake's he didn't. The news that the Awakeners were trying to take the countryside by pushing out or converting the aristocracy was troubling, but hardly unexpected. The fact that they were using Imperators to do it made things a sight more serious.

There were things that didn't add up about the daemonist's tale, however. He told them his father employed the Shacklemores to find him and bring him back to help Condred, but it sounded more like a kidnapping. The others believed him, but Murthians were adept at reading faces, and he saw a pain much deeper than the loss of his father and family home. Crake's story was an edited version: there were things he wasn't telling them.

Samandra's account was truthful, at least. When Crake hadn't returned, she'd asked about. It seemed she had a hard time believing Crake would skip out on her when they'd made plans. Well, that woman might be a little full of herself, but she was right. She remembered Crake's reaction when he saw the Shacklemores in the camp, so she went and asked them, and they told her where he'd been taken. They couldn't turn down a Century Knight.

'I'd heard my father had sent bounty hunters looking for me,' said Crake. 'I didn't know why, but I didn't want to go back. That's why I reacted that way. You'd know why if you met him.'

That was a lie. Silo knew it. And he saw in Jez's face that she knew it too. Whatever Crake thought the Shacklemores wanted him for, it wasn't for any family reunion. But the *Ketty Jay* was a place where a man might keep his secrets, and Silo wasn't about to pry.

When all the stories were done, they sat in the silence that followed new revelations.

'So what do we do now?' Malvery asked eventually. 'We tell the Archduke, right?' He was looking at Bree. Authority had shifted to her, as far as he was concerned. Divided loyalties in that man, that was certain. Silo would have to keep an eye on him, like he did with Ashua and Pelaru.

Bree sat back and spread her fingers out on the table. 'I gotta be honest, fellers. Me, I believe you. You might be a bunch of selfish bastards without the least regard for anything but the safety of your own precious arses, but even you lot aren't stupid enough to be on the Awakeners' side for real.'

'Er . . .' said Ashua. 'Thanks?'

'Problem is, you gotta convince the Archduke and his generals,' she continued. 'And you wouldn't believe how stubborn a bunch of dumb old men with medals can be. When we told 'em about what went down in Samarla, I swear they'd've called it desert fever or some such bullshit if we hadn't been Century Knights. Even then, they couldn't see why they needed to concern 'emselves, since we blew the place up. That little box of delivery orders you gave us, Doc, that was the only thing that convinced 'em. Men like that, they need proof before they'll do a damn thing.'

'Told you,' Ashua said to Malvery, and took a mouthful of coffee.

Malvery ignored her. 'But you can tell them, can't you? They'll believe you.'

'I ain't seen what you seen,' she said. 'I can vouch for you, but I can't lie to 'em. And, no offence, but you lot ain't much in the Archduke's good graces since you killed his son.'

Ashua choked and blasted a mouthful of coffee across the table into Crake's face. Crake took out a handkerchief and dabbed at his cheeks.

'That happens a lot,' he told Samandra by way of explanation.

'You killed his bloody *son*?' Ashua cried. 'Earl Hengar? Why didn't anyone tell me that before I joined this ham-arsed outfit?'

'Slipped my mind,' Frey said. He was looking steadily at Pelaru. 'Besides, it was an accident. You know we were set up.'

Silo was watching Pelaru as well. That may have been new information to him, or it might not. Either way, the whispermonger knew too much. It might become necessary to ensure he didn't leave the *Ketty Jay*. Ever.

'Look, whatever excuses you got don't improve the Archduke's disposition any,' said Samandra. 'You got off the death warrant 'cause you led us to Retribution Falls, but there's a long way from that to forgivin' you, and even longer to believin' you. Not when Kedmund Drave himself says he saw you fightin' on the Awakeners' side with his own eyes.'

'Oh, Cap'n,' said Crake, in the tone of a disappointed parent. 'You didn't.'

'I was chasing you through a warzone after you minced off in a strop!' Frey cried. 'It was that or get shot by some git in a dress.'

'I think they're called cassocks,' Ashua put in scathingly.

'Whatever.' Frey sat back and crossed his arms.

'Put yourselves in their shoes, Frey,' Samandra said. 'They're responsible for hundreds of thousands of troops. They have a war they think they can easily win. Are they really gonna go charging off after some secret weapon on the say-so of a bunch of pirates with a history of betraying them? Far as they're concerned, this could be an Awakener trap. They won't even listen.'

'So what will convince them?' Malvery asked.

'We need proof,' said Samandra. 'At the very least, one of us needs to see it for ourselves.' She indicated the Century Knights in the room.

'Piss on 'em if they won't listen to us!' Frey cried. 'We've warned you. Now what are we gonna do about Trinica?'

There was silence around the table again. The crew exchanged awkward glances. Slag, sensing a vacuum in the collective attention of the room, left his spot inside the oven and jumped up on to the table. He sat hopefully in the middle for a few moments, then when nobody stroked him he padded over to Jez and slipped down into her lap.

'Cap'n,' said Silo. 'She gone.'

'She's *not* gone!' he snapped. 'She's not gone! Not while she's still alive!'

'They put a daemon inside her, Cap'n,' said Malvery gently.

'And *he* can take it out!' Frey cried, thrusting a finger at Crake. 'Can't you?'

Crake looked pale. He swallowed. *You want to say no*, Silo thought. *Say it.*

'I've never heard of anyone converting an Imperator before,' Crake began weakly.

'Screw what you've heard of. You did it for your brother, right?'

'That's not the same. That was a different kind of daemon. Not half as strong as—'

But Frey wouldn't be argued with. 'You and me, we took down the Iron Jackal! You're saying it's stronger than that?' he cried in disbelief.

Crake looked down at the table. 'Maybe we can do it,' he said at length. 'But I wouldn't rate our chances.'

'Any chance is better than none.'

'No, Cap'n, listen. It's not as simple as just taking it out. I can't reverse what happened to Jez because the daemon is the only thing keeping her alive. If I took it out of her, she'd die. Now, if the Imperators kill their hosts the way the Manes do . . .'

'The Manes do not kill their hosts.' It was the clear, accented voice of Pelaru. 'I am a half-Mane, and I am alive.'

Frey seemed surprised to hear the Thacian come in on his side.

'I froze to death after I received the Invitation,' Jez added, emotionlessly. She was tickling behind Slag's ears. 'That's why my heart stopped. That's why I'm dead. It's 'cause of the Manes I got back up again.'

Frey stared at Crake expectantly. Crake could think of no more objections.

'Maybe,' he said again. 'But first you have to get her. You know what it's like with Imperators. We can't even get near them.'

'I can,' said Jez.

'I don't want her bloody head ripped off,' Frey snapped.

'Oh,' said Jez. 'Forget it, then.'

'I have a solution.' This was a new voice, one they hadn't heard before. Morben Kyne. His words came sheathed in strange harmonics: no doubt some effect created by the mouthpiece of his mask. 'Perhaps it will please all parties.'

'Spill it,' said Samandra.

Kyne stepped forward. Green artificial eyes glowed faintly from within his cowl. 'The Imperators are trusted implicitly within the Awakener organisation. Their loyalty is beyond question. Our spies suggest they are always present at meetings of the highest level, as bodyguards or observers. It has also been surmised that they can communicate with one another on a level that does not require physical speech.'

'Which is good, 'cause the Awakeners cut out their tongues,' said Samandra.

Frey thought of Trinica. No, they couldn't. She needed it to order her crew about. They *couldn't* . . .

Could they?

'The ability is limited, not like the simultaneous communication of the Manes,' said Kyne. 'But it's our guess that they all talk to each other, in a way.'

'So what are you saying?' Frey asked Kyne.

'It's likely that the Imperators are aware of the Awakeners' plans. The date and location of the attack, and so forth. Even the ones that were not present may have learned the information from others.'

'You're suggesting we capture one and question it?' Crake was incredulous.

'Didn't you just say we couldn't get near them?' This was Ashua.

'We can't,' Kyne said. 'But perhaps we can find a way to bring them to us.'

Crake seemed both terrified and excited by the prospect. 'Could we do it?'

'It will be dangerous, but maybe it can be done. I understand you yourself trapped and destroyed a powerful daemon in Samarla without using a sanctum. Did Miss Bree tell me right?'

'Well, yes, I . . .' Crake was nervous. He glanced at Jez, no doubt remembered the hash he'd made of things in the shrine below Korrene. 'Field daemonism is not really an exact science.'

'Then might we work on it together?' said Kyne. 'I would be interested in your theories.'

Crake was politely uncertain. 'Er . . . I . . . Well, yes, if you like. Do you know much about daemonism?'

Samandra snorted. 'Honey, he's *crawling* with daemons. Just about every item of clothing on that man's back is thralled. In fact, half the kit the Century Knights use was made by this feller. Not to put you down or anything, but he's the best daemonist in Vardia, and likely the world. Just be glad we got him on our side.'

Crake gaped. 'I . . . I didn't even sense them. For them to be so . . . Well, they must be *exquisitely* fashioned! Why, it'd be an *honour* to work with you!'

'If you're all quite finished admiring each other's arses,' Frey put in impatiently, 'how does any of this help Trinica?'

Crake was excited; the insult passed him by. 'When we have an Imperator, we can take readings from the daemon inside it. Once we have its frequencies, we'll know the frequencies for all the Imperators, since they're all possessed by the same type of daemon.'

'Like the Manes,' put in Samandra.

'Well, not quite,' said Crake gently. 'The Manes are all possessed by one single daemon, which has a tendril in each of them, so to speak. The Imperators are possessed by separate, identical daemons. When the Awakeners tried to copy the daemonist's experiment, they didn't get it exactly right.' He turned his attention back to Frey. 'It's like finding the key to a code. Once we've cracked it, we can fashion devices to negate them, so we're not crushed with fear whenever we get close. We can *fight* them then. And it will be a hundred times easier to extract that daemon from Trinica.'

Frey was staring intently at his fists, bunched on the table in front of him. Frustration was written on his face. 'Seems like a pretty damn roundabout way of getting to her.'

'You're welcome to try on your own if you want,' said Samandra. 'Me, I ain't in it for your suicide mission. Dracken's not here nor there to me. Far as I'm concerned, she took the Awakeners' coin and she got what she deserved. All I care about is gettin' proof of your story back to the Archduke. What you do after that is your own business.'

'It's the way it has to be done, Cap'n,' said Crake, with a shade more diplomacy. 'We have to negate her Imperator powers before we can get that daemon out of her. But there *is* hope.'

Frey rested his head in his hands. The others watched him, waiting for his response. Slag, in Jez's lap, gnawed at something between the toes of his forepaw.

He was tormented. Silo knew it. He knew this man better than anyone. Frey wanted to run after Trinica, to save her, because that was what his heart told him to do. But she was lost to him now, maybe for ever. And there was another part of him, a part that had won out many times, which wanted to throw it all up in the air and flee. To turn his back on all of this: the Coalition, Trinica, everybody.

Frey was a man who'd kept his world and his responsibilities small. Silo knew that path well. It was safer that way. But life had a way of involving a man in bigger things.

Frey lifted his head and looked at Silo. 'What do you think?' he asked. Once, he would never have consulted Silo about anything. He wouldn't have thought to. But things had changed, and they weren't changing back.

Silo weighed his words. As ever, he wouldn't be rushed. A man shouldn't speak if he didn't have something worth saying.

'Time was I thought I didn't have no stake in any o' this,' he said. 'Not this war, not your woman. Vards ain't my people, and Vardia ain't my land. Gonna be a foreigner here no matter what I do, so why take a side, right?' He lowered his head. 'But after last night, I been thinkin' different.'

He pushed away from the wall and began to pace round the table. 'Sammies been handin' over Azryx tech, 'cause they want the Awakeners in power so they can get to the aerium here. My bet is, once they get their fleet fuelled up, they won't come askin' no more. They reckon they can take this country like they took mine, they reckon the Awakeners are just a bunch o' priests couldn't run a country if their lives depended on it.'

There was an unfamiliar agitation in him. As if saying the words confirmed them in his mind. He began to speak louder, faster. He felt himself firing up. Mother, this was *truth*!

'But they wrong!' he said. 'These are *daemons*, damn it! They don't think like us. They ain't gonna rule this land, they gonna *enslave* it. They gonna turn your leaders one by one until there ain't nobody left to stand up to 'em, and by the time the Sammies come it's gonna be too late. You can't fight an army of daemons. It ain't gonna be Vardia that gets invaded, it's gonna be Samarla and Thace and every damn place else! There ain't gonna be no place to run. We don't stop this now, ain't just us gonna be goin' under. We fightin' for the *world* here. And I'm *damned* if I'm lettin' anyone make me a slave again!'

The whole room was staring at him. Even the cat had paused with its paw in its mouth, and was gazing at him in wonder as if he was an alien. After a moment, Frey turned his head to Malvery.

'Doc?'

'What he said,' said Malvery, thumbing at Silo.

'Ashua?'

'Shit, I'm inspired,' she said with a grin. 'Let's do it.'

'Jez?'

'To stop the Imperators? I'm in.'

'Harkins.'

Harkins saluted. 'Ready to fight for the Coalition, Cap'n!'

'Pelaru?' said Frey, and then caught himself. 'Oh, wait, I don't give a shit what you think. Alright, we go catch an Imperator. But after that, I'm going after Trinica. And you all better damn well back me up when I do. Fair enough?'

There were general mutters of reluctant agreement from the crew.

'Which leaves us with just one problem,' said Samandra. 'How do we lure an Imperator to us?'

Frey leaned forward, his face grim. 'As to that,' he said. 'I've got an idea.'

Twenty-Six

Old Flames – Lust – The Ghost in the Pipes –
Frey Disappoints – Politics

The sun beat down on Frey's shoulders, shining bright in a cloudless sky. The sea spread out before him, glittering in the midday heat. Insects creaked and hummed; birdsong filled the air. The Barabac Delta had been sultry even in winter, but here in the Feldspar Islands, further south and near the equator, there were no seasons to speak of. Just the same perfect day, over and over.

He stood on a stone balcony overlooking the Ordic Abyssal. Far below, waves rolled against the feet of the cliffs. At his back, tiered gardens rose up the slope, a private wonderland of shady paths, splashing brooks, covered walkways and secret arbours. Statues peeked from hidden nooks. Domed gazebos rose above the foliage. Along the coast to his right he could see the roof of a mansion, just visible through the trees.

Another time he might have found this place beautiful. It was the kind of paradise where a man might find contentment for a while. But there was no contentment here, and the beauty couldn't touch him. He felt cut off from the world. His body occupied a space, but he was connected to nothing. His responses were automatic, predetermined. Sometimes he felt like he was watching himself, a disinterested observer of someone else's life.

He existed, but nothing more.

What am I doing here? he thought to himself.

This wasn't how things were supposed to end up. He'd never asked for much. He'd never seriously coveted wealth and power. All he'd wanted was the freedom to do what he wanted. But somewhere along the line he'd acquired a crew that he cared about. Somehow he'd fallen back in love with a woman he thought he'd left behind.

And then he'd lost her. They'd forced a daemon into her body, into her *mind*. He tormented himself night and day by imagining how that felt. Was she still awake in there, screaming silently as the daemon pulled at her nerves like a puppeteer, making her limbs dance? Or had she been crushed by the onslaught, leaving nothing left of the woman he'd known? Would he ever get her back, or would the attempt claim his life and that of every friend he had?

There is hope. Crake had told him that. But he wasn't sure he could let himself believe it. Hope was a dangerous thing for all of them. Giving up now might save everyone. Everyone but Trinica, anyway.

This was why he never wanted responsibility for anyone but himself. It hurt too damned much when you lost them.

'Captain Darian Frey,' said a voice behind him. 'What a pleasant surprise.'

He turned away from the vista, and put a smile on his face for Amalicia Thade.

She was wearing a dark blue dress, cut low at the neck to show the necklace of precious stones that lay against her collarbone. Black hair tumbled over her shoulders. She was smiling, the easy smile of a young woman who knew how to use it as a weapon. Her skin and features were flawless, her eyes dark and mischievous. She was even more breathtaking than the last time he saw her, when he'd been aiming a gun at her head.

'Amalicia,' he said, warily. 'You look well.' Despite her appearance, he feared her a little. Not many people had beaten him up quite so savagely and frequently as Amalicia had.

'Marriage agrees with me, I think,' she said, holding out her hand to show him the ring on her finger. He made a pretence of admiring it.

'I heard,' he said. 'Congratulations. And where is your, er, husband?'

'Harbley's away on business, I'm afraid. I believe it's best you and he never meet, anyway. I don't think you'd get on.'

'Yeah, I'm pretty sure you're right.' Harbley Trove sounded like the kind of stuffed-arse ponce that Frey couldn't bear. Athletic, good-looking, heir to a vast fortune, he was rarely out of the gossip section of the broadsheets. Frey still remembered the day when Pinn came dancing gleefully up to the cockpit to show him the article. Amalicia had given up her fantasy of marrying a pirate captain and chosen a heroic aristocrat with a nose so proud and noble you could use it to mine for coal.

She touched his face lightly. 'You look terrible. Have you been sleeping?' she asked with false concern.

'It's been a rough couple of days,' he said neutrally.

'Shall we walk?' She offered her arm to him, and he took it. The touch brought back faint memories of sex. She'd been willing, unskilled and over-enthusiastic. It was hard to square up the squealing young woman he remembered with the elegant lady that walked beside him.

'I take it you haven't come to apologise,' she said.

'No,' he replied. 'But I reckon I should anyway. I never was all that good at getting out of situations like that.'

'You could have handled it better,' she said. 'But don't fret. Water under the bridge. I should thank you, actually.'

'Let's not go that far.'

'Well, if you hadn't run out on me, threatened to kill me and broken my heart, I'd never have met Harbley.'

'Glad it worked out for you, then,' he said. She was trying to draw some resentment or regret from him, eager to see him lament what he'd lost. He didn't have it in him to play along.

'It's good to see you again,' she said. But there was an ever-so-slight hint of frustration behind her smile, and she didn't quite mean it.

'You, too,' he said, and didn't mean it either.

They walked out of the sun and down a dappled avenue. Trees rustled overhead, and they passed a carved stone font that trickled with clear water.

'So, are you going to tell me to what I owe the pleasure of this visit?' Amalicia prompted.

Frey wondered how to put it. This whole idea was a bit of a long shot, but Frey hit more long shots than most. 'You remember when your father found out about us?' he said.

She laughed. 'How could I forget? He sent me to that awful hermitage.' Her voice hardened just a little. 'And you left me there for two years.'

'It took me that long to track you down,' Frey lied automatically.

She patted his hand. 'I suspect that's not quite the truth, Darian, but we'll let that go, shall we?'

Frey wasn't sure he liked her tone. The naïve, love-struck girl he'd known was gone for good by the sounds of it. That would make things harder.

'I was a shit to you,' he said, thinking that perhaps a little contrition was in order.

'Spare me,' she said. 'I deserved it for believing you. But let's not hash over the past any more. We're different people now. Or at least, I am.'

Frey wasn't done hashing, though. 'You hated that hermitage, didn't you?' he said. 'You hated that your father put you there. In fact, if I hadn't saved you, you'd have a Cipher tattooed on your forehead right now, and instead of these gardens you'd be in some skaggy corner of a backwoods village, preaching the faith.'

'If you're subtly implying that I owe you something, might I remind you that you saved me by getting my father killed?' she said, frosting over. 'And any debt you think I owe you has certainly been cancelled out by your behaviour since.'

Frey sensed that he'd gone too far, and backed up. 'Sorry,' he said. 'Just making a point. You're no friend of the Awakeners.'

'On the contrary,' she said. 'My family have been staunch Awakeners for generations. My father lost his life in their service. I myself was ready to enter the faith until his death made me head of my family. And Harbley is very devout. There's no one more loyal than I.'

But there was a wry look in her eye, and they both knew it wasn't true. Amalicia was a woman whose passions went unchecked. Love and hate burned uncontrollably in her. She maintained strong ties with the Awakeners for political reasons, but in her heart she loathed them, and her piety was a sham.

'Let's just say – hypothetically, that is – that there was a way to give the Awakeners a black eye for what you've been through,' he said. 'Would you be interested?'

'Darian!' she exclaimed. 'What reason do I possibly have to hate the Awakeners?'

'For turning your father into an overbearing arsepipe?' he suggested. 'You know it was that Awakener bullshit that made him a tyrant. You had your childhood ruined by it. And if it weren't for them, Gallian wouldn't have died at all. He was doing their work, remember?'

'You must think me a very vengeful person,' she said, with a wicked glint in her eye. 'But go on. As long as we're speaking hypothetically.'

'I need to get hold of an Imperator.'

Frey walked on a few more steps down the leafy avenue before he realised that she'd stopped. He looked back at her. She was staring at him, wide-eyed. 'Get hold?' she said, half-laughing in amazement. 'You want to *get hold* of an *Imperator*? May I ask what for?'

'Probably best you don't know the details,' he said. 'Considering.'

'I see,' she said. 'And what can I do to assist you in this frankly maniacal endeavour?'

'I need you to sell someone out to the Awakeners.'

She folded her arms. 'I'm waiting for an explanation.'

'You remember Crake?'

'Oh yes,' she said venomously. 'Your partner in crime.'

Ah, *there* was the old bitterness. Good. He was getting to her.

'Crake's father wouldn't bend to the Awakeners, so they sent an Imperator to put his son into a coma. Said he'd stay that way unless Rogibald supported them.'

That gave her pause. Like most aristocrats, she regarded the nobility as a sacred institution, exempt from the kind of treatment doled out to the poor. It shocked her to think of one of her own being treated in such a way.

'You're not lying to me?' she asked.

'You've seen stories of some mysterious plague in the broadsheets, maybe?'

'Perhaps,' she said warily.

'Look into it. It only affects aristocrats. Funny, that.'

'Only aristocrats that oppose the Awakeners,' she said. 'Which I don't.' But it was a weak defence and he saw that she knew it.

He shrugged. 'It's a slippery slope. How long do you think the aristocracy's going to remain safe under Awakener rule if they're already ransoming firstborns? How long before they come for your money and your mansions and whatever else you've got?'

That was a hit. She believed him, and it rocked her.

She began to walk again, a dazed look on her face. Almost absently she linked her arm with his, and they went on up the avenue together.

They followed a path around the island, passing rows of statues. There was the smell of salt on the breeze, and the trees rustled. Distantly, Frey could hear the surging of the sea. He said nothing, and left Amalicia to think.

'You're asking me to put myself in danger,' she said at last.

'I'm asking you to hedge your bets,' he said. 'Think what happens if the Awakeners lose the war. You can be sure the Archduke isn't going to look favourably on the families that supported them. But if he knew you'd helped him out. . .'

'If the *Awakeners* knew!' she said, alarmed.

'Who'll tell them? Me? Listen, you hardly have to do a thing. I'll even give you the name of the man you're going to screw over.'

'Darian,' she said, wincing.

'Sorry. Point is, all you have to say is that you heard something from someone. At worst, it's just bad information taken in good faith, and you were being loyal by reporting it. They can't fault you for that, can they?'

'And then what?' she asked. She was all but persuaded now; she was quibbling about the details, and she wanted to be reassured.

'They'll listen to you. They trust you. As long as you make it sound urgent enough, they'll send an Imperator to pay our man a visit, like they did with Crake's family.'

'And you'll be waiting.'

'Right.'

'And you won't tell anyone?'

'Only the Archduke, and only when the time's right. I've got enough contacts to get the word to him. Might be you get yourself a medal, if the Archduke wins. Family prestige, and all of that.'

'And the name of your victim?'

'Ebenward Plome.'

'Ha!' she said. 'He's been on their list for a while, no doubt. He's not been quiet about his opposition to the Awakeners. But he hardly ever leaves Thesk; they can't get to him there.'

'He isn't in Thesk right now. He's at the Tarlocks' place in the Splinters. Very remote. If someone were to tell them where he was, how vulnerable he is right now . . .'

'Ah,' she said. 'Now I begin to see.'

The path opened out into a paved area overhung by trees, a warm sanctuary in the foliage. In the centre was a small, circular building with a domed roof. Elaborate leaded windows were set into the dome. She went inside through an arched doorway, and he followed after her.

Their footsteps echoed as they entered the chamber. Soft light fell from above onto round walls painted with friezes and murals. In the middle of the tiled floor lay a gently bubbling pool with uneven sides. Crystals grew out of it, of many shapes and colours. They frosted its edge with spidery silicate webbing; they bulged from the water in amber clusters; they thrust upward in red shards. The heat and the moisture in the air gave the building an eerie, dreamlike quality, like a shrine to some forgotten god of nature.

'Isn't it wonderful?' said Amalicia, staring into the pool. 'Harbley says it's the minerals bubbling up from the deep earth that form the crystals.' She sighed. 'This is a very special place to me.'

Frey looked around. It was alright, he supposed. 'Amalicia,' he said. 'Will you help me?'

She turned away from the pool. Her cheeks were flushed and her breastbone had reddened. 'I'll help you,' she said. 'But I need you to help me with something first.'

She lifted her eyes to his, reached behind herself, and her dress slithered from her shoulders and fell in a pile around her ankles.

'Ah,' said Frey. His gaze drifted down to take in the sight of her. This was unexpected. 'Er . . . I thought you were happily married?'

'But he's away, Darian,' she said, stepping closer, pressing herself against him. 'And I'm so very lonely.'

Her scent was different.

Slag sniffed at the pipe, deep in the warm guts of the *Ketty Jay*. The ducts were still cooling after the recent flight; they pinged and ticked as they radiated their heat away. Normally, this was Slag's favourite time to snuggle up and sleep, cosy in the craft's embrace. But not today. He was far too excited.

He went further into the ducts, tracking her. It was the same cat, no doubt about it, but the invisible marks she left behind were deliciously different. They energised him and fired his blood. They made him feel young again.

He had to find her. It had become the only thing on his mind.

Whereas before he'd been merely intrigued, now he was desperate. He stalked her down maintenance crawl ways and through vents, sniffing at each mark she'd left. If it was stronger than the last, he hurried on. If it was weaker, he backtracked.

As the scent became more intense, so did the feelings it provoked. He was powerful, hungry, obsessed. He scampered from mark to mark, head clouded with a new and unfamiliar sensation. In all his long life, he'd never known anything like it.

When he found her, she was waiting for him. They circled in the faint glow of the duct lights, sniffing at each other. The smell of her drove him wild. Her manner was different now, her body language inviting him instead of pushing him away. It was her time, and Slag finally knew the feeling that had brought him here.

Lust.

Ashua looked up sharply, a mug of coffee halfway to her lips. 'What was that?'

Crake, who'd been steadily inching round the mess table to get out of the potential spray zone, looked bewildered. 'What was what?'

Malvery had his feet up on the table, eating a slab of dry cake that he'd found in the back of the pantry and resurrected through his own unique brand of culinary necromancy. 'Didn't hear a thing,' he said. He reached over to pour some more rum into his coffee.

Ashua listened again. She could have sworn she'd heard a baby crying. 'You fellers would tell me if the *Ketty Jay* was haunted, right?'

'Oh, definitely,' said Malvery through a mouthful of cake.

'First thing we'd do,' Crake agreed.

Ashua sat back and relaxed a little. Surely her imagination. No need to be nervy.

She sipped her coffee and let contentment find her again. Crake's return had settled them all to some degree. She was glad to have him back. Intelligent company was rare on the *Ketty Jay*, and she'd missed him, even if he currently spent more time with Samandra Bree than on his own craft. Malvery was happier than she'd seen him for months. They were working for the Coalition, albeit secretly: no more moral dilemmas for him.

In fact, everyone was so pleased to have their daemonist back that they barely mentioned Pinn at all, except to occasionally take the piss.

They all seemed confident that his bizarre infatuation with the Awakeners would wear off, and he'd turn up sooner or later. Or perhaps it hadn't sunk in that he'd gone yet. For her part, she didn't much care. All she minded was that the crew seemed to be sticking together.

That, and she'd negotiated herself a great big bonus from Bargo Ocken.

She heard the sound again and stiffened. 'Listen!' she said.

They listened, and they heard it too. A sound like a baby crying. This time she found the source: an air vent above the cooker. They all stared at it as the noise lengthened and dipped to a sinister croon.

'Um,' said Crake. He looked at Malvery. 'We don't *actually* have a ghost, do we?'

Malvery opened his mouth to reply, but suddenly the croon be-came a shocking yowl, making them all jump. Malvery and Crake looked at each other in bewilderment. Ashua burst out laughing.

'You never heard a pair of cats going at it before?' she asked.

'It ain't that I'm puzzled about,' said Malvery. 'Where'd Slag find himself a lady?'

'Got a whole crew full of romantics, don't you?' Ashua said, winking at Crake, who blushed.

There was another bloodcurdling shriek from the depths of the *Ketty Jay*.

'Didn't know the old fleabag had it in 'im,' said Malvery. He raised his mug towards the vent. 'Go on, lad! Give her what for!'

Ashua rolled her eyes. *Men.*

Frey pulled his trousers on. Amalicia gathered up her dress. They kept their backs to one another.

'That never happens,' Frey said.

'Apparently it does,' Amalicia replied tightly.

Frey had thought himself numbed to all feeling, but it turned out he was wrong. Shame got through his defences just fine.

Amalicia pulled her dress over her shoulders and sighed. She could barely conceal her irritation. 'I suppose it happens to every man once in a while,' she said. 'It just . . . never happened with me.'

Frey buttoned up his shirt. The chamber was too hot. Even the slow bubbling of the crystal pool oppressed him. He was wretched, scorched with embarrassment. He wanted to get away from her as fast as he could.

He felt betrayed. Happy, sad, drunk, high or depressed, he'd always performed. He'd done it with women of intimidating beauty and with women who looked like the back end of a rusty tractor. Whatever the circumstances, his equipment had never let him down. One of the great certainties of his world had been torn away from him today.

'Is it her?' Amalicia said from behind him. 'Is that why?'

He didn't trouble to ask how she knew about Trinica. There had been rumours circulating ever since Sakkan. No doubt she'd had her ear out.

Is it her? he thought. *Is it?* Suddenly he was angry. Was it the memory of her that stopped him, that last scream that still echoed in the dark places of his consciousness? Was it loyalty to her memory? Had she shackled him, without either of them knowing it? Had he shackled himself? Chained himself to a woman he might never be able to have, excluding all others?

That wasn't him! That wasn't Darian Frey! This wasn't even cheating, for rot's sake! They weren't even together!

And yet the sight of Amalicia naked hadn't stirred him. Her touch had produced no response. Something inside him had shut down, and he didn't know how to wake it up again.

Amalicia took his lack of reply as an affirmative. 'She must be quite a woman, this pirate queen of yours.'

He heard the poison in her voice. She'd never help him now. And without her, he didn't know how he could save Trinica. It was only in that moment that he realised how much had relied on this one woman, how slim his chances had been from the start.

'I should go,' he said, defeated. He needed to get out of her sight and never be seen by her again, to bury this incident in his memory and not tell another living soul.

'Wait,' she said, as he headed for the doorway. He stopped and looked back at her, crushed in on himself like a beaten dog. 'Eben-ward Plome, you said?'

He just stared at her dumbly.

She combed her fingers through her hair and threw it back over her shoulders. She was staring into the pool. 'I hear he's staying at the

Tarlocks' summer home in the Splinters right now. Such a disloyal, treacherous enemy of the Allsoul. He won't be there for long. Only a few days, perhaps.' She met his eyes briefly. 'It might be our only chance to turn him over to the side of the Awakeners.'

He could hardly credit what he was hearing. After everything he'd done to her, after this new humiliation, he'd never have expected the maturity necessary to choose politics over her emotions. She'd always been a spoilt child at heart, full of pique and rage. He felt an overwhelming surge of gratitude, and didn't know what to do with it.

'Thank you, Amalicia,' he said, his gaze on the floor. 'You're doing the right thing. If the Awakeners ever seize power, who knows what they'll do to the aristocracy.'

'Oh,' she said. 'No, that's not why I'm doing this.'

'So why?' he asked quietly.

'Hate,' she said, 'Pure and simple.' She gave him a small, vicious smile. 'I suppose I am a vengeful person after all.'

Twenty-Seven

Impaled – 'You Can't Deny His Whiskery Majesty' –
Pinn Gets Drunk – Hinges – Pinn Gets More Drunk

'Hey!'

Marinda froze. She looked slowly over her shoulder, like a child dreading the monster they imagine stands behind them.

'Wait up!' Pinn called, as he hurried across the clearing towards her.

He had to dodge his way through. This part of the Awakener camp was busy in the hot afternoon. Groups of sweltering men were loading cargo into aircraft. Cassocked figures hurried here and there, locked in agitated conversation. Teams of mercenaries carried out weapons checks while the mangroves stirred restlessly in the hot breeze from the south.

She must not have seen him, because she was walking away at some speed when he caught up with her.

'Hey! It's me!'

She turned around, brushed her hair back behind her ear self-consciously, levered an unconvincing smile onto her face. 'Artis,' she said. 'What a surprise.'

'Ta da!' he sang, spreading his arms wide. He wagged a finger at her. 'You are a hard woman to find.'

'Oh,' she said. 'It's the preparations, you see.'

Pinn looked about. Now that she mentioned it, he'd noticed a certain increase in activity over the last couple of days. He hadn't thought much of it, to be honest. He'd been preoccupied with his quest to find Marinda. The Awakener camp was a big place.

'What are we preparing for?' he asked.

'Leaving,' she said. 'Soon it will be time for the great assault, and we . . . What are you wearing?'

268

Pinn struck a pose, the better to show off his shabby, dirt-smeared beige cassock, an ill-fitting imitation of hers. He still had the Cipher painted on his head, though sweat had reduced it to a blue smear. 'You like it?' he asked. 'I'm a Speaker, like you!'

'Artis,' she said patiently. 'That's actually quite offensive.'

'Just thought I'd get into the spirit of things,' he said, unfazed by her disapproval. 'Can't blame me for being keen!'

She glanced about as if searching for escape. 'Well, it's very nice to see you again, but I really must be—'

'You weren't at the meeting place,' he said. 'Not yesterday or the day before! What about my lessons?'

'I, er, I understood that your crew had left. There was quite a stir about it. A lot of people were very angry, as I recall.'

'Not me!' said Pinn. 'I stayed. I'm a follower of the Allsoul, through and through.'

'I see,' she said. 'And a Prognosticator knows about this?'

'Oh, yeah,' he said. 'I've talked to three of them now. They said I was alright, 'cause I chose the Allsoul. Not like the others. That lot are traitors.'

She regarded him sceptically. Pinn wasn't quite sure if was telling the truth or not. His memory always was a bit fuzzy that way. He remembered running away into the swamp while everyone was occupied with shooting at the *Ketty Jay*. He remembered the flak exploding in the sky. After that, there was a lot of wandering about. It was easy to get lost in a camp this size. He'd slept rough one night; later on he'd just walked into a tent and taken a bunk and no one had disturbed him. He queued up and ate at mess tents. He got drunk at a makeshift bar that had set up its own still. A few people remarked on the fake Cipher on his forehead, but whatever he'd said had convinced them he was harmless. He thought he might have talked to a few of the higher-up Awakeners at some point, but that could have been his imagination. Well, anyway, they'd understand. After all, he'd stayed behind: how could they doubt his loyalty?

And all the time he'd been searching. Searching for Marinda. Those sweet, understanding eyes. That youthful, pretty smile. Those round, firm—

She caught him looking. His gaze flicked back up to her face. 'So how about my lesson?' he said, without missing a beat.

'Oh, I really couldn't. It's the preparations, you see. I have so much to do.'

' "Teach those who would be taught",' Pinn said, frowning and speaking in a deep voice to imitate the Prognosticator that had ordered her to give him lessons. He hadn't learned a thing in the time since, but he'd enjoyed staring at her a lot. 'Listen, I'll tell you what. You don't even need to give me a lesson today. *I'm* gonna give one to *you*. I'm gonna read the future!'

'You're, er . . . Pardon?'

'I'll show you!' he said. 'Come on! Where's that bowl of yours?'

He took her by the hand and dragged her off in the direction of a nearby tent. She protested weakly, but soon gave up. It was usually easier just to do what Pinn wanted. Reasoning with him was too exhausting.

There were a dozen or so crates in the tent, but it was mostly empty. Most of the supplies had been loaded into nearby aircraft. Part of the preparations Marinda kept talking about, Pinn guessed. He didn't care. He just wanted her to himself for a bit.

She had the bowl with her, of course; she always did. It was in a bag along with a flask of milk and her long, sharp needle, its tip blunted by cork. He had her hold the bowl and poured some milk into it, then he took the needle from her, pulled off the cork and held it up.

'Now I'm just going to prick your finger—' he began.

'No! Noooo, no, no,' she said, backing off. 'Dangerous. You shouldn't be doing that.'

'Come on, it can't be that hard.'

'There's a technique to it,' Marinda protested.

'Yeah, I saw your technique on that old lady you stabbed through the hand.'

Her face hardened. Pinn detected a bad move on his part. 'Er,' he said. 'What I mean is—'

'Wait!' she said. A slow smile spread across her lips. 'I have an idea. You want to read the future, you can read your own. *I'll* pierce *you*.'

Pinn suddenly felt a whole lot less enthusiastic about his grand plan to impress her. 'Erm,' he said.

'Come on, give me your hand,' Marinda said briskly. 'Here, hold the bowl and give me that needle. Now your finger. Come on!'

Before he knew quite how it had happened, Pinn found himself holding out his finger over the bowl of milk. He wished he'd thought faster, found some reason to argue. But she certainly seemed a lot more eager now.

'Okay,' he said. 'Just be gentle with meeeaaAAAAAHHH!'

She grabbed his hand and plunged the needle deep into his finger. The pain was spectacular. Pinn gritted his teeth to prevent himself from calling her something unforgivable.

'Oh, don't be a baby,' she said maliciously. She yanked his hand down and held it over the bowl. Blood squirted into the milk. It was terrifying to see that much come out at once. 'There you go. We need enough to get a good reading. You are a beginner, after all.'

As soon as he was decently able, he pulled his finger away and stuck it in his mouth. 'I said be gentle,' he complained as he sucked it.

She enjoyed that, he thought. *She actually enjoyed it.*

She took the bowl of bloody milk from him and set it on a crate. When she looked back at him, he was staring at her with the eyes of a wounded and pathetic animal. She sighed and softened a little.

'Give me your hand,' she said. Fearfully, he did so, but this time she only wanted to bind the wound with some dressing from her pack. He gazed at her fondly as she wrapped his finger. *So tender*, he thought.

'Now, then,' she said when she was done. 'Why don't you try to read your future? See if the Allsoul's gift is within you.' She was gentler now, perhaps guilty for jamming a needle in his finger so hard that he felt it in his elbow.

Pinn composed himself and walked solemnly over to the bowl. He bent over and studied it. 'Hmm,' he said.

The blood swirled slowly in the milk, forming arcs and clusters of spots. None of it meant shit to him. He was slightly disappointed – part of him had expected divine abilities – but not deterred. The plan didn't call for the intervention of the Allsoul, just a little creativity.

'I see it!' he said. 'I see it, clear as day! The Allsoul is speaking to me!'

'Are you sure?' Marinda asked doubtfully. She came up to his shoulder and peered into the bowl. 'What does it say?'

'It says . . . In the very near future . . .' Pinn traced the line of a swirl with his finger. 'You and I will go off into the undergrowth and bang like rabbits!'

Marinda burst out laughing. It wasn't quite the response Pinn had been expecting. He'd imagined something closer to a swoon.

'What?' he complained. 'You have to. The Allsoul said so. You can't deny His Whiskery Majesty.'

Marinda was holding her side and leaning against a crate. 'Stop!' she begged. 'Oh, dear, no! Don't say anything else!'

Pinn thought this was all pretty rude, and by the time she'd got herself under control, his mood had blackened to a thunderous sulk.

'Heretic,' he said peevishly.

She took a few deep breaths and wiped the tears from her eyes. 'Artis, you haven't done your research, have you? It's very sweet that you've got a crush on me . . . Wait, no, actually it's not, but anyway . . . Look, the thing is, Speakers are celibate.'

'Yes!' said Pinn, brightening. 'We *should* celebrate!'

'Celi*bate*,' said Marinda. 'Thoughts of lust distract the mind from communion with the Allsoul. Speakers don't have relations with anyone else.'

Pinn just stared at her. She'd said a bunch of words but they didn't seem to mean anything. She put it more plainly for his benefit.

'No sex,' she said. 'No kissing.'

'Hand job?' Pinn suggested hopefully.

'Not that either.'

'Shit,' said Pinn. 'Really?'

'I'm afraid so.'

Pinn considered that for a short while. He shifted his weight from one foot to the other. He frowned and *hmm*ed. Finally he arrived at the conclusion of his mighty cogitation.

'Your religion bites arse,' he said, and walked away.

After that, Pinn did what any hero would have done in his shoes. He headed for the bar.

The drinking tents had been set up mainly for the benefit of the mercs, who'd inevitably rampage if forced to stay sober for too long. Pinn stormed his way towards the central clearing of the Awakener camp, where the tents and stalls clustered thickest. On his way he pulled his cassock over his head and flung it into the mangroves. Damned thing was too hot to wear over his regular clothes anyway. He stopped at the edge of the path, where the swamp water lapped close, and wet his hands. Then he rubbed them all over his forehead until he'd reduced the smeared Cipher to a faint bluish smudge.

'Stupid bloody Awakener bloody shit bloody,' he muttered to himself as he walked.

The central clearing was busier than usual. Preparations for departure were in full swing, and the atmosphere was feverish with the anticipation of battle. There was a sense of time running out. People crowded the stalls and bars to spend their pay packets, to enjoy their last days in this company, to eat and drink and carouse in case they never got another chance. It all had the feeling of a particularly grubby and slightly dangerous fete.

The first drinking tent Pinn found was warm and muggy. A row of tables passed as a bar. Barrels and a still stood behind them, along with a crate of bottles and a rangy barman who looked like his face had melted in the heat. More barrels were placed upright around the tent to serve as tables. They were surrounded by stools, most of which were occupied even at this early hour. Pinn took a stool at the bar, ordered a grog and set to it.

Most of the first couple of hours were spent grinding his teeth and calling Marinda all the names he could think of. It took several drinks before he'd mellowed enough to stop hating her, and to start feeling sorry for himself.

He'd really made a mess of things this time. Here he was, in the middle of nowhere, with no idea where his mates were and no idea how to find them again. And all because of some stupid woman with a great big bloody tattoo on her forehead. What had he been thinking?

He pulled a crumpled piece of paper from his pocket and stared at it. His atrocious handwriting stared back at him. Each line had been crossed out.

Jurny.
Deth.
Dark hared stranger (not hot)
Find sumthin important
Trajedy on sum-one deer (emanda?)
You will beleeve!!

He balled it up in disgust and threw it over his shoulder. That was what he thought of prophecies. He could make prophecies too. He prophesised he was going to get hammered flatter than cowshit, and bollocks to anyone who tried to stop him.

Just then he caught sight of something on the ground by his stool. A crumpled ferrotype, that must have fallen from his pocket when he pulled out the piece of paper. With some effort he reached down and snagged it between his fingers, then brought it up to the bar and smoothed it out.

Looking back at him was Lisinda. Gentle, doe-eyed Lisinda. Lisinda of the soft hair and fulsome bosom. He'd crumpled up her picture on the way out of Korrene, meaning to deface it later, but he'd forgotten about it since then.

He gazed at her in wonder. It was almost as if fate had delivered her to him. She'd come to him in his time of need. A bit creased, but even so. A reminder. A message.

Lisinda.

He slammed his hands suddenly down on the bar. The barman stared at him.

'I've made a terrible mistake,' he announced.

There was only one thought in his mind as he blundered out of the tent and into the sunlight. Lisinda, Lisinda, Lisinda. Why hadn't he seen it before? *She* was the one for him. She'd *always* been the one. She didn't care about riches or great deeds. She'd loved him, and everything about him. And he loved her. He'd *always* loved her. He'd just forgotten about it till now.

Married or not, he was going to get her back.

The journey back to the clearing where he'd left his Skylance wasn't quite as short as he'd imagined. In fact, it took him the best part of three hours to get there, by which time he was sweaty, exhausted and beginning to get a hangover.

The early evening sun baked him steadily as he staggered down the dirt path that finally brought him to his destination. He stopped, wiped his knuckles across his brow and scanned his surroundings. There were the freighters whose crew had tried to stop the *Ketty Jay* escaping. There was the spot where the *Ketty Jay* had sat. And there . . .

A whimper escaped his lips.

There was the empty space where his Skylance had once stood.

★

Pinn lay in bed, his covers tucked up under his chin, wide-eyed in the dark. Six years old and scared.

The wind rattled the window in the frame. The house creaked. Shadows pooled, slicks of congealed dread.

Something awful was coming.

The first footstep on the stair. He clutched the blanket tight, squeezed his eyes shut, rolled on to his side so his back was to the door. Another step, and another. *Go away, I'm not here.*

But the footsteps came on relentlessly, up the stairs to the landing. They fell slow and heavy, closer and closer. The knowledge of the inevitable outcome squeezed his heart and pressed down on him hard.

The footsteps stopped outside the door.

Don't come in, don't come in.

The creak of a turning handle. The whine of hinges as the door opened.

He wanted to run. He wanted to shout. He wanted to throw off his blankets and show them he was awake. They couldn't get away with it if he could see them. They couldn't possibly do it if he could *see* them!

But nothing he did made any difference. It was always the same. He couldn't move or make a sound. He was forced to replay that night exactly as it had happened.

He lay there, pretending to be asleep. Long, delicate fingers ran through his hair; a palm rested gently against the side of his head.

'I love you,' his mother said, quietly.

Why had he pretended to be asleep that night? Maybe he'd planned to jump up and surprise her. Maybe he'd been angry about something and sulking. Whatever the reason, the sound of her voice drove it from his mind. It confused and frightened him. Those three words, never spoken before, now delivered in a tone of sadness and loss. He had the sense that something important was at hand, and he froze.

She got up and walked out of the room. He heard the whine of the hinges again. With that, the doom of his dream was complete. With that, she was gone for ever, without trace or reason.

The click of the latch as the door closed was like a gunshot. He jerked awake and sat upright. Standing in front of him was a lean, sag-faced man with straggly black hair turning to grey. He stared at the man.

The man stared back. Pinn took a few moments to work out who he was.

The barman. He was back on the same stool that he'd left earlier in the day when he went off to get his Skylance. His clothes had stuck to his skin in the tepid and moist air, but his mouth was dry.

He turned his head carefully to the left and surveyed the bar with the suspicious expression of a man who didn't quite know how he'd got to where he was, and was wondering if he'd been tricked somehow. It was dark outside, but hanging lanterns provided light. Fat moths circled them and occasionally managed to find a way inside, a decision they quickly regretted. The tent was noisy with conversation and the sound of night insects from the trees outside.

'You want another?' the barman asked.

Pinn made a wheeling motion with his hand. Keep 'em coming. The barman stuck a mug of grog in front of him.

'That one's on me,' said a voice to his right. Pinn rotated blearily and came face to face with a man who looked like he'd just shambled out of a burrow. He was short and squat, with long, shaggy hair that hung in unwashed clumps over a grizzled face of surpassing ugliness. Half his throat was covered with a disfiguring scar.

'Do I know you?' Pinn asked, squinting.

'Should think so,' came the surly reply. 'We crossed paths more than once.' He raised his mug and grunted. 'Balomon Crund. Bosun on the *Delirium Trigger*.'

Pinn vaguely remembered him, but he wasn't sure if his presence here was a good thing or not. Still, anyone who bought him a drink was alright as far as he was concerned. He clanked his pewter mug against Crund's and took a long pull to wash the sticky gunk from his mouth.

For a while they sat drinking in silence. Crund didn't seem much inclined to speak, which was odd, since buying a drink tended to imply that conversation would follow. Pinn began to feel slightly uneasy, but not enough to take his mind off his booze.

'Wasn't sure you'd still be here,' Crund said at last. 'Thought you'd run off with the rest of 'em. Couldn't think why you'd leave your craft behind though.'

'You know where it is?' Pinn asked sharply.

'Aye. They're gathering all the fighters ahead of the big take-off.

Engineers jacked it and they flew it off to put with the rest of 'em. Someone else'll be flying it, I suppose.'

'Not bloody likely!' said Pinn, steadying himself on the bar as he got to his feet. 'I'm gonna get it back!' His hand slipped off the edge of the bar and he fell off his stool and into Crund. Crund shoved him back onto his stool. 'Tomorrow!' Pinn finished with a flourish.

'So they gave you the boot? Your crew?'

Pinn snorted. 'I gave *them* the boot.'

'You an Awakener now, then?'

Pinn scowled. 'The Allsoul,' he raised his mug towards the roof of the tent, 'can pucker up and plant a great big sloppy kiss on my balls.'

The barman raised an eyebrow at that, then walked off towards the other end of the bar to serve somebody else. A cautionary voice in the drunken stew of Pinn's brain belatedly warned him to remember where he was, but nobody else appeared to have heard him over the din of conversation.

Suddenly he felt maudlin and sighed. 'I stayed behind. Did it for a woman. Probably shouldn't have.' He looked up. 'Speaking of women, how's old Chalk-face doing, anyway?' he asked. 'Isn't she a daemon or something these days?'

Crund's hand tightened around his mug, and his face became taut and grim. 'That's what I'm here about.' He fixed Pinn with a hard stare. 'We gotta talk.'

Twenty-Eight

Heavy Weather – Pelaru Speaks of Home –
Engines – Crake's Game – A Reversal

Snow blew against the window, sliding down the glass, piling on the sill. Jez stood there in her overalls, head tilted to one side, looking out. The fire at her back threw a warm yellow glow onto her legs and shoulders. The cold and dark was in front of her, the heat and light behind. She, being half-Mane, was neither hot nor cold, but somewhere in between. Where she'd always been.

The window was on the first floor, overlooking a cobbled courtyard with a fountain in its centre. Surrounding the courtyard were small, simple houses, stables, and a garage for vehicles. Lights glowed in some of the windows. Smoke wisped from chimney stacks, drifting into the grey-white void overhead. It was afternoon, but dark enough to be evening. To her right, a short marching arc of electric lights delineated the bridge.

Samandra Bree emerged from one of the houses and hurried across the courtyard. Jez watched her approach. Samandra was bundled up in a hide coat, furred hood pulled over her head. It was the first time Jez could recall seeing her without her tricorn hat. But then, this was winter in the Splinters; even Century Knights could freeze up here.

'Weather's closing in,' Malvery rumbled.

She shifted her gaze and took in the scene reflected in the glass. They were in a living room, bare and plain but still more homely than they were used to. Malvery was sitting on a stool by the fire, a bottle of grog hanging from one great paw. At a table nearby, Ashua was playing cards with Frey, Harkins and Colden Grudge. Silo sat at the end of the table, watching the gauges on a large brass device that hummed and grumbled at the borders of her consciousness.

Daemonism. Strong daemonism, courtesy of Morben Kyne. It set her teeth on edge.

'You think they'll come today?' Harkins asked nervously.

'Don't look like it now,' said Malvery.

'It's only been two days,' said Ashua, picking out a card from her hand. 'Could be weeks till they turn up, if they bother at all. Imperators probably have better things to do than chase down every dissident who gets ratted on by his peers.'

'Feels like it's been weeks already,' Frey muttered.

'That's 'cause you have the attention span of a brain-damaged seagull,' Ashua replied. 'Me, I'm *happy* they're taking their time. There's a mansion across the bridge with a wine cellar full to bursting, a cold room stocked with good meat, and a library bigger than I've ever seen.' She snapped down her card and scooped up the pile. 'I'm good.'

Frey cursed. 'Can't we play Rake again?' he complained.

The Cap'n wasn't taking the waiting well. She wondered how long it'd be before he decided that action – *any* action – was better than doing nothing at all. Before he broke his promise to the crew and set off after Trinica regardless of the consequences.

That was love. The kind that made you stupid. The kind she'd never felt, nor let anyone feel for her. She envied him that, whatever misery it brought him. He had something she'd never had.

But she had something else.

The door opened downstairs, and there was a gust of wind from outside. Samandra stamped in, trailing snow and flapping at herself. 'Cold as a corpse's arse out there,' she said. 'Fires are banked up. Should be good for a couple of hours. You're up next, Frey.'

Frey looked at his cards and said nothing.

'Are we gonna have to do this every day?' Malvery moaned.

'You want the houses lookin' occupied, don't you?' Bree replied. 'No one's gonna set down here if it don't look like the lights are on.' She walked over to Silo and peered over his shoulder at the gauges. 'Anything?'

'Nuh.'

Jez tried to shut out the daemonic hum from Kyne's device. It was a mix of machinery and aethereal power, running off electricity provided by a generator which fed the hamlet and the mansion nearby. The device was linked to large resonator masts placed all around the rim of the valley, set to detect engine noise. They were all linked up in a manner similar to Crake's earcuffs, but on a grander and more complex scale.

Kyne had access to some formidable technology, and by Samandra's account he was the best daemonist in the land. But even with his help, their plan was a risky one. Capturing an Imperator would be no easy matter. It was said they could stop a man's heart by willpower alone. Only a Mane could resist them, and then there was no question of capture; they awoke such primal hatred that neither Jez nor Pelaru would be able to stop themselves killing their targets.

Jez didn't much concern herself with plans any more. The struggles of the crew felt distant. Only occasionally did she involve herself with their wants and needs. The rest of the time she was simply there, doing what needed to be done, waiting for the right moment. The moment of certainty. The moment when she'd turn her back on the world, and leave them for ever.

The device was too distracting. She couldn't marshal her thoughts. She sensed the others watching her as she walked out of the room.

'. . . why do they put up with her anyway . . .'

'. . . gives me the chills, but it's Jez! Don't be so . . .'

'. . . gonna have to do something about . . .'

She took the stairs to the top floor, where there were two small bedrooms with several unmade beds between them. Some of the crew had been sleeping in the house. They had to take shifts watching the gauges on Kyne's machine, and it was easier to stay here than to trek back and forth to the *Ketty Jay*.

She went to the window of the back bedroom and opened it. A snowy rise, thick with bare black trees, lay before her. She clambered out and onto the sloping roof, moving swiftly and assuredly over the slippery surface. Sitting erect at the peak of the roof, waist deep in the snow, was Pelaru. She climbed up and sat next to him.

'I had hoped for some privacy,' he said, blinking away snow from his lashes. He was wearing a coat, but it was only to protect his fine clothes. He was Mane enough that he didn't feel the cold.

Jez ignored the hint. She had things she needed to talk to him about.

From up here, it was possible to see the whole of the grounds. The houses and stables and garages were for the servants that worked at the mansion during the summer. A skeleton staff of guards and caretakers looked after the place during the winter months. They were now under lock and key in the basement level of the mansion where they'd be out of the way and safe. They were being cared for well enough, and it was a bloodless ambush in the end. The guards had put down their weapons once Samandra Bree got involved. Her fame preceded her.

To her left she could see the lights of the landing pad glowing in the murk, away at the end of a short road. The Century Knights' aircraft was there, along with two smaller craft for the staff. The Tabington Wrath was a heavily armoured gunship, but it was expensive enough to be the choice of a paranoid rich man. The *Ketty Jay* and the Firecrow had been hidden elsewhere, in a clearing further down the valley, in case they were recognised.

To her right was the bridge to the mansion itself. The mansion stood on an island of rock in a shallow chasm that ran along the floor of the valley. During the summer months a meltwater river would run there, and the valley would be green. Now the valley was buried in snow, and the chasm yawned icily.

The mansion itself took up a third of the island, perched precariously on the edge of the drop. The rest was taken up by gardens – dead till spring – and a wide driveway to the bridge. Jez could barely see the mansion in the snow, only the lights of its windows. It looked dark and forbidding now, but she knew it was white and golden and fine in the sunlight.

'Have you ever visited Thace?' Pelaru said. 'I miss it. I miss Arath, her high gleaming spires, her shaded colonnades, her tree-lined boulevards. I miss the music and theatre and language. But what I miss most is the *togetherness*. For almost two thousand years, we've been the only true republic in Atalon. Every man and woman has their say. That unites us. Being Thacian unites us. We stand in the shadow of the great slave-owning nation over the mountains to the west, and we defy them.'

'You do more than defy them. You bombed the Samarlans' capital and killed their God-Emperor,' Jez pointed out. 'Twice.'

'Always in retaliation. Always after they tried to invade us.' His face darkened. 'We should have wiped the Divine Family out when we had the chance, but we wasted our time with peace settlements and politics.'

He glanced at Jez, and quickly away. It was hard for him to be near her, she knew that. The disappointment was too great. For Jez, it wasn't so hard. She'd already accepted that what they had wasn't what she'd thought it was. It was the love of kin. And there were many more like him, out there in the snow. Far to the North, beyond the Wrack. She heard them singing. They wanted her, and she was drawn to them.

'You know why I came to Vardia?' Pelaru said. 'I did it for my homeland. A Thacian wouldn't last five minutes in Samarla, so Vardia was the next best thing. I wanted to be a whispermonger, I wanted to know *everything*. And I dreamed that one day I might use that knowledge to protect the land I love.' He kicked at a chunk of snow and sent it sliding down the roof. 'What I've learned here . . . the Samarlans selling Azryx technology to the Awakeners . . . the Lord High Cryptographer a daemon . . . They cannot be allowed to win. My people need to know. Do you understand? My *people*!'

She did understand. 'I suppose we all have to pick a side, sooner or later,' she said. 'I assume you've let somebody know? Sent a letter or something?'

'I have my channels.'

'So why are you still here?'

'You know why,' he said, turning away angrily.

'Are you trying to save me?'

His jaw went tight. He sensed mockery, but she meant none.

'I don't need to be saved,' she said. 'I've made my choice.'

'You're giving up,' he said bitterly.

'I am what I am,' she said. 'Resisting it is pointless.' She wiped wet hair from her forehead. 'When were you planning to tell us about the relic you hid away in the *Ketty Jay*'s air vents?' she said.

To his credit, he showed no visible reaction, though his heart jumped hard. 'I wasn't,' he said. 'How did you find it?'

The cat, she thought. She'd found it while she was travelling with Slag, piggybacking his thoughts, sharing his simple world of savagery and instinct. But she said nothing of that. 'You do know what it is?'

'Of course I do,' he said. 'Osger knew. It was his field, and that particular object was his obsession. Rumour had it that it came into the possession of the Awakeners long ago. They recognised daemonism in it, and all daemonic objects they gathered to themselves. But they didn't know what they had. By the time anyone guessed, Korrene had been destroyed and the shrine was lost.'

'Until your explorer found it again.'

Pelaru gazed grimly out into the snow. 'I thought Osger was a fool to run off chasing a dream. I didn't believe anything was there. But I let him go to his death, and I didn't try hard enough to stop him.' He sighed and hung his head. 'And he was right. I recognised the relic when we searched the shrine. I was the fool.'

'And what do you plan to do with it, now you have it?'

'I will destroy it. Or if I can't, I will put it somewhere that nobody will ever find it.'

Jez thought about that. Yes, perhaps that was best. Better that than have it fall into the wrong hands. And yet—

'Hey! We got action!'

Jez's sensitive ears picked out the cry from the living room below. The Cap'n. She exchanged an urgent glance with Pelaru, and the two of them scrambled down off the roof. They swung back in through the window with preternatural agility and hurried to the living room, where they found the others loading their weapons.

Silo looked up as they entered. 'Engines,' he said, thumbing at Kyne's device. One of the gauges had jumped, the needle trembling near the halfway point. The two gauges next to it had roused slightly: they'd detected the peripheral sound.

'Must be small,' said Ashua. 'Maybe just a shuttle.'

'An Imperator, comin' on his own, if we're lucky,' said Bree.

'Our boys are gonna need more than luck,' Malvery said.

Frey pulled his earcuff from his pocket and clipped it on. 'Crake?' he said. 'Get ready. Shuttle coming in. We're on.'

Crake, his hand on his ear where the earcuff was attached, raised his head and looked at the others. 'They're coming,' he said.

Plome froze in the act of checking the resonators for the twelfth time. He gave a quick nod and stood up. The Chancellor was a squat, fat little man in his sixties. Stringy grey hair clung on around his temples, having given up the high ground. He drew out a hand-kerchief, mopped his brow and pate, then adjusted the pince-nez that perched on his nose.

'Well,' he said breathlessly. 'Time to man the battlements, as they say.'

Morben Kyne stood at a window on the far side of the chamber, hands linked behind his back, his hooded head bowed. He looked over his shoulder at the other two. Mechanical green eyes shone in a mask of brass.

'It's not too late to back out of this, Plome,' said Crake. 'We can handle it.'

Plome gave a nervous chuckle. 'Oh, now. You're not getting rid of me that easily. I may not be an adventurer or a Century Knight, but I am a daemonist.'

'Yes,' said Crake, and laid a hand on his friend's shoulder. 'We're all daemonists here.'

And it was daemonism that had brought them together and bound them in a common cause: the freebooter, the Century Knight and the politician. Plome had a seat in the House of Chancellors now; he had plenty to lose even if he got through today with his life and sanity. But the lure of the Art was strong. The opportunity to work with and learn from a man like Morben Kyne was too rare to resist. The chance to capture an Imperator, to do something never done before in daemonist lore, was a chance he couldn't pass up. They were all explorers in forbidden lands; discovery was their drug. Plome was not a brave man, but obsession brought its own kind of bravery.

'What we are facing here,' he said when Crake asked him to help them, 'is not only an assault on our liberties and our way of life, but an assault on free thought and free enquiry. I became a politician so that daemonists like us might one day be able to walk in the open without fear of being hanged. And I'm damned if I'll climb in a hole for the Awakeners.'

He didn't need to be here with them; it was enough to use his name as a lure. But he'd insisted on participating. Crake was faintly shamed by that. He'd always viewed Plome as rather a weak-willed sort, easily led: a good man but hardly a firebrand. Yet he was willing to nail his colours to the mast right then and there, to risk his life for his cause. Crake, in contrast, had spent months sitting on the fence. It had taken his father's death and the destruction of his home to tip him off it.

Plome had suggested the Tarlocks' summer house as a location for the trap. He'd visited his benefactors there before and knew it well.

After that, it had been up to the Cap'n to employ his wiles on Amalicia. None of it left a particularly good taste in Crake's mouth – he disliked endangering Plome, and he thought Amalicia had suffered enough at Frey's hands – but hard times called for hard decisions. The fate of the Coalition might be riding on the events that played out this afternoon.

The room they occupied was a small audience chamber with panelled wood walls, overlooked by paintings of family members. The dignified atmosphere had been ruined by the daemonist's pre-parations. Cables ran along the skirting boards, snaking between various devices in the corners. Clusters of batteries were piled up next to trolley racks containing oscillators, resonators and harmonis-ers. Damping rods and thick resonator masts stood against the walls, ready to throw out a web of frequencies. In the centre was a sum-moning circle with a double circle of smaller masts and spheres linked up to another resonator.

It was a cage within a cage. The instant an Imperator stepped into the room they'd hit him with a fluctuating barrage of frequencies and interference. Once the Imperator was disoriented and its power nullified, they could drive him into the circle, where he'd be thor-oughly disabled by a much more focused assault.

That, at least, was the theory. But first they had to get him into the room. And then they had to keep him there long enough to inter-rogate him.

Crake tried not to dwell on how much could go wrong. He'd almost got Jez killed last time with his seat-of-the-pants science. Field daemonism was a dangerous game.

But it's my *game*, Crake thought. Even Kyne listened to him when it came to field daemonism. Nobody had ever captured a daemon outside of a sanctum before, as far as he knew. Terrified as Crake was, he took pride in that. He'd always wanted to be a pioneer. He just never imagined it would be quite so life-threatening.

There were three entrances to the room, and two large windows in the other wall, looking out across the chasm. The lights of the hamlet were visible out there among the flurrying snowflakes, nestled in a hollow in the land, with tree-lined banks rising like shoulders around it. Crake suddenly wished he was out there, with the others. With Samandra.

'Do you think they can really kill you with their gaze?' Plome said, as he was gathering up his equipment. He gave a scared little laugh. 'Surely just a story to scare people, hmm?'

'Not just a story,' said Kyne, his voice full of strange harmonics. He was checking the large-bore pistol that he carried. 'Some are stronger than others. Some can frighten a man to death.'

'Oh,' said Plome.

Crake was strapping on a heavy backpack, containing the device which he'd newly dubbed his 'sonic flux emitter'. It wasn't quite as snappy as 'flux thrower,' but he thought it less vulnerable to mockery. It was wired to an improved battery given to him by Kyne, which lasted much longer than the old chemical things he'd been lugging about. 'The key is to hit the Imperator before he knows we're here,' he said. 'If he gets wind of us, he can use his power.'

'Right,' said Plome. He shouldered his own backpack.

Crake ran a mental inventory. He had wide-spectrum 'screamer' spheres on his belt, to disorient daemons. Damper spheres to negate their abilities. Small portable batteries for both. Then there was the sonic flux emitter, which he'd use to zero in on the Imperator's frequency and paralyse him with crippling pain. He carried that. The others had harmonic arc generators to ensnare the Imperator – *if* they could nail his frequency in time. And last but not least, they had dynamite.

Crake couldn't hit a barn door with a gun, and neither could Plome. Besides, if the Imperators were anything like Manes, it would take more than a couple of bullets in the chest to bring them down. Massive damage or a headshot would be necessary.

Their packs were bulky and cumbersome, and everything but the dynamite had to be wired in to the batteries that they carried with them. They wouldn't be able to move fast, and it was easy to get tangled up. Inelegant, but it was all they had. Even with Kyne providing the best equipment money could buy, their arsenal against the daemon was makeshift and clumsy.

'Ready?' Crake asked.

Nobody answered.

Through the lens of his spyglass, Frey watched the shuttle come slowly into view.

He was hunkered down with Silo in the snow, hidden among the bare trees near the edge of the chasm. Visibility was so poor, they'd been forced to throw on coats and get closer to get a good view of the mansion. He followed the small dark shadow as it took on form and substance, sliding out of the grey murk. The thin sound of its thrusters came to him on the wind.

'They've fallen for it,' he said.

For the first time since they'd escaped the Awakener base in the Barabac Delta, he felt excitement stir within him. These past days had been like living in a wasteland: dead horizons surrounded him. An empty hopelessness had sunk deep into his bones and made them heavy. Food and drink brought him no joy. Even Shine wasn't much help, and Ashua had smashed his last bottle anyway.

He felt a twinge of embarrassment as he remembered making a pass at her in his cabin, but a twinge was all it was. She, at least, had quickly shelved her resentment with the stoicism of a young woman who was used to it. She grew up around violent boys, after all: it probably wasn't the first time someone had tried it on.

The incident with Amalicia was far worse, but even that pain had faded quickly once he'd got away from her. It was hard to feel much of anything any more. Strong emotions were swallowed quickly, lost to the bleakness.

Trinica.

He'd been undone. He'd lost his chance. There would be no salvation for either of them. No restitution for what he'd done to her. She'd been taken and turned, and he didn't know whether he could take and turn her back. And even though he was desperate to rescue her, he'd never really believed it was possible. She was beyond his reach now. He just wanted to kill himself trying.

Yet now he saw the shuttle, he felt hope again. An Imperator – it *had* to be! And if Crake's wild plan came off, they'd have a way to fight the Imperators, and a way to recover the woman he loved. He didn't pretend to understand the method, but he trusted Crake enough to take him at his word.

With the spyglass fixed to his eye, he watched the shuttle come in. And he dared to believe again.

At least for a moment or two.

'Ain't right, Cap'n,' Silo said.

He took the spyglass away and wiped wet snow from his face. 'What isn't?'

'They comin' in the day,' he said. 'Crake's brother, they came at night. Took him out quiet, so no one knew. Look, they landin' on the roof. Anyone in that mansion, they'd be sure to hear 'em.'

Frey hadn't considered that. 'Maybe they don't always do it that way,' he said. 'Plome doesn't have children to use as leverage. Might be they plan to go scare him direct.'

'Might be,' said Silo. But he didn't sound convinced.

'What's up, Cap'n?' said Crake in his ear. Frey had forgotten about the earcuff.

'They're landing on the roof,' he said. He heard Crake relay the information to his companions.

The shuttle settled itself on the flat roof of the mansion, where there was a small, private landing pad for personal flyers. The shuttle couldn't have made it here on its own: it was too far from any town. That meant there was a mother craft somewhere in the mountains. Once they had the Imperator, they'd have to get gone before he was missed.

We're gonna be cutting this awful fine, he thought, and felt excitement spark in him again. Danger chased away the hollow feeling inside. Suddenly he wanted to get in there, face the Imperator, loose off a round or two. But this was Crake's show; he was only the support act.

They resumed their watch. Frey shifted in an attempt to relieve the chill. The ramp of the shuttle opened silently in the distance. A black-clad figure emerged. Frey felt the cold become a fraction more profound.

Then another one came out. And another behind that.

'Oh, shit,' Frey muttered.

'What?' snapped Crake in his ear. He was evidently on edge like the rest of them. 'Don't just say "Oh, shit." It's not very bloody specific.'

'There's three of them,' said Frey.

'*Three?*'

'Three Imperators, Crake! Is that specific enough for you?'

There was a babble of conversation in his ear. Frey tapped one boot anxiously against the other. Three Imperators. He'd never even seen three together before. You didn't send three Imperators to subdue one little aristocrat, no matter how much he'd pissed you off.

'You want Jez in there with you? Maybe Pelaru too? They can take care of—'

'No,' said Crake. 'Kyne thinks we can handle them.'

Frey heard a little scream of disbelief in the background, which he assumed was Plome.

'We've got to try, Cap'n. We're only going to get one chance at this. You put Jez in here and she'll slaughter the lot of them.'

'Rather them than you!' Frey said.

'Cap'n!' This was another voice. Malvery, who had the third earcuff. The fourth had been lost with Pinn. 'Cap'n, we got trouble!'

'I know! Weren't you listening?'

'*More* trouble, Cap'n. This contraption you left me sitting in front of, the gauges are going all over the place.'

It took Frey a moment to work out what he was talking about. Malvery was with the others in the living room of the house. Kyne's device was registering more engines.

'How many?' he demanded. 'How many aircraft?'

Malvery consulted with Samandra and came back to him quickly. 'Three. And by the way the gauges are going, they're big noisy bastards too. Comin' in at speed.'

Frey swore loudly and bitterly. Rage swelled up inside him. He pulled off his earcuff, balled his fist and thumped at the ground. 'Shit! Shit! Shit!'

Silo got to his feet and pulled his captain up. 'Ain't time for that, Cap'n. We gotta move!'

The two of them ran back up the road towards the house. Crake, Kyne and Plome would have to fend for themselves. Frey had his own problems.

They thought they were laying a trap for the Awakeners. But the Awakeners had laid a trap for them.

As he ran, he heard a sly, silken voice in his head. The voice of a woman he'd thought he knew. '*I suppose I am a vengeful person after all.*'

Well, he couldn't say Amalicia hadn't warned him.

Twenty-Nine

In the Snow – Too Many Enemies –
Kyne's Eyes – A Trap is Laid – Crake Reaches

By the time Frey and Silo reached the courtyard, they could hear the engines on the wind. The others were hurrying out of the house, bundled up in coats and carrying shotguns and pistols. Samandra was yelling at the crew, pointing them this way and that. Snow flurried round the hamlet, obscuring their vision and blowing in their eyes.

'Frey!' she cried as he arrived. 'You're with me! Come on!'

'Come on where?' Frey called back.

'Landing pad!'

Frey wasn't used to taking orders from anyone. Even in a crisis, he was roused to indignity. 'Now hold your arse for a second, Bree, this is *my* crew!'

Bree took a breath to swear at him, then decided diplomacy would be quicker. 'I need to get to that landing pad and get the Wrath airborne,' she explained. 'Rest of us need to dig in here ready for when they come at us. I could do with another pair of hands on board, and Grudge is better here with that cannon of his. Now you want to stay or come?'

'What about the *Ketty Jay* and the Firecrow? Bess is still locked up in the hold!'

'You ain't gonna make it to them in time!' she said.

She was right. Their best chance lay in getting the heavily armoured Wrath off the ground. The *Ketty Jay* and the Firecrow were on the other side of a forested rise, through heavy snow. But the road between here and the landing pad was dangerously exposed, and he wondered if they should scatter off into the trees instead of staying in the hamlet. That would leave the bridge undefended, though, and Crake and the others were in there, and—

'*Now*, Frey!' Samandra snapped.

The crew were looking at him expectantly. He made a decision. Any was better than none.

'We need to get to the landing pad and get the Wrath airborne,' he said with authority. 'Rest of you need to dig in here ready for when they come at us.'

Bree rolled her eyes, grabbed his arm and pulled him away towards the road. He heard Silo barking orders behind him, dividing up the crew into defensive positions.

Three Imperators. Three aircraft, and who knew how many guns and men? Frey and his crew knew something they shouldn't, and the Awakeners were going to make damned sure they didn't live to tell about it.

Frey and Samandra raced out of the hamlet, boots crunching in the snow. The road cut through the colourless landscape, winding between steep banks. On their left was a forest of bare trees; to their right, the trees had been cleared for meadows.

Frey caught sight of something out there in the whirling whiteness. A bulky grey shadow sinking towards the meadows. A troop transport, by the shape of it, probably packed with mercs or Sentinels or both.

'Malvery!' he yelled over the whine and roar of thrusters. 'They're coming at you from the south! Tell Silo!'

'Right-o,' said Malvery, and he sounded so matter-of-fact that Frey felt himself heartened. He believed in his crew, in their competence and spirit. Silo was a good leader; he'd left them in capable hands. No matter what the odds, they could win out. They always had a chance. He had to believe that.

'Frey! Heads up!' Samandra came to a halt, pointing at the sky. Ahead of them, coming from the direction of the landing pad, another craft was taking shape. It pushed out of the gloom, coming in low and steady. Frey stopped next to Samandra, peering at it, unsure of what sort of danger it represented. Was it, too, coming in to put down troops?

A gust of wind pushed the snow aside, and he saw it. His heart sank. It hung in the sky like some enormous bird of prey. A Bester-field Predator. A military grade attack craft. And they were right in its path.

He felt Samandra slam into him just as the Predator's rotary cannons opened up. They crashed into a snowdrift and a hail of bullets tore past them, throwing up a long cloud of powder. The Predator soared overhead, following the road towards the hamlet.

Frey found himself on his back on the bank, with Samandra lying on top of him, her face inches from hers. Even amid everything, the softness and warmth of her stirred him. He was inordinately pleased to find that he was still capable.

'Well, hello,' he said.

'In your dreams, pirate,' she said, and shoved herself off him and back to her feet.

'Hey! Crake's a pirate too, you know,' he said, as he pulled himself free of the drift.

He looked about, but he could barely see a thing for the snow-haze. He wasn't even certain which direction the landing pad was now. He'd got turned around. It was far too easy to get lost when every-thing was white.

'Which way's the—?'

She held out a hand to shut him up. The rotary cannons had started up again. They heard smashing glass and falling slates as the gunship fired on the hamlet. The sound sucked the humour out of him.

Voices came to them, snatches of barked orders. Soldiers or Sen-tinels, coming from the other direction. He caught a glimpse of grey figures slipping down the bank. The Awakeners had reached the road. Frey and Samandra had delayed too long; they were cut off from the landing pad.

Samandra grabbed him and thumbed at the north bank. They scrambled up it and into the naked forest, before the army of men coming down the other bank could catch sight of them and shoot them dead.

Silo ran through the kitchen with his head down. The window exploded inward; the counter-top was splintered and scored; the stove popped and clanged as it was riddled with holes. He skidded into cover in a doorway and crashed into Malvery, who had his hands over his head.

'This is pretty bloody unsporting behaviour!' Malvery yelled over the noise of the rotary cannons. 'What happened to picking on some-one your own size?'

Gallows humour was lost on Silo. Survival was a serious business to a Murthian. He searched the room, looking for better cover, angles of fire, anything that might help them. Years of living as a resistance fighter in Samarla had given him a talent for getting out of desperate situations, and this one was right up there with the best of them.

'There's another one!' Ashua cried, who was crouched by a window on the far side of the house, visible through the open door-way. 'They've got *two* gunships!'

Two of 'em. Mother. They gonna shred us from both sides.

'Soldiers coming in over the meadows!' Jez called.

Silo listened as the first aircraft swung away and began firing on another building. It was hovering over the courtyard, pounding the houses that surrounded it. Silo guessed the pilot didn't know exactly where they were, so they were cutting up the whole place in the hope of flushing them out.

He hurried through the doorway to the living room and hunkered down next to Jez. She and Ashua were at neighbouring windows overlooking the south slope, where the meadows ran out and the land tipped down to meet the back of the buildings. Off to the right was the hamlet's generator, attached by a cluster of pipes to a large cylindrical fuel tank.

Grey figures were hurrying across the meadows, carrying rifles. Dozens of them.

'Soon as they're close enough, let fly,' he said.

'I can go out there,' said Jez. She gave him a disturbingly hungry look and drew her lips back over her teeth. 'I can get among them.'

He felt a wave of repulsion at the feral leer on her face. 'Keep your post, Jez. Need you here.'

She stared at him for a long moment, then turned back to the window. It was a relief to have her eyes off him. No man or woman could put the scare on Silo, but Jez was different. She got you in the place where dreams and nightmares lived. Courage didn't mean a thing there.

'Soldiers headin' down the road to us!' Malvery called, his hand on his ear where the earcuff was affixed.

Damn it. Too many sides to defend. Too many enemies. If the

Awakeners overran the courtyard there would be no way out, no possibility of retreating into the trees to the north. He had to block them off.

'Doc!' he called, as he headed for the stairs. Malvery ran across the room and joined him. 'You two, don't move!' he shouted at Ashua and Jez as he left. 'We gotta hold the line!'

Harkins, Pelaru and Colden Grudge were strung out in positions along the south side of the hamlet, hidden among the buildings, waiting for the soldiers. It was the best he could do given the time that he had. They were already spread thin; now they'd have to spread themselves thinner.

He pushed open the door to the house and peered out. The gunship's cannons were loud enough to make him flinch. Bullets destroyed the flimsy walls of a shed; the roof collapsed with a crash. Overhead, above the gunship, an identical craft hove into view. Two Predators together, and the crew like mice hiding from cats. The second gunship let loose on the house where Kyne's device had been kept. The living room windows smashed in; stone and snow turned to powder beneath the assault.

Malvery jostled up to him and raised his shotgun, aiming at the gunship. Silo grabbed the barrel to stop him.

'Can't hurt 'em like that,' he said. 'It'd just bring 'em down on us.'

Malvery huffed in frustration. 'Where's Grudge and that damn great cannon of his?'

Silo would have liked an answer to that himself. But Grudge was smart. No sense giving away his position until he was sure he wouldn't be massacred in retaliation.

Better not wait too long, though, Silo thought, and he slipped out of the door. *Or there ain't gonna be anywhere left to hide.*

Just when Crake thought things couldn't get any worse, the lights went out.

'Well, that's exactly what I needed,' said Plome in a tiny voice.

Crake let his eyes adjust to the gloom. They were in a short corridor with three doorways leading off it. A large window at the end faced out across the chasm toward the hamlet. The cloud and snow was so thick that it was almost possible to forget it was still afternoon. The warmth of electric lamps was replaced by the grim cold glow from outside, and shadows clung thick to the corners.

The house was silent, but he could hear engines in the distance, and the chatter of machine guns, and the sound of collapsing walls. There were still a few lights on over the far side of the chasm. Perhaps the link between the generator in the hamlet and the mansion had been severed, some cable inadvertently cut amidst the wanton destruction. He wanted to believe that. Better than thinking the Imperators had done it on purpose.

He'd taken the earcuff from his ear. He needed all his concentration for the task ahead, and he couldn't do it if he was worrying about the others. About Samandra. She was the most capable person he knew, a woman for whom no challenge seemed too much, a character larger than life who could never be overcome. But he feared for her anyway.

'Maybe we should go back to the room,' Plome whispered. He'd been loath to leave the chamber they'd rigged up as a trap, and was looking for any excuse to return there. Like most daemonists, he felt powerless outside his sanctum.

Kyne had his head tipped back and was looking up at the ceiling. 'We can't trap three of them,' he said. 'We need to deal with two first.'

'Deal with?'

Kyne drew his large-bore pistol and fixed Plome with those green, faintly glowing eyes. 'Kill,' he said.

Plome swallowed and nodded. Clad head to toe in close-fitting brass armour, the Century Knight seemed barely human, a faceless force incapable of weakness. Crake hoped that was the case, anyway. He'd spent a few days working with Kyne on their preparations, and knew him to be formidably intelligent, but he'd still learned nothing of the true character of the man beneath the metal. Like many of the Archduke's elite, Kyne presented a public façade that was hard to penetrate.

The Century Knight was looking up at the ceiling again. 'They're staying together,' he said. 'I'd hoped to split them up, take them one at a time. But maybe it's better this way.'

There was a long creak from overhead. A foot on the floorboards. Crake felt something cold pass down his spine.

'I only hear one,' said Plome hopefully.

'But I *see* three,' said Kyne. 'Follow me.' He moved up the corridor, past the gaping Chancellor.

'He can see them? Through the damned *ceiling*?' Plome hissed at Crake.

Crake didn't know. Hard to tell how much of Kyne was real and how much was show. Was it possible that Kyne had thralled the eyepieces of his mask to allow him to see through solid objects? Was it their daemonic auras that he saw? The heat of their bodies? If so, his mastery of the Art must be breathtaking. But it might just as easily be some trickery that he was passing off as a miracle.

Following Kyne's lead, they made their way through the mansion. It was difficult to be stealthy with their clumsy backpacks, but there were rugs to muffle their footfalls. All Crake's senses were on edge. Tuned to the daemonic as he was, he felt keenly the presence of the Imperators, somewhere out of sight. The paranoia and unease was expected, but it didn't make the shadows any less threatening.

His mouth was full of the thin acid taste of fear. Three Imperators. Surely, to tackle them was suicide? He remembered the time he'd faced one in the corridors of a downed Awakener freighter, the way he'd cringed and puled in abject terror. He couldn't face that again. Kyne said they were capable of killing a man with their power, and Crake believed it.

But he didn't want to die. Not now he had so much to live for.

The man that first set foot on the *Ketty Jay* just over two and a half years ago had been a wretch. Hunted, riddled with guilt, he'd turned his back on the Art and sought only escape. How things had changed since. He'd had a hand in some of the most important events in the history of the Coalition. He'd seen things he hadn't known existed. He'd learned more of the Art through necessity and adventure than he'd ever learned from books.

And he'd met a woman he'd never have expected to love, or to love him back. A brash, vulgar, wonderful woman, who made him feel for the first time that there was something in the world more interesting and exciting than daemonism.

That was why he'd survive today. Three Imperators? He'd just have to beat them. Because he was damned if he'd die now, just when things were getting good.

Kyne held up a hand, bringing them to a halt. They were in a parlour furnished with low settees, a harpsichord, a card table and a Castles board. To their right was a stone fireplace. A fire burned low in the grate, throwing shadow shapes into the room. There were two doors other than the one they'd entered by. Both were open, showing dark rooms beyond.

'Here,' said Kyne. He motioned for them to hide.

The room was large and cluttered enough to provide ample opportunity for concealment. Plome scurried off behind the harpsichord. Kyne took position behind one of the doors – presumably the one he expected the Imperators to come through. Crake moved behind a large settee and knelt down on one knee. Easier to get up quickly with the heavy pack on his pack.

'As soon as they're in the room,' Kyne whispered. 'Hit them with everything you've got.' The strange harmonics surrounding his voice made it sound like it was coming from inside Crake's head. 'Start with the screamers. Dampers right after. I'll take care of two of them. The last one we catch with the harmonic arc generators.'

I'll take care of two of them. How could he be so confident? What did any of them know about the Imperators, really?

Well, they fell down if you tore their heads off. He'd seen that. So maybe a man like Kyne *could* take care of two of them. Maybe that cannon of his was thralled with something spectacular.

Maybe.

Silence fell, but for the faint sounds of combat that floated to them across the chasm, the low whistle of the mountain winds and the grizzling fire. Now they were no longer moving, the tension of the situation began to pile up inside them. Crake peered round the edge of the settee, into the shadowed room beyond the doorway. Dread was coming for them, dread greater that the mind could endure. He stared into the dark, convinced with the certainty of a frightened child that monsters lurked there.

A shadow moved. He froze. A product of his tormented imagination? He strained his eyes to see.

A burning log snapped like a gunshot in the grate. Crake jumped, but not as hard as Plome. The politician lurched halfway to his feet in fright. His arm wheeled as his backpack threatened to overbalance him. He teetered, then went down to his knees in an effort to correct himself. The weight of the pack tipped him forward, and he threw his hands out to stop himself bashing into the harpsichord. It moved as he touched it, its feet screeching across the parquet floor, and every string in its body resounded with a cacophonous din.

The clashing and chiming faded into an appalled and horrified silence. Nobody dared to move or breathe. Plome's eyes were as round as peeled eggs.

The shadows on the other side of the doorway seemed to thicken like treacle.

And then the terror came.

It bore down on Crake with almost physical force, a freezing weight heavy on his shoulders. Panic exploded in his breast. His mouth was dry, ears singing, heart thumping wildly. The darkness in the room had become the harbour of a thousand fears, but none greater than what waited beyond the doorway. There he sensed evil, so dense it dripped from the air.

He had to get away. It was a desperate need, the only thing in his mind: to run from that unseen malevolence. But he couldn't move. His muscles had gone weak. The harpsichord crashed again and he saw Plome flailing. The Chancellor tried to get to his feet, failed, and finally curled into an awkward ball, his pack like a protective shell. Even with all his thralled equipment, Kyne wasn't immune. The Century Knight staggered away from the doorway, clutching himself, and fell against the wall.

No help. No hope. No one to save him.

Crake went down on his hands and knees, nails clawing along the parquet floor. His fingers tangled in one of the many wires and cables that surrounded him, and something metal jerked loose from his belt and clattered loudly to the floor. He cringed from the noise. *Please-pleaseplease don't let them notice me.*

They didn't even need to be in the room. They just needed to know where their targets were. How could you fight something like that? How could you even try?

The fear was intensifying. His chest tightened, heart slamming against his ribs. It was difficult to draw breath.

They can kill you just by thinking about it.

His vision blurred with tears. He looked down between his hands and saw the object that had fallen from his belt. A metal sphere, attached by wires to a battery on his belt.

Damper sphere.

He heard the words in his head, but they didn't mean anything. He fell over on to his side. He couldn't support himself any more. Through the gap beneath the settee, he could see across the firelit room to the doorway. Something moved beyond it, a dark figure, sliding through the shadow.

Damper sphere.

And now the words connected through the fog in his mind, and found meaning. The damper sphere. It could stop the fear. It could take this unbearable feeling away.

With a monumental effort, he turned his head. His cheek was pressed to the floor. The damper sphere lay half a metre away from him. A small round button protruded from it. He tried to raise his arm and couldn't. There was no strength in him. His salvation lay right there and he couldn't reach it.

They're coming they're coming they're coming.

He wanted to be sick. He wanted to wet himself. Tears dripped from his eyes. His body shook and his bones felt liquid. His heart was slamming so hard and so fast that each beat became agony.

Reach, he told himself. *Reach for it.*

His vision was dimming, sparkles crowding in at the edges. He couldn't move. So cruel to die now, when he was so happy, when he had—

Samandra.

And he saw her, like a flashpan had gone off in his mind. Samandra, a vivacious, beautiful explosion of life. Samandra.

He gritted his teeth, body shuddering, lips a trembling snarl. He wouldn't give her up. He wouldn't. He *wouldn't!*

With a surge that was half terror and half fury, he brought his hand up and slapped it down on the button of the damper sphere.

The effect was immediate. The damper sphere vibrated and throbbed, throwing out a low buzzing hum, a mix of sonics that surrounded them in a null-field. The Imperator's influence was flung off him, the weight whipped away from his body. He gasped in a breath as the band round his chest loosened.

But though the power of the Imperators was lifted from him, genuine fear and fright remained. He had seconds to act before the damper ran out. Panicking, he scrabbled at his belt, found the screamer, hit it. A shriek cut through the air: wild sonics lashed the area. From the room beyond, he heard the Imperators howl, their voices lifting as one in a cold animal screech.

The sound was too much for him in his present state. All thought of defeating the enemy was gone; he just wanted to escape them. Without even looking at his companions, he blundered to his feet and ran, and ran, and ran.

Thirty

Trading Fire – Deserters – Ashua's Gamble –
Crake Slips the Net – Desperation

Ashua sighted down the barrel of the pistol, using both hands and the windowsill to steady her aim. It was a long shot, and the snow made it harder. She breathed out and squeezed the trigger.

Out there in the meadows, one of the grey hurrying figures toppled over and lay still.

She felt nothing for her target. He was just a shape, an anonymous man in a bulky coat, too distant from her life to cause her to care. It was a necessary detachment, born of a childhood in the slums. Life and death was cheap to her. Everyone's except her own.

To her left, at the other window, Jez was firing with mechanical speed. Her rifle cracked and snapped. Each time, a man went down.

There were too many to hold back for ever, Ashua knew that. But they could make the attack costly enough that the Awakeners might think again, pull back, try another tactic. They could buy time. That was the best they had, right now.

She took aim and fired again. This time she hit nothing. Her target kept coming, forging on through the snow, making a trench with his thighs. Someone shot at her from the meadow; a bullet smacked into the wall near the window, scattering brick shards. She ignored it. Her second shot dropped the man.

She ducked back into cover. Sporadic return fire was coming their way, but the meadows provided little protection and the defenders had an elevated position. She heard other guns firing along the line of houses which defended the hamlet. Pelaru and Harkins. Malvery's shotgun boomed from somewhere behind her, echoing through the courtyard, before it was covered up by the drill of rotary cannons.

Jez pulled back to reload. Ashua glanced across the bare living

301

room at her. Her teeth were gritted and her eyes bulged. Her hair had
escaped the rubber tube she used as a hairband and was hanging over
her face. She looked half crazed.

She caught Ashua's eye as she snapped the last bullet into the
breech and primed the rifle. Ashua looked away quickly. There was
something coiled and dangerous about Jez, something that might lash
out at any moment. Ashua didn't want any part of it.

Engines overhead. One of the gunships, moving above the house.
The low roar of thrusters filled the room, shaking the pipes. The
sound of it overwhelmed her; the size of their opposition seemed
suddenly immense.

We're not going to get out of this, are we?

The thought came treacherously, slipping a blade of doubt between
her ribs. If she could have run then, she might have done. If she had a
way to escape, she might have taken it. But there was nowhere to go.

The lack of options bolstered her courage. Easier to stand when
you were backed against a wall. She shook her head, spat an oath of
defiance. All her life, she'd fought to survive. She wouldn't fold now.

A moment later she was back at the window. The Awakeners had
multiplied out there. Some of them were tucked down in the snow,
aiming up at the houses. Others ran on, intending to storm the
defences by weight of numbers. Jez was making them pay a heavy
price. Ashua added her weapon to Jez's, and took down another two
men before ducking away to reload.

'There's too many,' Jez was muttering furiously. She punctuated
her words with rifle shots. 'There's too—' *Crack* '—damn—' *Crack*
'—many!'

Suddenly the world turned to noise and chaos, and Ashua flung
herself back as bullets smashed along the flank of the building, tearing
the windowsill to matchwood, setting the air sparkling with flying
shards of glass. She lay back against the wall that separated them from
the kitchen, stunned. Jez had crammed herself into the corner of the
room, eyes blazing, actually *drooling* like some damned carnivore in
sight of bloody meat. There was a screech of thrusters as the gunship
swung out over the meadow. It rotated in the air and lashed another
salvo across the row of buildings. Ashua scrambled to get out of the
way, but all she could do was press herself down behind a ragged

chair. Bullets whined through the room, but it was only a brief scattering before the pilot pulled away to focus attention elsewhere.

Ashua stayed where she was, chest heaving and heart pounding. That was too much. You couldn't fight that kind of firepower. The Awakeners had gunships on both sides of the houses now, and they were closing in on her location.

'This is bad,' she said to herself, in a frightened little-girl voice that she hadn't heard for a long time. 'This is really, really bad.'

Footsteps. Running footsteps, racing up the stairs that led into the kitchen. Alarmed, she slid around the wall to the doorway that linked the two rooms. She leaned round the corner and aimed her pistol.

A man in a coat burst into the kitchen, coming fast enough to shock her. She pulled the trigger.

Click.

Pelaru stared at her in amazement, frozen in place. Ashua stared back, wide-eyed. Now she realised: in the confusion of the gunship assault, she hadn't had time to reload.

The Thacian ran past, dismissing her, heading for Jez. Ashua let out a shaky breath.

I nearly shot him, she thought. *What if that had been Malvery?*

She pushed herself back against the wall. It was something solid, something she could rely on. She opened the chamber of her revolver and began pushing bullets in, keeping one eye on the whispermonger, who'd crouched down next to Jez.

'Jez!' he said. She didn't seem to be listening. 'Jez!' he snapped. She met his gaze. 'Don't,' he said firmly.

'There's too many,' she replied hoarsely.

Ashua snapped the chamber shut and hurried back to her window. The sill was shredded; now there was just a ragged hole, edged with brick and splinters. Snow blew in and settled among the pieces of broken glass. She cast about for a sight of the gunship, but it was lost in the whiteness.

The Awakeners were at the edge of the meadows now. Only a short slope separated them from the houses. She thrust her pistol out and began firing wildly. Two men jerked and collapsed, blood-spatters stark in the snow.

'Hey! Will someone get back to shooting?' she shouted.

Pelaru had Jez's head in his hands and was gazing hard into her eyes. Her teeth were bared; spit dripped from her chin. 'Control it,' he said. 'You're not invincible. You can't fight them all. Control it!'

'Damn it, I need *help!*' Ashua yelled. She loosed off another couple of shots, then retreated as a bullet nicked the hood of her coat.

Jez knocked Pelaru's hands away and shoved him back. He stumbled and tripped over his heels. As she stood there, hunched and savage, the full terror of her swept over Ashua. The Mane inside her had broken the surface. Her aspect changed, and in the dim light of the afternoon she looked like some nightmare phantasm. Then she threw down her rifle and leaped through the window.

'Jez!' Pelaru cried. He ran to the window and looked down.

The Awakeners were slow to react, puzzled by the sight of a woman in overalls leaping across the snow towards them. The nearest man barely had time to raise his gun before Jez drove her fist through his belly and out through his spine. She wrenched her arm free and shook him off, spraying a fan of red across the pristine white meadow. Then she lunged for another.

Some backed away or ran, others brought their guns to bear and fired wildly. But Jez was never where the bullets were; she flickered rapidly, fooling the eye. She flurried among them like the snow, and when she passed she left them headless or eviscerated.

Ashua watched, dumbfounded, as the Awakeners tried to keep up with her. One man shot his companion by accident while trying to draw a bead on the daemon on their midst. She fired off the last of her rounds into the back of an Awakener who wasn't even looking at her any more. All their attention was on Jez: the attack had faltered.

She dropped back to reload again. 'Hey, you wanna give her some help?' she said to Pelaru, who was standing by the window. Pelaru gave her a sharp glare. Then he jumped out of the window himself.

'Not like tha—' she began, but he was gone. She cursed, reloaded her gun and looked out of the window again. A blast of snowflakes chilled her face and made her blink rapidly. She'd lost sight of Jez, and caught only a glimpse of Pelaru before another squall took him away again. All that was left in their wake were bodies, the dark shapes of dead men punched into the snow, their liquids seeping out of them.

The weather had closed in hard and suddenly, and she was unsure which way the battle was going. She was alone, and felt momentarily lost. Could even Jez and Pelaru turn the tide, or would the Awakeners come back in force again, with only her pistol to oppose them? Silo and Malvery were elsewhere; she had no idea what Harkins was up to. The Cap'n would surely have been back by now if he'd managed to get the Wrath in the sky. So what was she supposed to do now?

Then she heard engines, the gunship coming back, and that decided her. She wasn't going to stick at her post when everyone else had abandoned theirs. She'd find the others, or find her own way out of this mess.

Keeping low, she scampered out of the living room and into the ruined kitchen. Through the smashed windows she could hear the other Predator, still patrolling above the courtyard. She peered out, and then ducked back as she saw it sliding through the air towards her. It had come low, and was almost level with her on the first floor. The pilot was checking the houses, looking for targets.

Pressed against the wall, she flexed her hand on the hilt of her pistol. What she wouldn't give to get just *one* of those flying bastards off her back. Was it worth trying for a lucky shot? To empty her gun at the cockpit, see if she could get the pilot through the windglass?

Her breathing quickened. The thought of it excited her. Fright had made her reckless. Yes. Rot and damn, yes! Fire off all five rounds then run. She'd do it. She'd take down that gunship, and then maybe they'd have a real chance.

She listened to the engines, waiting for the right moment, when the gunship had passed by.

Not yet . . . not yet . . . NOW!

She popped up and thrust her pistol through the window. But the gunship hadn't gone past her as she thought. It was right in front of her, a monster's face of cannons and metal, looking in. Blindly she fired, squeezing the trigger again and again. Bullets panged and sparked off the gunship's nose. Somehow she hit the cockpit, putting a hole in the windglass. The pilot, shocked and surprised, flinched away from the bullet and pulled the gunship aside. It slewed in the air and retreated a few metres.

She hadn't hit the pilot. She should have run then, but the enormity of her mistake struck her and rooted her to the spot. There was no way she was going to make it out of the building. In a second, the pilot would recover and press down on his guns. He'd drill the house to rubble with those rotary cannons.

On the far side of the courtyard, she saw a movement. On the first floor of a half-demolished shell of a house, Colden Grudge stepped into view, his enormous autocannon slung low on his hip. He tipped up its barrel, aimed it at the gunship, and pressed the trigger.

The autocannon thumped three times. Ashua threw herself down. The gunship exploded.

A wave of heat and flame and choking smoke blew through the kitchen. Shrapnel spun through the air and embedded itself in the far wall. She heard the gunship's engines cough and shriek as the great mass of metal fell out of the sky. It crashed into the fountain at the centre of the courtyard, crushing itself up like a ball before detonating in a final blast that sent parts of it flying off as far as the bridge.

When the echoes had died, she pulled herself up and looked down into the courtyard. There was no sign of Grudge. Only the flaming wreck of the gunship was left, belching smoke into the snowy sky.

A great surge of exhilaration swept through her, lifting her. She felt suddenly immortal. Dirtied and bruised, she lifted her fist and laughed wildly.

'That's what you get when you mess with us!' she screamed hoarsely at the broken gunship. 'Yeah! That's what you get!'

And she hurried off down the stairs to find her companions, buoyed by a new belief that they might just live through this after all.

Where are they? Where is everyone?

Crake fled through the darkened mansion. Panes of wan light striped chilly and still rooms. He clattered and shambled, fighting with his pack. Wires tangled his legs. He tore them away, pulled off the damper sphere that dragged along behind him. He fumbled at his belt and tugged at the screamer and its battery, fighting to remove them without breaking stride. After a short struggle, they came loose, and he tossed them aside too. They were useless now, their charge used up.

He broke out into a corridor. The sonic flux emitter in his backpack jogged and clashed against the battery inside. The pinecone transmitters sticking out of the top wobbled and jerked. It was a makeshift design, not built to withstand violent shaking. It wouldn't hold together long.

But it wasn't that which brought him up short in the end. It was the recollection that he had dynamite in his pocket. Wasn't that supposed to be dangerous if you shook it around too much? Or was that only when it was old? He didn't know, but the thought was enough to check his panicked run. He came to a halt, gasping, leaning on his knees.

Calm down, Grayther. Calm down.

Spit and blood, he was frightened. The first time he'd met an Imperator was bad enough, but then it had been one Imperator against a half-dozen targets or more. This was three Imperators against three, and the sheer *force* of them was awful. He was in no doubt that his heart would have given out under the stress if he'd been subjected to much more of that. The Imperators wouldn't have even needed to enter the room to kill their opponents.

He'd nearly died. The reality of that thought wormed its way into him.

What about the others? Did they get away? Plome wasn't exactly in great shape: had he even survived that first assault? Where were they now?

And where were the Imperators?

From outside he heard the sound of gunfire over the wind. They were still fighting out there. Good. It was when the gunfire stopped that he'd really begin to worry. He wanted to put his earcuff on, to found out what was going on, to see if Samandra and his friends were alright. He wanted the comfort of other voices. But he didn't dare. Imperators were somewhere nearby; he couldn't afford the distraction.

A creeping sense of dread began to build up behind him. His finely-tuned senses rang a warning. He looked over his shoulder. Was it his imagination, or was the darkness thickening at the end of the corridor? Was it just his fevered mind that told him the walls were closing in, ever so slightly? Did he hear a soft, gasping breath, like the last exhalation of a dying man?

Fear clawed its way up his throat from his belly, and he had to move again.

He went slower this time. Now that he had a lid on his panic, stealth was needed rather than speed. He wished he could shuck off his pack entirely, but the sonic flux emitter was his most potent weapon, and he couldn't abandon it.

He needed to find the others, that was all. Most importantly, he needed to find Kyne. He couldn't go up against the Imperators on his own.

But the house was silent, and if his companions were out there, they were staying quiet.

He slipped into a dining room dominated by a long table. Another fire was burning here, casting welcome warmth and light into the monochrome nightmare that Crake had found himself in. Feeding the flames to make the mansion look occupied had kept them busy during their preparations. A pointless ruse, in the end. The Awakeners had them outmanoeuvred from the start.

There were three doors from the dining room: one at each end and another between them. Crake snuck through the room, reached the door in the middle and looked through it.

Beyond was a corridor with several rooms and a stairway leading off it. At the end was a large rectangular window, its pane frosted and its sill piled with snow.

Silhouetted in the drab light from outside was a tall figure wearing a cloak and hood. Crake thought for an instant that it was Kyne.

It wasn't.

The terror hit him again, but he was already running, sprinting as fast as he could towards other side of the dining room. His muscles seized and the strength fell out of them, but his momentum carried him forward, and somehow he stumbled through the doorway and into the small sitting room beyond.

To his relief, his strength came back. The fear was huge but bearable. And the more distance he put between himself and the Imperator, the more it diminished. He crossed the room, out into a corridor, turned a corner.

It's lost me, he thought. *They cast their power like a net, and I slipped out from under it.*

The Imperator didn't know where he was for the moment, but he'd been seen. His pursuer would come hunting.

He reached into the side pocket of his pack and pulled out the control panel for the sonic flux emitter. It was a thin metal board with several dials and a switch, attached by wires to his pack. Like most daemonic equipment, it ate up power, and even with Kyne's specialised batteries it wouldn't last more than a couple of minutes. But the transmitters had quite a broadcast range. Maybe he could blast it out, find the Imperators' frequency quickly. When they started to scream, he'd know he had it. It would serve as a warning shot across their bows. Drive them back, make them think twice.

He just needed to know if it would work. He needed to know if he had any way to fight them. It was fear more than tactics that made him hit that switch.

Nothing happened.

He toggled it on and off again frantically. There should have at least been a hum of power from the pack.

The wires.

Some connection had come loose during all that running about. Maybe the battery, maybe something else. It was a haphazard, slip-shod design, but they hadn't exactly had the time to make something perfect. And now it wasn't working.

The darkness gathered through the doorway. The cold press of dread gathered with it. He heard a footstep.

Oh no, he thought, and fled again.

He ran through corridors and rooms, he ran downstairs when stairs presented themselves, but the Imperator was relentless. Whenever he stopped for breath, the air began to thicken behind him again, a nameless, primal horror bunching and growing there. Then he was forced to move on.

The mansion was large, and in his fright he became lost in it. He heard banging from somewhere below him, and remembered the staff locked in the basement. The gunfire and explosions from the hamlet had panicked them, and they wanted out. The fools: if they knew what waited out here, they'd stay quiet.

An idea had grown in him, that he might abandon the others and flee, out into the snow where his friends and his lover fought the Awakeners. Jez was there, at least. If the Imperators followed him, she could—

Wait! His eyes went wide. Jez! She could save them! The half-Manes, the best weapons they had against the Imperators, were out there on the battlefield.

Trying to catch the Imperators was the last thing on his mind now. He just wanted to live.

He stopped, felt in his pocket for the earcuff. Quickly he drew it out, put it to his ear.

An Imperator stepped round the corner.

Crake yelled, staggered backwards, tripped on his heels. The ear-cuff fell from his hands and rolled onto the floor. He threw out his hand to balance himself. It found a door handle, which turned beneath his grip. The door swung open and he fell through just as he felt the icy grip of the Imperator's power seize him again.

He swung the door shut behind him as he staggered into the room. It was a pantry, large and well stocked with deep shelves full of canned goods and preserves. A small window, high up, gave a little light. Crake was still off-balance as he wheeled in. He turned and fell on his side; there was a loud crash as the pack on his back took another heavy knock.

Panic. Blind panic. No way out. A closed room. No way out anywhere.

He scrambled backwards towards the far wall, reaching for his gun as he went, digging in his pockets, looking for anything that would prevent the awful thing outside from coming in. His searching hand closed on a hard waxy cylinder as his pack bumped up against the shelves, allowing no further retreat.

He pulled out a stick of dynamite from his pocket.

A desperate cry escaped his lips. Spittle flecked his beard. He reached into another pocket and tugged out a box of matches, which scattered as they came. He picked one up and struck it against the stone floor.

All he saw was a weapon. He was made automatic by terror, stripped down to survival instinct alone. The match flared, driving back the dark for an instant; he touched it to the fuse; then he flung the dynamite away from him with a futile blind motion, as a child might cast a stone at a man three times his size. The dynamite hit the door, bounced and rolled into the corner of the pantry, beneath the shelves, its fuse fizzing.

The fact that Crake was alone in a room with a lighted stick of dynamite was drowned out by the landslide of horror that came down on him. His throat tightened. He couldn't breathe. His heart wrenched against its moorings.

The handle turned, and slowly the door opened, and Crake knew that when he laid eyes on the creature that had come to claim him, he'd die on the spot. Yet when the Imperator stepped through, he realised he was wrong, that there was another level to terror previously unimagined. The Imperator turned his atrocious gaze upon Crake and pinned him there, and Crake mewled and whimpered and would have screamed if he could, but there was no breath left in his body. His heart was going like a machine gun, and it burned in his chest like he'd swallowed hot coals.

Then it was as if someone had clapped two hands over his ears, hard. As if he was a boy on a beach, hit by a wave too big to withstand, brought under where the world was a dull roar, to be dashed on the stones. His legs were seized and he flipped round so that he was thrown face-first into the shelves. The air was full of projectiles; he was battered from above by falling jars and cans. He covered his head as best he could, too shocked to make sense of what was happening.

Peace returned, except for the clink and clatter of falling glass and rolling cans.

He let out a breath. His heart was still pounding fit to burst. He listened to it slow, his back to the room. Every part of him was pummelled. His pulse and breath seemed amplified, but all external sounds were dull, as if his ears were clogged with cotton wool.

With numb fingers, he undid the belts that held his backpack to his body. He slipped his arm out and sat up and looked.

The room had been destroyed. Shelves had collapsed, shedding their contents. Glass was everywhere. A black and broken heap of leather and flesh lay on the floor by the door. There was little blood. But the monster was still, and the fear had gone.

Gritting his teeth in advance of the pain, Crake got to his feet. He could still do that, then. He looked at himself. He was bruised and cut everywhere, but with effort he could move everything. Dry-mouthed and battered, but alive.

'I killed you,' he croaked at the dead Imperator. He was almost as surprised by that as the Imperator must have been. 'I killed you.'

A defiant bravery crept over him, and any notion of escape was pushed aside. He still had breath in his body, and the enemy was proven fallible. He wouldn't call on the half-Manes. He didn't need them.

One down, he thought. *Two to go.*

Thirty-One

Bess, Unleashed – Frozen Up – Line of Sight –
The Runt of the Litter – A Slaughter

rey scrambled down a snow-laden bank, bullets clipping the trees behind him. The slope was steeper than it looked beneath the drifts; his heels skidded and he fell on his arse, slithering the rest of the way. He rolled onto his belly as he went, and ended up with his pistol out, aiming back up the slope.

A figure appeared in the flurrying murk. He was wearing a thick coat and furred hood, and was carrying a rifle. Frey shot him before he had a chance to use it.

He heard footsteps rasping in the snow. Two men came running round the side of the bank, having taken a shallower way down. One of them shouted and pointed at him. Frey rose up on his elbow and aimed at them through the stark black trees, but before he touched the trigger, two shotguns fired simultaneously and the men flailed and went down.

Samandra came jogging through the trees. She halted before him and spun her twin lever-action weapons, chambering new shells with a quick jerk of her wrists. Then she holstered them and offered a hand to Frey.

'Think that's the last of 'em,' she said, as she pulled him from the drift.

'Persistent sons of bitches, weren't they?'

'Reckon they got orders saying nobody leaves alive.'

'Well, I bloody am,' said Frey. 'Come on, can't be far now. Swear I've got frostbite.' He rubbed his hands together. They were numb and aching, but he couldn't aim worth shit wearing his gloves, so he was forced to endure it.

Samandra was listening to the distant gunfire. 'Strikes me my talents might be more use back there with them,' she said.

'By the time you get back there, there won't be anything left. We gotta do something about their air superiority, and I need you on the autocannon.'

She didn't argue the point any further. They hurried onward. Both were tired: ploughing through the snow was hard work. To their right the land rose, busy with the dark bristles of a hibernating forest. To their left there were no trees, just the howling emptiness of the gorge. Frey navigated by that.

As they went, he took his earcuff from his pocket and attached it with some difficulty. The snap of gunfire sounded in his ear, closer now, coming through Malvery's earcuff.

'Doc! How we doing?'

'Ain't good, Cap'n,' came the reply. 'Jez's gone berserk and the whispermonger's gone after her. We took down one gunship and the other's pulled back a bit, but there's a whole shitload of Awakeners crawlin' up our arses and we only got five guns.'

Five guns. He did a quick mental count. Ashua, Silo, Malvery, Harkins, Grudge. They were all still fighting, he realised with relief.

'Help's on the way,' he said. 'Keep your heads down. You heard from Crake?'

'You'd know if you ever put your bloody earcuff in,' said Malvery. 'No, not a peep.'

Frey couldn't think of anything else to say, so he said 'Good luck, mate.'

'Yeah, you too.'

The boom of Malvery's shotgun made him wince. He pulled out the earcuff and pocketed it again. Samandra was watching him, her eyes keen beneath the snow-specked fur lining of her hood.

'No news is good news, right?' he said to her.

Samandra said nothing.

They climbed another bank, and on the far side they found a clearing on the edge of the chasm, where the trees drew back and there was a stony hollow in the land. Looming out of the snow was the *Ketty Jay*, her blocky form solid and reassuring in the world of ghostly white.

Some of the tension went out of Frey as he saw her. A small part of him had been worrying that the Awakeners might have found her and surrounded her, as they had the Wrath on the landing pad.

There was a keypad on one of the *Ketty Jay*'s rear landing struts. Frey poked at the keys with trembling fingers. There was a thump inside the craft, and the squeaking of hydraulics as the ramp opened.

It had barely touched the ground before Bess came barrelling out of the darkened interior. She came to a halt at the bottom of the ramp, swinging her body left and right, looking for enemies. She'd been cooped up too long, and the sound of gunfire had made her agitated.

'That way,' said Frey, pointing back towards the hamlet. 'Anyone that isn't us, kick 'em all the way to the Wrack.'

Bess roared and thundered off into the trees.

'That's some precision strategy you got there,' Samandra commented as they headed up the ramp.

Frey turned on the lights in the hold and closed the ramp behind them. 'Every toolkit needs a hammer.'

They went quickly through the cargo hold, their breath steaming the air, and made their way up the stairs to the main passageway. Frey indicated the ladder leading up to the gunnery cupola as he went by.

'Up there,' he told her, already halfway to the cockpit.

Samandra slowed and looked up. 'I ain't got a clue how to work an autocannon,' she said.

'Just point it and pull the trigger,' Frey called over his shoulder. He jumped in the pilot seat and began flicking switches, beginning with the heaters.

'Why are there so many rum bottles up here?' Samandra's voice drifted through the cockpit door. He ignored her, tapped in the ignition code and hit the engines.

Nothing happened.

He tried again. This time the engines gave an asthmatic wheeze. Frey swore and started pumping the choke.

'Can't help noticing a distinct lack of any damn thing happenin', Frey,' Samandra shouted down. 'Why ain't we takin' off?'

'She's frozen up!' he yelled back. 'Gotta let the internals heat through, get the anti-freeze going.' He cursed himself. He should have had Silo out here keeping her warm. He never thought they'd need a quick launch.

'How long's *that* gonna take? Our guys ain't exactly got a surplus of time.'

314

'Not long!' he called back confidently. Then, under his breath: 'I hope.'

Crake went quietly through the mansion, listening as best he could through the ringing in his ears. There was an Imperator somewhere nearby. He felt it.

His hands were ready on the control panel of the sonic flux emitter. He'd fixed the broken connections, and now he was confident it would work as it should. Reasonably confident, anyway. There was no way of telling how much damage the device had suffered by being bashed about. No way except turning it on, anyway. And he wouldn't do that yet.

Before, he'd been scared. He hadn't been thinking straight. Turning on the device would likely have drawn the Imperators to him; he was lucky it hadn't worked. But now he'd killed one of his opponents, and the fight was back in him.

He'd reclaimed his earcuff from where it had fallen, but he hadn't put it in. He didn't need help from the crew. He could do this. He could take down the Imperators.

Every muscle was stiff, every movement painful. The skin of his face felt blasted and scoured. A dozen tiny cuts stretched and opened beneath the slashes in his clothes. He bore it all with a stoicism he'd never imagined he possessed.

He crept up to a doorway and looked through. The room beyond was lit by a fire in the grate. A harpsichord stood askew, a settee out of place, a card table on its side. This was the parlour where the Imperators had first attacked them. He'd come back to find his companions.

Nothing moved, but for the lunge and swing of the firelight. He crept into the room, walking softly. From here, he could see past the harpsichord. Behind it, in the corner, a dark lump lay.

A faint nausea trickled into his stomach. *Plome. Oh, no, Plome. I didn't want to drag you into this.*

But he'd done it anyway. He'd known the risks of asking his friend to be bait for the Imperators and he'd still gone ahead. Because the Awakeners had to be stopped.

He checked the room again and crept closer, crossing in front of the fire. Once the light was behind him, he could see a little better. He frowned. The lump was too small for Plome, and twisted in a strange way. Another step nearer, and he saw. A rug. A bunched-up rug, that had skidded into the corner, sent there by a running foot.

Plome was nowhere to be seen.

He let out a slow breath of relief. A quick check round the room found no sign of Kyne, either. They hadn't been killed here. They'd escaped, as he had.

That's good. That's great. Now all I need to do is find them.

He slipped out of the parlour and into a corridor. The fight was still in full swing outside. Once in a while, faint screams came to him on the skirling wind. Still he felt the crawling sense of a daemonic presence, somewhere in the dark, somewhere close.

He looked round a corner. A long corridor stretched away from him, with windows all along one side, looking out across the chasm at the white valley slopes. He was on the far side of the mansion from the hamlet, and out there was nothing. Bleak light struggled in, casting the shadow of the panes onto the polished floor.

Where are you? he thought, as he crept onward. His senses were on edge now, suspicion gnawing at him. The Imperator was close. Should he go back instead? But what if it was sneaking up behind him?

He passed an open doorway, and looked inside. Nothing. He walked on, and a moment later was seized from behind.

A hand clamped around his mouth. He was pulled backwards into the doorway, tottering on his heels. He tried to struggle, but suddenly he was grabbed and turned, and found himself face to face with *an Imperator.*

Morben Kyne, his green eyes shining beneath his hood, one finger held up to his mouth-grille in an urgent demand for silence. Crake's cry of alarm died in his throat. Slowly, Kyne pointed off through the wall, in the direction Crake had come from.

There's one of them following me.

Kyne had turned his head away from Crake, and was staring at the blank wall. Looking *through* it.

He can see them. He really can. Spit and blood, what knowledge he must have, what resources! A daemonist sanctioned by the Archduke! The things I could do, if I didn't have to hide away like a criminal. The things I could learn from him!

Kyne drew his large-bore pistol and stepped out into the corridor. Crake peered round the edge of the doorway. He could sense the presence of the approaching Imperator, the dread of it. Kyne aimed down the corridor, his arm out straight.

'Kyne!' Crake whispered. 'What are you doing? They'll bring down the terror on us before you get line of sight.'

Kyne didn't appear to have heard him. He was impassive, still as a statue. The dark at the end of the corridor began to curl and clot. Crake watched helplessly, half in hope and half in fear, because if the Imperator laid eyes on them it would all be over.

The bullet ignited as it left the chamber. A streak of blue flame shot down the corridor in an arc, slanting left towards the windows until, impossibly, it curved in its flight, swung the other way, *bent round the corner*. There was a dull explosion. Body parts and chunks of smoking flesh wheeled through the air, thumped onto the floor, smashed a window.

Kyne turned his head towards Crake, regarding him coldly with those mechanical eyes. 'I don't need line of sight,' he said.

Crake's face was slack with amazement. Thralled bullets. A weapon that sought out daemons. He'd never imagined such a thing. To make a bullet move like that! It was laughing in the face of physics!

Just around the corner, they found the rest of the Imperator. It wasn't much more than a pair of legs and a pelvis now. The corridor stank of burning meat.

Kyne looked down at the body. 'They caught me by surprise the first time,' he said. 'It won't happen again.' Then he raised his head and turned his masked face to Crake. 'Let's find Plome. We need to take the last one alive.'

Crake grinned.

In the whiteness she moved between them. She sensed them before they saw her. She anticipated the gunshots and was gone before the bullets arrived. She flickered in the whirling snow, a trick of the eye.

But when she reached them, oh, then she was all too real. Then they felt her, a hurricane of inhuman strength and flashing fangs. She bit and tore and took them apart, leaving them dismembered in the snow, lying in a blast-pattern of their own insides.

Jez's hair had come loose and it whipped around her face in wet

317

lashes. Her eyes were wild, her arms bloodied to the elbows, her teeth and chin and cheeks sodden with gore.

The howling of the Manes was loud in her head, rejoicing in her, celebrating her. The song of her brothers and sisters throbbed through her, beating in her ears as her heart once had.

This was freedom. To be, and nothing more.

'Jez?'

He called for her in a human voice. This strange one, this denier. He had the gift but he wouldn't open the box. He kept it closed and hidden away, and pretended it wasn't there. But look at him, coming through the snow! How fast he moved, how easily he evaded the enemy as he tracked her by the trail of dead. He was more than human now, and he could be more still; but he was afraid. Afraid to be what he was.

She loved him. She couldn't help but love her own. But she pitied him too, like the runt of the litter.

'Jez! Come back! You can't fight them all!'

But she didn't want to come back. There were more men on the way, a dozen of them, a concerted force sent against her. These were organised and determined men, not panicked prey. They found their courage in unity.

She recognised the danger, but it did nothing to deter her. She was drunk with slaughter, giddy with abandon. She was Mane, and only that. She'd chosen them and she embraced them entirely.

A dozen? She could take on twice that.

Behind her, rumbling and steaming in the snow, was the hamlet's generator. It stood some way apart from the other buildings, a knot of pipes and levers and tanks the size of a small barn. With that at her back, they couldn't get around her, and they'd be forced to watch their aim or risk blowing themselves up. Hesitation and uncertainty would undo them. She'd go among them like a wolf among sheep, and they'd scatter like their fellows.

'Jez!'

It was Pelaru, running out of the whipping snow. She ignored him, her eyes on the approaching men. They hadn't seen her yet; their sight was not as keen as hers. They were still searching.

He grabbed her arm and she turned her head sharply, teeth bared.

He didn't let her go. His fine clothes were sodden, all his poise and elegance gone, but still she softened at the sight of him.

'Please,' he said. 'There are too many. Your friends need you.'

She was unmoved. The words swept past her without meaning. 'Fight with me,' she said.

'They'll be overrun! We must help defend the hamlet until your captain can—'

Fight with me! This time she used her mind rather than her mouth, thrusting the thought at him like a sword held out for the taking.

But he didn't take it. He heard, and he recoiled. Mane speech horrified him. He let her go and stepped away, shocked.

She turned from him in disgust. Someone shouted nearby. They'd seen her. It was time.

Bullets flew as she sprang towards them. Some went wild, ringing dangerously off the pipes that surrounded the generator. A voice rose over the wind, barking orders, trying to minimise panic fire. A leader. She went for him first.

She dodged and flickered as she came, zigzagging out of the snow. Despite their discipline, fear seized them: fear of the daemon, fear of the Mane. She darted between them and pounced on their leader. He raised a pistol. Too slow. She had his throat out in an instant, and was gone before he'd even fallen.

'The sarge! She got the sarge!'

Their formation fell apart as she tore at them from the inside. They stumbled and swore and spun around, trying to catch sight of her. They tried to shoot her but ended up shooting each other instead. She howled with glee as she swept from prey to prey, leaving corpses in her wake, turning the snow red.

Was this the best they had?

And here came another one, waddling through the snow, made ungainly by his heavy backpack. And what was that in his hand?

Jez had fought in many battles, but never in a war. She knew guns, rifles, shotguns and hidden blades, but she'd never seen a flame-thrower before. By the time she realised the threat, it was too late. Even for her.

A jet of fire spewed from the nozzle of the flamethrower and into the melee, sweeping across the group. Scared out of his wits, the operator made no distinction between friend and foe. Jez could have evaded a bullet, but this cloud of burning death was beyond her. She leaped, but the fire caught her in mid-air, and suddenly the world turned to pain.

She crashed into the snow, shrieking. Her legs and torso were aflame. Her clothes were on fire, her skin was on fire. It was agony beyond endurance. She was incoherent with it, all thought lost in the blaze.

Men screamed nearby, flailing torches in the snow, trailing black smoke and the reek of cooking flesh. She thrashed wildly among them. Someone was firing a gun, shooting at anyone and anything.

The flamethrower operator spotted her, pointed the nozzle at her again. She saw him, and instinct made her turn away and cover herself. He squeezed the trigger and hit her full on.

Fire consumed her, roaring in her ears. Her hair burned. Her back blackened and bubbled. She tried to scream but drew scorching air into her lungs instead. The pain was everywhere, inside and out, an infinity of suffering, incomprehensible in scope.

Her body gave up control. She fell to her knees and tipped into the snow, which hissed and steamed as she hit it.

The jet of flame turned away from her, and there was Pelaru, beloved Pelaru, in his true form at last. He seized the flamethrower operator's head and tore it from his body. And as her sight died she saw him, the light within, the symphony of colours that he was. Even through the pain, her heart hurt with the beauty of it.

The headless man toppled, his finger still pressed on the trigger. The jet of fire swung through the air and licked across the skin of the generator, and the fuel tanks that powered it.

Pelaru's eyes met hers, and in that moment she knew him totally.

Then the fuel tanks exploded, and there was no more.

Thirty-Two

Thirty Seconds – Caged –
Where Few Have Dared to Tread – The Collar

C rake held his breath in the gloom of the darkened mansion. A
bead of sweat inched its icy way across his scalp.

A floorboard creaked.

'Now!'

Kyne's gloved hand slapped down on a button on the metal sphere
he was holding. Plome's palm came down on a sphere of his own. A
screamer and a damper, activated together. The silence was shattered
by a high-pitched screech and a dull throb, a non-noise that sucked
the echoes from the air.

In the next room, the Imperator let out a cry, a daemonic howl fit to
freeze bones. Crake hurried in, lumbering beneath the weight of his
back. The others were close on his heels. Crashing among the
furniture, a black-clad figure flailed wildly in the half-light.

'Thirty seconds!' Plome squeaked.

Crake swallowed down his fear and applied himself to the dials on
the portable control panel he held. Thirty seconds. Thirty seconds till
the batteries gave out, eaten up by the voracious devices that kept the
Imperator disorientated and choked off its power. Thirty seconds to
nail its frequencies with the sonic flux emitter.

Plome's eyes were wide, shining with terror behind his pince-nez.
He held up the damper, knuckles white, a pocket watch in his free
hand. Kyne had found him hiding in a cupboard. He was fortunate
the Imperator hadn't found him first.

How long had passed? How long?

The Imperator staggered to his feet. Kyne kicked his knee, knocking
him back down. He had his gun drawn and aimed, but if the devices
gave out, he might not get the chance to use it. The Imperator's

influence could crush a man instantly, pull all the strength from him, drive him to the floor.

Concentrate!

Crake turned the dials as slowly as he dared. He didn't need haste here, he needed precision. As he altered the frequency he kept half an eye on the shadowy figure in the centre of the room, watching for a reaction.

'Twenty!'

Had it been ten seconds already? Time was running too fast. The Imperator tried to stand and Kyne knocked him down again. He was tangled in its cloak and his hood had come off. His head was covered in black fabric, hiding the white maggot-like skin beneath. Crake stood back, turning the dials. Nothing.

'Ten!' Plome cried.

'Hurry it up, Crake!' Kyne warned.

Crake twisted too fast, swallowed, went back to his previous position and resumed scanning from there.

'Five! Four! Three!'

'Plome!' Kyne cried.

Plome fumbled at his belt and hit the screamer there. Kyne dropped the sphere he was holding and hit his damper. 'Thirty!' Plome cried again.

Each of them had been carrying a screamer and a damper. Crake had used his earlier. These were the last of them. When the batteries went dead, there would be nothing between them and the Imperator. They would die or Kyne would fire his weapon, but either way their struggle would have been meaningless.

The Imperator shrieked as if struck, spun away, clattered into a table which collapsed under him. Crake's eyes widened. He tuned his dials, watching to see which made the subject writhe. The Imperator's back arched.

Crake's hand jerked away from the dial. He hadn't realised how much it would seem like torture. Tormenting a daemon was so much easier when they weren't wearing a human form.

'Twenty!' Plome called.

Crake's misgivings were forgotten. He had the daemon speared through one of its primary frequencies; now he had to anchor it. He tuned more dials.

'Ten!'

The Imperator began to squeal and buck. Now he couldn't even get to his feet; he rolled and spasmed as if suffering some awful *grand mal* seizure.

'I've got it!' Crake said. 'I think I've got it! Go! Go!'

They pulled off the spheres they were carrying and tossed them aside. From their packs, each drew a metal cylinder with a pinecone-like set of rods on the end. The cylinders were connected by cables to the harmonic arc generators in their packs.

'Kyne! Two-twenty-four hundred in the mid-bass range!' Crake called, reading off his dial. 'Plome! Eight-eighty in the subsonic!'

With their free hands, they set the dials at their belts. Crake concentrated on the Imperator. He lashed and twisted like a landed fish, slithering through the darkened room. Without Kyne to keep watch, he was wary, as if he might lunge at any moment. But the sonic flux emitter was working, it was working the way it was *supposed* to work, and gradually Crake's fear was replaced by triumph. He was looking at the proof of his theory right here!

The first time he'd tried the harmonic arc generators, on the Iron Jackal, he'd been in possession of the daemon's frequencies. He'd been forearmed. Not this time. And yet he had the Imperator on a hook nonetheless. He was bruised and battered and he'd come way too close to death, but he *had* him!

'Ready!' Kyne said.

'Ready!' Plome agreed.

They'd moved round to either side of the prone Imperator. They held out their cylinders towards it.

'On my mark . . .' said Crake. 'Now!'

He hit the switch and deactivated the sonic flux emitter just as the others activated their own devices. The Imperator jumped to its feet and threw himself at Crake. He flinched away – he couldn't help it – but the Imperator never reached him. He froze before he got there, trapped in an invisible cage of frequencies.

Crake took a moment for a few gasping breaths. The Imperator raged against its confinement, but it couldn't break free. Plome and Kyne struggled to hold it. 'Together,' Crake reminded them. 'Move together. One on each side to maintain the cage. Go.'

He stepped out of the way. Kyne and Plome shuffled through the doorway, Kyne backing off and Plome following. As they moved, the cage between them moved too, and the Imperator was forced that way.

Crake went after them, his hand ready on the switch of the control panel in his hand. He wasn't sure how much juice his pack had left in it, but he'd need it if the Imperator broke out. He could see the effort it took Plome and Kyne to keep it where it was. Even the Iron Jackal hadn't fought that hard.

Then it struck him. Something he hadn't considered in his theory. The Iron Jackal was a pure daemon. It couldn't pass through the barrier that the harmonic arc generator set up. But an Imperator was a daemon sheathed in physical form. The sonics had no effect on the physical body, just the daemon inside.

He began to worry. Could the Imperator break through the barrier by muscle and momentum?

'How much time do we have?' Plome called, as they dragged it through darkened rooms, keeping a steady distance between them.

'Don't concern yourself with that,' said Kyne. 'The batteries will hold. Keep focused.'

'I can't *help* concerning myself!' Plome protested.

The Imperator bucked against his cage, jerking Plome's arm. Plome swallowed and forced it back, his pudgy hand trembling.

Crake went ahead into the audience chamber where they'd set their trap. It seemed like he'd aged half a lifetime since they were here last.

'Watch you don't trip on the cable across the doorway,' Crake warned them as he hurried over to a trolley rack of resonators. He crouched down in front of it, aching from the weight of his pack and the multiple cuts and bruises he'd sustained.

Kyne backed into the room. The Imperator was dragged through with him, stiff-legged and stumbling. Plome came last, pate glistening.

Crake hit the switch to activate the outer defences. A row of resonator masts against the wall hummed into life, sealing the room.

The Imperator sensed what Crake had done, saw the summoning circle in the middle of the room, and finally understood what they had in store. He redoubled his efforts to break away, struggling wildly. The force of it caused Plome to trip. He sidestepped and just about retained his balance, but his hand wavered: the harmonic arc cylinders were no longer aligned. For a moment the Imperator could move again. He lunged, trying to escape, but Kyne calmly shifted to his left and the Imperator froze again with a howl of frustration.

'Let's get this done,' said Kyne, his artificial green eyes burning into Plome's. Plome swallowed and nodded. Kyne backed into the summoning circle, stepping through the double row of rods and spheres. Plome stepped forward. The Imperator went with them, fighting every inch of the way.

Come on, come on! Crake thought to himself, his hand poised over another switch. *Hurry up!*

Kyne stepped out of the circle and tried pulling the Imperator in. Plome pushed from behind. The Imperator wavered on the threshold, resisting for all he was worth. Plome let out a cry of effort and exasperation. And then Kyne and Plome lurched, the Imperator stumbled forward, Crake hit the switch, and it was done.

Crake slumped to the floor, plonking himself on his arse. The Imperator howled and thrashed, but he was contained. Once a daemon was in the circle there was little chance of getting out of it, and there were enough batteries and backups here to keep him trapped for half an hour or more.

Exhaustion swept over him. He met Plome's eyes across the room. The politician looked dazed. Then the two of them began to laugh, little chuckles of disbelief.

They'd caught him. They'd actually caught an Imperator.

Plome walked unsteadily over to Crake and offered his hand. Crake let himself be pulled to his feet. Plome blew out his breath, gave Crake a nervous smile, and patted him on the arm.

'Well,' he said. 'That was hairy.'

'Welcome to the world of field daemonism, my friend,' said Crake, who was feeling expansive and elated. 'You've just gone where few have dared to tread.'

Plome mopped his brow and adjusted his pince-nez. 'Shouldn't say I'll be in a hurry to tread there again,' he said. Then his eyes glittered. 'But we got one, didn't we? We showed those bastards what real daemonists can do!'

'They'll write about us for years to come, just you see if they don't,' Crake replied.

Plome coughed. 'Yes, well. *After* daemonism is declared legal, I hope. I have my career to think of until then. Not to mention my neck.'

'We're not done yet,' said Kyne gravely, from the other side of the room. 'Crake, take the readings.'

His tone brought Crake down to earth again. He glanced at the Imperator, trapped in the circle, and was reminded what a dangerous creature they'd caught. He'd been overconfident in the past, and it had cost himself and others dear. Kyne was right: they were not done yet.

Plome helped him get his pack off his back, then shooed him away when Crake offered to return the favour. 'I can take care of myself. It's down to you two now. Go on.'

Crake went over to the oscillator, rolling his shoulders and stretching his back. It was a pleasurable agony. His muscles had stiffened and he hurt in two dozen places, and he still couldn't hear properly. A great tiredness had settled on him. After this, he planned to sleep for a week.

After this, he thought. He could finally believe there *would* be an afterwards. A time where he might find himself in Samandra's arms again.

The sound of gunfire outside filtered in through the grey windows and the whistling in his ears. Best not to think about that yet. There was still the matter of the battle outside. And even if he survived, Samandra might not.

No. She'll win through. She's like a force of nature. Nothing can stop her.

He told himself that, but the thought of her out there made his stomach knot, and he put it from his mind as best he could.

He knelt down gingerly in front of the oscillator and recorded the Imperator's primary resonances. Halfway through scribbling them down, he stopped as the enormity of the information in his hand hit him. This was the key to defeating the Imperators. To the population at large they were beings of supernatural power, divine enforcers like the will of the old gods made flesh. But the daemonists would show them otherwise.

He finished jotting down the frequencies and put them in his pocket. 'Got them,' he called over his shoulder. It seemed a weak line for an occasion so momentous.

Kyne, meanwhile, had finished his preparations. The Imperator was facing Plome and staring at him with an unwavering gaze, as if calculating the amount of pain he'd visit upon the politician when he got out of there. Kyne walked up behind the Imperator, reached into the summoning circle, and in one quick movement he seized the Imperator's wrist and snapped a manacle on it. The Imperator, surprised, tried to turn, but Kyne grabbed the other arm, twisted it behind his back, and secured the other wrist.

Crake was amazed that Kyne dared to reach into a summoning circle that way. Even though the daemon's power was nullified by the walls of the summoning circle, it seemed a reckless thing to do.

But Kyne wasn't finished. He grabbed a fold of the Imperator's mask in his fist. With one quick jerk he pulled it free, and the face of the Imperator was revealed.

Crake had seen one before, but it did little to prepare him. There was something instinctively repellent about them. Their cadaverous, pinched features and white skin made them corpselike. Their eyes had yellow irises like a bird of prey. Rancid gums and jagged teeth guarded a black lipless cave of a mouth. No tongue moved within.

'Spit and blood,' Plome gasped, and turned away.

This was where Kyne's expertise came to the fore. Crake had devised the method to catch the Imperator, but there was still one question remaining: how did you interrogate a creature who couldn't speak? Imperators had no tongues; they'd seen that in the past. Perhaps the Awakeners cut them out to preserve their secrets, or perhaps to keep them servile: it wouldn't do to give daemons a voice. Although, judging by what Crake had seen of the Lord High Cryptographer, it appeared they'd gained one anyway.

Kyne provided the answer to the question. A collar that made men speak the truth. It was something like Crake's golden tooth, but more powerful and focused. Kyne had used it in interrogations before; now he'd adapted it, thralling in a daemon that could read the vibrations of vocal cords and make them understandable. Once more, Crake was filled with admiration at the Century Knight's skill with daemonism. But then he remembered that his own rough artistry had done what even Kyne could not, and he felt a swell of pride.

'Now,' said Kyne. 'Let's see what he has to say for himself.'

Kyne picked up the collar, a simple loop of metal with a hinge and a clasp, and held it open as he approached the circle. The Imperator snapped his teeth, struggling against the manacles. Unmasked, trapped, he'd lost some of his dark grandeur. Kyne waited for the right moment, then with one assured movement he darted forward and snapped the collar shut around the Imperator's scrawny throat.

The Imperator immediately went rigid. Kyne stepped back and crossed his arms over his armoured chest. His eyes glowed piercingly beneath his hood.

'The Awakeners intend to launch an attack on the Coalition in the near future,' he said. 'You will tell me when and where. You will tell me the size and nature of their forces. You will tell me everything you know about it.'

The Imperator opened his mouth, gaped soundlessly, and shut it again.

'*You will speak*,' Kyne said, and suddenly the gloom felt heavier, and Kyne seemed to grow, to become menacing and dreadful. Crake almost spoke himself, such was the force of the command. He felt a powerful need to do as he was told.

His voice, Crake thought, as the words skittered away into silence and the harmonic echoes died. *He's thralled the mouthpiece of his mask. Samandra was right: he's crawling with daemons!*

The Imperator trembled with the effort of resistance. '*Speak!*' Kyne said again.

The Imperator shuddered. A line of red trickled from the corner of his mouth, shocking against the dead white skin of his face.

'*Speak!*' Kyne commanded.

The Imperator began to twitch and spasm. His mouth moved without sound. Drops of blood ran from his rotted nose.

'What's happening to it?' Plome cried.

'It's the same thing that happened to Condred,' said Crake. He should have anticipated this. 'The daemon's trying to destroy its host.'

'*Speak!*' thundered Kyne, and he loomed so large in Crake's mind that Crake took a step back in fear.

'*Thessssk . . .*' The words wheezed out of the Imperator like a slow breath through a harmonica, dragged from his lungs. '*Attack Thesssk . . . whole . . . fleet . . .*'

Thesk, the capital. They were planning an attack on the capital, the seat of the Archduke's power.

'*When?*' demanded Kyne.

The Imperator coughed up a gout of dark blood. It spattered Kyne's chest and masked face, and drooled down the Imperator's chin. Kyne didn't flinch. The Imperator was wavering on his feet, but the power of the collar and the summoning circle kept him upright.

'*When?*' Kyne said again.

'*Tomorrow . . .*' the Imperator said. '*TomoooooaaaccCKKK . . .*'

The Imperator's final word dried up into a rattling choke. Another flood of red spilled over his lips, his eyes rolled back, and he fell to his knees and tipped sideways, out of the circle, knocking aside rods and spheres as he fell. An unearthly screech sounded in their heads as his body passed through the protective flux, the last howl of the daemon as it was torn apart by the sonics. Then the Imperator hit the floor, lifeless and still.

Crake stared at the corpse, his chest heaving from the tension of the last few moments. Plome had his hand over his mouth. Kyne turned his head slowly towards them, green eyes like lamps in the dark. Outside, the sound of rifles cut through the silence.

Tomorrow. The Awakeners were going to attack the capital with all their strength, carrying an Azryx device capable of destroying the entire Coalition fleet. And they only had until tomorrow to stop it.

Thirty-Three

Holding the Line – Hand to Hand –
A Last Stand – P-12s

Silo backed off through the ruined room, Malvery at his side, both with shotguns held ready. All around them was the sound of movement: feet scraped, glass tinkled. An Awakener in a thick brown coat came lumbering through a doorway, carrying a rifle. Malvery fired, and he spun away in a cloud of blood and fabric.

Debris crunched underfoot, threatening to turn their ankles as they retreated. A section of the ceiling had caved in and boards hung down. To their left were jagged window frames that had once held glass. They were on the ground floor, and all Silo could see through the windows was the slope leading up to the meadows. That, and the man climbing in.

The Awakener was caught halfway in and halfway out. He'd got himself snagged on something and was frantically trying to pull his arm free. He looked up as Silo turned the barrel of his weapon on him, and Silo saw that he had wild black hair, and young terrified eyes. Then hair and eyes alike disappeared in the roar of Silo's shotgun.

'Swarmin' all over us down here!' Malvery said, still backing away.

Silo went to the doorway at the other side of the room and looked through. At the end of a short passageway, a door to the courtyard stood open, snow piling up against it. Malvery was right. They would have to abandon the buildings on the south side of the hamlet, facing the meadows where the lander had come down. Jez and Pelaru were nowhere to be found, Ashua had abandoned her post, and he'd sent Harkins to watch the trees to the north. They probably couldn't have held the south side anyway, not against this number.

'Awakeners keen on havin' us dead, that's for damn sure,' he said.

'Must've really got 'em worried,' Malvery replied, with a grim smile.

'Come on. Back to the others. We gonna hold that house, at least.'

They stopped for a moment in the doorway to the courtyard, to check that the coast was clear. The hamlet had been reduced to a warzone. The buildings were bullet-gnawed, roofs slumped and windows smashed. Snow had invaded them eagerly, and now gathered in cheerless living rooms and garages. The fountain in the centre of the courtyard had collapsed amid a tangle of metal that seeped black smoke: the remains of the gunship Grudge had taken down.

The wind picked up again, blowing a stinging flurry. Silo narrowed his eyes and ran for it. It was as good a time as any.

Somewhere to their left, past the burning wreckage of the gunship, was the bridge, the chasm, and the mansion beyond. All of that was lost to sight in the blizzard. To their right was a gap between the buildings where the road led away to the landing pad. The Awakeners had taken the pad and were pushing down the road, but they hadn't dared to enter the courtyard while the defenders held both sides of the hamlet.

Silo could hear the dull roar of engines nearby, an insidious reminder that another gunship still lurked out there. Grudge had made the pilot wary, and his autocannon was another reason the foot soldiers wouldn't enter the courtyard. He was hidden on the first floor of one of the buildings on the north side, covering the area from an elevated position. Silo approved of his tactics. The threat he posed kept the enemy off their backs more effectively than a dozen shotguns.

Somebody fired at them from the direction of the road, but the bullets were past and gone before they heard the shots, and they ignored them. They ran through the doorway of a stout stone house which had weathered the assault better than its neighbours. Inside was a short gloomy corridor with a doorway off to the left and narrow stairs heading up.

Malvery ran on while Silo paused and looked back, searching for signs of the gunship. Over the buildings on the south side of the courtyard, black smoke was billowing. The generator's fuel tanks had gone up. Something to do with Jez? Perhaps. He hoped she was keeping them busy out there.

He assessed his options, and found them meagre. It was only a matter of time before the enemy took up positions in the houses across the courtyard and started shooting at them. One of the houses had caught fire, either because of the explosion or because a burning log had spilled from its grate in the chaos. If the fire spread fast, it would make a more effective barrier of those houses than armed defenders ever could. But Silo didn't think they'd be around long enough for that to happen. Grudge could only hold the Awakeners back for so long, and by the sounds of the gunfire in the house behind him, their attackers were coming through the trees to the north as well.

They were surrounded, reduced to holding a single house. They needed help, and fast.

He shut the door and turned the key to lock it, then followed Malvery. The house had a similar layout to others in the hamlet. There were two rooms taking up the ground floor. At the front was a small living-space with a stove and a table; another doorway led to a bedroom in the back. Upstairs was a separate and larger apartment, with a kitchen and living room, and bedrooms above that. Simple accommodation for the servants and staff.

'We gotta get out of here!' Ashua called as he entered. She was in the back room, shooting through the windows.

'We ain't goin' anywhere!' he snapped. 'You already left one post, you ain't leavin' another!'

She didn't reply to that, but he could sense her resentment. Silo didn't care: he was angry at her for running. He'd been the one to vouch for her when the Cap'n wanted to kick her off the crew back in Samarla, and some part of him felt responsible for her behaviour. But much as she seemed intent on staying, he'd always had the sense that she'd drop them if it suited her. She hadn't the loyalty to the Cap'n that the others did. That made her unreliable.

'Comin' up the road!' called Malvery, who squatted by a window facing the courtyard.

Silo took position at the window next to him. The sight of the defenders abandoning the houses on the south side had encouraged the Awakeners. He could see their blurred shapes moving closer, sticking near the snowdrifts on either side of the road. A few speculative bullets came their way.

'Save your ammo,' said Silo. 'Won't hit anythin' at this range.'

'Right-o,' said Malvery. He patted the pockets of his coat, to check they were still bulging with shells. Silo glanced back at Ashua, who was covering the rear of the house with Harkins. They had a small ammo box between them. How long would that last, if the Awakeners came at them in force?

'You heard from the Cap'n?' he asked Malvery.

'He doesn't have his earcuff in, naturally,' said Malvery. He ducked away as a bullet ricocheted off the stone near his head. 'Might be in his pocket, but I can't hear bugger all over the sound of the wind and these pesky bastards trying to kill us.' He popped up and fired off a round.

'Ammo, Doc,' Silo reminded him.

'Sorry,' said Malvery. 'They're gathering out there.'

Silo cursed in Murthian. Where was the Cap'n? He could understand Frey's reluctance to use the earcuffs – like Frey, Silo hated the distraction in a gunfight, though it didn't appear to bother Malvery – but right now he needed to know when, or if, help was coming.

Suppose it don't matter, he told himself. *Ain't no place to run, anyways. Gonna hold this house as long as we can, and hope that's long enough.*

He heard fresh gunfire from the bedroom. Harkins and Ashua. 'Watch the road,' he told Malvery as he hurried through to the back.

'What in rot's name are we still doing here?' Ashua cried. She had her pistol steadied with both hands, and was firing into the trees. 'We need to fall back!'

Silo pressed himself up against the wall on the other side of the window, leaned out, and took a shot at a ghostly shape out there in the white world beyond. 'You gonna hold the damn line till I say otherwise,' he said.

'I didn't join this bloody crew to die in some frozen hole in the mountains!'

'Me neither. But here we are.'

There was a lull in the shooting. Neither of them could see a target. Ashua opened her mouth to protest further, but Silo got in first.

'Where you gonna go, huh? The mansion? Imperators there. That's if the gunship don't shoot us to pieces crossin' the bridge. The Cap'n's comin'. You might not believe it, but I do. So stay put.'

Ashua glared at him, a sullen fire in her eyes. Her defiance didn't fool him. She was afraid. She might be tough, but she'd never been in a war, never been under such sustained fire for so long. You never knew how someone might react when they were pinned down with no way out, not knowing if the next bullet coming would be the one to take them in the skull. She was on edge, liable to do something stupid.

He looked over at Harkins, who was at the next window, furiously concentrating on his task. Ashua needed something more than orders to steady her. Silo took a gamble.

'How about you, Harkins?' he called. 'You wanna run for it?'

'No, sir!' Harkins replied, without taking his eyes off the trees. Ashua looked startled.

'Why not?' Silo said.

Harkins turned his head. He was addressing Silo, but looking straight at Ashua. 'Because I'm no chickenshit,' he said levelly. 'Sir.'

Ashua spat on the floor and hunkered down to watch the trees again. Shame would keep her where she was. Silo gave Harkins a nod of respect and headed back to Malvery.

He'd seen something in Harkins these last few days. A new distance in his gaze, something firmer in his eye. He snapped to attention when spoken to, he didn't gripe or bitch like the others as he went about his work. He'd found a way to prop up his courage, and damn if he wasn't turning out to be useful in a gunfight at last. He still couldn't hit much with his pistol, but the Awakeners didn't know that.

Silo crouched next to Malvery, who was looking narrowly out at the road. Silo saw figures moving behind the windows across the courtyard.

'Don't like this,' said Malvery. 'They're waiting for something. Could do with getting Grudge to send a few shots their way, keep 'em on their toes.'

'That feller don't take no orders from me,' said Silo.

Malvery glanced at him. 'Heard what you did back there with Ashua,' he said. 'Cap'n made a smart pick having you as first mate. Ain't anyone else on the crew we'd listen to at a time like this.'

Silo shrugged a shoulder. 'You my people,' he said.

The bellow of engines alerted them a moment before the gunship came sweeping out of the blizzard, its cannons pointed right at them. Silo and Malvery scrambled away from the windows and flailed back towards cover as the front of the house was torn up. Splinters and powdered stone and plaster filled the air; the clatter of rotary cannons battered their ears. Silo hunkered in behind the stove. Malvery, having no better option, dived behind the sofa and made himself as small a target as his generous frame would allow.

The assault was over as quickly as it had begun. The gunship swung away and powered off into the blizzard, chased by Grudge's autocannon. It had been a swift attack, meant to catch them off guard.

Damn nearly did, as well.

'They're coming through at the back!' Ashua called. 'There's a lot of 'em!' Then she opened up with her pistol, and Harkins joined her.

Silo was about to run back there, but Malvery had slipped up to the front of the house and was looking through the ragged hole where one of the windows had been. 'We've got our own problems,' he said.

'Hold 'em!' Silo called back through the doorway.

'Yeah, I knew you were gonna say that,' he heard Ashua mutter as he ran over to Malvery. The doctor was already firing. A half-dozen men were spilling from the buildings on the south side and running across the courtyard, using the wreckage of the gunship as cover. Another eight or nine were running in from the road. Silo started shooting.

The gunship's attack had been a signal to come at the house from both sides. These weren't mercs: he could tell by the way they used their weapons, their inept understanding of cover. They were Sentinels. Mercs wouldn't run at a defended position with such abandon. They weren't suicidal.

Silo and Malvery dropped one, two, three of them. But they kept coming.

Malvery's shotgun ran dry. He tossed it to the floor, pulled out a stick of dynamite, and struck a match off the wall. Silo covered him till the fuse was lit, and then he lobbed it out through the window.

Some of the oncoming Awakeners saw it coming, tried to check their charge. Their companions crashed into the back of them, sending them stumbling forward in a tangle. The dynamite went off and sent them twisting and rolling away, living men turned to limp corpses.

Silo had ducked down to avoid the explosion; now he popped back up again and levelled his shotgun. It was seized by an Awakener who'd slipped close to the window along the wall. One hand on his shotgun barrel, the Awakener aimed a pistol at his face. Silo pulled his head aside, yanking his shotgun as he did so. It was enough to tug the Awakener off balance. The pistol went off by his ear, loud enough that it was like a punch, but the bullet missed.

Silo struggled with the Awakener, fighting to free his shotgun. The other man was strong, face weathered and teeth gritted beneath his furred hood. He was trying to get his arm through the window, get a good point-blank shot at Silo, but Silo was too close now. He was peripherally aware of Malvery frantically jamming another shell in his shotgun, but the doctor wouldn't be able to help him in time. So Silo lunged instead, shoving forward, using his weight. It took the Awakener by surprise. He swung the butt of the shotgun and caught the man a glancing blow on the jaw.

The Awakener staggered back from the window, but somehow he held on to the shotgun, bloody-mouthed and furious. The increased distance gave him space to aim his pistol, but then Malvery's shotgun boomed, and that ended it.

Suddenly the courtyard cobbles were being smashed, and men were smashed with them, limbs blasted into bloody smears on the snow as Grudge rained down autocannon fire from above. Silo didn't know what had taken him so long – perhaps they'd pinned him down once he'd revealed his position by firing at the gunship – but he was here now, and just in time. The Awakeners had been moments from overwhelming them at the windows; now they scattered and ran for their lives, knowing it was hopeless. Even the faithful had their limits.

Silo shot off the last of his rounds to discourage anyone who thought trying to climb inside would be the best way of escaping the death from above. The Awakeners on the south side had been driven back, but there was no respite for him. Seeing that the courtyard was safely covered, he scooped up a handful of shells and ran through to the other room.

He vaulted the bed and skidded into cover next to Ashua as a flurry of bullets clawed up the wall. Blinking brick dust from his eye, he reloaded and added his gun to Ashua's. The Awakeners were pouring from the trees now. The short slope of clear ground that led down from the snowy forest was littered with the dead, but it didn't deter the men behind.

They don't care 'bout their losses. Just keep comin' and comin'. They need us dead, and damn if it don't look like they gonna get their wish.

There was a fevered look in Ashua's eye, the dangerous gleam of someone backed into a corner. Harkins was frightened too, but he held his post at the window. Both of them knew this was a last stand. Both of them had decided to go down fighting.

An Awakener came skidding down the slope and lobbed a stick of dynamite at the windows. His aim was off: it hit the wall, bounced back, fell in the snow. Two of his companions tried to scramble away from it, but not fast enough.

There was a cry from Harkins. Silo saw him spin away from the window. His pilot's cap was gone; there was blood all over half his face. He staggered back and collapsed.

'Doc!' he shouted, as he crawled on his hands and knees under the windows.

'Busy here!' Malvery replied, and Silo heard Grudge's autocannon start up again. The Awakeners had regrouped and were coming back through the courtyard, autocannon or not.

Harkins' eyes were closed, and he wasn't moving. Silo didn't have time for more than a cursory glance at him. Men and women fell in battle all the time; Silo had seen more than his share of that. He'd grieve later, if he had to.

He took up Harkins' position by the window. Men rushed at him and he fired, primed his weapon, fired again. His movements became automatic, his enemies faceless, reduced from living, breathing people to simple threats that had to be removed. He fought as if in a dream. Sounds were dulled; he was deaf in one ear from the pistol shot. His body was at once incredibly tired and yet vital and strong. He killed and dodged and killed, and there was nothing but this moment, this fight. Nothing before or after. Only this.

Caught in that state, he was slow to recognise the dark shape that appeared among the trees at the top of the slope. It was only when she roared that he recognised Bess.

The sound of her shook the windowsills and rattled the pipes. She ploughed into the Awakeners from behind, swinging her great arms in all directions. The naked trees were smashed to matchwood. Men were swatted aside, crashing into trunks with bone-breaking force. She was like some mythical ogress, a force out of the primal dark come to life.

The Awakeners dissolved into confusion at the sight of her. Some of them scattered to the sides: some came on towards the windows, driven by fear of the beast in the trees.

Ashua fired dry, and was reloading when an Awakener lunged at her through the window. He tried to cram his rifle through to get a close-range shot, but got himself tangled up with her instead. Silo swung his shotgun around, but he couldn't fire without hitting Ashua. Instead he scooped up Harkins' pistol and tossed it through the air. Ashua caught it deftly in her left hand, jammed it in the Awakener's throat and pulled the trigger.

The Awakener pawed at her, gargling. She wrenched the rifle from his hand, put her boot in his chest and kicked him back out into the snow. Now with two weapons, she looked for a new target; but then her eyes widened, and she threw herself behind the bed. Silo turned back to the window in time to see Bess, who'd uprooted a tree, fling it down the slope towards them. He dived out of the way just before it hit the wall with an almighty boom, cracking the wall and crushing several Awakeners between the tree and the house.

'Fall back! Fall back!' he heard from outside, as he hunkered amid the falling dust from the ceiling, breathing hard. Caught between the guns in the house and the monster behind them, the Awakeners abandoned the assault at last. He heard them running, some of them screaming louder than the wounded left behind. Bess ran after them, bellowing.

Ashua got shakily to her feet. She climbed back over the bed and stared at the tree that now lay against the windows. An arm hung limply over the sill, its owner mangled just out of sight. She looked over at Silo, a crazed kind of disbelief on her face. 'The Cap'n came through,' she said.

'Don't he always?' Silo said. He got to his feet. 'You did good.'

A little smile touched the edge of her mouth. Then she saw Harkins, and it faded.

'I know,' he said. 'Stay here. You see anythin', yell.'

He went into the front room, where Malvery was lying against the wall, chest heaving, exhausted. The room stank of cordite. The quiet beyond the windows told Silo that the call for retreat had already spread to the courtyard, and that everywhere the Awakeners were routed.

'I do believe I heard the dulcet tones of Bess a moment ago,' said

Malvery, and chuckled. He lifted himself up and looked over his shoulder out the window. 'Look at 'em run.'

'Need you in the back, Doc,' said Silo. 'It's Harkins.'

Malvery became grim, and he got to his feet and hustled past Silo, through the doorway. Silo went to the windows. Beyond, the fires crackled and snapped, and snow was still falling, blanketing the bodies in the courtyard.

Thrusters sounded in the distance. Even muffled, he recognised the sound of Blackmore P-12s. The *Ketty Jay* was on her way.

I did what I could, Cap'n, he thought. *Rest is up to you.*

'I can't see shit up here!' Samandra yelled down from the cupola.

'You and me both!' Frey replied. It hadn't stopped him from flying recklessly fast. He'd wasted enough time already.

The *Ketty Jay* had been slow to wake in the cold. He'd only got her running by using a trick from the old days, before Trinica had his craft overhauled and everything started working as it should. His toe still hurt from that.

Below him and to starboard lay the hamlet. Half the south side was aflame. Nearby, the tangled remains of the generator burned bright in the gloom. He saw one wrecked gunship, but not the other. Belatedly it occurred to him that he should have asked Malvery what the situation was down there, but his earcuff was deep in his pocket and he couldn't spare the time to dig for it right now.

Is everyone alright down there? Is Crake? Am I already too late?

He slowed and banked to port, searching the blizzard for the second gunship. He spotted the landing pad where the Century Knights' aircraft waited, mantled in white. There were no troops in sight, but they'd left churned snow in their wake. He followed their tracks with his eye and found Bess, carving a trench across the meadows. Ahead of her, barely visible, frightened figures stumbled and hurried in the direction of the lander which had brought them here.

They're running, he thought, and hope fluttered inside him. *Did we win?*

'Frey! Ten o'clock!' Samandra called.

It was the second Predator, dropping out of the grey sky, guns angled downward. It wasn't facing them: the pilot hadn't seen them yet. The guns were trained on Bess.

Frey boosted the thrusters and hammered towards the Predator. Bess could hold up to small-arms fire well enough, but those cannons would take her to pieces. The pilot was intent on the target, lining up the shot, as Frey raced closer.

Hang on, hang on, just a second more.

But it was a second he didn't get. The pilot opened up, a hail of bullets lashed through the air, and Bess disappeared in a cloud of vaporised snow.

'No!' Frey cried, and he clamped his finger down on the trigger. Tracer fire spat from the *Ketty Jay*'s underslung machine guns, raking the Predator's flank, chewing up its ailerons. The craft slewed wildly to starboard, bringing the cockpit into Frey's line of fire. The windglass smashed and the pilot inside was chopped to meat. Still turning, the Predator dipped its head and its thrusters forced it down, grinding its nose into the earth. It crinkled and exploded in a rolling cloud of flame.

Frey slowed and banked hard, bringing the *Ketty Jay* around. He had to see what had become of Bess. He'd never been certain whether he thought of her as a living thing or a disposable object, but right then her safety was deeply important to him. He was still uncertain about the fate of his crew, and he dreaded to face his losses. Every survivor was precious. Even the golem.

Come on, Bess. You're a tough old girl. You'll be alright. Please be alright.

The snow filled his sight, flurrying against the windglass. The meadows were hazy with fog thrown up by the Predator's gun. He squinted, looking closer. Was that movement? Was that –?

Bess!

She came lumbering out of the cloud, turning left and right, searching for Awakeners with the puzzled enthusiasm of a child looking for lost toys. They were all out of sight now, leaving her bewildered but apparently unhurt. The gunship had missed.

Frey let out the breath he'd been holding.

'Aircraft!' Samandra shouted.

Frey tensed. The lander! How had it got airborne so quickly? It must have been already halfway to taking off by the time he arrived. They were leaving their men behind in their haste to flee.

Frantically he searched for it. If the lander got away, then all their efforts would be for nothing. The Awakeners would never imagine Frey's crew capable of capturing an Imperator and forcing information from them, but if the Century Knights were known to be involved, matters were different. The Sentinels would tell the Awakeners what had occurred, and the Awakeners would know their plans had been compromised and change them. But if nobody returned, the Awakeners would simply assume their ambush had failed, or something unforeseen had occurred on the way; there would be no cause to alter anything.

A growing bellow of engines. The lander came thundering out of the blizzard and over their heads, a dark slab of metal flung through the sky.

'Shoot it!' Frey cried, but the autocannon was already thumping. He hauled the *Ketty Jay* around, knowing it was already too late to catch them. He couldn't turn and accelerate in time, and if he lost sight of them in the snow he'd never find them again.

The back end of the lander came into view, its thrusters diminishing into the gloom. Autocannon shells flew after it. None of them came close to hitting the mark.

'You're worse than Malvery!' Frey shouted in exasperation. He hit the throttle, but the lander was already a grey blur, powering away over the hamlet. He watched it despairingly as it faded from view.

Just before it disappeared completely, its back end exploded.

Frey's eyes widened in surprise as a ball of flame consumed the lander's thrusters. It slowed and went into a shallow dive, sailing over the hamlet to disappear into the chasm beyond. There was an almighty detonation, and the chasm lit up along its length. After that, silence, but for the sound of the *Ketty Jay*'s Blackmore P-12s.

Frey braked to a hover and fell back in his chair. 'Good shot!' he called up to the cupola.

'Wasn't me, that's for damn sure. Can barely aim this thing,' said Samandra, a grin in her voice. 'Guess we can be sure that Colden is alive down there.'

Grudge. Grudge had taken it down. The thought of the Century

Knight brought the possibility of other survivors to mind. He dug out his earcuff and clipped it on.

'Malvery! Crake! You still there?'

'Just about,' said Crake. 'You ever blown yourself up with dynamite before? It's quite a thing.'

Frey laughed, relief making him lightheaded. 'You get 'em?'

'We got them. Got most of what we needed, too. But you're not going to like it.'

'Tell me later. Malvery?'

'Me, Silo and Ashua still kicking, Cap'n,' came the doctor's voice. Frey could have cheered for joy. 'Harkins took a hit, though.'

Frey's silent celebration stalled. 'Bad?'

'Got a bullet across his scalp. Bled like a stuck pig and it knocked him out, but he's come round now. Reckon he'll be fine. Feller's got a thicker skull than we gave him credit for.'

There was a fondness in Malvery's tone that warmed him. There was a bond between this crew, a kind of companionship he'd never known elsewhere. He was so immensely glad he hadn't lost that today.

Rot and damn, they'd really done it. They'd come through the Awakeners' ambush alive. He could scarcely believe it.

Up yours, Amalicia, he thought, giddy with triumph. *Nice try, but you lose.*

Then something brought him up short. The count wasn't right. Somebody was missing. It took him a shamefully long time to remember who.

'Hey,' he said. 'Anyone seen Jez?'

Thirty-Four

Clearing Up – An Argument – Frey Despairs –
Decision Time – 'Rest Up Now'

They found her in the snow, curled up in a foetal position. It was only by her size that he recognised her. She was smaller than the others.

Frey stared down at the blackened thing at his feet, and was numb. He thought Trinica had emptied him of grief, but now he found a greater emptiness still. Though she'd been distant of late, and sometimes he'd wished her away, he still remembered the old Jez.

He turned his face away. 'Take her to the infirmary,' he said to Malvery and Silo, who stood opposite. 'Least we can do is put her somewhere proper.'

Malvery nodded. There were furious tears glittering behind his green glasses. 'What about Pelaru?' he said through a thick throat.

They'd discovered Pelaru nearby, unburned, but with a jagged piece of shrapnel the size of a dagger driven through his skull.

'We don't owe him shit,' said Frey. 'Leave him.' It felt good to vent his spite on someone, even the dead.

He walked off, picking his way through the charred corpses. The snow was already covering up the scene, and melted slush was turning to ice. Nearby, the last of the Awakeners were being rounded up by Grudge and Kyne. The survivors had surrendered rather than freeze to death in the blizzard. They were being marched to the Wrath's hold, where there was a cell for criminals that the Century Knights captured on their travels. What their fate would be, Frey neither knew nor cared.

He walked towards the blazing mass of pipes and rent metal that was all that was left of the hamlet's generator. He stood so close that the heat on his skin became hard to bear, and his throat began to burn with the fumes. He welcomed the pain and the poison.

Jez was gone. The raw loss of that was almost too much to bear. This new tragedy was different to that of Trinica: more fundamental, closer to home. It wasn't only that Jez would never speak, laugh, move again – although that in itself was awful enough. It was the knowledge that something irreplaceable had been taken out of his world. Members of his crew had left and come back before, but there would be no coming back this time. The life he'd come to love had been forever altered.

He let out a trembling breath. Tears wanted to come, welling up from the void in his chest. He wouldn't let them. He stared into the fire and let the stinging of the fumes take the sting from his sorrow.

Jez. Damn it, why'd you do it?

Ashua had told him how Jez had gone alone into the fray, and how Pelaru had tried to stop her. She'd saved their lives more than once in the past that way, but never against such a number. He wondered, if he'd been there, if things would have been different. He wondered if he would have been able to stop her.

He felt like he'd abandoned her. He could have headed back to the hamlet when he found the road blocked off by Awakeners; instead he'd headed for the *Ketty Jay*. It seemed to make sense, but in doing so he'd left his crew to bear the brunt of the battle. And he'd taken too long, far too long to get back to them.

Don't. You're not responsible. You didn't even want to come here, remember?

But whatever he told himself, it was small solace. Jez was gone. Nothing would be the same.

He heard boots in the snow. They stopped some way behind him, held back by the heat. 'Frey,' said Samandra. 'We gotta talk.'

'Not now,' he said.

'Now is exactly when we gotta talk. This won't wait.'

He didn't have the energy to resist. He turned and walked past her, without meeting her eye, heading back to the *Ketty Jay*. Samandra sniffed, wiped her nose with the back of her hand, and followed after.

'Tomorrow?' Frey's voice was flat and dead.

Kyne stood in the corner of the mess, his mask expressionless, without mercy, offering no space for Frey's desolation. 'Tomorrow.

Maybe dawn, maybe dusk. Even if we set off now, we won't reach Thesk till past nightfall.'

'So go,' said Frey. 'You got what you wanted. You got your proof.'

'Not exactly, Cap'n,' said Crake. Anguish had made his face pale and puffy. Neither wanted to make decisions now, but Crake was slogging on anyway. 'The Imperator said there'd be an attack on Thesk tomorrow. He said nothing about the Azryx device.'

'But you got the readings, right? The readings we need to exorcise Trinica?'

Crake hesitated. 'Well, yes we did. But—'

'Then why should I care?'

Crake exchanged a glance with Samandra, who was sitting next to him at the table opposite Frey. Frey felt a bitter worm of resentment turn in his stomach. Look at them, the two of them, united. They had each other: who did he have?

'What we got ain't enough,' said Samandra. 'If they attack tomorrow, the whole Coalition fleet will pile in. That's what they want. They'll take out all our forces in one sweep.'

'Not if you warn them about the Azryx device.'

'We ain't *seen* any Azryx device.'

'*We've* seen it!' Frey shouted suddenly, banging his fist on the table. 'You were there in the Azryx city and you bloody well know what it can do! If the Archduke's too damn stupid to listen then he's welcome to kiss my arse and die with the rest of his pompous, shit-eating mob!' He lowered his voice to an angry snarl. 'You wanted us to give you proof? Well, we tried. And Jez is dead because of it.'

The room was silenced. Ashua scratched the back of her neck awkwardly. Silo showed nothing, as ever. Plome steepled his fingers and stared at them. The rest were elsewhere: Malvery was seeing to Harkins in the infirmary, where Jez's body also lay. Frey felt it there like a weight on his aircraft, a dense presence impossible to ignore.

'That's a real constructive attitude you got,' Samandra said, narrowing her eyes in sarcasm.

'Screw you,' said Frey. 'Wonder how constructive you'd feel if it were Grudge that got burnt to a cinder?'

'Quit your damn sulking! This is bigger than you!' she cried.

'Nothing's bigger than me!' he shouted back. 'Me is all I've got!'

Samandra opened her mouth to reply, but Crake put his hand on her wrist to stop her, and she subsided.

'Yeah, you're not so diplomatic, are you?' Frey sneered. He flicked a finger at Crake. 'Let him try.'

Crake seemed shocked by his tone. He didn't deserve to be treated like an enemy, but Frey wanted to lash out.

'Cap'n,' said Crake carefully. 'This is the future of our country we're talking about. Our entire way of life.'

'Last I heard, the Coalition had us all down as traitors. Change of government might be to our advantage, don't you think?'

'You don't mean that.'

'Don't I? You sure?'

'It's the only way to clear your names,' said Kyne. 'If you don't care about your own, think of your crew. You want to be hunted the rest of your days?'

Frey sat back and crossed his arms. It was a pitiful threat as far as he was concerned. 'By who? There won't *be* a Coalition if the Archduke sends his fleet up tomorrow.'

'All we're asking is that you come back to Thesk and tell the Archduke and commanders what you saw. Second-hand information won't be enough.'

'Wait, our word wasn't good enough before, but now it is?' Ashua said.

'Now we have no other choice,' said Kyne. 'And time has run out. Bree and Grudge will back you up as best they can. The generals might listen then.'

Frey began ticking points off his fingers. 'I killed the Archduke's son, or near enough as makes no difference. I came bloody close to killing Kedmund Drave. I ruined the Mentenforth Institute, the Archduke's private collection, and destroyed spit knows how many priceless relics. I reckon I'm not far off when I say the Archduke would love to see me and my crew dead.' He leaned forward, and anger seeped back into his voice. 'And you want me to go back there and *surrender*? To throw myself on their damned *mercy*? Maybe get us all hung? For what? On the off chance that the most powerful men in the country deign to climb down out of their arses long enough to hear me out?'

'If you're telling the truth, the conviction against you and your crew will likely be quashed.'

Frey laughed. 'Likely? That's quite a promise.'

'It's not my decision. I can't say what the Archduke will do.'

'Then the Archduke can rot.'

'Frey, you'll be comin' in of your own accord, with three Century Knights vouchin' for your good character,' said Samandra. 'Such as it is, anyway. They ain't gonna string you up.'

Frey was unconvinced, and it showed.

'We could make you, if we wanted,' said Kyne.

'You could try,' Frey replied darkly.

Crake leaned back in his chair and stared at Kyne steadily. 'Use that voice of yours, Kyne, and I'll know it,' he said. 'This is his choice.'

Frey was faintly surprised by that. He hadn't expected Crake to stand up for him in this matter. But then, Crake had always suffered from an unhealthy sense of fair play.

'No one's makin' anyone do anything,' said Bree, with a glance at her companion. 'Look, Frey. We all want the same thing here. We all want to stop the Awakeners, right?'

Frey looked around the room. He felt hunted. Most of the room was against him, it seemed. Everyone pushing him to do what was right, to put the good of the country over his own needs. How had it come to this? He'd resented the Coalition for most of his life; now he was supposed to swallow his pride and go crawling to them?

'We had a deal,' said Frey. 'I help you get the Imperators. You give me what I need to help Trinica. I kept my part of the bargain. Now you want to change the deal?' His gaze fell stonily on Crake. 'I need to get to her. And I need your help to get the daemon out of her. You gonna leave me to do it on my own?'

Crake swallowed. He let the daemonist squirm for a moment. 'Cap'n—' Crake said, but Frey held up his hand. He didn't want to hear whatever mealy-mouthed bullshit Crake had in store to make himself feel better about betrayal.

'Do any of you understand?' he said, his voice trembling with suppressed rage. 'The woman I—' He lost the word; it came out as a breath. He screwed his face into a grimace, determined to express the depth of what he felt. 'The woman I *love* is out there somewhere. Might be she's dead and something's walking round in her skin.

347

Might be they've cut out her tongue by now.' He felt frustrated tears prick at his eyes. They stood there, but didn't fall. 'Might be she's trapped in there with it, trapped in some . . . some *torment* I can't even begin to imagi—' His voice failed him again. He took a hard breath, let it hiss out through his teeth. 'Do *any* of you get that?'

There was silence. They knew better than to pretend they did.

'Cap'n,' said Silo at last, his deep voice calm. 'Whole Awakener fleet gonna be at Thesk tomorrow. Trinica gonna be with 'em, ain't she? Strikes me that whatever way you wanna go, it's all the same direction.'

Frey shut his eyes, trying to keep a lid on the emotions boiling up inside him. He hadn't considered that. He wasn't thinking straight.

'We need to do this, Frey,' said Crake. 'The whole civil war might rest on what we do right here and right now. If we don't give it our absolute best shot, we might be handing Vardia to the daemons tomorrow. We *have* to.'

Frey barely heard him. Why couldn't they all just bloody well leave him alone?

'You got a plan for how you're gonna get to her?' said Samandra, more gently than before.

Frey opened his eyes and looked up. 'What?'

'Y'know,' she said. 'How you're gonna get past the Awakeners, and then past her crew. How you're gonna subdue her or whatever. And then how you're gonna get her back to a sanctum where Grayther can do his stuff?' She turned to Crake. 'If it works, I mean. You didn't seem too confident about it before.'

Grayther didn't say anything, but his face said enough.

'No,' said Frey. All the anger had drained from him and now he was weary, so very weary. 'I thought I could lure her out, maybe . . .'

He trailed off lamely. Lure her? She probably didn't even know him any more. Yes, Crake might cobble together some daemonic device so he could tackle her, but his chances of even getting close were appallingly slender. He had no idea how to subdue her, for she wouldn't come willingly, and he could never smuggle her out past her crew. His only chance was getting her alone, and he couldn't see any way that could be done. The old Trinica he knew how to manipulate; but there was no telling what now walked in her place.

There was pity in Crake's eyes, and that was what crushed him. He saw his delusion mirrored on his friend's face. Suddenly it all seemed so absurd, so pointless, so pathetic. Love had made him wretched and desperate. But it was time to face the truth.

Trinica was gone, or beyond his reach. Jez was a blackened corpse in the infirmary. These things were irretrievable. And here he was among all these people, and all of them wanted something from him, leadership or sacrifice, decisions too important to delay. He felt crowded, panicked, suffocated . . . but most of all, he felt bone tired. And with that tiredness came a kind of bitter peace, an acceptance that turned the storms inside him to calm: the bleak cold calm of a stony desert.

Let the world do with him as it would. He didn't care.

He stood up slowly. There was a great weakness on him. His chair scraped against the floor as he pushed it back.

'Let's go to Thesk,' he said, and walked over to the ladder that would take him up and out of the mess.

'Cap'n,' said Crake. 'What are we going to do when we get there?'

Frey paused with one hand on a rung. He didn't look back. 'We're going to surrender,' he said.

Ashua was first out of the mess after Frey. She hurried down into the hold, her boots echoing in the silence, and had her hand on the lever of the cargo ramp before sense caught up with her.

What are you gonna do, Ashua? Where are you gonna go?

Well, there was the mansion. She wouldn't freeze to death, at least, although it'd be cold with the generator out. The staff had aircraft to put them in touch with civilisation. No doubt they'd be flying out as soon as the blizzard cleared, to summon help. Maybe she could hitch a ride. Maybe she could steal one.

And go where?

She closed her eyes, squeezed them shut against the fear. She wanted to run. She wanted to run so badly. To remain on the *Ketty Jay* meant going to Thesk, to seek forgiveness for something she hadn't even done. Presenting herself for the judgement of the rich and powerful so they could decide whether she was worthy to continue living.

This wasn't her way. Damn it, this wasn't even the *Cap'n's* way. If Frey hadn't been so broken down he'd have told them where to stick their absolution. Since when did they bow to anyone? Wasn't the whole point of being a freebooter to be free?

But Crake, oh, Crake with his bloody trust in authority. And Malvery too, and Harkins. She knew what they would have said, if they'd been there. The idiocy of patriotism enraged her. She had to get out.

Now her heart was fluttering, and she trembled. She couldn't breathe easily. Panic had her by the throat. She gritted her teeth and fought to pull herself back from the brink.

Easy, she said to herself. *What's wrong with you?*

But she knew what was wrong. She'd seen it before in the slums. After a kid made his first kill, or after someone had walked out of a fight unscathed that left everyone else dead. She was shaken up badly. The adrenaline of the battle had drained away, and now the shock was setting in.

She took her hand away from the lever. There were no solutions out there. Just white emptiness and cold.

Ocken! she thought suddenly. *Bargo Ocken! Than man owes you enough to set you up for a long time!*

The thought of him drove her to her sleeping-nook, where she'd hidden the communication device under her blankets, between the pipes. She let the fabric curtain fall behind her. Once closed in, she felt a little safer. She dug out the device and turned it over in her hands. A small brass cube, with a button on one face and a small glass light on another.

Get off this craft right now. Get in touch with Ocken. Take your payoff.

An ascending hum sounded from all around her, making the pipes vibrate. The engines were warming. The Cap'n was preparing for take-off.

Beyond the curtain of her nook, she heard footsteps as several people made their way down into the hold. Voices came to her, getting louder as they neared the bottom of the metal stairs.

'What about you? Are you coming with us?' said Crake.

'No, no, I don't think so.' She recognised the high, nervous tones of the politician, Plome. 'Can't see what help I'd be, to be honest. I shall stay here with the staff and see to things. They're not happy about being locked up like that. And someone needs to explain to the

Tarlocks what happened to their property. Not a job I relish, I tell you that!'

Bullshit, thought Ashua, who distrusted politicians of any kind. *You just don't want to be in Thesk when the fleet arrives tomorrow. Well, you might be a weasel, but you've got some sense at least.*

She should go. Nothing was stopping her. Nothing but herself.

Ashua thought of herself as a loner, but as far back as she could remember, she'd never been alone. A child couldn't survive on the streets of Rabban without help. Her earliest memories were peopled by benefactors and guardians. Adults who took pity on her, older children who fed and protected her, kids her own age who provided strength in numbers. Later there was Maddeus, father figure and employer both. Though she prowled the streets, tough as an alley-cat, she always had a home to go back to after he took her in.

And even when Maddeus sent her away, she had Shasiith, a city full of contacts and acquaintances to support her. When Shasiith had gone bad, when Jakeley Screed came after her and the Sammies were out for her blood, she'd jumped on board the *Ketty Jay* and found her support there.

But now there was nowhere left to go. And she found that she didn't want to leave anyway.

Her life had been filled with companions of necessity, her friend-ships more like alliances, easily broken when the need arose. Even Maddeus, distant intellectual Maddeus, had put her aside when it suited him. But in her time on the *Ketty Jay* she'd found people she liked and, more importantly, whom she trusted: Malvery, Crake, even the Cap'n when he wasn't being an arsewit. She respected Silo and was even sort of fond of Harkins. And Bess, well . . . she couldn't deny a certain affection for the golem, too. She'd always secretly wanted a pet.

She knew them now, and she'd seen how they were with one another. For all their bickering, they looked after each other, and the Cap'n looked after them. And she was part of that now. Maybe not as much as the others, but still. They wouldn't drop her if things got tough. If she needed help, they'd give it. She believed that, and it touched her. She'd never had that in her life before.

Walking out now felt like a betrayal. She could face the Cap'n, maybe, but not Crake and certainly not Malvery. She'd have to slip away, and would hurt them worse by doing so.

She didn't want to do that. But she didn't want to die, either. The war was coming to Thesk, and they were heading right to its heart. Even if they weren't treated as traitors, they'd be caught up in the fight. And this one would make the battle she'd just been through seem like a street-corner spat between children.

But it was that, or be alone.

The hydraulics kicked in with a thump, and the cargo ramp opened. A swirl of cold air stirred the curtain. It was bitter out there, but warm in her nook. The pipes radiated a drowsy heat, and she was protected in her hollow.

'Are you sure you can straighten things out with Drave and the Archduke?' Crake was saying as they walked down the ramp.

'Drave's a tough nut, but he ain't stupid. He'll listen to us,' said another voice: Samandra Bree. So the other footsteps must have been the other two Century Knights. ' 'Sides, honey, if he don't, there ain't gonna be much left worth survivin' for anyway.'

'That's a good point,' said Crake. 'I never thought of that.'

'Optimism,' said Samandra. 'Keeps me young.'

Their voices faded. When the ramp began to raise, she almost bolted. But she balled up a blanket in her fist and gripped it hard, willing herself not to move. Finally the ramp closed with a boom that echoed through the hold.

She relaxed her hand. So it was done. She'd made her choice. She'd passed through a gate, and it had shut behind her. She felt better for it.

She looked at the device in her hand. Leaving or not, she still had a job to do. If the Awakeners were heading for Thesk, then the Thacians needed to know. Pelaru might have already told his people about the Awakeners' secret weapon, but even if he had, he hadn't known when or where the strike would come. Perhaps Ocken could get the message to someone who could help. Perhaps the Thacians could make the Archduke listen to Frey's warnings. Vardia and Thace had been allies for a long time, united against Samarlan aggression. Thace wouldn't want to see Vardia fall to the Awakeners and end up an ally of Samarla. That would make their neighbours twice as dangerous.

So she'd send the message. She'd do what she could for the good of the country. And after that, she was going to find Malvery, and she was going to get really, really drunk.

The engine room had always been Silo's domain, and he went there once the *Ketty Jay* was airborne, to escape the prevailing mood. Here he could lose himself in the noise and heat, disappear among the walkways and pipes. Silo was a man comfortable with his own company, and right now he wanted no one else's.

Jez's death had hit them all hard. There was a sense of shock among the crew, but no time to grieve or heal. That was bad. Silo had seen his fair share of grief; he knew the kind of things it might make a man do, if he didn't get it out. But there'd be no quarter yet. They'd been caught in a whirlpool for a long time now, since way back in the days of Retribution Falls. Now they were nearing the centre. It was down to them whether they'd be swallowed or spat back out.

Well, what gonna come, gonna come, he thought. *Too late to pull out now.*

Each of the crew were dealing with the tragedy in their own way. Crake had thrown himself into his work. He was on the Wrath with Kyne, in the Century Knight's sanctum, using the readings they'd taken from the Imperator to knock up some countermeasures as best they could. And maybe when he was done, if there was time, he'd find solace in the Samandra's arms.

Harkins was flying the Firecrow. That was where he was happiest. Malvery was drinking, and Ashua was drinking with him for company. She didn't feel it like the others did, but she was there for the doc, and that was good. Malvery was the kind of man who needed to talk it out.

They'd survive. They'd get through. Silo had sorrow of his own, but his was more measured. Life as a slave, and later as a resistance fighter, had inured him somewhat to the pain of loss. Death was part of Murthian life, always at their shoulder. He'd honour his friend when the moment was right.

It was Frey that worried him. The Cap'n hadn't been all there since he came out of the Awakeners' base camp. This new blow might have been too much. He always was a self-destructive sort, but he'd always been defiant. Silo didn't like what he saw in the Cap'n's eyes at the mess table. It reminded him of people he'd known in the slave camps. The ones who'd been pushed too far, who'd lost too much. The ones who gave up, lay down and died.

At the base of the engine assembly was the curious device that Prognosticator Garin had attached while they were resident at the Awakener camp. Silo had taken the casing off some days before, but once he'd seen what was inside, he'd decided not to touch it. Most of it was familiar technology, but at the core was a small, spindle-shaped glass chamber. Coloured smoke swirled slowly inside, and little sparks of miniature lightning flashed within.

Azryx tech.

The tiny core was rigged up to simple broadcasting device. As to what it did, he had a good idea. They'd been fitting similar devices to every aircraft that joined the fleet. Common sense said that it had to be a countermeasure to their secret weapon. Otherwise, the Awakener fleet would fall out of the sky at the same time the Coalition fleet did. A guard they captured in the Azryx city told them once how the Sammies could fly certain craft in and out of it, ignoring the invisible field that sent delicate systems haywire. The Sammies must have sold that secret to the Awakeners too, along with the parts needed to make it work.

Having guessed its purpose, Silo didn't want to fiddle with it in case he broke it. He reckoned it might come in handy.

He made his way up stairs and along walkways, stopping here and there to check on the machinery. Everything was running smoothly now the *Ketty Jay* had warmed up.

Least something runnin' smoothly round here, he thought.

He spotted Slag among the pipes, curled up in his favourite spot. No doubt he'd been in the bowels of the craft the last few days, tucked up in the *Ketty Jay*'s core where the cold was kept at bay by heaters designed to protect the delicate machinery. Now the craft was running, he'd returned to the warmth of the engine room. The sight of him gave Silo a measure of comfort. In chaotic times, the cat was a reassuringly permanent fixture.

On impulse, he walked over to the pipes and reached out to tickle Slag behind the ears. Probably Slag would take a swipe at him for the liberty, but he was never fast enough these days.

Just before he touched him, he stopped. There was something profound in the cat's stillness. A creeping suspicion came over him.

He reached out and laid his hand on Slag's flank. It was cool, and no breath swelled it.

Silo bowed his head. He let out a long breath, let the surprise of it pass him by and the reality sink in. He knew death, knew that sense of departure when a living being became a framework. This one had been long expected, but still strange when it arrived. Eventually he felt a sort of peaceful melancholy, an acceptance of the inevitable.

'You lived more 'n your share,' he said slowly, his palm still flat against Slag's flank. 'Took on the world in your own way. Rest up now, old friend. You was a warrior. They never beat you.'

After that, he didn't have anything to say. He took his hand away, and stood back from the pipes, and looked around the engine room. It all seemed different now. Something vital had departed the *Ketty Jay*, something indefinable. Yesterday she'd been alive to him; now she was just machinery.

Better the crew don't know, he thought. *Not on top of everythin' else.*

'Rest up now,' he said again, this time quietly, almost to himself. He picked up the dead cat, cradling him gently in his arms, and headed off into the maze of the stairways and walkways, until the clank of boots on steel was lost in the roar of the engines.

Thirty-Five

*The Best Way to Kill a Mane – 'I'm Gettin' a Bad Feelin' About This' –
Drave's Revelations – Bruised*

Crake stood in the cockpit of the Wrath with Samandra by his side, and looked down on a sea of lights.

Grudge was in the pilot's seat, a hulking, silent presence. Kyne was still in his sanctum, finishing up a few things. The daemonists had done all they could in the time they had. They'd thralled several amulets with daemons that would theoretically negate the power of the Imperators. Crake went to the cockpit afterwards, to see Samandra, and to watch the city of Thesk come rolling out of the night.

He was tired down to the bone. The terror of the Imperators was only hours old, and he hadn't had a moment to rest since. Working with Kyne had energised him briefly – practising the Art always did – but now he felt twice as weary as before.

While he'd been occupied he'd avoided thinking about Jez, but now her fate weighed on him again. He saw her in his mind's eye, a small charred thing, lying in a black tarp body bag on the operating table in Malvery's infirmary. He'd seen her heal wounds with uncanny speed before, and it had always been impossible to tell whether she was dead or alive when comatose; but nobody was fooling themselves this time.

At least we know the best way to kill a Mane, he thought, with bitter irony.

He spared a thought for Pelaru, too. It seemed someone should. Belatedly, he remembered how he'd seen the whispermonger take an object from the shrine in Korrene, a metal casket that he seemed to recognise. Crake had meant to talk to him about that, but then the Shacklemores had kidnapped him and it had slipped his mind entirely. Well, that secret died with Pelaru. He didn't have the energy to care about it now.

But despite exhaustion and grief, he felt no despair. There was a rightness to things that he hadn't known for a long time. For once the crew of the *Ketty Jay* were doing something moral, something correct. He was in no doubt that the path they'd taken was the one they were meant to.

Malvery would have agreed, if he'd been in the meeting to lend his voice. Harkins too, he was sure. The Cap'n wasn't so keen, but he'd see in the end. Sometimes you had to trust in the higher powers, the institutions and hierarchies that Frey so despised. They couldn't take on the world on their own. And Crake wouldn't let Frey's irrational distrust of authority put the whole Coalition at risk.

Then there was Samandra. There was a rightness to her beyond all expectation. He'd never felt such certainty about a woman. She was gregarious where he was reserved, uncouth where he was refined, violent where he was gentle: the opposite of everything he thought he wanted. Yet they fit like puzzle pieces; their uneven edges locked them together.

His love for her was simple, uncomplicated by the expectations of his upbringing. He marvelled at his fortune that she should return his feelings. Would he have been capable of this, if not for his time on the *Ketty Jay*? Probably not. His sense of privilege would have prevented it. But he was a different man now.

Strange the way life takes us, he thought.

The city spread beneath them. Now they could see the lighted boulevards, the monuments, the bell towers and galleries. In the distance was the Archduke's palace, perched on a crag that rose high above the streets, a beautiful Third Age clutter of green copper domes and sloping rooftops of coloured slate. Coalition frigates slid through the sky and small personal flyers buzzed about. Crake watched them with dread in his heart. None of them knew the doom approaching them.

Seeing Thesk from above, as a net of stars cast out over the black earth, Crake felt all the beauty and fragility of the city and the civilisation it represented. He was suddenly terrified. Thesk was the pinnacle of Vardic culture, home to all its great museums and libraries. By this time tomorrow, it might all be different, the streets in ruin and the land in other hands. Science would be driven aside by superstition, humanity replaced by the inhuman.

It was too awful to contemplate.

'Think your brother's down there somewhere?' Samandra asked, catching his mood.

'I should think so,' he said. 'Somewhere.'

He'd thought often of Condred and his father these past few days. His brother was alive, at least. It was enough to know that. He didn't know if he'd see him again. He didn't know if they could ever truly be brothers with the ghost of Bess hanging over them.

For his father he felt little, just a small absence in his life. It was less than he expected, but then Rogibald had always been an icon rather than a person to him. His grief was more dutiful than genuine.

'Looks like we're gettin' an escort,' rumbled Grudge. Samandra leaned over the dash and he pointed. Several cruisers were approaching. The lead cruiser was flashing a message with its electroheliograph.

'Huh,' said Samandra. 'How'd they know we were comin'?'

Nobody had an answer. 'At least it's reassuring to know our side are so well-informed,' Crake offered.

But Samandra still wore a slight frown, and that made Crake uneasy too.

The Coalition cruisers slid into position around the Wrath and the *Ketty Jay*, and led them in towards the Archduke's palace. Perhaps it was meant for their protection, but Crake felt oppressed by the presence of the heavily armoured aircraft. Samandra paced the cockpit restlessly.

The Archduke's palace was modern, not like the dark stone piles that other dukes had as their ancestral homes. Its walls were a light beige, and it was peopled with statues. Elaborate clocks overlooked lawn-covered quads. A great building of steel and glass housed a tropical arboretum, and anti-aircraft cannons nestled in the courtyards.

There was a large walled landing pad near the gates on the sloping west side of the crag. They sank towards it; the cruisers stayed overhead. The Wrath landed first, and while Grudge was powering down the aircraft Crake watched the *Ketty Jay* land next to them. He wasn't used to seeing her from the outside, and was struck by how ungainly she looked: an ugly heap of angles, daubed with Awakener symbols, settling uncertainly on the ground. The Firecrow landed with a touch more grace. He looked for the Skylance, then remembered Pinn wasn't with them any more.

Almost as soon as the aircraft had landed, two dozen soldiers in the blue and grey of the Thesk militia came sallying through a gate, carrying rifles.

'I'm gettin' a bad feelin' about this,' Samandra muttered.

By the time Crake got outside, the crew of the *Ketty Jay* were already making trouble.

'Will you get that bloody gun out of my face?' Malvery bellowed at a pox-pitted soldier who was threatening him. 'We ain't the enemy!'

'Stay where you are!' an officious young sergeant barked at him. 'Tell your men to stay back, or we'll shoot!'

Malvery rolled his eyes. 'I ain't the Cap'n!' He thrust a finger at Frey. 'Talk to him!'

But Frey seemed disinterested and said nothing.

'Hold it down, Doc,' said Silo, in lieu of any leadership from Frey. 'Let's all step back till we know what they're about.'

'Is that a Murthian?' one of the soldiers asked. 'What in buggery's a Murthian doing here?'

'Can it, soldier!' the sergeant snapped. 'I want these prisoners rounded up and searched for weapons!'

'Prisoners?' Ashua cried.

Harkins was bullied over to stand with the others, and the soldiers began patting them down. Crake hoped they were at least sensible enough to have left their weapons aboard the *Ketty Jay*. Then, just when it looked like some sort of order was being established, Samandra came storming out of the Wrath.

'What the shit is this?' she yelled at the sergeant. 'These ain't prisoners! They're my guests! Who ordered all of—'

'*I* ordered it!' said Kedmund Drave, as he came striding through the ranks with four Century Knights at his back. He knew them all from the broadsheets: Eldrew Grissom and Mordric Jask – whom the others had met before – Celerity Blane and Graniel Thrate. The fact that there were so many together boded ill for someone.

Drave motioned to Grissom, who produced a device from his shabby duster. He brushed his straggly grey-white hair out of his face and panned the device around, watching the gauges. Then, without a word, he walked past the prisoners and up the ramp into the *Ketty Jay*'s hold.

Some kind of detection device, Crake thought. *But what's he detecting?*

A soldier seized Crake by the arm and pulled him over to stand by the others. Crake thought he was rather unnecessarily rough about it.

'Drave,' said Samandra, barely suppressing her anger. 'This lot came in of their own accord. I'm vouchin' for 'em. They've got important information for the Archduke.'

'Whatever they have to say can wait,' said Drave, his face stony.

'It *can't* wait, that's the point! Listen, we—'

'*You* listen, Miss Bree,' he said. 'These men and women are traitors and I intend to prove it. Your own judgement is in question here, and those of your fellow Knights. I'd keep quiet if I were you.'

'I ain't gonna stand here and let you accuse 'em of somethin' they ain't—'

She was interrupted by a sharp whistle from the *Ketty Jay*. Grissom emerged, holding up a small object. He tossed it over to Drave, who caught it out of the air. He looked down on it and gave a grim sneer of satisfaction. Then he brandished it in front of the crew.

'Anyone recognise this?' he challenged them.

Crake didn't. It was a brass cube with a press-stud on the top and a circle of glass on one face. It looked like something that might belong in his sanctum, but he was sure it wasn't his.

'No one?' Drave said. He swept up and down the line, and suddenly descended on Ashua like a hawk. He leaned down and pushed his broad scarred face close to hers. 'How about you?'

Ashua had gone very pale. Crake felt a stir of anger on her behalf. How dare he intimidate a young woman like that?

He swept away from her, holding up the device. 'As you may be aware, there's a civil war on. All of Pandraca's interested in how this plays out. Yorts, Sammies and Thacians; everyone wants to know which way the wind's blowing. And their spies are everywhere.' He turned back to the crew and ran his gaze across each of them. Crake felt a shiver as it passed over him.

'A few days ago we captured one of those spies. His name was Bargo Ocken.'

Ashua couldn't keep her reaction off her face. Crake noticed it. So did Drave.

'We found a device exactly like this on him,' Drave continued. 'It's a signalling device. Little bit of daemonist know-how. Works like an electroheliograph, except you don't have to be within sight. You press this stud,' he raised a finger to demonstrate, but didn't press, 'and a light comes on in the other boxes that are linked to it. You'll note, Miss Vode, that I said *boxes*. Plural. Ocken wasn't the only one receiving your messages.'

Crake, with a sinking feeling, began to understand. The others were looking at Ashua now, puzzlement and dawning disbelief on their faces. She kept her gaze fixed on Drave. It must have been easier to meet her accuser's eyes than her friends'.

'Do you understand me now, Miss Bree?' said Drave, turning back to Samandra. 'These scum you've been vouching for are traitors. Whatever they have to say is a lie. They've been feeding information to the Samarlans the whole t—'

'No!' Ashua blurted. 'It was the Thacians! Our allies! That's who I was talking to! Ocken worked for the Thacians!'

Drave gave her a long, slow stare. Then, as if speaking to a child, he said: 'Is that what he told you?'

The realisation of what she'd done took all the strength out of her, and she staggered. Crake caught her by instinct, and bore her up before she could fall. She met his eyes, and there was confusion and terror in them, and suddenly she was just a scared young woman instead of the tough street-rat that they all knew.

But Crake's heart had gone hard, and he let her go quickly and stepped back. Had the Ashua he'd known been a lie all along? Was she manipulating them even now? He could hardly believe it, and yet here she was, caught red-handed, a *traitor*.

She saw what was in his eyes and retreated from him, but there was nowhere to go. She was surrounded by the accusing gazes of the crew, all of them asking the same question. *Did you do it? Did you really?*

'It was the Thacians!' she insisted, desperation making her voice thin.

'You're a liar,' said Drave. 'Bargo Ocken works for a spyhunter called Jakeley Screed, and he works for the Sammies. You've been sending them highly sensitive information. I hope they paid you well, Miss Vode. You won't live to enjoy it.' He waved at the troops.

'They're all traitors and spies and enemies of the Coalition. Take them to the cells.'

'Oi! Not us! It's nothing to do with us!' Malvery bellowed, and suddenly everyone was pushing and shoving as the soldiers weighed in. Crake felt himself seized, his arm twisted painfully behind his back. He struggled, but cold iron was clamped on his wrist and he was cuffed. Someone barged into him and he got a smack on the nose from the side of their head. Stars blazed in front of his eyes.

This couldn't be right, he thought, dazed. This wasn't how it was supposed to be. They'd done the right thing: they'd gone to the authorities. Crake had practically *made* Frey go to the authorities. He'd always had faith in order and reason. Where was the order and reason in this?

They simply didn't have all the facts. That was the problem. He just had to make them understand, and all of this would be cleared up.

'Wait!' he cried over the tussle. 'Wait! We have to tell you what we found! The Awakeners are on their way! They're going to destroy the fleet!'

Drave held up the box. 'I've already heard all you have to say, traitor,' he said. 'And I'm not interested.'

Crake was wrenched forward then, and he found himself being propelled away from the aircraft, caught up in a tide of people. Faces and bodies surged in the electric light; breath steamed in the chill night air.

'I'll straighten this all out!' Bree shouted after him, an unfamiliar note of distress in her voice. 'Don't worry!'

Crake had no words worth saying back to her. He was shoved into position next to the Cap'n, who was handcuffed like he was, and the two of them were frogmarched towards the gate of the landing pad.

Frey threw him a filthy look. Crake turned away, ashamed.

Ashua sat against the wall of her cell, head hung and hugging her knees.

The lights were out, but nobody slept. She could hear the others shifting restlessly nearby, each in their own cells. They didn't talk between themselves, and she knew why. They didn't want to. Not while the traitor was listening.

The Samarlans. She'd been selling information to the Sammies all along. She wanted to feather her own nest because she didn't trust the crew would hold together, and in doing so, she'd condemned them all to death.

Stupid, stupid, stupid!

She needed to stay angry at herself. If she didn't, she'd think of other things. She'd think about how it might feel like when her legs dropped away and the rope snapped tight around her neck. She'd think about whether the noose would kill her instantly or if she'd have time to feel what was happening to her. Would her brain keep working, trapped there inside a skull attached to a useless body, filling her last instants with inconceivable horror?

She punched herself in the arm, hard. It was already bruised.

Jakeley Screed. That son of a bitch. He'd played her. And she'd fallen for it.

It was all so painfully simple. Dager Toyle, the man who'd originally employed her in Shasiith, was a Thacian spy. Screed had killed him and begun exterminating his network. Ashua thought she'd escaped, but she'd only bought herself some time. Screed had found her in the end, and when he did, he had a better use for her than just taking her out. She was in Vardia now, on the *Ketty Jay*, whose crew had acquired something of a reputation for mixing it up with the big players. Handily placed to feed the Sammies good information. So he sent Ocken to pose as one of Toyle's men, come to renew an old arrangement. He let Ashua believe he was dead, that it was safe again. And she, her eyes gleaming at the thought of all that money, never questioned it for a moment.

It wasn't her fault. She'd been tricked. She never meant the crew to be blamed for it. She'd never meant for them to find out.

Will you listen to yourself?

She punched herself in the same spot. The pain was enough to stop her breath for a moment. But she had to keep doing it, otherwise she might remember the expression on Malvery's face. The way he'd looked at her, the betrayal in his eyes. Or she might remember Crake, who could hardly bear to touch her. She'd remember the resentful glare the Cap'n gave her as he passed, reminding her whose fault it was that they were all getting arrested.

She sensed them out there, sitting in their cells in silence, because of her.

I'm sorry. I'm so, so sorry, she thought. But she couldn't say it. Apologies didn't mean shit in her world.

For a short while there, she'd felt like she had a family. But she'd been wrong. A few months didn't make a family. They didn't know her at all. Not well enough to understand why she did what she did. And they'd never trust her again. Because accidentally or not, she'd been spying for the Sammies. And, in the eyes of Malvery and Crake at least, there wasn't much she could do that was lower than that.

She punched herself again. She'd hurt like a bastard tomorrow. But she wouldn't hurt for long.

Thirty-Six

Gallows Talk – Bells – Hero of the Skies –
The Wrong End of a Whipping – 'It Ain't Over Till it's Done!'

The crew of the *Ketty Jay* stood in a line facing the grey morning, hands tied behind their backs and nooses round their necks. Side by side, as they'd always been.

Frey watched the sky as the judge droned on in the background, listing crimes real and imagined, filling up time with dreary accusations and pompous legalese. A biting chill was in the air. Clouds hung dark and heavy, muffling the weak winter sun. A flurry of thin sleet blew across the courtyard, leaving cold droplets on his skin.

There was a storm coming. He'd never been more certain of anything.

The witnesses assembled before the gallows platform were mainly soldiers, but there were familiar faces too. Samandra Bree, for one. She was handcuffed; it was the only way they'd let her stay after she went berserk at the sight of her lover at the end of a rope. She'd begged them in the end. Now she was quiet and pale, her face locked in an expression of abject fear, her eyes fixed only on Crake. There was something terrible in seeing a woman like that defanged.

Drave was there, of course, his arms folded beneath his broad chest, stern-faced and grim as rock. Grudge and Kyne were present, but under guard, as Samandra was. Their weapons had been taken from them until their reputations could be repaired. If it was shown that they'd been taken in by traitors, they'd be disciplined. Not that Frey much cared about that, given the circumstances.

He looked down at his feet with detached interest. Only a bolt kept the trapdoor he was standing on in place. Only that between him and oblivion. Seemed a precarious place to be.

'. . . and so it has been decreed that your loyalty to the Coalition and his Grace, the Archduke Monterick Arken, shall be determined on this day by such evidence as shall present itself, and on such evidence shall you be judged and your sentence carried out with all immediacy, or otherwise shall it commuted and judgement deferred to another day, for in such instance . . .'

Frey tuned out again. That was the nub of it, anyway. They were getting the formalities out of the way now, so the executioner could do his job once Drave gave the word. Drave had explained it to them in more straightforward terms.

'You're going to be up there just long enough to see the Awakener fleet destroyed, Frey,' he'd said. 'Just long enough to prove you're a liar. You can thank Kyne and Miss Bree that you've got even that much of a courtesy. I'd have seen you swinging by dawn.'

Unless the Awakener fleet *wasn't* destroyed, of course. Unless the Coalition fleet fell out of the sky. Then Frey would be proved right. Except then he'd be stuck in the middle of Thesk as the Awakener army invaded with overwhelming force, and they'd all likely end up killed in the carnage anyway.

Lose-lose, then. Still, it'd be worth it to see Drave's face.

The judge, a hangdog scarecrow of a man, snapped his book shut and stepped back. 'Anything to say?' Drave asked them.

'It's not too late, Drave!' Crake called out. He was sweating and trembling and looked like he was about to be sick, but he still found his voice. 'Tell the generals! Keep the fleet away! The Awakeners have a device that will destroy them all!'

Frey pitied his friend. There was something wide-eyed and hurt about him, the shock of a slapped child. He still wanted to believe in order and authority and the powers that be. He thought of the world as an upright, sensible place, where righteousness would prevail if only everyone tried hard enough. Frey knew otherwise. His only regret was that he hadn't been strong enough to deny Crake the chance to find out for himself.

'We know about the device, just like we know about the attack,' said Drave. 'We've known for some time. We have very good spies in the Century Knights; some of the best in the world. We know the Samarlans sold the device to the Awakeners, and that they smuggled it to the Barabac Delta and hid it there. And we know something else as well. *It doesn't work!*'

It was said with such damning conviction that Frey began to doubt it himself. Had they actually *seen* that particular device in action? No. They'd only heard what the scientists said to the Lord High Crypto-grapher, scientists who were just blowing smoke up the boss's arse to save their own necks. Hadn't they been griping about how it hadn't been tested enough? He'd assumed at the time that they were just being pernickety, crossing the 't's and dotting the 'i's, but now their lives were on the line, he wasn't so sure. Had it been tested at all? What had they actually said? He couldn't remember exactly.

'It *does* work!' Crake insisted. 'They got to your spies somehow. With Imperators, maybe. They want you to *think* it doesn't work so you'll bring the whole fleet to bear!'

'Now, there you're mistaken,' said Drave. 'They want us to think it *does* work so we *won't*. It took our best operatives months to dig out the date of the attack and uncover the news that the Azryx device wasn't working. But over the past week we've been getting all kinds of reports. Informants everywhere are saying the same thing: the device is operational. Awakeners have been defecting and giving themselves up just to bring us the news. Everyone has the same message: keep the fleet away from Thesk, or it'll be destroyed. Now doesn't that seem strange to you? News was so hard to come by, but all of a sudden it's so very easy. Almost as if the Awakeners wanted us to know it.'

Frey felt a grudging and bitter smile touch the edge of his mouth. The Awakeners had changed their tune a week ago. Just after the crew of the *Ketty Jay* escaped the Barabac Delta. *Well played, you slithery bastards.*

The Awakeners had tricked the Coalition into believing that their device didn't work. Then, when someone threatened to expose them, they flooded their information networks to make it seem they were desperate to convince their enemies of the opposite. The Coalition thought the Awakeners were bluffing them, but it was a double bluff. By the time Frey and his crew arrived with the truth, the Awakeners had already discredited it.

Add that to the fact that Drave had seen Frey fighting on the Awakener side with his own eyes, and Frey's frankly patchy history with the Coalition, and Frey could understand why they never had a hope of being believed. As far as Drave was concerned, they were just another bunch of pirates in the employ of the Awakeners, peddling false information so that Thesk would be undefended when the fleet arrived.

And maybe he was right. Maybe Frey and his crew had become unwitting patsies of the Awakeners, rushing to deliver their lies. Patriotic stupidity at its finest. And if so, the Coalition fleet would shoot the Awakeners down and they'd all hang.

He faced death with resignation. Despair had robbed him of will and energy. Failure had crushed him. It didn't even feel like he was really there, standing on the gallows. He felt disconnected from his own body. The immediacy of the danger didn't touch him.

Once, freedom was the most important thing to him, but he was a prisoner now. Later he'd come to care about his crew, but now he'd led one of them to her death and the rest to the noose. Only Pinn, the idiot, had got out in time. Lastly, he'd come to realise the depth of his feelings for Trinica. But he'd lost her too, and with her the chance to make amends for the death of their child and everything else he'd put her through.

Even if he survived to see another day, the idea of picking himself up again and going on with his life seemed an insurmountable effort. Better to end it here and now, perhaps. Better to let fortune wash him down whichever path it saw fit. He was done trying.

There was a commotion near the gates of the courtyard. A man in ducal livery stepped through, and announced loudly: 'His Grace, the Archduke Monterick Arken, Her Grace the Archduchess Eloithe, and the Lady Alixia!'

Even with nooses round their necks, Malvery, Harkins and Crake stood up straighter. He could see the hope in their eyes. The most powerful man in the land: surely *he* would set things to rights? Surely *he* wouldn't be so blind?

Stop hoping, Frey thought. *It only makes it worse.*

The crowd of soldiers moved aside, and the Archduke and his family came to stand before the gallows. Drave moved protectively to their side.

The Archduke wore a high-collared uniform and a heavy cloak of fur that rippled in the icy wind. He was tall and straight-backed, with dark red hair and a close-cropped beard. His wife was small, but her eyes were bright and fierce. Her dark hair blew about her face as she looked up at them, the baby Alixia swaddled in her arms.

The Archduke swept his gaze along the length of the platform, taking in each of the prisoners. Malvery, Harkins and Crake, standing to attention. Silo, statuesque, showing nothing as he stared straight ahead. Ashua, trying to stay strong but barely keeping it together. And finally Frey, who just gazed back at him blandly, unimpressed.

'This is him?' said the Archduke, in a rich and resonant bass voice.

'That's him,' said Drave.

The Archduke looked at Frey a long time. Frey returned the gaze insolently. The Archduke's face twitched with suppressed rage, and his eyes were hateful.

Finally the Archduke turned to Drave and nodded. Drave gave a tiny bow. The Archduke laid his hand on Eloithe's shoulder. She gave Frey a look of pure loathing and then allowed herself to be turned. Together they walked back towards the gate.

'Your Grace!' Crake called, his voice breaking as he did so. But the Archduke didn't stop, and the gates boomed closed behind him.

So that was what they'd come for. To look upon the face of the man who'd killed their son. They'd been cheated of their retribution the first time around, but they wouldn't be denied a second time.

Frey stared bleakly into the middle distance. Their pain was nothing to him. He'd pain enough of his own.

In the distance, a bell began to ring. More bells picked up the sound, until it spread across the city, a discordant clanging that rose from the streets to fill the air. The soldiers stirred.

'They're coming,' said Drave.

Pinn sang to himself over the sound of the engines, loud and off key and entirely without rhythm. He pumped his fist and swung his free arm around as if conducting himself. *'Arrr-tis Pinn! Hero of the skies! Ar-tis Pi-iiiiin! Heeeee-ro of the skiiiiiies!'*

All in all, Pinn was pretty happy about going to war.

The Awakener fleet seemed vast from close up. Pinn estimated its size as hundreds, possibly billions, of aircraft, though he allowed there might be some margin for error as he couldn't count very high at the best of times. There were patched-up rustbuckets and shining new fighter craft. There were crop-dusters and ex-military models, cargo haulers and thundering frigates and sleek high-end luxury liners. Anything that could fly – and some only barely could – had been pressed into service. Anything that could handle a gun had been fitted with one. Every scrap of might that the Awakeners had been able to muster was focused here, in one enormous convoy.

'*Heeeeeee-ro ooooooooof . . . THE SKIES!*' he finished with a flourish, and slumped back in his seat, out of breath and sweaty. He grinned at the ferrotype of Lisinda stuck to the dash. It had been creased and crumpled so thoroughly that he could barely make her out any more, but that didn't bother him. She'd always been prettier in real life anyway.

If only she could see him now. She'd dump that no-good husband of hers right there and then, and fly off with him into the sunset. That'd be a worthy ending to the book they'd write about his adventures. There wouldn't be a dry eye in Vardia.

Pinn had wanted to go to war ever since he was a boy. It was one of the great tragedies of his life that the Sammies called a truce to the Second Aerium War just days before he was old enough to enlist. He'd been in some pretty big scraps since then, but nothing like this. This was the real thing. This was properly epic.

The fact that he was fighting on the side of the Awakeners didn't much concern him. He wasn't the kind of person who thought about things like that. He'd abandoned the faith with the same speed and enthusiasm as he'd taken it up; in the end, he just wanted a scrap. Every chance to prove his superiority as a pilot was to be seized upon. And he reckoned you'd have to be a real idiot to be a pilot on the Coalition side today.

Unless you believed the rumours, of course. Over the last few days, word had leaked out about a secret weapon. Well, that was no news to Pinn – in fact, he may or may not have started the rumour himself while drunk – but more worrying were the new rumours that it didn't actually work. That troubled Pinn a little. He wasn't entirely sure who to believe: the high-ranking Awakeners who assured them that they'd seen victory in all their readings, or the grumbling mercs who'd suddenly realised they'd signed on to fight a Coalition Navy three times their size.

As the day of the attack got closer, dissent in the camp had grown. Tales were told by scared crews, of how their captains had gone off into the swamps and come back changed. Some captains, fearing they'd be next, tried to make a run for it. But the Awakeners were especially vigilant after the *Ketty Jay*'s escape, and the turncoats didn't get far.

An atmosphere of dread had begun to pervade the camp in its final days. Not least aboard the *Delirium Trigger*.

Pinn had found an unexpected drinking companion in Balomon Crund. The bosun of the *Delirium Trigger* was a dour and maudlin sort, not much given to conversation, but that was fine. Pinn would much rather talk *at* someone than *to* them, anyway. The few times Crund did have something to say, it was always on the same subject. The same woman Frey had been banging on about since Pinn could remember. Damn, it was tiresome listening to people talk about their sweethearts.

Pinn couldn't conceive of a relationship with a woman that didn't involve wanting to sleep with them. He'd even have given Jez a go, before he found out she was some bloody awful horror from beyond infinity. The same couldn't be said for Crund, though. The way he talked about his Cap'n, Pinn could tell. He was still devoted to her, even after what had happened, and it had left him broken-hearted.

Trinica had returned from the swamp a changed woman. She looked little different: ghastly white make-up, hair chopped, irises huge as coins and black as the void. But now it was more than a show. She'd become the part she'd played for her crew all these years. At last she was the terrible goddess they wanted.

Her mere presence in the room was enough to make the skin crawl. Nobody could argue with her: she reduced strong men to whimpering children. Her eyes had always been unnerving, but now nobody could stand her gaze. It bored into a man, stripped him to his core, dragged his secrets into the light.

There had been talk of mutiny before. Grumblings among the men. The Cap'n wasn't strong enough. She was sweet on that Frey feller, and it was making her soft. The first thing Trinica had done on her return was summon the head of those prospective mutineers to her cabin. The screams began soon after, and didn't stop for an hour. Nobody dared go in. They were not screams of pain: they were sounds beyond sanity.

When she was done, there was no more talk of mutiny.

Crund did his duties aboard the *Delirium Trigger*, but he could hardly bear to be there after that. It hurt too much to be around

Trinica. She wasn't the woman he'd known any more. So he escaped at every opportunity, and found Pinn in the bar more often than not, and together they drank to forget lost loves.

That first night, once they were good and hammered, Crund had charged Pinn with a task, and Pinn had made him a promise. He knew it was something important, except he couldn't quite remember what it was. Something to do with Frey. Something . . .

Lights began flashing all around, drawing him from his reverie. The electroheliographs on the surrounding aircraft were going crazy. He sat up, excited. That was the signal! The Coalition fleet was in sight!

Pinn was flying in the vanguard of the convoy, and he had a good view even through the clutter of aircraft surrounding him. Ahead of them, Thesk rose out of the hills beneath the louring clouds. A wide calm river flowed in from the east and then split and forked, dividing the city into three. It was deceptively calm from this distance, but the pilots had all been warned about the anti-aircraft batteries dotted around the city.

The Coalition fleet were not coming from the city, however. They were coming in from the sides. A pincer movement, designed to catch the enemy in the flanks, where they expected them to be weakest. It would be impossible to rearrange the convoy in time to respond.

But then, the Awakeners didn't intend to.

Pinn saw the fighters first, sleek, sharp Windblades swarming ahead of the bigger craft. The frigates came dipping down through the cloud behind them, vast slow ships of the air, bulky and bristling with cannons. In between were heavy assault craft, thickly armoured and deadly.

They came, and they kept coming, and when the horizon was dark with aircraft they kept coming still. The convoy, that had seemed so mighty, was dwarfed by its opposition. The entirety of the Coalition Navy, or near enough as made no difference; probably they still had skeleton forces elsewhere. The enemy pilots were highly trained and equipped with the best technology money could buy. The Awakeners were more than three-quarters volunteers.

But Pinn didn't care about the odds. That wasn't the kind of thing heroes worried over.

The formation started coming apart around him as fighters broke off to intercept the enemy. The plan was simple: stay near the convoy and defend it. Pinn could just about cope with remembering that. As soon as his way was clear, he peeled off to port and made his way out of the crowd and into open air. He'd need a bit of room for the fight.

Ahead of him, the Windblades were closing in. The Awakener fighters arrowed towards them. Pinn hunched over his flight stick, the cockpit rattling, thrusters roaring as he pushed them to their limits. A smile spread over his chubby face.

'Alright fellers,' he muttered. 'Who wants to be the first to feel Uncle Artis's toecap up their arse?'

One of the Windblades opened fire early, sending out a burst of tracers. It didn't get near Pinn, but it was enough to draw his attention.

'Think you just volunteered, mate,' he said. He angled his craft towards the overenthusiastic pilot, his finger hovering over the trigger.

The two clouds of fighters rushed towards each other, the gap closing rapidly with every second. Suddenly the air was full of gunfire as everyone let loose at once. Bullets whined and whipped past the cockpit. An aircraft to his right exploded.

Pinn kept his cool and held his course, waited that extra second, and pressed down on his guns. A trail of bullets scored across the nosecone of his target, shattered the canopy, raked up its back. The Windblade erupted in a ball of smoke and fire.

The two fronts of fighters met. Suddenly it wasn't bullets but aircraft lashing past him, engines screaming. Pinn screamed with them, mindless with joy. He banked and swooped, diving in among the enemy. Combat became a muddle, Awakener and Coalition craft all mixed together, dodging and shooting.

Pinn cackled with glee as he was slammed here and there by g-forces. He took down another Windblade, and another. The enemy barely noticed him in the confusion. His craft was frustratingly sluggish – too much time rotting in the swamp air, probably – but Pinn rose above it. He'd run rings round these losers even if he was flying one of those cannon-fodder junkers. He could fly anything!

He lost himself in the combat. Time slipped out of his grasp. He was action and reaction, riding adrenaline, hyper-alert. His senses were overcome by the noise of the engines, the flash of explosions, movement everywhere.

It was only when he heard the first of the anti-aircraft guns that he realised how near they'd got to Thesk. The convoy had been ploughing onward while the fighters scrapped around them; now they were close enough for the city's weapons to be deployed.

Pinn jumped in his seat as a freighter near the front of the convoy was ripped in half, belching flame as it fell away in pieces. Shells flew up from below and burst among the Awakener's heavy craft. The air filled with explosions.

The attacks were not all from below, either. The Coalition frigates had come within range now, and their guns began to smash into the convoy's flanks. The convoy fired back, but the distance was too extreme for accuracy, and the Navy had the better of it. Squeezed between the two halves of the fleet, battered by the city's weapons, the Awakeners began to take heavy losses.

And still they ploughed onward.

Deadly projectiles flew in all directions. Pinn climbed to get above the convoy and out of the way. The sight below him was not encouraging. The aircraft on the convoy's flanks were being torn apart. He saw another of the Awakeners' big freighters go down. Awakener outflyers battled with the Windblades in the sky all around him, but they were getting decimated.

Doubt began to nibble at Pinn's confidence. When were the Awakeners going to hit the button? When would the secret weapon come into play? Was it possible that the rumours were true? Was it possible that it really *didn't* work, that this whole thing had been a massive bluff, and the convoy was only slogging onward to its doom?

Then a Windblade shot across his flight path, and he was after it like a dog after a rabbit. It took him back into the thick of the fray. He dodged through the smoke of fresh kills, was showered in shrapnel. Explosions rocked him, setting him shuddering in his seat, pushing his craft this way and that. Two Awakener craft collided off his starboard wing, smashing head-on into each other in the confusion.

He hung on to the Windblade's tail as long as he could, but in the end he lost it. He banged the dash in frustration. The Coalition fighter was faster and more manoeuvrable. He wasn't used to being outclassed by an enemy's aircraft, and it made him petulant. He looked for another Windblade to destroy, to make himself feel better.

A detonation nearby rocked him. The Coalition frigates were alarmingly close now. He swung back towards the convoy. The Awakeners had put most of their junk freighters on the edges of the convoy to soak up the damage, but they weren't well armoured and didn't last long. It seemed like the whole outer layer of aircraft was ablaze. The convoy was getting shredded.

Pinn began to feel uneasy about this whole affair. Bad odds he could handle, but no one liked to be on the wrong end of a whipping. They were getting smashed from three sides and were barely even fighting back. He saw a few of the mid-sized craft trying to peel away from the Awakeners, intent on making a run for it. They didn't believe in the Awakeners' secret weapon. Maybe Pinn didn't, either. Maybe *he* should do what they were doing.

Bullets lashed through the air before his nose. He rolled and dived to avoid the attack. A couple of bullets punched his fuselage, but it was just a scratch. He levelled out and looked over his shoulder. A Windblade, coming in on his tail. No, *three* Windblades. The bastards were hunting in packs.

Alright, he thought. *If that's how you want it. Let's see you catch me.*

He threw his craft to starboard. And in that instant, something changed.

It felt like a ghost had passed through him. For the span of a heartbeat, time slowed and everything went silent. There was a huge sense of peace in his breast. His eyes found Lisinda's picture on his dash, and looked upon her fondly, as if she might be the last thing he ever saw.

Then the sensation was gone, and even though it was no longer inside him, he imagined he could feel it rippling outwards in a great sphere, with the convoy at its centre. Up into the sky, down towards the ground, spreading to encompass the combatants in the air and the city in the hills. There was nothing to be seen of it with the naked eye, except for its effects. Where it went, pandemonium followed.

The Azryx device had been activated. And it worked exactly as it was meant to.

The Windblades went first. They were already travelling at speed when their controls went haywire. One moment they were carving graceful paths through the air, the next they were corkscrewing wildly. In the crowded sky, they collided with one another and with Awakener fighters, or swatted themselves against the flanks of huge freighters.

Pinn evaded frantically as Windblades flew every which way and blazing pieces of aircraft rained down all around him. He ran a chicane of explosions, then hauled on his flight stick to get up above the carnage before he was taken down. G-forces pulled at him, crushing him into his seat, making his head light. A fighter plunged past his nose close enough that he almost stalled, but he rode it out, and then suddenly there was nothing around him but sky. He levelled out, high above the plane of the battle, and then looked down on the Coalition fleet.

There were no guns any more. Thesk's artillery had gone quiet. The Navy frigates dipped towards the earth in eerie, graceful silence as their aerium tanks vented, or ploughed into one another with stately momentum. The fighters, in contrast, were like fireflies, looping crazily, flashing where they exploded. A slow rain of burning metal was falling towards the hills and the city below, in thin fiery streams or colossal blazing chunks.

Pinn stared down in wonder, the flames reflected in his eyes as he drank in the sight greedily. From on high, the sheer scale of it was magnificent. He felt godlike. He'd never seen such beautiful destruction in all his born days.

'We won,' he whispered to himself. Then, louder: 'We won!'

The Coalition Navy fell into disorder and ruin behind them, and the Awakener convoy ploughed on towards the capital.

Crake watched from the gallows with tears in his eyes. All around him, soldiers were shouting, and there were cries of despair. But all he felt was terrible, terrible sadness.

Hundreds of aircraft. Thousands of lives. And we couldn't stop it.

The wind blew around the crag that the palace stood upon, bringing the sound of distant detonations as Coalition craft smashed into the earth. In the streets surrounding the palace, fires had begun. The battle had been fought to the east of the city, and most of the aircraft fell on the hills, but there had been a few flying overhead when the Azryx device was activated, and others had strayed from the battlefield. He watched as a light passenger craft made a shallow dive into a row of houses. It disappeared from view, and flame bloomed where it hit.

Rain began to fall. It came quick and heavy, as if someone had turned on a shower. Cold, stinging rain, falling on his face and shoulders, soaking him.

'*Drave!*' Malvery screamed in rage. '*Do you bloody well believe us now?*'

But Drave wasn't listening to him. He was shouting at the soldiers. 'To your positions! We have a city to defend!'

'Get me out of these shackles, Drave, you idiot son of a bitch!' Samandra yelled at him.

Drave motioned at a soldier, who ran over with the key and freed her. 'You three!' he said, motioning towards the Century Knights. 'With me! Protect the Archduke!'

Samandra ignored him. She shook off her shackles and ran up to the gallows, where she tugged the noose from around Crake's neck. He looked at her, shock and bewilderment in his eyes.

She read his thoughts. 'Hey!' she shouted. 'It ain't over! You hear? It ain't over till it's done!' And she kissed him, hard enough to hurt.

'Little help for the rest of us?' Malvery cried in exasperation, struggling to get his head out of his own noose.

Grudge and Kyne pushed past their guards and hurried to the gallows, where they took the nooses from around the necks of the *Ketty Jay*'s crew and untied the ropes that bound their hands.

'Century Knights!' Drave bellowed from the doorway, his face running with rain. 'Have you forgotten the oaths you swore?'

Grudge and Kyne looked at one another, then at Samandra. She was still staring into Crake's eyes, her hands on his cheeks. He saw her face in front of him, but he couldn't make sense of it all. Everything seemed dull and dreamlike to him. It couldn't be happening. It couldn't be. The fall of the Coalition. The end of everything he'd known.

'I gotta go,' she said to him. 'Sorry, honey. I gotta go. I swore an oath.'

'*Samandra Bree!*' Drave yelled. 'Are you a Century Knight or aren't you?'

She bit her lip. Tears welled, but didn't fall. 'I gotta go,' she said, and she ran. Crake reached for her, from instinct more than reason, but she was gone. By the time he looked around, the four Century Knights were on their way out of the courtyard. The soldiers had poured out with them. Only the crew were left, standing on the gallows, drenched by the hissing rain. None of them knew quite what to do with their newfound freedom.

'Well?' snapped Silo. 'Ain't none of us dead today. Get movin'!'

Malvery rounded on Ashua, who was standing a little way apart from the group. 'Her too?' he said. She flinched slightly at his tone.

'Ain't the time, Doc. She one of us till the Cap'n says otherwise.'

Malvery turned to Frey. 'Cap'n?'

Frey looked back at him, and his eyes were dead. 'Right now there's only one single thing in this world I give a shit about, and she's waiting on the landing pad.' He looked up into the grey, oppressive sky, and at the convoy of Awakener craft coming closer. 'Let's get out of this damn rain.'

Thirty-Seven

Vard Against Vard – The End of the Fairytale –
Harkins the Soldier – A Secret Weapon

By the time they reached the landing pad, the Awakeners were bombing the city.

Malvery huffed and puffed and cursed when he had the breath to do so. If only he was a younger man; younger and fitter and not so fond of drink. But the city needed him now. His country needed him. He pulled up his belt and staggered on in the wake of the others.

The landing pad was in chaos. Rain lashed the scene. Aircraft crew ran here and there, sodden grey ghosts in the downpour. Many hadn't been privy to the news of the Awakeners' secret weapon, and they had no idea why the Navy had fallen from the sky. Now they swarmed frantically over their aircraft, worrying at maintenance panels or stabbing buttons, unable to understand why the engines wouldn't start.

Beyond the high walls that surrounded the landing pad, past a squat tower with wrought-iron balconies and a copper dome, Malvery could see the Awakener fleet spreading over the city like a vast black hand. And he saw the bombs, little pellets of death tumbling from the bellies of the frigates towards the streets below.

They're bombing us! he thought in outrage. *Bombing their own people!*

The dull *crump* of distant explosions came to him, and made his blood boil. Vard against Vard. Countryman versus countryman, who so recently had fought side by side against the Sammies. He couldn't wrap his head around it. Not since the Ducal Rebellion had such a thing happened, one hundred and fifty years ago. And yet even as that civil war ended, the seeds were being sown for a new one. For it was the followers of the deposed king who became the first Awakeners, turning his mad scrawlings into prophecy. And that had brought them to this.

379

Malvery was a man who let life happen to him rather than imposing himself upon it. Yet this was too much, even for him. Good men and women, in their ignorance, were fighting on the side of daemons to depose their Archduke. It was madness, and it had to be stopped.

They ran across the landing pad towards the *Ketty Jay*. No one paid them any attention. He caught Ashua's eye as she ran alongside him, and there was fear of him in her gaze, and something like hope. She was puppyish in her shame, desperate for his forgiveness. But he looked away. She'd hurt him too much for that.

He'd begun to think of her as a daughter. He couldn't help it. Even that tattoo all over the side of her face looked to Malvery like the mark of an insecure adolescent staking her place in the world. He'd hugged her to his breast, and she'd bitten him.

Did you know what you were doing? he thought. *Were you working for the Sammies all along?*

He could hardly bear the sight of her. And yet each time he wounded her with his scorn, it stung him just as badly. What a damned soft-hearted old fool he was.

Frey ran up to a panel on one of the *Ketty Jay*'s landing struts and punched in a code. The cargo ramp hissed open, and they hurried in out of the rain. Malvery came last. He was halfway up the ramp when a flash of lightning flickered behind the clouds, illuminating a black frigate sliding through the sky in the distance. A rolling grumble of thunder passed overhead.

He knew that craft. The *Delirium Trigger*.

'Malvery! Get up here!' Frey called.

Malvery wiped the rain from his wet moustache and hurried inside.

Bess was standing immobile in the corner of the hold; Crake had put her to sleep during the journey to Thesk, and nothing but Crake's whistle would wake her up again. Silo had gone to a chest and was handing out weapons. They'd stashed their guns before arrival in order to indicate their peaceful intentions.

Frey was on the metal stairway leading to the main deck. 'Forget about them,' he told Silo. 'Doc, I need you on the autocannon.'

It took Malvery a moment to catch up. He'd assumed the *Ketty Jay* was out of commission, and they were just coming back for their weapons.

'We're taking off, Doc!' Frey said impatiently. 'Those things the

Awakeners fitted to our engines back in the camp? They cancel out the Azryx device. That's how the Awakeners are still up in the air.'

'Where are we going?' Harkins asked.

Frey looked surprised that he even had to answer that question. 'Away,' he said.

Malvery was again slow to take Frey's meaning, but this time it was for a different reason. He just couldn't conceive of running away from something as important as was happening here in Thesk.

'Cap'n,' he said. 'If the *Ketty Jay* can fly . . . Cap'n, we can't just take her and go! We have to—'

'We don't have to do a bloody thing!' Frey snapped. 'We tried to warn 'em and they tried to kill us. The Archduke, the generals, every overprivileged arseburp in this whole damn city can drown in their own shit for all I care. Present company excepted,' he added, nodding at Crake.

'Too kind,' Crake said uncertainly.

'Cap'n, you can't!' Malvery was aghast. 'They're gonna destroy the Coalition! Don't you get it? Daemons are gonna rule this land!'

'And adding our corpses to the pile is gonna achieve exactly *what?*' Frey cried. 'Listen, Doc, I get it. You're noble. You, Crake and Harkins, you're all very noble. But the fairytale's over now. I risked my neck for your principles, and those sons of bitches almost hung me by it. Well, I've got principles too, and they've kept me alive a lot longer than yours will. So I'm going. You can come with me, or you can piss off.'

The crew exchanged uncertain glances. They'd all been on the end of one of the Cap'n's rants before, but rarely with this level of bitterness and spite.

'What about Trinica?' Crake said.

Her name hit Frey like a blow, and took the wind out of him for a moment. The rage left his eyes, and something worse took its place. 'It's finished,' he said quietly. 'It's over. Everything's lost. And I'm done with the lot of it.'

Malvery strode over to the chest where Silo stood. 'Gimme my shotgun,' he said, holding out a hand. Silo slapped it into his palm. 'Shells,' he said, and Silo slung him a bag jangling with them. He pressed a shell into the chamber and primed it with a crunch.

'You're not coming, Doc?' Frey asked.

The tone of his voice caused Malvery to stop. The resignation there. This man was his friend. They'd been through so much together. Without the *Ketty Jay*, Malvery would likely have drunk himself to death. He knew Frey, knew exactly why he was acting this way. He wanted to be there to support him, to help him through it.

But here, now, there were more important things than Frey.

'I ain't coming,' he said.

Frey took the news without emotion. He turned to Crake. 'You?'

'Frey,' said Crake. 'Don't do this.'

'I'm leaving, Crake. Are you staying or coming?'

Crake met his gaze levelly. 'I can't leave.'

'Thought not,' said Frey. 'Your woman, eh?'

'It's more than that,' he said. 'And if I'm staying, Bess is too.'

'Naturally,' said Frey. 'What about you, Harkins?'

Harkins looked distraught. 'Cap'n . . . I mean . . . Shouldn't we oughta stay?'

'I'm not staying,' said Frey. He was adamant. 'Are you?'

Harkins turned to Malvery and Crake, as if they could help him out of his predicament. But they had no help to give him. He wavered a moment, and then his face hardened, he straightened his back and raised his head. He looked Frey in the eye and saluted.

'It's been an honour serving with you, Cap'n,' he said.

Frey nodded listlessly to himself. An agonising silence followed. They pitied him, standing there. Frey was a man who'd gambled on a losing hand, and he just kept on gambling bigger to get himself out of it. They'd lost crew members before, but nothing like this. This would split them apart for good. Nobody wanted to see the dissolution of the *Ketty Jay*'s crew, but the Cap'n had forced the issue. He'd dug in his heels, and made them choose between loyalty to him and loyalty to their country. Maybe, if he'd known the outcome, he'd never have tested them that way. But it was too late to back down now.

'Alright, then,' he said dismissively, turning away to ascend the stairs. 'Grab your guns and get off my aircraft. The rest of you—'

'I'm not coming,' said Ashua.

Frey stopped, his shoulders bunched with tension. 'You too?'

'Me too.'

'You're a traitor,' he said, and by the sound of it his teeth were gritted. 'You're a child of the slums and you spent most your life in

Samarla. They'll probably hang you anyway if you survive. What in rot's name do you owe them?'

'It's not them I owe,' she said. She turned her gaze to Crake, then to Malvery, and held it there with unexpected defiance. 'I'm no traitor,' she told him. 'I made a mistake. You ever made a mistake?'

The way she said it, it was as if she knew. About his friend Henvid Clack, about that night when Malvery operated while drunk, about the death that he'd never been able to forget. He looked at her then, with her muddy ginger hair spiky with rain, and she seemed so damned *young*. Just a girl, really. She'd gone her whole life fighting her own corner. Everyone she'd ever known had dropped her in the end. And it made him ashamed that he was on the verge of doing the same.

'Yeah,' he said. 'I made mistakes.'

'I thought they were Thacians,' she said. 'I was giving them information about the Sammies at first, the Awakeners later. Not the Vards. Doesn't make it right, but it makes it better.' She was trembling; he could see it. There wasn't much that scared her, but pushing the words out was harder than anything. 'I'll make it up to you. I'll fight with you here. If you want.'

Malvery swallowed. His throat had gone tight, and there were tears in his eyes. He turned away to hide it.

'Malvery?' said Crake. *What do you want to do? It's your call.*

Malvery waved a hand. 'Aye,' he said thickly. 'She's alright.'

Frey had turned round on the stairs to face them. He seemed like a man who'd taken too many blows, and was waiting for the *coup de grâce*. 'What about you, Silo?'

The Murthian had been watching the proceedings without visible emotion. Weighing things up, the way he did. Who knew what went on behind those eyes?

Go with him, Malvery thought. *For rot's sake, go with him. Don't leave the Cap'n alone after all he's done for us.*

Silo took a long time with his decision. No one rushed him. He wouldn't be rushed. At last he stirred and opened his mouth.

'Where we goin', Cap'n?'

Malvery let out a small sigh of relief. By now he'd mastered the swell of emotion that threatened to embarrass him. He fished green-lensed glasses from his breast pocket and popped them back on his nose.

'We've all made our choices, then,' said Frey, and his voice was dull with loss. 'I'm leaving right now, before the Awakener fleet gets here. Going north to Yortland, in case any of you change your minds. I suggest you get off the *Ketty Jay* while you still can.' He made to turn his back on them, but he hesitated. With some effort, he swallowed down pride and bile, and said 'Good luck, all of you. We had some times, didn't we?'

'We had some times,' Malvery agreed gravely.

'Frey . . .' said Crake. He was about to plead with the Cap'n to reconsider, but Malvery put a hand on his arm to stop him. It would do no good, and they both knew it.

Frey put his head down and walked on up the stairs. Malvery watched him go with a sense of desolation. Something had been done here that couldn't be undone.

He briefly wondered what would happen to his meagre things, his doctor's supplies, all the accoutrements of his old life. He wondered if he would have time to say goodbye to Jez, sewn up in a bag on the infirmary's operating table. He decided it didn't matter. None of it did. Nothing mattered but right now.

'Come on,' he said to them all. 'Get your guns.'

'But my books . . .' said Crake weakly. 'My equipment . . .'

'Don't reckon the Cap'n's in the mood to wait,' said Silo.

'Leave 'em,' said Malvery. 'Bess is what's important.'

Crake nodded reluctantly. He put his brass whistle to his lips and blew a silent note. In the dark, hollow depths of the armoured suit in the corner, two bright points like stars appeared. Bess stretched as she awoke.

They heard Frey powering up the engines as Silo handed them their weapons. The bombs were getting closer now. Crake reluctantly took a pistol and some ammo. When it came Ashua's turn, Silo held up her pistol and looked at her hard.

'Time was, Cap'n didn't want you on his crew,' he said. 'Only reason you got to stay was 'cause I vouched for you. Don't make no fool of me.'

Ashua took his words as seriously as they were intended. 'I'll make it right,' she said.

'See you do,' said Silo, and slapped the pistol into her hand.

The *Ketty Jay* creaked underneath them, and they felt the floor rise slightly. Time had run out. Malvery, Crake, Harkins, Ashua and Bess hurried down the ramp and off the *Ketty Jay*.

Outside, the rain was still pouring hard. Some of the pilots, attracted by the sound of engines, were heading across the landing pad towards them, evidently wondering why a craft with Awakeners sigils was taking off when they couldn't. They stopped being half so curious when they caught sight of the eight-foot metal golem coming out of it.

The *Ketty Jay* was lifting from the ground even before they'd hopped down. Silo pulled the lever to shut the ramp as soon as the last of them were off. Malvery looked back at the Murthian, and their eyes met through the closing gap.

I'll never see him again, he thought to himself. *Him or the Cap'n.*

Then the ramp closed, and he was shut out.

He caught an acrid whiff of aerium gas as the *Ketty Jay*'s skids left the landing pad. They stepped back as she drifted up into the air. The Coalition pilots raised their guns, uncertain whether to shoot at it or not. Frey didn't give them the chance. He engaged the thrusters while the *Ketty Jay* was still recklessly low. A blast of hot air shoved at the crew, blowing their coats and hair about.

Then the *Ketty Jay* roared off into the cloud and the rain and the storm, and dwindled until they saw it no more.

The pilots had turned their guns on the crew now, still unsure as to what had just happened. 'Point them guns elsewhere, you bunch of idiots! We're on your side!' Malvery bellowed. He won them over by sheer volume. 'Your aircraft ain't gonna work while the Awakeners are in the sky, and they'll be dropping troops on us any minute, like as not. Ain't you got anywhere more useful to be?'

The troops didn't argue with that. They dispersed, casting uneasy glances at Bess, who lumbered about restlessly. The fear in the air had set her on edge.

'I have to find Samandra,' said Crake.

'Sounds like a plan to me,' Malvery replied. 'Anyone's gonna be in the thick of it, it's her.'

'Not me,' said Harkins. 'I've got somewhere else to be.'

Malvery was surprised. Harkins' face was set and grim beneath his patched-up pilot's cap. 'Where are *you* going?'

Harkins pointed at the Firecrow, sitting silent in the hissing rain. 'There's one more aircraft that can still fly.'

Crake gaped. 'Harkins! You're not going up there?'

'I mean . . . I don't think I'll be much use down here, will I?'

'It's one against hundreds! It's suicide!'

Harkins had the look about him of a man walking on a frozen lake. Only the thin ice of discipline stood between him and the freezing depths of terror. But he was determined; Malvery saw that. And Malvery knew how much courage it took for a man like Harkins to make a stand.

'Malvery!' Crake said. 'Tell him! He can't go up there alone in that one little fighter!'

Harkins' gaze went nervously to Malvery. *Maybe he'd change his mind if I persuaded him,* Malvery thought. *But how much would it cost him if he backed down now? Better to live a coward, or die a hero? I know what the Cap'n would say. But he ain't here any more.*

Remembering his time in the Army during the First Aerium War, Malvery stood up straight, put his heels together, and saluted smartly from the elbow. 'Do your country proud, soldier,' he said.

Harkins had expected an argument. The doctor's unexpected support firmed his resolve instead. He returned Malvery's salute, gave him a quick and grateful smile, and then scampered off towards the Firecrow. Crake looked at Malvery, aghast.

'Man's gotta do what he's gotta do,' said Malvery. 'Seems like it's the day for that.'

'Turns out he really *isn't* a chickenshit,' said Ashua, almost to herself.

Malvery looked over at her. It still hurt him to do so. Forgiveness wouldn't come easy: there was a lot of disappointment and anger still to dilute. But she'd stayed with him, and she'd come as close as she ever would to an apology. She wanted to make it up to him. He had to let her try.

'The four of us, then,' he said. He hefted his shotgun. 'Let's get to it.'

★

Samandra found them, in the end, rather than the other way around. They were being held at gunpoint and surrounded by soldiers in a cobbled quad overlooked by an elaborate clock.

'Can't leave you alone for two minutes, can I?' she said as she strode through the circle of Coalition guards, rain pouring off her tricorn hat. 'Guns down, fellers. You don't want to make Bess nervous.'

It was good advice. Bess didn't like guns, and despite Crake's best efforts to soothe her, he wasn't sure he could do it much longer. Samandra had arrived just in time.

'They were asking for you,' said the sergeant. 'We didn't know who they were, but they had no uniforms, so . . .'

'Don't worry, you did good,' she told him. She put her hands on her hips and turned an exasperated face on her lover. 'Did you think you could just go running about the Archduke's palace with that walking junkpile in tow?' Then she broke into a smile and grabbed him by the lapels and kissed him.

All the sadness and distress he'd felt at the *Ketty Jay*'s departure melted away then, and he knew he'd done the right thing by staying. He was supposed to be here with her, he thought, as he tasted rainwater on her lips. Whatever happened next, this was where he belonged.

The moment was all too brief, and she let him go. 'Where's the rest of you?' she asked.

'It's just us,' said Crake.

'Ah,' said Samandra. Her face fell a little as she grasped the situation. 'Then you all better stick with me, if you don't want to get arrested again.'

She was evidently in a hurry, and they followed her through the palace grounds at a jog. Groups of soldiers ran past in the other direction; commanding officers shouted orders. Over the walls they could see the Awakener feet closing in from the east. They could hear the enemy's engines now, and the explosions were near enough to shake the ground beneath their feet.

'Sons of bitches are softening us up!' Samandra cried over the rain and thunder. 'They're puttin' troops down in the outer districts already. They'll take strategic points round the city, seize up our supply lines, try to force a surrender!'

'Then why,' Malvery puffed, 'are we running *away* from the fight?'
'You'll see,' said Samandra.

She led them through the maze of streets that sprawled around the Archduke's palace, high up on the great volcanic plug that overlooked Thesk. Soon they came to a small, out-of-the-way area with a neglected air about it. There she led them into a dead end yard, bordered on three sides by grim and worn walls of black stone. The last wall belonged to a building that looked like a storehouse or factory.

Waiting in the yard were Kyne and several soldiers. Kyne was holding an elaborately sculpted staff of twisted brass, as tall as he was, with a black orb cradled near its tip.

'Crake!' said the masked man. 'I'm glad you made it. You wouldn't want to miss this!'

'Feller's so damn dramatic,' Samandra said as an aside. 'Get on with it, Kyne!'

Kyne turned towards the building and held the staff in the air. Crake felt his senses prickle as a wave of daemonic energy passed over him. With a grinding of gears, a section of the wall sank into the ground.

The staff is the key, he thought to himself, excitement rising in his breast as the gap widened. *But the key to what?*

Inside, all was darkness. The wall rumbled out of sight. Crake peered into the void beyond.

Lightning flickered. Sharp light reflected off metal. And then something stirred within. A slow, huge movement, followed by another elsewhere. He heard a dull boom. A footstep.

They came out of the darkness and into the rain-swept and stormy morning. They clanked and creaked and stamped and steamed. There were dozens in there. Dozens and more.

Crake's mouth fell open. Bess made a curious cooing noise.

'Ladies and gentlemen,' said Samandra with a flourish. 'Meet our own secret weapon. The Archduke's golem army!'

Thirty-Eight

Harkins Alone – Pinn's War – Swansong –
The Wolverine – A Turn Up for the Books

We are many and we are one. Your wings are my wings. We
fly with one engine, we fight with one heart. I am the
Coalition Navy, and the Coalition Navy is me.

For the first time in Harkins' life, that was literally true.

He said the mantra over and over in his head as he flew away from
the Imperial palace and into the storm-hacked morning. Once, it had
been part of his daily ritual. They'd said it at roll-call every day. He'd
repeated it so many times that the words became automatic and
meaningless.

I am the Coalition Navy, he thought. *I'm all that's left.*

Encased in the cockpit of the Firecrow, surrounded by the warming
bellow of the thrusters and the howl of the wind, he was alone. The
Firecrow was painted with Awakener insignia, so he wouldn't be
attacked. He was an interloper among the enemy, far from help.
Whatever he did now, he'd do on his own.

He remembered his earcuff. Crake had given it back to him after
the battle at the Tarlock mansion, so he could keep in touch with the
Cap'n during the flight. Now he dug in his pocket and clipped in on,
hoping to hear voices. Something to relieve this sudden awful soli-
tude, this sense of being cast into the void.

Nothing. He heard rustles and muffled noises now and then, but
that was all. None of the others were wearing them. Still, he left the
earcuff on. Even those small sounds felt like company, and he'd take
what he could get up here in the slaty sky, hurtling through a hostile
world.

Fighters raced past beneath him, making low strafing runs along
the city streets. The populace were being punished for their resistance; Thesk was the sanctuary of the nonbelievers, and lessons had to

389

be learned. This was no peaceful coup, but a bloody invasion. In a stark blaze of lightning, he saw dozens of people fleeing along a boulevard towards the palace, swarming like insects far below.

Overhead and around him were the frigates and larger craft, their floods shining, blurred by a haze of rain-mist. They ploughed on through the sky, dropping bombs as they went, wounding the capital with fire and destruction. The sight of them drifting unopposed through Coalition skies offended him. With the anti-aircraft batteries choked off by the Azryx device, the Awakeners had no fear any more.

Well, Harkins would give them something to fear.

He slipped in behind a fighter that was just starting a bombing run. It was another Firecrow, all but identical to his. Since they were sold off by the Navy after the Second Aerium War to make way for the Windblades, Firecrows were everywhere, a cheap and reliable combat craft. But they were still dangerous, and many had found their way to the Awakener fleet.

Start with the best fighters, he told himself. *Leave the rustbuckets. Just do as much damage as you can.*

The pilot was oblivious to the threat. So safe and secure in his belief that the battle was won. He didn't even notice Harkins lining up on his tail. But in his mind's eye Harkins could still see the Coalition craft falling from the sky, thousands of fighting men and women wiped out in one appalling, cruel, dishonourable stroke. He felt rage bubbling up through him, thawing his fear. He felt the urge to be wanton and vicious.

His finger cradled the trigger. His teeth were gritted. He had the shot, and yet . . .

. . . and yet he didn't fire. Something held him back. Right now he was hidden; right now he still had the opportunity of escape. He could fly away and leave with his life. The moment he squeezed that trigger, he'd be starting something that could only end in his destruction.

Once, that would have been enough to cow him. Once his nerve would have broken at the thought of the Awakeners' retribution. But something had awakened in him now, a new awareness, and once realised it couldn't be ignored.

For a long time now, he'd lived in constant terror, shrinking away from everything and everyone. A miserable, confined existence, so afraid of death he was barely alive. And he couldn't do it any more. Better to live ten minutes as a wolf than ten years as a rabbit.

So Harkins bared his teeth, and pulled the trigger.

The pilot in the other Firecrow didn't have a chance. There was no time to evade. Harkins' guns chewed up his tail assembly, tearing through metal and blasting his rudder to pieces. The fighter slewed wildly, bullets tore along its fuselage, and it exploded.

Harkins pulled away, racing off through the sky. Other fighters were around, some near, some far. Had anyone seen him? He didn't know. The rain and gloom limited visibility, and the skies were still chaotic, with so many half-trained pilots flying about.

Well, it didn't matter. No going back now. A Kentickson Aeronaut came flying in from his starboard side, across his path. He swung around and took position on its tail. It was heading down for a strafing run. Harkins followed it down, and opened up on its back end. Tracer fire punched holes up its spine, and the fuel tank was hit. The holes smouldered, fizzed into life like a dynamite fuse, and seconds later the Aeronaut blew apart, sending shrapnel wheeling through the air.

He shot down another, and another, before the Awakeners started to pay attention. Even then, they couldn't catch him. He banked and looped, turning their best manoeuvres against them, running rings round the rookies and out-thinking the veterans. All around him, planes fell out of the sky. He flew with a freedom that he hadn't know since his glory days. There was nothing left to lose now, and he knew at last what Pinn had known every time he flew into battle. He knew what it was to be unafraid of death.

We are many and we are one, he thought to himself, and his hangdog face lit up in the muzzle flash of his machine guns.

Pinn's overwhelming impression was one of huge disappointment.

That was *it*? That was his war? A few minutes of wiping the sky with Coalition pilots, and then it was over? Granted, the end of the Coalition Navy had been spectacular, but his elation quickly gave way to boredom as the guns went quiet. Where was the fight against impossible odds, the hair-raising escapes, the suicidal bravery? Where was the *heroism*?

If this was the climax of the civil war and the end of the Coalition, then frankly, he felt robbed.

Below him, the city rumbled with explosions. Domes collapsed and grey, rain-battered buildings crumbled. Fighters swooped with blazing guns, sending citizens and militia scattering. The thought of attacking civilians didn't excite him much. There was no challenge there since the anti-aircraft guns had been disabled.

He flew on listlessly through the sky. Lisinda's creased portrait radiated disapproval from the dash.

'Well, I can't bloody help it if no one has the pods to fight me, can I?' he snapped at her in exasperation.

He spotted the Awakeners' flagship off to starboard, a long, rectangular craft, split at the ends like an old rotted beam. The Lord High Cryptographer was on board, they said. He remembered that moment in the Awakener base when he'd gazed upon the leader of the Awakeners, and felt something stir inside that had inspired him to abandon his friends. He fancied he could feel his presence now.

Nearby was a familiar shape: the black bulk of the *Delirium Trigger*, hanging in the sky. Other frigates had begun sending down landing shuttles full of troops, but the *Delirium Trigger* just hung there in the storm. Lightning flickered behind it, and thunder came down on the city like a fist.

The sight of Trinica's craft brought back a nagging memory, of sitting at a bar with Balomon Crund. They'd both been drunk, sloppy drunk, and Crund had leaned over, shoved his big shaggy head up close to Pinn's and said 'You gotta promise me something.'

The promise. That was right. Pinn wasn't normally one to treat a promise with much gravity, but this one had stuck in the back of his mind. What *had* he promised?

He stared at the *Delirium Trigger* as it slid past his wing, and tried to remember. Wisps of memory began to coalesce in his benighted mind. It seemed as if the answer was almost within his grasp when suddenly he saw a plume of flame light up the sky ahead of him.

He narrowed his eyes and looked closer. That wasn't a bomb; it was an explosion at altitude. As he watched, he saw two aircraft chasing off after another one. Tracer fire slid silently through the air.

Pinn became suddenly interested. Were they *fighting* over there?

He opened up the throttle and headed in that direction. The war had been a let down so far, but Pinn wasn't averse to feeding on scraps. Any battle was a good battle, as far as he was concerned.

Someone else was going to get the business end of Pinn's machine guns before the day was through.

Harkins rolled and climbed as tracer fire ripped through the sky behind him. There were two of them on his tail. One was a Firecrow, painted with Cipher decals as his own craft was. The other was a patchwork junker he didn't even recognise. They flew dangerously close to one another, jostling for position, each eager to be the one to take down the rogue in their midst.

Bad pilots, both of them. Harkins levelled out and gave them both a good few seconds to draw a bead on him, making himself a tempting target. Once he had them on the hook, he threw his craft to starboard. Both pilots reacted instinctively, banking to follow him, but they were flying too tight. The junker's wings clipped the Firecrow's and both of them went spinning away into the rainy gloom.

Lightning flickered and thunder rolled. Harkins allowed himself a sweaty grin. He was out on the edge of the Awakener fleet now, and he'd either lost or destroyed all his pursuers for the moment. Fire pumped through his veins. He was the assassin within, the hidden killer. Between the storm and the fact that his craft was painted up like an Awakener's, he'd avoided drawing the attention of too many pilots at once. Those that took an interest didn't know if he was the enemy, or his pursuers were. And there were dozens of identical Firecrows in the Awakeners' service. Once he stopped shooting, he became invisible again.

I am the Coalition Navy, and the Coalition Navy is me.

He'd head over to the other side of the convoy, start again. It would take them time to pick him up, and by then he'd be gone, harrying them elsewhere. He'd take the whole damned fleet down with him one by one if he had to!

Through the rain-streaked windglass of the cockpit, he caught sight of an aircraft ahead and above him, heading in his direction. He frowned, wiped at the glass, and then remembered the rain was on the outside. He narrowed his eyes and looked closer. There was something about that aircraft.

A gull-winged F-class Skylance, a racing craft bulked out with armour plate and fitted with underslung machine guns. He'd know that craft anywhere. There wasn't another one like it.

'Pinn!' he cried joyously. 'Hey! Pinn!'

The Skylance opened fire.

Harkins was shocked and slow to react, but his senses had been tuned by battle, and his instincts took over where thought failed him. He banked to starboard, swinging out of the path of the bullets, though not fast enough to avoid them entirely. Several glanced off the Firecrow's armour. Burning tracers fizzed past him and away.

'Pinn, you fat idiot! It's me!' he screamed. 'Put in your earcuff!'

But Pinn couldn't hear him. The Skylance plunged past him as Harkins swung away. He craned in his seat, trying to spot it again. He couldn't let Pinn come up on him from beneath.

What that moron up to? Why was he attacking? But of course, Harkins knew the answer. His Firecrow looked like every other Firecrow out there. Pinn had no idea who he was.

Harkins brought the Firecrow around, banking and diving, chasing the Skylance downward even as it started climbing back up towards him. There was a moment when he had a clear shot at the exposed cockpit, and he almost took it; but he hesitated. This was *Pinn*. However much of a disgusting fool he was, he was part of the *Ketty Jay*'s crew. Harkins couldn't just—

The Skylance fired early, catching him by surprise again. Harkins swung out of the way, pulling up hard. The blood drained from his head and his vision sparkled as g-forces dragged at him. He levelled up and raced behind a cargo freighter, putting it between him and his attacker. The huge craft was heavily damaged; fires blazed inside the holes in its hull.

Pinn! Why'd it have to be Pinn? Everywhere he went, everything he tried to do, Pinn was there to screw it up. His repulsive grinning face loomed large in all of Harkins' memories of the *Ketty Jay*. Pinn had always been his chief tormentor, merciless in his mockery, never offering a kind word. And the insults weren't even the worst of it. He'd been forced to share his quarters with that evil shit for years now, putting up with his stink and his snoring. That man had been the bane of his life from the moment Harkins laid eyes on him.

And now here he was to ruin things again, spoiling Harkins' swansong. Any nobility Harkins might have found in death would be lost now. Harkins would die ridiculous, shot down by his erstwhile crewmate who, in his blithe stupidity, would never even recognise what he'd done.

'Just piss off, Pinn!' he cried. 'Just leave me alone for once!'

But it wasn't going to happen. He flew out of cover behind the freighter and there, homing in on him, was the familiar shape of Pinn's Skylance. Harkins gritted his teeth. That son of a bitch wasn't going to give up.

'Alright,' he said. 'If that's the way you want it.'

He angled his Firecrow into the heart of the fleet and opened up his throttle. Ahead of him, the sky thickened with frigates and fighters. The flagship and the *Delirium Trigger* hung there, motionless, as other craft glided by like dull grey whales in the rain. Easier to fight in there, where it was tight. The Firecrow didn't have the Skylance's speed, but it was more manoeuvrable. And Pinn would have a harder time shooting at him if he didn't want to hit other Awakener craft. Harkins didn't have that handicap.

The Skylance raced to intercept him. Tracers whipped past him and he heard the rattle of guns. Thunder boomed. He banked behind a frigate, sweeping along its flank, blocking his pursuer's line of sight. Then he turned hard and dived, coming out under the frigate's belly, facing in the direction of the Skylance.

He pressed his triggers as soon as his enemy came into sight. No hesitation this time. But the Skylance rolled and plunged and the bullets hit nothing.

Harkins chased him down. He should have waited for a better shot. Pinn was too good a pilot to let himself get tagged at that range. His leering face appeared in Harkins' mind, distorted and made horrible by hate.

You're mine, he thought.

A heavy fighter, a Wolverine, came flying in on his port side. Its electroheliograph mast was flashing: *Cease fire. Cease fire.* Well, it was only a matter of time before someone else weighed in. Harkins ignored the Wolverine and shot past, the roar of his engines as loud as the roar of blood in his ears.

The air was busy with craft now. Harkins darted between them, tracking the Skylance through the storm. One of the frigates opened fire on them both, but they were small targets, almost impossible to hit at speed. They were past it and gone before the gunners got their range.

Using the big craft as cover, they chased after each other, turning and diving, climbing and rolling, playing hide-and-seek. Harkins lost the Skylance at one point, only to pop up again on its tail; but it got away from him, and he was surprised shortly after by a burst of gunfire that nearly took off his port wing. He escaped with a few holes, and was lucky not to have been hit in the fuel tanks.

Harkins flew with gritted teeth. Usually it was panic that fed his reactions; now it was anger. He knew that, however this ended, it would end in his death. But he wouldn't go out at Pinn's hands. After all that man had done to him, it would be too much.

He swung around, spotted the Skylance through the rain again. Pinn appeared to have lost him, and was searching. Harkins pushed the throttle and closed the gap. The Skylance was passing close to the port side of a frigate; Harkins raced up the starboard side, keeping the bigger craft between them, hoping to surprise Pinn at the far end.

When he emerged, the Skylance was nowhere to be seen.

Where'd he go?

Gunfire. Harkins jerked on the flight stick as tracers shredded the air, pinging off the Firecrow's armour, scoring its flank. The windglass of the cockpit cracked. Harkins caught a glimpse of his attacker before the two craft crossed paths and flew off in different directions.

Not Pinn, he realised, thoughts wild with alarm. *The Wolverine.*

He dived, still shaken, unsure how much damage he'd sustained. Suddenly he was beneath the belly of a frigate, its keel blurring past above him. A section of windglass rattled in its pane. If it cracked, he was done for: wind and rain would blind him.

Muzzle flash ahead. He looked up and his eyes widened in horror. The Skylance was there, roaring along the length of the frigate from the opposite direction, machine guns chattering, coming at him head-on. Harkins didn't even think of evading; he didn't have time to think at all. He pulled the trigger and let loose with everything he had.

For a single, endless second, the two aircraft shot towards each other, a hail of lead filling the air between them. But Harkins had the better aim. He saw the Skylance's nose chewed up by his bullets, saw it burst apart. He pulled the Firecrow away as the Skylance tipped upward and ploughed into the underside of the frigate, dragging a long line of fire all along its keel before exploding in one final, stunning detonation. Then Harkins was flying away into the rain, looking over his shoulder as the bow of the wounded frigate began to dip and the enormous craft went sinking towards the city below, its aerium tanks breached.

His head snapped round and he faced forward again. His heart pounded, and his skin was cold. Bloodshot eyes stared into the gloom ahead of him.

Pinn.

He'd killed Pinn. All those times he'd dreamed of doing it, and finally he had. The enormity of it piled onto him. All those times Pinn had mocked him. All that abuse.

Harkins' throat went dry. He'd just killed his best friend.

Something welled up within him, expanding from his thin belly up through his chest, swelling until it couldn't be contained any more. He let out a loud yell. His voice rang in the confines of the cockpit. He yelled until he was out of breath, then sucked in air and yelled again. A raw, wordless sound of uncontainable grief and fury.

Then, as abruptly as it had come, the feeling was gone. His mouth snapped shut; his eyes went hard. He yanked on the flight stick and slammed the Firecrow into a turn. He was looking for someone, anyone, to vent his feelings on.

Where are they? Where are they?

Tracer fire came flitting towards him. He took it as an invitation, and gunned the fighter down. Another one came for him at three o'clock. He swung round and flew straight towards it, reckless, un-caring. His guns rattled; his enemy fell from the sky.

Bullets from behind. He evaded automatically, then craned round in his seat to try to catch sight of whoever was on his tail. He couldn't, so he banked to starboard and shot behind a frigate instead, hoping to block them off. The frigate started up with its guns, but way too late; he was past it and away by then. He found himself on the tail of another fighter, one whose pilot seemed totally unaware of the battle going on around him.

Harkins didn't care. Conscript or volunteer, peasant or mercenary, armed or unarmed; they were all Awakeners to him. He pressed down on his guns, and the pilot died.

More bullets came from behind him. He looked back, and saw

there were two of them on his tail now. They were spreading out, working together to get angles on him. They knew how to fly, then. That was going to present a problem. He was attracting too many aircraft, flying wild. Asking for it.

He dodged and weaved, but they stayed on him. Fiery shells whipped past the cockpit. The Firecrow's engines screamed, and the cracked windglass of his canopy shivered and pinged.

Just let me get you in my sights, you bastards, he thought. But they were good, and they didn't let him turn. They hung in his blind spot, careful and methodical, and sent gunfire his way when they had the opportunity. Sooner or later they were going to nick him, and a few bullets in the right place was all it would take.

One of the frigates had found his range now, and started sending artillery his way. The Firecrow was shaken and shoved, and the cockpit hummed with the force of the detonations. Harkins barrel rolled and dived down towards a wallowing barque, hoping to put it between himself and the frigate. He cut in close to its flank, swung around behind it—

—and came face to face with the Wolverine, coming the other way. He'd swung right into its path, and was dead in its sights. His stomach plunged with the inevitable certainty of what would come next. The Wolverine opened fire—

—and exploded, ripped apart by gunfire from above. Harkins just stared as the heavy fighter blew to pieces in a belch of dirty flame, and a fighter craft went plunging past.

'*Waaaaa-hooo!*'

'*Pinn?*' Harkins almost screamed.

'Who else, you twitchy old freak?'

Harkins' brain refused to process what he was hearing. He flew away from the barque on automatic, out of range of the frigate. Who was this talking in his ear? Was it some trick of the daemon-thralled earcuff, channelling emanations from beyond the grave? He'd never trusted those damned things.

'But . . . but . . .'

'*But . . . but . . .*' Pinn mimicked cruelly. 'Thought it was you. I'd recognise your flying anywhere.'

'Why weren't you wearing your earcuff?!' It was the only thing Harkins could think of to say.

'Just put it in now,' said Pinn. 'Why, what's up?'

'I thought I killed you, that's what's up!'

Pinn howled with laughter. Harkins felt himself redden. He checked around himself and saw that the pursuit had fallen away. The pilots on his tail had been scared off by the artillery or by the prospect of an even fight. Probably mercs, then. The faithful wouldn't have given up so easily.

Now that he wasn't shooting, he was anonymous once again. He tried to find Pinn among the frigates in the rain. 'I shot down your Skylance!' he said, still trying to make sense of it all.

'That wasn't me in there!' Pinn crowed. 'You think you'd have got *me*? The Awakeners stole my craft and gave it to someone else. They gave me some old piece of shit instead, but I can still . . .' He tailed off as the penny finally dropped. '*You shot down my Skylance?*' he squawked.

'I thought you were flying it,' said Harkins, in his defence.

'You thought . . . you thought *what*? . . . You . . . ggnnaaa-RRRGH*HHHH*!'

Harkins felt a smile spread over his face as Pinn degenerated into incoherent animal noises of rage. He'd never heard Pinn so angry. And it was all on his account.

Well. That was a turn up for the books.

Pinn came up on his wing. He was flying a Linfordby Warrior, a pre-war fighter that had been ahead of its time but had been superseded by other models since. If Harkins looked closely, he thought he could see Pinn thrashing about in the cockpit, waving his arms and hitting the dashboard.

'You alright, Pinn?' he asked cheerily. 'Maybe you shouldn't have joined up with the Awakeners after all.'

Pinn fixed him with a deadly glare across the gap between them. Then suddenly, his tone changed, his anger forgotten. 'Wait, wait!' he said. 'Where's the Cap'n?'

'Cap'n's gone,' said Harkins. 'North, to Yortland.'

'He's *gone*?'

'Left not long ago.'

'We gotta catch him up!' said Pinn. 'He might come within range of these ear thingies if we throttle it!'

'Err . . .' said Harkins, half his mind on flying. 'Why?'

'Cause I think I know how to save the Coalition!' he said. 'Follow me! Artis Pinn, *Heeero of the SkiiiEEEEEES!*'

He banked his Warrior and belted off north, away from the fleet. Harkins, bewildered and full of excitement, could do nothing but go after him. Save the Coalition? However ridiculous his plan, if there was even a chance it had merit, he had to see it through.

It was only once he was far from Thesk that he realised he'd somehow survived his suicide mission.

Thirty-Nine

*North – Crund's Message –
Responsibility – The Ace of Skulls*

Frey listened to the steady exhalation of the *Ketty Jay*'s thrusters, the hum of her aerium engine, the creaking of her bulkheads. *This is all I need*, he said to himself. *I have everything I want right here.*

The words rang hollow in his mind, so he said them again to convince himself. Once, he wouldn't have needed convincing. Once he'd believed only Darian Frey mattered in the world, and he was content with that.

Maybe, with enough effort, he might believe it again.

Silo stood in the doorway of the cockpit, leaning against the bulkhead, arms crossed and head down. He hadn't said a word since they left. Frey wished he'd go away, back to the engine room where he spent most of his time. He felt judged. The Murthian's presence reminded him that he'd had a crew once. It was something he desperately needed to forget.

He gazed out with dull eyes at the cloudy morning. The storm was behind them now; the skies were calm and sunless. Less than half an hour ago, he'd been at the end of a rope. This particular day seemed a poor reward for survival, but he'd take what he could get.

Survival. That was what it was all about now. Survival, and nothing more.

Yortland would suit his mood: icy, empty and cruel, a hard place populated by hard people. He had a vague plan to track down Ugrik, the batshit insane son of the High Clan Chief who'd helped them find the Azryx city in Samarla a few months back. Ugrik ought to be able to set him up with some work. After that, well, he'd do what he'd always done. He'd get by.

Once Vardia was in the Awakeners' hands, Yortland would be the

401

only safe place left. No point heading for Thace; even if they let him in, it would be first on the invasion list once the Sammies got the aerium they craved. Maybe he'd make the run to New Vardia if the Great Storm Belt wasn't too bad. He'd find himself a quiet place with a game of Rake and a few suckers to fleece. That'd do him.

Trinica . . . Well, he wouldn't think of Trinica. She was lost in some hell where he couldn't reach her, and that was all there was to it. It took a lot for Frey to admit he was beaten, but that was the fact of the matter. Suck it up and move on.

There'd been a time when he had no aspirations and no possibility of disappointment, but these past few years he'd taken to fooling himself with delusions of grandeur and the pursuit of fame, riches and love. People said it was better to try and fail than to never try, but those people obviously hadn't failed hard enough. Hope had raised him higher than he'd ever have believed possible, but the fall from there was crippling.

You'll find another crew, he told himself. *There'll be other women.*

He said the words again in his head, to convince himself.

Silo, by the bulkhead, stirred and straightened. 'You're gonna want to hear this, Cap'n.'

'Hear what?' said Frey, who couldn't hear anything outside of the workings of the *Ketty Jay*.

Silo walked over, pulled the silver earcuff from his ear and held it out. Frey looked from the earcuff to his first mate and back again.

'Took it off the dash,' said Silo by way of explanation. 'Seemed you weren't usin' it.'

Frey was angered, for no reason he could understand. Silo had been listening for the voices of the crew as they departed, drawing out the connection to the very last. He wanted to know how they were faring. But the anger lasted only a moment before it was washed away by guilt. Frey knew how much it had cost Silo to come with him, how much faith and loyalty this man had shown by leaving the others behind. If Frey had been capable of love right then, he'd have loved him for that.

With some trepidation, he took the earcuff and clipped it on to his ear.

'—nyone listening? Cap'n? Can you hear us?'

'*Oi! Cap'n!*'

'It doesn't make it go further if you shout louder, you quarter-wit!'

'Ah, shut your clam trap. You don't know how these things work.'

Frey frowned in disbelief. Was that *Pinn*? Pinn and Harkins, bickering away like always? It didn't seem real. He listened to them yell at each other for a short while more. It was strangely comforting.

'I'm here,' he said at last.

'Cap'n!' they both cried together, and the joy in their voices made something twist in his chest.

'You decided to come with me, then?' he asked. Their presence felt like an endorsement. He'd made the right choice.

'What?' said Harkins. 'No, Cap'n, we came to bring you back.'

Frey's brief good feeling withered. 'I'm leaving, Harkins,' he said. 'I told you that.'

'Something I've got to tell you first,' said Pinn. 'A message from Balomon Crund.'

Crund? What did *he* want? The man had always hated him, jealous of Trinica's affection.

'He made me promise, Cap'n. If I could find you, I had to tell you. He said you're the only one outside the crew who ever gave a shit about Trinica. The only one who might be able to do something about it.'

'Just spill it, Pinn.'

'*Trinica's not gone*,' said Pinn. 'That's what he told me. He said he knows. The old Trinica's still in there, under the daemon.'

The words piled like stones onto Frey's heart. The dreadful weight of responsibility, expectation, obligation. Of all people, Balomon Crund was reaching out to him, asking him to save Trinica. He'd persuaded himself that there was no chance, that his love was a lost cause, and now here was Pinn to shatter that certainty and let in the vile, deceitful light of hope.

No. He wouldn't believe it. 'What does Crund know?' he said bitterly. 'What in damnation makes *him* so sure? What is it, a *feeling* he's got? Some bloody *intuition*? Why's he trying to lay this on me?'

Pinn seemed confused by Frey's tone. Perhaps he'd expected gratitude instead of scorn. 'Er . . .' he said. 'I don't know. He just said to tell you she's been carrying a book around.'

That caught him. 'What?'

'Yeah,' said Pinn. 'Some book you gave her. He says she started carrying it about after she got turned. Reading it sometimes.'

Frey went cold. There was only one book he could possibly mean. *The Silent Tide.* He'd given it to her in Samarla as a present over dinner, a token of love back before he'd even admitted his feelings to himself. And for a moment he was there again, on the veranda of the most expensive restaurant he'd ever sat in, with the river in the background and the city lights reflecting in its dark waters.

'What's it about?' he heard himself ask her, for he hadn't known himself. He couldn't even read the title; it was in Samarlan.

'It's a classic romance,' she replied, her eyes shining.

'Do they get it together at the end?'

'No,' she said. *'They die. It's a tragedy.'*

Frey's breath grew short. What would a daemon be doing reading a classic romance in Samarlan? There was only one explanation Frey could think of. Trinica, the *real* Trinica, had somehow exerted enough control to make it happen. Maybe she'd disguised its significance from the daemon; maybe the daemon thought it didn't matter. Or maybe it was just some old instinct, a last act of tough and stubborn love.

However he looked at it, it meant only one thing. A cry for help. Not from Crund, but from Trinica. A signal that had reached him, against all the odds, across thousands of miles, across the frontier of a war.

Tears welled in Frey's eyes, blurring his vision. She was alive in there, a prisoner in her own body. It was too awful to bear.

'That's not all, Cap'n!' Harkins enthused, oblivious to his reaction. 'Listen to this!'

'Oh, right,' said Pinn. 'Yeah! The Azryx device, the one that took out the Coalition Navy? Guess who's carrying it.'

'The *Delirium Trigger*!' Harkins cried gleefully.

'Oi! He was meant to *guess*!'

Frey pulled off the earcuff and cut their voices to silence. Now all he could hear was the *Ketty Jay*, the one precious constant all through his adult life. He stared out at the empty sky ahead.

Yes, of course, it made sense. Turn the captains of the biggest frigates into Imperators to keep them loyal, and then have them carry the Azryx device. The *Delirium Trigger* was the most formidable craft in the fleet, even more than the flagship. Naturally they'd put it there.

Frey felt the walls of the cockpit closing in on him. All he wanted was to be free. To fly off into nothingness and never to have to deal with pain or misery or suffering ever again. To cut his losses and fold his hand while he still could.

But life wouldn't let him. The same tides of fate that had brought him to this point were now trying to suck him back. As much as he tried to suppress it, a plan was forming in his mind. A way to save Trinica, and incidentally to save Thesk and the Coalition as well. A plan that only he could carry out.

It's not my responsibility, he thought. Then, with gritted teeth, he hit the dashboard with his fist. 'It's not my *responsibility!*'

Silo, standing by, said nothing.

But the crack that Pinn had made in his shell of denial was widening. Everything he'd stuffed inside came spilling out in a flood, filling him with breathless hope, panic, joy and resentment. He wanted to burst into tears; he wanted to kill somebody; he wanted to dance and rage all at the same time.

Was loving Trinica worth his death? Would a life not loving her be worth anything? Everything, *everything* rested on him. It wasn't fair. It wasn't fair to force him to a choice like that.

'Do you think we can do it, Silo?' he said quietly.

Silo could not have heard half the conversation that he'd had with Pinn and Harkins, but it didn't matter. He knew what Frey was talking about.

Frey waited. If he detected even a hint of doubt, the merest shred of uncertainty, then he was determined to hit the throttle and never look back. If he thought the man at his side had anything less than absolute faith, it wouldn't be enough to give him the courage he needed to do this. It wasn't the danger that frightened him; he'd faced danger plenty. It was the thought of getting back on the horse that had thrown him. It was the possibility of failure.

'Cap'n,' said Silo at length. 'I known you a long time now. And I ain't never met nobody so good at screwin' up a winnin' hand as you are.'

Frey blinked. He hadn't expected that.

'But I also ain't never met nobody so good at turnin' a losin' hand to winnin',' Silo continued. 'You took this crew o' outcasts and misfits, people who didn't have no place in the world, and you made us into somethin'. Don't you remember, Cap'n? We took down the Awakeners once already, back at Retribution Falls. Saved the Archduke's hide that time.' His voice became unexpectedly passionate as he went on; it wasn't something Frey was used to hearing from his first mate. 'We took on the *Manes*, Cap'n! We flew behind the Wrack and we looked 'em in the eye and we came back to tell about it. And after that, what d'you reckon we did? This team o' alcoholics and layabouts and shit knows what else that you pulled together? We found a damn *Azryx city* right in the heart of Samarla! We saw a Juggernaut! And what we brought back, it pretty much set off this whole war they all fightin' back there! None of us weren't nothin' on our own, but 'cause of you, we shook the damn world!'

He put his hand on Frey's shoulder. Frey felt the warm strength of it through his coat.

'We a losin' hand, Cap'n,' he said. 'But you the Ace of Skulls. Anyone can turn us to winnin', you can.'

Frey stared out through the windglass a long time. His face was grim, but there was something new in his eyes. Something that hadn't been there since they'd left the Awakener camp in the Barabac Delta.

Determination. Cold, hard purpose.

'Reckon some things are worth risking everything for,' said Frey.

'You damn right about that,' said Silo, as Frey began to turn the *Ketty Jay* around.

Forty

The Root of Courage – The Gate –
An Unsung Hero – Orders – New Arrivals

'The gate! They've opened the gate!'

The cry echoed along the streets, punctuated by gunfire. The narrow lanes and courtyards which surrounded the Archduke's palace were aswarm with men and things other than men. Massive shapes lunged through the rain, metal limbs screeching. Frigates hung close overhead, their enormous hulls filling the grey sky, trailing ropes like catfish tendrils. They wouldn't bomb the palace; its contents were too valuable. But they could drop Sentinels behind the defenders' positions.

'This way!' someone shouted, and the Coalition soldiers surged in that direction. Crake hurried along an alley with men jostling him on either side. The world seemed to have become very small. He was surrounded by a tiny bubble of reality; beyond it, everything was muffled and suspect. Samandra, Malvery and Ashua appeared at his side now and then, but he'd lose them just as quickly in the tide of soldiers. He spotted Grudge more often, and sometimes Celerity Blane, her blonde ringlets sodden, eyes narrow in a leonine face.

Gunfire pulled him up short at the corner. He pressed himself against the wet stone and peered round into a courtyard. Sentinels were dug in at one end, shooting out from behind a statue of Kendrick Arken, the first of the Archdukes. More of them were pouring in through an arch. The Century Knights didn't break stride; they raced out into the courtyard, heading for cover of their own. He saw his lover running, rolling, coming up with shotguns blasting. He saw Celerity Blane, astonishingly fast, rotary pistols chattering as they ate up bullets from her gunbelt. Colden Grudge came last with his great autocannon booming, tearing holes through the charging mob.

He wanted to be brave. He wanted to run out there, to fight by Samandra's side, to protect her. But something had rooted him to the corner. He couldn't go out into the open with all those bullets flying about. He wasn't a fighter, not this way. That was her department.

He looked over his shoulder, alerted by the thump and clank of a golem. Not Bess, though. This golem was larger even than her, a hulking armoured brute all rivets and plates. Its head was small and oval and smooth, without mouth or nose or ears. Mechanical eyes glared out from beneath a brow that had been fashioned in a menacing scowl.

It stamped past him, followed by another, and charged into the courtyard, heedless of the bullets. One of the golems headed for the archway, the other for the men behind the statue. The Awakeners tried to run, but the golems ploughed into them like cannonballs. Bones cracked beneath their huge flat feet; they shattered men left and right with their enormous fists. The leg of the statue was smashed away by one wild swing, and the stern figure of Kendrick Arken toppled to the ground in pieces. By the time the dust cleared, the Awakeners had fled.

Malvery came up next to him and gave him a hefty nudge with his elbow. 'You alright, mate?'

'Yes,' said Crake. 'It's just . . .' He waved out at the courtyard. 'All this.'

'I know,' said Malvery. 'Stick it out, eh? We'll drive 'em off with those golems on our side.'

'And then what?' Crake asked. 'What do we do then?'

Malvery's face was serious. 'That don't matter,' he said. 'Just do what you can.'

The crump and rumble of distant explosions could still be heard over the thunder and hissing rain. The ground trembled whenever a particularly big bomb hit. Even up on this crag, high above the city, they could feel Thesk's death throes through their soles.

Yes, he thought. *Just do what you can.*

He was frightened, and not only for himself. They could beat back the invaders from the palace, but they couldn't do it forever. Not with those frigates overhead. The Awakeners could land troops on top of them all day, and if the resistance proved too much, they'd simply forget about preserving Thesk's seat of power and start bombing. They'd annihilate the golems and bring down the walls.

Don't think about that. Think about now.

But he couldn't. He didn't have his crewmates' ability to ignore consequences and live in the moment. He'd often envied them that. They were so blithe in the face of danger.

Was that the root of courage? The art of forgetting what you'd lose if you failed?

Bess caught up with them, shambling to a halt nearby. She was dragging a dead Sentinel by his leg like a little girl with a doll. The Sentinel's head was dented on one side, the face aghast and purple.

'Put that down, Bess,' Crake said, faintly nauseated. Bess ignored him, her attention on the golems in the courtyard. She seemed bashful and subdued in their presence. They intimidated her.

Ashua hurried up, scrawny and soaked. She'd been off dealing with Awakeners in the streets behind them. The battle there was done, but only temporarily. No matter how hard they tried to drive the Awakeners out, more of them landed. Many of the Coalition troops had been held back to protect the palace, where the Archduke sheltered. The rest were out to make sure the Awakeners couldn't bring their ground forces through the streets and up to the palace doors.

'If they get a steady route up the road from the city, they can bring in armoured vehicles and rot knows what else,' Malvery growled. He slapped Crake on the shoulder. 'Come on. Still fightin' to be done yet.'

They hastened across the courtyard, following the others towards the gate which guarded the streets on the crag top. The Century Knights led the way. Samandra found Crake with her gaze before she disappeared through the arch. He would have liked her by his side, but he understood. She had a job to do. Matters here were too important to let herself be distracted by babysitting.

The fighting around the gate was fierce. A narrow road ran through the arch, lined with stables and shops on either side. Watchtowers stood there, and the battle was thickest near their base. A mob of Awakeners were trying to force their way up the road, driving ahead by sheer weight of numbers. Gun muzzles flashed; the air was punched with pistol reports; men screamed.

An Awakener gunship hovered overhead, seeking a clear shot at the

Coalition forces. More Century Knights were here: Eldrew Grissom, his duster whirling about him and his knives flashing; Graniel Thrate, the Sledgehammer. Golems weighed in, dashing men against the walls. Bess went with them, disregarding Crake's command to stay. The lure of the fight was too much for her.

Crake stayed close to the buildings and hurried up the street in short bursts. His palm was sweaty on his pistol grip. Ashua was close behind him. He wasn't sure how comfortable he felt about that. His head told him that she wasn't to be trusted, that she might well be on the side of the enemy. But it was hard for him to hate someone who'd so recently been a friend. There was too much empathy in him, too much capacity for self-doubt.

Besides, he had bigger things to worry about right now.

A pair of Sentinels appeared at the mouth of an alley behind them, a little way up the street. It was only because Crake was looking back at Ashua that he spotted them. He cried out a warning, thrust out his gun and fired three shots. Two window panes exploded and a nearby door jamb suffered a grievous wound. Other Coalition soldiers took care of the flesh-and-blood opponents.

'When this is done, I'm gonna teach you how to shoot that thing,' Ashua muttered, slipping past him to take the lead.

Crake felt himself flushing angrily. He'd take that from Malvery, but it didn't seem right to be disparaged by someone so recently accused of treachery. He'd expected a little more humility from someone who wanted to get back in his good books; but then, humility wasn't exactly Ashua's style.

There was a whine of engines as the gunship overhead adjusted itself, and then a rapid tattoo of cannon fire. Glass smashed, stone puffed, wood splintered as the street was strafed. A few Coalition soldiers, unlucky enough to be out of cover, danced and jerked as they were hit. One of the Coalition golems, undoubtedly the intended target, came apart in a screech of metal, and was left in a ruined, twisted pile on the cobbles.

Crake pressed himself back against the wall and covered his ears. He'd been in gunfights before, but even Sakkan hadn't been like this. The noise and movement and terror were overwhelming.

Then: a loud *thump-thump-thump*. An autocannon. The gunship's prow exploded, and the mutilated remainder slewed away to crash into a nearby rooftop. Men scattered as the building slumped into the street in a landslide of bricks and slate. Dust billowed up, a great cloud obscuring the gate.

Malvery roared with laughter. 'Seems they didn't get the memo about Grudge!' he cried. Passing soldiers smiled at that as they went racing down towards the gate, taking advantage of the cover provided by the dust cloud. Crake looked for Bess and couldn't find her. He applied himself to reloading his revolver while he had a moment's grace.

He was still bent over, slotting in the last of the bullets, when the horror came upon him.

Oh, no, he thought. *They're here.*

The gunfire stuttered into silence. Faces turned from grim determination to abject fear. Malvery, normally so stout-hearted, began to back away, whimpering. Ashua hunkered down into a ball and clung on to herself.

Crake's hand went to his chest. Against his skin he felt the chill touch of the metal amulet. One of the devices that he and Kyne had crafted to negate the power of the Imperators.

It doesn't work, he thought, as panic clutched at him. *It doesn't work!*

His legs went weak and he staggered. He put out a hand to steady himself, but his knees gave way. The weight of his failure took him down to the ground. All that they'd risked at the Tarlock mansion, the death of Jez and Pelaru, the Cap'n's dreams of saving his lover – all of it was worthless. The knowledge they'd gained of the Imperators meant nothing. Because the amulets didn't work.

In the dust cloud, something moved. A booted foot splashed into a puddle. Out of the rain and the swirling murk, a figure emerged, masked and cloaked, clad head to toe in black.

A golem thundered up the street towards the Imperator. He raised a gloved hand and the golem seized up and went crashing down in a heap.

We can't fight them. Not the Imperators. We can't win against them!

Crake spotted Samandra, on the other side of the street, pressed up against the wall where she'd scrambled. She was just visible on the edge of the settling dust, her face distorted in fright. The sight of that struck at him deeply. Those features should never be twisted that way, those eyes never so wide and so afraid. She was so strong and capable, stronger than him; to see her made helpless was an injustice against decency.

The amulet against Crake's chest was cold. Cold as ice. In fact, his whole body was going cold.

Just like it did when he used his tooth. Because the daemon was leaching his vitality.

Because the amulet was *working*.

From somewhere, he found strength. This fear was not supernatural. It was just that it was so potent he'd mistaken it for the Imperator's influence. No, this fear was honest and human, and it could be overcome.

His eyes fixed on Samandra, he gritted his teeth and willed himself to move. The effort was enormous, the distance insurmountable. But somehow, he got up from his knees, and he stood.

The Imperator turned its head slowly towards him, fixing him with its dreadful gaze. He put one foot in front of him, and then another. His throat was dry; his muscles trembled. It was like fighting against a current. But he came on, walking out into the street. Walking towards the Imperator.

The dust cloud was dispersing now, washed down by the rain. Behind the first Imperator, he saw a second one emerging. And behind that one were the Awakeners, a hundred troops with their guns, waiting for the cloud to clear so they could be sure their enemies had been subdued. So they could begin executing their helpless opponents.

The Imperator reached down to his belt and drew out a long black knife. He strode towards Crake with murderously efficient purpose, his sodden cloak flapping around him. The sight of that dark figure bearing down on him, the knowledge that he had seconds to live, almost rendered Crake immobile with fear.

Almost.

His arm leaden, his senses muffled, he raised his gun and pulled the trigger. The report was deafening in the silence.

The Imperator jerked and stopped mid-stride. For a moment, he just stood there. Then he staggered back a step, and looked down at the small hole in his chest. It wasn't bleeding.

When the Imperator looked up again, Crake had the gun aimed

point-blank at his forehead. He pulled the trigger again. The Imperator's head whiplashed back and he crumpled to the ground.

Crake breathed in, breathed out, and felt his fear turn to bitter and triumphant hatred. Then he turned hard eyes on the second Imperator, and went stalking across the street towards him.

Crake had never seen an Imperator display uncertainty before. His enemy looked around for help, drew his knife, held it without conviction. They relied so heavily on their fear-inducing powers that they had no other way to fight, and here was someone the Imperator had no power to affect. Crake felt his confidence rising with every step. He'd killed two Imperators now, three if he counted the one that died in the summoning circle. Usually he was a man with a surplus of conscience, but not where these creatures were concerned. They were less than animals to him. He found great satisfaction in exterminating them.

The Imperator lunged, but not at Crake. He darted to the side of the road, seized Samandra by the wrist, pulled her roughly to her feet. In a moment, he had his arm round her neck, her body held before him as a shield, the point of his knife against her nape.

Crake stopped dead. The Imperator glared at him, only his head and arm visible behind Samandra. He had no tongue to speak, but his intention was clear. *Come closer, and I'll kill her.* Five metres separated them: too far to reach her before he drove the knife home. Samandra whimpered, limp and unresisting, her courage destroyed by the Imperator's influence.

Crake's world had seemed close and confined during the fight; now it narrowed to a single moment. He was aware of many things: the pulse at Samandra's throat; the beating of his own heart; the falling rain and the Imperator's birdlike, yellow-irised eyes. And he knew that the dust cloud had become little more than a haze, and that Sentinels were already squinting through, wondering who the figure in the middle of the street was. They'd aim their guns and shoot, and he'd fall, and it would all be over.

Unless.

Crake was a meticulous man, a thoughtful man, a man who considered consequences and disdained recklessness. But in that instant, he knew what it was to be like the Cap'n, or Pinn, or even

Malvery. To know nothing of the future, to spurn it entirely, to be as careless and instinctive as an animal. To simply *do*, and nothing more.

In one quick movement, he raised his pistol and fired. The Imperator's head snapped back and smacked against the stone wall behind him. Then he slid to the ground, dead.

Crake saw Samandra's face clear as the Imperator's influence was broken. Her expression changed from fear to amazement. She looked down at the dead thing at her feet, then up at Crake, who was still aiming the revolver, his expression as amazed as hers.

'Good *shot!*' she said.

Suddenly there were thrusters overhead, and a hot downdraft blew around them and whipped about the streets, blasting the last of the dust away. Samandra's tricorn hat flapped and she had to grab it to keep it from flying off. She reached out and pulled Crake up against the wall, just before the air filled with bullets. But the bullets were not aimed at them; they were aimed at the gate, where the Awakeners had gathered. Crake heard the screams of the Sentinels as a hail of bullets cut through them.

'It's the *Ketty Jay!*' Malvery bellowed over the noise, and then laughed heartily and pointed to the sky. 'The Cap'n's back!'

The Sentinels quailed under the assault from the *Ketty Jay*'s machine guns. They saw the dead Imperators, saw the Coalition forces stirring back to life, and their dismay turned into a rout. They crowded back through the gate and began to run along the road that led off the crag. Frey let up on his guns, and the Coalition forces pushed the gates closed with a loud boom. A great cheer went up as the mechanical locks crashed back into place.

Crake staggered out into the street, dazed and weakened by his ordeal and the daemon in the amulet. He shielded his eyes from the rain and looked up, but the *Ketty Jay* was already turning, heading for the palace. Frey didn't seem to have noticed them down there among the ruin and the carnage.

Malvery slapped him on the back as he ran past, with Ashua chasing after him. 'Come on!' he said. 'Let's go see what he's got in mind!' And he ran off up the road towards the palace, cackling to himself. 'I knew he wouldn't let us down!' he cried, which Crake suspected was a lie.

Samandra appeared next to him, her eyes alight. 'Might not be such a bad idea at that,' she said. She tugged his arm and they made off after Malvery.

As the dizziness of the moment subsided, Crake suffered a moment of mild disappointment. The Cap'n's appearance had meant his own heroics had gone virtually unnoticed. But then, that was a daemonist's lot, he supposed: most of his triumphs happened in secret. Anyway, he'd never wanted for glory. All that mattered to him was that the woman he loved, the lusty, brash Samandra, was back as if she'd never gone.

Then she gave him a sidelong look and a smile of thanks. An acknowledgement, as from one comrade in battle to another. And that was enough.

'Cease fire!' Kedmund Drave was yelling, as Malvery burst into the courtyard. 'Cease fire!'

The soldiers put up their rifles uncertainly. Their bullets had done little good against the *Ketty Jay*'s armoured underbelly anyway, although they'd shot out a few of her floods. Now that he was no longer under attack, Frey began to descend. The soldiers watched with wary eyes as an aircraft painted with Awakener decals lowered itself into the heart of the palace grounds. Two aircraft hovered overhead. One was undoubtedly Harkins' Firecrow, which was incredible enough. The other . . .

Could that be *Pinn?*

Samandra came striding past Malvery and through the soldiers towards Drave. 'Convinced they're on our side yet?' she snapped at him scornfully. Drave just gave her a look and motioned at someone behind him. Morben Kyne appeared at the doorway to the courtyard, with the Archduke and his family. They waited at a safe distance as the *Ketty Jay* settled on her struts.

'That's the Cap'n! He'll always come back for his own!' Malvery declared to Ashua, as if it was something he'd said all along. He felt glad enough to forget Ashua's trespasses for the moment, and favoured her with grin. The grin she gave him in return warmed his heart more than he'd expected.

Suddenly, beyond all expectation, they were all back together again. Even Jez, in a way.

The cargo ramp came down. Forty soldiers and a half dozen

Century Knights primed their weapons. It seemed a bit much for the lone figure that came walking out onto the rain-wet flagstones. But Frey walked taller than when he'd left, and there was something in his eye that hadn't been there before.

The thunder overhead had gone silent. The storm had moved on, and only the driving rain was left. Beyond the courtyard, battles still raged, bombs still dropped and dark frigates ploughed the dreary sky. But here was a hush deep enough that Frey's boot heels could be heard scraping on the stone as he came to a halt.

Drave took a step forward, glaring imperiously at the newcomer. 'Captain Frey!' he said. 'In the name of the Archduke, I'm commandeering your aircraft. The Archduke and his family must be taken to safety. That's the highest priori—'

Frey spat on the ground at his feet. It was a blunt enough display of disrespect to render even Drave speechless.

'This is my aircraft, and she goes where I take her,' he said. 'So unless you've got a spare couple of hours to torture the ignition codes out of me – and the way this battle's going, I don't reckon you do – you'd best shut your mouth and listen up.'

Drave visibly expanded with rage. He sucked in a breath, and seemed like he was about to lunge; but Samandra slapped an open hand against his breastplate.

'Drave,' she said. 'Enough being an arsehole for one day, eh?'

Drave's eyes bulged. His face reddened. A vein at his temple pulsed. But though she was half a foot shorter than him, she stared him down. And Drave swallowed his fury and stepped back.

Frey gave him a look of disgust, then turned his head away dismissively, addressing the crowd. 'The Azryx device is on board the *Delirium Trigger*,' he said, his voice ringing out over the silent courtyard. 'That's where I'm going. If I can storm that frigate and take out the Azryx device, Thesk's anti-aircraft guns will be operational again. I figure with the entire Awakener convoy sitting over the city as they are, we'll be able to wipe them out with a surprise attack before they can get away. After that, there'll just be the troops on the ground to deal with, and I think we can handle them. What I need from you lot is one thing: take back the anti-aircraft emplacements, and be ready when they come back on. We'll get one shot at this.

Don't screw it up.' He swept the assembled soldiers with a commanding gaze. 'Any questions?'

Malvery felt his chest swell with pride, and he wasn't ashamed to find a tear gathering in his eye. 'That's the Cap'n,' he said again.

The soldiers stirred uneasily, exchanging glances with one another. The silence gathered and became oppressive. Then the crowd parted, and the Archduke walked through to stand next to Drave and Samandra in the rain, his flame-red hair plastered to his skull and his neat beard dripping. He gave Frey a long look. Frey looked back at him.

'Your Grace,' said Drave. 'This could all still be a trick to divide our forces. You and your family need to get to safety. The continuation of the Arken line is paramount.'

But the Archduke laid his hand on Drave's shoulder, and never took his eyes from Frey. 'No, old friend,' he said. 'If we lose here, we lose everything. I'll not leave my people to the mercy of daemons.'

He stepped forward, raised his voice, and spoke to Frey. 'Take what men and golems you need. Some of my Knights will accompany you. We will take care of matters on the ground.' Then he turned and addressed his troops, his voice becoming louder still. 'The battle is not yet lost! There is still hope to turn the tide! Will you fight now with us? Will you fight for Thesk, and the Coalition, and your mothers and brothers and friends?'

The cheer that went up at that shook the windows of the palace. Malvery, overwhelmed by the moment, gathered Ashua in his arms and hugged her. She gave a surprised little squeak as she was crushed and dumped breathlessly back to earth.

'I'll go with you!' called Samandra to Frey.

'You'll need me!' said Crake, hurrying out of the crowd. 'And Bess! And one of these!' He held up a tarnished brass amulet. 'My equipment's all still inside, right?'

'You're taking on Trinica, you'll need me too,' said Kyne. 'We'll bring golems.'

Others were volunteering now, more than they'd even need. Frey left Silo to sort them out. He embraced first Crake and then Malvery, who gave him a broad grin and laughed as he swept him up in a bear hug.

'Steady on, mate!' Frey said. 'Need all my ribs.' When Malvery had put him back down, he said: 'You coming too?'

Malvery gave him an apologetic shake of the head. 'Love to, Cap'n. But I'm gonna be more use down here. Gonna be a lot of wounded to tend to. We'll see about them guns.'

Frey seemed to understand. 'What about you?' he said to Ashua.

'Reckon I'll stick with this ox,' she said.

Frey looked at Malvery. 'She alright?' he asked.

'Aye,' Malvery said. 'She's alright.'

Frey nodded. 'Silo!' he called. The Murthian came over. 'I've got Century Knights, golems and daemonists coming up there with me. Need you to keep an eye on these two. Bring 'em back to me safe.' There was a question in Silo's eyes, but Frey was resolute. 'They're my crew,' he said. 'I wouldn't trust 'em to anyone else's command but yours.'

Silo dipped his head gravely. 'Understood, Cap'n.'

'Who's got that other earcuff?' Frey asked.

Malvery dug it out of his pocket and handed it to Silo. 'Reckon you ought to hold on to this,' he said. 'Let's all of us try not to lose touch again, eh?'

A cry went up from the south side of the courtyard. Soldiers pointed at the sky. Malvery hurried over as others gathered. Above the wall, near the horizon, a dark line could be seen against the clouds.

One of the soldiers had a spyglass to his eye. 'Aircraft!' he yelled. 'Hundreds of aircraft!'

'The rest of the Navy?' someone asked. 'We can't have had *every* craft here!' 'There ain't enough *left* of the Navy for that.'

'It's the Awakeners! They're bringing reinforcements!'

'Where did they get that many?'

But Morben Kyne stepped forward, peering into the sky with his mechanical eyes. 'It's not the Navy, and it's not the Awakeners either,' he said, his voice humming with strange harmonics. He lowered his head, and his hood fell across his face. 'It's the Samarlans.'

Forty-One

Dream Come True – A Wolf in Sheep's Clothing –
The Casket – Fighting on Deck – Bad Memories

'Cap'n,' said Pinn. 'Are you seeing what I'm seeing?'

'I see 'em, Pinn,' Frey said in his ear. 'Stay where you are, we'll be airborne in a sec.'

Pinn watched the approaching fleet from his vantage point above the palace, his forehead creased in a frown. He and Harkins were making slow circles while the Cap'n loaded up men in the courtyard below. They could have simply hovered, but it was too dangerous to hang still in the air. There were Awakener craft flying about, and frigates cruising nearby.

The sight of the Samarlan fleet was faintly dizzying. He'd seen Sammie craft before, over the Free Trade Zone, but never more than a few at a time. The aerium shortage in Samarla meant they couldn't afford to keep too many in the air. But how many were out there now? A thousand? More? They must have squeezed every last drop out of their reserves to raise this many craft.

'Why are the *Sammies* here?' he asked.

'That,' said Frey, 'is a bloody good question.'

He could make out the shape of the bigger craft now. They were smooth-sided, with sleek lines and pointed ends, and they slipped through the sky like sharks. The Sammies built their craft for beauty first and practicality second, and their elegant designs came at the expense of armour and aerodynamics. Theirs was an aesthetic culture; even their war-making was pretty.

The Awakeners had seen them too. The electroheliograph masts of their frigates were flashing. Pinn had never troubled to learn EHG code to any proficient degree, but every pilot understood the basic signals. From what he could make out, the Awakeners were just as puzzled as he was.

Pinn wasn't much for politics, but he dimly understood that the Sammies and the Awakeners were working together. The Sammies had sold the Azryx device to the Awakeners, after all. They wanted the Coalition gone so the new rulers would sell them aerium again.

Which was why it all came as a bit of a surprise when the Sammies opened fire.

Pinn stared in amazement as a row of silent flashes rippled along the length of the Sammie line, and the battered cargo freighters that guarded the flank of the Awakeners' convoy lit up in great blasts of flame. The Awakeners barely had time to register the attack before another salvo ripped into them, this one reaching deeper, hammering the frigates further in. Fighters went spinning away in pieces, blasted apart by the concussion of the heavy guns.

'Will someone tell me what in the name of buggery is going on?' Harkins yelled.

By the time the third salvo reached them, the Awakeners were reacting at last, but there was no organisation in their response. They had no plan for this, and no way to communicate orders fast enough. Some frigates broke formation, angling themselves to return fire. Other craft – those whose captains hadn't been turned into Imperators – made a break for escape. The fighters and bombers who'd been attacking the city swooped and swung about, their pilots confused and panicked.

'Are the Samarlans on our side now, or what?' Pinn asked.

'They're on their *own* side,' said Frey in exasperation. The *Ketty Jay* was lifting off from the courtyard now. 'And you two need to keep them off my back till I get to the *Delirium Trigger*.'

'What have they got against *us*? We're not even Awakeners!' Harkins cried.

'You've got Ciphers painted on your wings. Think they'll be able to tell the difference?'

But Pinn was hardly listening now. A sense of mounting excitement was building up within him. He could see a mass of Samarlan fighters racing towards the edge of the convoy, flying ahead of the big frigates, deadly darts shot at the heart of the Awakener ranks. He didn't care about the why and the what, or who was allied with who. All he cared about was one thing.

Once, there'd been a young man who wanted to go to war. He'd played with planes till he was old enough to fly them. He'd fantasised about being a hero. He'd dreamed of shooting the enemy out of the sky. But then the war had ended too soon, the enemy called it off, and that young man's dreams had been shattered.

And now at last, after all this time, the enemy had come to make amends.

A huge grin split his pudgy face. His piggy eyes twinkled. A hysterical cackle bubbled up out of his guts, and he threw back his head and let it out. Then he hit the throttle and yanked the flight stick, swinging his aircraft away from the palace and off through the rain.

Finally, *finally*, Pinn was going to get to kill him some Sammies.

'On the left! On the *left*!'

Frey threw the *Ketty Jay* to starboard, banking hard as a Sammie fighter swept past him, machine guns blazing. Samandra, who'd given the warning, went skidding across the cockpit and almost fetched up underneath the navigator's desk. She clambered back to her feet as Frey levelled up. The thumping of an autocannon sounded from above and behind them, and something exploded nearby. There was a Coalition soldier in the cupola, a trained gunner whose accuracy put Malvery and Samandra to shame. Frey never thought he'd see the day when he'd let Coalition hands touch any of the *Ketty Jay*'s controls, but these were strange times.

Fighter craft flitted about, whipping past like bullets. Sammies built their craft fragile but quick, and they were damned hard to get a bead on. The sky was dangerously crowded with big craft and little ones alike, everyone on their own trajectory, a panicked herd harassed by nimble predators. Aircraft smashed into each other. Shellfire detonated all around him.

Frey kept his head down and concentrated on threading the *Ketty Jay* safely through the chaos. Sammies or Awakeners, his mission hadn't changed. His object was the *Delirium Trigger* and Trinica. Let the world throw what obstacles it would in his path. He had one last chance to save her, and everyone else with her. His previous despair had fallen away; hope had lit a fire inside. Nothing was going to stop him now.

The Samarlans' betrayal was a master stroke. Their fleet was too precious to risk even a small part of it, their aerium too limited for even a short campaign in the air. So they'd sold the Azryx device to the Awakeners, and they'd let the Awakeners do all the work for them. The Awakeners had torn the country apart; the Awakeners had suffered the losses necessary to lure the Coalition Navy within range of the device.

And now the Samarlans came in with a surprise attack, having travelled unopposed across Vardic skies. A fleet of well-armed, highly-trained pilots against a group of mercenaries and volunteers, their forces already damaged and weakened. The Sammies had the same countermeasures as the Awakeners and the *Ketty Jay*, so the Azryx device didn't work on them. And if their timing seemed near-perfect, that was probably because someone on the inside had told them when and where the Awakener attack would occur.

That would be Ashua, then.

The Sammies weren't going to give Vardia to the Awakeners. That was never their plan. They didn't want to trade for their aerium any more. They were going to take it for themselves. And with the Coalition Navy out of the way, there wasn't a lot anyone could do about it.

If this was what future generations would call the Third Aerium War, it would be the shortest war in history.

The *Ketty Jay*'s thrusters screamed as Frey drove her towards the heart of the convoy, where the *Delirium Trigger* hung like a spider at the centre of a web. Pinn and Harkins swept around him, now ahead and now behind, chasing off Sammies, shooting them down when they could. Pinn's maniacal cackling was getting wearisome, but Frey kept the earcuff in all the same. For once he was glad of the noise in his ear. He hadn't realised what a comfort his crew were until he'd almost lost them.

The other frigates had gathered around the flagship and the *Delirium Trigger*, a hard core of artillery to defend the Lord High Cryptographer and his Azryx device. Cannons boomed, machine guns spat and autocannons pounded, tracking Sammie fighters as they lashed past in the rain. The sheer noise of it was terrifying. The *Ketty Jay* shook and shuddered as Frey fought to see through the rain sliding off the windglass.

Don't worry about me, he told them silently. *I'm an Awakener.*

And as far as they knew, he was. The *Ketty Jay*, with its Cipher decals showing proudly, slipped through the bombardment. The frigates had other targets.

'Pinn! Harkins! You've done your bit! Get out of here!' he said.

'No, sir!' said Harkins. 'Not while there's Sammies and Awakeners in the sky over Thesk!'

'I'm not even halfway done killin' these losers yet!' Pinn cried, with an edge of happy delirium in his voice.

'Alright,' said Frey. 'Stay safe. I want to see you both on the other side.'

Now he was above the core of the convoy, and he tipped the *Ketty Jay* into a dive and plunged in. The gathered frigates were like dark metal islands, floating in the sky. He darted between them; their flanks thundered past in a blur. Other Awakener fighters were in here with him, buzzing about like flies, sheltering behind the bigger craft. They ignored him, and he ignored them.

And then there she was, below him. A black shape in the rain, her huge bow emerging from behind another frigate, cannons roaring as she sent shells out towards the Sammies' capital craft. He closed in with reckless speed, coming in aft of her, and hit the airbrakes hard while dumping aerium from his tanks. Samandra grabbed the navigator's desk as the *Ketty Jay* decelerated, dropping down towards the *Delirium*'s main deck.

Either the gunners were busy with other matters, or they thought that nobody was foolish enough to try what Frey had in mind. By the time someone realised and swivelled one of the deck guns towards him, it was too late.

The *Ketty Jay* landed heavily and too fast, throwing Frey forward in his chair. She slammed onto her skids with a scream of metal, and magnetic clamps locked on. Frey felt a blaze of pain in his back as his spine was jolted, and Samandra went sprawling on her hands and knees. The *Ketty Jay*'s hydraulics howled as residual forward momentum threatened to rip her from her skids, and for a moment Frey thought she'd topple forward and collapse in a heap of twisted metal.

But then, just when it seemed she couldn't strain any further, she rocked back again and settled. When they looked up, the deck of the *Delirium Trigger* spread out before them, big enough for a dozen of his craft. Despite the gunner's best efforts, they were too low to be shot at: safety mechanisms prevented the cannons firing when they might hit their own aircraft.

'We're down,' said Frey.

Samandra looked up from the floor and tipped her tricorn hat back from where it had fallen over her face. 'You don't say,' she replied drily.

Frey released himself from the pilot's seat and snatched up his cutlass and pistols. Samandra was already out the door, heading down to the hold where the others waited ready. It would only be moments before the crew of the *Delirium Trigger* came swarming out on to the deck.

Frey took a breath. It wasn't the thought of the fight to come that scared him. It was the thought of facing Trinica.

Time to do this.

He went out into the corridor. Dull explosions from the battle outside rang through the *Ketty Jay*'s hull. The soldier in the cupola had descended the ladder and was disappearing down the stairs into the hold. Frey was about to follow him when something caught his eye further down the corridor.

The door of the infirmary was open. Something black was poking through the doorway, moving slightly.

Frey knew he didn't have time for it, but there was something urgent in the sight, something that needed investigating. He walked closer, warily, until it became clear that the black thing was a strip of tarp, quivering under the influence of the *Ketty Jay*'s air filters. He went to the doorway and looked inside.

The strip of tarp was part of a larger piece, a sack that lay on the floor near the door, which had been ripped open. It took him a moment to realise that it was the remains of the body bag they'd stored Jez's charred corpse in. Events had moved so fast that there hadn't even been time to bury her, so they'd left her on the operating table.

Frey looked from the empty table to the ripped body bag and back again. She wasn't there now.

He turned and ran, heading down to the hold, his mind awhirl. What did it mean? Had somebody been aboard and taken her while they were imprisoned?

Had she got up and *walked away*?

The cargo ramp was opening as he hurried down the stairs. Crake and Kyne were near the back of the assembled forces, wearing big backpacks and weighed down with daemonist paraphernalia. The Coalition soldiers clutched their weapons, taut with anticipation. Other Century Knights stood among them: Samandra Bree with her tricorn hat and her shotguns; Celerity Blane with her rotary machine-pistols, her face dirtied and eyes fierce; Eldrew Grissom, with his straggly grey hair and his duster full of blades. Colden Grudge had stayed behind; autocannons would be useless here, where the fighting would be at close quarters.

And then there were the golems, in the vanguard. Four of them, not counting Bess, who stood shyly at their side. Pale light from outside spilled onto metal skin as the ramp lowered and the sound of shellfire became louder and more immediate.

The ramp thumped down onto the deck, and they charged.

When the echoes of their battle-cries had died away, when the ramp had closed behind them and the hold stood empty and silent, then she emerged from the shadows.

Everything was pain. Every movement stabbed her with a dozen hot knives. Her vision was a blur, blobs of weak colour and nothing more. She existed in a state of torment.

And yet, she existed.

Jez took a shuffling step out into the light. Red eyes with yellow irises squinted out from a mask of carbonised flesh. One trembling arm was held uselessly before her chest, mottled and weeping with sores. Her overalls – more fireproof than her flesh – still clung to her in pieces. Bits of burnt skin flaked away from her as she moved.

All but the vestiges of reason had fled, driven away by agony. But there was purpose in her, a single goal that pushed her on. It was instinct that guided her now. She put one foot in front of the other, and made her excruciating way forward.

The damage had almost been too much, the shock to her system too great. She'd burned; her flesh had cooked. Had she been living, she would have been overwhelmed. As it was, she'd come within a hair's breadth of extinction.

But the damage, great as it was, was mostly on the outside. Manes whose bodies had become useless or inoperable were abandoned by the entity that linked them together, severed from the network. Jez's had just enough left to salvage.

So the daemon began rebuilding her patiently, replacing what needed replacing, changing what needed to be changed. Cell by cell it reconstructed her from the inside out. Even now, it was working: dead nerves were coming back to life; eyes that had boiled and split were swimming back into focus.

She was healing.

In her mind she heard the howls of her brethren. They called encouragement to her, they shared her pain. They told her she was not alone. Their voices gave her the strength to keep going.

Hidden in the dark recesses of the *Ketty Jay*'s cavernous hold, behind crates of machine parts and who knew what else, she found a vent. The grate was loose, but stiff enough to defeat her at first, weakened as she was. She slid her nails into the tiny gap between the grate and the bulkhead, nails that had grown longer and stronger than ever before. The second time she pulled, there was more strength in her. The vent came away with a shriek.

No breath inflated her thin chest. Her heart was still. She reached into the vent, and took hold of a large grey metal casket. It crashed to the floor as she pulled it out, too heavy for her to hold up.

A pair of eyes glittered in the blackness at the end of the vent. Already her eyesight had sharpened enough to make them out. There was a scrabble of claws, and the eyes disappeared.

A cat. She fought to concentrate through the singing in her head. Was it Slag? Slag, who'd guided her to this treasure in the first place? No, not him. He had departed; his mind was silent. Then it was the other cat. The female.

She couldn't hold on to the thought. It didn't seem important. All that was important was what was in the box, the thing that Osger had died looking for, that Pelaru had wanted to destroy. What a repellent idea that seemed now. She could no more destroy what was in the box than she could destroy herself. It was part of her, just as her brethren were part of her. Pelaru had never seen that. And though he'd died attempting to save her, she felt nothing for him. He'd chosen to remain apart, too fearful to embrace what he was. He didn't deserve her lament.

She opened the casket. Inside was a smooth sphere of deepest black. Silver lines ran all across its surface in curves and circles, crafted without symmetry or any pattern that the human mind could grasp. But she saw the pattern, and it was beautiful.

She reached inside and lifted it up, cupping it with both hands. It seemed to throb with energy. Her nerves crackled; the touch of it filled her with exhilaration. The voices in her head were overwhelming now, drowning out everything else. An immense compulsion came over her. The power in the sphere demanded to be used, demanded to be let free. She had no reason to deny it. And she knew how to do it, too.

This wasn't the first time she'd held a device like this in her hands. She'd used one before, in Sakkan, at the insistence of Captain Grist.

The Awakeners hadn't realised what they had in their shrine at Korrene until it was too late. By the time they did, by the time their spies had dug out the details of the tale of Captain Grist, the shrine was already lost, the city destroyed by an earthquake. Then the shrine had been found again, and the Awakeners rushed to reclaim it. But Osger had found it first. In following him, Pelaru obtained it. And now it had come to Jez.

It was a distress beacon, an alarm, taken from a Mane dreadnought some time in the distant past. It was a summons, a call to arms. It was Jez's way home.

They wanted to fight. She sensed it. As she lay dormant, the daemon had picked through her thoughts and divined what she knew. It had learned of a deadly threat, the potential of a daemon nation to the south. If the Awakeners took Vardia, they'd be within striking distance of the Wrack. And that was something that would not be borne.

Call us, they urged her. *Bring us. We are ready.*

She held the sphere to her scorched breast and bowed her head over it, gathering it to her like the most precious of infants. *Come and get me*, she thought, and she let the wild power loose.

The golems roared and raged, smashing through the crew of the *Delirium Trigger* as they fought on the rain-slick deck. Bess roared with them, stamping here and there on her stubby legs, swinging her huge arms. She tore away limbs and crushed the fallen. Bullets bounced off her armour, and slowed her not a bit. One of Trinica's pirates got the back of her hand and went sailing over the gunwale and out into the sky.

Frey aimed and fired, aimed and fired. His pistol was in one hand, his cutlass in the other. He shot at those men he couldn't reach and cut down those he could, his blade guided expertly by the daemon within. Overhead and around him, great frigates slid through the downpour, engines rumbling and cannons blasting away. Frey hacked and killed and shoved, teeth gritted. These men were in his path; that was all he cared about.

The pirates boiled up through a half-dozen hatches and doors that led belowdecks. Some of them tried to turn back when they saw the invaders, cowed by the sight of the raging metal monstrosities and the Century Knights that darted between them. They were pushed forward by the weight of people behind, and found themselves on the battlefield anyway. For most, fear of their mistress drove them up into the fight, careless of the odds. They were many, and they fought with the savagery of desperate men; but against the soldiers of the Coalition, the golems and the Knights, they were outmatched.

Frey heard Celerity Blane's pistols chattering. She never stopped moving, performing rolls and flips and aerials with a speed and skill verging on inhuman. Kyne lobbed something through the air at a group of pirates who'd taken cover on a higher deck. It was X-shaped, the size of a hand, and magnetic. It stuck to the hull where it hit, adhering to the barrier the pirates hid behind. An instant later there was a low pulse of bass sound, so deep that it was felt in the chest rather than heard through the ears. The pirates fell dead; they went out like lights.

'Over there!' Frey cried, pointing towards a nearby doorway that led down into the depths of the craft. It was crowded with corpses, but nobody defended it now.

He'd meant the shout for Crake and Kyne, but Samandra took it up too, and she went running over in that direction, shotguns crossed in front of her, firing to either side. Frey scampered low across the deck; Crake came scurrying behind him, labouring under his cumbersome pack. Most of the pirates were too busy with the golems to notice them.

Kyne met up with them at the doorway, along with several Coalition soldiers. Narrow stairs led to a dimly lit corridor below.

'Stand back,' said Kyne, and he sent another of his X-shaped devices spinning down there. It stuck to the floor; there was a dull bass pulse. 'Clear,' he said, and the soldiers began hurrying through. Frey was about to follow him when Crake grabbed his arm.

'What?' he said irritably, angry that anything should delay him in his mission to get to Trinica.

The expression on Crake's face stopped him. Crake was looking at the sky; Frey followed his gaze. A slow chill crept through him.

There was a disturbance in the layer of grey overhead. The clouds were darkening, swirling in a colossal slow circle, accelerating as they neared the centre. Here and there, pulses of light flashed in the blackness.

'Oh, you've got to be bloody joking me,' Frey murmured.

Some of the combatants on deck had stopped fighting and were staring upwards, transfixed. Like Frey, recognised it. They'd been at Sakkan that fateful day.

Lightning jumped across the maelstrom. The clouds churned faster, and the pulses of light got faster with them, gathering towards the centre. Faster the pulses came, and faster still until they were a dazzling flicker, and finally they burst in a blinding light too bright to bear.

When the light had faded, the clouds had collapsed inward, and there was a hole in the sky, a great swirling tunnel at the heart of the vortex. Frey felt fear then, for he knew what was at the other end. An icy waste, thousands of miles to the north behind the forbidding cloud-wall of the Wrack that shrouded the pole. A place where dead things built strange cities, from which few men had returned alive.

Frey ran down the stairs, into the belly of the *Delirium Trigger*, where his daemonic love waited for him in the gloom. He didn't wait to see the first of the dreadnoughts come sailing through the gap. He didn't need to. They'd be here, as inevitable as fate. And they'd bring death and terror with them.

The Manes were coming.

Forty-Two

Dreadnoughts & Blackhawks – Thrate & Crome –
The Crawler – Trinica's Cabin – The Belly of the Beast

There weren't many that hadn't heard tales of Sakkan, or of the Manes which haunted the northern shores and ravaged whole towns when the fogs came. But rumour couldn't compare to the sight of the first dreadnoughts coming through. Vast, black, tattered things; great anvils of riveted metal, tarnished and ugly, bristling with spikes and strung with a webwork of chains. The dark frigates of the Manes.

A supernatural fear fell upon the city. The terror of the raiders was not only due to reputation; the dreadnoughts seemed to broadcast it. Their mere presence was enough to send the citizens into even greater panic. More dreadnoughts came, and more, until they mottled the sky like corrupted flesh. From their hulls issued Blackhawk fighters, a swarm of flies rising from the rot. The Blackhawks had wings swept forward like the tines of a meat-fork, in defiance of the laws of aerodynamics, and they flew in tight clusters of three or six, so close together that they were practically touching. Yet their pilots moved as one, each knowing the others' minds, and they never crossed paths.

The dreadnoughts' cannons opened up, and the Blackhawks raced to attack.

The sky was filled with flame. Explosions large and small billowed and burst as far as the eye could see. Broken craft rained down on the city, trailing fire as they descended, destroying buildings and streets where they hit. It was like a battle out of myth, a titanic conflict between gods of old, while mortals scurried like mice in their shadows, fighting to hang on to their small lives.

'Can this possibly get any bloody *worse*?' Malvery roared in exasperation, crouched down in cover with one eye on the battle overhead.

Ashua held her hand out, palm up. 'At least the rain's easing off,' she said optimistically.

Silo popped up from behind their shield of rubble, aimed his shotgun, then ducked back without firing. 'Looks clear,' he said.

A half-dozen Coalition soldiers went hurrying past, shoulders hunched, splashing down the cobbled road. Silo broke cover and followed; the others stuck tight to him. They were moving faster and with less care than he'd like, but speed was of the essence. The Cap'n, if he succeeded, wouldn't be long in knocking out the Azryx device. By then, they had to have as many of the city's guns under their control as possible.

Course, if he don't succeed, all this effort ain't worth shit, Silo thought. But he trusted the Cap'n to do his part. Hard to stop a man like that, when he finally set his mind to something.

He kept his eyes peeled for ambush as they ran. He glimpsed movement through broken walls, figures flitting down cross-streets, but it was hard to tell the citizens from the enemy at a glance. Many of the Awakeners wore no uniform, just a Cipher painted or stitched somewhere on their clothes. They were all Vards: only the trappings differed.

Once this had been a proud and wealthy shopping street not far from People's Park in the lee of the great crag. Now its windows were smashed, its roofs bowed and fallen in, and flames flickered in the rubble behind unsteady façades. The street was full of debris left by the bombs. Bodies lay hidden among the ruins, an arm showing here, a head there, with blank eyes and bloodied hair. Some lay in plain view, bullet ridden. Silo jumped over them without a thought; they'd become scenery now.

Ahead of him were golems and soldiers, and Century Knights ran among them. The electroheliograph masts were down across the city, so runners had been sent to contact more distant pockets of resistance, while a portion of the palace forces split up to take back the nearest guns. Many of the anti-aircraft emplacements were gathered near the palace, the better to defend Thesk's heart. Some, presumably, were still under Coalition control, being fortified positions and easily defensible. But that left a lot which weren't. With three enemies overhead tearing chunks out of each other, a concerted attack from beneath would be devastating.

If they could win back the guns. If the Cap'n came through.

A gatling gun clattered ahead of them, followed by a volley of rifle fire. Silo hunkered down at the end of the street, where it opened into a square. There had once been a tall stone column at its centre, but it had broken midway up and toppled. A heaped bank of rubble pointed westward from its base, like the shadow of a sundial marking the hour of its own destruction.

The Awakeners had dug in here, Sentinels and mercs and peasant volunteers all jumbled up together. Desperate, frightened men, huddled behind piles of fallen stones, lashing out at anyone who came near. First the Sammie ambush, and now the Manes. They saw their great coup crumbling around them, and they had no plan of retreat.

Silo ducked as a bullet chipped the stone near his head. He waved Malvery and Ashua down, conscious of his promise to the Cap'n to bring them back safely. Snipers hid among the ruins, the tips of their rifles visible through crumbling window frames.

But neither snipers nor machine guns deterred the Archduke's golems. They thundered forward into the square, ploughing towards the barricades. Gatling guns pocked their armour, and bullets sparked on stone. Dynamite was thrown from behind the Awakener barricades. It cost one of the golems a foot and sent another one reeling.

Silo heard a percussive *thwip-thwip-thwip* noise from above. He looked up, and caught a momentary glimpse of a slender, dark figure on the rooftops. She was clad in armour that covered her whole body, moulded tight to her form, and was carrying a long-barrelled rifle of exquisite design. He spotted her only for an instant, and then lost her again: the colours of her armour shifted with the background, camouflaging her, making her indistinct.

That was all he saw of Zalexa Crome, the Century Knights' infamous assassin. But where there had been Awakener snipers before, men lay limp with their arms hanging over the sills.

The soldiers ran in after the golems. With them went Graniel Thrate, looking half golem himself in his massive suit of thralled armour, a black metal sledgehammer in one hand and an enormous gun in the other. Bullets whipped back and forth across the square as the Coalition soldiers attempted to storm the enemy positions.

Then there was a low rumble, and the pebbles on the barricade under Silo's nose began to jitter and dance. With a growl of engines, an armoured vehicle burst into the square, shunting a slide of rubble before it. It was squat and boxy, with a short, wide cannon turret on its humped back, and it ran on enormous metal tracks.

'Oh, shit!' said Ashua. 'A Crawler! The militia used to set them on us in Rabban when things got *really* bad!'

She was drowned out by the explosion as the Crawler fired its cannon. They covered their heads and crushed themselves down as chips of stone peppered them. Silo's ears were ringing when he came back up again. Through the dust, he saw the mangled wreckage of a golem lying in the centre of the square, surrounded by the bodies of soldiers.

The Crawler pushed onward, its tracks crushing the dead beneath it. Bullets pinged off its armour as the cannon turret swivelled. Coalition soldiers scattered in frantic retreat. Then the cannon boomed again, and the soldiers went flying, some in pieces.

The Awakeners rallied, spraying the square with bullets. The Coalition forces fell back before the armoured Crawler. Silo and the others helped cover their retreat, shooting at the enemy to keep them occupied.

'We gotta get to the other side of that square!' Malvery cried. 'The anti-aircraft gun's right over there! Used to get the tram past it on the way to my surgery.'

'Ain't goin' anywhere with that Crawler there,' Silo said, but then he saw someone come lunging out of cover. Graniel Thrate, his head made tiny his enormous armour, sprinting across the square towards the Crawler. It swivelled its cannon, but too slow. He shoulder-charged it in the side with the force of a steam train, and to Silo's amazement he drove a great dent into it, collapsing its wheel as-sembly. The tracks on that side dragged uselessly as the Crawler was pushed back, skidding across the flagstones. It crashed into a low wall and tipped a little, its tracks lifting off the ground. Thrate got his hands under it and, with neck muscles straining, he hauled it upward. It rolled over the wall and crashed down onto its turret with calamit-ous screech of metal, and there it lay still.

Ashua stared open-mouthed. Even Silo looked amazed. It was hard to imagine, with warriors like that, how the Coalition had let itself get into such a desperate position.

'That,' said Malvery, adjusting his glasses, 'was impressive.'

'Attack!' shouted one of the Coalition commanders, and his troops surged forward again. This time Silo, Malvery and Ashua joined the charge.

Now it was the Awakeners' turn to retreat. They turned tail and fled as the remaining golems smashed through their barricades. Graniel Thrate was among them, swinging his sledgehammer left and right, broken men flying like rag dolls. Others dropped dead from neat headshots, the work of the invisible Zalexa Crome, somewhere up on the rooftops.

Silo, Ashua and Malvery ran with them, picking targets where they could. Silo saw a bearded merc, caught up in the suicidal desperation of a last stand, come running out from cover with his guns blazing. He wanted to die. Silo gave him his wish.

In a flurry, it was over, and the square was clear. They took a moment to breathe, to survey the carnage and destruction that surrounded them. All around, once beautiful buildings were scorched and shattered. The elegance of this great city had been lost in blood and fire. Silo saw the hurt in Malvery's eyes. This had been his home for most of his life.

The Coalition troops were pursuing the Awakeners out of the square, in the direction of the anti-aircraft gun. Malvery turned his attention to the men lying on the ground, searching for wounded.

'Later, Doc,' Silo said, motioning towards to the retreating troops. 'We need your gun now.'

'There's people here I can help . . .' Malvery said, though his protest was weak.

'Can't save everyone,' said Silo.

Then Ashua screamed.

Silo knew it was bad before he even saw it. Ashua wasn't one to scream. He looked round, and the world decelerated, everything moving in slow motion.

Not just bad. Worse than that.

He'd been so caught up in the battle on the ground that he'd virtually forgotten about the fight overhead. But now the sound of engines was suddenly loud in his ears. Looming in his vision, filling up the sky, the blazing prow of a frigate rushed down towards them, trailing fire. Like a colossal meteor, like the fist of a god.

It crashed into the city a dozen streets away, hitting at a shallow angle. Flame blasted up into the air. It ploughed through stone and steel, carving a vast trench through the buildings, getting louder and louder as it bore down on Silo. A gargantuan beast of smoke and dust and screaming metal and crashing stone, charging him.

Too massive for any of them to avoid. Too fast to do anything about it. All they could do was stand there, locked in a single moment of terror and resignation.

Mother, he thought. *I'm comin' home.*

His thoughts were lost in a deafening hurricane of wind and sound, and a wave of heat and force hit him.

After that, nothing.

The dark metal corridors of the *Delirium Trigger* rang with the shouts of men and the sound of combat. Frey pushed through the press of soldiers, his face a grim mask lit starkly by the muzzle flash of his pistol as he fired. There was momentum in him now. His bridges had burned. Going back would be pointless. There was nothing to go back to.

Sammies. Manes. Awakeners. Treason. All the rack and ruin of his life. And one chance to set things right.

It was too close down here for golems. The *Delirium Trigger*'s upper decks were a maze of narrow passageways, barely wide enough for two men to walk abreast. The air was stifling, and it reeked of cordite and sweat and blood and the shit in dead men's pants. Frey shot a pirate through the lung as he came running out of a doorway, and stepped over his gurgling body without even looking down.

He pulled open a sliding door, thrust his gun inside and found only silence. Soldiers shoved past him down the corridor. He stepped inside to get out of the way. His ears had been hammered by the reports of shotguns and pistols; this was a place of relative peace, with the distant detonations and the screams of the wounded muffled by thick bulkheads.

It was Trinica's cabin, where he'd been heading all along. Once he'd thought it oppressive, with its dark wood panels, brass and iron fixtures and overwrought frowning sconces. A grave and serious room. Now he drank it in with his eyes. In all the world, this was the only place she'd put her mark on. The only place that bore anything of her spirit.

There was her bookshelf, full of academic tomes and literature in both Vardic and Samarlan. There was her chair, and her massive desk next to the sloping window. Light from explosions outside flickered across charts that had been laid out there, and the book that lay across them. A beautifully embossed book.

A book he recognised.

'Cap'n!' said Crake. He was standing in the doorway, encumbered by his heavy pack. Frey held up a hand to silence him. He was aware of the need to hurry. This was more important.

He moved slowly across the room. When he got to the desk, he reached out and turned the book over so that he could see the title. It was in Samarlan, but it didn't matter. He recognised it anyway.

The Silent Tide.

So it was true. Balomon Crund hadn't been lying to him. Trinica had been carrying this book with her, reading it. In spite of the daemon that controlled her, she'd managed this. A cry for help. A message in a bottle.

'Cap'n?' Crake asked again, uncertainly.

He left the book, turned, and hurried back out. Crake moved aside as he pushed through. 'Come on,' he said sharply. 'She needs me.'

They made their way onward, catching up with Kyne and Samandra, who'd hung back to wait for them. The other soldiers had moved up the corridor and were engaged in a new battle. They were about to follow when a blast rocked the *Delirium Trigger*, sending Crake tottering into the wall.

'Not Samarlan,' said Kyne. 'Must be the Manes getting through. Seems it's the Awakener convoy they're after. I doubt it'll hold for long.'

'Sounds like the end of the world out there,' said Crake.

'Might well turn out to be the case,' Samandra commented.

'Hey,' said Frey. 'Stairs.' He pointed down a cross-corridor, where a set of stairs were just about visible halfway along.

'We should stay with the soldiers, Cap'n,' Crake said nervously.

'Soldiers are too damn slow,' said Frey, starting up the corridor. He glanced over his shoulder at Kyne and Samandra. 'You're Century Knights, aren't you?'

Samandra looked at Crake and shrugged. 'I'm all good with reckless.'

Frey touched his hand against his chest as they descended. The amulet that Crake had given him was cold against his skin. It seemed a pretty poor defence against what was to come. He didn't have a great deal of faith in daemonism at the best of times, but Crake's skills had served him well in the past, and he'd put his trust in worse things before.

He had to believe. That was all there was to it.

The lower decks had wider corridors than the ones above. There was nobody in sight when they emerged, and it was eerily still. It seemed that the majority of the pirates had gone to fight off the boarders. Frey looked left and right suspiciously, his pistol in one hand and his cutlass in the other, listening. The lights here were dim, and the seething gloom was a hot threat.

The daemon, he thought. He could sense it, warping the edges of his consciousness, tingeing the scene with paranoia. She was close.

He looked back at Crake, who nodded in confirmation. He felt it too.

They moved on warily, heading for the hold. The *Delirium Trigger* seemed to breathe like some vast beast. He heard the clanking of her iron heart, the hiss of her vents, felt her shudder as another shell exploded close by. At any moment, he expected an attack. Yet for all the gunfire and explosions that echoed through the hollow corridors, nothing came for them. Nothing until—

'Frey!'

He whirled, his arm outstretched and his pistol aimed. As he fired, he caught a glimpse of an ugly face ducking back from a doorway, framed by a dirty mop of black hair. The sound of the gun bounced away down the passageway, and the darkness in the corners seemed to blacken, as if some terrible thing had just turned its attention their way.

'It's me, you fool!' growled a voice from the doorway. 'Balomon Crund!'

Frey was breathing hard. He was more keyed up than he'd realised. 'What do you want?' he said.

Crund showed an empty hand, then poked his head out again. 'It's this way!' he said. He looked up the corridor. 'Quick, they'll have heard you! They're waiting by the door to the hold!'

Frey hesitated. He'd never been liked by Crund, and they'd been enemies more than allies. He didn't trust him as far as he could throw him.

'I brought you here, didn't I?' he snarled, angry that Frey should doubt him. 'There's another way in! A side door!'

There were running footsteps coming from up the corridor. 'Reckon he ain't lyin' about his mates, at least,' said Samandra. She spun her shotguns around in her hands; they crunched as they were primed. 'Sounds like a lot of 'em.'

Still Frey didn't move. Still he wasn't sure. He'd been betrayed too many times by Trinica and her crew.

'You *can* save her, can't you?' Crund asked, and there was something imploring in his eyes, something desperate. It was that look that decided Frey in the end. He saw himself in that: a man caught up in his devotion, helpless against it. A man like that would do anything. He might even betray his mistress for her own good.

'Yeah,' said Frey. 'I can save her.' And he went after Crund through the doorway, with Crake and Kyne on his tail, their packs clanking and clattering. Samandra followed them through.

'They seen us,' she said. 'Be quick.'

They ran through narrow, dark chambers full of steaming pipes. Orange lights gave glimpses of deeply shadowed faces, eyes fierce and intent. Bullets skipped off the metalwork, forcing them to duck. Samandra, bringing up the rear, dropped into a crouch behind the cover of a pipe and started shooting back at their pursuers.

'Keep goin'!' she called over the gunfire. 'I'll take care of this lot!'

'Samandra!' Crake cried. He came to a halt, reluctant to leave her behind. She spared him a moment, and the two of them locked eyes across the room.

'This is your show now, honey,' she said. 'Do your stuff.'

Kyne grabbed his arm and pulled him onward. They heard Samandra's shotguns blasting away as they left.

'She's a Century Knight,' said Kyne as they ran. 'Don't worry about her. Worry about what's ahead.'

Balomon, who'd been lumbering in front of them like some shaggy troll, suddenly halted at a narrow metal door. 'Through here,' he said, and tapped a code into a keypad. The door slid open, and they stepped through.

The *Delirium Trigger*'s cargo hold was a cavern of dark, grimy metal, its roof supported by enormous girders that acted as pillars, running round the outside edge. It was cool here, and water dripped from the ceiling, where the outline of a loading hatch was faintly visible. Electric lamps shone weakly from the walls, but they struggled to illuminate such a large space.

Between and behind the pillars, a dizzying range of equipment and loot was stacked and lashed together. There were ammo crates, chests of ducats and tanks of liquid aerium. Shadowy vehicles lurked behind piles of spare parts. Near the back was an enormous bronze head as large as a man.

But it was what was in the centre of the hold that drew their eyes. There, a space had been cleared, and there stood the Azryx device that had destroyed the Coalition fleet.

Frey felt a crawling dread. Here in the belly of the *Delirium Trigger*, it was more sinister than the first time he'd seen it. An ill, mesmerising light washed out from the towering cylinder at its heart. The lightning that flickered inside the swirling gas suggested a pattern, some snickering code to mock him. The bone-like material that encased the cylinder seemed like a growth, some awful tumour crawling up the glass-like casement. The inscriptions on the brassy towers at its four corners were warnings in an ancient tongue.

The door they'd entered by slid shut behind them, muffling the sound of Samandra's guns. They whirled; Crake raced to the door. 'The code!' he urged. Crund tapped in the code on the keypad. Nothing happened. 'They've trapped us in here!'

The atmosphere in the room thickened, shadows swarmed and the temperature dropped. Frey slowly turned his head, looking over his shoulder. From behind the Azryx device, a lean figure stepped into view, half-lit by the bruised glow from the cylinder.

'Hello, Trinica,' he said.

Forty-Three

Back from the Dead – Silo's Command –
The Charge – A Pitiful Epitaph

S ilo's eyes flickered open.

He was face down on the ground. Cold, wet stone pushed into his cheek. His head rang like a struck bell, his neck was agonisingly stiff, and his limbs and torso blazed with pain.

He wasn't sure where he was or what had happened to him. Automatically, he tried to rise. The pain made him grunt, but he pushed through it, and forced himself up onto his knees. The effort set off a pounding in his skull, which faded as quickly as it came.

Blinking, he looked about. He knelt amidst a broken landscape of stone and dust and flame. Hot winds blew smoke around him. People staggered here and there, like the wandering souls of the damned; vague blurred shadows, shouting things he couldn't understand.

The frigate.

The memory of the enormous aircraft plunging towards him brought him another step closer to making sense of things. He was at the edge of a wide, shallow trench which had been scored through the city. Some way distant, a mountain of twisted metal smoked and flamed. In its wake, no building was left standing. The far side of the square had been entirely destroyed, but the near side, where Silo had been thrown, was still partially intact.

It had passed them by, then. But not by much. And it had taken a heavy toll.

He got to his feet, dazed. None of it seemed real. Bodies lay everywhere, red and black and twisted. Lipless jaws yawned, showing charred teeth. The air reeked of cooking flesh and prothane.

Malvery stumbled past him, moaning. The doctor didn't even seem to see him. Instead he fell to his knees a few metres away, where a limp figure was lying beside the remains of a wall.

It took a few seconds for his stunned brain to slot her into place. Ashua.

Concern and alarm drove him to movement. He made his way over to Malvery on leaden legs. The distance exhausted him; he was forced to his knees again. There was no strength in his body. It had been knocked out of him along with his wits.

Malvery had Ashua in his arms, supporting her shoulders and head in the crook of his elbow while he felt for a pulse at her throat. Blood stained her short ginger hair and ran down her tattooed face; her skin was pallid and dirty.

'Come on, come on, come on,' Malvery was muttering frantically, broken glasses still hanging askew on his bulbous nose. He patted her face. 'Don't play games now. You ain't dead. You ain't!'

He looked around as if for help, and found Silo there. 'I can't see where she got hit,' he said hoarsely, and he brushed back her hair to try to find a wound. There was something close to panic in his voice. He was as shell-shocked as Silo was. 'I can't find the wound!'

Silo just stared at her. She wasn't moving. Malvery craned his neck and searched among the wandering ghosts that surrounded them, as if there was anyone more qualified than he to give aid.

'Doc . . .' Silo croaked. His throat felt like it had been scorched.

'I think she might've cracked her skull,' Malvery muttered. 'I think there might be a crack there.'

He put on big hand on her head, feeling clumsily around. At his touch, Ashua bucked and fell out of his grip. Malvery gasped and tried to gather her up, but she kicked out and fought him off, and ended up scrambling away on her arse, with one hand held to the side of her head.

'*Ow!*' she said pointedly, scowling at him. 'That bloody hurts!'

'You're alive!' Malvery cried out in delight.

'Course I'm alive,' Ashua said. She was slurring her words, and sounded drunk. 'Reckon I'd rather not be, though.' She stared about dreamily. 'Crawler hit us?'

Malvery laughed, and went over to her and gave her an awkward hug. She winced as he squeezed her, but she didn't protest. She laid her head on his shoulder, and let herself be held.

Silo got to his feet again, and this time found that he had more strength in his legs. The sense of dislocation was lessening moment by moment; he was returning to himself. There was something he was meant to do here, he just couldn't remember what.

Above him, through the drifting black haze, he saw a great swirling vortex and explosions in the sky. They sounded distant and hollow, as if they were no part of the world he occupied here on the ground. But the longer he looked, the more the picture came together.

The Awakeners had been mostly scattered or destroyed now, but the core of the convoy remained. A dozen battered frigates hung static around the flagship, hemmed in by the Samarlans. But the Samarlans weren't attacking them any more; instead, they were *defending* them from the Manes on their flank, whose terrible dreadnoughts were still arriving. The Awakener convoy struggled and fought, but they were bereft of leadership or tactics. They could do little but harass the craft that surrounded them.

Why are the Sammies helpin' the Awakeners? Silo thought; but the answer came to him almost as soon as he'd posed the question. The Awakeners had the Azryx device. The Sammies must have known the Awakeners would guard the device at the heart of their fleet, and didn't want to risk it being destroyed. They wanted the city guns neutralised until they could get their landing parties down to secure them; it was worth taking a few casualties for that.

The guns, he thought, and suddenly he remembered it all. He lurched away across the blasted square, stepping over rubble and bits of bodies.

The guns were their only hope now. With the Awakeners all but out of the game, it was between the Manes and the Sammies as to who would control the skies. Once the victor had beaten their opponents, they'd descend on the city in force. The Samarlans with their troops, or the Manes with their howling hordes. Slavery or conversion. Not much of a choice.

What were the Manes doing here? He didn't know; nor did he know who'd summoned them. But if they hadn't, the Sammies would have swarmed all over the city by now. The Manes' intervention might just have bought the Coalition the time they needed.

'Fall back!' someone was shouting in the distance. 'Fall back to the palace!'

Silo frowned, not sure if he'd heard the order right. A bloodied young soldier went stumbling past him, his uniform ragged and a wounded hand held to his chest. Silo grabbed him by his shoulder.

'Where you goin'?' he asked.

The soldier stared at him, bewilderment in his eyes. 'The palace,' he said, as if it was obvious.

'You're goin' back?' Silo asked in amazement. 'You still got your gun, ain't you?'

The soldier surveyed the scene of destruction around him. 'Going back to the palace,' he muttered blankly.

'They're dug in, you mad bloody Murthian!' said another soldier. 'Let him go.'

Silo let the young soldier wander off. The man who'd addressed him was in his late twenties, with a short moustache and a thick head of black hair mussed by the battle. Other than that, he looked relatively unharmed. 'You seen the commander? Any sergeants?'

'No,' said Silo. 'Where's the gun?'

'It's over there,' the soldier replied, pointing across the obliterated square. Through the flames, it was just possible to make out the barrel of an anti-aircraft gun tilted upward. 'They've dug in, didn't you hear? They retreated back up that road and shut the damn gates.'

Silo looked at him levelly. 'Show me,' he said.

Maybe it was something in his tone, or the determination in his eyes, but the soldier did as he was told. 'Come on, then,' he said, and he led Silo away.

'Fall back!' someone was shouting behind him. 'Gather up! We're falling back to the palace!' They saw a golem wandering aimlessly, a dim giant without direction, searching for opponents.

The soldier, who introduced himself as Eltenby, guided Silo through the wreckage and bodies. On the far side of the square was a swathe of smouldering rubble where a row of buildings had been demolished. Beyond was a shallow rise in the land, and the anti-aircraft emplacement sat on top of that, surrounded by a wall. It had escaped the destruction. A short uphill stretch of clear ground led to the gate.

'There,' said Eltenby, pointing. 'You can see them on the wall. The only way in is through that gate. They have another gatling gun up there, a three hundred and sixty degree field of vision and open terrain all around. Anyone tries to approach from any side, they'll cut us down.'

Silo narrowed his eyes. 'Not all of us,' he said. 'We gotta take that gun.'

Eltenby stared at him in surprise. 'Are all your people as crazy as you?'

Silo didn't bother to answer that. He got to his feet and stalked back across the square. Somewhere, a man was still shouting, 'Gather up! Fall back!' Silo headed towards the sound, with Eltenby tagging after him. The soldier seemed interested to see what Silo would do.

Silo found the owner of the voice behind a pile of rubble. He was a stocky man with short blond hair and broad, scowling features, and he was directing soldiers back up the road towards the palace. Silo wasn't clear on the ranks of the Coalition Army, but he knew enough to see that this man wasn't much higher than a grunt. If any commanding officers had survived, he couldn't see them.

The sight of the soldiers leaving inspired anger in Silo. He didn't know where it came from; usually he was good at mastering his emotions. But this . . . This was *wrong*. He felt it powerfully, and it took him over.

'Hey!' he yelled. 'Hey! Where you goin'? We ain't done here!'

Several dozen soldiers, most of them dirtied and carrying wounds, stopped and looked back at him.

'You all goin' home?' he cried. 'Ain't you noticed there's a war on?'

'Shut your mouth, foreigner,' sneered a soldier as he passed. 'Bet you can't wait for your masters to get here.'

Silo's eyes blazed, and he grabbed the soldier by the front of his uniform and dragged him close, until they were face to face. The man smirked nervously, but he couldn't meet Silo's gaze, and he wilted. Silo shoved him away.

'Ain't nobody the master o' me,' he snarled. He raised his voice, addressing the others. 'I *am* a foreigner. This ain't even my land. So how come I'm the only one here got any guts?'

'Fall back to the palace!' shouted the stocky soldier, ignoring him.

But Silo wasn't in the mood to be ignored. 'There ain't *time* to fall back to the palace!' he roared. The other soldiers had stopped retreating now; he had their attention, at least for the moment.

He pointed up to the sky, where the remnants of the Awakener convoy huddled within the Samarlan swarm. 'There's a man up there riskin' his life to save this damn city! A man who got a million reasons not to give a shit, but he doin' it anyway! And he gonna take out the Awakeners' secret weapon, and we gonna have the use of those anti-aircraft guns again, and then we gonna rip those Sammie bastards all to pieces! But first we gotta *take that gun*! You all got them orders, didn't you? Didn't the Archduke himself give you that job?'

'The sarge is gone,' one of the soldiers protested.

'Who in rot's name is in command now, anyway?' someone else called. 'Where's Thrate?'

'Thrate's gone too. I saw it. He was right in the path when that frigate came down.'

The news hit them hard. One of the Century Knights? Those men and women were the heroes of the Coalition. The best of them were legends. It didn't seem possible that one of them could have been erased like that.

'You don't need no commanding officer!' Silo shouted. 'And you don't need no Century Knights! You just gotta pick up your guns and fight! This is your *home*!'

There was silence among the soldiers. Even the stocky soldier had fallen quiet. Some of the men were shamefaced, some furious. They exchanged glances, each trying to divine what their neighbour thought, seeking consensus.

'Shit, I'm with you,' said a loud voice, and Malvery walked up to stand next to him.

'Me, too,' said Ashua. Her tattooed face was smeared with blood, but she joined them all the same.

Eltenby looked around at his companions in disbelief. When nobody else spoke, he stepped forward. 'Are we going to let a foreigner show us how to fight?' he asked them. 'Are we going to let a man from Murthia defend our country?'

'They're dug in! They got gates and walls and a gatling gun!' came the protest, but it fell on stony ground now. There was a murmuring among the soldiers. Their pride had been pricked, and they were shaking off the shock of the frigate crash.

'Who cares what they've got?' someone shouted. 'We're the Coalition Army!' A rough cheer went up at that.

'I ain't running from a bunch of peasants and witchdoctors!' came another voice.

'Let's show those rotting Sammies the kind of welcome we give in Vardia!'

Soon they were all firing each other up, yelling slogans and taunts. The camaraderie of warriors, momentarily broken by disaster, knitted them back together. Silo felt it too; he knew the strength of it, from his desperate days as a resistance fighter in Samarla, when he'd been second-in-command to a small army.

Exhilaration filled him. They were all on his side now; they looked to him to lead. The colour of his skin, the set of his features didn't matter. He was an idea, not a person any more. A lens to focus them, to channel their hurt and fear, their bravery and their fury.

'Let's take back that gun!' he shouted, and this time they shouted with him.

They went hustling across the square towards the anti-aircraft emplacement, gathering stragglers on the way. Once the majority had turned, the rest came. By the time they reached the smouldering barrier of banked rubble, they were seventy or more, and there was a golem with them.

'Those things understand us?' Silo asked Eltenby, as the huge metal creature lumbered up alongside.

'As far as I can tell,' Eltenby replied.

'We're gonna need him,' he said.

He turned to address the others. 'Once we get over this rubble, they'll be shootin' at us,' he said. 'Ain't much cover out there, so hit the ground runnin' and *keep* runnin'. Golem's gonna lead. We get to the gate, and he gonna damn well knock it down! Now load up your weapons. Once we go, we ain't comin' back!'

The soldiers began stuffing rounds into their pistols. Some were pale and grey, some with taut faces. They were scared, now it came to it. Any sane man would be. But they took their courage from their companions.

Malvery and Ashua were standing near Silo, loading up with the rest of them. The doctor kept casting worried glances at Ashua, until finally she shook her head irritably and said: '*What?*'

'Maybe you ought to sit this one out,' said Malvery. He waved vaguely at her head. 'Might be you have concussion.'

'I'm not sitting out shit,' Ashua said, and went back to filling the chambers of her revolver.

'I just mean . . .' said Malvery. 'You know, if you're doing this to prove something . . . I mean, you don't have to . . .'

'I *do*,' she snapped. She leaned close and prodded him in the chest. 'Yeah, I do. Because somewhere inside you, you've still got doubts. You're still wondering if I'm for real, or if I was playing you all along.' She shoved him angrily. 'So if it takes some dumb-shit death or glory charge to convince you, then that's what I'll do. 'Cause I'm damned if I'm letting you cast me off for one little mistake.'

Malvery opened his mouth to reply, then didn't. He harumphed and looked ashamed.

'Besides,' she said. 'Sammies screwed me good. Reckon a few shots up their arse from that anti-aircraft gun is the least I owe them.'

Silo pressed the last of the shells into his shotgun and levered it back and forth to prime it. He remembered how the Cap'n had charged him to bring Malvery and Ashua back safe. But there were more important things than safety.

'Go!' he shouted. 'Go! Go! Go!'

The golem roared, and the men yelled and howled, fired up with anticipation and fear. They went scrambling up the rubble slope, the golem in the lead, and Silo went up with them. Rocks shifted beneath his feet; he had to clamber, and was cut. But the slope rolled back, and he reached the crest, and then he was slipping and sliding down the other side, bouncing from foothold to foothold, and the sound of the guns began.

By the time his boots hit solid ground, he was past caring whether anyone was following him. Strength pounded through him, and he was hot with rage. His breath came loud in his ears. He felt powerful, invincible, ready to throw himself into death's teeth.

Bullets pocked and whined around him. He'd get hit by one, or he wouldn't. Nothing he could do about it but run.

Ahead of them lay a shallow rise, with a cracked road, scorched grass and little else until it met the stone ring of the anti-aircraft emplacement. Atop the walls, Sentinels aimed and fired with their rifles, and a gatling gun sat on a tripod, waiting for them to come into range. The sky above flashed and boomed as the Samarlans and the Manes traded cannon fire.

The golem led the way. More men caught up with Silo as they came off the rubble slope and on to the rise. They gathered into a charge, picking up momentum as they ran. A thunder of boots, the rasp of uniforms and the clatter of buckles and guns. Each person in their own private world, vision narrowed by adrenaline; each part of the mass, driven on by the crowd, taking strength from their allies. Someone shouted a wild battle-cry. A few soldiers fired at the Awakeners, hopeful shots, wasting ammo. Using their guns to boost their courage.

A man to Silo's left was cut down, punched through the chest, blood puffing from a hole in his back. He stumbled to a halt, a puzzled look on his face, and pitched over. Silo heard another man fall behind him, screaming, wounded in a limb. The Sentinels' shots were increasingly accurate now, and though they ran hard enough to burst their lungs, the emplacement seemed to come no nearer.

Then came the sound that each of them had dreaded and none had dared think about. The killing rattle of the gatling gun, spitting bullets down onto them from its position above the gate. Suddenly the scuff and whip of rifle shot became a hail, chopping up the ground, smacking into earth and flesh. Screams came from everywhere, choked gurgles and short yelps, swiftly cut short. Men to either side of Silo went down. Someone lost a finger. The back of one man's head blew out, and Silo saw shards of white bone among the red.

The chaos overtook him. Silo tripped, running too fast for his own feet; he fell and skidded on his knees. A man behind him grabbed the back of his coat, tried to pull him up. Silo was dragged roughly forward instead, scrabbling to get his feet back under him. Then the man who was dragging him shuddered and fell onto his shoulders. Silo slipped out from underneath, skinning one hand on the road as he pushed himself upright. Somehow he managed to avoid falling flat on his face, and he stumbled on up the rise.

Most of the soldiers had overtaken him. He saw Malvery labouring near the rear of the crowd, too fat and unfit to outpace the others. Ashua was ahead of them both, her mouth stretched in a savage yell, eyes fixed on her destination. The dead were left in their wake, lifeless limbs flopping as they rolled to a halt.

The gatling gun swept across the group ahead of him. The golem sparked and sang as bullets hammered into it, but it charged on

THE ACE OF SKULLS

through them without pause. The people to either side of it weren't so lucky. He saw men jerking as they were hit, saw them stagger and collapse. They fell like wheat before a scythe, and Ashua went down with them. She tumbled and hit the ground hard, rolling several times before she came to a stop.

Malvery gave a wordless cry of anguish. He surged forward and ran to her, heedless of the bullets flying around him. She was dragging herself up off the ground as he reached her, slack-eyed, leg-shot, her face lax with shock. He slung an arm round her shoulder, lifted her and propelled her on towards the gate, one foot dragging behind her.

Malvery knew what Silo knew: there was no turning back. Their only hope for survival lay in reaching the emplacement.

But they were too far away. Hope drained from Silo as he saw the distance still left to cover. Ahead of him, the soldiers were falling. So many, and so fast. He saw Eltenby die, red holes appearing in his back as he juddered and clawed at the air. And he knew then that there would be no escape for anybody. Even if they retreated now, they'd be cut down as they fled.

The cold horror of despair sank into him. What had he been thinking? What in damnation had driven him to such folly?

He'd always been a survivor, a man who did what was necessary to look out for himself and his own. Ashua was the same, and so was the Cap'n. Yet somehow they'd all become swept up in this, pushed to acts of foolish bravery by a sense of something bigger than they were. The unity of shared conflict had overwhelmed them, and they'd bought into the game when they should have stayed out of it.

War was a trick. An illusion to make men do things they couldn't ordinarily do. For all the patriotic talk, all the glorious fervour of a righteous cause, every man and woman faced their deaths alone. It was only when you were staring at the end that you realised all that camaraderie didn't mean a damn, but by then it was too late to take it back.

You the Ace of Skulls, he heard himself say to the Cap'n. How naïve and stupid it sounded now. If he hadn't said that, the *Ketty Jay* would have flown on. He wouldn't have been here, and he would never have led these soldiers and his friends to their deaths.

Shoulda kept your mouth shut, he thought. What a pitiful epitaph that would make.

449

Then the sound of the gatling gun changed. No longer was it firing into the front ranks of the attackers, but tipping backwards, sending bullets harmlessly into the air. Now it was spinning to a halt, and Silo looked up through the sweat that stung his eyes and saw that there was nobody manning it any more.

One of the Sentinels on the wall ran over to the gatling, seized its handles and tilted it down towards the road once more. Before he could press the trigger, blood sprayed from the back of his head, and he toppled backwards out of sight. The man to right of him looked across in puzzlement. An instant later, his head snapped back and he slumped forward over the rampart.

Despair turned to fierce exultation as Silo accelerated once again. He overtook Malvery and Ashua, catching up the golem at the head of the charge. If he looked over his shoulder, he'd see nothing but rubble and broken buildings; but then, Zalexa Crome was legendarily hard to spot. Somewhere back there the Century Knight was alive and kicking, her sniper rifle trained on the Awakeners. All of a sudden, they had a chance.

His doubts were thrown aside. A primal yell tore from his throat, a cry of savagery and triumph. He was flooded with new energy, driven by the promise of survival, of getting to grips with his tormentors and exacting revenge upon them for the murder they'd wreaked.

The riflemen fell into disarray as they saw their companions killed by some invisible assailant. They scrambled to get off the wall. More than half the Coalition troops lay dead in the road behind Silo, but the rest of them still lived, and they charged the emplacement with the golem at their head.

The golem bellowed and shoulder-charged the gate at full pelt, crashing into it like a freight train. Wood splintered and metal buckled. The gate crashed inward; the bar that secured it cracked in half. That first blow almost destroyed the gate entirely. The golem pulled itself free and drew back one colossal fist to finish the job. With one mighty swing, the gate was torn from its hinges and fell backwards.

Now the way was clear, the Coalition soldiers flooded past the golem, and Silo was swept along with them. Inside was a circular courtyard surrounding the massive anti-aircraft gun, which sat idle, pointing uselessly at the sky. There were Awakeners in the courtyard, and some on the walkway on the inside of the wall. The Coalition soldiers ran in headlong, guns blazing.

Silo found himself in amidst a close press of men. Allies and enemies jostled him. A figure in a cassock appeared out of the crowd, and Silo emptied his shotgun into the man's belly. Blood spattered his face. He wiped his eyes, got his vision back, and cracked his shotgun butt down on the crown of a merc who was facing away from him.

A few riflemen up on the wall sent bullets into the fray, but they were still being plagued by Zalexa Crome, and one by one they went toppling off to crash down on the heads of the men below. The golem wrenched the gate up off the floor and hefted it at a group of mercs who were shooting into the crowd from across the courtyard. It spun through the air, end over end, and though they did their best to scramble out of the way, their best wasn't good enough.

Dynamite went off somewhere. Silo felt the force of it, saw a group of men thrown aside, Awakener and Coalition alike. A Sentinel fell at his feet, half his face purple with bruising, eyes so bloodshot there were no whites left. Silo pumped his shotgun. A Speaker in a white cassock came running at him with a knife. Silo fired, and the man was blown backwards, crashed into someone else and knocked them to the ground too. A Coalition soldier nearby screamed and fell. Maybe Silo had hit him; he couldn't tell. All this shooting in close combat was dangerous, but he'd long gone past the point of being sensible. He killed, and killed, and that was all.

Somewhere in the middle of it all, he found himself searching breathlessly for targets, and there were none to be found. The gunfire petered out and fell quiet. Silo saw men falling to their knees, holding their hands up in surrender. There were desperate, disbelieving smiles on the face of the Coalition soldiers. Silo looked around and found Malvery near the gate, a smoking shotgun in one hand, supporting Ashua with his free arm. Ashua hopped on one leg, but she was alive, and holding a revolver of her own. They'd come late, but they'd been there at the end.

Silo stood there, chest heaving, his shotgun hanging loosely in his hand. There were perhaps twenty soldiers left of the seventy who'd begun the charge, and a handful of Awakeners, but in that moment it didn't matter. He hadn't let the Cap'n down. His crew were safe, and they had the gun.

He lifted his shotgun over his head and gave a hoarse bellow of exhausted triumph. The other men joined their voices to his, a rousing cry that lifted up to the battle-hammered skies above, where the great aircraft fought on in ignorance of what they'd done.

A small victory in the grand scheme of things, and won with great sacrifice, but it was a victory. It was a foreigner's victory, *Silo*'s victory, and all those cheers were for him.

Forty-Four

Trinica – 'It's Only Fear' – Some Dread Edifice –
WANTED – Phantoms, in the End

~ *D arian* ~

His name was like the exhalation of a ghost, a hoarse whisper that came from all around him, seeping from the shadows of the *Delirium Trigger*'s hold.

He stepped out from behind the metal pillars and into the cavernous central space. His pistols and cutlass were in his belt, but his hands hung by his side, palm up and empty.

'I'm here,' he said.

She stood there in the sick glow of the Azryx device, half in darkness and half in light. She was as he'd expected her, dressed in close-fitting black. A corpse-white head floated like an apparition above her shoulders, her hair hacked into clumps. Blood red lipstick was smeared across chin and cheek. She'd lost one of her contact lenses, and now her eyes were mismatched, one pupil black and huge and the other . . .

The other had changed. Once that eye had been green. Once he'd known every fleck and flaw of it. But even in the uneasy luminescence cast by the swirling gases, he could see the colour had changed. It was bright yellow, an eagle's eye. The eye of an Imperator.

Her sheer presence was oppressive. The air was heavy with dread, and his skin crept. The darkness beyond the pillars was full of furtive movements glimpsed from the corner of his eye. The steady drip of water from the ceiling had become sinister. Susurrant murmurings chased around the edges of the room.

Here was the dark goddess she'd always pretended to be. Here was the legendary terror of the skies, Trinica Dracken, the pirate queen.

But it wasn't his Trinica.

~ *You've come to save her* ~ breathed the voice. He heard a slow, croaking chuckle, the dry wheeze of something ancient and rotten. The mockery in the daemon's tone slid off him. Usually, being near Trinica disarmed him, made him awkward and uncertain. Not now. He didn't see the woman he loved, but the creature that held her, and he was filled with cold purpose, his will like the tempered edge of a blade.

He heard Crake and Kyne move up warily alongside. Balomon Crund wasn't with them; he'd scurried off to the periphery of the hold, afraid of his mistress's wrath. Crake pressed a thin metal collar into his hand. 'Remember the plan, Cap'n,' he murmured. 'We can do this.'

Yes, the plan. Crake and Kyne would subdue her long enough for Frey to snap the collar round her throat. The collar would suppress the daemon and keep Trinica quiescent until they could get her to a sanctum and drive it out. *If* it worked. The last Imperator they'd tried that trick on had died in agony. Kyne had assured him they had a better chance this time: now they knew the Imperators' frequency, he'd been able to tune the collar accurately. But the Century Knight wouldn't lie, either. If it wasn't suppressed correctly or destroyed quickly, the daemon in Trinica would kill her before they could get it out.

It was a gamble, and the stakes had never been higher. But Frey was a man accustomed to long odds.

Trinica lowered her head, her face falling into shadow, and a moment later the fear hit. Frey felt the weight of it push down on him. Freezing fingers clutched at his heart and panic coiled in his belly. He heard Crund scream from somewhere in the darkness at the edge of the hold. Crake's amulet was useless; nothing could withstand the awful, crushing, maddening horror of the Imperators. His breath became short, and he took a step back in panic. He wanted to run, as far and fast as he could.

Then he felt a warm hand on his back, preventing him from moving any further. He looked across and saw Crake there, his friend. The daemonist's eyes were calm.

'You can beat it,' Crake said. 'It's only fear.'

Frey took strength from Crake's composure. If Crake could master it, he could too. The amulet *was* working; he could feel it now. The chill in his heart was the amulet, sucking at him. He took in a breath, blew it out through pursed lips, and felt himself steady. Crake nodded at him, and gave him a reassuring pat on the back.

'There you go,' he said.

Frey raised his head, and looked the daemon in the eye. 'That the best you've got?' he asked.

Kyne held up a metal sphere and pressed the stud with his thumb. A piercing shriek cut through the hold, and Trinica shrieked with it. She stumbled back against the Azryx machine, clutching at her head, pawing at the air. The sight of her in such pain would have been more than Frey could bear in other times, but it didn't move him now. It was a necessary cruelty. Whatever it took to get that creature out of her.

Kyne and Crake moved past him, splitting up to take position either side of Trinica. Each had a cylinder in one hand, with a pinecone arrangement of small rods at the tip, linked by a cable to the cumbersome backpacks they wore. Frey had forgotten what they were called, but he remembered how they'd worked on the Iron Jackal. They could cage a daemon between them, but care was needed. If the operators didn't stand exactly opposite each other, the daemon could slip out.

Kyne was still holding up the screamer with his free hand. Trinica thrashed and writhed and threw herself about; she slipped to the floor and scrambled back up again, a wild creature tortured. In the strange light it was like some hellish dance. As Kyne and Crake manoeuvred to get an angle on her, Frey advanced steadily, the collar open in his hand. He caught a glimpse of Crund's frightened face by one of the girder pillars, before the bosun looked away. Crund couldn't stand to watch his mistress's suffering, but Frey didn't have the luxury of mercy. He pushed his feelings down and shut them away tight. He'd do what he had to.

Kyne thrust out his arm, pointed the cylinder at Trinica and pressed the stud on it. She shrieked with new vigour, stumbling away from him as if repelled. But Crake was waiting on the other side with a cylinder of his own. Suddenly she was trapped, paralysed, strait-jacketed by invisible frequencies.

Kyne tossed the screamer aside and took hold of the cylinder with both hands, struggling against Trinica's efforts to escape. 'Now, Frey!' he cried.

Frey stepped towards her, the jaws of the collar ready to snap shut on her neck. Her mismatched eyes were fixed on it. Her face, the face he'd loved for so long, was contorted in fear. For a moment, the look she wore shook his resolve. What if he killed her? What if this collar was a death sentence as sure as a bullet to the head, and she knew it?

Well, what if it was? Better than this half-life, her body in thrall to a daemon. He knew what she'd have him do, and he loved her enough to do it. No matter what it cost him.

'Now!' Kyne said again.

He reached forward to snap the collar round her neck.

The Mane shell that exploded against the *Delirium Trigger*'s flank was a big one, and it scored a direct hit. Even with all her armour, she shuddered violently and listed hard in the air. Everyone in her hold staggered with the impact. Crake threw out an arm for balance; the cylinders went out of alignment; the cage was broken. Frey saw the danger and lunged, but Trinica pulled her head back and the collar clicked shut on nothing.

She darted towards Kyne. Her hand lashed out, and came away trailing a thin chain: Kyne's amulet, torn from his neck. Now unprotected, the Century Knight gave a yell of terror, distorted through the mouthpiece of his mask. He flailed backwards, tripped to the floor and went scrambling away on his hands and knees.

Crake grabbed for her, clumsily trying to pin her arms. She slipped from his grip and smashed him across the face with a backhand fist. The daemonist's eyes went dull, and he collapsed to the ground, out cold.

Trinica's head snapped around and she fixed Frey with a freezing gaze. He withered before her, and backed away slowly, the collar held uselessly in one hand. There was no way he'd get it on her now.

She bared her teeth. Her breath hissed through them. She'd been hurt, and she wasn't playing around any more. There was deadly intent in her eyes.

~ Darian ~

Not knowing what else to do, Frey pulled a pistol from his belt and held it out shakily. She looked at it with a puzzled frown, and then cocked her head to one side, as if to say: *Really?* Fast as a snake, she knocked it from his hand and it went skidding away across the floor, into the shadows.

Frey stumbled back a step, but she was on him in an instant. He felt himself lifted with inhuman strength, pulled up by the lapels of his coat. Then he was flung bodily through the air, twisting, helpless. He hit a stack of crates, and pain blasted his senses. The impact knocked the breath from his lungs. He was battered from above as more crates came down on top on him. The edge of one of them struck him on his crown, sending him reeling close to unconsciousness. He came back to himself, half-buried in boxes, his head swimming and his vision blurred, his body ablaze with agony.

Somewhere out there was a threat. He blinked and tried to clear his mind, searching the gloomy hold. There: a blurred figure, walking slowly towards him. Trinica. The daemon. Trinica.

Get up. Get up, or you're gonna die. Get up, or you'll fail her.

He fought to rise. The crates on his back shifted and toppled, but the effort was too much. He slumped back to the ground.

Trinica approached without hurry. He could hear the soft rasp of her breath, the tap of her boots on the metal floor, the drip of water from above. Behind her, the Azryx device rose like some dread edifice to the forbidden goddess of the *Delirium Trigger*, encased in bone. Decay and rot swirled at its heart.

There was no one to help him. Crake was out of it, Kyne and Crund reduced to cringing cowards by her daemonic power. He struggled to get to his feet, not knowing what he'd do once he got there, only that he wouldn't die on his knees. This time there were no crates on his back. He got halfway before her hands seized him again, and he was pulled up, and brought face to face with her.

She dangled something in front of him, too close to focus on. Kyne's amulet.

~ How? ~

Somehow, that single word expressed all its intention. The daemon wanted to know how they'd learned to negate its powers. But more, it wanted to know how this had all come to pass. How had the Awakeners been defeated? Where had it all gone wrong? Why were the Manes here? Who was he, this Captain Frey that had plagued them for so long? It would learn, and it would share that knowledge, and next time there would be no mistake.

~How? ~ she demanded, though her lips never moved.

Frey began to laugh. Hysteria brought it out of him, and though it hurt like bastardy to do it, it felt good all the same. 'You want to know what's going on?' he said. 'Sweetheart, you're asking the wrong feller.' He coughed and gave her a shit-eating grin. 'I just work here.'

She snarled, and with one quick movement she threw him across the room. He tumbled and turned in the air, his senses a whirling blur of vertigo and fright, dominated by the awful anticipation of impact.

He smashed into one of the great girders that held up the roof of the hold. Something gave as he hit; the snap of bone resounded through the hollow room. He crashed to the floor in a pile. He couldn't catch his breath; his mouth flooded, and tasted like tin. He retched and blood splattered the floor. The dizzying agony as his stomach clenched made his head go light and his vision sparkle.

He managed to inhale. Razors scored his back. Something was broken inside. Couple of ribs, maybe worse.

Shit, shit, shit.

Each new movement brought new pain. He wanted to lie still and surrender himself to whatever was to come. Instead he gritted bloody teeth and forced his trembling limbs into action. It seemed like he'd spent his whole life getting back to his feet, and he wasn't stopping now. Even when he didn't have anything else, he had defiance.

That was the thing about underdogs. They never knew when they were beaten.

He'd made it to his hands and knees by the time she reached him. He raised his head and looked at her, like a battered dog before its mistress, waiting for another blow.

Come on, Trinica, he thought. *I know you're in there. Fight it. Help me. Fight it.*

She raised her foot and brought her heel down hard on his left hand. He tried to scream as bone splintered, but all he could manage was a silent wheeze. He snatched his hand back and clutched it to his chest. It had become a clumsy mitten of meat encasing a jumble of broken crockery, burning like it was on fire.

Unable to hold himself up any more, he lost his balance and fell onto his side. The jolt brought tears to his eyes. The pain was more than he'd thought it possible to suffer. He lay there curled up, wishing for the dark of unconsciousness, but there was no respite. He coughed again, and more blood came up.

I'm dying. Oh shit, I'm dying.

He was hauled up by his lapels once more, and held up before her. He wasn't sure he had the strength to stand on his own, but he shuffled his feet, dragged his ankles, got his boots under him. His head lolled on his neck, and his breath came in rasps; the effort to draw in air was immense. He choked on the blood filling his mouth. Punctured lung? Ruptured spleen? Did it matter any more?

The daemon bared its teeth. ~ *How?* ~

Trinica's face swam before him. No, not Trinica. The ghost of her, the nemesis he'd fashioned to torment him. Maybe it was always heading to this, ever since that day he left her standing pregnant in front of the wedding party, and never showed up. Everything since had sprung from that single act of selfishness. Earl Hengar's death, Retribution Falls, the Mane attack on Sakkan, the destruction of the Azryx city in Samarla, the civil war; all mere sideshows to the main attraction: his elaborate and extended self-punishment for that one moment of youthful idiocy. For the death of his unborn child and what he'd done to the woman who'd carried it.

He'd fought so hard to win her back. He'd dreamed of the chance to atone. But in the end it had been a fool's chase. There would be no forgiveness for him. There was only the vengeance he deserved, and it was fitting that it should be delivered at her hands.

Finish it, then, he thought, and he waited for the end.

But there was no new blow, and he wasn't thrown again. Instead he felt a creeping sensation along his scalp, slipping through the bone until it was inside his skull, dirty little fingers grubbing at his brain. Those mismatched eyes bored into his. Horror took him, and he tried to pull away; but she clamped his jaw roughly in one hand, and he couldn't.

Pictures were forming in his head. Memories, uncovering themselves against his will, scenes from the buried past brought out into the light.

Not that, he begged her silently. *Not that.*

His thoughts, his desires, his innermost feelings. All his regret and shame, all his triumph and glory. Every secret he'd guarded in a lifetime of secrecy. The daemon was peeling him back in layers, digging into him, dragging him out in pieces to be scrutinised and cast aside. It was reading his mind.

He couldn't bear it. He couldn't bear to be seen without illusion, to have his life autopsied before him. The physical pain he'd suffered was nothing compared to this.

He saw childish rebellions at the orphanage. He saw the day he'd first brought Slag on board the *Ketty Jay*, a mewling kitten, there for luck and for dealing with all those damned rats. He saw himself arguing with Trinica about the wedding and the baby, a young man who didn't even understand why he was angry. He saw himself charming women and then leaving them, saw himself cutting deals with low-lifes and ripping off the weak. He saw moments of tender camaraderie with his crew.

His life was laid out in his mind, exposed to an alien regard, and it was terrible. In that merciless light, he was no longer special. Everything precious was cheapened and made tawdry. Every failing, stripped of excuses or equivocation, showed up stark and shameful. Viewed coldly, his history seemed wretched, the tale of a cheat and a philanderer, a narcissist and a liar. A man of small importance, always trying to be something greater than he was, doomed to defeat and doomed never to realise it.

No, he thought. *No, I was worth something. I was! I lived!*

A picture came to his mind then. A picture of himself, a ferrotype on a handbill, *WANTED* printed in large letters above him. He was young and smiling in it. They'd distributed that handbill all over Vardia after the death of Earl Hengar, back when Duke Grephen and Gallian Thade were trying to frame him, back when the Awakeners were first trying their hand at insurrection.

He'd been enraged when he first saw it, because that portrait they'd taken was only a part of a larger ferrotype, one he hadn't wished to be reminded of at the time. But now he unfolded it in his memory, and found himself standing in a meadow with mountains behind him, and Trinica there, clinging to his arm and laughing. Laughing at the camera they'd set up on a tripod, laughing with unforced delight, laughing just to laugh. Laughing because she was a young woman in the throes of first love, brimming with a pure, naïve, dreamer's passion, and she knew nothing of the troubles of the world.

He held on to that picture, forced his thoughts upon it. The daemon was trying to tug him away, to move on to other things, but he wouldn't let it go. He clutched it tight in his mind, and the picture opened out again until it was no longer a picture but a scene.

Now he stood in the meadow with her, the sun warm on his back and the hiss of the long grass in his ears and clean mountain air in his lungs. He felt as he'd felt then, when he'd lived in a time free of responsibility and commitment, when he was just a cargo pilot who'd fallen for the boss's daughter. A time when he'd been filled with the heady joy of love without precedent, and he'd felt like an explorer on an uncharted frontier.

In that moment, he'd loved her completely. It filled his mind, crowding out everything else. This place, this time. He never wanted to leave it. He never *should* have left it. And while he held on to it, nothing else could get in; not the past or the future, and not the cruel eye of the daemon. Nothing could sully this memory. It was untouchable. It was perfect.

And somewhere in the bittersweet bliss of reverie, he became aware that the daemon was no longer pawing at his consciousness. Trinica no longer gripped his jaw, and her face had changed. Instead of the hateful creature that inhabited her body he saw *her* staring out at him. Those odd-coloured eyes shimmered with sorrow; her stained and smeared lips trembled.

He wanted her to look at him for ever, but she had only seconds. She'd mastered the daemon briefly, but it wouldn't stay down for long. With her terrified gaze, she implored him.

Ignoring the pain that wracked him, he laid his left forearm on her shoulder to steady himself, his shattered hand dangling uselessly at the end. He leaned in close, so that his bloodied lips brushed her ear, and he could feel the flutter of the pulse at her throat.

'I love you,' he said. And he drove the point of his cutlass into her with all the strength in his body.

A soft whimper escaped her as the blade passed through her and thrust out of her back. Her eyes, still fixed on his, tautened with the agony of it. She took in half a breath, and then her eyes rolled up, her head tipped back and her legs gave way.

He caught her with his left arm, clutched her to him and kept her there as she jerked and shuddered. The air warped and bent, distorting their surroundings like a fairground mirror; aethereal screeches filled the hold; a hurricane raged around them. He held on to her with one arm as if she was the only thing that would stop him from being blown away. With his other, he gripped tight the hilt of the cutlass.

He'd slain her once before with this blade, back in the Azryx city, when the Iron Jackal had taken on her form as a ploy to delay him. The daemon in his cutlass had destroyed the daemon then, just as it fought the daemon inside her now. But that had been a deception; this time it was real. To save her, he'd killed her.

He'd killed her.

The wind died and the screams died with them, and still he held Trinica. He held her till the shivers stopped and the trembling ceased and she hung there in the circle of his arm, her cheek against his shoulder, her eyes closed. He held her till the silence returned.

It was that silence, in the end, that broke him. The absence. He took in a breath, not caring how his broken ribs stabbed at him, and he let out a raw cry of rage and anguish that echoed from the cold walls of the hold. He pulled the blade from his lover's body and threw it aside, and with Trinica still held against him he drew his second pistol and fired it over her shoulder at the Azryx device: once, twice, three times. The transparent casing that kept the gas inside cracked in two places, and a chunk of the bonelike exterior was blown away, revealing strange machinery which sparked with dangerous energy. He fired till his drum was empty, and kept firing after that, and would have gone on if a gloved hand hadn't closed around the revolver and taken it from his hand. He turned his head and glared into the impassive mask of Morben Kyne.

'It's over,' said Kyne.

Frey pulled Trinica hard against him, encircling her with both arms now, and sobbed helplessly, like a child. He felt her blood seeping through his shirt; or maybe it was his. He didn't know. He didn't know where his wounds ended and hers began any more. He just knew that she was gone, and that knowledge was everything.

The light in the hold dimmed and changed. The gas in the Azryx device had begun to change colour, moving from shades of putrescence and bile to a deep arterial red. Gangrenous black swirls appeared at its heart, and little worms of lightning crawled around the cracks in the casing, questing fingers seeking a way out. One of the cracks shot out a new branch, doubling in length under the stress from inside. A low pulsing sound was coming from the device, threatening in tone, getting louder.

'We have to go,' Kyne told him, his voice a flat buzz.

But Frey didn't want to go anywhere. He didn't care about the device, or the war, or the dull boom of artillery from beyond the *Delirium Trigger*'s hull. He'd been emptied out. All he wanted was to bring Trinica back, as if by force of will he could undo what had been done.

But he'd learned enough of the world to know better. There were no second chances, just illusions to grasp for. Phantoms, in the end.

He heard a strangled cry, and there was Balomon Crund, his swart face aghast. Behind him was Crake, gazing at his captain with sorrow in his eyes. Frey couldn't stand it; he had to look away. Let them leave him here with her. Let him stay in this place, and be done with it.

There was a banging on the door they'd come through. Crake seemed grateful for the distraction, and he hurried over. 'Crund. The code for the keypad,' he said. When the bosun didn't reply, Crake snapped at him. 'Crund!'

Crund grunted a few numbers at Crake, and he punched them in. The door opened this time, and Samandra came through.

' 'Bout time!' she said. 'What's the idea, locking me out there? I had to shoot ten of the bastards before they got the idea and buggered off . . .' She tailed away as she saw the look on Crake's face, and then noticed Frey and Trinica, standing in the centre of the hold. It might have been the end of a slow dance, the last lovers clinging to each other, reluctant to quit the floor. But the music was over now.

The pulse from the Azryx device was getting louder. Crake ducked in fright as an arc of lightning crackled and jumped across the hold to feel its way up one of the pillars. The air stank of burnt ozone, and the hair on the backs of Frey's hands stood up on end.

Samandra eyed the machine uncertainly. 'Er, fellers? Remember what happened when we took out that generator back in the Azryx city? This might not be a hundredth the size, but damned if I want to be near it when it goes.'

Crake walked over to Frey. He reached down and picked up the cutlass. 'Frey,' he said.

'Leave me,' Frey whispered.

'I can't do that, Cap'n.'

'I said *leave me!*' he shouted.

And then Trinica coughed, and blood ran from her lips down the side of his neck.

The two men exchanged a look of pure disbelief. Crund shouted: 'She's alive!'

Frey felt himself ignite. 'She's still alive,' he said. 'She's still *alive!*'

'Well, it was a daemon blade you stabbed her with,' said Crake. 'I mean, it always did know what you wanted. Maybe it missed the vital organs on purp—'

'Stop explainin', honey,' Samandra told him gently. 'Ain't really the time.'

'She's alive!' cried Frey again. He hadn't heard a word of what Crake had just said. He was dazed by the sheer wonderful, impossible joy of it.

'Well, if you want her to stay that way we best get out of here and get her to a doc,' said Samandra. 'Give her here, Frey, you look like you can barely walk.'

'I'll carry her!' said Crund fiercely. When Frey hesitated, the bosun pulled her from his arms. Frey staggered, and Crake slung his arm round his friend to stop him from falling. The pain of his bruises and his shifting ribs stole the breath from him, but he forced it down, stayed on his feet, spat out the blood that kept coming up into his mouth. Balomon picked up Trinica with ease, holding her like a baby in his brawny arms.

Another bolt of lightning snapped across the hold, and a pile of crates exploded. 'Let's get goin'!' Samandra cried. Together, they hurried towards the exit as fast as they were able, while behind them the Azryx device began to tear itself apart.

She's alive, Frey thought. *She's alive. She's alive.*

But for how much longer?

Forty-Five

Bleeding Out – A Farewell in Her Eyes –
'What'd I Miss?' – Getting Sentimental – A Debt is Paid

The *Delirium Trigger* shook and groaned as they hurried through the gloomy corridors up towards the light, carrying their wounded. An explosion boomed through the hull and she keeled to port, sending them careering into a wall. Running footsteps sounded from around corners, the rough shouts of soldiers and pirates. Occasional gunshots could be heard.

They stopped to bind Trinica's wounds once they were a safe distance from the hold. It was a delay they could hardly afford, but Crake didn't complain. He saw the desperation in Frey, the haggard hope on his face. He didn't think as much of Trinica as the Cap'n did, but he knew love. If Trinica bled out before they got her to a doctor, no victory would make up for it. The Cap'n had got them here; they all owed him.

It was a quick job, and they were almost done when a trio of pirates came hurrying round the corner. Samandra and Kyne had their weapons up in an instant. The pirates were about to raise their own guns when Balomon Crund barked at them.

'Hold there!'

Their eyes fell on him, and Trinica lying next to him.

'Cap'n's down,' he snarled. 'The *Trigger*'s goin' with her. Abandon ship! Get to the shuttles! Abandon ship, you jackals!'

They didn't need another prompt. The pirates backed away warily, turned tail and ran. Crund picked Trinica up and they set off again.

Crake had his arm round Frey, and the Cap'n's broken hand flopped over his shoulder. His breath was laboured and short. He did his best not to make a sound, but the occasional suppressed grunt and gasp told of the pain he was in. Blood kept coming up in his mouth, and however much he spat out there was always more.

Bleeding inside, thought Crake, and a cold fear sank into him. *Hold on, Cap'n. You can make it.*

But his weight seemed to increase as Crake dragged him along, and Crake knew it was because Frey was weakening, supporting himself less and less with his legs.

You can make it.

They'd almost reached the deck when the explosions from outside multiplied sharply. The sound of detonations became constant, now far, now near, a thundering percussion rolling around in the distance, which occasionally sprang loud upon them and rattled their teeth.

'Do believe that's the anti-aircraft cannons,' Samandra muttered. 'Could've done with them holding off a mite longer.'

So the Azryx device had failed. How much longer before that failure became catastrophic, and it obliterated them? Crake didn't dare think. Any moment could be their last, every passing second a gamble against mounting odds, and oblivion waited at the end. To even consider it might crack him.

There was still chaos on deck, but the combat had ceased. The *Delirium Trigger*'s crew – what was left of them – had given up the fight and were making their escape. The sky was full of fire and smoke. Anti-aircraft shells burst all around them in deafening, shattering blooms. Tracer fire chattered up into the night. Great looming frigates sank through the air, their guts ablaze, the drone of their engines descending with them. The Coalition soldiers had battened down, pressed against the gunwales, sheltering themselves from the barrage.

Celerity Blane raced over to them as they emerged through the doorway. She gave Samandra a harried smile and then looked at Crake. 'All here? Good,' she said in a jaunty aristocratic accent. 'Now how about we open up that aircraft and get out of here, eh? Before we all die, I mean.'

'Reckon someone's already ahead of you,' said Samandra, looking past her. And Crake saw that the cargo ramp of the *Ketty Jay* was indeed opening up, which was strange, because there was nobody standing near the keypad on the landing strut, and nobody but the crew knew the access code. Frey had made sure of it, in case anyone got any ideas about leaving without them.

So someone was opening it from the *inside*?

The ramp touched down. Some of the soldiers had already seen it and were hurrying that way, but they came skidding to a halt and then backed off, their guns ready. Stumbling out of the aircraft was a small, blackened figure, a charred scarecrow that limped onto the deck.

Crake stared, unable to believe his eyes.

'No!' Frey cried, his voice bubbling with blood. He spat and hauled in a breath. 'Nobody shoot!' he yelled with as much volume as he could manage.

'Put them guns down!' Samandra shouted, with considerably more.

The soldiers didn't put their guns down, but they didn't fire either. They fell back, moving aside for the stranger. Some of them scrambled to get away. Crake could feel the fear emanating from her even at this distance. Not like the focused power of the Imperators, just the instinctive terror caused by the presence of a daemon.

Onward she came, looking to her left and right, staring curiously at the people around her as if she wasn't quite sure what they were all doing there. As she advanced, pieces fell from her, great burned scabs peeling away from her face and limbs, leaving her moist and raw beneath. She walked hunched over, like a wounded animal, and as more of her flaked away Crake saw more of what lay beneath.

A gaunt body in ragged overalls. Sallow skin, stretched taut like parchment over her bones. Teeth long and pointed. Fingernails like talons. Eyes a mix of yellow and red. A ghoul of the skies. A Mane.

Jez, and yet not Jez. Not any more.

Then the soldiers cried out and cringed down, and even Samandra stepped back and swore under her breath. As the wreck of a nearby Awakener frigate dipped out of sight, a great black prow broke through the smoke with a bellow of engines. A colossal mass of dirty metal and spikes and rivets, ploughing towards them through a hole in the convoy, ignoring the explosions all around it. Thick chains trailed in its wake like great tendrils, dangling behind and beneath it. The sight of it oppressed them, robbed their courage, nailed them to the spot.

A Mane Dreadnought. And it was coming right for them.

At the sight of it, Jez began staggering forward faster, heading towards the aft end of the *Delirium Trigger*'s deck. She'd found strength from somewhere; her limp hampered her less. She let out a screech as she went, something inhuman, which cut through the air and froze Crake's blood.

She's turned. She's really turned at last.

As if she'd heard his thoughts, she stumbled to a halt, and turned her head and stared right at him. She looked from him to the Cap'n and back again. And horrible though it was, her face softened a little, and for a moment Crake saw in her the old Jez he'd known. His friend and companion. The woman he'd shared his darkest secret with.

He raised an arm in farewell. She just gazed at him, her head tilted slightly to the side. But though she gave him no more sign than that, he thought he read a farewell in her eyes all the same.

Then she turned and sprinted across the deck. The soldiers cowered as the dreadnought swooped across the *Delirium Trigger*, its keel roaring by mere metres overhead. A foul-smelling wind whipped around them, stinking of oil and decay. Crake saw a nightmarish blur of faces gathered at the gunwale, and heard the howling and shrieking of the Manes as they pawed the air with sharp-fingered hands. Then the chains that dragged behind the dreadnought smashed into the deck, lashing across the *Delirium Trigger*'s back like whips, ploughing her with furrows. Jez sprang, and for a moment was lost within the forest of whirling chains; then the dreadnought was past, flying away into the sky, and Jez was clinging on to one of them. Crake watched in awe as she climbed, scampering up the links towards the Manes above, who reached down with long scrawny arms to help her on board.

She was lost to sight behind another frigate, and the dreadnought carried her away.

'Can someone explain what exactly happened just then?' asked Celerity, her eyes wide.

'She's gone to be with her people,' said Crake, sadly.

The explosion that tore through the *Delirium Trigger* knocked them all off their feet. Crake fell beneath Frey; the Cap'n screamed with the pain of the impact. Quickly Crake pulled him up, no time for sympathy, dragging him towards the *Ketty Jay*. The *Delirium Trigger* was beginning to list. A hit in the aerium tanks from the anti-aircraft guns. She wouldn't be in the air much longer. If the Azryx device didn't take her out, her impact with the ground would.

The soldiers were running for the *Ketty Jay* with a kind of controlled panic. Samandra ran ahead of them into the craft, while Kyne took Frey's other arm and helped to haul him across the deck. The Cap'n was dazed with pain, eyes swimming in and out of focus. Behind them came Crund, carrying his mistress.

Another blast shook the deck as they were hurrying up the cargo ramp. Crake stumbled into a hydraulic strut, but he kept his feet this time. On into the hold they went, where the soldiers were securing themselves to anything they could grab. He saw Grissom in there, Bess too, but he didn't have time to stop.

'Shut that ramp!' he called over his shoulder at Celerity, who was the last one inside. The *Ketty Jay* was tilting with the *Delirium Trigger*, locked to the deck by its magnetic skids. Anything not tied down had started to slide across the hold.

They found Samandra in the cockpit, in the pilot's seat, frantically hitting buttons. 'What's the damn ignition code?' she cried.

Frey pushed Crake and Kyne off him, stumbled to the pilot's seat and hauled her out of it. 'Nobody flies the *Ketty Jay* but me,' he snarled through bloody lips. Then he lowered himself into the seat, punched in the code and hit the controls to flood the aerium tanks. The *Ketty Jay* began lifting up on her struts, metal groaning and creaking. Frey disengaged the magnetic skids, and she floated free.

'Hang on,' he said, and he hit the thrusters.

Crake wasn't hanging on. He tripped out through the door of the cockpit and sprawled full-length into the corridor. Samandra called after him, but Crake didn't answer. Instead, he got to his feet and clambered up the ladder to the cupola. The Azryx device was going to blow at any moment. He didn't want to be hit by something and never see it coming. He was compelled to look, as if by looking he could somehow avoid it.

At the top, he clambered into the gunner's seat amid the acrid debris of empty rum bottles and the musty smell of Malvery. The violence outside was staggering, the detonations without end. The whole sky was exploding; tracer bullets stitched the air. As they pulled away from the Awakener convoy, he could see Samarlan frigates being ripped apart, their weak armour no match for the city's guns. The *Ketty Jay* was battered, shaken this way and that.

He looked out in terror. How could anything survive this? How could they possibly live through it?

Because of the frigates. Because they're shooting at the big craft. Not at us.

He clung to that thought.

A flash caught his eye. The *Delirium Trigger* was shrinking behind them, diminishing amidst the pandemonium, but as he looked he saw an arc of strange lightning flash across its surface. A jagged streak shot out and hit another frigate nearby, crawling along its surface. Crake flinched as the frigate exploded, tearing itself apart from nose to stern.

Now there was more lightning coming from the *Delirium Trigger*, questing fingers reaching out, crackling over its body and jumping to other craft, catching passing fighters and obliterating them. The Awakeners' flagship began to pull away, its pilot having seen the danger. As its long, ungainly shape began to turn in the air, lightning jumped from the *Delirium Trigger*, striking it once, twice, and then with a sustained burst that crawled and writhed up its flank. Explosions ripped along the craft, unzipping it from stern to bow, and then it broke apart in the centre and went toppling earthward like two blazing halves of a snapped stick.

The Lord High Cryptographer was on that! Crake thought. Then he crushed himself down in his seat as the lightning became more frantic and the dark shape of the *Delirium Trigger* disappeared inside a sparkling, crawling cocoon.

Go faster, Cap'n! Faster!

A blue sphere of rolling lightning swelled out from the *Delirium Trigger*. It expanded fast, sending out arcs in all directions as it went, writhing tentacles of destruction. Anything on its edge was annihilated and then swallowed. Frigates, two dozen or more, disappeared in flame. The entire Awakener convoy was consumed, and then the Samarlan frigates that surrounded it. The ball of energy grew and grew until it filled Crake's sight, reflected in his terrified eyes, and it seemed they could never outpace it, and it would engulf them as it had all the rest.

But then it slowed, and receded, diminishing as the *Ketty Jay* carried him away. Finally, there was only a hole in the grey sky where the Awakener convoy had been. Where the *Delirium Trigger* and the Azryx device and the Lord High Cryptographer had existed a moment before, now there was only air. The Awakener high command were less than dust, destroyed by their own weapon.

Crake let himself breathe out again.

'What'd I miss?' said a voice below him. Samandra was climbing up the ladder, hoping to squeeze herself up into the cupola, eager to see.

'Oh,' said Crake, still staring out at the end of the Awakeners. 'Nothing much.'

'They're retreating!'

Malvery paused in his labours just long enough to glance at the sky. Hard to tell what was what up there, amid all the fire and ruin. But the Sammies were getting shredded, he could tell that much. Smoking shells of aircraft crashed down on the city below. Caught between the Manes and the anti-aircraft guns, they'd suffered atrocious losses. Nothing more than they deserved, in Malvery's opinion.

'The Manes!' said the soldier, seeing that Malvery didn't understand. 'Look! They're pulling back!' He laughed. 'They don't like the taste of our guns any more than the Sammies do!'

'Don't worry about what's up there,' said Malvery. 'We've got work to do down here. Give me a hand, now.'

Between them, they lifting the groaning man from the road and put him on to a makeshift stretcher made of bloodied Awakener cassocks tied between two rifles. Malvery scanned the road for any last signs of movement, but saw none. This was the third casualty they'd rescued from the killing ground in front of the anti-aircraft emplacement. The rest were beyond saving.

His eyes roamed over the scattered dead, their bodies chewed up in the jaws of the gatling gun. Beyond lay the wrecked frigate and the smouldering trench it had cut in its wake. Further on, he could see the Archduke's palace high on the crag, smashed aircraft raining down like meteors around it, fiery explosions blooming in distant streets. Thesk, his city, made apocalyptic. He'd never believed it possible, never thought he'd see the day. Such loss, such *waste*.

And yet, as he hauled up the stretcher and they carried their burden away, he felt pride along with his sorrow. Pride for the Cap'n, for Silo, for himself and all the crew of the *Ketty Jay*. And pride for Ashua, who'd stood with them till the end, and scared him silly doing it. If she'd been killed, he'd never have forgiven himself.

But she hadn't. And the Awakeners were wiped out, and the

Sammies were defeated. Now the Manes had turned tail, heading back through the vortex to their icy cities beyond the Wrack. Neither Sammies nor Manes had been able to land troops. Only the Awakeners had men in the city, and they'd put up no further resistance.

The battle was won. Whatever the cost, the battle was won. A fierce heat grew in his breast at the thought, a furnace glow from within.

They'd won. Vardia had won.

The anti-aircraft gun was still booming as they carried the wounded man through the gate and laid him down in the courtyard with the others. The sound of it was deafening, but against the roar of war it was only one more noise among many. As the gate shut behind them, Malvery saw Silo up on the wall, bellowing orders, organising the defence of the perimeter. He was taking no chances. No one was recapturing that gun after the price they'd paid to get it.

'Anything I can do?' Ashua asked as she limped over, an Awakener rifle as her crutch. She was pale, but lively enough, considering. The bullet had gone right through her thigh. There wasn't much Malvery could do but disinfect it and bind it up. With the right drugs, she'd be fine.

'Just keep your weight off that leg,' said Malvery.

'Aye aye, Doc.'

He turned his attention to the wounded man and began cutting away the uniform with a blade so he could assess the damage. Eventually, when Ashua showed no sign of moving, he harrumphed.

'You were brave out there,' he said awkwardly.

'You too,' she replied.

He hummed and hawed as he looked in his bag for a new spool of catgut to make stitches. 'I oughta apologise,' he said. 'The way I treated you.'

'S'okay,' said Ashua. 'Bloody stupid thing I did. Still . . .' She looked up at the sky. 'At least I'm the one responsible for the annihilation of the Sammies' entire air force, eh? In fact, if they hadn't turned up, the Awakeners would probably have overrun this city by now.' She took on a thoughtful tone. 'You might even say I'm . . . well, a hero.'

'Don't push it, girl,' Malvery growled. He raised an eyebrow and glared at her. 'However it turned out, you were still—' Then he saw the expression on her face, and realised she was joking. He shook his head and gave her an exasperated smile. 'What am I gonna do with you, eh?'

Ashua laid a hand on his shoulder. 'You'll look out for me, Doc. And I'll do the same for you.'

Malvery felt himself well up at that, and blinked back tears. *Foolish old man*, he thought. *Getting sentimental.*

'Doc!' yelled Silo, as he came hurrying down from the wall to the courtyard. 'It's the Cap'n!'

'He's alright?' Ashua asked.

'He comin' in on our location! Tell the gunner not to fire on him!'

'I'm on it,' said Ashua, and limped off with as much speed as she could manage.

Silo came to a halt next to Malvery, who was still working on the wounded man, assisted by the soldier who'd helped carry him. 'What about Pinn and Harkins?' Malvery asked.

'They good. Pulled out when the anti-aircraft guns kicked up. Been drivin' me crazy listenin' to 'em ever since I put the cuff back in. Had some competition goin' on, how many Sammies they could shoot down.'

'Who won?'

'Both of 'em, near as I can tell.' He spotted the *Ketty Jay* swooping down through the flak, and waved at some nearby soldier. 'Clear a space there! Cap'n's back, damn it! Cap'n's comin' back!'

The *Ketty Jay*'s cargo ramp touched the floor of the courtyard, and the men and women in the hold poured out. Soldiers hugged each other and thumped their comrades' backs. Grissom and Celerity Blane strode out with their heads held high. Bess larked with the other golems, her childish enthusiasm infecting them.

But then a voice rose over the others. 'Make way! Make way, there!' It was Balomon Crund, with Trinica Dracken in his arms. And behind him came Frey, supported by Crake and Kyne, with Samandra Bree at their heels. The crowd parted for them, and they came out into the courtyard, emerging into the grey daylight surrounded by the tinny stink of vented aerium gas.

'Malvery!' Crake shouted. 'Doc!'

Frey could barely see through the agony. His vision had become blurred and his legs had no strength in them. It was hard to tell one pain from another. His torso was an aching mass. He still couldn't draw breath properly. But he had a purpose, a focus, and that kept him moving.

Malvery got up from the ground, where he'd been tending to casualties, and came hurrying over. The doctor's moustached face loomed in Frey's vision.

'Frey,' he said in horror. 'What in buggery happened to you?'

'Forget about me,' he said, and gritted his teeth as something shifted and stabbed inside him. 'Her! Save her!'

Malvery looked at Trinica. 'Put her on the floor,' he told Crund, and then he crouched next to her and looked beneath the crude dressing they'd wrapped around her wound. 'What happened to her?'

'Cap'n put a cutlass through her,' said Crake.

'You *what?*' Malvery said. He was feeling her pulse. 'Second thought, I don't even wanna know.' He put the dressing back. 'Frey, this is too bad. I can't—'

'I don't wanna hear it, Doc. Make it happen.'

'She needs blood. Now.'

'Give her mine!'

'You ain't got enough to give.'

'Do what I say, damn it!' Frey cried, then was seized by a coughing fit and spat blood on the ground.

'Cap'n!' Malvery barked, and the volume of his voice shocked Frey into silence. 'If you ain't compatible, you'll kill her. Likely you'll kill yourself tryin' anyway. And even if you are compatible, I don't rate my chances. Let me save *you!* Or if not you, there's plenty people round here I *can* save. I'm a doctor, alright? I know what I'm doing!'

'Take *my* blood!' said Crund.

'No!' said Frey. 'What if you're not compatible?'

'What if *you're* not?' Malvery said.

'I *am!*' Frey snarled. 'We were tested . . . After we knew about the baby . . . Doctor took my blood for . . .'

'What baby?' Malvery said, but Frey ignored him. There wasn't time to argue! Didn't he see that?

'We're *compatible*,' he said through gritted teeth. 'We've always been . . . compatible.'

'Frey, I can't. It'll kill you. I can't do that!'

Frey found a burst of strength, fuelled by frustration, and he seized

Malvery by the front of his jumper and pulled him close. 'Doc,' he said. 'If you ever . . . If you were ever a friend to me . . . You gotta do this now. This is everything, you hear? This is *everything*.'

Malvery's face was a picture of doubt. This went against everything he believed, as a doctor and as a person. Frey knew what Malvery thought of his obsession. Shit, Malvery didn't even *like* Trinica very much. But Frey had to do this, and he couldn't do it without Malvery's help.

He owed Trinica a life. And he aimed to give her one.

'It won't save her,' Malvery said, but there was defeat in his voice and Frey knew he'd won.

'Gotta try,' said Frey. 'Gotta try.'

Malvery wrestled with his conscience a moment more, but in the end he lowered his head, and his brow clouded. 'Get her inside,' he said. 'I'll do what I can.'

The others knew better than to try to stop him, and for that Frey was deeply grateful. He couldn't fight any more battles. He let them take him into a room off the courtyard, where they put him on a table, and they laid Trinica out next to him. She was still, and looked so small; the rise and fall of her breast was hardly perceptible. But he felt no terror of her now. The daemon inside her had been destroyed, beaten by the daemon in his blade. Even if she died now, she died herself, unconquered.

He was dimly aware of Malvery returning with supplies he'd taken from the *Ketty Jay*. He saw the doctor laying out jars and tubes, heard him snapping instructions at Crake, who was assisting him. They assembled the apparatus for the transfusion, blurred ghosts fussing in the background.

He stared up at the ceiling. Wetness trickled down his cheek. A tear, leaking from the corner of his eye. He didn't want to leave this life. He loved it too much. It had treated him appallingly at times, and he'd abused it in return, but at that moment it seemed the most wonderful and precious of things. He couldn't stand the loss of it.

But he'd lived. He'd made a difference. And now he could say with honesty that he'd done his damnedest.

There was that. At least there was that.

He felt the bite of a needle at his inner elbow. He turned his head, and saw a transparent rubber tube stretching from him to a glass jar

---

that lay between him and Trinica on the table. The jar was connected to a rubber bulb which Malvery was squeezing rapidly. At the other end of the apparatus was a needle in Trinica's arm.

'Make a fist,' said Malvery to Frey. 'Crake, give him something to squeeze. It'll help the blood through.'

Frey had little enough strength in his body, but he crawled his hand across the the table, and took up Trinica's. And he squeezed her cold fingers as hard as he could manage.

'Reckon that'll do,' said Malvery, through a thick throat.

Frey felt very far away from everything now. It was as if he were watching the scene from the end of a long tunnel. His body no longer seemed his own. He observed with detached fascination as the rich, dark blood began to fill the jar, *his* blood. He saw it slip along the tubes, and finally into Trinica, a glistening red thread between him and her.

A great calm washed over him, a sense of rightness. He felt complete. Then his eyes fluttered closed, and he was gone.

Forty-Six

Eulogy – A Better Ending – The Lowdown –
Stars and Crosses – The End of an Era

T he funeral was held on a high hillside on a bright chill morning. A nipping wind blew about the mourners, stirring their coats against them. Long thin clouds raced across the sky. In the distance lay the city of Thesk, slumped and shattered but still undefeated, and the Archduke's palace stood proud at its heart.

It was a lonely spot, and there were only eight at the graveside including Bess. She held a bunch of mountain flowers in one huge hand, with a great sod of earth hanging off them where she'd torn them from the ground. The rest were all crew, except for Samandra Bree, who'd come with Crake. Harkins sniffed quietly and Pinn had his collar up and his shoulders hunched, his grim face barely visible. Silo was impassive as ever. Ashua stood silently with her arms crossed.

Before them all stood Malvery. He'd volunteered for the eulogy. It seemed the least he could do.

'What can you say when a part of your life ain't there any more?' he said, his voice low and heavy. 'Words don't change much. Best you can do is remind yourself why it is you miss 'em.'

He paused for a long time. Bess stirred uncertainly.

'He was a fighter,' Malvery said at last. 'You gotta give him that. Can't ever say he was lucky in love, but he found it in the end, and that's more than most of us can expect. He could be an arsy bastard at times, but mostly he made us laugh, and he always seemed to be there when you needed him.' He gave a deep sigh and lowered his head. 'He was the heart and soul of us. There wouldn't have been a *Ketty Jay* without him.'

He went down on one knee and placed one hand on the grave marker. It was an old plate from the engine room, scratched with a name and some dates.

'We'll never forget him,' said Malvery. 'He was a damn fine cat.'

Afterwards, as they made their way back to the shuttle, Crake said 'Shame the Cap'n couldn't be here. He'd have liked to see Slag off with the rest of us.'

'Would've been nice,' Malvery agreed. 'But he ain't gonna be out of hospital for another month at least and, to be fair, that cat was starting to reek.'

Frey crept warily through the corridors of the hospital, eyes and ears alert. His bare feet were cold on the polished floor, but he moved in silence, and that was what was important. He couldn't go fast, but he could go smart. Nurse Crowsnitch had become predictable, her patrols too regular. This time there'd be no stopping him. Nobody was making *him* take it easy for his own good.

If he was honest, Nurse Crowsnitch sort of had a point. It wasn't exactly easy to breathe with his ribs bandaged tight beneath his gown, and his short excursions tired him out. He blamed it on having to lug around the heavy cast they'd put over his hand, but he was also ready to admit the small possibility that he might need some time to recover from the grievous wounds he'd sustained in the *Delirium Trigger*'s hold.

But Frey was not a man who could easily amuse himself, and recuperation was purgatory to him. There was only so long he could stare at brown and cream walls. Brown and cream: the colours of boredom. It was too much to take. And besides, making trouble was in his nature.

A click of heels, echoing down the corridor. He froze, listening. Crowsnitch! Had she outwitted him?

But the footsteps receded, heading away from him, and he relaxed. *Not this time, lady*, he thought, but he picked up his pace and hurried the rest of the way to his destination.

It was a tiny ward with four beds, all of them occupied. Mailey, the pretty young librarian with the broken leg, was the only one awake. She wiggled her fingers at him as he slipped in and closed the door carefully. He gave her a sheepish smile, tiptoed over to another bed and gingerly lowered himself into a nearby chair.

Trinica was in the bed, lying on her side, her head pillowed and facing him, her eyes closed. He checked that she was still breathing;

he could never settle until he was sure. But yes, there was the slight rise of the blankets around her body, and there was the faint sigh of air over her lips. Her existence was still a miracle to him. He had to reassure himself with each visit that she was really there.

Her face was drawn and wan in sleep, and there were lines where there hadn't been in his memory. She'd lost weight, and she'd never carried much to begin with. There was no make-up on her now. Her hair had been cut short to make the best of the hacked-up mess she'd arrived with. But she was here, and she was beautiful, and she was his.

She stirred, and her left hand moved and found the cast they'd put over his own shattered hand. On her finger was a ring, a simple silver ring he'd given her once, and which she'd once given back to him. Now she wore it again.

Her eyes opened and found his. Even after weeks, the sight of them was still a faint surprise. Gone was the green he knew. Her irises were now yellow as corn. At least one of the changes the daemon had wreaked in her had been permanent.

She smiled at him. 'You again.'

'What do you mean?' he protested. 'I've been here all night.'

'Liar.'

'Ask Mailey!'

'It's true,' Mailey piped up. 'Never left your side.'

Trinica chuckled weakly. 'Quite a conspiracy you two have going.'

Frey reached into a drawer by the bed and brought out a book, its leather cover delicately embossed. 'Ready for the next chapter?'

'Yes, please!' said Mailey, clapping her hands.

Frey and Trinica exchanged a glance, the kind of knowing, indulgent look shared by new lovers, for whom the whole world has become a delightful joke. He opened the book in his lap at the marked page. A mass of Samarlan characters stared back at him. He didn't recognise a single one of them.

'*The Silent Tide*,' he announced. 'Being the adventures of the brave and attractive Captain Frey and the slightly less brave and not quite so attractive Captain Trinica Dracken.'

'Narcissism is such an endearing trait, Darian.'

'Chapter Four,' he said. He tilted his head as he studied the page. 'You know, I think I like romances better when I don't understand them.'

'You're actually holding it upside down.'

'You want to hear this story or not?'

'Oh, yes,' she said. She settled down deeper into her pillow, and her eyes shone as she watched him. 'I think I'm going to like the ending better this time around.'

They held the ceremony in the great hall of the Archduke's palace, in the presence of all the dukes of Vardia. Beneath the vaulted ceilings and the great brass candelabras, under the stony gaze of leaders and thinkers and artists of ages past, the heroes of the civil war were honoured. Generals and aristocrats lined the pews, and the entire House of Chancellors was in attendance. The men were straight-backed in crisp jackets and starched collars; the ladies were resplendent in their finery. Trumpets sounded, bright flags lined the walls, and the Archduke himself handed out medals amid all the pomp a triumphant country could muster.

Really, it was all a bit much for Frey.

He stood at the back, in the gallery, overlooking the main floor. With him were dozens of other people who weren't important or official enough to merit a seat. That included Trinica and, surprisingly, Samandra Bree. 'Century Knights don't get medals,' was all she'd said when he asked.

Another group of soldiers were led on to the dais. The Archduke passed along the line, announcing each man's name and pinning a medal on his chest. The ceremony had been going on for an hour now, and Frey was bored stupid. His clothes were too tight on him, and everything itched. He hated formal wear; he always felt he deserved to be laughed at when he was dressed up. Trinica told him it suited him, but he still wasn't sure if she was making fun or not.

For her part, Trinica wore aristocratic guise as one who'd been born to it. In her long red dress, she was transformed. A silver necklace hung against her pale collarbones and she wore a small jewelled wristlet. Hard to imagine a woman so elegant had ever reaved the skies.

He leaned over to her. 'You reckon this is gonna go on much longer?'

'Days, I expect.'

Frey groaned. He scanned the crowd idly. He spotted Plome down among the Chancellors, clapping away enthusiastically, but it was telling that there was no sign of Amalicia Thade. Those aristocrats who'd sided with the Awakeners would be finding life considerably less easy from here on in.

Well, let her thrive or fail as she would. He didn't bear her any ill will. He probably deserved what she did to him, so he counted them even.

He turned to Samandra. She cleaned up amazingly well for a foul-mouthed tomboy killing machine. In a black dress and long gloves, with her hair clipped back and falling down her back in waves, she was as unrecognisable as Trinica.

'So give me the lowdown,' he said. 'What did I miss in hospital?'

Samandra, who was equally bored, leaned closer and kept her voice low. 'Things have been pretty interesting round here lately,' she said. 'The Awakeners . . . well. The Archduke can't stop people believin' what they like, but he can stop the Awakeners sellin' it to 'em. All their assets, we got. No more shrines allowed, no more hermitages, no more Speakers, even out in the country. Kyne's been headin' up a task force to hunt down any Imperators left. Most of 'em suicided before he could get hold of 'em, but he grabbed one an' neutralised it, then put it out on public show. Let the people know the truth of it, sort of thing. That convinced a lot o' folk.'

'You think they're gone for good?'

She shrugged. 'Can't say. There's always gonna be some underground stuff, but the Awakeners have always been aggressive self-promoters. Now they can't do that. Reckon we'll see how much their ideas are worth when they can't shove 'em down anyone's throat any more.' She picked something off the back of her neck and flicked it away, which didn't seem very ladylike considering her outfit. 'They say the diehards are headin' for the colonies, shippin' out for New Vardia before the Storm Belt gets impassable. Good luck to 'em, I say. Long as they ain't here.'

Frey gave a grunt of agreement. 'What about the Sammies?'

'That's a whole other can o' worms. They invaded us, even if they fudged it. People were sayin' we should invade 'em right back, now their navy's gone. Seemed to forget we don't have much more than a scrap of a navy left ourselves. Politicians came up with some plans: we were gonna use mercs to embargo the Free Trade Zone properly, crack down hard on aerium smuggling, make damn sure those Sammie bastards never got a drop from us again. But then guess who waded in?'

Frey had already heard the rumour. 'Thace.'

'Uh-huh. Reckon they got tired of waitin' for Samarla to get round to invading them and decided to do it first. They got the only fleet in town now, and they know them Sammies are just gonna tool up and do it again if they ain't stamped on hard. Lucky they're on our side.'

'Samarla and Thace are really at war, then?'

'Oh, yeah. Don't know that anyone can take a land as big as Samarla, but I wouldn't be surprised if they took a damn good chunk of it. Still, good news for your mate Silo.'

'How so?'

'You know Thacians. Life, liberty, equality, all o' that. Think they'll stand for slavery in their territories? Might be we get to see the first free Murthian population in five hundred years. Not to mention the Daks, though they way they act I wonder if they *like* bein' slaves.'

'Damn,' said Frey in amazement. 'That's quite a thing.'

'See what you set off?' she said, nudging him. 'Not bad for a bunch of reprobates with a galaxy of personality disorders.'

'Aren't you dating one of those reprobates?'

She snorted. 'Someone has to keep you classy.'

Frey barked a laugh, and somebody shushed him. Then Trinica touched his arm and pointed down at the dais. 'There they are!' she said.

And there they were, taking their places before the Archduke. Malvery, Crake, Harkins and Pinn, and finally Silo. They stood there stiffly, all shiny buttons and dazzling shoes, hair and beards combed and cut – those who had them. Even Frey had to admit, they didn't look half bad.

Archduke Monterick approached Malvery first. 'For extraordinary bravery in the service of your fellow soldiers,' he said. 'For your vital part in bringing Vardia information about the enemy, and thereby saving uncountable lives; Althazar Malvery, I present you with the Legion of Vardia medal, to go with your Duke's Cross. Your country counts you as one of its most treasured sons.'

And I owe you my life, thought Frey. *And more importantly, I owe you hers. Damn if you're not the best surgeon in Vardia, old mate.*

Applause filled the hall as the Archduke pinned the medal next to the one Malvery already had. The doctor kept his face as composed as he could, but even at this distance Frey could see Malvery glowing so fiercely with pride that you could have roasted a chicken on him.

'Grayther Crake!' said the Archduke, moving along the line. 'Few men have pushed the boundaries of our knowledge with such dedication and at such terrible risk to themselves. Your research and sacrifice were crucial in bringing the Imperators to heel, and for that, I award you the Ducal Star, for your magnificent contribution to science.'

'I notice he never quite said *daemonism*,' Trinica muttered.

'That'll come in time,' said Samandra. 'Can't change people's minds overnight, but I reckon it ain't gonna be long before daemonism ain't such a dirty word no more.'

'Jandrew Harkins!' the Archduke continued. 'For outstanding bravery in the air, I present you with the Coalition Navy's highest honour, the Iron Wing!'

The gallery applauded with gusto. Frey whistled through his fingers until Trinica hit him.

'Artis Pinn!' said the Archduke. 'For a selfless act of espionage, for infiltrating the Awakener ranks at great personal risk in order to return with critically important intelligence, the People's Medal!'

'How in rot's name did he swing that?' Samandra murmured.

'Pinn just won a medal for intelligence,' Frey said, shaking his head as he clapped. 'I don't want to live on this planet any more.'

Then the Archduke moved to stand before Silo. There was a short pause as the Archduke regarded him, and seemed deep in thought.

'Wait for it,' said Frey. 'This'll be a treat.'

'Silopethkai Auramaktama Faillinana!' the Archduke boomed.

Frey's jaw dropped. 'I'll be damned. That feller's good!'

'Your leadership in battle is an inspiration to all Vards,' the Archduke said. 'When all seemed lost, you gave us strength. Never before has a Vardic duke or monarch awarded a medal to a Murthian, but I do so today. You have shown us that courage knows no race nor borders. I give you the Duke's Cross, in recognition of your gallantry!'

The riot of applause that followed shook the doors of the hall. Chancellor Plome was the first in the pews to stand, and with him went the House of Chancellors, and then everyone was on their feet, and cheers swelled up like a tide and roared through the chamber. The men of the *Ketty Jay* couldn't keep their composure, and broke out in great beaming smiles. Frey clapped until his hands were sore, and by the time they began walking down off the dais, he was all but exhausted.

'You're not sad you didn't get one?' Trinica asked him.

Frey blew out his lips. 'What would I do with a medal? I'm surprised that lot got one, to be honest. After what happened with Earl Hengar, I mean. Pretty gracious of him, I'd say.'

'Reckon too many people heard about what you fellers did,' said Samandra. 'He sorta had to. But with regards to Hengar, they were just followin' orders. You were givin' 'em. It'd be a bit much for him to take, honourin' you.'

'Pity Ashua couldn't be here, though. She'd have liked to see the doc get his.'

'That'd also be a bit much,' said Samandra. 'Traitor to the country, whether she meant it or not. She can count herself lucky she got a pardon.'

'Yeah,' said Frey, with a meaningful glance at the woman next to him. 'Not like that evil pirate Trinica Dracken.'

Samandra just looked ahead. 'Far as I know, she died on the *Delirium Trigger*, just like her bosun. Funny that your new lady looks a bit like her without the make-up, though. What are the chances?'

'It is remarkable, isn't it?' Trinica agreed.

They heard a shriek from the hall. Frey looked down and saw a stocky young blonde woman in peasant dress struggling with the guards. Suddenly she broke free and ran up the aisle towards the side of the dais, where the crew of the *Ketty Jay* had descended. Before anyone could stop her, she ran up to Pinn, seized him by his chubby cheeks and planted an enormous kiss on his lips.

'Oh, sweet rot and damnation,' Samandra said in horror, a hand over her mouth. 'What am I seeing here? Is someone actually *kissing* Pinn?'

Then the woman broke away from him, and Frey got a look at her. Yes, he knew that placid, bovine country face. He'd seen her ferro-type a hundred times, forced on him by Pinn whenever he was in his cups. It just didn't seem possible.

'*Lisinda!*' cried Pinn.

'I think . . . er . . . I think that's his sweetheart,' said Frey. 'Like, the original one.'

'Didn't he abandon her five years ago or something?' Trinica asked.

'Yeah,' said Frey. 'Well, I mean, he left her a note saying he'd be back when he was famous and rich or something, but we all thought . . . Well . . .' Frey just stared. 'Do you think she really just . . . I mean, she actually *waited* for him? For *him*?' He threw up his hands. 'I dunno. I give up.'

There was a brief debacle as Lisinda was dragged away by the guards, with Pinn still attached to her, noisily trying to slurp at her face. After that, the ceremony resumed, and Frey got restless again.

'What happens next?' he asked Samandra.

'Next? Oh, there's a drinks reception in the palace with the great and good. Dukes and duchesses waitin' to congratulate you, Chancellors shakin' hands, the Press takin' your picture, wine, lobsters, all o' that.'

'Ah,' said Frey. He shuffled his feet, looked from one lady to the other, scratched his cheek. 'You wanna just round everyone up, find a bar and get slaughtered?'

'I'm in,' said Trinica immediately.

'Thought you'd never say it,' Samandra added, already on her way out the door.

Malvery roared with laughter and crashed his mug of ale so hard against Samandra's that he showered everyone in the booth.

'And that's for the Century bloody Knights! Legends, the lot o' you!'

'Adrek! Keep 'em coming!' Samandra hollered.

Adrek, barman and proprietor of The Wayfarers tavern, was already on his way with another tray. 'Steady now!' he said, as he put down their drinks.

'Ah, come on, Adrek!' Samandra cried. 'How many times you get this many heroes in your bar all at once? Look at all them medals!'

'You hear that?' Pinn asked Lisinda, who was nestled inside his arm. 'Heroes!'

There was another cheer, and they swept up their drinks from the tray and crashed them together, wasting half the round immediately.

485

Arkin chuckled. Despite having a Century Knight as a regular patron, the barman seemed rather star-struck. Or maybe it was just that he was relieved his establishment was still standing, and was prepared to indulge those he held responsible for saving it. Either way, he was in a good mood, and the drinks were on him tonight.

The Wayfarers was Samandra's drinking hole, a place that managed to be simultaneously large and cramped, with walls panelled in dark wood and many niches and secluded booths. Fires kept the winter chill away, and yellow light glittered on rippled green glass in the partitions. They'd changed from formal wear into clothes more suited to the occasion, but those who had medals still wore them anyway, pinned to coats and shirts. They'd earned them, and they were damned well going to show them off.

They toasted the Coalition, and themselves, and then gave a more solemn toast to absent friends and absent pets. They told each other stories of their adventures as if they hadn't all been there, and fell about at the punchlines. They even half-listened as Pinn extolled the virtues of his sweetheart, pointing out her flawless skin, her depthless eyes, her bountiful bosom. She giggled and hiccupped and seemed not the slightest bit embarrassed by it all.

'Well, of course I waited for him!' she told them. 'He went off to find fame and fortune, all to be worthy of me! So romantic! But when the broadsheets put up the list of who was going to get a medal, and I saw his name there, well . . . I had to see! So I thought I'd surprise him!'

'And you know what else?' Pinn cried incredulously. 'You know that letter I got from her ages ago, the one that said she was married? Well, it wasn't even *from* her! She was never even married!'

Frey looked at Malvery. 'Fancy,' he said, deadpan. Malvery coughed into his fist and concentrated very hard on his pint.

They drank and they laughed until Frey thought he'd burst with joy. To be here now, with his friends and with Trinica by his side – it was more than he could ever have hoped for. There was Ashua, her eyes bright; there was Crake, cracking a joke. Malvery guffawed and Pinn japed. Even Harkins and Silo were having fun. And though Jez wasn't with them, he imagined her out there somewhere, with her people, and he wondered if she might be happier than they could ever have made her.

Balomon Crund wasn't with them. He'd signed on with the first freebooter crew out of Thesk. It was enough for him that Trinica was safe; he couldn't bear seeing her anyone else's arms. That wasn't what she was to him. But Frey raised a mug to the scarred bosun anyway, and the rest did too. Without him, none of them would have been here.

For a time, it was if they floated in a sphere of perfect contentment, and everything outside was fuzzy and unimportant. And then Crake said:

'So what are you all going to do now, then?'

His words brought them back to earth. The spectre of the future cut into the moment, the carefree atmosphere was gone, and they became serious. This drunken celebration wouldn't last for ever. At least some of the crew of the *Ketty Jay* would be departing. An era was at an end.

They all knew about Crake. He'd declared that he was staying in Thesk, to study daemonism under Morben Kyne, and to be with Samandra. He'd evolved his field daemonism method while on the crew of the *Ketty Jay*, but now he believed he'd reached the limit of what he could do with a makeshift sanctum. The chance to learn from Kyne was too good to pass up.

Plus, there was the question of Bess, and Thesk was a better environment for her than the *Ketty Jay*. There was even talk of having her socialise with the other golems of the Archduke's army. She'd taken to hanging around them whenever she could, and they seemed to accept her.

'The daemons in the golems talk to each other, and to her,' Crake had told them. 'I think she might actually be able to make friends with them, in some way.'

So the question of Crake was settled. Now Frey looked around the faces of the people at the booth to see who else had outgrown him and his aircraft.

'The, er, the Navy wants to take me back,' said Harkins. 'Turns out I'm one of the most experienced pilots they've got, now. Might be I'll be an instructor.' He looked downcast. 'Sorry, Cap'n. I think I want that. Think I work better with rules and discipline, and the *Ketty Jay* . . .'

'Yeah,' said Frey, with a rueful grin. 'We don't have much of either.'

The others laughed uneasily. But Frey put a hand across the table. 'I'll be sorry to see you go, Harkins. You can keep the Firecrow, if you want. Won't be much good to me, and you thrashed it so hard I can't even sell it anyhow.'

'Thanks for understanding, Cap'n,' said Harkins, and he shook Frey by his good hand.

'I'm going back home with Lisinda!' Pinn declared loudly, oblivious to the sombre mood. 'Done my stuff! I'm a bona fide hero! Reckon it's time to settle down with a good woman.' He looked into Lisinda's adoring eyes. 'Maybe even raise a couple of kids.'

Malvery spluttered into his mug of ale and covered his face in froth.

Crake, Pinn, Harkins. 'How about the rest of you?' Frey asked. He felt Trinica take his hand under the table. He didn't know what he wanted them to say. He didn't know what he wanted to do. His whole life had been a game of Rake, with steadily ascending stakes; he'd never thought about what would happen after he won.

Malvery spoke up first. 'Well, that sorta depends on you, Cap'n.' He inclined his head towards Trinica. 'Seems like your circumstances changed more than most. There's your lady; you got her. So what are *you* gonna do?'

Frey looked at Trinica, seeking a reaction. She put her hands up in the air. 'Oh, no! Don't put this on me! You make your own choice, Darian, and I'll go where you go. I'm homeless and don't have a ducat to my name; the Coalition seized all my assets, remember?'

'That's kinda fair, considering where you got 'em,' said Samandra. 'Consider it the price for us forgettin' Trinica Dracken ever existed.'

'See?' said Trinica to Frey. 'I don't exist.' But the wink she gave him suggested that the Coalition hadn't quite found *all* of her rainy day money.

Frey sat back, puffed out his cheeks and ran a hand through his hair. So, the decision was all his? But he didn't *want* to make it on his own. It wasn't just about him any more. It was about everyone.

'Well, I still got the *Ketty Jay*,' he said, with a shrug. 'You fellers even *want* to tag along any more? Doc, weren't you thinking of opening up a practice in Thesk or something?'

'Cap'n,' said Malvery. 'More people get shot around you per hour than any other location in Vardia. Reckon I'm more use by your side than anywhere else. Besides, someone's got to keep an eye on you.'

'And someone's got to keep an eye on *you*!' Ashua said.

'Someone gotta keep an eye on *all* o' you,' said Silo. 'I'm with you, Cap'n. Medal or no medal, I ain't got no other place I belong more 'n' on that aircraft.'

Frey began to get excited. Malvery, Ashua, Silo, himself . . . and Trinica. Well, that was pretty much a crew, wasn't it? 'So what are we gonna do?' he asked them. 'Where are we gonna go?'

'Who cares?' said Malvery. 'Let's go hunt down Peleshar, that island that disappeared! Your mad mate Ugrik said he had a plan to find it, didn't he?'

'New Vardia!' Ashua said. 'I always fancied the frontier!'

'Since when?' Malvery asked.

'Since thirty seconds ago. Damn, we'll go join Red Arcus and be rebels!'

'You're just pissed 'cause you didn't get a medal,' said Pinn, waggling his medal at her.

'Alright then, let's go to Samarla!' Ashua said, laughing. 'Give the Thacians a hand, see if we can't help out some of Silo's folk.'

'Hey, hey, hey!' said Crake, holding up his hands for silence. 'Can I throw a wild idea in here? Don't any of you want to, you know, take it easy for a while? Do some honest trading, maybe? Go on holiday?'

They all looked at one another across the table. Then a grin spread across Crake's face, and Malvery roared with laughter and clashed his mug against Crake's. Suddenly they were all shouting over each other, boasting, joking, making plans and dreaming possibilities. Frey sat back and slid his arm around Trinica; she leaned into him, and he knew everything was alright, that the future was theirs for the taking.

Everything he'd always dreaded had come upon him: responsibility, commitment, the weight of expectations. And yet here he was with the woman he loved at his side and the world at his feet. He was freer than he'd ever felt. He could go anywhere, do anything, be anyone. And he'd never been happier than now.

'You think we can do it?' he said to her quietly, as the rest of them argued and hollered and jostled. 'You and me? You think we can ever forget what we did to each other, make it how it was, begin again?'

She took his face in her hands and kissed him. His friends whooped and cheered like louts. And when she let him go, she looked deeply into his eyes, and there on her lips was a little heartbreaking smile of hope.

'Yes, Darian,' she said. 'Let's begin again.'

Epilogue

In the gloomy, gaping silence of the *Ketty Jay*'s hold, tiny claws clicked on metal.

It was a small rat, not like the great monsters of old, but it had courage beyond its size. It came out tentatively and slipped along a narrow pipe with its body held low, then clambered down the bulkhead to the floor. Once there, it stood on its hind legs and raised itself, sniffing the air.

Instinct told it to be careful. It was a foolish rat that braved the open spaces with the Adversary about.

But things had changed of late. The terrible stench of their tormentor had faded from the vents and ducts and the deep places. The scourge of generations had departed, it seemed, and the rats grew bold. They sensed the balance of power in their world had shifted.

The rat ran out into the hold, stopped, sniffed around again. The chill air held the promise of great bounty. It could smell edible things inside some of those crates. The ducts were meagre hunting grounds, but here was the promised land they'd been denied for so long. It scuttled off, following the scent.

This one was only the first; there would be others, and more after them. The rats would come, and they'd feed, and they'd breed. The *Ketty Jay* would be theirs again.

A thumping of paws came quick from the shadows. The rat turned to flee back the way it had come, but the cat sensed its plan and intercepted it. Claws like blades plunged into its side. Fanged jaws snapped shut on its throat.

It was a foolish rat that braved the open spaces with the Adversary about.

The ugly mottled cat tore and gulped at the flesh, and licked the blood from her black and orange fur. She was not a big tom like Slag had been, but she was learning that these little rats were not beyond her. There were many of them, and that was good, for she was often hungry now.

She ate every morsel she could strip from the carcass, and left the remains where they lay. Then she padded away across the hold, back towards the little nest she'd made in a far dark corner. She went to sleep with the taste of the hunt still on her tongue, and the warm presence of new life quickening in her belly.